FYODOR DOSTOEVSKY, one of the finest psychologists in world literature, was born in Moscow in 1821. Introduced to literature from the age of three, he was very close to his parents and 'nanny'. His literary upbringing was influenced by Alena Frolovna, his nanny, who would read to him fairy tales, heroic sagas, and legends. As a student too, he was drawn to Romantic and Gothic fiction, especially the works of Sir Walter Scott, Nikolay Karamzin, Ann Radcliffe, Alexander Pushkin, and Friedrich Schiller among others. Unlike his contemporary writers, Dostoevsky was not born into the landed gentry. Therefore, his literary works foregrounded the lives of "accidental families" and of "the insulted and the humiliated". His stories explored human psychology in the turbulent socio-political atmosphere of 19th-century Russia.

His first novel, *Poor Folk,* was published in 1846 when he was 25. This gained him entry into St. Petersburg's literary circles. In 1849, he was arrested for being part of a literary group that discussed 'banned' books of Tsarist Russia. His most acclaimed works include *Crime and Punishment* (1866), *The Idiot* (1869), *Demons* (1872) and *The Brothers Karamazov* (1880). *Notes from Underground* (1864), his novella, is considered one of the earliest works of existentialist literature.

Dostoevsky's books have been translated into more than 170 languages. His writings inspired prominent authors of later generations including Anton Chekhov, Friedrich Nietzsche, and Jean-Paul Sartre.

The Idiot

Fyodor Dostoevsky

Om Books International

Reprinted in 2025

Om Books International

Corporate & Editorial Office
A-12, Sector 64, Noida 201 301
Uttar Pradesh, India
Phone: +91 120 477 4100
Email: editorial@ombooks.com
Website: www.ombooksinternational.com

Sales Office
107, Ansari Road, Darya Ganj,
New Delhi 110 002, India
Phone: +91 11 4000 9000
Email: sales@ombooks.com
Website: www.ombooks.com

ISBN: 978-93-5276-674-1

Printed in India

10 9 8 6 5 4

CONTENTS

PART ONE

Chapter 1

At nine o'clock in the morning, towards the end of November, the Warsaw train was approaching Petersburg at full speed. It was thawing, and so damp and foggy that it was difficult to distinguish anything ten paces from the line to right or left of the carriage windows. Some of the passengers were returning from abroad, but the third-class compartments were most crowded, chiefly with people of humble rank, who had come a shorter distance on business. All of course were tired and shivering, their eyes were heavy after the night's journey, and all their faces were pale and yellow to match the fog.

In one of the third-class carriages, two passengers had, from early dawn, been sitting facing one another by the window. Both were young men, not very well dressed, and travelling with little luggage; both were of rather striking appearance, and both showed a desire to enter into conversation. If they had both known what was remarkable in one another at that moment, they would have been surprised at the chance which had so strangely brought them opposite one another in a third-class carriage of the Warsaw train. One of them was a short man about twenty-seven, with almost black curly hair and small, grey, fiery eyes. He had a broad and flat nose and high cheek bones. His thin lips were continually curved in an insolent, mocking and even malicious smile. But the high and well-shaped forehead redeemed the ignoble lines of the lower part of the face. What was particularly striking about the young man's face was its deathlike pallor, which gave him a look of exhaustion in spite of his sturdy figure, and at the same time an almost painfully passionate expression, out of keeping with his coarse and insolent smile and the hard and conceited look in his eyes. He was warmly dressed in a full, black, sheepskin-lined overcoat, and had not felt the cold at night, while his shivering neighbour had been exposed to the chill and damp of a Russian November night, for which he was evidently unprepared. He had a fairly thick and full cloak with a big hood, such as is often used in winter by travellers abroad in Switzerland, or the North of Italy, who are not of course proposing such a journey as that from Eydtkuhnen to Petersburg. But what was quite suitable and satisfactory in Italy turned out not quite sufficient for Russia. The owner of the cloak was a young man, also twenty-six or twenty-seven years old, above the average in height, with very fair thick hair, with sunken cheeks and a thin, pointed, almost white beard. His eyes were large, blue and dreamy; there was something gentle, though heavy-looking in their expression, something of that strange look from which some people can recognise at the first glance a victim of epilepsy. Yet the young man's face was pleasing, thin and clean-cut, though colourless, and at this moment blue with cold. He carried a little bundle tied up in an old faded silk handkerchief, apparently containing all his belongings. He wore thick-soled shoes and gaiters, all in the foreign style. His dark-haired neighbour in the sheepskin observed all this, partly from having nothing to do, and at last, with an indelicate smile, in which satisfaction at the misfortunes of others is sometimes so unceremoniously and casually expressed, he asked: 'Chilly?'

And he twitched his shoulders.

'Very,' answered his neighbour, with extraordinary readiness, 'and to think it's thawing too. What if it were freezing? I didn't expect it to be so cold at home. I've got out of the way of it.'

'From abroad, eh?'

'Yes, from Switzerland.'

'Phew! You don't say so!' The dark-haired man whistled and laughed.

They fell into talk. The readiness of the fair young man in the Swiss cloak to answer all his companion's enquiries was remarkable. He betrayed no suspicion of the extreme impertinence of some of his misplaced and idle questions. He told him he had been a long while, over four years, away from Russia, that he had been sent abroad for his health on account of a strange nervous disease, something of the nature of epilepsy or St Vitus's dance, attacks of twitching and trembling. The dark man smiled several times as he listened, and laughed, especially when, in answer to his enquiry, 'Well, have they cured you?' his companion answered, 'No, they haven't.'

'Ha! You must have wasted a lot of money over it, and we believe in them over here,' the dark man observed sarcastically,

'Perfectly true!' interposed a badly dressed, heavily built man of about forty, with a red nose and pimpled face, sitting beside them.

He seemed to be some sort of petty official, with the typical failings of his class. 'Perfectly true, they only absorb all the resources of Russia for nothing!'

'Oh, you are quite mistaken in my case!' the patient from Switzerland replied in a gentle and conciliatory voice. 'I can't dispute your opinion, of course, because I don't know all about it, but my doctor shared his last penny with me for the journey here; and he's been keeping me for nearly two years at his expense.'

'Why, had you no one to pay for you?' asked the dark man.

'No, Mr Pavlishtchev, who used to pay for me there, died two years ago. I've written since to Petersburg, to Madame Epanchin, a distant relation of mine, but I've had no answer. So I've come ...'

'Where are you going then?'

'You mean, where am I going to stay? ... I really don't know yet... Somewhere ...'

'You've not made up your mind yet?' And both his listeners laughed again.

'And I shouldn't wonder if that bundle is all you've got in the world?' queried the dark man.

'I wouldn't mind betting it is,' chimed in the red-nosed official with a gleeful air, 'and that he's nothing else in the luggage van, though poverty is no vice, one must admit.'

It appeared that this was the case; the fair-haired young man acknowledged it at once with peculiar readiness.

'Your bundle has some value, anyway,' the petty official went on, when they had laughed to their heart's content (strange to say, the owner of the bundle began to laugh too, looking at them, and that increased their mirth), 'and though one may safely bet there is no gold in it, neither French, German, nor Dutch – one may be sure of that, if only from the gaiters you have got on over your foreign shoes – yet if you can add to your bundle a relation such as Madame Epanchin, the General's lady, the bundle acquires a very different value, that is if Madame Epanchin really is related to you, and you are not labouring under a delusion, a mistake that often happens ... through excess of imagination.'

'Ah, you've guessed right again,' the fair young man assented. 'It really is almost a mistake, that's to say, she is almost no relation, so much so that I really was not at all surprised at getting no answer. It was what I expected.'

'You simply wasted the money for the stamps. H'm! ... Anyway you are straightforward and simple-hearted, and that's to your credit. H'm! ... I know General Epanchin, for he is a man everyone knows; and I used to know Mr Pavlishtchev, too, who paid your expenses in Switzerland, that is if it was Nikolay Andreyevitch Pavlishtchev, for there were two of them, cousins. The other lives in the Crimea. The late Nikolay Andreyevitch was a worthy man and well connected, and he'd four thousand serfs in his day...'

'That's right, Nikolay Andreyevitch was his name.'

And as he answered, the young man looked intently and searchingly at the omniscient gentleman.

Such omniscient gentlemen are to be found pretty often in a certain stratum of society. They know everything. All the restless curiosity and faculties of their mind are irresistibly bent in one direction, no doubt from lack of more important ideas and interests in life, as the critic of today would explain. But the words, 'they know everything,' must be taken in a rather limited sense: in what department so-and-so serves, who are his friends, what his income is, where he was governor, who his wife is and what dowry she brought him, who are his first cousins and who are his second cousins, and everything of that sort. For the most part these omniscient gentlemen are out at elbow, and receive a salary of seventeen roubles a month. The people of whose lives they know every detail would be at a loss to imagine their motives. Yet many of them get positive consolation out of this knowledge, which amounts to a complete science, and derive from it self-respect and their highest spiritual gratification. And indeed it is a fascinating science. I have seen learned men, literary men, poets, politicians, who sought and found in that science their loftiest comfort and their ultimate goal, and have indeed made their career only by means of it.

During this part of the conversation the dark young man had been yawning and looking aimlessly out of window, impatiently expecting the end of the journey. He was preoccupied, extremely so, in fact, almost agitated. His behaviour indeed was somewhat strange; sometimes he seemed to be listening without hearing, and looking without seeing. He would laugh sometimes not knowing, or forgetting, what he was laughing at.

'Excuse me, whom have I the honour'... the pimply gentleman said suddenly, addressing the fair young man with the bundle.

'Prince Lyov Nikolayevitch Myshkin is my name,' the latter replied with prompt and unhesitating readiness.

'Prince Myshkin? Lyov Nikolayevitch? I don't know it. I don't believe I've ever heard it,' the official responded, thoughtfully. 'I don't mean the surname, it's an historical name, it's to be found in Karamzin's *History*, and with good reason; I mean you personally, and indeed there are no Prince Myshkins to be met anywhere, one never hears of them.'

'I should think not,' Myshkin answered at once, 'there are no Prince Myshkins now except me; I believe I am the last of them. And as for our fathers and grandfathers, some of them were no more than peasant proprietors. My father was a sublieutenant in the army, yet General Epanchin's wife was somehow Princess Myshkin; she was the last of her lot, too ...'

'Ha-ha-ha! The last of her lot! Ha-ha! How funnily you put it,' chuckled the official.

The dark man grinned too. Myshkin was rather surprised that he had perpetrated a joke, and indeed it was a feeble one.

'Believe me, I said it without thinking,' he explained at last, wondering.

'To be sure, to be sure you did,' the official assented good-humouredly.

'And have you been studying, too, with the professor out there, Prince?' asked the dark man suddenly.

'Yes ... I have.'

'But I've never studied anything.'

'Well, I only did a little, you know,' added Myshkin almost apologetically. 'I couldn't be taught systematically, because of my illness.'

'Do you know the Rogozhins?' the dark man asked quickly.

'No, I don't know them at all. I know very few people in Russia. Are you a Rogozhin?'

'Yes, my name is Rogozhin, Parfyon.'

'Parfyon? One of those Rogozhins …' the official began, with increased gravity.

'Yes, one of those, one of the same,' the dark man interrupted quickly, with uncivil impatience. He had not once addressed the pimply gentleman indeed, but from the beginning had spoken only to Myshkin.

'But… how is that?' The official was petrified with amazement, and his eyes seemed almost starting out of his head. His whole face immediately assumed an expression of reverence and servility, almost of awe. 'Related to the Semyon Parfenovitch Rogozhin, who died a month ago and left a fortune of two and a half million roubles?'

'And how do you know he left two and a half millions?' the dark man interrupted, not deigning even now to glance towards the official.

'Look at him!' he winked to Myshkin, indicating him, 'What do they gain by cringing upon one at once? But it's true that my father has been dead a month, and here I am, coming home from Pskov almost without boots to my feet. My brother, the rascal, and my mother haven't sent me a penny nor a word – nothing! As if I were a dog! I've been lying ill with fever at Pskov for the last month.'

'And now you are coming in for a tidy million, at the lowest reckoning, Oh! Lord!' the official flung up his hands.

'What is it to him, tell me that?' said Rogozhin, nodding irritably and angrily towards him again. 'Why, I am not going to give you a farthing of it, you may stand on your head before me, if you like.'

'I will, I will.'

'You see! But I won't give you anything, I won't, if you dance for a whole week.'

'Well, don't! Why should you? Don't! But I shall dance, I shall leave my wife and little children and dance before you. I must do homage! I must!'

'Hang you!' the dark man spat. 'Five weeks ago, like you with nothing but a bundle,' he said, addressing the prince, 'I ran away from my father to my aunt's at Pskov. And there I fell ill and he died while I was away. He kicked the bucket. Eternal memory to the deceased, but he almost killed me! Would you believe it, Prince, yes, by God! If I hadn't run away then, he would have killed me on the spot.'

'Did you make him very angry?' asked the prince, looking with special interest at the millionaire in the sheepskin. But though there may have been something remarkable in the million and in coming into an inheritance, Myshkin was surprised and interested at something else as well. And Rogozhin himself for some reason talked readily to the prince, though indeed his need of conversation seemed rather physical than mental, arising more from preoccupation than frankness, from agitation and excitement, for the sake of looking at someone and exercising his tongue. He seemed to be still ill or at least feverish. As for the petty official, he was simply hanging on Rogozhin, hardly daring to breathe, and catching at each word, as though he hoped to find a diamond.

'Angry he certainly was, and perhaps with reason,' answered Rogozhin, 'but it was my brother's doing more than anything. My mother I can't blame, she is an old woman, spends her time reading the lives of the saints, sitting with old women; and what brother Semyon says is law. And why didn't he let me know in time? I understand it! It's true, I was unconscious at the time. They say a telegram was sent, too, but it was sent to my aunt. And she has been a widow for thirty years and she spends her time with crazy pilgrims from morning till night. She is not a nun exactly, but something worse. She was frightened by the telegram, and took it to the police station without opening it, and there it lies to this day. Only Vassily Vassilitch Konyov was the saving of me, he wrote me all about it. At night my brother cut off the solid gold tassels from the brocaded pall on my father's coffin. "Think what a lot of money they are worth," said he. For that alone he can be sent to Siberia if I like, for it's sacrilege. Hey there, you scarecrow,' he turned to the official, 'is that the law – is it sacrilege?'

'It is sacrilege, it is,' the latter assented at once.

'Is it a matter of Siberia?'

'Siberia, to be sure! Siberia at once.'

'They think I am still ill,' Rogozhin went on to Myshkin, 'but without a word to anyone, I got into the carriage, ill as I was, and I am on my way home. You'll have to open the door to me, brother Semyon Semyonovitch! He turned my father against me, I know. But it's true I did anger my father over Nastasya Filippovna. That was my own doing. I was in fault there.'

'Over Nastasya Filippovna?' the official pronounced with servility, seeming to deliberate.

'Why, you don't know her!' Rogozhin shouted impatiently.

'Yes, I do!' answered the man, triumphantly.

'Upon my word! But there are lots of Nastasya Filippovnas. And what an insolent brute you are, let me tell you! I knew some brute like this would hang on to me at once,' he continued to Myshkin.

'But perhaps I do know!' said the official, fidgeting. 'Lebedyev knows! You are pleased to reproach me, your excellency, but what if I prove it? Yes, I mean that very Nastasya Filippovna, on account of whom your parent tried to give you a lesson with his stick. Nastasya Filippovna's name is Barashkov, and she's a lady, so to speak, of high position, and even a princess in her own way, and she is connected with a man called Totsky – Afanasy Ivanovitch – with him and no one else, a man of property and great fortune, a member of companies and societies, and he's great friends with General Epanchin on that account...'

'Aha! So that's it, is it?' Rogozhin was genuinely surprised at last. 'Ugh, hang it, he actually does know!'

'He knows everything! Lebedyev knows everything! I went about with young Alexandre Lihatchov for two months, your excellency, and it was after his father's death too, and I know my way about, so to say, so that he couldn't stir a step without Lebedyev. Now he is in the debtor's prison, but then I had every opportunity to know Armance and Coralie, and Princess Patsky and Nastasya Filippovna, and much else besides.'

'Nastasya Filippovna? Why, did Lihatchov ...' Rogozhin looked angrily at him. His lips positively twitched and turned white.

'Not at all! Not at all! Not in the least!' the official assured him with nervous haste. 'Lihatchov couldn't get at her for any money! No, she is not an Armance. She has nobody but Totsky. And of an evening she sits in her own box at the Grand or the French theatre. The officers may talk a lot about her, but even they can say nothing against her. "That's the famous Nastasya Filippovna," they say, and that's all. But nothing further, for there is nothing.'

'That's all true,' Rogozhin confirmed, frowning gloomily. 'Zalyozhev said so at the time. I was running across the Nevsky, Prince, in my father's three year-old coat and she came out of a shop and got into her carriage. I was all aflame in an instant. I met Zalyozhev. He is quite another sort – got up like a hairdressers assistant, with an eyeglass in his eye, while at my father's house we wear tarred boots and are kept on Lenten soup. "She's no match for you, my boy," he said, "she is a princess. Her name is Nastasya Filippovna Barashkov, and she is living with Totsky, and Totsky doesn't know how to get rid of her, for he's just reached the proper time of life, fifty-five, so that he wants to marry the greatest beauty in Petersburg." Then he told me that I could see Nastasya Filippovna that day at the Grand Theatre – at the ballet; she'd be in her box in the *baignoire*. As for going to the ballet, if anyone at home had tried that on, father would have settled it – he would have killed one. But I did slip in for an hour though, and saw Nastasya Filippovna again; I didn't sleep all that night. Next morning my late father gave me two five per cent bonds for five thousand roubles each. "Go and sell them," he said, "and take seven thousand five hundred to Andreyev's office, and pay the account, and bring back what's left of the ten thousand straight to me; I shall wait for you." I cashed the bonds, took the money, but I didn't go to Andreyev's. I went straight to the English shop, and picked out a pair of earrings with a diamond nearly as big as a nut in each of them. I gave the whole ten thousand for it and left owing four hundred; I gave them my name and they trusted me. I went with the earrings to Zalyozhev; I told him, and said, "Let us go to Nastasya Filippovna's, brother." We set off. I don't know and can't remember what was under my feet, what was before me or about me. We went straight into her drawing-room, she came in to us herself. I didn't tell at the time who I was, but Zalyozhev said, "This is from Parfyon Rogozhin, in memory of his meeting you yesterday; graciously accept it." She opened it, looked and smiled: Thank your friend Mr Rogozhin for his kind attention." She bowed and went out. Well, why didn't I die on the spot! I went to her because I thought I shouldn't come back alive. And what mortified me most of all was that that beast Zalyozhev took it all to himself. I am short and badly dressed, and I stood, without a word, staring at her because I was ashamed, and he's in the height of fashion, curled and pomaded, rosy and in a check tie – he was all bows and graces, and I am sure she must have taken him for me! "Well," said I, as he went out, "don't you dare dream now of anything, do you understand?" He laughed. "And how are you going to account for the money to your father now?" I felt like throwing myself into the water, I must own, instead of going home, but I thought "What did anything matter after all?" and I went home in desperation like a damned soul.'

'Ech! Ugh!' The petty official wriggled. He positively shuddered. 'And you know the deceased gentleman was ready to do for a man for ten roubles, let alone ten thousand,' he added, nodding to the prince.

Myshkin scrutinised Rogozhin with interest; the latter seemed paler than ever at that moment.

'Ready to do for a man!' repeated Rogozhin. 'What do you know about it? He found it all out at once,' he went on, addressing Myshkin, 'and Zalyozhev went gossiping about it to everybody. My father took me and locked me up upstairs and was at me for a whole hour. "This is only a preface," he said, "but I'll come in to say good night to you!" And what do you think? The old man went to Nastasya Filippovna's, bowed down to the ground before her, wept and besought her; she brought out the box at last and flung it to him. 'Here are your earrings, you old grey-beard," she said, "and they are ten times more precious to me now since Parfyon faced such a storm to get them for me. Greet Parfyon Semyonovitch and thank him for me," she said. And meanwhile I'd obtained twenty roubles from Seryozha Protushin, and with my mother's blessing set off by train to Pskov, and I arrived in a fever. The old women began reading the Lives of the Saints over me, and I sat there drunk. I spent my last farthing in the taverns and lay senseless all night in the street, and by morning I was delirious, and to make matters better the dogs gnawed me in the night. I had a narrow squeak.'

'Well, well, now Nastasya Filippovna will sing another tune,' the official chuckled, rubbing his hands. 'What are earrings now, Sir! Now we can make up for it with such earrings ...'

'But if you say another word about Nastasya Filippovna, as there is a God above, I'll thrash you, though you used to go about with Lihatchov!' cried Rogozhin, seizing him violently by the arm.

'Well, if you thrash me you won't turn me away! Thrash me, that's just how you'll keep me! By thrashing me you'll have put your seal on me ... Why, here we are!'

They had in fact reached the station. Though Rogozhin said he had come away in secret, several men were waiting for him. They shouted and waved their caps to him.

'I say, Zalyozhev here too!' muttered Rogozhin, gazing at them with a triumphant and almost malicious-looking smile, and he turned suddenly to Myshkin. 'Prince, I don't know why I've taken to you. Perhaps because I've met you at such a moment, though

I've met him too (he indicated Lebedyev) and I haven't taken to him. Come and see me, Prince. We'll take off those gaiters of yours, we'll put you into a first-rate fur coat, I'll get you a first-class dress-coat, a white waistcoat, or what you like, I'll fill your pockets with money!... We'll go and see Nastasya Filippovna! Will you come?'

'Listen, Prince Lyov Nikolayevitch!' Lebedyev chimed in solemnly and impressively. 'Don't miss the chance, oh, don't miss the chance!'

Prince Myshkin stood up, courteously held out his hand to Rogozhin and said cordially: 'I will come with the greatest of pleasure and thank you very much for liking me. I may come today even, if I've time. For I tell you frankly I've taken a great liking to you myself, I liked you particularly when you were telling about the diamond earrings. I liked you before that, too, though you look gloomy. Thank you, too, for the clothes and the fur coat you promise me, for I certainly shall need clothes and a fur coat directly. As for money, I have scarcely a farthing at the moment.'

'There will be money, there will be money by the evening, come!'

'There will, there will!' the official assented, 'by evening, before sunset there will be!'

'And women, Prince, are you very keen on them? Let me know to start with!'

'I, N-no! You see ... Perhaps you don't know that, owing to my illness, I know nothing of women.'

'Well, if that's how it is,' cried Rogozhin, 'you are a regular blessed innocent, and God loves such as you.'

'And the Lord God loves such as you,' the official repeated.

'And you follow me,' said Rogozhin to Lebedyev.

And they all got out of the carriage. Lebedyev had ended by gaining his point. The noisy group soon disappeared in the direction of Voznesensky Prospect. The prince had to go towards Liteyny. It was damp and rainy; Myshkin asked his way of passers-by – it appeared that he had two miles to go, and he decided to take a cab.

Chapter 2

General Epanchin lived in a house of his own not far from Liteyny. Besides this magnificent house – five-sixths of its rooms were let in flats – he had another huge house in Sadovy Street, which was also a large source of revenue to him. He owned also a considerable and profitable estate close to Petersburg, and a factory of some sort in the district. In former days the general, as everyone knew, had been a shareholder in government monopolies. Now he had shares and a considerable influence in the control of some well-established companies. He had the reputation of being a very busy man of large fortune and wide connexions. In certain positions he knew how to make himself indispensable, for instance, in his own department of the government. Yet it was known that Ivan Fyodorovitch Epanchin was a man of no education and the son of a simple soldier. The latter fact, of course, could only be to his credit; yet though the general was an intelligent man, he was not free from some very pardonable little weaknesses and disliked allusions to certain subjects. But he was unquestionably an intelligent and capable man. He made it a principle, for instance, not to put himself forward, to efface himself where necessary, and he was valued by many people just for his unpretentiousness, just because he always knew his place. But if only those who said this of him could have known what was passing sometimes in the soul of Ivan Fyodorovitch, who knew his place so well! Though he really had practical knowledge and experience and some very remarkable abilities, he preferred to appear to be carrying out the ideas of others rather than the promptings of his own intellect, to pose as a man 'disinterestedly devoted' and – to fall in with the spirit of the age – a warm-hearted Russian. There were some amusing stories told about him in this connexion, but the general was never disconcerted by these stories. Besides, he was always successful, even at cards, and he played for very high stakes and far from attempting to conceal this little, as he called it, weakness, which was pecuniarily and in other ways profitable to him, he intentionally made a display of it. He mixed in very varied society, though only, of course, with people of consequence. But he had everything before him, he had plenty of time, plenty of time for everything, and everything was bound to come in its due time. And in years, too, the general was what is called in the prime of life, fifty-six, not more, and we know that that is the very flower of manhood; the age at which real life begins. His good health, his complexion, his sound though black teeth, his sturdy, solid figure, his preoccupied air at his office in the morning and his good-humoured countenance in the evening at cards or at 'his grace's' – all contributed to his success in the present and in the future, and strewed his excellency's path with roses.

The general had a family of blooming children. All was not roses there, indeed, but there was much on which his excellency's fondest hopes and plans had long been earnestly and deeply concentrated. And, after all, what plans are graver and more sacred than a father's? What should a man cling to, if not to his family?

The general's family consisted of a wife and three grown-up daughters. The general had married many years before, when only a lieutenant, a girl of almost his own age, who was not distinguished either by beauty or education, and with whom he had received only a dowry of fifty souls, which served, however, as a stepping-stone to his fortune in later days. But the general never in after years complained of his early marriage, he never regarded it as the error of his luckless youth, and he so respected his wife, and at times so feared her, indeed, that he positively loved her. His wife was a Princess Myshkin, of an ancient though by no means brilliant family, and she had a great opinion of herself on account of her birth. An influential person, one of those patrons whose patronage costs them nothing, had consented to interest himself in the young princess's marriage. He had opened a way for the young officer and had given him a helping hand along it, though indeed no hand was needed, a glance was enough and would not have been thrown away! With few exceptions the husband and wife had spent their whole life in harmony together. At an early age Madame Epanchin, as a princess by birth, the last of her family, possibly, too, through her personal qualities, had succeeded in finding influential friends in the highest circles. In later years, through her husband's wealth and consequence in the service, she began to feel almost at home in those exalted regions.

It was during these years that the general's three daughters – Alexandra, Adelaïda and Aglaia – had grown up. They were only

Epanchins, it's true, but of noble rank on their mother's side, with considerable dowries and a father who was expected to rise to a very high position sooner or later, and what was also an important matter, they were all three remarkably good-looking, even the eldest, Alexandra, who was already turned twenty-five. The second was twenty-three and the youngest, Aglaia, was only just twenty. This youngest one was quite a beauty and was beginning to attract much attention in society. But that was not everything; all three were distinguished by education, cleverness and talent. Everyone knew that they were remarkably fond of one another and always hung together. People even talked of sacrifices made by the two elder sisters for the sake of the youngest, who was the idol of the house. They were not fond of showing themselves off in society and were modest to a fault. No one could reproach them with haughtiness or conceit, yet they were known to be proud and to understand their own value. The eldest was a musician, the second painted remarkably well, but this had not been generally known till lately and had only come out accidentally. In a word, a great deal was said in praise of them. But there were hostile critics. People talked with horror of the number of books they had read. They were in no hurry to get married; they valued belonging to a certain circle in society, yet not to excess. This was the more remarkable as everyone knew the attitude, the character, the aims and the desires of their father.

It was about eleven o'clock when Myshkin rang at the general's flat, which was on the first floor, and was a modest one considering his position. A liveried servant opened the door and Myshkin had much ado to explain his appearance to the man who, from the first, looked suspiciously at him and his bundle. At last, on his repeated and definite assertion that he really was Prince Myshkin and that he absolutely must see the general on urgent business, the wondering servant conducted him into a little anteroom leading to the waiting-room that adjoined the general's study, and handed him over to another servant, whose duty it was to wait in the morning in the anteroom and to announce visitors to the general. This second servant, who wore a tailcoat, was a man over forty, with an anxious countenance. He was his excellency's special attendant who ushered visitors into the study and so knew his own importance.

'Step into the waiting-room and leave your bundle here,' he said, seating himself in his armchair with deliberation and dignity, and looking with stern surprise at Myshkin, who had sat down on a chair beside him with his bundle in his hands.

'If you'll allow me,' said Myshkin, 'I'd rather wait here with you; what am I to do in there alone?'

'You can't stay in the anteroom for you are a visitor, in other words a guest. Do you want to see the general himself?'

The servant obviously found it difficult to bring himself to admit such a visitor and decided to question him once more.

'Yes, I have business...' Myshkin began.

'I don't ask you what business – my duty is only to announce you. But I've told you already, without the secretary's leave I am not going to announce you.'

The man's suspicion grew more and more marked: the prince was too unlike the ordinary run of visitors. Though at a certain hour the general used often, almost every day in fact, to receive visitors of the most varied description, especially on business, yet in spite of the latitude of his instructions the attendant felt great hesitation; the secretary's opinion was essential before he showed him in.

'Are you really ... from abroad?' he asked, almost in spite of himself, and was confused.

He had been about perhaps to ask, 'Are you really Prince Myshkin?'

'Yes, I have only just come from the station. I think you were going to ask, "Am I really Prince Myshkin?" but you didn't ask from politeness.'

'Hm!' grunted the astounded servant.

'I assure you that I haven't told you a lie and you won't get into trouble on my account. And you need not be surprised at my looking like this and having a bundle; I am not in very flourishing circumstances just now.'

'Hm! I have no apprehension on that score, you know. It's my duty to announce you, and the secretary will see you, unless you ... that's just the difficulty ... You are not asking the general for assistance, if I may make bold to enquire?'

'Oh no, you can rest assured of that. My business is different.'

'You must excuse me, but I asked looking at you. Wait for the secretary; his excellency is engaged with the colonel at present and then the secretary... from the company ... is coming.'

'Then, if I have to wait a long while, I should like to ask you if there is anywhere I could smoke? I've got a pipe and tobacco.'

'Smoke?' repeated the attendant, glancing at him with scornful surprise as though he could scarcely believe his ears. 'Smoke? No, you can't smoke here; you ought to be ashamed to think of such a thing. Ha-ha! It's a queer business.'

'Oh, I didn't mean in this room; I know that, I would have gone anywhere else you showed me, for I haven't had a smoke for three hours. I am used to it. But it's as you please, there's a saying, you know, "At Rome one must..." '

'Well, how am I going to announce a fellow like you?' the attendant could not help muttering. 'In the first place you have no business to be here, you ought to be sitting in the waiting-room, for you are a visitor, in other words a guest, and I shall be blamed for it... You are not thinking of staying with the family?' he added, glancing once more at the bundle, which evidently disturbed him.

'No, I don't think so. Even if they invite me, I shan't stay. I've simply come to make their acquaintance, that's all.'

'What? To make their acquaintance?' the attendant repeated with amazement and redoubled suspiciousness. 'Why, you said at first you'd come on business?'

'Oh, it's hardly business. Though I have business, if you like, but only to ask advice; I've come chiefly to introduce myself, because I am Prince Myshkin and Madame Epanchin is a Princess Myshkin, the last of them, and there are no Myshkins left but she and I.'

'Then you are a relation?' the startled lackey was positively alarmed.

'Hardly that either. Still, to stretch a point, I am a relation, but so distant that it's not worth counting. I wrote to Madame Epanchin from abroad, but she didn't answer me. Yet I thought I must make her acquaintance on my return. I tell you all this that you may have no doubt about me, for I see you are still uneasy. Announce Prince Myshkin, and the name itself will be a sufficient reason for my visit. If I am received – well and good, if not, it's perhaps just as well. But I don't think they can refuse to see me. Madame Epanchin will surely want to see the last representative of the elder branch of her family. She thinks a great deal of her family, as I have heard on good authority!'

The prince's conversation seemed simple enough, yet its very simplicity only made it more inappropriate in the present case, and the experienced attendant could not but feel that what was perfectly suitable from man to man was utterly unsuitable from a visitor to a manservant. And since servants ate far more intelligent than their masters usually suppose, it struck the man that there were two explanations: either the prince was some sort of impostor who had come to beg of the general, or he was simply a little bit soft and had no sense of dignity, for a prince with his wits about him and a sense of his own dignity, would not sit in an anteroom and talk to a servant about his affairs. So in either case he might get into trouble over him.

'Anyway, it would be better if you'd walk into the waiting room,' he observed, as impressively as possible.

'But if I had been there, I wouldn't have explained it all to you,' said Myshkin, laughing good-humouredly, 'and you would still have been anxious, looking at my cloak and bundle. Now, perhaps, you needn't wait for the secretary, but can go and announce me to the general.'

'I can't announce a visitor like you without the secretary; besides, his excellency gave special orders just now that he was not to be disturbed for anyone while he is with the colonel. Gavril Ardalionovitch goes in without being announced.'

'An official?'

'Gavril Ardalionovitch? No. He is in the service of the company. You might put your bundle here.'

'I was meaning to, if I may. And I think I'll take off my cloak too.'

'Of course, you couldn't go in in your cloak.'

Myshkin stood up and hurriedly took off his cloak, remaining in a fairly decent, well-cut, though worn, short jacket. A steel chain was visible on his waistcoat, and on the chain was a silver Geneva watch.

Though the prince was a bit soft – the footman had made up his mind that he was so – yet he felt it unseemly to keep up a conversation with a visitor. Moreover, he could not help feeling a sort of liking for the prince, though from another point of view he aroused in him a feeling of strong and coarse indignation.

'And Madame Epanchin, when does she see visitors?' asked Myshkin, sitting down again in the same place.

'That's not my business. She sees visitors at different times according to who they are. The dressmaker is admitted at eleven even, Gavril Ardalionovitch is admitted earlier than other people, even to early lunch.'

'Your rooms here are kept warmer than abroad,' observed Myshkin, 'but it's warmer out of doors there than here. A Russian who is not used to it can hardly live in their houses in the winter.'

'Don't they heat them?'

'No, and the houses are differently built, that is to say the stoves and windows are different.'

'Hm! Have you been away long?'

'Four years. But I was almost all the time at the same place in the country.'

'You've grown strange to our ways?'

'Yes, that's true. Would you believe it, I am surprised to find I haven't forgotten how to speak Russian. As I talk to you, I keep thinking "Why, I am speaking Russian nicely." Perhaps that's why I talk so much. Ever since yesterday I keep longing to talk Russian.'

'Hm! Ha! Used you to live in Petersburg?' *In* spite of his efforts the lackey could not resist being drawn into such a polite and affable conversation.

'In Petersburg? I've scarcely been there at all, only on my way to other places. I knew nothing of the town before, and now I hear there's so much new in it: that anyone who knew it would have to get to know it afresh. People talk a great deal about the new Courts of Justice now.'

'Hm!... Courts of justice ... It's true there are Courts of justice. And how is it abroad, are their courts better than ours?'

'I don't know. I've heard a great deal that's good about ours. We've no capital punishment, you know.'

'Why, do they execute people there then?'

'Yes. I saw it in France, at Lyons. Dr Schneider took me with him.'

'Do they hang them?'

'No, in France they always cut oft their heads.'

'Do they scream?'

'How could they? It's done in an instant. They make the man lie down and then a great knife is brought down by a heavy, powerful machine, called the guillotine... The head falls off before one has time to wink. The preparations are horrible. When they read the sentence, get the man ready, bind him, lead him to the scaffold – that's what's awful! Crowds assemble, even women, though they don't like women to look on ...'

'It's not a thing for them!'

'Of course not, of course not! Such a horrible thing!... The criminal was an intelligent, middle-aged man, strong and courageous, called Legros. But I assure you, though you may not believe me, when he mounted the scaffold he was weeping and was as white as paper. Isn't it incredible? Isn't it awful? Who cries for fear? I'd no idea that a grown man, not a child, a man who never cried, a man of forty-five could cry for fear! What must be passing in the soul at such a moment; to what anguish it must be brought! It's an outrage on the soul, that's what it is! It is written "Thou shalt not kill," so because he has killed, are we to kill him? No, that's impossible. It's a month since I saw that, but I seem to see it before my eyes still. I've dreamt of it half a dozen times.'

Myshkin was quite moved as he spoke, a faint colour came into his pale face, though his voice was still gentle. The footman followed him with sympathetic interest, so that he seemed sorry for him to stop. He, too, was perhaps a man of imagination and strainings after thought.

'It's a good thing at least that there is not much pain,' he observed, 'when the head falls off.'

'Do you know,' Myshkin answered warmly, 'you've just made that observation and everyone says the same, and the guillotine was invented with that object. But the idea occurred to me at the time that perhaps it made it worse. That will seem to you an absurd and wild idea, but if one has some imagination, one may suppose even that. Think! If there were torture, for instance, there would be suffering and wounds, bodily agony, and so all that would distract the mind from spiritual suffering, so that one would only be tortured by wounds till one died. But the chief and worst pain may not be in the bodily suffering but in one's knowing for certain that in an hour, and then in ten minutes, and then in half a minute, and then now, at the very moment, the soul will leave the body and that one will cease to be a man and that that's bound to happen; the worst part of it is that it's *certain*. When you lay your head down under the knife and hear the knife slide over your head, that quarter of a second is the most terrible of all. You know this is not only my fancy, many people have said the same. I believe that so thoroughly that I'll tell you what I think. To kill for murder is punishment incomparably worse than the crime itself. Murder by legal sentence is immeasurably more terrible than murder by brigands. Anyone murdered by brigands, whose throat is cut at night in a wood, or something of that sort, must surely hope to escape till the very last minute. There have been instances when a man has still hoped for escape, running or begging for mercy after his throat was cut. But in the other case all that last hope, which makes dying ten times as easy, is taken away *for certain.* There is the sentence, and the whole awful torture lies in the fact that there is certainly no escape, and there is no torture in the world more terrible. You may lead a soldier out and set him facing the cannon in battle and fire at him and he'll still hope, but read a sentence of certain death over that same soldier, and he will go out of his mind or burst into tears. Who can tell whether human nature is able to bear this without madness? 'Why this hideous, useless, unnecessary outrage? Perhaps there is some man who has been sentenced to death, been exposed to this torture and has then been told "you can go, you are pardoned." Perhaps such a man could tell us. It was of this torture and of this agony that Christ spoke, too. No, you can't treat a man like that!'

Though the footman would not have been able to express himself like Myshkin, he understood most, if not all, of the speech; that was evident from the softened expression of his face.

'If you are so desirous of smoking,' he observed, 'you might be able to, perhaps, only you would have to make haste about it. For his excellency might ask for you all of a sudden and you wouldn't be here. You see the door under the stairs, go in there and there's a little room on the right; you can smoke there, only you must open the window, for it's against the rules ...'

But Myshkin had not time to go and smoke. A young man with papers in his hands suddenly appeared in the anteroom. The footman began helping him off with his coat. The young man looked askance at Myshkin.

'This gentleman, Gavril Ardalionovitch,' the footman began, confidentially and almost familiarly, 'announces himself as Prince Myshkin and a relation of the mistress; he has just arrived from abroad with the bundle in his hand, only ...'

Myshkin could not catch the rest. As the footman began to whisper, Gavril Ardalionovitch listened attentively and looked with great interest at the prince. He ceased listening at last and approached him impatiently.

'You are Prince Myshkin?' he asked with extreme politeness and cordiality.

He was a very good-looking, well-built young man, also about eight-and-twenty, of medium height, with fair hair, a small, Napoleonic beard and a clever and very handsome face. Only his smile, with all its affability, was a trifle too subtle; it displayed teeth too pearl-like and even; in spite of his gaiety and apparent good-nature there was something too intent and searching in his eyes.

'He must look quite different when he is alone and perhaps he never laughs at all,' was what Myshkin felt.

The prince briefly explained all he could, saying almost the same as he had to the footman and before that to Rogozhin. Meanwhile Gavril Ardalionovitch seemed recalling something.

'Was it you,' he asked, 'who sent a letter to Lizaveta Prokofyevna a year ago, or even less, from Switzerland, I think?'

'Yes.'

'Then they know about you here and will certainly remember you. You want to see his excellency? I'll announce you at once ... He will be at liberty directly. Only you ought ... you had better step into the waiting-room ... Why is the gentleman here?' he asked the servant sternly.

'I tell you, he wouldn't himself...'

At that moment the door from the study was thrown open and a military man with a portfolio in his hand bowed himself out, talking loudly.

'You are there, Ganya,' cried a voice from the study, 'come here.'

Gavril Ardalionovitch nodded to Myshkin and went hastily into the study.

Two minutes later the door was opened again and the musical and affable voice of Gavril Ardalionovitch was heard: 'Prince, please come in.'

Chapter 3

General Ivan Fyodorovitch Epanchin stood in the middle of the room and looked with extreme curiosity at the young man as he entered. He even took two steps towards him. Myshkin went up to him and introduced himself.

'Quite so,' said the general, 'what can I do for you?'

'I have no urgent business, my object is simply to make your acquaintance. I should be sorry to disturb you, as I don't know your arrangements, or when you see visitors ... But I have only just come from the station ... I've come from Switzerland.'

The general was on the point of smiling, but on second thoughts he checked himself. Then he thought again, screwed up his eyes, scrutinised his visitor again from head to foot, then rapidly motioned him to a chair, sat down himself a little on one side of him, and turned to him in impatient expectation. Ganya was standing in the corner at the bureau, sorting papers.

'I have little time for making acquaintances as a rule,' observed the general, 'but as you have no doubt some object...'

'That's just what I expected,' Myshkin interrupted, 'that you would look for some special object in my visit. But I assure you I have no personal object except the pleasure of making your acquaintance.'

'It is of course a great pleasure to me too, but life is not all play, you know, one has work sometimes as well Moreover, so far, I haven't been able to discover anything in common between us ... any reason, so to speak

'There certainly is no reason, and very little in common, of course. For my being Prince Myshkin and Madame Epanchin's being of the same family is no reason, to be sure. I quite understand that. And yet it's only that that has brought me. It's more than four years since I was in Russia, and I left in such a state – almost out of my mind. I knew nothing then and less than ever now. I need to know good people; there is also a matter of business I must attend to, and I don't know to whom to apply. The thought struck me at Berlin that you were almost relations, and so I would begin with you; we might perhaps be of use to one another – you to me and I to you – if you were good people, and I had heard that you were good people.'

'I am very much obliged to you,' said the general, surprised. 'Allow me to enquire where are you staying?'

'I am not staying anywhere as yet.'

'So you've come straight from the train to me? And...with luggage?'

'All the luggage I have is a little bundle of my linen, I've nothing else; I generally carry it in my hand. I shall have time to take a room this evening.'

'So you still intend to take a room at a hotel?'

'Oh yes, of course.'

'From your words I was led to suppose that you had come to stay here.'

'That might be, but only on your invitation. I confess, though, I wouldn't stay even on your invitation, not for any reason, but simply... because I'm like that.'

'Then it's quite as well that I haven't invited you, and am not going to invite you. Allow me, Prince, so as to make things clear once for all: since we have agreed already that there can be no talk of relationship between us, though it would of course be very flattering for me, there's nothing but...'

'Nothing but to get up and go?' Myshkin got up, laughing with positive mirthfulness, in spite of all the apparent difficulty of his position. 'And would you believe it, General, although I know nothing of practical life, nor of the customs here, yet I felt sure that this was how it was bound to be. Perhaps it is better so. And you didn't answer my letter, then ... Well, goodbye, and forgive me for troubling you.'

Myshkin's face was so cordial at that moment, and his smile so free from the slightest shade of anything like concealed ill-will, that the general was suddenly arrested and seemed suddenly to look at his visitor from a different point of view; the change of attitude took place all in a minute.

'But do you know, Prince,' he said in a quite different voice, 'I don't know you, after all, and Lizaveta Prokofyevna will perhaps like to have a look at one who bears her name ... Stay a little, if you will, and if you have time.'

'Oh, I've plenty of time, my time is entirely my own.' And Myshkin at once laid his soft round hat on the table. 'I confess I was expecting that Lizaveta Prokofyevna might remember that I had written to her. Your servant, while I was waiting just now, suspected I'd come to beg for assistance. I noticed that, and no doubt you've given strict orders on the subject. But I've really not come for that, I've really only come to get to know people. But I am only afraid I am in your way, and that worries me.'

'Well, Prince,' said the general, with a good-humoured smile, 'if you really are the sort of person you seem to be, it will be pleasant to make your acquaintance, only I am a busy man, you see, and I'll sit down again directly to look through and sign some things, and then I'm going to his grace's, and then to the office, so though I am glad to see people ... nice ones, that is, but... I am so sure, however, that you are a man of very good breeding, that... And how old are you, Prince?'

'Twenty-six.'

'Oh, I supposed you were much younger.'

'Yes, I am told I look younger than my age. I shall soon learn not to be in your way, for I very much dislike being in the way. And I fancy, besides, that we seem such different people ... through various circumstances, that we cannot perhaps have many points in common. But yet I don't believe in that last idea myself, for it often only seems that there are no points in common, when there really are some ... it's just laziness that makes people classify themselves according to appearances, and fail to find anything in common ... But perhaps I am boring you? You seem...'

'Two words; have you any means at all? Or do you intend to take up some kind of work? Excuse my asking.'

'Certainly, I quite appreciate and understand your question. I have for the moment no means and no occupation either, but I must have. The money I have had was not my own, it was given me for the journey by Schneider, the professor who has been treating me and teaching me in Switzerland. He gave me just enough for the journey, so that now I have only a few farthings left. There is one thing, though, and I need advice about it, but...'

'Tell me, how do you intend to live meanwhile, and what are your plans?' interrupted the general.

'I wanted to get work of some sort.'

'Oh, so you are a philosopher, but are you aware of any talents, of any ability whatever in yourself, of any sort by which you can earn your living? Excuse me again.'

'Oh, please don't apologise. No, I fancy I've no talents or special abilities; quite the contrary in fact, for I am an invalid and have not had a systematic education. As to my living, I fancy...'

Again the general interrupted, and began questioning him again. The prince told him all that has been told already. It appeared that the general had heard of his deceased benefactor, Pavlishtchev, and had even known him personally. Why Pavlishtchev had interested himself in his education the prince could not explain; possibly it was simply from a friendship of long standing with his father. Myshkin lost his parents when he was a small child. He had grown up and spent all his life in the country, as his health made country air essential. Pavlishtchev had put him in charge of some old ladies, relations of his, and had engaged for him first a governess and then a tutor. Myshkin said that, although he remembered everything, there was much in his past life he could not explain, because he had never fully understood it. Frequent attacks of his illness had made him almost an idiot (Myshkin used that word 'idiot'). He said that Pavlishtchev had met in Berlin Professor Schneider, a Swiss, who was a specialist in such diseases and had an institution in Switzerland in the canton of Valais, where he had patients suffering even from idiocy and insanity, and treated them on his own method with cold water and gymnastics, training them also, and superintending their mental development generally. Pavlishtchev had sent him to Switzerland to this doctor nearly five years ago, and had died suddenly two years ago, making no provision for him. Schneider had kept him and continued his treatment for those two years, and although he had not completely-cured him, he had greatly improved his condition. Finally, at his own wish, and in consequence of something that had happened, he had sent him now to Russia. The general was very much surprised. 'And you have no one in Russia, absolutely no one?' he asked.

'At the moment no one, but I hope ... I have received a letter...'

'Have you, anyway,' the general broke in, not hearing the last phrase, 'have you at least been trained for something, and would your affliction not prevent your taking, for instance, some easy post?'

'Oh, it would certainly not prevent me. And I should be very glad of a post, for I want to see what I am fit for. I have been studying for the last four years without a break, though on his special system, not quite on the regular plan. And I managed to read a great deal of Russian, too.'

'Russian? Then you know the Russian grammar and can write without mistakes?'

'Oh, yes, perfectly.'

'That's good; and your handwriting?'

'My writing is excellent. Perhaps I may call that a talent, I am quite a calligraphist. Let me write you something as a specimen,' said Myshkin warmly.

'By all means. It's quite essential, in fact... And I like your readiness, Prince; you are very nice, I must say.'

'You've got such splendid writing materials, and what numbers of pens and pencils, and what splendid thick paper… And what a jolly study! I know that landscape, it's a view in Switzerland. I am sure the artist painted it from nature, and I am certain I've seen the place – it's in the canton of Uri…'

'Very probably, though it was bought here. Ganya, give the prince some paper; there are pens and paper, write at that little table. What's that?' asked the general, turning to Ganya, who had meanwhile taken from his portfolio and handed him a large photograph. 'Ah, Nastasya Filippovna! Did she send it you, she, she herself?' he asked Ganya eagerly and with great curiosity.

'She gave it me just now, when I went with my congratulations. I've been begging her for it a long time. I don't know whether it wasn't a hint on her part at my coming empty-handed on such a day,' added Ganya, with an unpleasant smile.

'Oh, no,' said the general with conviction. 'What a way of looking at things you have! She'd not be likely to hint… and she is not mercenary either. Besides, what sort of present could you make her, that's a matter of thousands! You might give her your portrait, perhaps? And, by the way, hasn't she asked for your portrait yet?'

'No, she hasn't; and perhaps she never will. You remember the party this evening, Ivan Fyodorovitch, of course? You are one of those particularly invited.'

'Oh, I remember, to be sure I remember, and I am coming. I should think so, it's her twenty-fifth birthday. Hm! Do you know, Ganya, I don't mind telling you a secret. Prepare yourself. She promised Afanasy Ivanovitch and me that at the party this evening she would say the final word: to be or not to be. So mind you are prepared.'

Ganya was suddenly so taken aback that he turned a little pale.

'Did she say that positively?' he asked, and there was a quaver in his voice.

'She gave us her promise the day before yesterday. We both pressed her till she gave way. But she asked me not to tell you beforehand.'

The general looked steadily at Ganya; he was evidently not pleased at his discomfiture.

'Remember, Ivan Fyodorovitch,' Ganya said, hesitating and uneasy, 'that she has left me quite at liberty till she makes up her mind, and that even then the decision rests with me.'

'Do you mean to say you ... do you mean to say...' the general was suddenly alarmed.

'I mean nothing.'

'Good heavens, what sort of position will you put us in?'

'I haven't refused, you know. I know I have expressed myself badly...'

'The idea of your refusing!' said the general with vexation, which he did not even care to conceal. 'It's not a question of your *not* refusing, my boy, but of your readiness, of the pleasure and the gladness with which you will receive her promise ... How are things going at home?'

'What does that matter? I decide everything at home. Only father is playing the fool as usual, but you know what a perfect disgrace he has become. I never speak to him, but I do keep him in check; and if it were not for my mother I would turn him out of the house. Mother does nothing but cry, of course; my sister is angry, but I told them straight out at last that I can do what I like with myself, and that I wish to be ... master in the house. I put it all very clearly to my sister, while my mother was there.'

'I still fail to understand it, my boy,' observed the general meditatively, with a slight motion of his hands and shrug of his shoulders. 'Nina Alexandrovna kept sighing and moaning when she came the other day, you remember. What's the matter? I asked. It appeared that it would mean *dishonour* to them. Where does the dishonour come in, allow me to ask? What can anyone reproach Nastasya Filippovna with? What can anyone bring up against her? Not that she has been living with Totsky, surely? That's such nonsense, under the circumstances, especially. "You wouldn't let her be introduced to your daughters," she says. Well, what next! She is a person! How can she fail to see, how can she fail to understand...'

'Her own position?' Ganya prompted the embarrassed general. 'She does understand it; don't be angry with her. But I did give her a good lesson not to meddle in other people's affairs. Yet the only thing that keeps them quiet at home is that the final word has not yet been said, but there's a storm brewing. If it's finally settled today, it will be sure to break out.'

Myshkin heard all this conversation sitting in the corner writing his specimen copy. He finished, went to the table and presented his page.

'So that's Nastasya Filippovna!' he observed, looking attentively and curiously at the photograph. 'Wonderfully beautiful,' he added warmly at once.

The portrait was indeed that of a wonderfully beautiful woman. She had been photographed in a black silk dress of an extremely simple and elegant cut; her hair, which looked as though it were dark brown, was arranged in a simple homely style; her eyes were dark and deep, her brow was pensive; her expression was passionate, and, as it were, disdainful. She was rather thin in the face and perhaps pale.

Ganya and the general stared at Myshkin in surprise.

'Nastasya Filippovna? Surely you don't know Nastasya Filippovna already?' queried the general.

'Yes, I've only been twenty-four hours in Russia, and already I know a beauty like that,' answered Myshkin.

And then he described his meeting with Rogozhin, and repeated the story he had told him.

'Here's something new!' said the general, uneasy again. He had listened to the story with the greatest attention and looked searchingly at Ganya.

'Most likely nothing but vulgar fooling,' muttered Ganya, who was also somewhat disconcerted. 'A young merchant's spree. I've heard something about him before.'

'And so have I, my boy,' put in the general. 'Nastasya Filippovna told the whole story of the earrings at the time. But now it's a different matter. It may really mean millions and ... a passion. A low passion, perhaps, but still there's the note of passion about it, and we know what these gentlemen are capable of when they are infatuated ... Hm! ... I only hope nothing sensational will come of it,' the general concluded thoughtfully.

'You are afraid of his millions?' asked Ganya with a smirk.

'And you are not, of course?'

'How did he strike you, Prince,' asked Ganya, turning suddenly to him. 'Is he a serious person or simply a silly fool? What is your opinion?'

There was something peculiar taking place in Ganya as he was asking his question. It was as though a new and peculiar idea was kindled in his brain, and flashed impatiently in his eyes. The general, who was simply and genuinely uneasy, also looked askance at the prince, but did not seem to expect much from his answers.

'I don't know what to tell you,' answered Myshkin, 'only I fancied that there was a great deal of passion in him, and even a sort of morbid passion. And he seems still quite ill, too. It's quite possible that he'll be laid up in a day or two again, especially if he begins carousing.'

'What? You fancied that?' the general caught at this idea.

'Yes.'

'Yet something sensational may well happen, not in a day or two, but before tonight, something may turn up perhaps today,' said Ganya to the general, with a grin.

'Hm! ... Of course ... Very likely, and then it will all depend on how it strikes her,' said the general.

'And you know what she is like sometimes?'

'Like what, do you mean?' the general pounced at him, roused to extreme perturbation. 'Listen, Ganya, please don't contradict her much today ... and try to be, you know...in fact, to please her... Hm!... Why are you grinning like that? Listen, Gavril Ardalionovitch, it won't be out of place, not at all so, to ask now what are we working for? You understand that as regards any personal advantage to me in the matter, I am quite at rest; in one way or another I shall settle it. Totsky has made up his mind once for all, so I am perfectly secure, and therefore all I desire now is simply your advantage. You can see that for yourself. Can you mistrust me? Besides, you are a man...a man...in fact a man of sense, and I was relying upon you...since in the present case... that...that...'

'That's the chief thing,' put in Ganya again, coming to the assistance of the hesitating general, and twisting his lips into a malignant smile, which he did not even try to conceal. He looked the general straight in the face with his feverish eyes, as though he wanted him to read in his eyes all that was in his mind. The general crimsoned and was angry.

'Quite so, sense is the chief thing!' he assented, looking sharply at Ganya. 'You are a funny person, Gavril Ardalionovitch! You seem pleased about this young merchant, I observe, as though he might be a way out of it for you. But in this affair it's just by your sense you ought to have been guided from the first. In this affair you ought to understand and to act honestly and straightforwardly with both sides, or else to have given warning beforehand, to avoid compromising others, especially as you've had plenty of time to do so, and there's still time, indeed, now,' (the general raised his eyebrows, significantly) 'although there are only a few hours left. Do you understand? Do you understand? Will you or won't you? If you won't, say so – and please yourself. Nobody is coercing you, Gavril Ardalionovitch, nobody is dragging you into a trap, that is, if you look on it as a trap.'

'I will,' said Ganya in a low voice, but firmly. He dropped his eyes and sank into gloomy silence.

The general was satisfied. He had been carried away by anger, but he evidently regretted that he had gone so far. He turned suddenly to Myshkin, and his face seemed to betray an uneasy consciousness that the prince had been there and had at least heard what was said. But he was instantly reassured; a glance at Myshkin was enough to reassure anyone.

'Oho!' cried the general, looking at the specimen of the handwriting presented him by Myshkin. 'That's a prize copy! And a splendid one! Look, Ganya, what skill!'

On the thick sheet of vellum the prince had written in medieval Russian characters the sentence, 'The humble Abbot Pafnuty has put his hand thereto.'

'That,' Myshkin explained with extraordinary pleasure and eagerness, 'that's the precise signature of the Abbot Pafnuty, copied from a fourteenth-century manuscript. Our old abbots and bishops used to sign their names beautifully, and sometimes with what taste, with what exactitude! Haven't you Pogodin's collection, General? And here I've written in another style; this is the large round French writing of last century, some letters were quite different. It was the writing of the market-place, the writing of professional scribes imitated from their samples. I had one. You'll admit that it has points. Look at those round o's and a's. I have adapted the French writing to the Russian alphabet, which was very difficult, but the result is successful. There's another splendid and original writing – see the phrase "Perseverance overcomes all obstacles" – that's Russian handwriting, a professional or perhaps military scribe's; that's how government instructions to an important person are written. That's a round handwriting, too, a splendid black writing, written thick but with remarkable taste. A specialist in penmanship would disapprove of those flourishes, or rather those attempts at flourishes, those unfinished tails – you see them – but yet you know they give it a character, and you really see the very soul of the military scribe peeping out in them, the longing to break out in some way and to find expression for his talent, and the military collar tight round his neck, and discipline, too, is in the handwriting – it's lovely! I was so struck with a specimen of it lately, I came on it by chance, and fancy where – in Switzerland! Now this is a simple, ordinary, English handwriting. Art can go no further, it's all exquisite, tiny beads, pearls; it's all finished. But here is a variation, and again a French one, I got it from a French commercial traveller. It's the same style as the English, but the black strokes are a trifle blacker and thicker than in the English, and you see the proportion is spoiled. Notice, too, the oval is a trifle rounder, and the flourish is admitted, too, and a flourish is a most perilous thing! A flourish requires extraordinary taste, but if only it's successful, if symmetry is attained, the writing is so incomparable that one may simply fall in love with it.'

'Oho! But you go into such niceties!' laughed the general, 'You are not simply a good penman, my dear fellow, you are an artist! Eh, Ganya?'

'Marvellous,' said Ganya, 'and he recognises his vocation too,' he added, with a sarcastic laugh.

'You may laugh, but there's a career in it,' said the general. 'Do you know, Prince, to what personage we'll get you to write now? Why, you can count on thirty-five roubles a month from the start. But it's half-past twelve,' he added, glancing at the clock. 'To business, Prince, for I must make haste and perhaps I may not see you again today. Sit down for a minute. I have explained already that I cannot see you very often, but I am sincerely anxious to help you a little, a little of course, that is, in what's essential, and then for the rest you must do as you please. I'll find you a job in the office, not a difficult one, but needing accuracy. Now for the next thing. In the home, that is, the family of Gavril Ardalionovitch Ivolgin, this young friend of mine with whom I beg you to become acquainted – his mother and sister have set apart two or three furnished rooms, and let them with board and attendance to specially recommended lodgers. I am sure Nina Alexandrovna will accept my recommendation. For you it will be a godsend, Prince, for you will not be alone, but, so to speak, in the bosom of a family, and to my thinking you ought not to be alone at first in such a town as Petersburg. Nina Alexandrovna and Varvara Ardalionovna, her daughter, are ladies for whom I have the greatest respect. Nina

Alexandrovna is the wife of a retired general who was a comrade of mine when I was first in the service, though owing to circumstances I've broken off all relations with him. That doesn't prevent me, however, from respecting him in a certain sense. I tell you all this, Prince that you may understand that I recommend you personally, and so I make myself in a sense responsible for you. The terms are extremely moderate, and I hope that your salary will soon be quite sufficient to meet them. Of course a man wants pocket-money, too, if only a little, but you won't be angry with me, Prince, if I tell you that you'd be better off without pocket-money, and, indeed, without any money in your pocket. I speak from tire impression I have of you. But as your purse is quite empty now, allow me to lend you twenty-five roubles for your immediate expenses. You can repay me afterwards, of course, and if you are as sincere and genuine a person as you appear to be, no misunderstandings can arise between us. I have a motive for interesting myself in your welfare; you will know of it later. You see I am perfectly straightforward with you. I hope, Ganya, you've nothing against the prince's being installed in your house?'

'Oh, quite the contrary. And my mother will be delighted,' Ganya assented politely and obligingly.

'You've only one room let, I think. That, what's his name … Ferd… ter…'

' Ferdyshtchenko.'

'Oh, yes. I don't like your Ferdyshtchenko, he is a dirty clown. And I can't understand why Nastasya Filippovna encourages him so? Is he really a relation of hers?'

'Oh, no, that's only a joke! There's not a trace of relationship.'

'Well, hang him! Well, Prince, are you satisfied?'

Thank you, General, you have been very kind to me, especially as I haven't even asked for help; I don't say that from pride; I really didn't know where to lay my head. It's true Rogozhin invited me just now.'

'Rogozhin? Oh, no, I would advise you as a father, or, if you prefer, as a friend, to forget Mr Rogozhin. And altogether I would advise you to stick to the family which you are entering.'

'Since you are so kind,' began the prince, 'I have one piece of business. I have received the news …'

'Excuse me,' broke in the general, 'I haven't a minute more now. I'll go and tell Lizaveta Prokofyevna about you; if she wishes to see you at once (I will try to give her a good impression of you) I advise you to make use of the opportunity and gain her good graces, for Lizaveta Prokofyevna can be of great use to you: you bear her name. If she doesn't wish to, there's nothing for it, some other time perhaps. And you, Ganya, look through these accounts meantime, Fedoseyev and I have been struggling with them. You mustn't forget to include them.'

The general went out, and so Myshkin did not succeed in telling him about the business which he had four times essayed to speak of in vain. Ganya lighted a cigarette and offered one to Myshkin. The latter accepted it, but refrained from conversation for fear of interrupting him. He began looking about the study. But Ganya scarcely glanced at the sheet covered with figures, which the general had indicated to him. He was preoccupied; his smile, his expression, his thoughtfulness weighed on Myshkin even more when they were left alone. All at once Ganya approached Myshkin, who was at that moment standing before the portrait of Nastasya Filippovna, gazing at it.

'So you admire a woman like that, Prince?' he asked him suddenly, looking searchingly at him and as though with some peculiar intention.

'It's a wonderful face,' he answered, 'and I feel sure her story is not an ordinary one. The face is cheerful, but she has passed through terrible suffering, hasn't she? Her eyes tell one that, the cheek bones, these points under her eyes. It's a proud face, awfully proud, but I don't know whether she is kind-hearted. Ah, if she were! That would redeem it all!'

'And would you marry such a woman?' Ganya went on, his feverish eyes fixed upon him.

'I can't marry anyone, I am an invalid,' said Myshkin.

'And would Rogozhin marry her? What do you think?'

'Marry her! He might tomorrow, I dare say he'd marry her and in a week perhaps murder her.'

He had no sooner uttered this than Ganya shuddered so violently that Myshkin almost cried out.

'What's the matter?' he asked, seizing his hand.

'Your excellency! His excellency begs you to come to her excellency,' the footman announced, appearing at the door.

Myshkin followed the footman.

Chapter 4

The three daughters of General Epanchin were blooming, healthy, well-grown young women, with magnificent shoulders, well-developed chests and strong, almost masculine, arms; and naturally with their health and strength they were fond of a good dinner and had no desire to conceal the fact. Their mamma sometimes looked askance at the frankness of their appetite, but though her views were always received with a show of respect by her daughters, some of her opinions had long ceased to carry the unquestioned authority of early years, so much so that the three girls, always acting in concert, were continually too strong for their mother, and for the sake of her own dignity she found it more expedient to yield without opposition. Her temperament, it is true, often prevented her from following the dictates of good sense; Lizaveta Prokofyevna was becoming more capricious and impatient every year. She was even becoming rather eccentric, but as her well-trained and submissive husband was always at hand, her pent-up moods were usually vented upon him, and then domestic harmony was restored and all went well again.

Madam Epanchin herself had not lost her appetite, how ever, and as a rule she joined her daughters at half-past twelve at a substantial lunch almost equivalent to a dinner. The young ladies drank a cup of coffee earlier, in their beds as soon as they waked, at ten o'clock precisely. They liked this custom and had adopted it once for all. At half-past twelve the table was laid in the little dining-room next to their mamma's apartments, and occasionally when the general had time, he joined this family party at lunch. Besides tea, coffee, cheese, honey, butter, a special sort of fritters beloved by the lady of the house, cutlets, and so on, strong hot soup was also served.

On the morning when our story begins, the whole family was gathered together in the dining-room waiting for the general, who had promised to appear at half-past twelve. If he had been even a moment late, he would have been sent for, but he made his appearance punctually. Going up to his wife to wish her good-morning and kiss her hand, he noticed something special in her face. And although he had had a presentiment the night before that it would be so, owing to an 'incident' (his favourite expression), and had been uneasy on this score as he fell asleep, yet now he was alarmed again. His daughters went up to kiss him; though they were not angry with him, there was something special about them too. The general had, it is true, become excessively suspicious of late. But as he was a husband and father of experience and dexterity, he promptly took his measures.

It will perhaps help to make our story clearer, if we break off here and introduce some direct explanations of the circumstances and relations in which we find General Epanchin's family at the beginning of our tale. We have just said that the general, though not a man of much education, but, as he expressed it, a self-taught man, was an experienced husband and a dexterous father; he had, for instance, made it a principle not to hurry his daughters into marriage – that is, not to pester and worry them by over-anxiety for their happiness, as so many parents unconsciously and naturally do, even in the most sensible families in which grown-up daughters are accumulating. He even succeeded in bringing over Lizaveta Prokofyevna to his principle, though it was difficult to carry out – difficult because it was unnatural. But the general's arguments were exceedingly weighty and founded on palpable facts. Moreover, left to their own will and decision, the girls would inevitably be bound to realise the position themselves, and then things would go smoothly, for they would set to work willingly, give up being capricious and excessively fastidious. All that would be left for the parents to do would be to keep an unflagging and, as far as possible, unnoticeable watch over them, that they might make no strange choice and show no unnatural inclination; and then to seize a fitting moment to come to their assistance with all their strength and influence to bring things to a finish. The mere fact, too, that their fortune and social consequence was growing every year in geometrical progression made the girls gain in the marriage market as time went on.

But all these incontestable facts were confronted by another fact. The eldest daughter, Alexandra, suddenly and quite unexpectedly indeed (as always happens) reached the age of twenty-five. Almost at the same moment Afanasy Ivanovitch Totsky, a man in the best society, of the highest connexions, and extraordinary wealth, again expressed his long-cherished desire to marry. He was a man of five-and-fifty, of artistic temperament and extraordinary refinement. He wanted to make a good marriage; he was a great admirer of feminine beauty. As he had been for some time on terms of the closest friendship with General Epanchin, especially since they had both taken part in the same financial enterprises, he had broached the subject, so to speak, by asking his friendly advice and guidance. Would a proposal of marriage to one of his daughters be considered? A break in the quiet and happy course of the general's family life was evidently at hand.

The beauty of the family was, as we have said already, unquestionably the youngest, Aglaia. But even Totsky, a man of extraordinary egoism, realised that it was useless for him to look in that direction and that Aglaia was not for him. Perhaps the somewhat blind love and the over-ardent affection of the sisters exaggerated the position, but they had settled among themselves in a most simple-hearted fashion that Aglaia's fate was not to be an ordinary fate, but the highest possible ideal of earthly bliss. Aglaia's future husband was to be a paragon of all perfections and achievements, as well as the possessor of vast wealth. The sisters had even agreed between themselves, without saying much about it, that if necessary they would sacrifice their interests for the sake of Aglaia. Her dowry was to be colossal, unheard-of. The parents knew of this compact on the part of the two elder sisters, and so when Totsky asked advice, they scarcely doubted that one of the elder sisters would consent to crown their hopes, especially as Afanasy Ivanovitch would not be exacting on the score of dowry. The general with his knowledge of life attached the greatest value to Totsky's proposal from the first. As owing to certain special circumstances, Totsky was obliged to be extremely circumspect in his behaviour, and was merely feeling his way, the parents only presented the question to their daughters as a remote proposition. They received in response a satisfactory, though not absolutely definite, assurance that the eldest, Alexandra, might perhaps not refuse him. She was a good-natured and sensible girl, very easy to get on with, though she had a will of her own. It was conceivable that she was perfectly ready to marry Totsky; and if she gave her word, she would keep to it honourably. She was not fond of show, with her there would be no risk of violent change and disturbance, and she might well bring sweetness and peace into her husband's life. She was very handsome, though not particularly striking. What could be better for Totsky?

Yet the project was still at the tentative stage. It had been mutually agreed in a friendly way between Totsky and the general that they should take no final and irrevocable step for a time. The parents had not even begun to speak quite openly on the subject to their daughters; there were signs of a discordant element: Madame Epanchin, the mother, was for some reason evincing dissatisfaction, and that was a matter of great importance. There was one serious obstacle, one complicated and troublesome factor, which might ruin the whole business completely .

This complicated and troublesome 'factor' had as Totsky himself expressed it, come on to the scene a long time – some eighteen years – before.

Afanasy Ivanovitch had one of his finest estates in a central province of Russia. His nearest neighbour was the owner of a small and poverty-stricken property, and was a man remarkable for his continual and almost incredible ill-luck. He was a retired officer of good family – better, in fact, than Totsky's own – by name Filip Alexandrovitch Barashkov. Burdened with debts and mortgages, he managed after working fearfully hard, almost like a peasant, to get his land into a more or less satisfactory condition. At the smallest success he was extraordinarily elated. Radiant with hope, he went for a few days to the little district town to see and, if possible, come to an agreement with one of his chief creditors. He had been two days in the town when the elder of his little village rode in with his beard burnt off and his cheek scarred, and informed him that the place had been burnt down the day before, just at midday, and 'that his lady had graciously been burnt, but his children were unhurt.' This surprise was too much even for Barashkov, accustomed as he was to the buffeting of fortune. He went out of his mind and died in delirium a month later. The ruined property with its beggared peasants was sold to pay his debts. Afanasy Ivanovitch Totsky in the generosity of his heart undertook to bring up and educate Barashkov's children, two little girls of six and seven. They were brought up with the children of Totsky's steward, a retired government clerk with a large family, and, moreover, a German. The younger child died of whooping cough, and little Nastasya was left alone. Totsky lived abroad and soon completely forgot her existence. Five years later it occurred to him on his way elsewhere to look in on his estate, and he noticed in the family of his German steward a charming child, a girl about twelve, playful, sweet, clever and promising to become extremely beautiful. On that subject Afanasy Ivanovitch was an unerring connoisseur. He only spent a few days on his estate, but he made arrangements for a great change in the girl's education. A respectable and cultivated elderly Swiss governess, experienced in the higher education of girls and competent to teach various subjects besides French, was engaged for her. She was installed in Totsky's country house, and little Nastasya began to receive an education on the broadest lines. Just four years later this education was over; the governess left, and a lady who lived near another estate of Totsky's in another remote province came, by his instructions, and took Nastasya away. On this estate there was also a small recently built wooden house. It was very elegantly furnished, and the place was appropriately called 'The Pleasaunce'. The lady brought Nastasya straight to this little house, and as she was a childless widow, living only three-quarters of a mile away, she installed herself in the house with her. An old housekeeper and an experienced young maid were there to wait on Nastasya. In the house she found musical instruments, a choice library for a young girl, pictures, engravings, pencils, paints and brushes, a thoroughbred lapdog, and within a fortnight Afanasy Ivanovitch himself made his appearance ... Since then he had been particularly fond of that remote property in the steppes and had spent two or three months there every summer. So passed a fairly long time – four years, calmly and happily in tasteful and elegant surroundings.

It happened once at the beginning of winter, four months after one of Totsky's summer visits, which had on that occasion lasted only a fortnight, a rumour was circulated, or rather reached Nastasya Filippovna, that Afanasy Ivanovitch was going to be married in Petersburg to a beautiful heiress of good family – that he was, in fact, making a wealthy and brilliant match. The rumour turned out to be not quite correct in some details. The supposed marriage was only a project, still very vague, but it was a turning-point in Nastasya Filippovna's life. She displayed great determination and quite unexpected strength of will. Without wasting time on reflection, she left her little house in the country and suddenly made her appearance in Petersburg, entirely alone, going straight to Totsky. He was amazed, and, as soon as he began to speak to her, he found almost from the first word that he had completely to abandon the language, the intonations, the logic, the subjects of the agreeable and refined conversations that had been so successful hitherto – everything, everything! He saw sitting before him an entirely different woman, not in the least like the girl he had left only that July.

This new woman turned out, in the first place, to know and understand a great deal – so much that one could not but marvel where she had got such knowledge and how she could have arrived at such definite ideas. (Surely not from her young girl's library!) What was more, she understood many things in their legal aspect and had a positive knowledge, if not of the world, at least of how some things are done in the world; moreover, she had not the same character as before. There was nothing of the timidity, the schoolgirlish uncertainty, sometimes fascinating in its original simplicity and playfulness, sometimes melancholy and dreamy, astonished, mistrustful, tearful and uneasy.

Yes, it was a new and surprising creature who laughed in his face and stung him with venomous sarcasms, openly declaring that she had never had any feeling in her heart for him except contempt – contempt and loathing which had come upon her immediately after her first surprise. This new woman announced that it was a matter of absolute indifference to her if he married at once anyone he chose, but she had come to prevent his making that marriage, and would not allow it from spite, simply because she chose not to, and that therefore so it must be – 'if only that I may have a good laugh at you, for I too want to laugh now.'

That at least was what she said, she did not perhaps utter all that was in her mind. But while this new Nastasya Filippovna laughed and talked like this, Afanasy Ivanovitch was deliberating on the position and, as far as he could, collecting his somewhat shattered ideas. This deliberation took him some time; he was weighing things and making up his mind for a fortnight. But at the end of that fortnight he had reached a decision.

Afanasy Ivanovitch was at that time a man of fifty, his character was set and his habits formed. His position in the world and in society had long been established on the most secure foundations. He loved and prized himself, his peace and comfort, above everything in the world, as befits a man of the highest breeding. No destructive, no dubious element could be admitted into that splendid edifice which his whole life had been building up. On the other hand, his experience and deep insight told Totsky very quickly and quite correctly that he had to do with a creature quite out of the ordinary – a creature who would not only threaten but certainly act, and, what was more, would stick at nothing, especially as she prized nothing in life and so could not be tempted. Evidently there was something else in it: there were indications of a chaotic ferment at work in mind and heart, something like romantic indignation – God knows why and with whom! – An insatiable and exaggerated passion of contempt; in fact, something highly ridiculous and inadmissible in good society, and bound to be a regular nuisance to any well-bred man. Of course, with Totsky's wealth and connexions he could at once have got rid of the annoyance by some trifling and quite pardonable piece of villainy. On the other hand, it was evident that Nastasya Filippovna was hardly in a position to do much harm, in a legal sense, for instance. She could not even create a scandal of any consequence, because it was so easy to circumvent her. But all that only applied if Nastasya Filippovna should think fit to behave as people do behave in such circumstances without departing too widely from the regular course. But here Totsky's keen eye served him well: he was clever enough to see that Nastasya Filippovna fully realised that she could not harm him by means of the law, but that there was something very different in her mind and … in her flashing eyes. As she valued nothing and herself least of all (it needed much intelligence and insight in a sceptical and worldly cynic, such as he was, to realise that she had long ceased to care what became of her, and to believe in the earnestness of this feeling), Nastasya Filippovna was quite capable of facing hopeless ruin and disgrace, prison and Siberia, only to humiliate the man for whom she cherished such an inhuman aversion. Afanasy Ivanovitch never concealed the fact that he was somewhat a coward, or rather perhaps highly conservative. If he had known, for instance, that he would be murdered at the altar on his wedding day, or that anything of that sort, exceedingly unseemly, ridiculous, impossible in society, would happen, he would certainly have been alarmed, but not so much of being killed or wounded, or of having someone spit in his face in public, or of anything of that kind, as of the unnatural and vulgar form of the insult. And that was just what Nastasya

Filippovna threatened, though she said nothing about it. He knew that she had studied him and understood him thoroughly and so knew how to wound him. And as his marriage had been merely a project, Afanasy Ivanovitch submitted and gave way to Nastasya Filippovna.

There was another consideration which helped him to this decision: it was difficult to imagine how unlike in face this new Nastasya Filippovna was to the old one. She had been only a very pretty young girl, but now ... Totsky could not forgive himself for having failed for four years to see what was in that face. Much no doubt was due to the inward and sudden change in their relative attitudes. He remembered, however, that there had been moments even in the past when strange ideas had come into his mind, looking at those eyes. There was a promise in them of something deep. The look in those eyes seemed dark and mysterious. They seemed to be asking a riddle. He had often wondered during the last two years at the change in Nastasya Filippovna's complexion. She had become fearfully pale and, strange to say, was even handsomer for it. Totsky, like all gentlemen who have lived freely in their day, felt contemptuously how cheaply he had obtained this virginal soul. But of late he had been rather shaken in this feeling. He had in any case made up his mind in the previous spring to lose no time in marrying Nastasya Filippovna off with a good dowry to some sensible and decent fellow serving in another province. (Oh, how horribly and maliciously Nastasya Filippovna laughed at the idea now!) But now Afanasy Ivanovitch, fascinated by her novelty, positively imagined that he might again make use of this woman. He decided to settle Nastasya Filippovna in Petersburg and to surround her with luxury and comfort. If not one thing, he would have the other. He might even gratify his vanity and gain glory in a certain circle by means of her. Afanasy Ivanovitch greatly prized his reputation in that line.

Five years of life in Petersburg had followed, and of course many things had become clear in that time. Totsky's position was not an agreeable one. The worst of it was that, hating been once intimidated, he could never quite regain his confidence. He was afraid and could not even tell why he was afraid – he was simply afraid of Nastasya Filippovna. For some time during the first two years he suspected that Nastasya Filippovna wanted to marry him herself, but did not speak from her extraordinary pride and was obstinately waiting for him to make an offer. It would have been a strange demand, but he had become suspicious; he frowned and brooded unpleasantly. To his great and (such is the heart of man!) somewhat unpleasant surprise, he was convinced by something that happened that, even if he made the offer, he would not be accepted. It was a long while before he could understand this. It seemed to him that there was only one possible explanation: that the pride of the 'offended and fantastic woman' had reached such a pitch of frenzy that she preferred to express her scorn once for all by refusing him, to securing her future position and mounting to inaccessible heights of grandeur. The worst of it was that Nastasya Filippovna got the upper hand of him in a shocking way. She was not influenced by mercenary considerations either, however large the bait, and though she accepted the luxury offered her, she lived very modestly and had scarcely saved anything during those five years. Totsky ventured upon very subtle tactics to break his chains; he began, with skilful assistance, trying to tempt her with all sorts of temptations of the most idealistic kind. But the ideals in the form of princes, hussars, secretaries from the embassies, poets, novelists, even Socialists – none of them made the least impression on Nastasya Filippovna, as though she had a stone for a heart and her feelings had been withered and dried up for ever. She lived a rather secluded life, reading and even studying; she was fond of music. She had few friends; she associated with the wives of petty officials, poor and ridiculous people, was acquainted with two actresses and some old women, was very fond of the family of a respectable teacher, and the numerous members of this family loved her and gave her a warm welcome. She would often have five or six friends to see her in the evening. Totsky visited her frequently and regularly. General Epanchin had with some difficulty made her acquaintance of late. At the same time a young government clerk, called Ferdyshtchenko, a drunken and ill-bred buffoon, who affected to be funny, had made her acquaintance with no difficulty whatever. Another of her circle was a strange young man, called Ptitsyn, modest, precise and of highly polished manners, who had risen from poverty and become a moneylender. At last Gavril Ardalionovitch was introduced to her… Nastasya Filippovna ended by gaining a strange reputation. Everyone had heard of her beauty, but that was all. No one could boast of her favours, no one had anything to tell of her. This reputation, her education, her elegant manners, her wit, all confirmed Totsky in a certain plan of his. It was at this moment that General Epanchin began to take so active a part in the affair.

When Totsky had so courteously approached him, asking for his advice as a friend in regard to one of his daughters, he had in the noblest way made the general a full and candid confession. He told him that he had made up his mind not to stick at any means to gain his freedom; that he would not feel safe even if Nastasya Filippovna assured him herself that she would leave him in peace for the future; that words meant little to him, that he needed the fullest guarantees. They talked things over and determined to act together. It was decided to try the gentlest means first and to play, so to speak, on the 'finer chords of her heart.' They went together to Nastasya Filippovna, and Totsky spoke straight away of the intolerable misery of his position. He blamed himself for everything; he said frankly that he could not repent of his original offence, for he was an inveterate sensualist and could not control himself, but that now he wanted to marry, and the whole possibility of this highly suitable and distinguished marriage was *in* her hands: in a word, he rested all his hopes on her generous heart. Then General Epanchin, as the father, began to speak and he talked reasonably, avoiding sentimentality. He only mentioned that he fully admitted her right to decide Afanasy Ivanovitch's fate, and made clever display of his own humility, pointing out that the fate of his daughter, and perhaps of his two other daughters, was now depending on her decision. To Nastasya Filippovna's question what it was they wanted of her, Totsky with the same bald directness confessed that she had given him such a scare five years before that he could not feel quite safe even now till Nastasya Filippovna was herself married. He added at once that this proposition, would, of course, be absurd on his part, if he had not some foundation for it. He had observed and knew for a fact that a young man of good birth and respectable family, Gavril Ardalionovitch Ivolgin, who was an acquaintance she welcomed in her house, loved her and had long loved her passionately, and would of course give half his life for the bare hope of winning her affection. Gavril Ardalionovitch had confessed as much to him – Totsky – in a friendly way long ago, in the simplicity of his pure young heart, and Ivan Fyodorovitch, who had befriended the young man, had long known of his passion. Finally, he said that if he – Totsky – were not mistaken, Nastasya

Filippovna must herself have long been aware of the young man's love; and he fancied indeed that she looked on it indulgently. It was of course, he said, harder for him than anyone to speak of this, but if Nastasya Filippovna would allow that he – Totsky – had at least some thought for her . good, as well as a selfish desire to arrange for his own comfort, she would realise that it had for some time been strange and painful to him to see her loneliness, which was all due to vague depression and complete disbelief in the possibility of a new life, which might spring up with new aims in love and marriage; that it was throwing away talents perhaps of the most brilliant, a wanton brooding over grief – that it was, in fact, a sort of sentimentality unworthy of the good sense and noble heart of Nastasya Filippovna. Repeating that it was harder for him than for anyone to speak of it, he finished up by saying he could not help hoping that Nastasya Filippovna would not meet him with contempt, if he expressed a genuine desire to guarantee her future and offered her the sum of seventy-five thousand roubles. He added in explanation that that sum was already secured to her in his will; that, in fact, it was not a question of compensation of any sort… though, indeed, why refuse to admit and forgive in him a human desire to do something to ease his conscience – and so on and so on, as is always said in such circumstances. Afanasy Ivanovitch spoke elegantly and at length. He added, as though in passing, the interesting information that he had not dropped a word about the seventy-five thousand, and that no one, not even Ivan Fyodorovitch sitting here, knew of it.

Nastasya Filippovna's answer astounded the two friends. She showed no trace of her former irony, her former hostility and hatred, of the laughter which even in recollection sent a cold shiver down Totsky's spine; on the contrary, she seemed glad of the opportunity of speaking to someone with frankness and friendliness. She acknowledged that she had long been wanting to ask for friendly advice and that only her pride had hindered her, but once the ice was broken, nothing could be better. At first, with a mournful smile and then with a gay and playful laugh, she confessed that there could in any case be no such storm as in the past; that she had for some time past looked at things differently, and that, although there was no change in her heart, she had been compelled to accept many things as accomplished facts; that what was done could not be undone, that what was past was over, so much so that she wondered at Afanasy Ivanovitch's still being uneasy. Then she turned to Ivan Fyodorovitch and with a very deferential air said that she had long ago heard a great deal about his daughters and entertained a profound and sincere respect for them. The very idea that she could be in any way of service to them would be a source of pride and gladness to her. It was true that she was depressed and dreary, very dreary; Afanasy Ivanovitch had guessed her dreams; she longed to begin a new life, finding new aims in children and home-life, if not in love. As for Gavril Ardalionovitch, she could scarcely speak. She thought it was true that he loved her; she believed that she too might care for him, if she could believe in the reality of his attachment, but even if he were sincere, he was very young; it was hard for her to make up her mind. What she liked best of all about him was that he was working and supporting his family without assistance. She had heard that he was a man of energy and pride, eager to make his way, to make his career. She had heard too that his mother, Nina Alexandrovna, was an excellent woman, highly respected; that his sister, Varvara Ardalionovna, was a very remarkable girl of great character; she had heard a great deal about her from Ptitsyn. She had heard that they had borne their misfortunes bravely. She would be very glad to make their acquaintance, but it was a question whether they would welcome her into their family. She would say nothing against the possibility of such a marriage, but she must think more about it; she would beg them not to hurry her. As for the seventy-five thousand, there was no need for Afanasy Ivanovitch to make so much of speaking about it. She knew the value of money and would certainly take it. She thanked Afanasy Ivanovitch for his delicacy in not having spoken of the money to Gavril Ardalionovitch, or even to the general, but why should not the young man know about it? There was no need for her to be ashamed of accepting this money on entering their family. In any case she had no intention of apologising to anyone for anything, and wished that to be known. She would not marry Gavril Ardalionovitch, until she was certain that neither he nor his family had any hidden feeling about her. In any case she did not consider herself to blame in any way; Gavril Ardalionovitch had much better know on what footing she had been living for those five years in Petersburg, on what terms she had been with Afanasy Ivanovitch, and whether she had laid by any money. If she accepted the money now it was not as payment for the loss of her maidenly honour, for which she was in no way to blame, but simply as a compensation for her ruined life.

She grew so hot and angry saying this (which was very natural, however) that General Epanchin was much pleased, and considered the matter settled. But Totsky, having once been so thoroughly scared, was not quite confident even now, and was for a long time afraid that there might be a snake under the flowers. But negotiations had been opened; the point on which the whole scheme of the two friends rested, the possibility of Nastasya Filippovna's being attracted by Ganya, became more and more clear and definite, so that even Totsky began to believe at times in the possibility of success. Meanwhile Nastasya Filippovna came to an understanding with Ganya; very little was said, as though the subject were painful to her delicacy. She recognised and sanctioned his love, however, but insisted that she would not bind herself in any way; that she reserved for herself till the marriage (if marriage there were) the right to say *no* up to the very last moment, and she gave Ganya equal freedom. Ganya soon afterwards learned by a lucky chance that Nastasya Filippovna knew in full detail all about his family's hostility to the marriage and to her personally, and the scenes at home to which it gave rise. She had not spoken of this to him, though he was expecting it daily.

There is much more to be told of all the gossip and complications arising from the proposed match and the negotiations for it, but we have been anticipating things already, and some of these complications were no more than vague rumours. It was said, for instance, that Totsky had found out that Nastasya Filippovna had some undefined and secret understanding with the general's daughters – a wildly improbable story. But another story he could not help believing, and it haunted him like a nightmare. He heard for a fact that Nastasya Filippovna was fully aware that Ganya was marrying her only for money; that Ganya had a bad, mercenary, impatient, envious heart, and that his vanity was grotesque and beyond all bounds; that though Ganya had really been passionately striving to conquer Nastasya Filippovna, yet after the two elder men had determined to exploit the incipient passion on both sides for their own purposes, and to buy Ganya by selling to him Nastasya Filippovna in lawful wedlock, he began to hate her like a nightmare. Passion and hatred were strangely mingled in his soul, and although he did after painful hesitation give his consent to marry the 'disreputable hussy,' he swore in his heart to make her pay bitterly for it and 'to take it out of her' afterwards, as he was said to have expressed it himself. It was rumoured Nastasya Filippovna knew all this and had some secret plan up her sleeve. Totsky was in such a panic that he even gave up confiding his uneasiness to Epanchin, but there were moments when, like a weak man, he readily regained his spirits and took quite a cheerful view. He was greatly relieved, for instance, when Nastasya Filippovna promised the two friends that she would give them her final decision on the evening of her birthday.

On the other hand, the strangest and most incredible rumour concerning no less honoured a person than Ivan Fyodorovitch appeared, alas! More and more well founded as time went on.

At the first blush it sounded perfectly wild. It was difficult to believe that Ivan Fyodorovich at his venerable time of life, with his excellent understanding and his practical knowledge of the world, and all the rest of it, could have fallen under Nastasya Filippovna's spell himself, and that it had come to such a pitch that this caprice had almost become a passion. What he was hoping for it was difficult to imagine; possibly for assistance from Ganya himself. Totsky suspected something of the kind, at any rate; he suspected the existence of some tacit agreement between the general and Ganya, resting on their comprehension of each other. But it is well known that a man carried away by passion, especially a man getting on in years, is quite blind, and prone to find grounds for hope where there are none; what's more, he loses his judgement and acts like a foolish child, however great an intellect he may have. It was known that the general had procured for Nastasya Filippovna's birthday some magnificent pearls, costing an immense sum, as a present from himself, and had thought a great deal about this present, though he knew that Nastasya Filippovna was not mercenary. On the day before the birthday he was in a perfect fever, though he successfully concealed his emotion. It was of those pearls that Madame Epanchin had heard. Lizaveta Prokofyevna had, it is true, many years' experience of her husband's flightiness, and had in fact got almost accustomed to it, but it was impossible to let such an incident pass; the rumour about the pearls made a great impression upon her. The general detected this beforehand; some words had been uttered on the previous day; he foresaw a momentous explanation coming, and dreaded it.

That was why he was particularly unwilling to lunch in the bosom of his family on the morning on which our story begins. Before Myshkin's appearance he had decided to escape on the pretext of urgent business. Making his escape often meant in the general's case simply running away. He wanted to gain that day at least, and above all that evening, undisturbed by unpleasantness. And suddenly the prince had turned up so appropriately. 'A perfect godsend!' thought the general to himself, as he went in to meet his wife.

Chapter 5

Madame Epanchin was jealous of the dignity of her family. What must it have been for her to hear without the slightest preparation that this Prince Myshkin, the last of the family, of whom she had heard something already, was no better than a poor idiot, was almost a beggar, and was ready to accept charity! The general reckoned on making an effect, impressing her at once, turning her attention in another direction and avoiding the question of the pearls under cover of this sensation.

When anything extraordinary happened, Madame Epanchin used to open her eyes very wide, and, throwing back her whole person, she would stare vaguely before her without uttering a word. She was a woman of large build and of the same age as her husband, with dark hair, still thick, though getting very grey. She was rather thin, with a somewhat aquiline nose, sunken yellow cheeks, and thin drawn-in lips. Her forehead was high but narrow; her large grey eyes had sometimes a most unexpected expression. She had once had the weakness to fancy that her eyes were particularly effective, and nothing had been able to efface the conviction.

'Receive him? You receive him now, at once?' And the lady opened her eyes to their very widest, gazing at Ivan Fyodorovitch, as he fidgeted before her.

'Oh, as far as that goes, there's no need of ceremony, if only you don't mind seeing him, my dear,' the general hastened to explain. 'He is quite a child and such a pathetic figure, he has some sort of fits. He has just arrived from Switzerland – came straight from the station. He is queerly dressed, like a German, and not a penny, literally; he is almost crying. I gave him twenty-five roubles, and want to find him some little post as a clerk in our office. And I beg you, *Mesdames*, to offer him lunch, for I think he is hungry too ...'

'You amaze me!' Madame Epanchin went on as before. 'Hungry and fits! What sort of fits?'

'Oh, they don't occur so frequently; and, besides, he is like a child, but well educated. I should like to ask you, *Mesdames*' – he addressed his daughters again – 'to put him through an examination; it would be as well to know what he is fit for.'

'An ex-am-in-a-tion?' drawled his wife, and in the utmost astonishment she rolled her eyes from her husband to her daughters and back again.

'Oh, my dear, don't take it in that sense ... but of course it's just as you please. I was meaning to be friendly to him and introduce him to the family, because it's almost an act of charity.'

'Introduce him to the family? From Switzerland?'

'That's no drawback, but, I repeat again, it's as you like. I thought of it because, in the first place, he is of the same name, and perhaps a relation; and besides, he's nowhere to lay his head. I supposed it would be rather interesting to you to see him, in fact, because after all he belongs to the same family.'

'Of course, *Maman*, if one needn't stand on ceremony with him. Besides he must be hungry after the journey; why not give him something to eat, if he has nowhere to go?' said the eldest girl, Alexandra.

'And if he is a perfect child, too. We could have a game of blind man's buff with him."

'Blind man's buff! What do you mean?'

'Oh, *Maman*, please leave off pretending!' Aglaia interrupted in vexation.

The second daughter, Adelaïda, who was of mirthful disposition, could not restrain herself and burst out laughing.

'Send for him, Papa, *Maman* gives you leave,' Aglaia decided.

The general rang, and told the servant to call the prince.

'But on condition he has a napkin tied round his neck when he sits at the table,' his wife insisted. 'Call Fyodor or Mavra ... to stand behind his chair and look after him while he eats. I only trust he is quiet when he has a fit. Does he wave his arms?'

'Oh, quite the opposite, he is very well bred and has charming manners; he is just a little simple sometimes. But here he is. Come, let me introduce Prince Myshkin, the last of the name, your namesake and perhaps your kinsman; make him welcome and be kind to him. Lunch will be served directly, Prince, so do us the honour ... But excuse me, I must hurry off, I am late.'

'We know where you are hurrying off to,' observed his wife majestically.

'I am in a hurry – I am in a hurry, my dear; I am late. Give him your albums, *Mesdames,* let him write something there for you, his handwriting is something exquisite. You should see how he wrote out for me in the old-world characters "The Abbot Pafnuty put his hand thereto." ... Well, goodbye.'

'Pafnuty? The abbot? Stop a minute – stop a minute. Where are you off to, and who is this Pafnuty?' his wife called with distinct annoyance and almost agitation after her escaping spouse.

'Yes, yes, my dear, it was an abbot who lived in old days ... But I am off to the Count's, I ought to have been there long ago; he fixed the hour himself... Goodbye for the present, Prince.'

The general retired with rapid steps.

'I know what count he is going to see,' Lizaveta Prokofyevna pronounced sharply, and she turned her eyes irritably to the prince. 'What was it?' she began peevishly and grumpily, trying to remember. 'Well, what was it? Ah, yes, what abbot?...'

'Maman,' Alexandra was beginning; and Aglaia even stamped her foot.

'Don't interfere with me, Alexandra Ivanovna,' snapped the mother. 'I want to know too. Sit here, Prince, here on this easy-chair, opposite me; no, here. Move into the sun, nearer the light, so that I may see you. Well, what abbot?'

'The Abbot Pafnuty,' answered Myshkin attentively and seriously.

'Pafnuty? That's interesting. Well, what about him?'

The lady asked her questions impatiently, rapidly, sharply, keeping her eyes fixed on the prince; and when Myshkin answered, she nodded her head at every word.

'The Abbot Pafnuty of the fourteenth century,' began Myshkin. 'He was at the head of a monastery on the Volga in what is now the province of Kostroma. He was famous for his holy life. He visited the Tatars, helped in the management of public affairs, and signed some document. I've seen a copy of the signature. I liked the handwriting and I imitated it. When the general wanted to see my writing just now so as to find me a job, I wrote several phrases in different handwritings, and among others I wrote "the Abbot Pafnuty put his hand thereto" in the abbot's own handwriting. The general liked it very much, and so he spoke of it just now.'

'Aglaia,' said Madame Epanchin, 'remember Pafnuty, or better write it down, else I always forget. But I thought it would be more interesting. Where is this signature?'

'I think it was left in the general's study, on the table.'

'Send at once and fetch it.'

'Hadn't I better write it again for you, if you like?'

'Of course, *Maman*,' said Alexandra. 'But now we had better have lunch, we are hungry.'

'Quite so,' assented her mother. 'Come along, Prince. Are you very hungry?'

'Yes, I've begun to be very hungry now, and I am very grateful to you.'

'It's a very good thing that you are polite, and I notice you are not nearly such a ... queer creature as you were described. Come along. Sit here, facing me.' She insisted on making Myshkin sit down when they went into the dining-room. 'I want to look at you. Alexandra, Adelaïda, help the prince to something. He is really not such an ... invalid, is he? Perhaps the table-napkin is not necessary... Used you to have a napkin tied round your neck at mealtimes, Prince?'

'Long ago, when I was seven, I believe I did, but now I usually have my napkin on my knee at mealtimes.'

'Quite right. And your fits?'

'Fits?' The prince was a little surprised. 'My fits don't happen very often now. But I don't know; I am told the climate here will make me worse.'

'He speaks well,' said the lady, turning to her daughters; she still nodded her head at every word Myshkin uttered. 'I didn't expect it. So it was all stuff and nonsense, as usual. Help yourself, Prince, and tell me where you were born and where you've been brought up? I want to know all about you; you interest me extremely.'

Myshkin thanked her, and while eating with excellent appetite began again repeating the story he had repeated several times that morning. The lady was more and more pleased with him; the girls too listened rather attentively. They worked out the relationship; it turned out that Myshkin knew his family-tree fairly well. But in spite of their efforts they could make out scarcely any connexion between him and Madame Epanchin. Among the grandfathers and the grandmothers a distant kinship might be discovered. The lady was particularly delighted with this dry subject, for she scarcely ever had a chance of indulging her tastes by discussing her pedigree. So she got up from table quite excited.

'Come, all of you, into our assembly-room,' she said, 'and we'll have coffee there. We have a room where we all meet,' she said to Myshkin, as she led him there. 'My little drawing-room, where we assemble and sit when we are alone and each of us does her work. Alexandra, my eldest daughter here, plays the piano or reads or sews; Adelaïda paints landscapes and portraits (and can never finish anything); and Aglaia sits doing nothing. I am not much good at work either; I can never get anything done. Well, here we are. Sit here, Prince by the fire and tell me something. I want to know how you tell a story. I want to be fully convinced, and when I see old Princess Byelokonsky, I shall tell her all about you. I want them all to be interested in you too. Come, tell me something.'

'But, *Maman*, it's very queer to tell a story like that,' observed Adelaïda, who had by now set up her easel, taken out her brushes and palette, and was setting to work copying from an engraving a landscape she had begun long ago.

Alexandra and Aglaia sat down on a little sofa and, folding their arms, prepared to listen to the conversation. Myshkin observed that he was a centre of attention on all sides.

'I would never say anything if I were told to like that,' observed Aglaia.

'Why not? What is there queer about it? Why shouldn't he tell me something? He has a tongue. I want to know how he can describe things. Come, anything. Tell us how you liked Switzerland, your first impression of it. You will see, he'll begin directly, and begin well too.'

'It was a strong impression'... Myshkin was beginning.

'There, you see,' the eager lady broke in, addressing her daughters, 'he has begun.'

'Do let him speak at least, *Maman*,' said Alexandra, checking her. 'This prince may be a great rogue and not an idiot at all,' she whispered to Aglaia.

'No doubt of it; I've seen that a long while,' answered Aglaia. 'And it's horrid of him to play a part. Is he trying to gain something by it?'

'My first impression was a very strong one,' Myshkin repeated. 'When I was brought from Russia through various German towns, I simply looked about in silence and, I remember, asked no questions. That was after a long series of violent and painful attacks of my illness, and when my complaint was at its worst and my fits frequent, I always sank into complete stupefaction. I lost my memory, and though my brain worked, the logical sequence of ideas seemed broken. I couldn't connect more than two or three ideas together. That's how it seems to me. When the fits became less frequent and violent, I became strong and healthy again as I am now. I remember I was insufferably sad; I wanted to cry. I was all the while lost in wonder and uneasiness. What affected me most was that everything was *strange*; I realised that. I was crushed by the strangeness of it. I was finally roused from this gloomy state, I remember, one evening on reaching Switzerland at Bale, and I was roused by the bray of an ass in the market-place. I was immensely struck with the ass, and for some reason extraordinarily pleased with it, and suddenly everything seemed to clear up in my head.'

'An ass? That's odd,' observed Lizaveta Prokofyevna. 'Yet there's nothing odd about it; one of us may even fall in love with an ass,' she observed, looking wrathfully at the laughing girls. 'It's happened in mythology. Go on, Prince.'

'I've been awfully fond of asses ever since; they have a special attraction for me. I began to ask about them because I'd never seen one before, and I understood at once what a useful creature it was – industrious, strong, patient, cheap, long-suffering. And so, through the ass, all Switzerland began to attract me, so that my melancholy passed completely.'

'That's all very strange, but you can pass over the ass; let's come to something else. Why do you keep laughing, Aglaia? And you, Adelaïda? The prince told us splendidly about the ass. He has seen it himself, but what have you seen? You've never been abroad.'

'I have seen an ass, *Maman*' said Adelaïda.

'And I've even heard one,' asserted Aglaia.

The three girls laughed again. Myshkin laughed with them.

'That's too bad of you,' observed the lady. 'You must excuse them, Prince, they are good-natured. I am always quarrelling with them, but I love them. They are flighty, thoughtless madcaps.'

'Why?' laughed Myshkin. 'I should have done the same in their place. But still I stand up for the ass; the ass is a good-natured and useful creature.'

'And are you good-natured, Prince? I ask from curiosity,' enquired Madame Epanchin.

They all laughed again.

'That hateful ass again! I wasn't thinking about it,' cried the lady. 'Believe me, Prince, I spoke without any ...'

'Hint? Oh, I believe you certainly.' And Myshkin went on laughing.

'I am glad you are laughing. I see you are a very good-natured young man,' said Lizaveta Prokofyevna.

'Sometimes not good-natured,' answered Myshkin.

'I am good-natured,' the lady put in unexpectedly, 'and if you like I am always good-natured, you may say; it's my one failing, for one oughtn't to be always good-natured. I get angry often with these girls, and still more with Ivan Fyodorovitch, but the worst of it is that I am always more good-natured when I am angry. Just before you came in I was angry and pretended that I didn't and couldn't understand anything. I am like that sometimes; like a child. Aglaia pulled me up. Thank you for the lesson, Aglaia. But it's all nonsense. I am not quite such a fool as I seem and as my daughters would like to make me out. I have a will of my own and am not easily put to shame. But I say this without malice. Come here, Aglaia, give me a kiss, there ... that's fondling enough,' she observed, when Aglaia had with real feeling kissed her on the lips and on the hand. 'Go on, Prince. Perhaps you will remember something more interesting than an ass.'

'I don't understand how anyone can describe straight off like that,' Adelaïda observed again. 'I couldn't think of anything.'

'But the prince will think of something, for he is extremely clever – at least ten times as clever as you are, very likely twelve times. I hope you will feel it after this. Prove it to them, Prince, go on. You really can pass over the ass now. What did you see abroad besides the ass?'

'It was clever about the ass too,' observed Alexandra. 'It was interesting what the prince told us of his invalid condition and how one external shock made everything pleasant to him. I've always been interested to know how people go out of their minds and recover again. Especially when it happens all of a sudden.'

'Yes, yes,' cried her mother eagerly. 'I see that you can be clever sometimes too. Well, come, stop laughing. You were speaking of Swiss scenery, Prince, I think. Well?'

'We reached Lucerne and I was taken to the lake. I felt how beautiful it was, but I felt dreadfully depressed by it,' said Myshkin.

'Why?' asked Alexandra.

'I don't know why. I always feel depressed and uneasy at the sight of such a landscape for the first time; I feel both happy and uneasy. But that was all while I was still ill.'

'I should awfully like to see it,' said Adelaïda. 'I can't understand why we don't go abroad. I haven't been able to find subjects for painting for the last two years. The East and the South have been painted long ago. Find me a subject for a picture, Prince.'

'I know nothing about it. I should have thought you've only to see and to paint.'

'I don't know how to see things.'

'Why do you keep talking in riddles? I can't make head or tail of it,' interrupted her mother. 'What do you mean by not knowing how to see? You've got eyes; see with them. If you can't see here, you won't learn how to abroad. Better tell us how you saw things yourself, Prince.'

'Yes, that would be better,' added Adelaïda. 'The prince has learnt to see things abroad.'

'I don't know. I simply got better abroad; I don't know whether I learnt to see things. But I was almost all the time very happy.'

'Happy? You know how to be happy?' cried Aglaia. 'Then how can you say you didn't learn to see things? You might teach us, even.'

'Please do!' laughed Adelaïda.

'I can't teach anything,' Myshkin laughed too. 'I spent almost all my time abroad in the same Swiss village. I rarely went excursions, and only to a short distance. What could I teach you? At first I was simply not dull; I soon began to grow stronger. Then every day became precious to me, and more precious as time went on, so that I began to notice it. I used to go to bed very happy and get up happier still. But it would be hard to say why.'

'So you didn't want to go away? You had no desire to go anywhere?' asked Alexandra.

'At the beginning, quite at the beginning, I had, and I used to become very restless. I was continually thinking of the life I would lead: I wanted to know what life had in store for me. I was particularly restless at some moments. You know there are such moments, especially in solitude. There was a small waterfall there; it fell from a height on the mountain, such a tiny thread, almost perpendicular – foaming, white and splashing. Though it fell from a great height it didn't seem so high; it was the third of a mile away, but it only looked about fifty paces. I used to like listening to the sound of it at night. At such moments I was sometimes overcome with great restlessness; sometimes too at midday I wandered on the mountains, and stood alone halfway up a mountain surrounded by great ancient resinous pine trees; on the crest of the rock an old medieval castle in ruins; our little village far, far below, scarcely visible; bright sunshine, blue sky, and the terrible stillness. At such times I felt something was drawing me away, and I kept fancying that if I walked straight on, far, far away and reached that line where sky and earth meet, there I should find the key to the mystery, there I should see a new life a thousand times richer and more turbulent than ours. I dreamed of some great town like Naples, full of palaces, noise, roar, life. And I dreamed of all sorts of things, indeed. But afterwards I fancied one might find a wealth of life even in prison.'

'That last edifying reflection I read when I was twelve in my "Reader," ' said Aglaia.

'That's all philosophy,' observed Adelaïda. 'You are a philosopher and have come to instruct us.'

'Perhaps you are right,' smiled Myshkin. 'I am really a philosopher perhaps, and – who knows? – perhaps I really have a notion of instructing ... That's possible, truly.'

'And your philosophy is just like Yevlampia Nikolayevna's,' Aglaia put in again. 'She is the widow of a clerk, who comes to see us, rather like a poor relation. Cheapness is her one object in life – to live as cheaply as possible, and she talks of nothing but farthings. And yet she has money, you know; she is sly. That's like your wealth of life in prison; perhaps, too, your four years of happiness in the country for which you bartered your Naples; and you seem to have gained by the bargain, though it was a petty one.'

'There may be two opinions about life in prison,' said Myshkin. 'A man who spent twelve years in prison told me something. He was one of the invalids in the care of my professor. He had fits;

he was sometimes restless, wept, and even tried to kill himself. His life in prison had been a very sad one, I assure you, but not at all petty. Yet he had no friends but a spider and a tree that grew under his window… But I'd better tell you how I met another man last year. There was one very strange circumstance about it – strange because such things rarely happen. This man had once been led out with others to the scaffold and a sentence of death was read over him. He was to be shot for a political offence. Twenty moments later a reprieve was read to them, and they were condemned to another punishment instead. Yet the interval between those two sentences, twenty minutes or at least a quarter of an hour, he passed in the fullest conviction that he would die in a few minutes. I was always eager to listen when he recalled his sensations at that time, and I often questioned him about it. He remembered it all with extraordinary distinctness and used to say that he never would forget those minutes. Twenty paces from the scaffold, round which soldiers and other people were standing, there were three posts stuck in the ground, as there were several criminals. The three first were led up, bound to the posts, the death-dress (a long white gown) was put on, and white caps were pulled over their eyes so that they should not see the guns; then a company of several soldiers was drawn up against each post. My friend was the eighth on the list, so he had to be one of the third set. The priest went to each in turn with a cross. He had only five minutes more to live. He told me that those five minutes seemed to him an infinite time, a vast wealth; he felt that he had so many lives left in those five minutes that there was no need yet to think of the last moment, so much so that he divided his time up. He set aside time to take leave of his comrades, two minutes for that; then he kept another two minutes to think for the last time; and then a minute to look about him for the last time. He remembered very well having divided his time like that. He was dying at twenty-seven, strong and healthy. As he took leave of his comrades, he remembered asking one of them a somewhat irrelevant question and being particularly interested in the answer. Then when he had said goodbye, the two minutes came that he had set apart for *thinking* to himself. He knew beforehand what he would think about. He wanted to realise as quickly and clearly as possible how it could be that now he existed and was living and in three minutes he would be *something* – someone or something. But what? Where? He meant to decide all that in those two minutes! Not far off there was a church, and the gilt roof was glittering in the bright sunshine. He remembered that he stared very persistently at that roof and the light flashing from it; he could not tear himself away from the light. It seemed to him that those rays were his new nature and that in three minutes he would somehow melt into them … The uncertainty and feeling of aversion for that new thing which would be and was just coming was awful. But he said that nothing was so dreadful at that time as the continual thought, "What if I were not to die! What if I could go back to life – what eternity! And it would all be mine! I would turn every minute into an age; I would lose nothing, I would count every minute as it passed, I would not waste one!" He said that this idea turned to such a fury at last that he longed to be shot quickly.'

Myshkin suddenly ceased speaking; everyone expected him to go on and draw some conclusion.

'Have you finished?' asked Aglaia.

'What? Yes,' said Myshkin, rousing himself from momentary dreaminess.

'But what did you tell that story for?'

'Oh … something in our talk reminded me of it…'

'You are very disconnected,' observed Alexandra. 'You probably meant to show, Prince, that not one instant of life can be considered petty, and that sometimes five minutes is a precious treasure. That's all very laudable, but let me ask, how did that friend who told you such horrors … he was reprieved, so he was presented with that 'eternity of life.' What did he do with that wealth afterwards? Did he live counting each moment?'

'Oh no, he told me himself. I asked him about that too. He didn't live like that at all; he wasted many, many minutes.'

'Well, there you have it tried. So it seems it's impossible really to live "counting each moment." For some reason it's impossible.'

'Yes, for some reason it is impossible,' repeated Myshkin. 'I thought so myself… and yet I somehow can't believe it…'

'Then you think you will live more wisely than anyone?' said Aglaia. 'Yes, I have thought that too sometimes.'

'And you think so still?'

'Yes … I think so still,' answered Myshkin, looking at Aglaia with the same gentle and even timid smile, but he laughed again at once and looked gaily at her.

'That's modest,' said Aglaia almost irritably.

'But how brave you are, you laugh! But I was so impressed by his story that I dreamt of it afterwards. I... dreamt of that five minutes Once more he looked earnestly and searchingly from one to another of his listeners.

'You are not angry with me for anything?' he asked suddenly, seeming embarrassed, but looking them straight in the face.

'What for?' cried the three young ladies in surprise.

'Why, because I seem all the while to be preaching to you.'

They all laughed.

'If you are angry, don't be,' he said. 'I know for myself that I have lived less than others and that I know less of life than anyone. Perhaps I talk very queerly at times ...'

And he was overwhelmed with confusion.

'If you're happy, as you say, you must have lived more, not less, than others. Why do you make a pretence and apologise?' Aglaia persisted naggingly. 'And please don't mind about preaching to us; it's no sign of superiority on your part. With your quietism one might fill a hundred years of life with happiness. If one shows you an execution or if one holds out one's finger to you, you will draw equally edifying reflections from both and be quite satisfied. Life is easy like that.'

'I can't make out why you are so cross,' said Madame Epanchin, who had been watching the speakers' faces for some time, 'and I can't make out what you are talking about either. Why a finger? What nonsense! The prince talks splendidly, only rather sadly. Why do you discourage him? When he began he was laughing, and now he is quite glum.'

'It's all right, *Maman*. But it's a pity you haven't seen an execution, Prince, I should like to have asked you one question.'

'I have seen an execution,' answered Myshkin.

'You have?' cried Aglaia. 'I ought to have guessed it. That's the last straw! If you've seen that, how can you say that you were happy all the time? Didn't I tell you the truth?'

'But do they have executions in your village?' asked Adelaïda.

'I saw it at Lyons. I visited the town with Schneider; he took me with him. We chanced upon it directly we arrived.'

'Well, did you like it? Was there much that was edifying and instructive?' asked Aglaia.

'I did not like it at all and I was rather ill afterwards, but I must confess I was riveted to the spot; I could not take my eyes off it.'

'I couldn't have taken my eyes off it either,' said Aglaia.

'They don't like women to look on at it; they even write about such women in the papers.'

'I suppose, if they consider that it's not fit for women, they mean to infer (and so justify it) that it is fit for men. I congratulate them on their logic. And you think so too, no doubt.'

'Tell us about the execution,' Adelaïda interrupted.

'I don't feel at all inclined to now.' Myshkin was confused and almost frowned.

'You seem to grudge telling us about it,' Aglaia said tauntingly.

'No, but I've just been describing that execution.'

'Describing it to whom?'

'To your footman while I was waiting …'

'To which footman?' he heard on all sides.

'The one who sits in the entry, with grey hair and a red face. I sat in the entry waiting to see Ivan Fyodorovitch.'

'That's odd,' said the general's wife.

'The prince is a democrat,' Aglaia rapped out. 'Well, if you told Alexey about it, you can't refuse us.'

'I simply must hear about it,' said Adelaïda.

'One thought came into my mind just now,' Myshkin said to her, growing rather more eager again (he seemed easily roused to confiding eagerness), 'when you asked me for a subject for a picture, to suggest that you should paint the face of the condemned man the moment before the blade falls, when he is still standing on the scaffold before he lies down on the plank.'

'The face? The face alone?' asked Adelaïda. 'That would be a strange subject. And what sort of picture would it make?'

'I don't know. Why not?' Myshkin insisted warmly. 'I saw a picture like that at Bale not long ago. I should like to tell you about it… I'll tell you about it someday … It struck me very much.'

'You shall certainly tell us afterwards about the picture at Bale,' said Adelaïda; 'and now explain the picture of this execution. Can you tell me how you imagine it to yourself? How is one to draw the face? Is it to be only the face? What sort of a face is it?'

'It's practically the minute before death,' Myshkin began with perfect readiness, carried away by his memories and to all appearance instantly forgetting everything else, 'that moment when he has just mounted the ladder and has just stepped on to the scaffold. Then he glanced in my direction. I looked at his face and I understood it all ... But how can one describe it? I wish, I do wish that you or someone would paint it. It would be best if it were you. I thought at the time that a picture of it would do good. You know one has to imagine everything that has been before – everything, everything. He has been in prison awaiting execution for a week at least; he has been reckoning on the usual formalities, on the sentence being forwarded somewhere for signature and not coming back again for a week. But now by some chance this business was over sooner. At five o'clock in the morning he was asleep. It was at the end of October; at five o'clock it was still cold and dark. The superintendent of the prison came in quietly with the guard and touched him carefully on the shoulder. He sat up, leaning on his elbow, saw the light, asked "What's the matter?" "The execution is at ten o'clock." He was half awake and couldn't take it in, and began objecting that the sentence wouldn't be ready for a week. But when he was fully awake he left off protesting and was silent – so I was told. Then he said, "But it's hard it should be so sudden ..." And again he was silent and wouldn't say anything more. The next three or four hours are spent on the usual things: seeing the priest, breakfast at which he is given wine, coffee and beef (isn't that a mockery? Only think how cruel it is! Yet on the other hand, would you believe it, these innocent people act in good faith and are convinced that it's humane); then the toilet (do you know what a criminal's toilet is?); and at last they take him through the town to the scaffold ... I think that he too must have thought he had an endless time left to live, while he was being driven through the town. He must have thought on the way, 'There's a long time left, three streets more. I shall pass through this one, then through the next, then there's that one left where there's a baker's on the right ... It'll be a long time before we get to the baker's!"

'There were crowds of people, there was noise and shouting; ten thousand faces, ten thousand eyes – all that he has had to bear, and, worst of all, the thought, "They are ten thousand, but not one of them is being executed, and I am to be executed." Well, all that is preparatory. There is a ladder to the scaffold. Suddenly at the foot of the ladder he began to cry, and he was a strong manly fellow; he had been a great criminal, I was told. The priest never left him for a moment; he drove with him in the cart and talked with him all the while. I doubt whether he heard; he might begin listening and would not understand more than two words. So it must have been.

At last he began going up the ladder; his legs were tied together so that he could only move with tiny steps. The priest, who must have been an intelligent man, left off speaking and only gave him the cross to kiss. At the foot of the ladder he was very pale, and when he was at the top and standing on the scaffold, he became as white as paper, as white as writing paper. His legs must have grown weak and wooden, and I expect he felt sick – as though something were choking him and that made a sort of tickling in his throat. Have you ever felt that when you were frightened, or in awful moments when all your reason is left, but it has no power? I think that if one is faced by inevitable destruction – if a house is falling upon you, for instance – one must feel a great longing to sit down, close one's eyes and wait, come what may... When that weakness was beginning, the priest with a rapid movement hastily put the cross to his lips – a little plain silver cross – he kept putting it to his lips every minute. And every time the cross touched his lips, he opened his eyes and seemed for a few seconds to come to life again, and his legs moved. He kissed the cross greedily; he made haste to kiss, as though in haste not to forget to provide himself with something in case of need, but I doubt whether he had any religious feeling at the time. And so it was till he was laid on the plank ... It's strange that people rarely faint at these last moments. On the contrary, the brain is extraordinarily lively and must be working at a tremendous rate – at a tremendous rate, like a machine at full speed. I fancy that there is a continual throbbing of ideas of all sorts, always unfinished and perhaps absurd too, quite irrelevant ideas: "That man is looking at me. He has a wart on his forehead. One of the executioner's buttons is rusty" ... and yet all the while one knows and remembers everything. There is one point which can never be forgotten, and one can't faint, and everything moves and turns about it, about that point. And only think that it must be like that up to the last quarter of a second, when his head lies on the block and he waits and ... *knows,* and suddenly hears above him the clang of the iron! He must hear that! If I were lying there, I should listen on purpose and hear. It may last only the tenth part of a second, but one would be sure to hear it. And only fancy, it's still disputed whether, when the head is cut off, it knows for a second after that it has been cut off! What an idea! And what if it knows it for five seconds!

'Paint the scaffold so that only the last step can be distinctly seen in the foreground and the criminal having just stepped on it;

his head, his face as white as paper; the priest holding up the cross, the man greedily putting forward his blue lips and looking – and aware of everything. The cross and the head – that's the picture. The priest's face and the executioner's, his two attendants and a few heads and eyes below might be painted in the background, in half light, as the setting ... That's the picture!'

Myshkin ceased speaking and looked at them all.

'That's nothing like quietism, certainly,' said Alexandra to herself.

'And now tell us how you were in love,' said Adelaïda.

Myshkin looked at her with astonishment.

'Listen,' Adelaïda said, seeming rather hurried. 'You promised to tell us about the Bale picture, but now I should like to hear how you have been in love. Don't deny it, you must have been. Besides, as soon as you begin describing anything, you cease to be a philosopher.'

'As soon as you have finished telling us anything, you seem to be ashamed of what you've said,' Aglaia observed suddenly. 'Why is that?'

'How stupid that is!' snapped her mother, looking indignantly at Aglaia.

'It's not clever,' Alexandra assented.

'Don't believe her, Prince,' said Madame Epanchin, turning to him. 'She does it on purpose from a sort of malice; she has really not been so badly brought up. Don't think the worse of them for teasing you like this; they must be up to some mischief. But they like you already, I know. I know their faces.'

'I know their faces too,' said Myshkin with peculiar emphasis.

'What do you mean?' asked Adelaïda curiously.

'What do you know about our faces?' the two others enquired too.

But Myshkin did not speak and was grave. They all waited for his answer.

'I'll tell you afterwards,' he said gently and gravely.

'You are trying to rouse our curiosity,' cried Aglaia. 'And what solemnity!'

'Very well,' Adelaïda interposed hurriedly again, 'but if you are such a connoisseur in faces, you certainly must have been in love, so I guessed right. Tell us about it.'

'I haven't been in love,' answered Myshkin as gently and gravely as before. 'I... have been happy in a different way.'

'How? In what?'

'Very well, I'll tell you,' said Myshkin, as though meditating profoundly.

Chapter 6

'You are all looking at me with such interest,' began Myshkin, 'that if I didn't satisfy it you might be angry with me. No, I am joking,' he added quickly, with a smile. 'There were lots of children there, and I was always with the children, only with the children. They were the children of the village, a whole crowd of schoolchildren. It was not that I taught them. Oh, no, there was a schoolmaster for that – Jules Thibaut. I did teach them too, perhaps, but for the most part I was simply with them, and all those four years were spent in their company. I wanted nothing else. I used to tell them everything; I concealed nothing from them. Their fathers and relations were all cross with me, for the children couldn't get on without me at last, and were always flocking round me, and the schoolmaster at last became my chief enemy. I made many enemies there, and all on account of the children. Even Schneider reproved me. And what were they afraid of? Children can be told anything – anything. I've always been struck by seeing how little grownup people understand children, how little parents even understand their own children. Nothing should be concealed from children on the pretext that they are little and that it is too early for them to understand. What a miserable and unfortunate idea! And how readily the children detect that their fathers consider them too little to understand anything, though they understand everything. Grown-up people do not know that a child can give exceedingly good advice even in the most difficult case. Oh, dear! When that pretty little bird looks at you, happy and confiding, it's a shame for you to deceive it. I call them birds because there's nothing better than a bird in the world. What really set all the village against me was something that happened ... but Thibaut was simply envious of me. At first he used to shake his head and wonder how it was the children understood everything from me and scarcely anything from him; and then he began laughing at me when I told him that neither of us could teach them anything, but that they can teach us. And how could he be envious of me and say things against me, when he spent his life with children himself! The soul is healed by being with children ... There was one patient in Schneider's institution, a very unhappy man. I doubt whether there could be any unhappiness equal to his. He was there to be treated for insanity. In my opinion he was not mad, it was simply that he was frightfully miserable; that was all that was the matter with him. And if only you knew what our children were to him in the end ... But I'd better tell you about that patient another time. I'll tell you now how it all began. At first the children didn't take to me. I was so big, I am always so clumsy; I know I am ugly too ... and then I was a foreigner. The children used to laugh at me at first, and they began throwing stones at me after they saw me kiss Marie. And I only kissed her once ... No, don't laugh.' Myshkin made haste to check the smile on the faces of his listeners. 'It was not a question of love. If only you knew what an unhappy being she was, you would be very sorry for her, as I was. She lived in our village. Her mother was an old woman. One of the two windows of their tumbledown little house was set apart, by permission of the village authorities, and from it the old woman was allowed to sell laces, thread, tobacco and soap. It all came to a few halfpence, and that was what she lived on. She was an invalid; her legs were all swollen so that she could not move from her seat. Marie was her daughter, a girl of twenty, weak and thin. She had been consumptive for a long time, but she went from house to house doing hard work – scrubbing floors, washing, sweeping out yards and minding cattle. A French commercial traveller seduced her and took her away, and a week later deserted her and went off on the sly. She made her way home begging, all mud-stained and in rags with her shoes coming to pieces. She was a week walking back, spent the nights in the fields and caught a fearful cold. Her feet were covered with sores, her hands were chapped and swollen. She wasn't pretty before, though; only her eyes were gentle, kind and innocent. She was extremely silent. Once when she was at work she began singing, and I remember everyone was surprised and began laughing. "Marie singing! What Marie singing!" She was fearfully abashed and did not open her lips again. People were still kind to her in those days, but when she came back broken down and ill, no one had any sympathy for her. How cruel people are in that way! What hard ideas they have about such things! Her mother, to begin with, received her with anger and contempt: "You have disgraced me." She was the first to abandon her to shame. As soon as they heard in the village that Marie had come home, everyone went to have a look at her, and almost all the village assembled in the old woman's cottage – old men, children, women, girls, everyone – an eager, hurrying crowd. Marie was lying on the ground at the old woman's feet, hungry and in rags, and she was weeping. When they all ran in, she hid her face in her dishevelled hair and lay face downwards on the floor. They all stared at her, as though she were a reptile; the old people blamed and upbraided her, the young people laughed; the women reviled and abused her and looked at her with loathing, as though she had been a spider. Her mother allowed it all; she sat there nodding her head and approving. The mother was very ill at the time and almost dying: two months later she did die. She knew she was dying, but up to the time of her death she didn't dream of being reconciled to her daughter. She didn't speak one word to her, turned her out to sleep in the entry, scarcely gave her anything to eat. She had to be constantly bathing her bad legs in hot water. Marie bathed her legs every day and waited on her. She accepted all her services in silence and never said a kind word to her. Marie put up with everything, and afterwards when I made her acquaintance, I noticed that she thought it all right and looked on herself as the lowest of the low. When the old mother was completely bedridden, the old women of the village came to sit up with her in turns, as their custom is. Then they gave up feeding Marie altogether, and in the village everyone drove her away and no one would even give her work, as before. Everyone, as it were, spat on her, and the men no longer looked on her as a woman even; they would say all sorts of nasty things to her. Sometimes, though not often, when the men got drunk on Sunday, they would amuse themselves by throwing farthings to her, just flinging them on the ground. Marie would pick them up without a word. She had begun to spit blood by that time. At last her clothes were in absolute tatters, so that she was ashamed to show herself in the village. She had gone barefoot since she came back. Then the children particularly, the whole troop of them – there were about forty schoolchildren – began jeering, and even throwing dirt at her. She asked the cowherd to let her look after the cows, but he drove her away. Then she began going off for the whole day with the flock of her own accord, without permission. As she was of great use to the cowherd, and he noticed it, he no longer drove her away, and sometimes even gave her bread and cheese, what was left from his dinner. He looked upon this as a great kindness on his part. When her mother died, the pastor did not scruple to heap shame on Marie in church before all the people. Marie stood crying by the coffin, as she was, in her rags. A crowd of people had collected to look at her standing by the coffin and crying. Then the pastor – he was a young man, and his whole ambition was to become a great preacher – pointed to Marie and, addressing them all, said, "Here you see the cause of this worthy woman's death" (and it was not true, for the woman had been ill for two years); "here she stands before you and dares not look at you, for she has been marked out by the finger of God; here she is, barefoot and ragged – a warning to all who lose their virtue! Who is she? Her daughter!" and so on in the same style. And, would you believe it, this infamy pleased almost everyone! But… then things took a different turn. The children took a line of their own, for by then they were all on my side, and had begun to love Marie.

'This was how it happened … I wanted to do something for Marie. She was badly in want of money, but I never had a farthing at that time. I had a little diamond pin, and I sold it to a pedler who went from village to village buying and selling old clothes. He gave me eight francs, and it was certainly worth forty. I was a long time trying to meet Marie alone. At last we met by a hedge outside the village, on a by-path to the mountain, behind a tree. Then I gave her the eight francs and told her to take care of it, because I should have no more. Then I kissed her and said that she mustn't think I had any evil intent, and that I kissed her not because I was in love with her, but because I was very sorry for her, and that I had never, from the very beginning, thought of her as guilty but only as unhappy. I wanted very much to comfort her at once and to persuade her that she shouldn't consider herself below everyone, but I think she didn't understand. I saw that at once, though she scarcely spoke all the time and stood before me looking down and horribly abashed. When I had finished, she kissed my hand, and I at once took her hand and would have kissed it, but she pulled it away. It was then the children saw us, the whole lot of them. I learnt afterwards that they had been keeping watch on me for some time. They began whistling, clapping their hands and laughing, and Marie ran away. I tried to speak to them, but they began throwing stones at me. The same day everyone knew of it, the whole village. The whole brunt of it fell on Marie again; they began to dislike her more than ever. I even heard that they wanted to have her punished by the authorities, but, thank goodness, that didn't come off. But the children gave her no peace: they teased her more than ever and threw dirt at her; they chased her, she ran away from them, she with her weak lungs, panting and gasping for breath. They ran after her, shouting and reviling her. Once I positively had a fight with them. Then I began talking to them; I talked to them every day as much as I could. They sometimes stopped and listened, though they still abused me. I told them how unhappy Marie was; soon they left off abusing me and walked away in silence. Little by little, we began talking together. I concealed nothing from them, I told them the whole story. They listened with great interest and soon began to be sorry for Marie. Some of them greeted her in a friendly way when they met. It's the custom there when you meet people, whether you know them or not, to bow and wash them good-morning. I can fancy how astonished Marie was. One day two little girls got some things to eat and gave them to her; they came and told me of it. They told me that Marie cried, and that now they loved her very much. Soon all of them began to love her, and at the same time they began to love me too. They took to coming to see me often, and always asked me to tell them stories. I think I must have told them well, for they were very fond of listening to me. And afterwards I read and studied simply to have things to tell them, and for the remaining three years I used to tell them stories. Later on, when everybody blamed me – and even Schneider – for talking to them like grown-up people and concealing nothing from them, I said that it was a shame to deceive them; that they understood everything anyway, however much things were concealed from them, and that they learnt it perhaps in a bad way, but not so from me. One need only remember one's own childhood. They did not agree … I kissed Marie a fortnight before her mother died; by the time the pastor delivered his harangue, all the children had come over to my side. I at once told them of the pastor's action and explained it to them. They were all angry with him, and some of them were so enraged that they threw stones and broke his windows. I stopped them for that was wrong, but everyone in the village heard of it at once, and they began to accuse me of corrupting the children. Then they all realised that the children loved Marie, and were dreadfully horrified, but Marie was happy. The children were forbidden to meet her, but they ran out to where she kept the herds, nearly half a mile from the village. They carried her dainties, and some simply ran out to hug and kiss her, say *"Je vous aime, Marie,"* and ran back as fast as their legs would carry them. Marie was almost beside herself at such unlooked-for happiness; she had never dreamed of the possibility of it. She was shamefaced and joyful. What the children liked doing most, especially the girls, was running to tell her that I loved her and had talked to them a great deal about her. They told her that I told them all about her, and that now they loved her and pitied her and always would feel the same. Then they would run to me, and with such joyful, busy faces tell me that they had just seen Marie and that Marie sent her greetings to me. In the evenings I used to walk to the waterfall; there was one spot there quite hidden from the village and surrounded by poplars. There they would gather round me in the evening, some even coming secretly. I think they got immense enjoyment out of my love for Marie, and that was the only point in which I deceived them. I didn't tell them that they were mistaken, that I was not in love with Marie, but simply very sorry for her. I saw that they wanted to have it as they imagined and had settled among themselves, and so I said nothing and let it seem that they guessed right. And what delicacy and tenderness were shown by those little hearts! They couldn't bear to think that while their dear Leon loved Marie she should be so badly dressed and without shoes. Would you believe it, they managed to get her shoes and stockings and linen, and even a dress of some sort. How they managed to do it I can't make out. The whole troop worked. When I questioned them, they only laughed merrily, and the girls clapped their hands and kissed me. I sometimes went to see Marie secretly too. She was by that time very ill and could scarcely walk. In the end she gave up working for the herdsman, but yet she went out every morning with the cattle. She used to sit a little apart. There was a ledge jutting out in an overhanging, almost vertical rock there. She used to sit out of sight on the stone, right in the corner, and she sat there almost without moving all day, from early morning till the cattle went home.

She was by then so weak from consumption that she sat most of the time with her eyes shut and her head leaning against the rock and dozed, breathing painfully. Her face was as thin as a skeleton's, and the sweat stood out on her brow and temples. That was how I always found her. I used to come for a moment, and I too did not want to be seen. As soon as I appeared, Marie would start, open her eyes and fall to kissing my hands. I no longer tried to take them away, for it was a happiness to her. All the while I sat with her she trembled and wept. She did indeed try sometimes to speak, but it was difficult to understand her. She seemed like a crazy creature in terrible excitement and delight. Sometimes the children came with me. At such times they generally stood a little way off and kept watch to protect us from anyone or anything, and that was an extraordinary pleasure to them. When we went away, Marie was again left alone with her eyes shut and her head leaning against the rock, dreaming perhaps of something. One morning she could no longer go out with the cows and remained at home in her deserted cottage. The children heard of it at once, and almost all of them went to ask after her that day. She lay in bed, entirely alone. For two days she was tended only by the children, who ran in to her by turns, but when the news reached the village that Marie was really dying, the old women went to sit with her and look after her. I think the villagers had begun to pity Marie; anyway, they left off scolding the children and preventing them from seeing her, as they had done before. Marie was drowsy all the time, but her sleep was broken – she coughed terribly. The old women drove the children away, but they ran under the window sometimes only for a moment, just to say, *"Bonjour, notre bonne Marie."* And as soon as she caught sight of them or heard them, she seemed to revive and, regardless of the old women, she would try to raise herself on her elbow, nod to them and thank them. They used to bring her dainties as before, but she scarcely ate anything. I assure you that, thanks to them, she died almost happy. Thanks to them she forgot her bitter trouble; they brought her, as it were, forgiveness, for up to the very end she looked upon herself as a great sinner. They were like birds beating their wings against her window and calling to her every morning, *"Nous t'aimons, Marie."* She died very soon. I had expected her to last much longer. The day before her death I went to her at sunset; I think she knew me, and I pressed her hand for the last time. How wasted it was! And next morning they came to me and said that Marie was dead. Then the children could not be restrained. They decked her coffin with flowers and put a wreath on her head. The pastor did no dishonour to the dead in the church. There were not many people at the funeral, only a few, attracted by curiosity, but when the coffin had to be carried out, the children all rushed forward to carry it themselves. Though they were not strong enough to bear the weight of it alone, they helped to carry it, and all ran after the coffin, crying. Marie's grave has been kept by the children ever since; they planted roses round it and deck it with flowers every year.

'But it was after the funeral that I was most persecuted by the villagers on account of the children. The pastor and the schoolmaster were at the bottom of it. The children were strictly forbidden even to meet me, and Schneider made it his duty to see that this prohibition was effectual. But we did see each other all the same; we communicated from a distance by signs. They used to send me little notes. In the end things were smoothed over, but it was very nice at that time. This persecution brought me nearer to the children than ever. In the last year I was almost reconciled to Thibaut and the pastor. And Schneider argued a great deal with me about my pernicious "system" with children. As though I had a system! At last Schneider uttered a very strange thought – it was just before I went away. He told me that he had come to the conclusion that I was a complete child myself, altogether a child; that it was only in face and figure that I was like a grown-up person, but that in development, in soul, in character, and perhaps in intelligence, I was not grown up, and that so I should remain, if I lived to be sixty. I laughed very much. He was wrong, of course, for I am not a child. But in one thing he is right: I don't like being with grown-up people. I've known that a long time. I don't like it because I don't know how to get on with them. Whatever they say to me, however kind they are to me, I always feel somehow oppressed with them, and I am awfully glad when I can get away to my companions; and my companions have always been children, not because I am a child myself, but simply because I always was attracted by children. When I was first in the village, at the time when I used to take melancholy walks in the mountains alone, when I sometimes, especially at midday, met the whole noisy troop running out of school with their satchels and slates, with shouts and games and laughter, my whole soul went out to them at once. I don't know how it was, but I had a sort of intense happy sensation at every meeting with them. I stood still and laughed with happiness, looking at their little legs for ever flying along, at the boys and girls running together, at their laughter and their tears (for many of them managed to fight, cry, make it up and begin playing again on the way home from school), and then I forgot all my mournful thoughts. Afterwards, for the last three years, I couldn't even understand how and why people are sad. My whole life was centred on the children.

'I never reckoned on leaving the village, and it did not enter my mind that I should one day come back here to Russia. I thought I would always stay there. But I saw at last that Schneider couldn't go on keeping me; and then something turned up, so important apparently that Schneider himself urged me to go, and answered for me that I was coming. I shall see into it and take advice. My life will perhaps be quite changed, but that doesn't matter. What does matter is that my whole life is already changed. I left a great deal there – too much. It's all gone. As I sat in the train, I thought, "Now I am going among people. I know nothing, perhaps, but a new life has begun for me." I determined to do my work resolutely and honestly. I may find it dull and difficult among people. In the first place, I resolved to be courteous and open with everyone. "No one will expect more than that of me. Perhaps here, too, they will look on me as a child, but no matter." Everyone looks on me as an idiot, too, for some reason. I was so ill at one time that I really was almost like an idiot. But can I be an idiot now, when I am able to see for myself that people look upon me as an idiot? As I come in, I think. "I see they look upon me as an idiot, and yet I am sensible and they don't guess it." … I often have that thought.

'It was only at Berlin, when I got some little letters which they had already managed to write me, I realised how I loved the children. It's very painful getting the first letter! How distressed they were seeing me off! They'd been preparing for my going for a month beforehand. *"Leon s'en va, Leon s'en va pour toujours!"* We met every evening as before at the waterfall and talked of our parting. Sometimes we were as merry as before; only when we separated at night, they kissed and hugged me warmly, which they had not done previously. Some of them ran in secret to see me by themselves, simply to kiss and hug me alone, not before all the others. When I was setting off, they all, the whole flock of them, went with me to the station. The railway station was about a mile from our village. They tried not to cry, but some of them could not control themselves and wailed aloud, especially the girls. We made haste so as not to be late, but every now and then one of them would rush out of the crowd to throw his little arms round me and kiss me, and would stop the whole procession simply for that. And although we were in a hurry, we all stopped and waited for him to say goodbye. When I'd taken my seat and the train had started, they all shouted "Hurrah!" and stood waiting there till the train was out of sight. I gazed at them too ... Do you know, when I came in here and looked at your sweet faces – I notice people's faces very much now – and heard your first words, my heart felt light for the first time since then. I thought then that perhaps I really was a lucky person. I know that one doesn't often meet people whom one likes from the first, yet here I've come straight from the railway station and I meet you. I know very well that one's ashamed to talk of one's feelings to everyone, but I talk to you without feeling ashamed. I am an unsociable person and very likely I may not come to you again for a long time. Don't take that as a slight. I don't say it because I don't value your friendship, and please don't think that I have taken offence at something. You asked me about your faces and what I noticed in them. I shall be delighted to tell you that. You have a happy face, Adelaïda Ivanovna, the most sympathetic of the three. Besides your being very good-looking, one feels when one looks at you, "She has the face of a kind sister." You approach one simply and gaily, but you are quick to see into the heart. That's how your face strikes me. You, Alexandra Ivanovna, have a fine and very sweet face too, but perhaps you have some secret trouble. Your heart is certainly of the kindest, but you are not light-hearted. There's a peculiar something in your face, such as we see in Holbein's *Madonna in Dresden*, Well, so much for your face. Am I good at guessing? You took me to be so yourselves. But from your face, Lizaveta Prokofyevna,' he turned suddenly to Madame Epanchin, 'from your face I feel positively certain that you are a perfect child in everything, everything, in good and bad alike, in spite of your age. You are not angry with me for saying so? You know what I think of children. And don't think it's from simplicity that I have spoken so openly about your faces. Oh no, not at all! Perhaps I have my own idea in doing it.'

Chapter 7

When Myshkin ceased speaking, they were all looking at him gaily, even Aglaia, and particularly Lizaveta Prokofyevna.

'Well, they have put you through your examination,' she cried. 'Well, young ladies, you thought you were going to patronise him as a poor relation, but he scarcely deigns to accept you, and only with the proviso that he won't come often! It makes us look silly, especially Ivan Fyodorovitch, and I am glad of it. Bravo, Prince! We were told to put you through an examination. And as for what you said about my face, it's perfectly true: I am a child, and I know it. I knew that before you told me; you put my own thoughts into words for me. I believe your character's like mine exactly, like two drops of water, and I am glad of it. Only you are a man and I am a woman and haven't been to Switzerland: that's the only difference.'

'Don't be in a hurry, *Maman,*' cried Aglaia. 'The prince admitted that he had a special motive in all he has confessed and was not speaking simply.'

'Yes, yes,' laughed the others.

'Don't tease him, my dears, he is shrewder maybe than all the three of you together. You will see. But why do you say nothing about Aglaia, Prince? Aglaia is waiting, and so am I.'

'I can't say anything at once, I'll speak later.'

'Why? I should have thought she couldn't be overlooked.'

'Oh no, she couldn't. You are exceedingly beautiful, Aglaia Ivanovna. You are so beautiful that one is afraid to look at you.'

'Is that all? What about her qualities?' Madame Epanchin persisted.

'It's difficult to judge beauty; I am not ready yet. Beauty is a riddle.'

'That's as good as setting Aglaia a riddle,' said Adelaïda. 'Guess it, Aglaia. But she is beautiful, Prince?'

'Extremely,' answered the prince with warmth, looking enthusiastically at Aglaia. 'Almost as beautiful as Nastasya Filippovna, though her face is quite different.'

All looked at one another in surprise.

'As who-o-o?' gasped Madame Epanchin. 'As Nastasya Filippovna? Where have you seen Nastasya Filippovna? What Nastasya Filippovna?'

'Gavril Ardalionovitch was showing her portrait to Ivan Fyodorovitch just now.'

'What! He brought Ivan Fyodorovitch her portrait?'

'To show it to him. Nastasya Filippovna had given it to Gavril Ardalionovitch today, and he brought it to show.'

'I want to see it!' Madame Epanchin cried eagerly. 'Where is the photograph? If it was given him, he must have got it, and he must still be in the study. He always comes to work on Wednesdays and never leaves before four. Call him at once. No, I am not dying to see him. Do me a favour, dear prince. Go to the study, take the photograph from him and bring it here. Tell him we want to look at it, please.'

'He is nice, but too simple,' said Adelaïda, when the prince had gone.

'Yes, somewhat too much so,' Alexandra agreed; 'so that it makes him a little absurd, in fact.'

Neither of them seemed to be saying all she thought.

He got out of it very well, though, over our faces,' said Aglaia. 'He flattered us all, even Mamma.'

'Don't be witty, please,' cried her mother. 'He did not flatter me, though I was flattered.'

'You think he was sly?' asked Adelaïda.

'I fancy he is not so simple.'

'Get along with you,' said her mother, getting angry. 'To my thinking you are more absurd than he is. He is simple, but he's got all his wits about him, in the most honourable sense, of course. Exactly like me.'

'It was certainly a mistake to have spoken about the photograph,' Myshkin reflected as he went to the study, feeling a little conscience-stricken. 'But perhaps it was a good thing I spoke of it...'

A strange, though still vague idea was beginning to take shape in his mind.

Gavril Ardalionovitch was still sitting in the study absorbed in his papers. It was clear he did not receive his salary from the company for nothing. He was terribly disconcerted when the prince asked him for the portrait and told him how they had come to hear about it.

'E-ech! What need had you to chatter about it?' he cried in angry vexation. 'You know nothing about it… Idiot!' he muttered to himself.

'I am sorry. I did it without thinking; it happened to come up. I said that Aglaia was almost as handsome as Nastasya Filippovna.'

Ganya begged him to tell him exactly what had happened. Myshkin did so. Ganya looked at him sarcastically again.

'You've got Nastasya Filippovna on the brain …' he muttered, but paused and sank into thought.

He was evidently upset. Myshkin reminded him of the photograph.

'Listen, Prince,' Ganya said suddenly, as though an idea had struck him. 'I want to ask a great favour of you … but I really I don't know.'

He broke off, embarrassed. He seemed struggling with himself and trying to make up his mind. Myshkin waited in silence. Ganya scanned him once more with intent and searching eyes.

'Prince,' he began again, 'they are angry with me now… in there … owing to a strange … and absurd incident, for which I am not to blame. In fact, there's no need to go into it. I think they are rather vexed with me in there, so that for a time I don't want to go in without being invited. But there is something I absolutely must say to Aglaia Ivanovna. I have written a few words, on the chance' – he held a tiny folded note in his hand – 'and I don't know how to give it to her. Won't you take it for me and give it to her at once, but to Aglaia Ivanovna alone, so that no one sees it? You understand? It's no very terrible secret, nothing of that sort… but… Will you do it?'

'I don't quite like doing it,' answered Myshkin.

'Oh, Prince, it's horribly important for me!' Ganya began entreating him. 'She will perhaps answer … Believe me, it's only at the last extremity, at the last extremity that I could have recourse to… By whom else could I send it? It's very important… dreadfully important…'

Ganya was terribly afraid that Myshkin would not consent and looked in his eyes with cringing entreaty.

'Very well, I'll give it her.'

'Only so that no one sees it,' Ganya besought him, delighted. 'And another thing, I can rely on your word of honour, of course, Prince?'

'I won't show it to anyone,' said Myshkin.

'The note is not sealed, but...' Ganya was beginning in his anxiety, but he broke off in confusion.

'Oh, I won't read it,' answered Myshkin quite simply. He took the photograph and went out of the study.

As soon as Ganya was left alone, he clutched at his head.

'One word from her and I... and I will break it off, perhaps.'

He could not settle down to his papers again for excitement and suspense, and began pacing from one corner of the room to the other.

Myshkin pondered as he went. The task laid upon him impressed him unpleasantly. The thought of a letter from Ganya to Aglaia was unpleasant too. But when he was the length of two rooms from the drawing-room, he stopped short, as though recollecting something. He looked round, went to the window nearer to the light, and began looking at the portrait of Nastasya Filippovna.

He seemed trying to decipher something that had struck him before, hidden in that face. The impression it had made had scarcely left him, and now he was in a hurry to verify it again. He was now even more struck by the face, which was extraordinary from its beauty and from something else in it. There was a look of unbounded pride and contempt, almost hatred, in that face, and at the same time something confiding, something wonderfully simple-hearted. The contrast of these two elements roused a feeling almost of compassion. Her dazzling beauty was positively unbearable – the beauty of a pale face, almost sunken cheeks and glowing eyes – a strange beauty! Myshkin gazed at it for a minute, then started suddenly, looked round him, hurriedly raised the portrait to his lips and kissed it. When he walked into the drawing-room a minute later, his face was perfectly calm.

But he had hardly entered the dining-room (which was separated by one room from the drawing-room) when he almost ran against Aglaia, who was coming out. She was alone.

'Gavril Ardalionovitch asked me to give you this,' said Myshkin, handing her the note.

Aglaia stood still, took the note, and looked strangely at Myshkin. There was not the slightest embarrassment in her expression. There was only a shade of wonder in her eyes, and that seemed only in reference to Myshkin. Aglaia's eyes seemed to ask him to account for having got mixed up in this affair with Ganya, and to ask him calmly and haughtily. They looked at one another for two or three seconds. Then something ironical seemed to come into her face; with a slight smile she walked away.

Madame Epanchin gazed for some moments in silence, with a shade of nonchalance, at the photograph of Nastasya Filippovna, which she held affectedly at arm's length.

'Yes, good-looking,' she pronounced at last, 'very good-looking indeed. I've seen her twice, only at a distance. That's the sort of beauty you appreciate, then?' she suddenly said to Myshkin.

'Yes, it is ...' answered Myshkin with some effort.

'You mean, just that sort of beauty?'

'Just that sort.'

'Why?'

'In that face ... there is so much suffering,' answered Myshkin, as it were involuntarily speaking to himself, not in answer to her question.

'But perhaps you are talking nonsense,' Madame Epanchin concluded, and with a haughty gesture she flung the photograph down on the table.

Alexandra took it. Adelaïda went up to her and they looked at it together. At that moment Aglaia came back into the drawing-room.

'What power!' Adelaïda cried suddenly, looking eagerly over her sister's shoulder at the portrait.

'Where? What power?' her mother asked sharply.

'Such beauty is power,' said Adelaïda warmly. 'With beauty like that one might turn the world upside down.'

She walked thoughtfully away to her easel. Aglaia only glanced cursorily at the portrait, screwed up her eyes, pouted, walked away and sat down clasping her hands.

Madame Epanchin rang the bell.

'Call Gavril Ardalionovitch here; he is in the study,' she told the servant who answered it.

'Maman,' cried Alexandra significantly.

'I want to say a few words to him – that's enough!' her mother snapped out, cutting short her protest. She was evidently irritated. 'We have nothing but secrets here, Prince, you see – nothing but secrets. It has to be so, it's a sort of etiquette; it's stupid. And in a matter which above everything needs frankness, openness and straightforwardness. There are marriages being arranged. I don't like these marriages...'

'*Maman,* what are you saying?' Alexandra again made haste to check her.

'What is it, dear daughter? Do you like it yourself? As for the prince's hearing it, we are friends. He and I are, anyway. God seeks men, good ones of course, but He does not want the wicked and capricious. Capricious especially, who say one thing one day and something else another. Do you understand, Alexandra Ivanovna? They say I am queer, Prince, but I can tell what people are like. For the heart is the great thing, and the rest is all nonsense. One must have sense too, of course ... perhaps sense is the great thing really. Don't smile, Aglaia, I am not contradicting myself: a fool with a heart and no sense is just as unhappy as a fool with sense and no heart. It's an old truth. I am a fool with a heart and no sense, and you are a fool with sense and no heart, and so we are both unhappy and miserable.'

'What are you so unhappy about, *Maman?*' Adelaïda could not resist asking. She seemed the only one of the company who had not lost her good-humour.

'Learned daughters, in the first place,' retorted her mother curtly, 'and as that's enough of itself, there's no need to go into other causes. Words enough have been wasted. We shall see how you two (I don't count Aglaia) will manage with your sense and your talk, and whether you will be happy with your fine gentleman, most admirable Alexandra Ivanovna. Ah!' she exclaimed, seeing Ganya enter, 'here comes another matrimonial alliance. Good-day!' she said in response to Ganya's bow, without asking him to sit down. 'You are contemplating marriage?'

'Marriage? How? What marriage?' muttered Gavril Ardalionovitch, dumbfounded. He was terribly disconcerted.

'Are you getting married, I ask you, if you prefer that expression?'

'N-no ... I... N-no ...' Gavril Ardalionovitch lied and a flush of shame overspread his face.

He stole a glance at Aglaia, who was sitting a little apart, and hurriedly looked away again. Aglaia looked coldly, intently and calmly at him, steadily watching his confusion.

'No? You said no?' the ruthless lady persisted. 'Enough, I shall remember that today, Wednesday morning, you have said "No" in answer to my question. What is today – Wednesday?'

'I think so, *Maman,*' answered Adelaïda.

'They never know the days. What day of the month is it?'

'The twenty-seventh,' answered Ganya.

'The twenty-seventh. Just as well for some reasons. Goodbye. I think you've a great deal to do, and it's time for me to dress and go out. Take your photograph. Give my kind regards to your unhappy mother. Goodbye for the present, dear prince. Come and see us often. I am going to see old Princess Byelokonsky on purpose to tell her about you. And listen, my dear, I believe it's simply for my sake God has brought you to Petersburg from Switzerland. Perhaps you may have other work to do, but it was chiefly for my sake. That was just God's design. Goodbye, dears. Alexandra, come to my room, my dear.'

Madame Epanchin went out. Ganya, crestfallen, confused, angry, picked up the photograph from the table and turned with a wry smile to Myshkin.

'Prince, I am just going home. If you've not changed your mind about boarding with us, I will take you, for you don't even know the address.'

'Stay a little, Prince,' said Aglaia, suddenly getting up from her chair. 'You must write in my album. Papa said you had a fine handwriting. I'll bring it you directly.'

And she went out.

'Goodbye for the present, Prince, I am going too,' said Adelaïda.

She pressed Myshkin's hand warmly, smiling kindly and cordially to him, and went away. She did not look at Ganya.

'That was your doing,' snarled Ganya, falling upon Myshkin as soon as everyone had gone. 'You've been babbling to them of my getting married!' he muttered in a rapid whisper, with a furious face and an angry gleam in his eyes. 'You are a shameless chatterbox!'

'I assure you, you are mistaken,' Myshkin answered calmly and politely. 'I didn't even know you were going to be married.'

'You heard Ivan Fyodorovitch say this morning that everything would be settled tonight at Nastasya Filippovna's. You repeated it. You are lying! From whom could they have found out? Damn it all, who could have told them except you? Didn't the old woman hint it to me?'

'You must know best who told them, if you really think they hinted at it. I haven't said a word about it.'

'Did you give the note? An answer?' Ganya interrupted with feverish impatience.

But at that very moment Aglaia came back and Myshkin hadn't time to answer.

'Here, Prince,' she said, laying the album on the table, 'choose a page and write me something. Here is a pen, a new one too. You don't mind it's being a steel one? I hear that calligraphists never use steel pens.'

Talking to Myshkin, she seemed not to notice Ganya's presence. But while the prince was fixing his pen, looking for a page and making ready, Ganya went up to the fireplace where Aglaia was standing, on Myshkin's right hand. With a quavering, breaking voice he said almost in her ear: 'One word – one word only from you and I am saved.'

Myshkin turned round quickly and looked at them both. There was real despair in Ganya's face; he seemed to have uttered those words in desperation without thinking. Aglaia looked at him for a few seconds with exactly the same calm wonder with which she had looked on the prince. And this calm wonder, this surprise, as though she were completely at a loss to understand what was said to her, seemed more terrible to Ganya at that moment than the most withering contempt.

'What am I to write?' asked Myshkin.

'I will dictate you,' said Aglaia, turning to him. 'Are you ready? Write: 'I don't make bargains'; then write the day and the month. Show me.'

Myshkin handed her the album.

'Excellent! You've written it wonderfully. You have an exquisite handwriting. Thank you. Goodbye, Prince. Stay,' she added, as though suddenly recollecting something. 'Come along, I want to give you something for a keepsake.'

Myshkin followed her, but in the dining-room Aglaia stood still. 'Read this,' she said, handing him Ganya's note.

Myshkin took the note and looked wonderingly at Aglaia.

'I know you haven't read it, and that man cannot have confided in you. Read it, I want you to read it.'

The note had evidently been written in haste.

> Today my fate will be decided, you know in what way. Today I must give my word irre0vocably. I have no claim on your sympathy; I dare not have any hope. But once you uttered a word – one word, and that word lighted the

dark night of my life and has been my beacon ever since. Speak one such word again now and you will save me from ruin! Only say to me, 'Break off everything,' and I will break it all off today. Oh, what will it cost you to say that! That word I only ask for as a sign of your sympathy and compassion for me. Only that – only that! Nothing more, nothing! I dare not dream of hope, for I am not worthy of it. But after a word from you I can accept my poverty again; I shall joyfully endure my hopeless lot. I shall face the struggle; I shall be glad of it; I shall rise up again with renewed strength.

Send me that word of sympathy (only sympathy, I swear)! Do not be angry with the audacity of a desperate and drowning man for making a last effort to save himself from perdition.

G. I.

'This man assures me,' said Aglaia abruptly, when Myshkin had finished reading it, 'that the words "break it all off," will not compromise me and will bind me to nothing, and gives me a written guarantee of it, as you see, in this note. Observe how naïvely he hastened to underline certain words, and how coarsely his secret thought shows through it. Yet he knows that if he broke it all off of himself, without a word from me, without even speaking of it to me, without expecting anything from me, I should have felt differently to him and perhaps might have become his friend. He knows that for a fact. But he has a dirty soul. He knows it, but can't bring himself to it; he knows it, but still he asks for a guarantee. He can't act on faith. He wants me to give him hope of my hand, to make up for the hundred thousand. As for my words in the past of which he speaks in his note, and which he says have lighted up his life, it's simply an insolent lie. I merely pitied him once. But he is insolent and shameless. He at once conceived a notion that hope was possible for him. I saw it at once. Since then he has begun trying to catch me; he is trying to catch me even now. *But* enough. Take the note and give it back to him as soon as you are out of the house; not before, of course.'

'And what answer am I to give him?'

'Nothing, of course. That's the best answer. So you are going to live in his house?'

'Ivan Fyodorovitch himself advised me to this morning,' said Myshkin.

'Then be on your guard with him, I warn you. He won't forgive you for taking him back his note.'

Aglaia pressed Myshkin's hand lightly and walked away. Her face was grave and frowning. She did not even smile when she bowed to him at parting.

'I am just coming; I'll only get my bundle,' said Myshkin to Ganya, 'and we will go.'

Ganya stamped with impatience. His face looked black with fury. At last both went out into the street, Myshkin with his bundle in his hand.

'The answer? The answer?' cried Ganya, pouncing upon him. 'What did she say to you? Did you give her the letter?'

Myshkin gave him the note without a word. Ganya was petrified.

'What? My letter?' he cried. 'He didn't give it to her. Ach, I might have expected it! Ach, d-d-damnation! I see how it was she didn't understand just now. But how could you – how could you have failed to give it? Oh, d-damna ...'

'Excuse me, on the contrary, I succeeded in giving your note at once, the very minute you'd given it me, and exactly as you asked me to. It's in my hands again because Aglaia Ivanovna gave it back to me just now.'

'When? When?'

'As soon as I'd finished writing in her album, when she called me. You heard her? We went into the dining-room, she gave me the note, told me to read it and to give it to you back.'

'To read it?' Ganya shouted almost at the top of his voice. 'To read it?

You've read it?'

And in amazement he stood stock still again in the middle of the pavement, so astounded that he positively gaped.

'Yes, I've just read it.'

'And she gave it you – gave it you herself to read? Herself?'

'Yes; and I assure you I shouldn't have read it unless she'd asked me to.'

Ganya was silent for a minute, reflecting with painful effort. But suddenly he cried: 'Impossible! She couldn't have told you to read it. You are lying! You read it of yourself.'

'I am speaking the truth,' answered Myshkin in the same perfectly untroubled voice, 'and I assure you I am very sorry that it is so distasteful to you.'

'But, you luckless creature, she must have said something at the time. Surely she made some answer?'

'Yes, of course.'

'Tell me, then, tell me! Oh, damn it!'

And Ganya twice stamped his right foot, wearing a galosh, on the pavement.

'When I'd finished reading it, she told me that you were trying to catch her; that you wanted to compromise her so that she might give you hopes of her hand, and that, secure of that, you wouldn't lose by abandoning your hopes of a hundred thousand. That if you had done so without bargaining with her and had broken it off without asking for a guarantee from her beforehand, she would perhaps have become your friend. I believe that's all. Oh, something more. When I asked, after I'd taken the letter, what was the answer, she said that no answer was the best answer. I think that was it. You must excuse me if I've forgotten her exact words and only repeat it as I understood it.'

Ganya was overcome by intense anger and his fury burst out without restraint.

'Ah, so that's it!' he snarled. 'So my notes are thrown out of the window! Mr, she won't make bargains – then I will! And we shall see! I have other things to fall back upon … We shall see! I'll make her smart for it!'

His face was pale and distorted; he foamed at the mouth; he shook his fist. So they walked for some steps. He behaved exactly as though he were alone in his room and made no attempt to keep up appearances before Myshkin, as though he looked upon him as absolutely of no consequence. But suddenly he reflected and pulled himself up.

'But how is it,' he said suddenly, addressing Myshkin, 'how is it you' – ('an idiot,' he added to himself) – 'are suddenly trusted with such confidence after two hours' acquaintanceship? How is it?'

Envy was all that was wanted to complete his suffering, and it suddenly stung him to the heart.

'That I can't explain,' answered Myshkin.

Ganya looked wrathfully at him.

'Was it to make you a present of her confidence that she called you into the dining-room? She was going to give you something.'

'That's just how I understand it.'

'But, damn it all, why! What have you done? How have you won their hearts? Listen.' He was violently agitated and in a terrible ferment; all his ideas seemed hopelessly scattered. 'Listen. Can't you remember what you've been talking about – every word from the beginning, and give some sort of account of it? Don't you remember noticing anything?'

'Certainly I can,' answered Myshkin. 'At the beginning when I first went in and made their acquaintance, we began talking about Switzerland.'

'Confound Switzerland!'

'Then we talked of capital punishment.'

'Capital punishment?'

'Yes, something suggested it... Then I told them how I spent three years out there, and the story of a poor village girl...'

'Damn the poor village girl! What else?'

Ganya was raging with impatience.

'Then how Schneider told me his opinion of my character, and how he forced me to ...'

'Hang Schneider and damn his opinion of you! What else?'

'Then something led up to my speaking of faces, or rather of the expression of faces, and I said that Aglaia Ivanovna was almost as beautiful as Nastasya Filippovna. And that was how I came to mention the portrait...'

'But you didn't repeat – you didn't repeat what you heard this morning in the study? You didn't? You didn't?'

'I tell you again I did not.'

'How the devil then... Bah! Did Aglaia show the note to the old lady?'

'I can assure you positively that she did not do that. I was there all the while, and she hadn't the time to.'

'But perhaps you missed something... Oh, d-damned idiot!' he exclaimed, completely beside himself. 'He can't even tell anything properly.'

Ganya, having once begun to be abusive and meeting no resistance, lost all restraint, as is always the case with certain sorts of people. A little more and he would have begun to spit, he was so furious. But his fury made him blind, or he would have understood long ago that this 'idiot,' whom he was treating so rudely, was sometimes rather quick and subtle in understanding and could give an extremely satisfactory account of things. But something unexpected happened all at once.

'I must tell you, Gavril Ardalionovitch,' Myshkin said suddenly, 'that I was once so ill that I really was almost an idiot, but I've got over that long ago, and so I rather dislike it when people call me an idiot to my face. Though I can excuse it in you in consideration of your ill-luck, but in your vexation you've been abusive to me twice already. I don't like that at all, especially so suddenly at first acquaintance; and so, as we are just at the crossroads, hadn't we better part? You go to the right to your home, and I go to the left. I've got twenty-five roubles, and I shall be sure to find some lodging-house.'

Ganya was dreadfully disconcerted, and even flushed with shame at meeting with such an unexpected rebuff.

'Excuse me, Prince,' he cried warmly, dropping his offensive tone for one of extreme politeness. 'For mercy's sake, forgive me! You see what trouble I'm in. You know scarcely anything of it as yet, but if you knew all, I am sure you would feel there was some excuse for me. Though, of course, it is inexcusable…'

'Oh, I don't need so much apology,' Myshkin hastened to answer. 'I understand that it's very horrid for you and that's why you are rude. Well, let's go to your house; I'll come with pleasure.'

'No, I can't let him go like that now,' Ganya was thinking to himself, looking resentfully at Myshkin on the way. 'The rogue got it all out of me, and then removed his mask… There's something behind it. But we shall see! Everything will be decided – everything! Today!'

They were by now standing opposite the house.

Chapter 8

Ganya's flat was on the third storey, on a very clean, light, spacious staircase, and consisted of six or seven rooms, big and little. Though the flat was ordinary enough, it seemed somewhat beyond the means of a clerk with a family, even with an income of two thousand roubles a year. But it had been taken by Ganya and his family not more than two months before with a view to taking boarders, to the intense annoyance of Ganya himself, to satisfy the urgent desires of his mother and sister, who were anxious to be of use and to increase the family income a little. Ganya scowled and called taking boarders degrading. It made him feel ashamed in the society where he was accustomed to appear as a somewhat brilliant young man with a future before him. All such concessions to the inevitable and all the cramped conditions of his life were a deep inner wound. For some time past he had become extremely and quite disproportionately irritable over every trifle, and if he still consented to submit and to put up with it for a time, it was only because he was resolved to change it all in the immediate future. But that very change, that very way of escape on which he had determined, involved a formidable difficulty – a difficulty the solution of which threatened to be more troublesome and harassing than all that had gone before.

The flat was divided by a passage, into which they stepped at once on entering. On one side of the passage were the three rooms which were intended for 'specially recommended' boarders. On the same side of the passage, at the farthest end, next to the kitchen, was a fourth room, smaller than the rest, which was occupied by the father of the family, the retired General Ivolgin. He slept on a wide sofa, and was obliged to go in and out of the flat through the kitchen and by the back staircase. Ganya's brother, Kolya, a schoolboy of thirteen, shared the same room. He too had to be packed away in it, to do his lessons there, to sleep in ragged sheets on another sofa, very old, short and narrow, and above all to wait on his father and to keep an eye on him, which was becoming more and more necessary. Myshkin was given the middle one of the three rooms; the first on the right was occupied by Ferdyshtchenko, and the one on the left was empty. But Ganya led Myshkin first into the other half of the flat, which consisted of a dining room, of a drawing-room which was a drawing-room only in the morning, being transformed later in the day into Ganya's study and bedroom; and of a third room, very small and always shut up, where the mother and daughter slept. It was a tight fit, in fact, in the flat. Ganya could only grind his teeth and say nothing. Though he was and wished to be respectful to his mother, it could be seen from the first minute that he was a great despot in his family.

Nina Alexandrovna was not alone in the drawing-room. Her daughter was with her, and both ladies were busy with some knitting while talking to a visitor, Ivan Petrovitch Ptitsyn. Nina Alexandrovna looked about fifty, with a thin and sunken face and dark rings under her eyes. She looked in delicate health and somewhat melancholy, but her face and expression were rather pleasing. At the first word one could see that she was of an earnest disposition and had genuine dignity. In spite of her melancholy air one felt that she had firmness and even determination. She was very modestly dressed in some dark colour in an elderly style, but her manner, her conversation, all her ways betrayed that she was a woman who had seen better days.

Varvara Ardalionovna was a girl of twenty-three, of middle height, rather thin. Her face, though not very beautiful, possessed the secret of charm without beauty and was extraordinarily attractive. She was very like her mother and was dressed in almost the same way, showing absolutely no desire to be smart. Her grey eyes might have been at times very merry and caressing, if they had not as a rule looked grave and thoughtful; too much so, especially of late. Her face too showed firmness and decision; in fact it suggested an even more vigorous and enterprising determination than her mother's. Varvara Ardalionovna was rather hot-tempered, and her brother was sometimes positively afraid of her temper. The visitor with them now, Ivan Petrovitch Ptitsyn, was a little afraid of her too. He was a young man, not yet thirty, modestly but elegantly dressed, with a pleasant but rather too solemn manner. His dark brown beard showed that he was not in the government service. He could talk cleverly and well, but was more often silent. He made a pleasant impression on the whole. He was obviously attracted by Varvara Ardalionovna and did not conceal his feelings. She treated him in a friendly way, but put off answering certain questions, and did not like them. But Ptitsyn was far from losing courage. Nina Alexandrovna was cordial to him and had of late begun to confide in him. It was known, moreover, that he was trying to make his fortune by lending money at high interest on more or less good security. He was a great friend of Ganya's.

Ganya greeted his mother very frigidly, did not greet his sister at all, and after abruptly introducing Myshkin and giving a minute account of him, he at once drew Ptitsyn out of the room. Nina

Alexandrovna said a few friendly words to Myshkin and told Kolya, who peeped in at the door, to conduct him to the middle room. Kolya was a boy with a merry and rather pleasant face and a confiding and simple manner.

'Where is your luggage?' he asked Myshkin, as they went into the room.

'I have a bundle. I left it in the passage.'

'I'll bring it you directly. We have only the cook and Matryona, so I help too. Varya looks after everything and gets cross. Ganya says *you've* come from Switzerland today.'

'Yes.'

'Is it nice in Switzerland?'

'Very.'

'Mountains?'

'Yes.'

'I'll bring you your bundles directly.'

Varvara Ardalionovna came in.

'Matryona will make your bed directly. Have you a trunk?'

'No, a bundle. Your brother has gone to fetch it; it's in the passage.'

'There's *no* bundle there except this little one. Where have you put it?' asked Kolya, coming back into the room.

'I haven't any but that,' answered Myshkin, taking his bundle.

'A-ah! I was wondering whether they hadn't been carried off by Ferdyshtchenko.'

'Don't talk nonsense,' said Varya sternly. Even to Myshkin she spoke shortly and with bare civility.

'*Chère Babette,* you might treat me more tenderly, I am not Ptitsyn.'

'One can see you still want whipping, Kolya, you are so stupid. You can ask Matryona for anything you want. Dinner is at half-past four. You can dine with us or in your own room, as you prefer. Come, Kolya, don't be in the way.'

'Let us go, you determined character.'

As they went out they came upon Ganya.

'Is father at home?' Ganya asked Kolya, and on receiving an affirmative reply he whispered something in his ear. Kolya nodded and followed his sister out.

'One word, Prince. I forgot to mention it with all this … business. I've a request to make. Be so good, if it won't be a great bother to you – don't gossip here of what has just passed between Aglaia and me, nor *there* of what you'll find here, because there's degradation enough here too. Damn it all, though! … Restrain yourself for today, anyway.'

'I assure you that I gossiped much less than you think,' said Myshkin, with some irritation at Ganya's reproaches.

Their relations were obviously becoming more and more strained.

'Well, I have had to put up with enough today through you. Anyway, I beg you to keep quiet.'

'You must notice besides, Gavril Ardalionovitch, I was not bound in any way; and why shouldn't I have spoken of the photograph? You didn't ask me not to.'

'Oh dear, oh dear! What a horrid room!' observed Ganya, looking round him contemptuously. 'Dark and looking into the yard. You've come to us at a bad time from every point of view. But that's not my business, I don't let the rooms.'

Ptitsyn peeped in and called Ganya, who hurriedly left Myshkin and went out. There was something more he wanted to say, but he was obviously ill at ease and seemed ashamed to say it. He had found fault with the room to cover his embarrassment.

As soon as Myshkin had washed and made himself a little tidier, the door opened again and another person looked in. This was a gentleman about thirty, tall and broad, with a huge curly red head. His face was red and fleshy, his lips were thick, his nose was broad and flat. He had little ironical eyes lost in fat, that looked as if they were always winking. The whole countenance produced an impression of insolence. He was rather dirtily dressed.

He first opened the door only far enough to poke his head in. The head looked about the room for five seconds, then the door began slowly opening and the whole person came into view in the doorway. Yet the visitor did not come in, but, screwing up his eyes, still stared at Myshkin from the doorway. At last he closed the door behind him, came nearer, sat down on a chair, took Myshkin's hand, and made him sit on the sofa near him.

'Ferdyshtchenko,' he said, looking intently and enquiringly at Myshkin.

'What of it?' answered Myshkin, almost laughing.

'A boarder,' said Ferdyshtchenko, looking at him as before.

'Do you want to make my acquaintance?'

'E-ech,' said the visitor, sighing and ruffling up his hair, and he began staring in the opposite corner. 'Have you money?' he asked, turning suddenly to Myshkin.

'A little.'

'How much?'

'Twenty-five roubles.'

'Show me.'

Myshkin took the twenty-five-rouble note out of his waistcoat pocket and handed it to Ferdyshtchenko, who unfolded it, looked at it, turned it over, then held it to the light.

'That's rather strange,' he said, seeming to reflect. 'Why do they turn mud colour? These twenty-five-rouble notes often turn an awful colour, while others fade. Take it.'

Myshkin took back his note. Ferdyshtchenko got up from his chair. 'I've come in to warn you, in the first place, not to lend me money, for I shall be sure to ask you to.'

'Very well.'

'Do you mean to pay here?'

'Yes.'

'Well, I don't. Thanks. I'm the next door on the right. Did you notice it? Try not to come and see me too often; I shall come and see you, you needn't be afraid. Have you seen the general?'

'No.'

'Nor heard him either?'

'Of course not.'

'Well, you'll see him and hear him. What's more, he tries to borrow even of me. *Avis au lecteur*. Goodbye. Can one exist with such a name as Ferdyshtchenko? Eh?'

'Why not?'

'Goodbye.'

And he went to the door. Myshkin learnt later that this gentleman felt it incumbent upon him to amaze everyone by his originality and liveliness, but never succeeded in doing so. Some people he impressed unfavourably, which was a real mortification to him. Yet he did not relinquish his efforts. At the door he succeeded in retrieving his position, so to speak, by stumbling against a gentleman who was coming in. Letting this fresh visitor, who was a stranger to Myshkin, into the room, he winked warningly several times behind his back, and so made a fairly effective exit.

The other gentleman was a tall and corpulent man of fifty-five or more, with a fleshy, bloated, purple-red face, set off by thick grey whiskers and moustache. He had large, rather prominent eyes. His appearance would have been rather impressive, if it had not been for something neglected, slovenly, even unclean about him. He was wearing shabby indoor clothes, an old frock-coat with elbows almost in holes and dirty linen. At close quarters he smelt a little of vodka, but his manner was impressive and rather studied. He betrayed a jealous desire to display his dignity.

The gentleman approached Myshkin deliberately, with an affable smile. He took his hand silently and, holding it for some time in his, looked into Myshkin's face as though recognising familiar features.

'It's he! He!' he pronounced softly but solemnly. 'His living picture! I heard them utter a dear and familiar name and it brought back a past that is gone for ever … Prince Myshkin?'

'Yes.'

'General Ivolgin, retired from service and unfortunate. Your name and your father's, may I venture to ask?'

'Lyov Nikolayevitch.'

'Yes, yes! Son of my friend, the companion of my childhood, I may say, Nikolay Petrovitch?'

'My father's name was Nikolay Lyovitch.'

'Lyovitch,' the general corrected himself, but without haste and with complete assurance, as though he had not in the least forgotten it, but had uttered the wrong name by accident. He sat down, and taking Myshkin's hand he too made him sit down beside him. 'I used to carry you in my arms.'

'Is it possible?' said Myshkin. 'My father died twenty years ago.'

'Yes, it's twenty years – twenty years and three months. We were at school together; I went straight into the army.'

'My father was in the army too: sublieutenant in the Vassilkovsky regiment.'

'In the Byelomirsky. He was transferred to the Byelomirsky just before his death. I was at his bedside and blessed him for eternity. Your mother …'

The general paused, as though arrested by painful memory.

'Yes, she died six months later from a chill,' said Myshkin.

'It was not a chill – not a chill. You may trust an old man's words. I was there; I buried her too. It was grief at the loss of her husband; not a chill. Yes, I remember the princess too. Ah, youth! It was for her sake that the prince and I, friends from childhood, were on the point of becoming each other's murderers.'

Myshkin began to listen with a certain scepticism.

'I was passionately in love with your mother when she was betrothed – betrothed to my friend. The prince observed it and it was a blow to him. He came to me early in the morning before seven o'clock, and waked me up. I dressed in amazement. There was silence on both sides; I understood it all. He pulled two pistols out of his pocket. Across a handkerchief, without witnesses. What need of witnesses when within five minutes we should have sent each other into eternity? We loaded, stretched the handkerchief, aimed the pistols at each other's hearts and gazed in each other's faces. Suddenly tears gushed from the eyes of both; our hands trembled. Of both – of both at once. Then naturally followed embraces and a conflict in mutual generosity. The prince cried, "She is yours." I cried, "No, yours." In fact… in fact… you've come to live with us?'

'Yes, for a little time perhaps,' said Myshkin, seeming to hesitate.

'Mother asks you to come to her, Prince,' cried Kolya, looking in at the door.

Myshkin got up to go, but the general put his right hand on his shoulder and affectionately made him sit down again.

'As a true friend of your father's I want to warn you,' said the general. 'You can see for yourself I have suffered, through a tragic catastrophe, but without trial. Without trial! Nina Alexandrovna is a rare woman. Varvara Ardalionovna, my daughter, is a rare daughter. We are driven by circumstances to take boarders – an incredible downfall! I, who was on the eve of becoming a governor-general!… But you we shall always be glad to receive. And meanwhile there is a tragedy in my house!'

Myshkin looked at him enquiringly and with great curiosity.

'A marriage is being arranged, and a strange marriage. A marriage between a woman of doubtful character and a young man who might be a *kammerjunker*. That woman is to be brought into the house where are my daughter and my wife! But as long as I breathe, she shall not enter it! I will lie down on the threshold and she must walk over me. Ganya I scarcely speak to now; I avoid meeting him, indeed. I warn you beforehand; since you'll be living with us, you'll see it anyway. But you are the son of my friend and I have the right to hope …'

'Prince, will you be so good as to come into the drawing-room?' Nina Alexandrovna herself appeared in the doorway and called him.

'Only fancy, my dear,' cried the general, 'it appears that I used to dandle the prince in my arms!'

Nina Alexandrovna glanced reproachfully at the general and searchingly at Myshkin, but did not say a word. Myshkin followed her, but as soon as they had entered the drawing-room and sat down, and Nina Alexandrovna had begun in an undertone and very rapidly telling Myshkin something, the general himself made his appearance. Nina Alexandrovna ceased speaking instantly and, with evident annoyance, bent over her knitting. The general perhaps observed this annoyance, but was still in excellent spirits.

'The son of my friend,' he cried, addressing Nina Alexandrovna. 'And so unexpectedly! I'd long given up all idea … My dear, surely you must remember Nikolay Lyovitch? He was still at… Tver when you were there.'

'I don't remember Nikolay Lyovitch. Is that your father?' she asked Myshkin.

'Yes. I don't think it was at Tver he died, though, but at Elisavetgrad,' Myshkin observed timidly to the general. 'I was told so by Pavlishtchev.'

'It was at Tver,' persisted the general. 'He was transferred to Tver just before his death, and before his illness showed itself, in fact. You were too little to remember the removal or the journey. Pavlishtchev may easily have forgotten, though he was an excellent man.'

'Did you know Pavlishtchev too?'

'He was a rare man, but I was on the spot. I blessed him on his deathbed.'

'My father died while he was awaiting trial,' Myshkin observed again; 'though I've never been able to find out what he was accused of. He died in a hospital.'

'Oh, that was about the case of the private Kolpakov, and there's no doubt that the prince would have been acquitted.'

'Was that so? Are you sure?' asked Myshkin with marked interest.

'I should think so!' cried the general. 'The court broke up without coming to a decision. It was an incredible case! A mysterious case, one may say. Captain Larionov, the commander of the company, died; the prince was appointed for a time to take his duty. Good. The private Kolpakov committed a theft – stole boot-leather from a comrade and spent it on drink. Good. The prince – in the presence, observe, of the sergeant and the corporal – gave Kolpakov a blowing-up and threatened to have him flogged. Very good. Kolpakov went to the barracks, lay down on his bed, and died a quarter of an hour afterwards. Excellent. But it was so unexpected, it was quite incredible. Anyway, Kolpakov was buried. The prince reported the matter and Kolpakov's name was removed from the lists. One would have thought it was all right. But just six months later at the brigade review the private Kolpakov turns up, as though nothing had happened, in the third company of the second battalion of the Novozemlyansky infantry regiment of the same brigade and of the same division.'

'What?' cried Myshkin, beside himself with astonishment.

'It's not so, it's a mistake,' said Nina Alexandrovna, addressing him suddenly and looking at him almost with anguish. *'Mon mari se trompe.'*

'But, my dear, *se trompe* – it's easy to say. How do you explain a case like that? Everyone was dumbfounded. I should have been the first to say *qu'on se trompe.* But unhappily I was a witness and was on the commission myself. All who had seen him testified that this was the same private Kolpakov who had been buried six months before with the usual parade and the beating of drums. It was an unusual incident, almost incredible, I admit, but ...'

'Father, your dinner is ready,' announced Varvara Ardalionovna, entering the room.

'Ah, that's capital, excellent! I am certainly hungry... But it was, one may even say, a psychological incident...'

'The soup will be cold again,' said Varya impatiently.

'I am coming, I am coming,' muttered the general as he went out of the room. 'And in spite of all enquiries,' he was heard saying in the corridor.

'You must overlook a great deal in Ardalion Alexandrovitch, if you stay with us,' said Nina Alexandrovna to Myshkin. 'But he won't be much in your way; he even dines alone. All have their failings, you know, and their ... peculiarities, some perhaps even more than those who are usually looked down upon for it. One special favour I will ask of you. If my husband ever applies to you for payment, tell him, please, that you've already paid me.

Of course, anything you give to Ardalion Alexandrovitch will be taken off your bill, but I ask you simply to avoid muddling our accounts ... What is it, Varya?'

Varya came back into the room and without speaking handed her mother a portrait of Nastasya Filippovna. Nina Alexandrovna started, and examined it for some time – at first, it seemed, with dismay, and then with overwhelming and bitter emotion. At last she looked enquiringly at Varya.

'A present to him today from herself,' said Varya, 'and this evening everything will be settled.'

'This evening!' Nina Alexandrovna repeated in a low voice, as though in despair. 'Well, there can be no more doubt about it then, and no hope left. She announced her decision by giving the portrait... But did he show it to you himself?' she added with surprise.

'You know that we've scarcely spoken a word for the last month. Ptitsyn told me all about it, and the portrait was lying on the floor by the table; I picked it up.'

'Prince,' said Nina Alexandrovna, addressing him suddenly, 'I wanted to ask you (that was why I asked you to come to me), have you known my son long? I believe he told me you'd only arrived from somewhere today.'

Myshkin gave a brief account of himself, leaving out the greater part. Nina Alexandrovna and Varya listened.

'I am not trying to find out anything about Gavril Ardalionovitch in questioning you,' observed Nina Alexandrovna. 'You must make no mistake on that score. If there is anything he can't tell me about himself, I don't want to learn it without his knowledge. I ask you, because just now when you'd gone out, Ganya answered, when I asked him about you: "He knows everything; you needn't stand on ceremony with him." What does that mean? That is, I should like to know to what extent...'

Ganya and Ptitsyn suddenly came in. Nina Alexandrovna instantly ceased speaking. Myshkin remained sitting beside her, while Varya moved away. Nastasya Filippovna's photograph was left lying in the most conspicuous place on Nina Alexandrovna's work-table, just in front of her. Ganya saw it and frowned. He picked it up with an air of annoyance and flung it on his writing-table at the other end of the room.

'Is it today, Ganya?' his mother asked suddenly.

'Is what – today?' Ganya was startled, and all at once he flew at Myshkin. 'Ah, I understand! Your doing again! It seems to be a regular disease in you. Can't you keep quiet? But let me tell you, your excellency …'

'It's my fault, Ganya, no one else's,' interposed Ptitsyn.

Ganya looked at him enquiringly.

'It's better so, Ganya, especially as on one side the affair is settled,' muttered Ptitsyn; and moving away, he sat down at the table, and taking out of his pocket a piece of paper covered with writing in pencil, he began looking at it intently.

Ganya stood sullenly, in uneasy expectation of a family scene. It did not even occur to him to apologise to Myshkin.

'If everything is settled, then Ivan Petrovitch is certainly right,' observed Nina Alexandrovna. 'Don't scowl, please, Ganya, and don't be angry. I am not going to ask you anything you don't care to tell me of yourself, and I assure you I am completely resigned. Please don't be uneasy.'

She went on with her work as she said this and seemed to be really calm. Ganya was surprised, but was prudently silent, looking at his mother and waiting for her to say something more definite. He had suffered too much from domestic quarrels already. Nina Alexandrovna noticed this prudence, and added with a bitter smile: 'You are still doubtful and do not believe me. Don't be uneasy, there shall be no more tears and entreaties, on my part anyway. All I want is that you may be happy, and you know that. I submit to the inevitable, but my heart will always be with you whether we remain together or whether we part. Of course I only answer for myself; you can't expect the same from your sister …'

'Ah, Varya again!' cried Ganya, looking with hatred and mockery at his sister. 'Mother, I swear again what I promised you already! No one shall ever dare to be wanting in respect to you so long as I am here, so long as I am alive. Whoever may be concerned, I shall insist on the utmost respect being shown to you from anyone who enters our doors.'

Ganya was so relieved that he looked with an almost conciliatory, almost affectionate, expression at his mother.

'I was not afraid for myself, Ganya, you knows I've not been anxious and worried all this time on my own account. I am told that today everything will be settled. What will be settled?'

'She promised to let me know tonight whether she agrees or not,' answered Ganya.

'For almost three weeks we have avoided speaking of it, and it has been better so. Now that everything is settled, I will allow myself to ask one question only. How can she give you her consent and her portrait when you don't love her? How, with a woman so...so ...'

'Experienced, you mean?'

'I didn't mean to put it in that way. Can you have hoodwinked her so completely?'

A note of intense exasperation was suddenly audible in the question. Ganya stood still, thought a minute, and with undisguised irony said: 'You are carried away, mother, and can't control yourself again. And that's how it always begins and then gets hotter and hotter with us. You said that there should be no questions asked and no reproaches and they've begun already! We'd better drop it; we'd better, really. Your intentions were good, anyway ... I will never desert you under any circumstances. Any other man would have run away from such a sister. See how she is looking at me now! Let us make an end of it. I was feeling so relieved ... And how do you know I am deceiving Nastasya Filippovna? As for Varya, she can please herself, and that's all about it. Well, that's quite enough now.'

Ganya got hotter with every word and paced aimlessly about the room. Such conversations quickly touched the sore spot in every member of the family.

'I have said that, if she comes into the house, I shall go out of it, and I too shall keep my word,' said Varya.

'Out of obstinacy!' cried Ganya. 'And it's out of obstinacy that you won't be married either. Don't snort at me! I don't care a damn for it, Varvara Ardalionovna! You can carry out your plan at once, if you like. I am sick of you. What! You have made up your mind to leave us at last, Prince, have you?' he cried to Myshkin, seeing him get up from his place.

Ganya's voice betrayed that pitch of irritation when a man almost revels in his own irritability, gives himself up to it without restraint and almost with growing enjoyment, regardless of consequences. Myshkin looked round at the door to answer the insult, but seeing from Ganya's exasperated face that another word would be too much for him, he turned and went out in silence.

A few minutes later he heard from their voices in the drawing-room that the conversation had become even noisier and more unreserved in his absence.

He crossed the dining-room into the hall on the way to his room. As he passed the front door, he heard and noticed someone outside making desperate efforts to ring the bell. But something seemed to have gone wrong with the bell, it only shook without making a sound. Myshkin unbolted the door, opened it, and stepped back in amazement, startled. Nastasya Filippovna stood before him. He knew her at once from her photograph. There was a gleam of annoyance in her eyes when she saw him. She walked quickly into the hall, pushing him out of her way, and said angrily, flinging off her fur coat: 'If you are too lazy to mend the bell, you might at least be in the hall when people knock. Now he's dropped my coat, the duffer!'

The coat was indeed lying on the floor. Nastasya Filippovna without waiting for him to help her off with it, had flung it on his arm from behind without looking, but Myshkin was not quick enough to catch it.

'They ought to turn you off. Go along and announce me.'

Myshkin was about to say something, but was so abashed that he could not, and, carrying the coat which he had picked up from the floor, he walked towards the drawing-room.

'Well, now he is taking my coat with him! Why are you carrying my coat away? Ha, ha, ha! Are you crazy?'

Myshkin went back and stared at her, as though he were petrified. When she laughed he smiled too, but still he could not speak. At the first moment when he opened the door to her, he was pale; now the colour rushed to his face.

'What an idiot!' Nastasya Filippovna cried out, stamping her foot in indignation. 'Where are you going now? What name are you going to take in?'

'Nastasya Filippovna,' muttered Myshkin.

'How do you know me?' She asked him quickly. 'I've never seen you. Go along, take in my name. What's the shouting about in there?'

'They are quarrelling,' said Myshkin, and he went into the drawing-room.

He went in at a rather critical moment. Nina Alexandrovna was on the point of entirely forgetting that 'she was resigned to everything'; she was defending Varya, however. Ptitsyn too was standing by Varya's side; he had left his pencilled note. Varya herself was not overawed; indeed, she was not a girl of the timid sort, but her brother's rudeness became coarser and more insufferable at every word. In such circumstances she usually left off speaking and only kept her eyes fixed on her brother in ironical silence. By this proceeding she was able, she knew, to drive her brother out of all bounds. At that moment Myshkin entered the room and announced: 'Nastasya Filippovna.'

Chapter 9

There was complete silence in the room; everyone stared at Myshkin as though they didn't understand him and didn't want to understand him. Ganya was numb with horror. The arrival of Nastasya Filippovna, and especially at this juncture, was the strangest and most disturbing surprise for everyone. The very fact that Nastasya Filippovna had for the first time thought fit to call on them was astounding. Hitherto she had been so haughty that she had not in talking to Ganya even expressed a desire to make the acquaintance of his family, and of late had made no allusion to them at all, as though they were non-existent. Though Ganya was to some extent relieved at avoiding so difficult a subject, yet in his heart he treasured it up against her. In any case he would rather have expected biting and ironical remarks from her about his family than a visit to them. He knew for a fact that she was aware of all that was going on in his home in regard to his engagement and of the attitude of his family towards her. Her visit *now,* after the present of her photograph and on her birthday, the day on which she had promised to decide his fate, was almost equivalent to the decision itself.

The stupefaction with which all stared at Myshkin did not last long. Nastasya Filippovna herself appeared at the drawing-room door and again slightly pushed him aside as she entered the room.

'At last I have managed to get in. Why do you tie up the bell?' she said good-humouredly, giving her hand to Ganya, who rushed to meet her. 'Why do you look so upset? Introduce me, please.'

Ganya, utterly disconcerted, introduced her first to Varya, and the two women exchanged strange looks before holding out their hands to each other. Nastasya Filippovna, however, laughed and masked her feelings with a show of good humour, but Varya did not care to mask hers, and looked at her with gloomy intensity. Her countenance showed no trace even of the smile required by simple politeness. Ganya was aghast; it was useless to entreat, and there was no time indeed, and he flung at Varya such a menacing glance that she saw from it what the moment meant to her brother. She seemed to make up her mind to give in to him, and faintly smiled at Nastasya Filippovna. (All of the family were still very fond of one another.) The position was somewhat improved by Nina Alexandrovna, whom Ganya, helplessly confused, introduced after his sister. He even made the introduction to Nastasya Filippovna instead of to his mother. But no sooner had Nina Alexandrovna begun to speak of the 'great pleasure,' &c., when Nastasya Filippovna, paying no attention to her, turned hurriedly to Ganya and, sitting down, without waiting to be asked, on a little sofa in the corner by the window, she cried out: 'Where's your study? And ... where are the lodgers? You take lodgers, don't you?'

Ganya flushed horribly and was stammering some answer, but Nastasya Filippovna added at once: 'Wherever do you keep lodgers here? You've no study even. Does it pay?' she asked, suddenly addressing Nina Alexandrovna.

'It's rather troublesome,' the latter replied. 'Of course it must pay to some extent, but we've only just...'

But Nastasya Filippovna was not listening again: she stared at Ganya, laughed, and shouted to him: 'What do you look like! My goodness! What do you look like at this minute!'

Her laughter lasted several minutes, and Ganya's face certainly was terribly distorted. His stupefaction, his comic crestfallen confusion had suddenly left him. But he turned fearfully pale, his lips worked convulsively. He bent a silent, intent and evil look on the face of his visitor, who still went on laughing.

There was another observer who had scarcely recovered from his amazement at the sight of Nastasya Filippovna, but though he stood dumbfounded in the same place by the drawing-room door, yet he noticed Ganya's pallor and the ominous change in his face. That observer was Myshkin. Almost frightened, he instinctively stepped forward.

'Drink some water,' he murmured to Ganya, 'and don't look like that.'

It was evident that he spoke on the impulse of the moment, without ulterior motive or intention. But his words produced an extraordinary effect. All Ganya's spite seemed suddenly turned against him. He seized him by the shoulder and looked at him in silence with hatred and resentment, as though unable to utter a word. It caused a general commotion; Nina Alexandrovna even uttered a faint cry. Ptitsyn stepped forward uneasily; Kolya and Ferdyshtchenko, who were coming in at the door, stopped short in amazement. Only Varya still looked sullen, yet she was watching intently. She did not sit down, but stood beside her mother with her arms folded across her bosom.

But Ganya checked himself at once, almost at the first moment, and laughed nervously. He regained his self-pos session completely.

'Why, are you a doctor, Prince?' he cried as simply and good-humouredly as he could. 'He positively frightened me. Nastasya Filippovna, may I introduce? This is a rare personality, though I've only known him since the morning.'

Nastasya Filippovna looked at Myshkin in astonishment.

'Prince? He is a prince? Only fancy, I took him for the footman just now and sent him in to announce me! Ha, ha, ha!'

'No harm done – no harm done,' put in Ferdyshtchenko, going up to her quickly, relieved that they had begun to laugh. 'No harm: *se non e vero* ...'

'And I was almost swearing at you, Prince! Forgive me, please. Ferdyshtchenko, how do you come to be here at such an hour? I did not expect to meet you here, anyway. Who? What prince? Myshkin?' she questioned Ganya, who, still holding Myshkin by the shoulder, had by now introduced him.

'Our boarder,' repeated Ganya.

It was obvious that they presented him and almost thrust him upon Nastasya Filippovna as a curiosity, as a means of escape from a false position. Myshkin distinctly caught the word 'idiot' pronounced behind his back, probably by Ferdyshtchenko, as though in explanation to Nastasya Filippovna.

'Tell me, why didn't you undeceive me just now when I made such a dreadful mistake about you?' Nastasya Filippovna went on, scanning Myshkin from head to foot in a most unceremonious fashion.

She waited with impatience for an answer, as though she were sure the answer would be so stupid as to make them laugh.

'I was surprised at seeing you so suddenly,' Myshkin muttered.

'And how did you know it was I? Where have you seen me before? But how is it? Really, it seems as though I had seen him somewhere. And tell me why were you so astonished just now? What is there so amazing about me?'

'Come now, come,' Ferdyshtchenko went on, simpering. 'Come now! Oh Lord, the things I'd say in answer to such a question! Come!... We shall think you are a duffer next, Prince!'

'I should say them too in your place,' said Myshkin, laughing, to Ferdyshtchenko. 'I was very much struck today by your portrait,' he went on, addressing Nastasya Filippovna. 'Then I talked to the Epanchins about you; and early this morning in the train, before I reached Petersburg, Parfyon Rogozhin told me a great deal about you ... And at the very minute I opened the door to you, I was thinking about you too, and then suddenly you appeared.'

'And how did you recognise that it was I?'

'From the photograph, and ...'

'And what?'

'And you were just as I had imagined you ... I feel as though I had seen you somewhere too.'

'Where – where?'

'I feel as though I had seen your eyes somewhere ... but that's impossible. That's nonsense ... I've never been here before. Perhaps in a dream ...'

'Bravo, Prince!' cried Ferdyshtchenko. 'Yes, I take back my *"se non e vero."* But it's all his innocence,' he added regretfully.

Myshkin had uttered his few sentences in an uneasy voice, often stopping to take breath. Everything about him suggested strong emotion. Nastasya Filippovna looked at him with interest, but she was not laughing now.

At that moment a new voice, speaking loudly behind the group that stood close round Myshkin and Nastasya Filippovna, seemed to cleave a way through the company and part it in two. Facing Nastasya Filippovna stood the head of the family, General Ivolgin himself. He wore an evening coat and had a clean shirt-front; his moustaches were dyed.

This was more than Ganya could endure.

Ambitious and vain to a hypersensitive, morbid degree, he had been seeking for the last two months for any sort of means by which he could build up a more presentable and gentlemanly mode of life. Yet he felt himself without experience, and perhaps likely to go astray in the path he had chosen. At home, where he was a despot, he had taken up in despair an attitude of complete cynicism, but he dared not maintain this position before Nastasya Filippovna, who had held him in suspense till the last minute and ruthlessly kept the upper hand of him. 'The impatient beggar,' as Nastasya Filippovna had called him, so he had been told, had sworn by every oath that he would make her pay bitterly for it afterwards. Yet at the same time he had sometimes dreamed like a child of reconciling all incongruities. Now, after all that, he had to drink this bitter cup too, at such a moment above all! One more unforeseen torture – most terrible of all for a vain man – the agony of blushing for his own kindred, in his own house, had fallen to his lot.

'Is the reward itself worth it?' flashed through Ganya's mind at that moment.

At that instant there was happening what had been his nightmare for those two months, what had frozen him with horror and made him burn with shame: the meeting had come at last between his father and Nastasya Filippovna. He had sometimes tormented himself by trying to imagine the general at the wedding, but he never could fill in the agonising picture and made haste to put it out of his mind. Perhaps he exaggerated his misfortune out of all proportion. But that is always the way with vain people. In the course of those two months he had considered the matter thoroughly and had decided at all costs to suppress his parent for a time at least and to get him, if necessary, out of Petersburg, with or without his mother's consent. Ten minutes earlier, when Nastasya Filippovna made her entrance, he was so taken aback, so dumbfounded, that he forgot the possibility of Ardalion Alexandrovitch's appearance on the scene and had taken no steps to prevent it. And behold, here was the general before them all, and solemnly got up for the occasion too in a dress-coat, at the very moment when Nastasya Filippovna was 'only seeking some pretext to cover him and his family with ridicule' (of that he felt convinced). Indeed, what could her visit mean, if not that? Had she come to make friends with his mother and sister, or to insult them in his house? But from the attitude of both parties there could be no doubt on that subject: his mother and his sister were sitting on one side like outcasts, while Nastasya Filippovna seemed positively to have forgotten that they were in the same room with her. And if she behaved like that, it was pretty certain she had some object in it.

Ferdyshtchenko took hold of the general and led him up.

'Ardalion Alexandrovitch Ivolgin,' said the general with dignity, bowing and smiling. 'An old soldier in misfortune and the father of a family which is happy in the prospect of including such a charming ...'

He did not finish. Ferdyshtchenko quickly set a chair for him, and the general, who was rather weak on his legs at that moment so soon after dinner, fairly plumped, or rather fell, into it. But that did not disconcert him. He took up his position directly facing Nastasya Filippovna, and with an agreeable simper he deliberately and gallantly raised her fingers to his lips. It was at all times difficult to disconcert the general. Except for a certain slovenliness, his exterior was still fairly presentable, a fact of which he was thoroughly well aware. He had in the past moved at times in very good society, from which he had been finally excluded only two or three years before. Since then he had abandoned himself to some of his weaknesses, unchecked. But he still retained his easy and agreeable manner.

Nastasya Filippovna seemed highly delighted at the advent of General Ivolgin, of whom of course she had heard.

'I've heard that my son ...' began Ardalion Alexandrovitch.

'Yes, your son! You are a pretty one too, his papa! Why do you never come and see me? Do you shut yourself up, or is it your son's doing? You at least might come to see me without compromising anyone.'

'Children of the nineteenth century and their parents...' the general began again.

'Nastasya Filippovna, please excuse Ardalion Alexandrovitch for a moment, someone is asking to see him,' said Nina Alexandrovna in a loud voice.

'Excuse him! Why, but I've heard so much about him, I've been wanting to see him for so long! And what business has he? He is retired? You won't leave me, General? You won't go away?'

'I promise you he shall come and see you, but now he needs rest.'

'Ardalion Alexandrovitch, they say you need rest,' cried Nastasya Filippovna, displeased and pouting like a frivolous and silly woman deprived of a toy.

The general did his best to make his position more foolish than before.

'My dear! My dear!' he said reproachfully, addressing his wife solemnly and laying his hand on his heart.

'Won't you come away, mother?' said Varya aloud.

'No, Varya, I'll sit it out to the end.'

Nastasya Filippovna could not have failed to hear the question and the answer, but it seemed only to increase her gaiety. She showered questions upon the general again, and in five minutes the general was in a most triumphant state of mind and holding forth amidst the loud laughter of the company.

Kolya pulled Myshkin by the lapel of his coat.

'You get him away somehow. This is impossible! Please do!' There were tears of indignation in the poor boy's eyes. 'Oh, that beast Ganya!' he muttered to himself.

'I used indeed to be an intimate friend of Ivan Fyodorovitch Epanchin's,' the general babbled on in reply to Nastasya Filippovna's question. 'He, I, and the late Prince Lyov Nikolayevitch Myshkin, whose son I have embraced today after twenty years' separation, we were three inseparables, a regular cavalcade, so to say – like the three musketeers, Athos, Porthos, and Aramis. But one is in his grave, alas! Struck down by slander and a bullet; another is before you and is still struggling with slanders and bullets

'With bullets?' cried Nastasya Filippovna.

'They are here, in my bosom, and were received under the walls of Kars,and in bad weather I am conscious of them. In all other respects I live like a philosopher, I walk, I play draughts at my café like any bourgeois retired from business, and read the *Indépendance.* But with Epanchin, our Porthos, I've had nothing to do since the scandal two years ago on the railway about a lapdog.'

'About a lapdog? What was it?' asked Nastasya Filippovna with marked curiosity. 'About a lapdog? Let me see ... and on the railway too,' she repeated, as though recollecting something.

'Oh, it was a stupid affair, not worth repeating. It was all about Princess Byelokonsky's governess, Mistress Schmidt. But ... it's not worth repeating.'

'But you must tell me!' cried Nastasya Filippovna gaily.

'And I've never heard it before,' observed Ferdyshtchenko. *'C'est du nouveau.'*

'Ardalion Alexandrovitch!' came again beseechingly from Nina Alexandrovna.

'Father, there's someone to see you!' cried Kolya.

'It's a stupid story and can be told in two words,' began the general complacently. 'Two years ago – yes, nearly two, just after the opening of the new railway – I was already in civilian dress then and busy about an affair of great importance in connection with my giving up the service. I took a first-class ticket, went in, sat down and began to smoke. Or rather I went on smoking; I had lighted my cigar before. I was alone in the compartment. Smoking was not prohibited, nor was it allowed; it was sort of half allowed, as it usually is. Of course it depends on the person. The window was down. Just before the whistle sounded, two ladies with a lapdog seated themselves just opposite me. They were late. One of them was dressed in gorgeous style in light blue; the other more soberly in black silk with a cape. They were nice-looking, had a disdainful air, and talked English. I took no notice, of course, and went on smoking. I did hesitate, but I went on smoking close to the window for the window was open. The lapdog was lying on the pale blue lady's knee. It was a tiny creature no bigger than my fist, black with white paws, quite a curiosity. It had a silver collar with a motto on it. I did nothing. But I noticed the ladies seemed annoyed, at my cigar, no doubt. One of them stared at me through her tortoiseshell lorgnette. I did nothing again, for they said nothing. If they'd said anything, warned me, asked me – there is such a thing as language after all! But they were silent... Suddenly, without the slightest preface – I assure you without the slightest, as though she had suddenly taken leave of her senses – the pale blue one snatched the cigar out of my hand and flung it out of the window. The train was racing along. I gazed at her aghast. A savage woman, yes, positively a woman of quite a savage type; yet a plump, comfortable looking, tall, fair woman, with rosy cheeks (too rosy, in fact). Her eyes glared at me. Without uttering a word and with extraordinary courtesy, the most perfect, the most refined courtesy, I delicately picked up the lapdog by the collar in two fingers and flung it out of the window after the cigar! It uttered one squeal. The train was still racing on.'

'You are a monster!' exclaimed Nastasya Filippovna, laughing and clapping her hands like a child.

'Bravo, bravo!' cried Ferdyshtchenko.

Ptitsyn too smiled, though he also had been extremely put out by the general's entrance. Even Kolya laughed and cried 'Bravo!' too.

'And I was right, perfectly right,' the triumphant general continued warmly. 'For if cigars are forbidden in a railway carriage, dogs are even more so.'

'Bravo, father!' cried Kolya gleefully. 'Splendid! I should certainly, certainly have done the same.'

'But what did the lady do?' Nastasya Filippovna asked impatiently.

'She? Ah, that's where the unpleasantness comes in,' the general went on, frowning. 'Without uttering a word and without the slightest warning she slapped me on the cheek. A savage woman, quite a savage type.'

'And you?'

The general dropped his eyes, raised his eyebrows, shrugged his shoulders, pursed up his lips, flung up his hands, paused, then suddenly pronounced: 'I was carried away.'

'And hurt her – hurt her?'

'On my honour, I did not. A scandalous scene followed, but I did not hurt her. I simply waved my arm once, solely to wave her back. But as the devil would have it, the pale blue one turned out to be English, a governess or some sort of family friend of Princess Byelokonsky, and the one in black, as it appeared, was the eldest of the princess's daughters, an old maid of five-and thirty. And you know what terms Madame Epanchin is on with the Byelokonsky family. All the six princesses fainted, tears, mourning for the pet lapdog, screams on the part of the English governess – a perfect Bedlam! Of course I went to apologise, to express my penitence, wrote a letter. They refused to see me or my letter. And Epanchin quarrelled with me, refused me admittance, turned me out.'

'But allow me. How do you explain this?' Nastasya Filippovna asked suddenly. 'Five or six days ago I read in the *Indépendance* – I always read the *Indépendance* – exactly the same story. Precisely the same story! It happened on one of the Rhine railways between a Frenchman and an Englishwoman. The cigar was snatched in the same way; the lapdog was thrown out of window too. It ended in the same way. Her dress was pale blue even!'

The general flushed terribly. Kolya blushed too and squeezed his head in his hands. Ptitsyn turned away quickly. Ferdyshtchenko was the only one who went on laughing. There is no need to speak of Ganya: he had stood all the time in mute and insufferable agony.

'I assure you,' muttered the general, 'that the very same thing happened to me.'

'Father really had some trouble with Mrs Schmidt, the governess at the Byelokonsky's,' cried Kolya. 'I remember it.'

'What! Exactly the same? The very same story at the opposite ends of Europe and alike in every detail, even to the pale blue dress,' persisted the merciless lady. 'I'll send you the *Indépendance Belge.*'

'But note,' the general still persisted, 'that the incident occurred to me two years ago.'

'Ah, there is that!' Nastasya Filippovna laughed as though she were in hysterics.

'Father, I beg you, come out and let me have a word with you,' said Ganya in a shaking and harassed voice, mechanically taking his father by the shoulder.

There was a gleam of infinite hatred in his eyes.

At that moment there was a violent ring at the front door – a ring that might well have pulled down the bell. It betokened an exceptional visit. Kolya ran to open the door.

Chapter 10

There seemed a great deal of noise and many people in the entry. From the drawing-room it sounded as though several people had already come in and more were still coming. Several voices were talking and shouting at once. There was shouting and talking on the staircase also; the door opening on it had evidently not been closed. The visit seemed to be a very strange one. They all looked at each other. Ganya rushed into the dining-room, but several visitors had already entered it.

'Ah, here he is the Judas!' cried a voice that Myshkin knew. 'How are you, Ganya, you scoundrel?'

'Here he is, here he is himself!' another voice chimed in.

Myshkin could not be mistaken: the first voice was Rogozhin's, the second Lebedyev's.

Ganya stood petrified and gazing at them in silence in the doorway from the drawing-room, not hindering ten or twelve persons from following Parfyon Rogozhin into the dining-room. The party was an exceedingly mixed one, and not only incongruous but disorderly. Some of them walked in as they were, in their overcoats and furs. None were quite drunk, however, though they all seemed extremely exhilarated. They seemed to need each other's moral support to enter; not one would have had the effrontery to enter alone, but they all seemed to push one another in. Even Rogozhin walked diffidently at the head of the party, but he had some intention, and he seemed in a state of gloomy and irritated preoccupation. The others only made a chorus or band of supporters. Besides Lebedyev, there was Zalyozhev, who had flung off his overcoat in the entry and walked in swaggering and jaunty with his hair curled. There were two or three more of the same sort, evidently young merchants; a man in a semi-military greatcoat; a very fat little man who kept laughing continually; an immense man over six feet, also very stout, extremely taciturn and morose, who evidently put his faith in his fists. There was a medical student, and a little Pole who had somehow attached himself to the party. Two unknown ladies peeped in at the front door, but did not venture to come in. Kolya slammed the door in their faces and latched it.

'How are you, Ganya, you scoundrel? You didn't expect Parfyon Rogozhin, did you?' repeated Rogozhin, going to the drawing-room door and facing Ganya.

But at that moment he caught sight of Nastasya Filippovna, who sat facing him in the drawing-room. Evidently nothing was further from his thoughts than meeting her here, for the sight of her had an extraordinary effect on him. He turned so pale that his lips went blue.

'Then it's true,' he said quietly, as though to himself, looking absolutely distracted. 'It's the end! ... Well ... you shall pay for it!' he snarled, suddenly looking with extreme fury at Ganya. 'Well... ach!'

He gasped for breath, he could hardly speak. Mechanically he moved into the drawing-room, but as he went in, he suddenly saw Nina Alexandrovna and Varya, and stopped somewhat embarrassed, in spite of his emotion. After him came Lebedyev who followed him about like a shadow and was very drunk; then the student, the gentleman with the fists, Zalyozhev, bowing to right and left, and last of all the little fat man squeezed himself in. The presence of the ladies was still a check on them, and it was evidently an unwelcome constraint, which would of course have broken down if they had once been set off, if some pretext for shouting and beginning a row had arisen. Then all the ladies in the world would not have hindered them.

'What, you here too, Prince?' Rogozhin said absently, somewhat surprised at meeting Myshkin. 'Still in your gaiters, e-ech!' he sighed, forgetting Myshkin's existence and looking towards Nastasya Filippovna again, moving closer to her as though drawn by a magnet.

Nastasya Filippovna too looked with uneasy curiosity at the visitors.

Ganya recovered himself at last.

'But allow me. What does this mean?' he began in a loud voice, looking severely at the newcomers and addressing himself principally to Rogozhin. 'This isn't a stable, gentlemen, my mother and sister are here.'

'We see your mother and sister are here,' muttered Rogozhin through his teeth.

'That can be seen, that your mother and sister are here.' Lebedyev felt called upon to second the statement.

The gentleman with the fists, feeling no doubt that the moment had arrived, began growing something.

'But upon my word!' cried Ganya, suddenly exploding and raising his voice immoderately. 'First, I beg you all to go into the dining-room, and secondly, kindly let me know ...'

'Fancy, he doesn't know!' said Rogozhin, with an angry grin, not budging from where he stood. 'Don't you know Rogozhin?'

'I've certainly met you somewhere, but...'

'Met me somewhere! Why,I lost two hundred roubles of my father's money to you three months ago. The old man died without finding it out. You enticed me into it and Kniff cheated. Don't you recognise me? Ptitsyn was a witness of it. If I were to show you three roubles out of my pocket, you'd crawl on all fours to Vassilyevsky for it – that's the sort of chap you are! That's the sort of soul you've got! And I've come here now to buy you for money. Never mind my having come with such boots on. I've got a lot of money now, brother, I can buy the whole of you and your livestock too. I can buy you all up, if I like! I'll buy up everything!' Rogozhin grew more and more excited and seemed more and more drunk. 'E-ech!' he cried. 'Nastasya Filippovna, don't turn me away. Tell me one thing: are you going to marry him, or not?'

Rogozhin put this question desperately, as though appealing to a deity, but with the courage of a man condemned to death who has nothing to lose. In deadly anguish he awaited her reply.

With haughty and sarcastic eyes, Nastasya Filippovna looked him up and down. But she glanced at Varya and Nina Alexandrovna, looked at Ganya, and suddenly changed her tone.

'Certainly not! What's the matter with you? And what has put it into your head to ask such a question?' she answered quietly and gravely and as it seemed with some surprise.

'No? No!' cried Rogozhin, almost frantic with delight. 'Then you are not? But they told me ... Ach! ... Nastasya Filippovna, they say that you are engaged to Ganya. To him! As though that were possible! I told them all it was impossible. I can buy him up for a hundred roubles. If I were to give him a thousand, three thousand, to retire, he would run off on his wedding day and leave his bride to me. That's right, isn't it, Ganya, you scoundrel? You'd take the three thousand, wouldn't you? Here's the money – here you have it! I came to get you to sign the agreement to do it. I said I'll buy him off and I will buy him off!'

'Get out of the room, you are drunk!' cried Ganya, who had been flushing and growing pale by turns.

His outburst was followed by a sudden explosion from several persons at once: the whole crew of Rogozhin's followers were only awaiting the signal for battle. With intense solicitude Lebedyev was whispering something in Rogozhin's ear.

'That's true, clerk!' answered Rogozhin. 'True, you drunken soul! Ech, here goes! Nastasya Filippovna,' he cried, gazing at her like a maniac, passing from timidity to the extreme of audacity, 'here are eighteen thousand roubles!' and he tossed on the table before her a roll of notes wrapped in white paper and tied with string. 'There! And ... and there's more to come!'

He did not venture to say what he wanted.

'No, no, no!' Lebedyev whispered to him with an air of dismay.

It could be divined that he was horrified at the magnitude of the sum and was urging him to try his luck with a much smaller one.

'No, brother, you are a fool; you don't know how to behave here ... and it seems as though I am a fool like you!' Rogozhin started, and checked himself as he met the flashing eyes of Nastasya Filippovna. 'E-ech! I've made a mess of it, listening to you,' he added with intense regret.

Nastasya Filippovna suddenly laughed as she looked at Rogozhin's downcast face.

'Eighteen thousand to me? Ah, one can see he is a peasant!' she added with insolent familiarity, and she got up from the sofa, as though to go away.

Ganya had watched the whole scene with a sinking heart.

'Forty thousand, then – forty, not eighteen!' cried Rogozhin. 'Ptitsyn and Biskup promised to get me forty thousand by seven o'clock. Forty thousand! Cash down!'

The scene had become scandalous in the extreme, but Nastasya Filippovna stayed on and still went on laughing, as though she were intentionally prolonging it. Nina Alexandrovna and Varya had also risen from their places and waited in silent dismay to see how much further it would go. Varya's eyes glittered but the effect of it all on Nina Alexandrovna was painful; she trembled and seemed on the point of fainting.

'A hundred, then, if that's it! I'll give you a hundred thousand today. Ptitsyn, lend it me, it'll be worth your while!'

'You are mad,' Ptitsyn whispered suddenly, going up to him quickly and taking him by the hand. 'You are mad! They'll send for the police! Where are you?'

'He is drunk and boasting,' said Nastasya Filippovna, as though taunting him.

'I am not boasting, I'll get the money before evening. Ptitsyn, lend it me, you money-grubber! Ask what you like for it. Get me a hundred thousand this evening! I'll show that I won't stick at anything.' Rogozhin was in an ecstasy of excitement.,

'What is the meaning of this, pray?' Ardalion Alexandrovitch, deeply stirred, suddenly cried in a menacing voice, going up to Rogozhin.

The suddenness of the old man's outburst, after his complete silence till that moment, made it very comic. There was laughter.

'Whom have we here?' laughed Rogozhin. 'Come along, old fellow, we'll make you drunk.'

'This is too disgusting!' cried Kolya, shedding tears of shame and vexation.

'Is there no one among you who will take this shameless woman away?' exclaimed Varya, quivering all over with anger.

'They call me a shameless woman,' Nastasya Filippovna answered back with contemptuous gaiety. 'And I came like a fool to invite them to my party this evening. That's how your sister treats me, Gavril Ardalionovitch!'

For some time Ganya stood as though thunderstruck at his sister's outburst, but seeing that Nastasya Filippovna really was going this time, he rushed frantically at Varya and seized her arm in a fury.

'What have you done?' he cried, looking at her, as though he would have withered her on the spot.

He was utterly beside himself and hardly knew what he was doing.

'What have I done? Where are you dragging me? Is it to beg her pardon for having insulted your mother and for having come here to disgrace your family, you base creature?' Varya cried again, looking with triumphant defiance at her brother.

For some instant they stood so, facing one another. Ganya still kept hold of her arm. Twice Varya tried with all her might to pull herself free, but suddenly losing all self-control, she spat in her brother's face.

'What a girl!' cried Nastasya Filippovna. 'Bravo! Ptitsyn, I congratulate you!'

Everything danced before Ganya's eyes, and, completely forgetting himself, he struck at his sister with all his might. He would have hit her on the face, but suddenly another hand caught Ganya's. Myshkin stood between him and his sister.

'Don't, that's enough,' he brought out insistently, though he was shaking all over with violent emotion.

'Are you always going to get in my way?' roared Ganya. He let go Varya's arm and, mad with rage, gave Myshkin a violent slap in the face with the hand thus freed.

'Ah!' cried Kolya, clasping his hands. 'My God!'

Exclamations were heard on all sides. Myshkin turned pale. He looked Ganya straight in the face with strange and reproachful eyes; his lips quivered, trying to articulate something; they were twisted into a sort of strange and utterly incongruous smile.

'Well, you may … but her … I won't let you,' he said softly at last.

But suddenly he broke down, left Ganya, hid his face in his hands, moved away to a corner, stood with his face to the wall, and in a breaking voice said, 'Oh, how ashamed you will be of what you've done!'

Ganya did, indeed, stand looking utterly crushed. Kolya rushed to hug and kiss Myshkin. He was followed by Rogozhin, Varya, Ptitsyn, Nina Alexandrovna – all the party, even the general, who all crowded about Myshkin.

'Never mind, never mind,' muttered Myshkin in all directions, still with the same incongruous smile.

'And he will regret it,' cried Rogozhin. 'You will be ashamed, Ganya, that you have insulted such a … sheep' (he could not find another word). 'Prince darling, drop them; curse them and come along. I'll show you what a friend Rogozhin can be.'

Nastasya Filippovna too was very much impressed by Ganya's action and Myshkin's answer. Her usually pale and melancholy face, which had seemed all along so out of keeping with her affected laughter, was evidently stirred by a new feeling. Yet she still seemed unwilling to betray it and to be trying to maintain a sarcastic expression.

'I certainly have seen his face somewhere,' she said, speaking quite earnestly now, suddenly recalling her former question.

'Aren't you ashamed? Surely you are not what you are pretending to be now? It isn't possible!' cried Myshkin suddenly with deep and heartfelt reproach.

Nastasya Filippovna was surprised, and smiled, seeming to hide something under her smile. She looked at Ganya, rather confused, and walked out of the drawing-room. But before reaching the entry, she turned sharply, went quickly up to Nina Alexandrovna, took her hand and raised it to her lips.

'I really am not like this, he is right,' she said in a rapid eager whisper, flushing hotly; and turning round, she walked out so quickly that no one had time to realise what she had come back for. All that was seen was that she whispered something to Nina Alexandrovna and seemed to have kissed her hand. But Varya saw and heard it all, and watched her go out, wondering.

Ganya recovered himself and rushed to see Nastasya Filippovna out. But she had already gone. He overtook her on the stairs.

'Don't come with me,' she cried to him. 'Goodbye till this evening. You must come, do you hear?'

He returned, confused and dejected, a painful uncertainty weighed on his heart, more bitter than ever now. The figure of Myshkin too haunted him ... He was so absorbed that he scarcely noticed Rogozhin's crew passing him and shoving against him in the doorway, as they hurried by on their way out of the flat. They were all loudly discussing something. Rogozhin walked with Ptitsyn, talking of something important and apparently urgent.

'You've lost the game, Ganya!' he cried, as he passed him.

Ganya looked after him uneasily.

Chapter 11

Myshkin went out of the drawing-room and shut himself up in his room. Kolya ran in at once to try and soothe him. The poor boy seemed unable to keep away from him now.

'You've done well to come away,' he said. 'There will be a worse upset there now than ever. And it's like that every day with us; it's all on account of that Nastasya Filippovna.'

'There are so many sources of distress in your family, Kolya,' Myshkin observed.

'Yes, there are. There's no denying it. It's all our own fault. But I have a great friend who is even more unfortunate. Would you like to meet him?'

'Very much. Is he a comrade of yours?'

'Yes, almost like a comrade. I'll tell you all about it afterwards ... But Nastasya Filippovna is handsome, don't you think? I've never seen her before, though I've tried hard to. I was simply dazzled. I'd forgive Ganya everything, if he were in love with her. But why is he taking money? That's what's horrid.'

'Yes, I don't much like your brother.'

'Well, I should think not! As if you could, after ... But you know I can't endure those ideas. Some madman, or fool, or scoundrel in a fit of madness, gives you a slap in the face and a man is disgraced for life, and cannot wipe out the insult except in blood, unless the other man goes down on his knees and asks his pardon. In my opinion it's absurd and it's tyranny. Lermontov's drama, *The Masquerade,* is based on that, and I think it's stupid. Or rather, I mean, not natural. But he wrote it almost in his childhood.'

'I liked your sister very much.'

'The way she spat in Ganya's mug! She is a plucky one. But you didn't spit at him, and I am sure it was not for want of pluck. But here she is – speak of the devil... I knew she'd come. She is generous, though she has faults.'

'You've no business here,' said Varya, pouncing on him first of all. 'Go to father. Is he bothering you, Prince?'

'Not at all, quite the contrary.'

'Now then, elder sister, you are off! That's the worst of her. And, by the way, I thought that father'd be sure to go off with Rogozhin. He is penitent now, I expect. I must see what he is about, I suppose,' added Kolya, going out.

'Thank God, I got mother away and put her to bed, and there was no fresh trouble! Ganya is ashamed and very depressed. And he may well be. What a lesson!... I've come to thank you again and to ask you, did you know Nastasya Filippovna before?'

'No, I didn't.'

'Then what made you tell her to her face that she was "not like this"? And you seem to have guessed right. I believe she really isn't. I can't make her out, though. Of course her object was to insult us, that's clear. I've heard a great deal that's queer about her before. But if she came to invite us, how could she behave like that to mother? Ptitsyn knows her well. He says he would hardly have known her today. And with Rogozhin! It's impossible for anyone with self-respect to talk like that in the house of one's ... Mother too is very worried about you.'

'Never mind that!' said Myshkin, with a gesture of his hand.

'And how was it she obeyed you? ...'

'In what way?'

'You told her she ought to be ashamed and she changed at once. You have an influence over her, Prince,' added Varya, with a faint smile.

The door opened and to their great surprise Ganya entered. He did not even hesitate at the sight of Varya. For a moment he stood in the doorway, then resolutely went up to Myshkin.

'Prince, I behaved like a scoundrel. Forgive me, my dear fellow,' he said suddenly with strong feeling.

There was a look of great pain in his face. Myshkin looked at him in wonder and did not answer at once.

'Come, forgive me – forgive me!' Ganya urged impatiently. 'I am ready to kiss your hand, if you like.'

Myshkin was greatly impressed and put both his arms round Ganya without speaking. They kissed each other with sincere feeling.

'I had no idea – no idea you were like this,' said Myshkin at last, drawing a deep breath. 'I thought you were ... incapable of it.'

'Owning my fault? ... And what made me think this morning you were an idiot! You notice what other people never see. One could talk to you, but... better not talk at all.'

'Here is someone whose pardon you ought to ask too,' said Myshkin, pointing to Varya.

'No, they are all my enemies. You may be sure, Prince, I've made many attempts. There's no true forgiveness from them,' broke hotly from Ganya.

And he turned away from Varya.

'Yes, I will forgive you!' said Varya suddenly.

'And will you go to Nastasya Filippovna's tonight?'

'Yes, I will if you wish it, but you had better judge for yourself whether it's not out of the question for me to go now.'

'She is not like this, you know. You see what riddles she sets us. It's her tricks.'

And Ganya laughed viciously.

'I know for myself that she is not like this and that this is all her tricks. But what does she mean? Besides, Ganya, think what does she take you for, herself? She may have kissed mother's hand, this may all be some sort of trickery, but you know she was laughing at you all the same. It's not worth seventy-five thousand, it really isn't, brother! You are still capable of honourable feelings, that's why I speak to you. Don't you go either. Be on your guard! It can't end well.'

Saying this, Varya, much excited, went quickly out of the room.

'That's how they all are,' said Ganya, smiling. 'And can they suppose I don't know that myself? Why, I know much more than they do.'

So saying, Ganya sat down on, evidently disposed to prolong his visit.

'If you know it yourself,' asked Myshkin rather timidly, 'how can you have chosen such misery, knowing it really is not worth seventy-five thousand?'

'I am not talking of that,' muttered Ganya. 'But tell me, by the way, what do you think – I want to know your opinion particularly – is such "misery" worth seventy-five thousand, or no?'

'I don't think it's worth it.'

'Oh, I knew you'd say that! And is such a marriage shameful?'

'Very shameful.'

'Well, let me tell you that I am going to marry her, and there's no doubt about it now. I was hesitating a little while ago, but there's no doubt now. Don't speak! I know what you want to say.'

'I was not going to say what you think. I am greatly surprised at your immense confidence.'

'In what? What confidence?'

'Why, that Nastasya Filippovna is sure to marry you and that the matter is settled, and secondly, that if she does marry you, the seventy-five thousand will come into your pocket. But of course there's a great deal in it I know nothing about.'

Ganya moved nearer to Myshkin.

'Certainly, you don't know all,' he said. 'Why else should I put on such chains?'

'I think it often happens that people marry for money and the money remains with the wife.'

'N-no, that won't be so with us ... In this case there are ... there are circumstances,' muttered Ganya, musing uneasily. 'But as for her answer, there is no doubt about that,' he added quickly. 'What makes you think that she'll refuse me?'

'I know nothing about it except what I've seen; and what Varvara Ardalionovna said just now

'Ah! That was nonsense. They don't know what else to say. She was laughing at Rogozhin, you may take my word for that. I saw it; that was obvious. At first I was frightened, but now I see through it. Or is it the way she behaved to mother, father and Varya?'

'And to you too.'

'Well, perhaps, but that's only a feminine paying off of old scores, nothing else. She is a fearfully irritable, touchy and vain woman. Like some clerk who has been passed over in the service. She wanted to show herself and all her contempt for them ... and for me too. That's true, I don't deny it ... And yet she will marry me, all the same. You don't know what queer antics human vanity will lead to. You see, she looks on me as a scoundrel because I take her, another man's mistress, so openly for her money, and doesn't know that other men would have taken her in after a more scoundrelly fashion than I, would have stuck to her and begun pouring out liberal and progressive ideas to her, dragging in the woman question; and she would have gone into their snares like a thread into the needle. They would have made the vain little fool believe (and so easily) that she was espoused only "for her noble heart and her misfortune," though it would have been for money just the same. I don't find favour because I don't care to sham; and that's what I ought to do. But what is she doing herself? Isn't it just the same? So what right has she to despise me and to get up games like these? Because I show some pride and won't give in. Oh well, we shall see!'

'Can you have loved her till this happened?'

'I did love her at first. But that's enough. There are women who are good for nothing but mistresses. I don't say that she has been my mistress. If she'll behave quietly, I'll behave quietly, but if she's mutinous, I shall abandon her at once and take the money with me. I don't want to be ridiculous; above all, I don't want to be ridiculous.'

'I keep fancying Nastasya Filippovna is clever,' observed Myshkin cautiously. 'Why should she go into the trap when she sees beforehand what misery it will mean for her? You see, she might marry someone else. That's what's so surprising to me.'

'Well, there are reasons. You don't know everything, Prince... It's... Besides, she is persuaded that I love her to madness, I assure you. Moreover, I strongly suspect that she loves me too after her own fashion – like the saying, you know, "whom I love I chastise." She will look on me as a knave all her life (and perhaps that's what she wants), and yet she'll love me in her own way. She is preparing herself for that, it's her character. She is a very Russian woman, I tell you. But I've got a little surprise in store for her. That scene with Varya just now happened accidentally, but it's to my advantage: she's seen my attachment now and convinced herself of it and of my being ready to break all ties for her sake. So I am not such a fool, you may be sure. By the way, you don't imagine I am usually such a gossip, do you? Perhaps I really am doing wrong in confiding in you, dear prince. But it's because you are the first honourable man I've come across, that I pounced on you. Don't think I say that as a joke. You are not angry for what happened just now, are you? This is the first time for the last two years, perhaps, that I have spoken from my heart. There are terribly few honest people here; none more honest than Ptitsyn. I believe you are laughing, aren't you? Scoundrels love honest men. Don't you know that? And of course I am … though how am I a scoundrel, tell me that, on your conscience? Why do they all follow her lead in calling me a scoundrel? And, do you know, I follow their example and hers and call myself a scoundrel too! That's what's scoundrelly, really scoundrelly!'

'I shall never again look on you as a scoundrel,' said Myshkin. 'Just now I thought of you as quite wicked, and you have so rejoiced me all of a sudden. It's a lesson to me not to judge without experience. Now I see that you can't be considered wicked, nor even a really demoralised man. In my opinion you are simply one of the most ordinary men that could possibly be, only perhaps very weak and not at all original.'

Ganya smiled sarcastically to himself, but did not speak. Myshkin saw that his opinion displeased him and was embarrassed. He too was silent.

'Has father asked you for money?' Ganya enquired.

'No.'

'If he does, don't give it him. But he once was a decent person, I remember. He used to visit people of good standing. And how quickly they pass away, these decent people, when they are old! The slightest change of circumstances and there's nothing left of them, it's all gone in a flash. He used not to tell such lies in old days, I assure you. In old days he was only rather over-enthusiastic – and see what it's come to now! Of course drink's at the bottom of it. Do you know, he keeps a mistress? He has become something worse than a harmless liar now. I can't understand my mother's long-suffering. Has he told you about the siege of Kars? Or how his grey trace-horse began to talk? He doesn't even stick at that.'

And Ganya suddenly roared with laughter.

'Why do you look at me like that?' he asked Myshkin suddenly.

'I am surprised at your laughing so genuinely. You still have the laugh of a child. You came in to make your peace with me just now and said, "if you like I'll kiss your hand" – just as a child would make it up. So you are still capable of such phrases and such impulses. And then you begin a regular harangue about this black business and this seventy-five thousand. It all seems somehow absurd and incredible.'

'What do you argue from that?'

'Aren't you acting too heedlessly? Oughtn't you to look about you first? Varvara Ardalionovna is right, perhaps.'

'Ah, morality! That I am a silly boy, I know that myself,' Ganya interposed hotly, 'if only from my talking about such things with you. It's not for mercenary reasons I am making this marriage, Prince,' he continued, as though, stung by the vanity of youth, he could not resist speaking. 'I should certainly be out of my reckoning if so, for I am still too weak in mind and character. It's because I am carried away by passion, because I have one chief object. You think that as soon as I get seventy-five thousand I shall run and buy a carriage. No, I shall wear out my coat of the year before last and drop all my club acquaintances. There are few people of perseverance among us, though we are all money-grubbers. And I want to be persevering. The great thing is to do it thoroughly; that's the whole problem. At seventeen Ptitsyn used to sleep in the street and sell penknives. He began with a farthing and now he has sixty thousand, but what toils he went through to get it! But I shall skip those toils and begin straight off with a capital. In fifteen years people will say, "There goes Ivolgin, the king of the Jews." You tell me I am not an original person. Observe, dear prince, that nothing offends a man of our day and our race more than to tell him that he is not original, that he is weak-willed, has no particular talents and is an ordinary person. You haven't even given me credit for being a first-rate scoundrel, and you know I was ready to annihilate you for it just now. You offended me more than Epanchin, who, without discussion, without having tried to tempt me, in the simplicity of his heart, note that, believes me capable of selling my wife. That has made me savage for a long time, and I want money. When I have money, I shall become a highly original man. What's most low and hateful about money is that even talent can be bought with it, and will be, till the end of the world. You'll say that this is all childish or, perhaps, romantic. Well, it will be the more fun for me, and I shall do what I want. Anyway, I shall persevere and carry it through. *Rira bien qui rira le dernier.* What makes Epanchin insult me like that? Spite, is it? Never! It's simply because I am of so little consequence. But then

... That's enough though, it's time to be off. Kolya has poked his nose in at the door twice already, he is calling you to dinner. And I am going out. I shall look in on you sometimes. You will be all right with us; they will make you quite one of the family now. Mind you don't give me away. I believe that you and I shall either be friends or enemies. And what do you think, Prince, if I had kissed your hand (as I sincerely offered to do), would that have made me your enemy afterwards?'

'It would have been sure to, but not for always. You could not have kept it up afterwards, you would have forgiven me,' Myshkin decided, with a laugh, after a moment's thought.

'Aha! One must be more on one's guard with you. Damn it all, you have put a drop of venom in that too! And who knows, perhaps you are an enemy? By the way – ha, ha, ha! – I forgot to ask you, was I right in fancying that you were rather too much taken with Nastasya Filippovna, eh?'

'Yes... I like her.'

'In love with her?'

'N-no.'

'But he is blushing and unhappy. Well, never mind, never mind, I won't laugh. But do you know she is a woman of virtuous life? Can you believe that? You imagine she is living with that man, Totsky? Not a bit of it. Not for ever so long. And did you notice that she is awfully awkward, and that she was embarrassed for some seconds today? Yes, really. It's just people like that who are fond of dominating others. Well, goodbye.'

'Ganya went out in a good humour and much more at his ease than he had been when he entered. Myshkin remained motionless for ten minutes, thinking.

Kolya poked his head in at the door again.

'I don't want any dinner, Kolya, I had such a good lunch at the Epanchins'.'

Kolya came in altogether and gave Myshkin a note. It was folded and sealed and was from the general. Kolya's face showed how much he disliked giving it him, Myshkin read it, got up and took his hat.

'It's not two steps away,' said Kolya in confusion. 'He is sitting there now over a bottle. How he manages to get credit there I can't conceive. Prince, darling, don't tell my people that I've given you the note. I've sworn a thousand times not to pass on these notes, but I am sorry for him. And I say, please don't stand on ceremony with him; give him some trifle and let that be the end of it.'

'I had a notion of going to him myself, Kolya; I want to see your father ... about something. Come along.'

Chapter 12

Kolya led Myshkin into Liteyny Street, not far away, to a café on the ground floor with a billiard-room. Here in a room apart, in the right-hand corner, Ardalion Alexandrovitch was installed, as though an habitual visitor. He had a bottle on a little table before him and was actually holding a copy of the *Indépendance Belge* in his hands. He was expecting Myshkin. He laid aside the newspaper as soon as he saw him and began a long and heated explanation, of which Myshkin, however, could make very little, for the general was already far from sober.

'I haven't got ten roubles,' Myshkin cut him short, 'but here is a note for twenty-five. Change it and give me fifteen, or else I shall be left without a farthing myself.'

'Oh, certainly, and you may be sure I'll do so immediately.'

'I've come to you with a request, too,General. You've never been to Nastasya Filippovna's?'

'Me? Me never been? You say that to me? Just occasionally, my dear fellow, several times,' cried the general in an access of triumphant and complacent mockery. 'But I broke off the acquaintance myself, for I don't wish to encourage an unseemly alliance. You've seen for yourself, you've been witness this morning. I've done all a father can do, a mild and indulgent father, that is. Now a very different father must come on to the scene, and then we shall see whether an old warrior who has served with honour will triumph over the intrigue, or whether a shameless cocotte shall force her way into an honourable family.'

'I was going to ask you whether you could take me as a friend to Nastasya Filippovna's this evening. I must go today, but I don't know how I can get there. I was introduced today, but not invited; this evening she has a party. But I don't mind disregarding convention a little; I don't mind being laughed at, if only I can get in.'

'That's precisely, precisely my own idea, my young friend,' cried the general enthusiastically. 'I didn't ask you to come on account of that trifle,' he went on, appropriating the money, however, and putting it in his pocket. 'I sent for you precisely to ask you to be my companion in an expedition to Nastasya Filippovna's, or rather an expedition against Nastasya Filippovna. General Ivolgin and Prince Myshkin! How will that strike her? On the pretext of a civility on her name-day, I will announce my will at last – indirectly, not straight out, but it will be just as effective as though directly. Then Ganya will see for himself what he must do. He must choose between his father who has seen honourable service and … so to say … and so on, or … But what will be, must be! Your idea is a very happy one. At nine o'clock we will start, we've plenty of time.'

'Where does she live?'

'A long way from here, close to the Great Theatre, at Mitovtsov's house, almost in the square, on the first floor … It won't be a large party, though it is her name-day, and it will break up early …'

It was getting on in the evening. Myshkin sat listening and waiting for the general, who began an extraordinary number of anecdotes and did not finish one of them. On Myshkin's arrival he asked for another bottle, and it took him an hour to finish it; then he asked for a third, and finished it too. It may well be believed that by that time the general had narrated almost the whole of his history.

At last Myshkin got up and said he could not wait any longer. The general emptied the last drops out of the bottle, stood up and walked out of the room very unsteadily. Myshkin was in despair. He could not understand how he could have believed in him so foolishly. As a matter of fact he never had believed in him; he had simply reckoned on the general as a means of getting to Nastasya Filippovna, even at the cost of some impropriety. But he had not anticipated anything very scandalous. The general turned out to be thoroughly drunk; he was overwhelmingly eloquent and talked without ceasing, with feeling and on the verge of tears. He insisted continually that the misbehaviour of all the members of his family had brought about their ruin, and that it was high time to put a stop to it.

They reached Liteyny Street at last. It was still thawing. A warm, muggy, depressing wind whistled up and down the streets; carriages splashed through the mud. The horses' hoofs struck the flags with a metallic ring. Crowds of wet and dejected people slouched along the pavements, here and there a drunken man among them.

'Do you see those first floors lighted up?' said the general. 'My old comrades live all about here, and I – I who have seen more service and faced more hardships than any of them, I trudge on foot to the lodging of a woman of doubtful reputation! I, a man who has thirteen bullets in his breast! ... You don't believe it? And yet it was solely on my account Dr Pirogov telegraphed to Paris and for a while abandoned Sevastopol at the time of the siege, and Nelaton, the Paris court doctor, succeeded in obtaining a free pass in the name of science and got into the besieged city on purpose to examine me. The highest authorities are cognisant of the fact. "Ah, that's the Ivolgin who has thirteen bullets in him!" ... That's how they speak of me. Do you see that house, Prince? In the first floor there lives Sokolovitch, an old friend of mine, with his honourable and numerous family. That household and three families living in the Nevsky Prospect and two in Morskaya make up my present circle – that is, of my personal acquaintances. Nina Alexandrovna resigned herself to circumstances long ago. But I still remember the past ... and still refresh myself, so to speak, in the cultured society of my old comrades and subordinates who worship me to this day. That General Sokolovitch (I haven't been to call on him for some little time, by the way, and haven't seen Anna Fyodorovna) ... You know, dear prince, when one doesn't entertain oneself, one is apt insensibly to drop out of visiting others. But yet... hm!... You don't seem to believe me... But why not introduce the son of the dearest friend of my youth and companion of my childhood into this delightful family? General Ivolgin and Prince Myshkin! You will see an exquisite girl, not one indeed – two, even three ornaments of Petersburg and of society: beauty, culture, enlightenment... the woman question, poetry – all united in a happy varied combination, to say nothing of a dowry of eighty thousand roubles in hard cash for each of them, which is never a drawback in spite of any feminist or social questions ... In fact I must, I certainly must introduce you. General Ivolgin and Prince Myshkin! A sensation, in fact.'

'At once? Now? But you've forgotten ...' began Myshkin.

'I've forgotten nothing – nothing. Come along! This way, up this magnificent staircase. I wonder why there's no porter, but ... it's a holiday and the porter has taken himself off. They've not dismissed the drunken fellow yet. This Sokolovitch is indebted for the whole happiness of his life and career to me – to me and no one else. But here we are.'

Myshkin made no further protest and to avoid irritating the general he followed him submissively, confidently hoping that General Sokolovitch and all his family would gradually evaporate like a mirage and turn out to be non-existent, so that they could quietly retrace their steps downstairs. But to his horror this hope began to fail him: the general led him up the stairs like a man who really had friends living there, and every minute he put in some biographical or topographical detail with mathematical exactitude. At last, when they had reached the first floor and stopped on the right before the door of a luxurious flat and the general had hold of the bell, Myshkin made up his mind to make his escape, but one strange circumstance held him for a moment.

'You've made a mistake, General,' he said, 'the name on the door is Kulakov, and you want Sokolovitch.'

'Kulukov… Kulakov means nothing. The flat is Sokolovitch's, and it's Sokolovitch I shall ask for. Hang Kulakov!… Here is someone coming.'

The door was opened indeed. A footman peeped out and announced that the master and mistress were not at home.

'What a pity – what a pity! Just how things always happen,' Ardalion Alexandrovitch repeated several times with profound regret. 'Tell them, my boy, that General Ivolgin and Prince Myshkin wished to present their respects in person and regret extremely, extremely…'

At that moment from an inner room another person peeped towards the open door, apparently a housekeeper, or perhaps a governess, a lady about forty in a dark dress. She approached inquisitively and mistrustfully, hearing the names of General Ivolgin and Prince Myshkin.

'Marya Alexandrovna is not at home,' she pronounced scrutinising the general carefully. 'She has gone out with the young lady, Alexandra Mihailovna, to her grandmother's.'

'Alexandra Mihailovna too! Good heavens, how unfortunate! Would you believe it, madam, that is always my luck! I humbly beg you to give my compliments, and beg Alexandrova Mihailovna to remember … in fact give her my earnest wishes for what she wished for herself on Thursday evening, listening to a Ballade of Chopin's; she will remember. My earnest wishes! General Ivolgin and Prince Myshkin!'

'I won't forget,' said the lady with more confidence, as she bowed them out.

As they went downstairs, the general continued with undiminished warmth regretting that they had not found them in and that Myshkin had missed making such a delightful acquaintance.

'Do you know, my dear boy, I am something of a poet in soul. Have you noticed that? But … but I do believe we may have called at the wrong flat,' he concluded suddenly and quite unexpectedly. 'The Sokolovitches, I remember now, live in a different house; and I fancy, too, they are in Moscow now. Yes, I made a slight mistake, but no matter.'

'There's only one thing I want to know,' Myshkin observed disconsolately. 'Must I give up reckoning on you altogether, and hadn't I better go alone?'

'Give up? Reckoning? Alone? But whatever for, when this is for me a vital undertaking on which so much of the future of my family depends? No, my young friend, you don't know Ivolgin. To say "Ivolgin" is to say "a rock"; you can build on Ivolgin as you can on a rock, that's what they used to say in the squadron in which I began my service. I have only just to call in for one minute on the way at the house where my soul has for years found consolation after my trials and anxieties

'You want to go home?'

'No! I want to go and see Madame Terentyev, the widow of Captain Terentyev, one of my subordinate officers … and a friend of mine, too. Here at Madame Terentyev's I am refreshed in spirit, and here I bring my daily cares and my family troubles … and as today I am weighed down by a heavy moral burden, I…'

'I am afraid I was awfully stupid to have troubled you this evening,' murmured Myshkin. 'Besides, you're … Goodbye!'

'But I cannot, I really cannot let you go, my young friend,' cried the general. 'A widow, a mother of a family, and she draws from her heart strings which re-echo through all my being. A visit to her is a matter of five minutes; I don't stand on ceremony in the house, I almost live there. I will wash, make myself a little tidy, and then we'll drive to the Great Theatre. I assure you I need you the whole evening. Here, in this house, here we are. Ah, Kolya, you here already! Is Marfa Borissovna at home, or have you only just come?'

'Oh no,' answered Kolya, who had just met them in the gateway, 'I've been here a long time, with Ippolit. He is worse, he was in bed this morning. I've just been to a shop to get some cards. Marfa Borissovna is expecting you. Only, father, you are in a state!' Kolya finished up, watching the way his father walked and stood. 'Well, come along.'

The meeting with Kolya induced Myshkin to accompany the general to Marfa Borissovna's, but only for one minute. Myshkin wanted Kolya; he made up his mind to give up the general in any case, and could not forgive himself for having rested his hopes on him. They were a long time climbing up to the fourth storey by a back staircase.

'Do you want to introduce the prince?' Kolya asked on the way.

'Yes, my dear, to introduce him: General Ivolgin and Prince Myshkin. But what is… how is… Marfa Borissovna?…'

'Do you know, father, you'd better not go! She'll give it to you! There has been no sign of you for three days and she is expecting the money. Why did you promise her money? You are always doing things like that! Now you've got to get out of it!'

On the fourth storey they stopped before a low door. The general was evidently downcast, and pushed Myshkin in front of him.

'I'll stay here,' he muttered. 'I want to surprise her.'

Kolya went in first. The general's surprise missed fire, for a lady peeped out of the door. She was heavily rouged and painted, wore slippers and a dressing-jacket, had her hair plaited in pigtails, and was about forty. As soon as the lady saw him, she promptly screamed, 'Here he is, the base, viperish man! My heart misgave me it was he!'

'Come in, it's all right,' the general muttered to Myshkin, still trying to laugh it off with a guileless air.

But it was not all right. They had hardly passed through a dark, low-pitched passage into a narrow sitting-room, furnished with half a dozen rush-bottom chairs and two card-tables, when the lady of the house returned at once to the charge in a peevish tone of habitual complaint.

'Aren't you ashamed – aren't you ashamed, you savage and tyrant of my family, tyrant and monster? You have robbed me of everything! You have sucked me dry and are still not content, you vampire! I will put up with you no longer, you shameless, dishonourable man!'

'Marfa Borissovna – Marfa Borissovna, this is Prince Myshkin – General Ivolgin and Prince Myshkin,' muttered the general, trembling and overwhelmed.

'Would you believe it,' said the captain's widow, turning suddenly to Myshkin, 'would you believe that this shameless man has not spared my orphan children! He's robbed us of everything, carried off everything, sold and pawned everything and left us nothing! What am I to do with your IOUs, designing and unscrupulous man? Answer, you deceiver; answer, you devouring monster! How, how am I to nourish my orphan children? And here he comes in drunk and can't stand on his legs! ... What have I done to call down the wrath of God? Answer, base and hideous hypocrite!'

But the general was not equal to the occasion.

'Marfa Borissovna, twenty-five roubles... all I can, thanks to a generous friend. Prince, I was cruelly mistaken! Such is ... life. But now... excuse me, I feel weak,' said the general, standing in the middle of the room and bowing in all directions. 'I am weak, forgive me! Lenotchka, a pillow ... dear child!'

Lenotchka, a girl about eight years old, ran at once to fetch a pillow and put it on the hard sofa covered with ragged American leather. The general sat down, intending to say much more, but as soon as he touched the sofa, he turned on his side facing the wall, and sank into the sleep of the just. Marfa Borissovna mournfully and ceremoniously motioned Myshkin to a chair at one of the card-tables. She sat down facing him, with her right cheek on her hand, and began looking at Myshkin in silence. Three little children, two girls and a boy, of whom Lenotchka was the eldest, went up to the table, laid their arms on it, and all three also stared at Myshkin.

Kolya made his appearance from the next room.

'I am very glad I've met you here, Kolya,' said Myshkin to him. 'Can't you help me? I must be at Nastasya Filippovna's. I asked Ardalion Alexandrovitch to take me there, but you see he is asleep. Will you take me there, for I don't know the streets, nor the way? I have the address though, by the Great Theatre, Mytovtsov's house.'

'Nastasya Filippovna? But she has never lived near the Great Theatre, and father's never been at Nastasya Filippovna's, if you care to know. It's strange you should have expected anything of him. She lives near Vladimirsky Street, at the Five Corners; it's much nearer here. Do you want to go at once? It's half-past nine. If you like, I'll take you there.'

Myshkin and Kolya went out at once. Myshkin (alas!) had nothing with which to pay for a cab, so they had to walk.

'I wanted to introduce you to Ippolit,' said Kolya; 'he is the eldest son of the widow in the dressing-jacket. He was in the other room. He is ill and has been in bed all day. But he is so queer. He is frightfully touchy, and I fancied he'd feel ashamed with you because of your coming at such a moment… I am not so much ashamed as he is, anyway, because it's my father but his mother. It does make a difference, for there's no dishonour for the male sex in such a position. But maybe it's only a prejudice that one sex is more privileged than the other in such cases. Ippolit is a splendid fellow, but he is a slave to certain prejudices.'

'You say he is in consumption?'

'Yes; I think the best thing for him would be to die soon. If I were in his place, I should certainly wish I were dead. He is sorry for his brother and sisters, the little ones you saw. If it were possible, if we only had the money, he and I would have taken a flat together and have left our families. That's our dream. And do you know, when I told him just now what happened to you, he flew into a regular rage and said that a man who accepts a blow without fighting a duel is a scoundrel. But he is frightfully irritable; I've given up arguing with him. So Nastasya Filippovna invited you at once, did she?'

'That's just it, she didn't.'

'How is it you are going, then?' cried Kolya, and he stopped short in the middle of the pavement. 'And… in such clothes! You know, it's an evening party.'

'Goodness knows how I shall *go* in. If they let me in, all right; if they don't, there's no help for it. As for clothes, what can I do?'

'Have you some object in going? Or are you only going just *pour passer le temps* in "honourable society"?'

'No, I really… that is, I am going with an object… it's difficult to put into words, but…'

'Oh, well, what it is exactly is your affair. What I care to know is that you are not simply inviting yourself to a party in the fascinating society of cocottes, generals and moneylenders. If it had been so, you must excuse me, Prince, I should have laughed at you and despised you. Honest people are terribly scarce here, so that there's really nobody one can respect. One can't help looking down on people, and they all insist on respect; Varya especially. And have you noticed, Prince, that we are all adventurers nowadays? And particularly among us, in Russia, in our beloved country. And how it's all come about, I don't understand. The foundations seemed so firm, but what do we see now? Everyone is talking and writing about it, showing it up. In Russia everyone is showing things up. Our parents are the first to go back on themselves, and are ashamed of their old morals. You have a father in Moscow teaching his son not to stick at *anything* to get money; we know it from the papers. Just look at my general; what has he come to? And yet you know, it seems to me that my general is an honest man. Yes, I really think so! It's nothing but irregularity and wine; it really is so. I feel sorry for him, in fact, only I am afraid to say so, because everyone laughs. But I really am sorry for him. And what is there in them, the sensible people? They are all money-grubbers, every one of them. Ippolit justifies usury, he says it's right; he talks about an economic upheaval, the ebb and flow of capital, confound them! It vexes me to hear it from him, but he is exasperated. Only fancy, his mother, the captain's widow, you know, gets money from the general and lends it him at high interest! It's a horrible disgrace! And do you know that mother – my mother, I mean, Nina Alexandrovna – helps Ippolit with money, clothes and everything, and provides for the children partly too, through Ippolit, because they are neglected. And Varya helps too.'

'There, you see, you say that there are no strong, honest people, that we are all money-grubbers, but there you have strong people – your mother and Varya. Don't you think to help like that and in such circumstances is a proof of moral strength?'

'Varya does it from vanity, to show off, so as not to be inferior to mother, but mother really is… I respect it in her. Yes, I respect that and think it right. Even Ippolit feels it, and he is bitter against almost everyone. At first he laughed, and called it low on my mother's part, but now he begins to feel it sometimes. Hm! So you call that strength. I shall make a note of that. Ganya doesn't know it, or he would call it conniving at things.'

'Ganya doesn't know, then? There seems to be a great deal Ganya doesn't know,' said Myshkin, pondering.

'Do you know, Prince, I like you very much. I can't forget what happened to you this afternoon.'

'And I like you very much too, Kolya.'

'Listen. How do you intend to live here? I shall soon get a job and be earning something. Let us live together, you and me and Ippolit. We'll take a flat and will let the general come and see us.'

'I shall be delighted. But we'll see. I feel very much upset just now. What? Are we there? Is this the house? What a magnificent entrance! And a hall-porter! Well, Kolya, I don't know what will come of it.'

Myshkin stood still as though in bewilderment.

'You will tell me about it tomorrow. Don't be too frightened. God give you good luck, for I think as you do about everything. Goodbye! I'll go back there and tell Ippolit. There's no doubt she will see you, don't be uneasy. She is very original. It's the first floor on this staircase, the porter will show you.'

Chapter 13

Myshkin felt very uneasy as he went up, and did all he could to give himself courage. 'The worst that can happen,' he thought, 'is that she will refuse to see me and will think something bad of me; or perhaps she'll see me and laugh in my face ... Eh, never mind.' And in fact the prospect did not alarm him very much, but to the question what he would do and why he was going there he could find no satisfactory answer. It would hardly be altogether the right thing, even if he were to catch a favourable opportunity, to say to Nastasya Filippovna, 'Don't marry that man, don't be your own destruction. He doesn't love you, it's your money he loves, he told me so himself; and Aglaia Epanchin told me so too, and I have come to tell you.'

There was another unanswered question before him, and such a vital one that Myshkin was afraid to consider it; he could not, dared not, even admit it; he did not know how to formulate it, he flushed and trembled at the mere thought of it. But in spite of all these doubts and apprehensions he ended by going in and asking for Nastasa Filippovna.

Nastasya Filippovna lived in a really magnificent, though not very large, flat. There had been one time, at the beginning of her five years in Petersburg, when Afanasy Ivanovitch had been particularly lavish in his expenditure on her. He had still had hopes of her love in those days, and had dreamed of tempting her chiefly by luxury and comfort, knowing how easily habits of luxury are acquired and how difficult they are to give up afterwards, when luxury gradually passes into necessity. In this respect Totsky clung to the good old tradition, without modifying it in any way, having an unbounded respect for the supreme power of the appeal to the senses. Nastasya Filippovna did not refuse luxury – she liked it, indeed – but strange as it seemed, she was not in the least a slave to it; apparently she could have done without it at any moment; she even took the trouble to say so plainly on several occasions, which made an unpleasant impression on Totsky. There was much, however, in Nastasya Filippovna which struck him unpleasantly, and subsequently even moved him to contempt. Apart from the inelegance of the class of people with whom she sometimes associated and to whom she must therefore have been attracted, she displayed other very strange propensities. She showed a sort of savage mingling of two tastes, a capacity for being satisfied and putting up with things and means of which one would have supposed that a well-bred and refined person would not admit the existence. In fact, if Nastasya Filippovna had displayed an elegant and charming ignorance of the fact, for instance, that peasant women were not in a position to wear the *batiste* garments that she did, Afanasy Ivanovitch would probably have been extremely pleased. The whole plan of Nastasya Filippovna's education had been from the beginning elaborated with a view to such a result by Totsky, who was a very subtle person in his own line. But, alas! The finished product was a strange one. In spite of that, Nastasya Filippovna had, and always kept, something which at times impressed even Totsky himself by its extraordinary and fascinating originality, by a sort of power. It sometimes enchanted him even now, when all his former designs on Nastasya Filippovna had collapsed.

Myshkin was met by a maid (Nastasya Filippovna kept only women servants). He asked her to take his name in, and to his surprise the girl showed no wonder, and she betrayed no hesitation at the sight of his dirty boots, his wide-brimmed hat, his sleeveless cloak, and his embarrassed air. She took off his cloak, asked him to wait in the reception-room, and went at once to announce him.

Nastasya Filippovna's party consisted of the circle she always had about her. The guests were few in number, indeed, compared with similar birthday parties of previous years. In the first place, Afanasy Ivanovitch Totsky and Ivan Fyodorovitch Epanchin were present. Both were amiable but secretly uneasy and in ill-disguised apprehension of the promised declaration in regard to Ganya. Ganya of course was there too. He too was very gloomy and preoccupied, almost rude in fact. Most of the evening he stood apart at some distance and did not speak. He had not ventured to bring Varya, and Nastasya Filippovna made no reference to her, but immediately after greeting Ganya she alluded to his scene with Myshkin. General Epanchin, who had not heard of it, was much interested. Then Ganya drily and with restraint, but perfectly openly, told what had happened that afternoon and how he had gone to the prince to beg his pardon. He warmly expressed the opinion that it was strange and unaccountable to call the prince 'an idiot,' that he thought him quite the opposite – a man, in fact, who knew very well what he was about.

Nastasya Filippovna listened to this dictum with great attention and watched Ganya curiously, but the conversation passed immediately to Rogozhin, as a leading figure in the scene at Ganya's. Totsky and Epanchin were much interested to hear about him too. It appeared that the person who knew most about Rogozhin was Ptitsyn, who had been with him and busy in his service till nine o'clock that evening. Rogozhin had insisted on their obtaining a hundred thousand roubles that day. 'It's true he was drunk,' observed Ptitsyn, 'but I believe he has secured the hundred thousand, difficult as it seems. Only I am not sure whether he will get it today, and whether he'll get it all. Several people are at work for him – Kinder, Trepalov, Biskup. He doesn't mind what interest he gives, of course, as he is drunk and in the first flush of fortune,' said Ptitsyn in conclusion.

All this information was received with interest, though it seemed to depress some, and Nastasya Filippovna was silent, obviously not caring to say what she felt. Ganya too was mute. Epanchin was secretly almost more uneasy than anyone. The pearls he had presented that morning had been accepted with rather a frigid politeness and even a shade of mockery. Ferdyshtchenko alone of all the party was in a festive holiday mood. He laughed aloud at times for no special reason, simply because he had taken up the part of jester. Totsky himself, who had the reputation of a witty and elegant storyteller, and had usually led the conversation at these parties, was evidently out of humour and ill at ease, which was unlike him. The other guests, who were, however, few in number, were not merely incapable of lively conversation, but positively unable at times to say anything at all. One poor old teacher had been invited, goodness knows why; then there was an unknown and very *young* man, fearfully shy and absolutely mute the whole evening; a lively lady of forty, probably an actress; and an exceedingly handsome, exceedingly well and richly dressed, and extraordinarily taciturn young lady.

Myshkin's appearance therefore was positively welcome. The announcement of his name caused surprise and some queer smiles, especially as from Nastasya Filippovna's air of surprise it was clear that she had not dreamed of inviting him. But after the first moment of wonder she showed at once so much pleasure that most of the party promptly prepared to meet the unexpected visitor with mirth and laughter.

'Though it's his innocence,' pronounced Ivan Fyodorovitch Epanchin, 'and it's rather dangerous to encourage such tendencies, it's really not amiss at the moment that he has taken it into his head to turn up, even in such an original manner. He may perhaps amuse us, as far as I can judge of him at least.'

'Especially as he has invited himself,' Ferdyshtchenko put in at once.

'Well, what of that?' asked the general drily. He detested Ferdyshtchenko.

'Why, that he must pay for his entrance!' explained the latter.

'Oh, Prince Myshkin is not Ferdyshtchenko, anyway,' the general could not resist saying. He could never reconcile himself to the thought that he was in the same company and on an equal footing with Ferdyshtchenko.

'Aïe, General, spare Ferdyshtchenko,' replied the latter, simpering. 'I am here in a special position.'

'What special position are you in?'

'Last time I had the honour of explaining it exactly to the company. I'll repeat it again to your excellency. You see, your excellency, everyone has wit, but I have no wit. To make up for it I've asked leave to speak the truth, for everyone knows that it's only people who have no wit who speak the truth. Besides, I am a very vindictive man, and that is because I have no wit. I put up with every insult, but only till my antagonist comes to grief. As soon as he comes to grief, I remember it, and at once avenge myself in some way. "I kick," as Ivan Petrovitch Ptitsyn has said of me; though he, of course, never kicks anyone. Do you know Krylov's fable, your excellency, "The Lion and the Ass"? Well, that's you and me; it's written about us.'

'You are talking nonsense again, I think, Ferdyschtchenko,' said the general, boiling over.

'What do you mean, your excellency?' retorted Ferdyshtchenko, who had reckoned on being able to retort and so lengthen out his twaddle. 'Don't be uneasy, your excellency, I know my place. If I say, "You and I are the lion and the ass in Krylov's fable," I take the part of the ass on myself, of course, and your excellency is the lion, as in Krylov's fable:

> The mighty lion, the terror of the woods,
> With growing years had lost his youthful strength.

I, your excellency, am the ass.'

'There I agree,' the general dropped incautiously.

All this, of course, was coarsely and intentionally done, but it seemed to be the accepted thing for Ferdyshtchenko to be allowed to play the fool.

'I am only kept and only received here that I may talk in this way,' Ferdyshtchenko had once exclaimed. 'Can such a person as I am be received? I understand that. Can a person like me be set beside a refined gentleman like Afanasy Ivanovitch? One is driven to the only explanation, that they do it because it's inconceivable,'

But though it was coarse, it was sometimes cutting, very cutting, indeed, and that was what Nastasya Filippovna seemed to like. Those who wanted to visit her had to make up their minds to put up with Ferdyshtchenko. He perhaps guessed the truth, that he was received because his presence had from the first been insufferable to Totsky. Ganya too endured unspeakable misery at his hands, and in that way Ferdyshtchenko was able to be of great use to Nastasya Filippovna.

'The prince will begin by singing us a fashionable song,' Ferdyshtchenko concluded, looking to see what Nastasya Filippovna would say.

'I don't think so, Ferdyshtchenko, and please don't get excited,' she said drily.

'A-ah! If he is under special protection, I will be indulgent too.'

But Nastasya Filippovna got up not listening to him, and went forward herself to meet Myshkin.

'I am sorry,' she said, suddenly appearing before him, 'that I forgot to invite you this afternoon, and I am very glad that you give me an opportunity of thanking you and telling you how well you've done to come.'

As she spoke, she looked intently at Myshkin, trying to find some explanation of his coming.

Myshkin would perhaps have made some reply to her friendly words, but he was so dazzled and overwhelmed that he could not utter a word. Nastasya Filippovna noticed this with satisfaction. That evening she was in full dress and her appearance was very striking. She took him by the hand and led him to the company.

At the door of the drawing-room Myshkin suddenly stopped, and with extraordinary emotion whispered hurriedly, 'Everything is perfection in you ... even your being thin and pale ... One would not like to imagine you different... I had such a longing to come to you ... I... forgive me!'

'Don't ask forgiveness,' laughed Nastasya Filippovna; 'that would destroy all the strangeness and originality. It's true what they say that you are a strange man. So you look upon me as perfection, do you?'

'Yes.'

'Though you are first-rate at guessing, you are mistaken. I'll remind you of that today...'

She introduced Myshkin to her guests, to more than half of whom he was already known. Totsky at once said something cordial. The whole company seemed to revive, they all began talking and laughing. Nastasya Filippovna made Myshkin sit down beside her.

'But after all what is there wonderful in the prince's having come?' Ferdyshtchenko cried louder than all of them. 'It's a clear case, it speaks for itself!'

'It's too clear and speaks too plainly for itself,' put in Ganya who had been silent till then. 'I've been observing the prince today almost continuously from the very instant when he saw Nastasya Filippovna's portrait for the first time this morning on Ivan Fyodorovitch's table. I remember distinctly that I thought of something even then, which I am quite convinced of now, and which the prince confessed himself, by the way.'

This whole speech Ganya uttered quite seriously, without a hint of playfulness, in a gloomy tone which sounded strange.

'I've made you no confession,' replied Myshkin, flushing. 'I simply answered your question.'

'Bravo! Bravo!' shouted Ferdyshtchenko. 'That's sincere anyway-it's sly and sincere too!'

Everyone laughed aloud.

'Don't shout, Ferdyshtchenko,' Ptitsyn observed to him in an undertone, with disgust.

'I should not have expected such an enterprise of you, Prince,' remarked Ivan Fyodorovitch. 'One wouldn't have thought you were that sort of fellow. Why, I looked on you as a philosopher. Ah, the sly dog!'

'And to judge from the way the prince blushes at an innocent jest like an innocent young girl, I conclude that, like an honourable young man, he is cherishing the most laudable intentions in his heart,' the aged teacher, a toothless old man of seventy suddenly said, or rather mumbled, to the general surprise, for no one had expected him to open his lips that evening.

Everyone laughed more than ever. The old man, probably imagining that they were laughing at his wit, laughed more and more heartily as he looked at them, till he ended by coughing violently. Nastasya Filippovna, who had an unaccountable affection for all such queer old men and women, and for crazy people even, began looking after him at once, kissed him, and ordered some more tea for him. She told the servant who came in to bring her a cloak, in which she wrapped herself, and then to put more wood on the fire. She asked what time it was, and the servant answered that it was half-past ten.

'Friends, would you like some champagne?' Nastasya Filippovna suggested suddenly. 'I've got some ready. Perhaps it will make you more cheerful. Please don't stand on ceremony.'

The offer of wine, especially in such a naïve way, seemed very strange from Nastasya Filippovna. Everyone knew the rigid standard of decorum maintained at her previous parties.

The company was becoming more lively, but not in the same way as usual. The wine was, however, accepted, first by General Epanchin himself, secondly by the sprightly lady, the old man, Ferdyshtchenko, and after them by the rest. Totsky too took his glass, hoping to modify the novel tone of the company by giving it as far as possible the character of pleasant playfulness. Only Ganya drank nothing.

Nastasya Filippovna had taken a glass of champagne, and declared that she would drink three that evening. It was difficult to understand her strange and at times abrupt and sudden sallies, her hysterical and causeless laughter, alternating with silent and even morose depression. Some of her visitors suspected that she was feverish. They began to notice at last that she too seemed expecting something, frequently looked at her watch, and was becoming impatient and preoccupied.

'You seem to be a little feverish?' asked the sprightly lady.

'Not a little, but very much. That's why I wrapped myself up in my cloak,' replied Nastasya Filippovna, who really was turning pale and seemed at times trying to suppress a violent shiver.

They were all concerned and made a movement.

'Shouldn't we let our hostess rest?' said Totsky, looking at Ivan Fyodorovitch.

'Certainly not. I beg you to stay; I need your presence especially today,' Nastasya Filippovna observed suddenly, with a significant emphasis.

And as almost all the guests knew that a very important decision was to be made that evening, her words seemed pregnant with meaning. General Epanchin and Totsky exchanged glances once more. Ganya twitched convulsively.

'It would be a good thing to play some *petit-jeu,'* observed the sprightly lady.

'I know a new splendid *petit-jeu'* put in Ferdyshtchenko. 'Though it was only played once, and even then it was not successful.'

'What was it?' asked the sprightly lady.

'A party of us were together one day – we'd been drinking, it's true – and suddenly someone made the suggestion that each one of us, without leaving the table, should tell something he had done, something that he himself honestly considered the worst of all the evil actions of his life. But it was to be done honestly, that was the point, that it was to be honest, no lying.'

'A strange idea!' said the general.

'Nothing could be stranger, your excellency, but that's the best of it.'

'Ridiculous idea,' said Totsky. 'But I can understand it – it's just a form of bragging.'

'Perhaps that was just what we wanted, Afanasy Ivanovitch.'

'But such a *petit-jeu* would set us crying, instead of laughing,' observed the sprightly lady.

'It's quite impossible and absurd,' Ptitsyn chimed in.

'Was it successful?' asked Nastasya Filippovna.

'Well, no, it was a failure. Everyone certainly did tell something; many of them told the truth, and, would you believe it, some of them positively enjoyed telling it. But afterwards everyone was ashamed; they couldn't keep it up. On the whole, though, it was very amusing, in a way, of course.'

'It really would be nice,' observed Nastasya Filippovna, suddenly growing eager. 'Let's try it, gentlemen. We really are not very lively. If each of us would consent to tell something... of that sort... of course, voluntarily. No one is forced to do it, eh? Perhaps we could keep it up. It would be awfully original, anyway.'

'It's a stroke of genius!' said Ferdvshtchenko. 'Ladies are excluded, however; men must begin. We'll cast lots, as we did then. We must – we must! If anyone really doesn't want to, of course he needn't, but that's being very disagreeable. Throw your lots into my hat here, gentlemen; the prince shall draw them. Nothing could be simpler – to describe the worst thing you've done in your life, that's awfully easy, gentlemen! You'll see. If anyone forgets, I'll undertake to remind him.'

The idea seemed a very queer one and almost everyone disliked it. Some frowned, some smiled slyly. Some protested but faintly; Ivan Fyodorovitch, for instance, who was loth to oppose Nastasya Filippovna, and noticed how attracted she was by this strange idea, perhaps simply because it was strange and almost impossible. Nastasya Filippovna was always self-willed and inconsiderate when once she had expressed a desire, even though it were the veriest caprice, of no benefit to her. And now she seemed hysterical, ran to and fro and laughed spasmodically and violently, especially at Totsky's uneasy protests. Her dark eyes glittered, there was a hectic flush on her pale cheeks. The dejected and disgusted air of some of her visitors possibly increased her ironical desire to play the game. Perhaps the cynicism and the cruelty of the idea was just what attracted her. Some of the party were persuaded that she had a special object in it. Yet they assented; it was curious, anyway, and to many people the prospect was alluring. Ferdyshtchenko was the most excited of all.

'What if it's something one can't tell... before ladies?' observed the silent youth timidly.

'Why, don't tell it, then. There are plenty of wicked actions without that,' answered Ferdyshtchenko. 'Ach, you young people!'

'But I don't know which of my actions I consider the worst,' put in the sprightly lady.

'Ladies are exempted from the obligation,' repeated Ferdyshtchenko; 'but only from the obligation: anything of their own inspiration will be accepted with gratitude. Men are exempt as well, if they object too much.'

'But what proof is there that I shan't tell lies?' enquired Ganya. 'And if I do, the whole point of the game is lost. And who wouldn't tell lies? Everyone is sure to.'

'Why, that's one thing that's fascinating to see what sort of lies a man will tell. There's no particular danger of your telling lies, Ganya, for we all know your worst action as it is. But just fancy, gentlemen,' Ferdyshtchenko cried with sudden inspiration, 'only think with what eyes we shall look at one another tomorrow, for instance, after we've told our tales!'

'But is this possible? Are you really in earnest, Nastasya Filippovna?' Totsky asked with dignity.

'If you are afraid of wolves, you mustn't go into the forest,' observed Nastasya Filippovna sneeringly.

'But let me ask you, Mr Ferdyshtchenko, what sort of *petit-jeu* can one make out of this?' Totsky went on, more and more uneasy. 'I assure you that such things are never successful. You say yourself that it has been unsuccessful once already.'

'Unsuccessful! Why, last time I told the story of how I stole three roubles, I simply told it straight off.'

'I dare say. But I suppose there was no possibility of your telling it so that it seemed like the truth, and that you were believed? Gavril Ardalionovitch has observed very justly that with the slightest hint of falsehood the whole point of the game is lost. Telling the truth is only possible by accident through a special sort of boastfulness, in the worst possible taste, inconceivable and utterly unsuitable here.'

'But what a subtle person you are, Afanasy Ivanovitch!' cried Ferdyshtchenko. 'You positively surprise me! Only fancy, gentlemen, by observing that I couldn't tell the story of my thieving so as to make it like the truth, Afanasy Ivanovitch hints in the subtlest way that I couldn't really have stolen (for it would have been bad form to have said so aloud); though perhaps he is privately convinced that Ferdyshtchenko may very well have been a thief. But to business, gentlemen, to business. The lots are collected and you've put in yours too, Afanasy Ivanovitch, so no one has refused. Prince, draw!'

Without a word Myshkin put his hand into the hat and the first lot he drew was Ferdyshtchenko's, the second Ptitsyn's, the third General Epanchin's, the fourth Totsky's, the fifth his own, the sixth Ganya's, and so on. The ladies had not put in lots.

'Good heavens, what a misfortune!' cried Ferdyshtchenko. 'I thought that the first would be the prince, and then the general. But, thank God, Ivan Petrovitch comes after me, and I shall be rewarded. Well, gentlemen, I am bound of course to set a good example, but what I regret most of all at this moment is that I am a person of no consequence and not distinguished in any way – not even of decent rank. Of what interest is it to anyone that Ferdyshtchenko should have done something horrid? And what is my worst action? There's an *embarras de richesse*. Shall I tell of the same theft again, to convince Afanasy Ivanovitch that one may steal without being a thief?'

'You are also convincing me, Mr Ferdyshtchenko, that it's possible to enjoy, even to revel in describing one's nasty actions, even though one is not asked about them. But... Excuse me, Mr Ferdyshtchenko.'

'Begin, Ferdyshtchenko, you are chattering too much and will never finish,' Nastasya Filippovna insisted with irritable impatience.

Everyone noticed that after her hysterical laughter she had suddenly become actually ill-humoured, peevish and irritable; yet she persisted obstinately and imperiously in her wild caprice. Afanasy Ivanovitch was horribly uncomfortable. He was furious too at Ivan Fyodorovitch, who sat sipping champagne, as though there were nothing the matter; perhaps reckoning on telling something when his turn came.

Chapter 14

'I've no wit, Nastasya Filippovna, that's what makes me talk too much,' cried Ferdyshtchenko, beginning his story. 'If I were as witty as Afanasy Ivanovitch or Ivan Petrovitch, I should have sat still and held my tongue tonight, like Afanasy Ivanovitch and Ivan Petrovitch. Prince, let me ask you, what do you think? Don't you think that there are many more men in the world thieves than not thieves, and that there isn't a man in the world so honest that he has never once in his life stolen anything? That's my idea, from which I don't conclude, however, that all men are thieves; though, goodness knows, I've often been tempted to. What do you think?'

'Ugh! How stupidly you tell your story!' commented the sprightly lady, whose name was Darya Alexeyevna. 'And what nonsense! It's impossible that everyone should have stolen something. I've never stolen anything.'

'You've never stolen anything, Darya Alexeyevna, but what will the prince say? He is blushing all over.'

'I think what you say is true, only you exaggerate very much,' said Myshkin, who really was for some reason blushing.

'And you, Prince, have never stolen anything yourself?'

'Oh dear, oh dear! How absurd this is! What are you thinking about Mr Ferdyshtchenko,' the general interposed.

'You are simply ashamed to tell it when it comes to the point, so you try to drag the prince in, because he can't take his own part,' Darya Alexeyevna snapped out.

'Ferdyshtchenko, tell your story or hold your tongue, and don't drag in other people. You put one out of all patience,' said Nastasya Filippovna sharply and irritably.

'In a minute, Nastasya Filippovna, but since the prince has confessed – for I insist that the prince has as good as confessed – what would anyone else (to mention no names) say, if he wanted to tell the truth for once? As for me, gentlemen, there's no need to tell more; it's very simple and stupid and nasty. But I assure you I am not a thief; I don't know how I came to steal. It happened the year before last, one Sunday, at Semyon Ivanovitch's villa; he had friends dining with him. After dinner the gentlemen were sitting over their wine. It occurred to me to ask the daughter, a young lady called Marya Semyonovna, to play the piano. I walked through the corner room. On Marya Ivanovna's work-table lay a green paper note for three roubles. She must have taken it out for the housekeeping. There was no one in the room. I took the note and put it in my pocket, what for I can't say. What came over me I don't know. Only I hastily went back and sat down at the table. I sat on there, expecting something, in considerable excitement. I chattered away without stopping, told anecdotes, laughed. Afterwards I joined the ladies. About half an hour later they missed the note and began questioning the maids. They suspected one called Darya. I showed extraordinary interest and sympathy, and I remember that, when Darya was utterly overcome, I began persuading her to confess, assuring her that her mistress would be kind; and I did that aloud, before everyone. Everyone looked on, and I felt extraordinary pleasure in the fact that I was preaching to her while the note lay in my pocket. I spent those three roubles drinking in a restaurant that night. I went in and asked for a bottle of Lafitte. I never asked for a bottle like that, by itself; I wanted to spend the money at once. I felt no particular pangs of conscience at the time, nor have I since. I shouldn't do it again, certainly; you may believe that or not, as you like, I don't care. Well, that's all'

'But there's no doubt that's not the worst thing you've ever done,' said Darya Alexeyevna with aversion.

'That's a pathological incident, not an action,' observed Totsky.

'And the servant?' asked Nastasya Filippovna, not disguising her intense disgust.

'The servant was turned away next day, of course. The family was strict.'

'And you let that happen?'

'That's good! Why, could I have gone and told of myself?' chuckled Ferdyshtchenko, though he seemed struck by the extremely unpleasant impression made on all by his story.

'How loathsome!' cried Nastasya Filippovna.

'Why, you want to hear of a man's worst action, and yet you expect something brilliant! A man's worst actions are always loathsome, Nastasya Filippovna; we shall hear that directly from Ivan Petrovitch. And a great many people are brilliant on the outside and want to seem virtuous because they have their own carriage. All sorts of people keep a carriage. And by what means?...'

Ferdyshtchenko, in fact, was quite carried away, and flew into a sudden rage, positively forgetting himself and overstepping all bounds; his whole face twitched with anger. Strange as it seems, he apparently had expected a very different reception of his story. These errors of taste, this special sort of bragging, as Totsky had called it, happened very frequently with Ferdyshtchenko, and were quite in his character.

Nastasya Filippovna positively quivered with fury and looked intently at Ferdyshtchenko. He was instantly quelled and relapsed into silence, almost cold with fear; he had gone too far.

'Hadn't we better make an end of it?' Totsky asked artfully.

'It's my turn, but I claim my right of exemption and shall not speak,' said Ptitsyn resolutely.

'Don't you want to?'

'I can't, Nastasya Filippovna; and in fact I look upon such a *petit-jeu* as out of the question.'

'General, I believe it's your turn,' said Nastasya Filippovna, turning to Epanchin. 'If you refuse, too, you will throw us all out, and I shall be sorry, for I was reckoning on finishing it by telling an incident from my own life. Only I wanted to do that after you and Afanasy Ivanovitch, for you must give me confidence,' she added, laughing.

'Oh, if you promise to,' cried the general fervently, 'I am ready to tell you of my whole life; and I confess I have got my story ready for my turn...'

'And from his excellency's air alone one may judge of the peculiar creative pleasure with which he has worked up his anecdote,' Ferdyshtchenko ventured to observe with a sarcastic smile, though he was still rather ill at ease.

Nastasya Filippovna glanced at the general, and she too smiled to herself. But her depression and irritability were obviously increasing every moment. Totsky was more alarmed than ever at her promise to tell something herself.

'It has happened to me, friends, as to everyone, to commit actions in my life that were not very pretty,' began the general: 'but it's strange that I regard tire brief incident which I'll describe directly as the basest action of my life. It's almost thirty-five years ago, yet I can never escape a twinge at heart, so to say, at recalling it. It was an extremely foolish business, however I was at that time only a lieutenant and was working my way up in the army. Well, we all know what a lieutenant is – young blood and ardour, but a miserable screw. I had an orderly in those days called Nikifor, who was awfully zealous on my behalf. He saved, sewed, scrubbed and cleaned, and even stole right and left anything he could lay his hands on to help our housekeeping. He was a most faithful and honest man. I was strict, of course, but just. We happened to stay for some time in a little town. I had lodgings in a suburb in the house of the widow of a retired sublieutenant. The old lady was eighty or thereabouts. She lived in a little ancient tumbledown wooden house, and was so poor she didn't even keep a servant. What was worse though, she had at one time had a numerous family and relations. Some had died, others were scattered, while others had forgotten the old woman. Her husband she had buried forty-five years before. Some years previously a niece used to live with her, a hunchback woman, as wicked as a witch, so people said, she had even bitten the old woman's finger. But she too was dead, so that the old lady had been struggling on for three years quite alone. I was frightfully bored there, and she was so silly one could get nothing out of her. At last she stole a cock of mine. The matter has never been cleared up to this day, but there was no one else could have done it. We quarrelled over the cock – quarrelled in earnest; and it happened that as soon as I asked I was transferred to other quarters, to a suburb the other side of the town, in the house of a merchant with a large family and a big beard, as I remember him. Nikifor and I were delighted to move. I left the old lady indignantly. Three days later I came in from drill and Nikifor informed me: "We were wrong, your honour, to leave our bowl at our old lady's; I have nothing to put the soup in." I was surprised, of course. "How so? How was it the bowl was left behind?" Nikifor, surprised, went on to report that when we were leaving the landlady had not given him our bowl, because I had broken her pot; that she had kept our bowl in place of her pot, and that she had pretended I had suggested it. Such meanness on her part naturally made me furious; it would make any young officer's blood boil. I leapt up and flew out. I was beside myself, so to say, when I got to the old woman's. I saw her sitting in the passage, huddled up in the corner all alone, as though to get out of the sun, her cheek propped on her hand. I poured out a stream of abuse, calling her all sorts of names, you know, in regular Russian style. Only there seemed something strange as I looked at her: she sat with her face turned to me, her eyes round and staring, and answered not a word. And she looked at me in such a queer way, she seemed to be swaying. At last I calmed down. I looked at her, I questioned her – not a word. I stood hesitating: flies were buzzing, the sun was setting, there was stillness. Completely disconcerted, I walked away. Before I got home I was summoned to the major's; then I had to go to the company, so I didn't get home till it was quite evening. Nikifor's first words were, "Do you know, your honour, that our landlady is dead?" "When did she die?" "Why, this evening, an hour and a half ago." So that at the very time I was abusing her, she was passing away. It made such an impression on me that, I assure you, I couldn't get over it. The thought of it haunted me; I dream of it at night. I am not superstitious, of course, but two days after I went to church to the funeral. In fact, as time goes on it seems to haunt me more. Not that it haunts me exactly, but now and then one pictures it and feels uncomfortable. I've come to the conclusion that the sting of it lies in this. In the first place, it was a woman – so to speak, a fellow-creature, a *humane* creature, as they call it nowadays. She had lived, lived a long life, lived too long. At one time she had had children, a husband, family and relations – all this bubbling, so to say, smiling, so to say, life about her; and then all at once complete blank, everything gone, she left alone like...some fly accursed from the beginning of time. And then at last God had brought her to the end, as the sun was setting, on a quiet summer evening my old woman too was passing away – a theme for pious reflection, to be sure. And then at that very moment, instead of a tear to see her off, so to say, a reckless young lieutenant, swaggering arms akimbo, escorts her from the surface of the earth to the Russian tune of violent swearing over a lost bowl! Of course I was to blame, and, though from the length of years and change in my nature, I've long looked at my action as though it had been another man's, I still regret it. So that, I repeat, it seems positively queer to me, for if I were to blame, I was not altogether so. Why should she have taken it into her head to die at that moment? Of course there is only one explanation, that what I did was in a certain sense pathological. Yet I couldn't be at peace till, fifteen years ago, I provided for two incurable old women in the almshouse, so as to soften the last days of their earthly existence by comfortable surroundings. I think of bequeathing a sum of money to make it a permanent charity. Well, that's all about it. I repeat that I may have done wrong in many things in my life, but this incident I honestly consider my worst action.'

'And, instead of the worst, your excellency has described one of your good actions. You've cheated Ferdyshtchenko,' commented Ferdyshtchenko.

'Yes, General, I never imagined you had such a good heart after all. I am almost sorry,' Nastasya Filippovna dropped carelessly.

'Sorry! What for?' asked the general with an affable laugh, and not without complacency he sipped his champagne.

But it was Totsky's turn, and he too had prepared himself. Everyone thought that he would not, like Ptitsyn, refuse, and everyone for certain reasons awaited his confession with curiosity; at the same time they were watching Nastasya Filippovna.

With an extraordinary air of dignity, which was in keeping with his stately appearance, Afanasy Ivanovitch began in his quiet, polite voice to tell one of his 'charming anecdotes.' He was, by the way, a man of fine appearance and dignified carriage, tall, rather stout, a little bald and turning grey. He had soft pendulous, rosy cheeks and false teeth. He wore his clothes loose and well cut, and his linen was always exquisite. His plump white hands were pleasant to look at. On the first finger of his right hand he wore a costly diamond ring.

All the while he was telling his story, Nastasya Filippovna was staring intently at the lace frill of her sleeve, and kept pinching it with two fingers of her left hand. She didn't even once glance at the speaker.

'What makes my task easier,' began Afanasy Ivanovitch, 'is the absolute obligation of describing the very basest action of my life. In that case there can be no hesitation; conscience and the prompting of the heart dictate at once what one must tell. I confess with bitterness that among all the innumerable, perhaps frivolous and thoughtless actions of my life there is one the impression of which has lain almost too heavily on my mind. It happened nearly twenty years ago. I was staying then in the country with Platon Ordyntsev. He had just been elected marshal of nobility and had come down with his young wife, Anfisa Alexeyevna, to spend his winter holidays there. It was a few days before her birthday and two dances had been arranged. At that time that charming novel of Dumas *fils, La Dame aux Camélias*, was in the height of fashion and was just making a great sensation in society. It's a work which, in my opinion, is not destined to die or tarnish with age. In the provinces all the ladies were in ecstasies over it – those, at least, who had read it. The charm of the novel, the originality of the situation of the principal character, that enchanting world analysed so subtly, and all the fascinating incidents scattered about the book (for instance, the use of the nosegays of white and pink camellias alternately) – all these charming details, in fact, and the whole *ensemble* made an overwhelming sensation. Camellias became extraordinarily fashionable, everyone wanted them, everyone was trying to get them. I ask you, is it possible to get many camellias in a country district when everyone is asking for them for dances, even when there are not many dances? Petya Vorhovsky was breaking his heart at the time, poor fellow, over Anfisa Alexeyevna. I really don't know whether there was anything between them – that is, I mean whether he had any real grounds for hope. The poor fellow was crazy to get camellias for Anfisa Alexeyevna by the night of the ball. The Countess Sotsky, a visitor from Petersburg staying with the governor's wife, and Sofya Bezpalov were, we knew for certain, coming with nosegays of white ones. Anfisa Alexeyevna longed to create a special sensation with red ones. Poor Platon was almost driven distracted – of course, he was the husband. He promised to procure the flowers; and what do you think? On the very eve of the ball they were snapped up by Katerina Alexandrovna, a terrible rival of Anfisa Alexeyevna in everything. They were at daggers drawn. Of course it was a case of hysterics and fainting fits. It was all over with Platon. You may well believe that if Petya had been able to contrive a bouquet somehow at that interesting moment, his chances would have greatly improved. A woman's gratitude in such cases is boundless. He flew about like a madman, but it was an impossible achievement, and it was no use talking about it. All at once I met him at eleven o'clock on the evening before the birthday and the ball given by Madame Zubkov, a neighbour of Ordyntsev's. He was beaming. "What is it?" "I have found it. Eureka!" "Well, my dear boy, you do surprise me! Where? How?" "At Yekshaisk, a little town fifteen miles away, not in our district. There's a merchant of the old style, a rich man called Trepalov, living there with his old wife. Instead of children they keep canaries. They've both a passion for flowers, and he has camellias."

"Why, it may not be true. And what if he won't give you them?" "I shall fall on my knees and grovel at his feet till he does. I won't go away without!" "When are you going?" "Tomorrow at daybreak, at five o'clock." "Well, good luck to you!" And, you know, I felt so pleased on his account. I went back to the Ordyntsev's. One o'clock at night came and, you know, I was still thinking about it. I meant to go to bed, when suddenly a very original idea came to me. I made my way to the kitchen. I waked Savely, the coachman, gave him fifteen roubles, and said, "Let me have the horses in half an hour." Half an hour later, of course, the sledge was at the gate. Anfisa Alexeyevna, I was told, had a migraine, she was feverish and delirious. I got in and drove off. Before five o'clock I was at Yekshaisk, at the inn. I waited till daybreak, and only till daybreak. By seven o'clock I was at Trepalov's. I said this and that, and asked, "Have you any camellias? My good kind sir, help me, save me! I bow down at your feet!" The old man was tall, grey-headed, severe – a terrible old man. "No, no! On no account. I can't consent." I plumped down at his feet. I positively flopped on the floor. "What are you doing, Sir? What are you about?" He was almost alarmed. "A human life is at stake!" I shouted to him. "Well, take them if that's so, in God's name." I did cut those red camellias! They were wonderful, exquisite; there was a little greenhouse full of them. The old man sighed. I pulled out a hundred roubles. "No, Sir, don't insult me in such a way." "In that case, my worthy sir, devote that hundred roubles to the hospital here for the food and expenses there." "Well, that," said the old man, "is a different matter, that's a good and noble work and pleasing to God. I will present that money to the hospital as a health-offering for you." And, you know, I liked that old Russian; he was, so to speak, Russian to the backbone, *de la vraie souche!* Delighted at my success, I set off homewards. I went back a roundabout way to avoid meeting Petya. As soon as I arrived I sent the bouquet up to Anfisa Alexeyevna to greet her when she waked. You can imagine her delight, her gratitude, her tears of gratitude. Platon, who the day before had been at his last gasp, was sobbing on my breast. Alas! All husbands have been the same since the creation of… lawful matrimony. I won't venture to say more, but poor Petya's chances were completely over after that episode. I expected at first that he would murder me when he found out, and made ready to meet him, but what happened I would never have believed. He fainted; by the evening he was delirious, and next day he had brain fever and was sobbing like a child and in convulsions. A month later, as soon as he was well again, he volunteered for the Caucasus. It turned out quite a romance. It ended by his being killed in the Crimea. By that time his brother, Stepan Vorhovsky, was in command of a regiment; he had distinguished himself. I confess I had pricks of conscience even many years afterwards. Why, with what object had I dealt him such a blow? And it's not as though I'd been in love myself at the time. It was simple mischief for the sake of flirtation, nothing more. If I hadn't snatched that bouquet from him – who knows? – the man might have been alive to this day; he might have been happy, he might have been successful, and it would not have entered his head to go to fight the Turks!'

Afanasy Ivanovitch ceased speaking with the same stately dignity with which he had begun his story. The company noticed that there was a peculiar light in Nastasya Filippovna's eyes and her lips quivered as he finished. Everyone was watching them with curiosity.

'They've cheated Ferdyshtchenko! How they have cheated! This really is cheating!' cried Ferdyshtchenko in a lachrymose voice, realising that he could and must say something.

'And whose fault was it that you didn't know better? You should learn from these clever people!' Darya Alexeyevna, an old and faithful friend and ally of Totsky's, snapped out almost triumphantly.

'You are right, Afanasy Ivanovitch, the game is a very boring one and we must end it quickly,' Nastasya Filippovna commented carelessly. 'I'll tell you myself what I promised, and let us have a game of cards.'

'But the promised anecdote first of all,' the general assented warmly.

'Prince,' Nastasya Filippovna turned sharply and unexpectedly to Myshkin, 'my old friends here, General Epanchin and Afanasy Ivanovitch, want me to be married. Tell me what you think. Shall I be married or not? As you say, I will do.'

Afanasy Ivanovitch turned pale; the general was petrified. Everyone stared and craned forward. Ganya stood rooted to the spot.

'To … to whom?' asked Myshkin in a sinking voice.

'To Gavril Ardalionovitch Ivolgin,' Nastasya Filippovna went on in the same harsh, firm and distinct voice.

Several seconds of silence followed. Myshkin seemed struggling to speak and unable to pronounce a word, as though there were some awful weight on his chest.

'N-no … don't marry him,' he whispered at last, and breathed painfully.

'So it shall be then. Gavril Ardalionovitch,' she addressed him imperiously and, as it were, triumphantly, 'you have heard the prince's decision? Well, that is my answer, and let it be the end of the matter once for all!'

'Nastasya Filippovna!' said Totsky in a trembling voice.

'Nastasya Filippovna!' pronounced the general in a persuasive but agitated voice.

There was a general stir and commotion.

'What is the matter, friends?' she went on, looking at her guests, as though surprised. 'Why are you so upset? And how distressed you all look!'

'But … remember, Nastasya Filippovna,' Totsky muttered, faltering, 'you have made a promise quite voluntarily, and might have partly spared … Tam at a loss and… of course, perplexed, but … in short, at such a minute and before… before people… and to do it all like this, to end a serious matter by such a *petit-jeu* – a matter affecting the honour and the heart… a matter involving

'I don't understand you, Afanasy Ivanovitch. You really don't know what you are sating. In the first place, what do you mean by "before people"? Are we not in the company of dear and intimate friends? And why *petit-jeu?* I really meant to tell my anecdote, and here I have told it. Isn't it a nice one? And why do you say that it's not serious? Isn't this serious? You heard me say to the prince "As you say, so it shall be." Had he said "Yes," I would have given my consent at once. But he said "No," and I refused. Isn't that serious? My whole life was hanging in the balance. What could be more serious?'

'But the prince – what's the prince to do with it? And what is the prince after all?' muttered the general, almost unable to restrain his indignation at the offensive authority given to the prince.

'Why, what the prince has to do with it is that he is the first man I have met in my whole life that I have believed in as a sincere friend. He believed in me at first sight and I in him.'

'I have only to thank Nastasya Filippovna for the extraordinary delicacy with which she … has treated me,' Ganya, pale and with twitching lips, articulated at last in a quivering voice. 'It was of course the fitting way, but… the prince … the prince in this matter! …'

'Is after the seventy-five thousand, do you mean?' Nastasya Filippovna broke in suddenly. 'Did you mean to say that? Don't deny it, you certainly meant to say that. Afanasy Ivanovitch, I had forgotten to add, take back that seventy-five thousand, and let me assure you that I set you free for nothing. It's enough! It's time you too were free. Nine years and three months! Tomorrow, a new leaf, but today is my birthday, and I am doing what I like for the first time in my whole life. General, you too take back your pearls; give them to your wife; here they are. Tomorrow I shall leave this flat for good, and there will be no more parties, friends.'

Saying this, she suddenly got up, as though she meant to go away.

'Nastasya Filippovna! Nastasya Filippovna!' was heard on all sides. Everyone was in excitement, all rose from their seats and surrounded her. All had listened uneasily to her impetuous, feverish, frantic words. They all felt that there was something wrong; no one could explain it, no one could make it out. At that moment there was a violent ring at the bell, exactly as there had been at Ganya's flat that afternoon.

'A-ah! Here's the way out! At last! It's half-past eleven!' cried Nastasya Filippovna. 'I beg you to be seated, friends. Here is the way out!'

Saying this, she sat down herself. A strange laugh quivered on her lips. She sat in silent and feverish expectation, looking towards the door.

'Rogozhin and his hundred thousand, not a doubt of it!' Ptitsyn muttered to himself.

Chapter 15

Katya, the maid, came in, much alarmed.

'Goodness knows what's the matter, Nastasya Filippovna! A dozen men have broken in, and they are all drunk. They ask to be shown in. They say it's Rogozhin, and that you know.'

'That's right, Katya; show them all in at once.'

'You don't mean ... all of them, Nastasya Filippovna? They are in a disgraceful state – shocking!'

'Let them all in, Katya, every one of them; don't be afraid, or they'll come in without your showing. What an uproar they are making, just as they did this afternoon! Perhaps you are offended, friends' – she turned to her guests – 'at my receiving such company in your presence? I am very sorry, and beg your pardon, but I can't help it, and I am very, very anxious you should all consent to be my witnesses at this final scene; though, of course, you must please yourselves ...'

The guests were still astonished, looking at one another and whispering. But it was perfectly clear that all this had been calculated and arranged beforehand, and that although Nastasya Filippovna had certainly gone out of her senses, she could not be turned from her intention now. Everyone was in agonies of curiosity. Besides, there was no one present likely to be alarmed. There were only two ladies in the party: Darya Alexeyvna, a sprightly lady who had seen the seamy side of life and could not be easily put out of countenance, and the handsome but silent stranger. But the silent stranger could hardly have understood what was passing: she was a German who had not long been in Russia and knew not a word of Russian, and she seemed to be as stupid as she was handsome. She was a novelty and it had become a fashion to invite her to certain parties, sumptuously attired, with her hair dressed as though for a show, and to seat her in the drawing-room as a charming decoration, just as people sometimes borrow from their friends for a special occasion a picture, a statue, a vase, or a fire-screen. As for the men, Ptitsyn, for instance, was a friend of Rogozhin's. Ferdyshtchenko was in his element. Ganya could not recover himself, yet he had a vague but irresistible impulse to stay out his ignominy to the end. The old teacher, who had only a dim notion of what was going forward, was almost in tears and literally trembling with fear, noticing an exceptional agitation around him and in Nastasya Filippovna, whom he adored as though she had been his grandchild. But he would sooner have died than have deserted her at such a moment. As for Totsky, he would, of course, not have cared to compromise himself by such adventures, but he was too much interested in the matter, though it was taking such a crazy turn. Moreover, Nastasya Filippovna had dropped two or three words for his benefit, which made him feel he could not go home till the matter was cleared up. He resolved to remain to the end and to keep perfectly silent, confining himself to observation, which indeed was the only course consistent with dignity. General Epanchin, who had only just been offended by the unceremonious and ridiculous return of his present might of course feel still more insulted by these strange eccentricities, or perhaps by the entrance of Rogozhin. A man in his position had indeed demeaned himself too far by sitting down by the side of Ptitsyn and Ferdyshtchenko. For, however much passion might influence him, it might well at last have been overcome by a sense of obligation, by a feeling of duty, of his rank and importance and self-respect generally, so that Rogozhin and his companions were in any case inadmissible in the presence of his excellency.

'Ach! General,' Nastasya Filippovna interrupted him at once, as soon as he made his protest. 'I had forgotten! But, believe me, I had thought of you before. If it's such an offence to you, I won't insist on keeping you; though I am very anxious to have you particularly beside me at this moment. In any case I thank you very much for your friendship and flattering notice, but if you are afraid …'

'Allow me, Nastasya Filippovna,' cried the general in a rush of chivalrous feeling. 'To whom are you saying this? Only from devotion to you I will remain at your side now, and if there is any danger … Besides, I must confess I am extremely interested. I only meant to say that they will spoil your carpets and perhaps break something … And you ought not to see them at all, to my thinking, Nastasya Filippovna.'

'Rogozhin himself,' Ferdyshtchenko announced.

'What do you think, Afanasy Ivanovitch,' the general managed to whisper to him in haste, 'hasn't she taken leave of her senses? I mean not allegorically, but in the literal, medical sense. Eh?'

'I've told you that she's always been disposed that way,' Totsky whispered slyly.

'And she is in a fever too …'

Rogozhin was accompanied by almost the same followers as in the afternoon. There were only two additions to the company: one a worthless old man, once the editor of a disreputable, libellous paper, of whom the story went that for drink he had once pawned his false teeth; and a retired sublieutenant, the rival by trade and calling of the gentleman with the fists. He was utterly unknown to all Rogozhin's party, but had been picked up in the street on the sunny side of the Nevsky Prospect, where he used to stop the passers-by, begging assistance in the language of Marlinsky, slyly alleging that he used to give away as much as fifteen roubles at once in his time. The two rivals at once took up a hostile attitude to one another. The gentleman with the fists considered himself affronted by this addition to the party. Being silent by nature, he merely growled at times like a bear and with profound contempt looked at the tricks by which his rival, who turned out to be a man of the world and a diplomatist, tried to ingratiate himself and win favour. The sublieutenant promised, to judge by appearances, more skill and dexterity 'at work' than strength, and he was shorter than the fisted gentleman. Delicately and without entering into open competition, though he boasted shockingly, he hinted several times at the superiority of English boxing. He seemed, in fact, a thoroughgoing champion of Western culture. The fisted gentleman only smiled contemptuously and huffily, not deigning to contradict his rival openly, though at times he showed him silently, as though by chance, or rather moved into the foreground, a thoroughly national argument – a huge, sinewy, gnarled fist covered with a sort of reddish down. It was made perfectly clear to everyone that, if this truly national argument were accurately brought to bear on any subject, it would reduce it to pulp.

Thanks to the efforts of Rogozhin, who had all day long been looking forward to his visit to Nastasya Filippovna, none of the party were completely drunk. He himself was by now nearly sober, but almost stupefied with the number of sensations he had passed through in that chaotic day, that was unlike anything he had experienced in his life before. One thing only had remained constantly in his mind and his heart at every minute, every instant. For the sake of that one thing he had spent the whole time between five o'clock in the afternoon and eleven o'clock at night in continual misery and anxiety, worrying, with Kinders and Biskups, Jews and money lenders, who were driven almost distracted too, rushing about like mad on his errands. They had, anyway, succeeded in raising the hundred thousand roubles, of which Nastasya Filippovna had mockingly dropped a passing and quite vague hint. But the money had been lent at a rate of interest of which even Biskup himself did not venture to speak to Kinder above a bashful whisper.

As in the afternoon, Rogozhin stepped forward first; the rest followed him, somewhat uneasy, though fully conscious of their advantages. What they were most frightened of – goodness knows why – was Nastasya Filippovna. Some of them almost expected that they would all be promptly 'kicked downstairs' and among these was the dandy and lady-killer Zalyozhev. But others – and the fisted gentleman was conspicuous among them – cherished at heart profound though unspoken contempt, and even hatred, for Nastasya Filippovna, and had come to her house as though to take it by storm. But the magnificence of the first two rooms, the articles they had never seen or heard of before, the choice furniture and pictures, and the life-size statue of Venus, roused in them an overwhelming sentiment of respect and almost of fear. This did not, however, prevent them all from gradually crowding with insolent curiosity into the drawing-room after Rogozhin. But when the fisted gentleman, his rival, and some of the others noticed General Epanchin among the guests, they were for the first moment so crestfallen that they positively beat a retreat to the other room. Lebedyev, however, was among the more fearless and resolute, and he stepped forward almost beside Rogozhin, having grasped the true significance of a fortune of a million four hundred thousand, a hundred thousand of it in hard cash. It must be observed, however, that all of them, even the knowing Lebedyev, were a little uncertain of the precise limits of their powers and did not know whether they were really able to do just as they liked or not. Lebedyev was ready to swear at certain moments that they were, but at other moments he felt uneasily impelled to remind himself of several pre-eminently cheering and reassuring articles of the legal code.

On Rogozhin himself Nastasya Filippovna made a very different impression from that produced on his companions. As soon as the curtain over the door was raised and he saw her, everything else ceased to exist for him, as it had that morning, and even more completely than it had that morning. He turned pale, and for an instant stopped short. It might be conjectured that his heart was beating violently. He gazed for some seconds timidly and desperately at Nastasya Filippovna without taking his eyes off her. Suddenly, as though lost to all reason, almost staggering as he moved, he went up to the table. On the way he stumbled against Ptitsyn's chair and trod with his huge dirty boots on the lace trimming of the dumb German beauty's magnificent light blue dress. He did not apologise, and indeed he did not notice it. He laid on the table a strange object, which he was holding before him in both hands when he entered the drawing-room. It was a thick roll of paper, six inches thick and eight inches long, stoutly and tightly wrapped up in a copy of the *Financial News*, tied round and round and twice across with string, as loaves of sugar are tied up. Then he stood still without uttering a word and let his hands fall, as though awaiting his sentence. He was dressed exactly as before, except for a new bright red and green silk scarf round his neck, a huge diamond pin in the form of a beetle stuck in it, and a massive diamond ring on a finger of his grubby right hand.

Lebedyev stopped short three paces from the table; the others, as I have said, were gradually making their way into the drawing-room. Katya and Pasha, Nastasya Filippovna's maids, had run up too to look under the lifted curtain in great amazement and alarm.

'What's this?' asked Nastasya Filippovna, scanning Rogozhin intently and curiously and glancing towards 'the object.'

'A hundred thousand!' answered Rogozhin almost in a whisper.

'Ah, so he's kept his word! What a man! Sit down, please, here on this chair; I shall have something to say to you later. Who is with you? All the same party? Well, let them come in and sit down; they can sit on that sofa and this other sofa here. Here are two armchairs ... What's the matter with them, don't they want to?'

Some of them were in fact completely overcome with confusion; they beat a retreat and settled down to wait in the other room. But others remained and sat down as they were invited, only rather further from the table, and for the most part in out-of-the-way corners. Some of them still wished to efface themselves, but others regained their effrontery with incredible rapidity, as time went on. Rogozhin too sat down on the chair assigned him, but he did not sit there long; he stood up and did not sit down again. By degrees he began to scrutinise and distinguish the visitors. Seeing Ganya, he smiled malignantly and whispered to himself 'Hullo!' He gazed at the general and Totsky without shyness or special interest. But when he noticed Myshkin beside Nastasya Filippovna, he was extremely amazed and could not take his eyes off him for a long time; he seemed at a loss to explain his presence. It may well have been that he was at moments in actual delirium. Besides the violent emotions he had gone through that day, he had spent all the previous night in the train and had been almost forty-eight hours without sleep.

'This, friends, is a hundred thousand roubles,' said Nastasya Filippovna, addressing the company with a sort of feverish impatient defiance, 'in this dirty bundle. This afternoon he shouted like a madman that he would bring me a hundred thousand this evening, and I've been expecting him all the time. He was bidding for me: he began at eighteen, then he suddenly passed at one bound to forty, and then this hundred here. He's kept his word! Oh dear, oh dear! How pale he is! … It all happened at Ganya's this afternoon. I went to pay his mother a visit, in my future home, and there his sister shouted in my face, "Won't they turn this shameless creature out!" and she spat in her brother Ganya's face. She is a girl of character!'

'Nastasya Filippovna!' General Epanchin articulated reproachfully.

He was beginning to understand the situation in his own way.

'What's the matter, General? Is it improper? Let's give up humbugging! What if I used to sit in the box at the French theatre like an inaccessible paragon of virtue; what if I did run like a wild thing from all who have been pursuing me for the last five years, and wore the airs of proud innocence – it was all because I was a silly fool! Here in your presence he has come in and put a hundred thousand on the table, after my five years of innocence, and no doubt they've troikas outside waiting for me. He prices me at a hundred thousand. Ganya, I see you are still angry with me. Could you really have meant to make me one of your family? Me, Rogozhin's woman? What did the prince say just now?'

'I didn't say you were Rogozhin's. You don't belong to Rogozhin,' Myshkin articulated in a shaking voice.

'Nastasya Filippovna, give over, my dear, give over, darling,' Darya Alexeyevna said suddenly, unable to restrain herself. 'If they make you so miserable, why think about them? And can you really mean to go off with a fellow like that, even for a hundred thousand? It's true it's a hundred thousand, that's something. You take the hundred thousand and send him about his business; that's the way to treat them. Ech! If I were in your place I'd send them all… upon my word!'

Darya Alexeyevna was moved to positive anger. She was a very good-natured and impressionable woman.

'Don't be angry, Darya Alexeyevna,' Nastasya Filippovna laughed to her. 'I did not speak to him in anger. Did I reproach him? I simply can't understand what folly possessed me to want to enter an honourable family. I've seen his mother; I kissed her hand. And the pranks I played at your flat this afternoon, Ganya, were on purpose to see for the last time how far you could go. You surprised me, really. I expected a good deal, but not that. Would you actually have married me, knowing that he was giving me such pearls almost on the eve of your wedding and I was accepting them? And Rogozhin! Why, in your home, in the presence of your mother and sister he was bidding for me; and even after that you came here to make a match of it and nearly brought your sister! Can Rogozhin have been right when he said that you'd crawl on all fours to the other end of Petersburg for three roubles?'

'Yes, he would too!' Rogozhin brought out suddenly, speaking quietly, but with an air of profound conviction.

'It would be a different matter if you were starving, but I am told you get a good salary. And, apart from the disgrace and everything else, to think of bringing a wife you hate into your house (for you do hate me, I know that)! Yes, now I do believe that such a man would murder anyone for money! Everyone is possessed with such a greed nowadays, they are all so overwhelmed by the idea of money that they seem to have gone mad. The very children take to money-lending! A man winds silk round his razor, makes it firm, comes from behind and cuts his friend's throat like a sheep's, as I read lately. Well, you are a shameless fellow! I am a shameless woman, but you are worse. I say nothing about that bouquet-holder...'

'Is this you – is this you, Nastasya Filippovna!' General Epanchin clasped his hands in genuine distress. 'You, so refined, with such delicate ideas – and now! What language! What expressions!'

'I am tipsy now, General,' Nastasya Filippovna laughed suddenly. 'I want to have my fling! This is my day, my holiday, my red-letter day; I've been waiting for it a long time! Darya Alexeyevna, do you see this bouquet-holder, this *monsieur aux camélias*? There he sits laughing at us ...'

'I am not laughing, Nastasya Filippovna, I am only listening with the greatest attention,' Totsky protested with dignity.

'Why have I been tormenting him for the last five years and not letting him go? Was he worth it? He is just what he ought to be ... Most likely he reckons I have treated him badly too. He gave me education, he kept me like a countess, and the money – the money wasted on me! He looked me out a respectable husband in the country in those days, and now Ganya here; and, would you believe it, I have not lived with him for the last five years, and yet have taken his money and thought I had a right to! I've been so completely lost to all sense! You say, take the hundred thousand and get rid of him, if it's horrid. And it really is horrid ... I might have been married long ago, and not to Ganya either, but that would have been just as horrid too. And why have I wasted five years in my anger? And would you believe it, four years ago I thought at times whether I hadn't better marry my Afanasy Ivanovitch outright? I thought of it out of spite. I had all sorts of ideas in my head at that time; and, you know, I could have brought him to it. He used to urge it himself though you mayn't believe it. He was lying, it's true, but he is easily tempted, he can't restrain himself. But afterwards, thank God, I thought he wasn't worth such anger! And I suddenly felt so disgusted with him then that, if he had besought me, I wouldn't have married him. And for the last five years I've been keeping up this farce. No, I'd better be in my proper place, in the streets! I must either have a spree with Rogozhin or go out as a washerwoman tomorrow. For I've nothing of my own. If I go away, I shall give up everything of his, I shall leave every rag behind. And who'll take one with nothing? Ask Ganya there if he'll have me! Why, even Ferdyshtchenko wouldn't!'

'Perhaps Ferdyshtchenko wouldn't, Nastasya Filippovna. I am a candid person,' interposed Ferdyshtchenko; 'but the prince would take you. You sit here and complain, but you should look at the prince. I've been watching him a long time.'

Nastasya Filippovna turned with curiosity to Myshkin.

'Is that true?' she asked.

'It's true,' whispered Myshkin,

'Will you take me as I am, with nothing?'

'I will, Nastasya Filippovna.'

'Here's a new development,' muttered the general. 'I might have expected it.'

Myshkin looked with a stern, mournful and penetrating gaze into the face of Nastasya Filippovna, who was still scanning him.

'Here's a find!' she said suddenly, turning again to Darya Alexeyevna. 'And simply from goodness of heart, too; I know him. I have found a benefactor! But maybe it's true what they say about him, that he is … *not quite*. What are you going to live on if you are so in love that you, a prince, are ready to marry Rogozhin's woman?'

'I am going to marry an honest woman, Nastasya Filippovna, not Rogozhin's woman,' said Myshkin.

'Do you mean that I am an honest woman?'

'Yes.'

'Oh, all those notions… come out of novels! Those are old-fashioned fancies, Prince darling; nowadays the world has grown wiser. And how can you get married? You want a nurse to look after you!'

Myshkin got up and in a shaking, timid voice, but with an air of intense conviction, pronounced, 'I know nothing about it, Nastasya Filippovna. I've seen nothing of life. You are right there, but … I consider that you will be doing me an honour, not I you. I am nothing, and you have suffered and have come pure out of that hell, and that is a great deal. Why, then, are you ashamed, and ready to go off with Rogozhin? It's fever … You have given back seventy thousand to Mr Totsky and you say that you will give up everything – everything here. No one here would do that. I… Nastasya Filippovna … I love you! I would die for you, Nastasya Filippovna! I won't let anyone say a word about you. If we are poor, I'll work, Nastasya Filippovna …'

At the last word a snigger was heard from Ferdyshtchenko and Lebedyev, and even the general gave a sort of snort of great dissatisfaction. Ptitsyn and Totsky could not help smiling, but controlled themselves. The others simply gaped with astonishment.

'… But perhaps *we* shan't be poor, but very rich, Nastasya Filippovna,' Myshkin went on in the same timid voice. 'I don't know for certain, and I am sorry that I haven't been able all day to find out about it, but I had a letter from Moscow while I was in Switzerland, from a certain Mr Salazkin, and he informed me that I may receive a very large inheritance. Here is the letter …'

Myshkin did in fact produce a letter from his pocket.

'Isn't he raving!' muttered the general. 'This is a perfect madhouse!'

For an instant there was silence.

'I believe you said, Prince, that the letter was from Salazkin?' asked Ptitsyn. 'He is a man very well known in his own circle; he is a very distinguished lawyer, and, if it is really he who sends you the news, you may put complete trust in it. Fortunately I know his handwriting, for I had business with him lately … If you would let me have a look at it, I might tell you.'

With a shaking hand Myshkin held out the letter without a word.

'What now? What now?' the general cried, looking at everybody like one possessed. 'Can it really be an inheritance?'

Everyone fixed their eyes on Ptitsyn as he read the letter. The general curiosity had received a new and violent stimulus. Ferdyshtchenko could not keep still; Rogozhin looked on with amazement and great anxiety, turning his eyes from Myshkin to Ptitsyn. Darya Alexeyevna seemed on tenterhooks of expectation. Even Lebedyev could not help coming out of his corner and bending himself into a triangle, peeped at the letter over Ptitsyn's shoulder with the air of a man expecting a blow for doing so.

Chapter 16

'It's a genuine thing,' Ptitsyn announced at last, folding up the letter and handing it to Myshkin. 'By the uncontested will of your aunt you will come into a very large fortune without any difficulty.'

'Impossible!' the general fired off like a pistol-shot.

Everyone was agape with astonishment again.

Ptitsyn explained, addressing his remarks chiefly to General Epanchin, that Myshkin had five months previously lost an aunt, whom he had never know personally, the elder sister of his mother and the daughter of a Moscow merchant of the third guild, called Papushin, who had died bankrupt and in poverty. But the elder brother of this Papushin, who had also died lately, had been a well-known rich merchant. His two only sons had both died in the same month a year before. The shock of their loss had led to the old man's illness and death shortly after. He was a widower and had no heirs in the world but his niece, Myshkin's aunt, who was quite a poor woman without a home of her own. At the time she inherited the fortune she was almost dying of dropsy, but she had at once tried to find Myshkin, putting the matter into Salazkin's hands, and she had had time to make her will. Apparently neither Myshkin nor the doctor in whose charge he was in Switzerland had cared to wait for an official notification or to make enquiries, and the prince, with Salazkin's letter in his pocket, had decided to set off himself.

'However, I can only tell you,' Ptitsyn concluded, addressing Myshkin, 'that this is certainly true and incontestable, and everything Salazkin says to you as to the authenticity and certainty of your fortune you may take as equal to hard cash in your pocket. I congratulate you, Prince! You too wall perhaps come in for a million and a half – possibly more. Papushin was a very rich merchant.'

'Bravo! the last of the Myshkins!' yelled Ferdyshtchenko.

'Hurrah!' croaked Lebedyev in a drunken voice.

'And I lent him twenty-five roubles this morning, poor fellow! Ha, ha, ha! It's a fairy tale, that's what it is,' said the general, almost stupefied with astonishment. 'Well, I congratulate you-I congratulate you.'

And he got up and went to embrace Myshkin. The others too rose and also pressed round Myshkin. Even those who had retreated behind the curtain came into the drawing-room. There was a confused hubbub of talk and exclamations, there were even clamours for champagne; everyone was in fuss and excitement. For an instant they almost forgot Nastasya Filippovna and that she was, anyway, the hostess. But gradually and almost simultaneously the thought occurred to all that Myshkin had just made her an offer of marriage. So that the position struck them as three times as mad and extraordinary as before. Greatly astonished, Totsky shrugged his shoulders; he was almost the only person still sitting, the rest of the company were crowding round the table in disorder.

People asserted afterwards that it was at this moment Nastasya Filippovna went mad. She was still sitting down, and for some time looked about her with a strange and wondering gaze, as though she could not take it in and were trying to grasp what had happened. Then she suddenly turned to Myshkin and with a menacing frown stared intently at him, but that was only for a moment; perhaps she suddenly fancied that it was all a joke, a mockery. But Myshkin's face reassured her. She pondered, then smiled again vaguely, as though not knowing why.

'Then I am really a princess,' she whispered to herself, as it were mockingly, and, chancing to look at Darya Alexeyevna, she laughed. 'It's a surprising ending ... I ... didn't expect it ... But why are you all standing, friends? Please sit down. Congratulate me and the prince! I think someone asked for champagne. Ferdyshtchenko, go and order it. Katya, Pasha' – she suddenly caught sight of her maids in the doorway – 'come here. I am going to be married. Did you hear? To the prince. He has a million and a half; he is Prince Myshkin, and is marrying me.'

'And a good thing too, my dear; it's high time! It's not a chance to miss,' cried Darya Alexeyevna, tremendously moved by what had passed.

'Sit down beside me, Prince,' Nastasya Filippovna went on. 'That's right. And here they are bringing the wine. Congratulate us, friends!'

'Hurrah!' shouted a number of voices.

Many of them were crowding round the wine, and among these were almost all Rogozhin's followers. But though they shouted and were prepared to shout, yet many of them, in spite of the strangeness of the circumstances and the surroundings, realised that the situation had changed. Others were bewildered and waited mistrustfully. Many whispered to one another that this was quite an ordinary affair, that princes marry all sorts of women, even girls out of gypsy camps. Rogozhin himself stood staring, his face twisted into a fixed and puzzled smile.

'Prince, my dear fellow, think what you are doing,' General Epanchin whispered with horror, coming up sideways and pulling Myshkin by his sleeve.

Nastasya Filippovna noticed this and laughed.

'No, General! I am a princess myself now, do you hear? The prince won't let me be insulted. Afanasy Ivanovitch, you too congratulate me. I can sit down beside your wife now everywhere. What do you think, it's a good bargain a husband like that? A million and a half, and a prince and an idiot into the bargain, they say. What could be better? Real life is only just beginning for me now. You are too late, Rogozhin! Take away your money; I am marrying the prince, and I am richer than you are!'

But Rogozhin had grasped the situation. There was a look of unspeakable suffering in his face. He clasped his hands and a groan broke from his breast.

'Give her up!' he shouted to Myshkin.

There was laughter.

'Give her up for you?' Darya Alexeyevna pronounced triumphantly. 'He plumped the money down on the table, the lout! The prince is marrying her, but you only came in to make an upset!'

'I'll marry her too! I'll marry her at once, this minute! I'll give up everything ...'

'Get along! You're a drunkard out of a tavern. You ought to be turned out,' Darya Alexeyevna repeated indignantly.

The laughter was louder than before.

'Do you hear, Prince?' said Nastasya Filippovna, turning to him. 'That's how a peasant bids for your bride!'

'He is drunk,' said Myshkin. 'He loves you very much.'

'And won't you feel ashamed afterwards that your bride almost went off with Rogozhin?'

'You were in a fever, you are in a fever now, almost delirious.'

'And won't you feel ashamed when people tell you afterwards that your wife used to live with Totsky as his kept mistress?'

'No, I shan't be ashamed ... It wasn't your doing that you were with Totsky.'

'And you will never reproach me with it?'

'Never.'

'Be careful; don't answer for your whole life!'

'Nastasya Filippovna,' said Myshkin softly and as it were with compassion, 'I told you just now that I would take your consent as an honour, and that you are doing me an honour, not I you. You smiled at those words, and I heard people laughing about us. I may have expressed myself very absurdly and have been absurd myself, but I thought all the time that I... understood the meaning of honour, and I am sure I spoke the truth. You wanted to ruin yourself just now irrevocably, for you'd never have forgiven yourself for it afterwards. But you are not to blame for anything. Your life cannot be altogether ruined. What does it matter that Rogozhin did come to you and Gavril Ardalionovitch tried to deceive you? Why will you go on dwelling on it? Few people would do what you have done, I tell you that again. As for your meaning to go with Rogozhin, you were ill when you meant to do it. You are ill now, and you had much better go to bed. You would have gone off to be a washerwoman next day; you wouldn't have stayed with Rogozhin. You are proud, Nastasya Filippovna, but perhaps you are so unhappy as really to think yourself to blame. You want a lot of looking after, Nastasya Filippovna. I will look after you. I saw your portrait this morning and I felt as though I recognised a face that I knew. I felt as though you had called to me already … I shall respect you all my life Nastasya Filippovna.'

Myshkin finished suddenly, seeming all at once to recollect himself. He blushed, becoming conscious of the sort of people in whose presence he was saying this.

Ptitsyn bent his head and looked on the ground, abashed. Totsky thought to himself, 'He is an idiot, but he knows that flattery is the best way to get at people; it's instinct!' Myshkin noticed too in the corner Ganya's eyes glaring at him, as though they would wither him up.

'There's a kind-hearted man!' Darya Alexeyevna pronounced, much touched.

'A man of refinement, but doomed to ruin,' the general whispered in an undertone.

Totsky took his hat and was about to get up and slip away. He and the general glanced at one another, meaning to leave together.

'Thank you, Prince. No one has ever talked to me like that before,' said Nastasya Filippovna. 'They've always been trying to buy me, but no decent man has ever thought of marrying me. Did you hear, Afanasy Ivanovitch? What did you think of all the prince said? It was almost improper, don't you think? … Rogozhin, don't go away yet! But you are not going, I see. Perhaps I shall come with you after all. Where did you mean to take me?'

'To Ekaterinhof,' Lebedyev reported from the corner. Rogozhin simply started and gazed open-eyed at her, as though he could not believe his senses. He was completely stupefied, as though he had had a violent blow on the head.

'What are you thinking about, my dear? You really are ill. Have you taken leave of your senses?' cried Darya Alexeyevna, alarmed.

'Did you really think I meant it?' laughed Nastasya Filippovna, jumping up from the sofa. 'Ruin a child like that? That's more in Afanasy Ivanovitch's line: he is fond of children! Come along, Rogozhin! Get your money ready! Never mind about wanting to marry me, let me have the money all the same. Perhaps I shan't marry you after all. You thought if you married me, you'd keep your money? A likely idea! I am a shameless hussy! I've been Totsky's concubine … You ought to marry Aglaia Epanchin now, Prince, instead of Nastasya Filippovna, or you'll have Ferdyshtchenko pointing the finger of scorn at you! You may not be afraid, but I shall be afraid of ruining you, and of your reproaching me with it afterwards. As for your saying that I am doing you an honour, Totsky knows all about that. And you've just missed Aglaia Epanchin, Ganya, do you know? If you hadn't haggled with her, she would have married you. You are all like that; you should make your choice once for all – disreputable women or respectable ones! Or you are sure to get mixed … I say, the general is staring; his mouth is open.'

'This is Sodom – Sodom!' said the general, shrugging his shoulders.

He too got up from the sofa. Everyone stood up again. Nastasya Filippovna seemed in a perfect frenzy.

'Is it possible?' moaned Myshkin, wringing his hands.

'Did you think I meant it? I am proud myself, perhaps, although I am a shameless hussv. You called me perfection this evening; a fine sort of perfection who, simply to boast of trampling on a million and a princedom, is going into the gutter! What sort of wife should I make you after that? Afanasy Ivanovitch, I really have flung away a million, you know! How could you drink I should be glad to many Ganya for the sake of your seventy-five thousand? You can take back your seventy-five thousand, Afanasy Ivanovitch. You didn't rise to a hundred; Rogozhin has cut you out. I'll comfort Ganya myself; I've thought how to. But now I want some fun, I'm a street wench! I've been ten years in prison, now I'm going to enjoy myself. Come, Rogozhin, get ready, let's go!'

'Let's go!' roared Rogozhin, almost frantic with delight. 'Hey, you, wine! Ough!'

'Have plenty of wine ready, I want to drink. And wall there be music?'

'Yes, yes. Don't go near her!' cried Rogozhin frantically, seeing Darya Alexeyevna approaching Nastasya Filippovna. 'She is mine! It's all mine! My queen! It's the end!'

He was gasping with joy. He walked round Nastasya Filippovna, shouting to everyone, 'Don't come near her!' His whole retinue had by now flocked into the drawing-room. Some were drinking, some were shouting and laughing, all were in the greatest excitement and completely at their ease. Ferdyshtchenko began trying to fraternise with them. General Epanchin and Totsky again attempted to effect a hasty retreat. Ganya too had his hat in his hand, but he stood in silence and still seemed unable to tear himself away from the scene before him.

'Don't come near her!' cried Rogozhin.

'Why are you bellowing?' Nastasya Filippovna laughed at him. 'I am still the mistress here; if I like, I can still kick you out. I haven't taken your money yet, there it lies still; give it here, the whole bundle! Is there a hundred thousand in that bundle? Ough, how nasty! What's the matter with you, Darya Alexeyevna? Would you have had me ruin him?' – she pointed to Myshkin. 'How can he be married? He wants a nurse to look after him. The general there will be his nurse; see how he is hanging upon him! Look, Prince, your betrothed takes the money because she is a low woman, and you wanted to marry her! But why are you crying? Are you sorry? You ought to laugh as I do.' – Nastasya Filippovna went on, though there were two large tears glistening on her cheeks. – 'Trust to time; it will all pass! Better to think twice now than after … But why are you all crying? Here's Katya crying too! What's the matter with you, Katya dear? I'll leave a lot to you and Pasha, I've settled it already; and now goodbye! I've made an honest girl like you wait on a low creature like me … It's better so, Prince, it's really better; you'd have despised me later on, and we should not have been happy. Don't swear, I don't believe it! And how stupid it would have been! … No, better part as friends, or no good would have come of it, for I am something of a dreamer myself, you know. Haven't I dreamed of you myself? You are right, I dreamed of you long ago, when I lived five years all alone in his country home. I used to think and dream, think and dream, and I was always imagining someone like you, kind, good and honest, and so stupid that he would come forward all of a sudden and say, "You are not to blame, Nastasya Filippovna, and I adore you." I used to dream like that, till I nearly went out of my mind … And then this man would come, stay two months in the year, bringing shame, dishonour, corruption, degradation, and go away. So that a thousand times I wanted to fling myself into the pond, but I was a poor creature, I hadn't the courage; and now … Rogozhin, are you ready?'

'Ready! Don't come near her!'

'Ready!' shouted several voices.

'The troikas are waiting with bells!'

Nastasya Filippovna snatched up the bundle of notes.

'Ganya, an idea has occurred to me. I want to compensate you, for why should you lose everything? Rogozhin, would he crawl on all fours to the other end of Petersburg for three roubles?'

'He would.'

'Then listen, Ganya; I want to see into your soul for the last time. You have been torturing me for three months past, now it's my turn. You see this roll, there are a hundred thousand roubles in it! I'm just going to throw it into the fire, before everyone, all are witnesses. As soon as the fire has got it all alight, put your hands into the fire, only without gloves, with your bare hands and turn back your sleeves, and pull the bundle out of the fire. If you can pull it out, it's yours, the whole hundred thousand. You'll only burn your fingers a little – but it's a hundred thousand, think of it! It won't take long to pull out. And I shall admire your spirit, seeing how you put your hands into the fire for my money. All are witnesses that the bundle shall be yours. And if you don't, then it will burn; I won't let anyone touch it. Stand away! Everyone stand back! It's my money! It's my wages for a night with Rogozhin. Is it my money, Rogozhin?'

'Yours, my joy! Yours, my queen!'

'Then all stand back, I may do what I like! Don't interfere! Ferdyshtchenko, make up the fire!'

'Nastasya Filippovna, I can't raise my hands to it,' answered Ferdyshtchenko, dumbfounded.

'Ech!' cried Nastasya Filippovna. She snatched up the *tongs*, separated two smouldering chunks of wood, and as soon as the fire flared up, she flung the bundle into it.

There was an outcry from all the party; many even crossed themselves.

'She's gone out of her mind! She is mad!' they shouted.

'Oughtn't we...oughtn't we...to tie her up?'the general whispered to Ptitsyn, 'or send for the ... She is mad, isn't she, isn't she?'

'N-no, perhaps it isn't quite madness,' Ptitsyn whispered, trembling and white as a handkerchief, unable to take his eyes off the smouldering roll of notes.

'She is mad! She's mad, isn't she?' the general persisted to Totsky.

'As I told you, she is a woman of glaring effects,' muttered Afanasy Ivanovitch, also somewhat pale.

'But come, you know, it's a hundred thousand!'

'Good heavens!' was heard on all sides. Everyone crowded round the fireplace, everyone pressed forward to see, everyone exclaimed. Some even jumped on chairs to look over each other's heads. Darya Alexeyevna whisked away into the other room and whispered in alarm with Katya and Pasha. The beautiful German had fled.

'Madam! Royal lady! Omnipotent lady!' wailed Lebedyev, crawling on his knees in front of Nastasya Filippovna, stretching out his hands to the fire. 'A hundred thousand – a hundred thousand! I saw the notes myself, they were rolled up before me. Lady! Gracious lady! Tell me to pick them out! I'll get right in, I'll put my grey head in! ... My wife is sick and bedridden; I've thirteen children, all orphans; I buried my father last week, he had nothing to eat, Nastasya Filippovna!'

And he tried to get to the fire.

'Get away!' cried Nastasya Filippovna, shoving him off. 'All stand back! Ganya, why are you standing still? Don't be shy, pick it out! It's your luck!'

But Ganya had suffered too much that day and was not ready for this last unexpected ordeal. The crowd parted in front of him and he remained face to face with Nastasya Filippovna, three steps from her. She was standing close by the fire, waiting, with intent, glowing eyes fixed upon him. Ganya stood in his evening dress with his arms folded and his gloves and hat in his hand, gazing mutely at the fire. A frenzied smile strayed on his chalk-white face. It is true that he couldn't take his eyes off the fire, off the smouldering roll of notes, but something new seemed to have risen up in his soul: he seemed to have vowed to endure the ordeal. He did not move from his place. In a few instants it became clear to everyone that he was not going to touch the notes.

'I say, if it's burnt they'll all cry shame on you!' Nastasya Filippovna shouted to him. 'You'll hang yourself afterwards! I am in earnest.'

The fire which had flamed up at first between two smouldering brands was smothered by the bundle being thrown on to it. But a little blue flame still lingered on the lower side at the end of one log. At last the long thin tongue of flame licked the bundle too; the fire caught it and ran upwards at the corners. Suddenly the whole bundle flared up in the fireplace and a bright flame shot up. Everyone drew a deep breath.

'Lady!' Lebedyev vociferated again, pushing forward, but Rogozhin dragged and pushed him back once more.

Rogozhin seemed petrified in a fixed stare at Nastasya Filippovna. He could not take his eyes off her; he was drunk with delight, he was in the seventh heaven.

'That's like a queen!' he kept repeating, addressing himself to everyone near. 'That's style!' he kept shouting, beside himself. 'Which of you pickpockets would do a thing like that, eh?'

Myshkin looked on, mournful and silent.

'I'd pull it out with my teeth for a paltry thousand,' suggested Ferdyshtchenko.

'I could pull it out with my teeth too,' the fisted gentleman groaned in the rear, in genuine despair. 'D-damn it all! It's burning, it's all on fire!' he shouted, seeing the flame.

'It's burning – it's burning!' they all cried with one voice, almost everyone making a dash to the fire.

'Ganya, don't show off! For the last time I say it!'

'Pick it out!' roared Ferdyshtchenko, rushing to Ganya in a positive frenzy and pulling him by the sleeve. 'Pull it out, you conceited jackanapes! It'll be burnt! Oh, d-damn you!'

Ganya pushed Ferdyshtchenko violently away, turned, and walked to the door. But before he had taken two steps, he staggered and fell in a heap on the floor.

'Fainting!' they cried.

'Dear lady, it will be burnt!' wailed Lebedyev.

'It'll burn for nothing!' they were roaring on all sides.

'Katya, Pasha, water for him, spirit!' shouted Nastasya Filippovna.

She picked up the tongs and pulled out the notes. All the outside wrappings were burnt and in ashes, but it could be seen at once that the inside of the roll was untouched. The bundle was wrapped up in three thicknesses of newspaper and the notes were unhurt. Everyone breathed more freely.

'Only a poor little thousand spoiled perhaps and the rest are all safe,' Lebedyev commented with great feeling.

'It's all his! The whole roll is his! Do you hear, friends?' Nastasya Filippovna declared, laying the roll of notes beside Ganya. 'He wouldn't do it, he stood the test, so his vanity is even greater than his love of money. It's no matter, he'll come to. But for this he might have murdered someone ... There, he's coming to himself. General, Ivan Petrovitch, Darya Alexeyevna, Katya, Pasha, Rogozhin, do you hear? The notes are his – Ganya's. I give it him to do as he likes with, as compensation for… whatever it is! Tell him! Let it lie there by him… Rogozhin, march! Goodbye, Prince! You are the first man I have seen in my life! Goodbye, Afanasy Ivanovitch, *merci!*'

The crowd of Rogozhin's followers passed through the rooms to the front door after Rogozhin and Nastasya Filippovna, with hubbub, clamour and shouts. In the hall the maids gave her her fur coat; the cook Marfa ran in from the kitchen. Nastasya Filippovna kissed them all.

'But can you be leaving us altogether, dear lady? But where are you going? And on your birthday, too, such a day!' the weeping girls asked, kissing her hands.

'To the gutter, Katya – you heard that's my proper place – or else to be a washerwoman. I've done with Afanasy Ivanovitch. Greet him for me, and don't remember evil against me …'

Myshkin rushed headlong to the street door, where all the party were getting into four troikas with bells. General Epanchin succeeded in overtaking him on the staircase.

'Pray think what you are doing, Prince!' he said, seizing his arm. 'Give it up! You see what she is. I speak as a father.'

Myshkin looked at him, but without uttering a word broke away and ran downstairs.

At the street door, from which the troikas had just started, the general saw Myshkin call the first sledge and shout to the driver: 'To Ekaterinhof; follow the troikas!' Then the general's grey horse drew up and the general drove home with new hopes and plans and the pearls, which in spite of everything he had not forgotten to take with him. Among his plans the fascinating figure of Nastasya Filippovna flitted two or three times. The general sighed.

'I am sorry – genuinely sorry. She is a lost woman! A mad woman!… But the prince is not for Nastasya Filippovna now … so it's perhaps a good thing it's turned out as it has.'

A few edifying words summing up the situation were uttered by two guests of Nastasya Filippovna's, who decided to walk a little way.

'Do you know, Afanasy Ivanovitch, they say something of the sort is done among the Japanese,' observed Ivan Petrovitch Ptitsyn. 'They say anyone who has received an insult goes to his enemy and says, 'You have wronged me, and in revenge I've come to cut open my stomach before you,' and with those words actually does rip open his stomach before his enemy, and probably feels great satisfaction in doing so, as though it really were a vengeance. There are strange people in the world, Afanasy Ivanovitch!'

'And you think there was something of the sort in this case too?' Totsky responded, with a smile. 'Hm!… That's clever, though … and you've made an excellent comparison. But you've seen for yourself, my dear Ivan Petrovitch, that I've done all I could; I can't do more than I can, you'll admit. But you must admit too that that woman has some first-rate points … some brilliant qualities. I felt tempted to cry out to her, if only I could have demeaned myself to do it in that Bedlam, that she herself is my best apology for all her accusations. Who wouldn't have been fascinated sometimes by that woman so that he would forget reason and … everything? You see, that lout Rogozhin plumped down his load of money at her feet! True, all that happened just now was something ephemeral, romantic and unseemly, but there was colour in it and originality, you must admit that. My God, what might not be made of such a character, with such beauty! But in spite of all effort, in spite of her education even – it's all lost! She is an uncut diamond – I've said so several times.'

And Afanasy Ivanovitch sighed deeply.

PART TWO

Chapter 1

Two days after the strange incident at Nastasya Filippovna's party with which we concluded the first part of our story, Prince Myshkin was hurrying on his way to Moscow to receive his unexpected fortune. It was said that there might be other reasons for his hasty departure, but of this and of Myshkin's adventures during his absence from Petersburg we can give little information. Myshkin was away just six months, and even those who had reason to be interested in his fate could find out very little at that time. Though rumours did reach them indeed at rare intervals, they were for the most part strange ones and almost always contradictory. The Epanchin family, of course, took more interest in Myshkin than anyone else, though he went away without even taking leave of them. General Epanchin did see him two or three times; they had some serious conversation. But though the general saw him, he did not mention it to his family. And indeed at first, for almost a month after Myshkin had gone, his name was avoided by the Epanchins altogether. Only Madame Epanchin had pronounced at the very beginning 'that she had been cruelly mistaken in the prince.' Then two or three days later she added vaguely, not mentioning Myshkin's name, 'that the most striking thing in her life was the way she was continually being mistaken in people.' And finally, ten days later, she wound up by adding sententiously when she was vexed with her daughters, 'We have made mistakes enough. We'll have no more of them.'

We must add that for some time there was rather an unpleasant feeling in the house. There was a sense of oppression, of strain, of some unspoken dissension; everyone wore a frown. The general was busy day and night, absorbed in his work. His household hardly got a glimpse of him; he had rarely been seen more active and occupied, especially in his official work. As for the young ladies, no word was spoken by them openly. Perhaps even when they were alone together, very little was said. They were proud, haughty girls and reserved even with one another, though they understood each other not only at a word but at a glance, so that sometimes there was no need to say much.

There was only one conclusion that might have been drawn by a disinterested observer, if there had happened to be such a one – namely, that to judge from the above-mentioned facts, few as they were, Myshkin had succeeded in making a marked impression on the Epanchin family, though he had only been once among them, and then for a short time. Perhaps the feeling he had inspired was simply curiosity aroused by certain eccentric adventures of Myshkin's. However that might be, the impression remained.

Little by little, the rumours that had circulated about the town were lost in the darkness of uncertainty. A story was told indeed of some little prince who was a simpleton (no one could be sure of his name), who had suddenly come into a vast fortune and married a Frenchwoman, a notorious dancer of the *cancan* from the Chateau-de-Fleurs in Paris. But others declared that it was a general who had come in for a fortune, and that the man who had married the notorious French *cancan* dancer was a young Russian merchant of untold wealth, and that at his wedding, from pure bravado, he had when drunk burnt in a candle lottery tickets to the value of seven hundred thousand roubles. But all these rumours soon died away, a result to which circumstances greatly contributed. Mr Rogozhin's followers, for instance, many of whom might have had something to say, had all gone in his wake to Moscow, a week after an awful orgy at the Ekaterinhof Vauxhall, in which Nastasya Filippovna took part. The few persons who were interested in the subject learnt from certain reports that Nastasya Filippovna had run off and disappeared the day after this orgy, and she seems to have been traced to Moscow, so that Rogozhin's departure to Aloscow seemed to fall in with this rumour.

There were rumours too with regard to Gavril Ardalionovitch Ivolgin, who was also pretty well known in his own circle. But something happened to him which quickly softened and in the end completely stopped all unpleasant stories about him: he fell seriously ill and unable to go to his office, much less into society. He recovered after a month's illness, but for some reason resigned his position in the office of the joint stock company and was replaced by another man. He had not once been to the Epanchins' house either, so another clerk undertook the duties of secretary to the general. Gavril Ardalionovitch's enemies might have assumed that he was so crestfallen at all that had happened to him as to be ashamed to go out into the street, but he was really ill, and sank into a state of hypochondria; he grew moody and irritable. Varvara Ardalionovna was married to Ptitsyn that winter. All who knew them put the marriage down to the fact that Ganya was unwilling to return to his duties, and was not only unable to keep his family, but was even in need of assistance and almost of care himself.

It may be observed in parenthesis that no mention was made in the Epanchin family of Gavril Ardalionovitch either, as though such a man had never been seen in their house, nor had indeed existed in the world at all. Yet meantime everyone in the family learnt – and very shortly indeed – one remarkable fact concerning him. On the fatal night after his unpleasant experience with Nastasya Filippovna, Ganya did not go to bed on returning home, but awaited Myshkin's return with feverish impatience. Myshkin, who had gone to Ekaterinhof, came home at six o'clock next morning. Then Ganya went into his room and laid on the table before him the roll of scorched notes presented to him by Nastasya Filippovna while he lay fainting. He begged Myshkin to give this present back to her at the first opportunity. When Ganya went into Myshkin's room, he was in a hostile and almost desperate mood, but some words must have been exchanged between them, after which Ganya stayed two hours with Myshkin, sobbing bitterly all the time. They parted on affectionate terms.

This story, which reached the Epanchins, turned out to be perfectly correct. It was strange, of course, that such facts could so soon come out and be generally known; all that had happened at Nastasya Filippovna's, for instance, became known at the Epanchins' almost the next day, and fairly accurately. As for the facts concerning Gavril Ardalionovitch, it might have been supposed that they had been carried to the Epanchins' by Varvara Ardalionovna, who suddenly became a frequent visitor and an intimate friend of the girls, to the great astonishment of Lizaveta Prokofyevna. But though Varvara Ardalionovna thought fit for some reason to make such friends with the Epanchins, yet she certainly would not have talked to them about her brother. She too was rather a proud woman in her own way, although she did seek the intimacy of people who had almost turned her brother out. She had been acquainted with the Epanchin girls before, but she had seen them rarely. She hardly ever showed herself in the drawing-room even now, however, and went in, or rather slipped in, by the back staircase. Lizaveta Prokofyevna had never cared for her and did not care for her now, though she had a great respect for her mother, Nina Alexandrovna. She wondered, was angry, and put down their intimacy with Varya to the whims and self-will of her daughters, who 'did not know what to think of to oppose her.' But Varya continued to visit them, both before and after her marriage.

A month after Myshkin's departure, however, Madame Epanchin received a letter from old Princess Byelokonsky, who had gone a fortnight before to Moscow to stay with her eldest married daughter, and this letter had a marked effect upon her, though she said nothing of it to her daughters or to Ivan Fyodorovitch, but from various signs it was evident to them that she was much excited, even agitated, by it. She began talking rather strangely to her daughters and always of such extraordinary subjects; she was evidently longing to open her heart, but for some reason restrained herself. She was affectionate to everyone on the day she received the letter, she even kissed Adelaïda and Aglaia; she owned herself in fault in regard to them, but they could not make out how. She even became indulgent to Ivan Fyodorovitch, who had been in her bad books for the past month. Next day, of course, she was extremely angry at her own sentimentality, and managed to quarrel with everyone before dinner, but the horizon cleared again towards the evening. For a whole week she continued to be in a fairly good humour, which had not been the case for a long time past.

But a week later a second letter came from Princess Byelokonsky, and this time Madame Epanchin made up her mind to speak out. She announced solemnly that 'old Byelokonsky' (she never called the princess anything else when she spoke of her behind her back) gave her comforting news about that... 'queer fellow, that prince, you know.' The old lady had traced him in Moscow, had enquired about him, and had found out something very good. Myshkin had been to see her himself at last, and had made an extremely good impression on her, as was evident from the fact that she invited him to come and see her every morning between one and two. 'He has been hanging about there every day, and she is not sick of him yet,' Madame Epanchin concluded, adding that through 'the old woman' the prince had been received in two or three good families. 'It's a good thing that he doesn't stick at home and isn't shy like a noodle.'

The girls to whom all this was imparted noticed at once that their mamma was concealing a great deal in the letter. Perhaps they learnt this from Varvara Ardalionovna, who might and probably did know everything Ptitsyn knew about Myshkin and his stay in Moscow. And Ptitsyn was in a position to know more than anyone else. But he was an exceedingly silent man in regard to business matters, though of course he used to talk to Varya. Madame Epanchin conceived a greater dislike than ever for Varya on account of it.

But anyway the ice was broken, and it became suddenly possible to speak of Myshkin aloud. Moreover, the great interest he had awakened and the extraordinary impression he had left on the Epanchins were once more apparent. The mother was astonished, indeed, at the effect that her news from Moscow had on her daughters. And the daughters too wondered at their mamma, who, after declaring that 'the most striking thing in her life was the way she was continually being mistaken in people,' had yet procured for the prince the protection of the 'powerful' old Princess Byelokonsky, though it must have cost her much begging and praying, for the 'old woman' was difficult to prevail upon in such cases.

But as soon as the ice was broken and there was a change in the wind, the general too hastened to express himself. It appeared that he too had been taking an exceptional interest in Myshkin. But he discussed only 'the business aspect of the question.' It appeared that in the interests of the prince he had asked two very trustworthy and, in their own way, influential persons in Moscow to keep an eye on him, and still more on Salazkin, who had charge of his affairs. All that had been said about the fortune – 'about the fact of the fortune, that is to say – had turned out to be true, but the fortune itself had turned out to be much less considerable than had been rumoured at first. The property was partly in an involved condition: there were, it appeared, debts; other claimants turned up too, and in spite of the advice given him Myshkin had behaved in a most unbusinesslike way. 'God bless him, of course!' Now when the ice of silence was broken, the general was glad to express his feelings 'in all sincerity of heart,' for though 'the fellow was a bit *lacking* , still he did deserve it. Yet he had done something stupid. Creditors of the late merchant's had sent in claims, for instance, based on questionable or worthless documents; and some of them, getting wind of the prince's character, had even come forward without any documents at all; and – would you believe it? – the prince had satisfied almost all of them in spite of his friends' representations that all these wretches of creditors had absolutely no claim on him; and his only reason for satisfying them was that some of them actually had been unfairly treated.

Madame Epanchin observed that old Byelokonsky had written something of the sort to her, and that 'it was stupid, very stupid. There's no curing a fool,' she added harshly, but it could be seen from her face how pleased she was at the conduct of this 'fool.' In the end the general saw that his wife cared for Myshkin, as though he were her son, and had begun to be unaccountably affectionate to Aglaia. Seeing this, Ivan Fyodorovitch assumed for a time a peculiarly businesslike air.

But this pleasant state of things did not last long. A fortnight passed and again there was a sudden change. Madame Epanchin looked cross, and, after some shrugging of the shoulders, General Epanchin resigned himself again to the 'ice of silence.'

The fact was that only a fortnight before he had privately received some brief and not quite clear, though authentic, information that Nastasya Filippovna, who had at first disappeared in Moscow, then been found there by Rogozhin, and had then again disappeared and been found again, had at last almost promised to marry him, and, behold! Only a fortnight later his excellency had suddenly learnt that Nastasya Filippovna had run away for the third time, almost on her wedding day, and had disappeared somewhere in the provinces, and that Prince Myshkin had vanished at the same time, leaving all his business in Salazkin's charge, 'Whether with her, or simply in pursuit of her, is not known, but there's something in it,' the general concluded.

Lizaveta Prokofyevna too had received some unpleasant news. The upshot of it was that two months after the prince had gone almost every" rumour about him had died down in Petersburg, and the 'ice of silence' was again unbroken in the Epanchin family. Varya, however, still visited the girls.

To make an end of all these rumours and explanations we will add that there were many changes in the Epanchin household in the spring, so that it was difficult not to forget the prince who sent no news of himself and perhaps did not care to do so. During the winter they gradually came to the decision to spend the summer abroad, Lizaveta Prokofyevna and her daughters, that is. It was, of course, impossible for the general to waste his time on 'frivolous diversion.' This decision was due to the urgent and persistent efforts of the girls, who were thoroughly persuaded that their parents did not want to take them abroad because they were so taken up with trying to marry them and find them husbands. Possibly the parents were convinced at last that husbands might be met with even abroad, and that travel for one summer, far from upsetting plans, might even perhaps 'be of use'. This is the place to mention that the proposed marriage of Afanasy Ivanovitch Totsky and the eldest of the girls had been broken off, and the formal offer of his hand had never been made. This had somehow happened of itself without much talk and without any family quarrel. The project had suddenly been dropped on both sides at the time of Myshkin's departure. This circumstance had been one of the causes of the ill-humour prevailing in the Epanchin family, though the mother had declared at the time that she was so glad that 'she could have crossed herself with both hands at once.' Though the general was in disfavour and knew that he was to blame, yet he felt aggrieved for a long time. He was sorry to lose Afanasy Ivanovitch – 'such a fortune and such a sharp fellow!' Not long afterwards the general learnt that Totsky had been fascinated by a Frenchwoman of the highest society, a marquise and a *légitimiste*; that they were going to be married, and that Afanasy Ivanovitch was to be taken to Paris and then to Brittany. 'Well, with the Frenchwoman he is lost to us,' concluded the general. The Epanchins were preparing to set off before summer, when suddenly a circumstance occurred which changed all their plans, and the tour was put off again, to the great delight of the general and his wife. A certain Prince S— came from Moscow to Petersburg, a well-known man and well known for his excellent qualities. He was one of those modern men, one may even say reformers, who are honest, modest, genuinely and intelligently desirous of the public weal, always working and distinguished by a rare and happy faculty of finding work. Not courting public notice, avoiding the bitterness and verbosity of party strife, the prince had a thorough understanding of contemporary movements, though he did not regard himself as a leader. He had been in the government service; afterwards he had been an active member of a Zemstvo. He was, moreover, a correspondent of several learned societies. In collaboration with a well-known expert, he had collected facts and made enquiries which led to an improvement in the scheme for a very important new railway line. He was about thirty-five. He was a man 'of the highest society,' and had, moreover, a 'good, serious, and unmistakable fortune,' in the words of General Epanchin, who happened to have to do with Prince S— about rather important business and made his acquaintance in the house of the count who was the chief of General Epanchin's department. Prince S— had a certain interest in Russian 'practical men' and never avoided their society. It came to pass that the prince was introduced to the general's family. Adelaïda Ivanovna, the second of the sisters, made a considerable impression upon him. Before the end of the winter he made her an offer. Adelaïda liked him extremely; Lizaveta Prokofyevna liked him too; General Epanchin was delighted. The foreign tour was of course put off. The wedding was fixed for the spring.

The tour might still have come off in the middle of the summer or towards the end of it, if only as a brief visit for a month or two to console the mother and the remaining daughters for the loss of Adelaïda. But something fresh happened. Towards the end of the spring (Adelaïda's wedding was deferred till the middle of the summer) Prince S — introduced to the Epanchins one of his own family, whom he knew very well, though he was only a distant relation. This was Yevgeny Pavlovitch Radomsky, a young man of twenty-eight, an Imperial aide-de-camp, extremely handsome and of good family. He was witty, brilliant, 'modern', 'of extreme education', and almost too fabulously wealthy. As to the latter point, General Epanchin was always very careful. He made enquiries: 'There does seem to be something in it; though, of course, one ought to make sure.' This young and promising aide-de-camp was highly recommended by old Princess Byelokonsky from Moscow. But one rumour about him was rather disturbing: there were tales of *liaisons*, of 'conquests', and broken hearts. Seeing Aglaia, he became assiduous in his visits to the Epanchins'. Nothing indeed had been said as yet, no hint even had been dropped, yet it seemed to the parents that it would be out of the question to go abroad that summer. Aglaia herself was of a different opinion.

All this was happening just before our hero's second entry on the scene of our story. By that time, to judge by appearances, poor Prince Myshkin had been completely forgotten in Petersburg. If he had suddenly appeared now among those who had known him, he would seem to have fallen from heaven. We will add one other fact and so complete our introduction.

After Myshkin's departure Kolya Ivolgin had at first spent his time as before – that is to say, he went to school, visited his friend Ippolit, looked after his father, and helped Varya in the house and ran her errands. But the boarders were soon all gone. Ferdyshtchenko went away three days after the evening at Nastasya Filippovna's and soon disappeared completely, so that nothing was known about him; it was said, though not on good authority, that he was drinking. Myshkin had gone away to Moscow, and there were no more boarders. Later on, when Varya was married, Nina Alexandrovna and Ganya moved with her to Ptitsyn's house at the other end of Petersburg. As for General Ivolgin, a quite unforeseen event befell him about the same time: he was put in the debtors' prison. This was the doing of his friend, the captain's widow, on account of various bills he had given her to the value of two thousand roubles. It was a complete surprise to him, and the poor general was 'undoubtedly the victim of his unfounded faith in the generosity of the human heart, speaking generally.' Having adopted the soothing habit of signing promises to pay and IOUs, he had never conceived that they could ever lead to anything; he had always supposed that it was *all right*. It turned out not to be all right. 'How can one put faith in mankind after that? How is one to show generous confidence?' he used to exclaim bitterly, sitting with his new friends in prison over a bottle of wine, and telling them anecdotes of the siege of Kars and the soldier who rose from the dead. It suited him capitally, however. Ptitsyn and Varya maintained that it was the very place for him; Ganya quite agreed with them. Only poor Nina Alexandrovna shed bitter tears in secret (at which her household positively wondered), and, ill as she always was, she dragged herself as often as she could to visit her husband.

But from the time of the 'general's mishap,' as Kolya expressed it – and, in fact, from the time of his sister's marriage – Kolya had got quite out of hand and things had come to such a pass that he rarely even slept at home. They heard that he had made a number of new acquaintances; moreover, he became far too well known in the debtors' prison. Nina Alexandrovna could not get on there without him; at home now they did not even worry him with questions. Varya, who had been so severe with him before, did not pester him now with the slightest enquiry about his wanderings; and, to the surprise of the rest of the household, Ganya, in spite of his hypochondria, sometimes talked and behaved in quite a friendly way to him; and this was something quite new, for Ganya at twenty-seven had naturally never taken any friendly interest in his fifteen-year-old brother. He had treated him rudely and had insisted on all the family's being severe with him, and was always threatening to pull his ears, which drove Kolya 'beyond the utmost limits of human endurance.' One might have imagined that Kolya had become positively indispensable to Ganya. He had been somewhat impressed by Ganya's returning that money; for that he was ready to forgive him a great deal.

Three months had passed since Myshkin's departure, when the Ivolgin family heard that Kolya had suddenly made the acquaintance of the Epanchins and had been made very welcome by the young ladies. Varya soon heard of this, though it was not through her that Kolya came to know them, but of his own accord. The Epanchins gradually grew fond of him. Lizaveta Prokofyevna did not take to him at all at first, but afterwards she began to make much of him 'for his frankness and because he doesn't flatter.' That Kolya did not flatter was perfectly true. He managed to be quite independent and on a perfectly equal footing with them, though he sometimes read books and papers to Madame Epanchin, but he was always ready to be of use. Once or twice, however, he quarrelled seriously with Lizaveta Prokofyevna and told her that she was a despot and that he would not set foot again in her house. The first time the quarrel arose on 'the woman question,' and the second time there was a difference of opinion as to the best time of the year for catching greenfinches. Strange as it may appear, two days after the quarrel, Madame Epanchin sent a note round to him by a footman begging him to come. Kolya did not stand on his dignity and went at once. Aglaia alone, for some reason, had no liking for him and kept him at a distance. Yet it was Aglaia that he was destined to astonish. At Easter he seized an opportunity when they were alone, and handed her a letter, saying nothing but that he was told to give it to her alone. Aglaia stared menacingly at the 'conceited little upstart,' but Kolya went out without waiting further. She opened the letter and read:

> Once you honoured me with your confidence. Perhaps you have quite forgotten me now. How has it happened that I am writing to you? I don't know, but I felt an irresistible desire to remind you, just you, of my existence. How often I have wanted you all three! But of all three I saw only you. I need you -I need you very much. I have nothing to write to you about myself, have nothing to tell. That's not what I want to do; I have a great desire that you should be happy. Are you happy? That was all I wanted to say to you.
>
> Your brother,
> L. Myshkin

Reading that brief and rather incoherent letter, Aglaia flushed all over and fell to musing. It would be hard to say what she was thinking of. Among other things she asked herself whether she should show it to anyone. She felt somehow ashamed to. But she ended by throwing the letter into her table drawer with a strange and ironical smile. But the next day she took it out again and put it into a thick, strongly bound book (she always did this with her papers so that she might find them more readily when she wanted them). And not till a week after did she happen to notice what the book was. It was *Don Quixote de La Mancha*. Aglaia burst out laughing for some unknown reason. It is not known whether she showed the note to her sisters.

But even while she was reading the letter she wondered: can that conceited and boastful puppy be chosen as a correspondent by the prince, and perhaps his only correspondent here? With a show of exaggerated carelessness she began to cross-examine Kolya. But though the boy was always quick to take offence, this time he did not in the least notice her carelessness. Very briefly and rather drily he explained that, although he had given Myshkin his permanent address when the latter was leaving Petersburg and had offered to do what he could for him, this was the first commission he had given him, and the first letter he had received from him, and in support of his words he showed her a letter addressed to him from

Myshkin. Aglaia did not scruple to read it. The letter to Kolya ran as follows:

> Dear Kolya, will you be so good as to give the enclosed sealed letter to Aglaia Ivanovna? Hoping you are all well,
>
> Your loving,
> L. Myshkin

'It's ridiculous to trust a chit like you!' Aglaia said huffily, handing Kolya back his letter, and she walked contemptuously by him.

This was more than Kolya could endure, when he had even asked Ganya, without telling him why, to lend him his new green scarf for the occasion. He was bitterly offended.

Chapter 2

It was the beginning of June and the weather had been unusually fine in Petersburg for a whole week. The Epanchins had a luxurious summer villa of their own at Pavlovsk. Lizaveta Prokofyevna became suddenly excited and bestirred herself, and after less than two days of bustle they moved there.

Two or three days after they had left, Prince Lyov Nikolayevitch Myshkin arrived by a morning train from Moscow. No one met him at the station, but as he got out of the carriage he suddenly had a vision of strange glowing eyes fixed upon him in the crowd that met the train. When he looked more attentively, he could not discover them again. It could only have been a fancy, but it left an unpleasant impression. And apart from that, Myshkin was sad and thoughtful and seemed worried about something.

The cab drove up to a hotel near Liteyny. The hotel was by no means a good one, and Myshkin took two small, dark and badly furnished rooms in it. He washed and changed his clothes, asked for nothing, and went out hurriedly, as though afraid of losing time or of not finding someone at home.

If anyone who had known him six months before, on his first arrival in Petersburg, had seen him now, he might well have thought him greatly changed for the better in appearance. Yet this was scarcely true. It was only his dress that was quite different; his clothes were all new and had been cut by a good Moscow tailor. But there was something wrong even with his clothes: they were rather too fashionable (as clothes always are from conscientious but not very talented tailors), yet worn by a man who was obviously indifferent to his appearance, so that anyone too prone to laughter might perhaps have found something to smile at in Myshkin's appearance. But people will laugh at all sorts of things.

Myshkin took a cab and drove to Peski. He had no difficulty in finding a small wooden house in one of the streets there. To his surprise it turned out to be a pretty little house, clean, kept in excellent order, and with a front garden full of flowers. The windows on the street were open, and from them came the continuous sound of a harsh voice, as though someone were reading aloud or making a speech; the voice was sometimes interrupted by a chorus of ringing laughter. Myshkin went into the yard, mounted the steps and asked for Mr Lebedyev.

'He is in there,' answered the cook who opened the door to him, with her sleeves tucked up to her elbows. She pointed to the 'drawing-room'.

The drawing-room had walls covered with dark blue paper and was furnished neatly with some effort at smartness – that is, it contained a sofa and a round table, a bronze clock under a glass case, a narrow looking-glass on the wall, and a small old-fashioned chandelier hanging by a bronze chain from the ceiling and adorned with lustres. In the middle of the room, with his back to the door, stood Mr Lebedyev himself. He was wearing a waistcoat, but had discarded his coat in deference to the weather, and, striking himself on the chest, he was declaiming bitterly on some subject. His audience consisted of a boy of fifteen with a merry and intelligent face and a book in his hands; a young girl about twenty, dressed in mourning and carrying a baby in her arms; a girl of thirteen, also in mourning, who was laughing violently with her mouth wide open; and another very strange-looking figure lying on the sofa, a rather handsome, dark lad of twenty with thick long hair, large black eyes, and with just a hint of beard and whiskers on his face. He seemed to be frequently interrupting Lebedyev in his harangue and arguing with him; and this no doubt was what provoked the laughter of the others.

'Lukyan Timofeyitch! Lukyan Timofeyitch, I say! Look here! ... Well, botheration take you!' And, waving her hands, the cook went out red with anger.

Lebedyev looked round, and seeing Myshkin, stood for some time as though thunderstruck. Then he rushed to him with an ingratiating smile, but before he reached him he stood still again, murmuring, 'Il—il— illustrious prince!'

But suddenly, as though unable to rise to the position, he turned round and, apropos of nothing, rushed first at the girl in mourning with the baby in her arms, so that she was startled and drew back, but he left her at once and flew at the younger girl, who was standing in the doorway leading into the next room with traces of laughter still on her smiling lips. She was scared by his shout and bolted to the kitchen. Lebedyev stamped his feet at her to add to her alarm, but meeting the eye of Myshkin, who looked on embarrassed, he brought out in explanation, 'To show ... respect. Ha-ha-ha!'

'There's no need of all this ...' Myshkin was beginning.

'One minute – one minute – one minute ... like a hurricane!'

And Lebedyev vanished quickly from the room. Myshkin looked with surprise at the girl, at the boy, and at the figure on the sofa; they were all laughing. Myshkin laughed too.

'He's gone to put his coat on,' said the boy.

'How annoying!' Myshkin began, 'and I expected ... Tell me, is he...'

'You think he is drunk?' cried a voice from the sofa. 'Not a bit of it! Three or four glasses, five perhaps, but what's that? – The regular thing.'

Myshkin turned to the voice from the sofa, but the girl began speaking, and, with a most candid air on her charming face, she said, 'He never drinks much in the morning. If you have come to see him on business, you had better speak to him now, it's the best time. When he comes back in the evening, he is sometimes drunk, though now he more often cries in the evening and reads the Bible to us, for it's only five weeks since mother died.'

'He ran away because it was hard for him to answer you,' laughed the young man on the sofa. 'I'll bet anything that he is cheating you already and is hatching something now.'

'Only five weeks! Only five weeks!' Lebedyev said, coming back with his coat on, blinking and pulling his handkerchief out of his pocket to wipe his tears. 'We are alone in the world!'

'But why have you come in all in rags?' said the girl. 'Why, behind the door there lies your new coat. Didn't you see it?'

'Hold your tongue, dragonfly!' Lebedyev shouted at her. 'Oo, you!' He stamped his feet at her.

But this time she only laughed.

'Why are you trying to frighten me? I am not Tanya. I shall not run away. But you will wake Lubotchka and frighten her into convulsions... What's the use of shouting?'

'God forbid! Don't say such a thing!' Lebedyev was terribly alarmed all at once, and flying up to the baby, who was asleep in his daughter's arms, made the sign of the cross over it several times with a frightened face. 'God save and preserve her! That's my baby daughter, Lubov,' he added, addressing Myshkin, 'born in most lawful wedlock of my newly departed wife Elena, who died in childbirth. And this is my daughter Vera in mourning. And that – that – oh, that...'

'What! he can't go on?' cried the young man. 'Go on, don't be shy!'

'Your excellency,' Lebedyev cried with a sort of rush, 'have you read in the papers of the murder of the Zhemarin family?'

'Yes,' answered Myshkin with some surprise.

'Well, that's the actual murderer of the Zhemarin family, there he is!'

'What do you mean?' said Myshkin.

'That is, allegorically speaking, the future second murderer of a future Zhemarin family, if such there be. He is preparing himself for it...'

Everybody laughed. It occurred to Myshkin that Lebedyev really might be playing the fool because he foresaw the questions he would ask, and, not knowing what answer to make, was trying to gain time.

'He is a rebel! He is plotting!' shouted Lebedyev, as though unable to restrain himself. 'Tell me, can I have I the right to recognise such a foul-mouthed fellow such a strumpet, so to speak, and monster, as my own nephew, the only son of my deceased sister Anisya?'

'Oh, shut up, you drunken fellow! Would you believe it, Prince, he's going in for being a lawyer now – pleads cases in the court. He's become so eloquent, he talks in high-flown language to his children at home. He made a speech before the justices of the peace five days ago, and whom do you think he defended? Not a poor woman who begged and besought him to, who had been robbed by a rascally moneylender of five hundred roubles, all she had in the world, but that very moneylender, a Jew called Zaidler, just because he promised him fifty roubles ...'

'Fifty roubles if I won the case, only five if I lost it,' Lebedyev explained suddenly in quite a different tone, as though he had not been shouting at all.

'Well, he made a fool of himself, of course. Things are different nowadays; they only laughed at him. But he was awfully pleased with himself. "Remember, O judges who are no respecters of persons," says he, "that a sorrowful, bedridden old man living by his honest toil is losing his last crust of bread. Remember the wise words of the lawgiver: 'Let mercy prevail in the court.' " And, would you believe it, he says over that very speech to us here every morning, word for word, just as he spoke it? Just before you came in, he was reading it for the fifth time, he was so pleased with it. He is licking his lips over it. And now he wants to defend someone else. You are Prince Myshkin, I believe? Kolya told me he had never met anyone cleverer than you in the world...'

'Yes, yes, and there is no one cleverer in the world,' Lebedyev chimed in at once.

'Well, he is lying, we know. Kolya loves you, but this man wants to make up to you. But I don't intend to flatter you at all, let me assure you. You have some sense – judge between him and me. Would you like the prince to judge between us?' He addressed himself to his uncle. 'I am glad you've turned up, Prince, indeed.'

'Yes,' cried Lebedyev resolutely, and he unconsciously looked round at the audience, which began to gather about him again.

'Why, what is it?' asked Myshkin, frowning a little.

His head ached and he felt more and more convinced that Lebedyev was cheating him and glad to gain time.

'This is the statement of the case. I am his nephew. That was not a lie, though he is always lying. I haven't finished my studies, but I mean to, and I will, for I have character. Meanwhile I've taken a job on the railway at twenty-five roubles a month. I admit, moreover, that he has helped me two or three times. I had twenty roubles and I lost them. Would you believe it, Prince, I was so low, so base, that I lost them gambling?'

'To a wretch – a wretch whom you ought not to have paid!' shouted Lebedyev.

'Yes, to a wretch, but whom I ought to have paid,' the young man went on. 'That he is a wretch I'll bear witness to, and not because he beat me. He is an officer who has been turned out of the army, Prince – a discharged lieutenant, one of Rogozhin's crew, and he teaches boxing. They are all scattered now since Rogozhin got rid of them. But the worst of it is that I knew he was a wretch, a scoundrel, and a thief, and yet I sat down to play with him, and when I had lost my last rouble (we were playing *palki*) I thought to myself, "If I lose, I'll go to my uncle Lukyan and bow down to him; he won't refuse me." That was low – yes, that really was low! That was conscious meanness!'

'Yes, that was certainly conscious meanness,' repeated Lebedyev.

'Well, don't crow over me; wait a bit,' his nephew shouted testily. 'He is only too pleased. I came here to him, Prince, and owned up. I acted honourably, I did not spare myself. I abused myself before him all I could – all here are witnesses. In order to take that job on the railway it is necessary for me to have some sort of a rig-out, for I am in absolute rags. Just look at my boots! I couldn't turn up like that, and if I don't turn up at the proper time, someone else will get the job, and then I shall be stranded again; and when should I get another chance? Now I am only asking him for fifteen roubles and I promise that I will never ask him for anything else again; and, what's more, before the end of the first three months I'll pay him back every farthing of it. I'll keep my word. I can live on bread and kvas for months together, for I have plenty of will. I shall get seventy-five roubles for three months. With what I borrowed before, I shall owe him thirty-five, so I shall have enough to pay him. Let him fix what interest he likes, damn him! Doesn't he know me? Ask him, Prince, when he has helped me before, haven't I paid him back? Why won't he help me now? He is angry because I paid that lieutenant, there's no other reason. You see what he is – a regular dog in the manger!'

'And he won't go away!' cried Lebedyev. 'He lies here and won't go away.'

'I told you so. I won't go till you give it me. You are smiling, Prince. You seem to think I am in the wrong?'

'I am not smiling, but to my thinking you certainly are rather in the wrong,' Myshkin answered unwillingly.

'Say straight out that I am altogether wrong; don't shuffle. What do you mean by "rather"?'

'If you like, you are altogether wrong.'

'If I like! That's absurd! Do you suppose that I don't know myself that it's rather a doubtful line to take: that it's his money, it's for him to decide, and it's an act of violence on my part? But you … know nothing much of life, Prince. There's no good in sparing men like him a lesson. They need a lesson. My conscience is clear. On my conscience, he will be none the worse for it; I shall pay him back with interest. He has got moral satisfaction out of it too: he has seen my humiliation. What more does he want? What's the use of him if he doesn't help people? Look at what he does himself! Ask him how he treats others and how he takes people in! How did he manage to buy this house? I'll bet you anything he has cheated you before now, and is already scheming to cheat you again. You smile. Don't you believe it?'

'It seems to me that all this hasn't much to do with your business,' observed Myshkin.

'I've been lying here for the last three days, and what goings on I've seen!' cried the young man, not heeding. 'Would you believe it, he suspects that angel, that motherless girl there, my cousin and his daughter, and every night he searches her room for lovers! He comes in here on the sly and peeps under my sofa too. He is crazy with suspiciousness; he sees thieves in every corner. He jumps up every minute in the night, looking at the windows to see if they are properly fastened, trying the doors, peeping into the oven, and he'll do this half a dozen times in the night. At the court he defends robbers, but he gets up three times in the night to say his prayers on his knees here in the drawing-room, and bangs his forehead on the floor for half an hour at a time. And what prayers for everyone, what pious lamentations, when he is drunk! He prayed for the rest of the soul of the Countess du Barry; I've heard it with my own ears; Kolya heard it too. He is perfectly cracked!'

'Do you see, do you hear how he slanders me, Prince?' cried Lebedyev, flushing and really angry. 'And he doesn't know that, drunken and degraded swindler and beggar though I may be, my one good deed was that I wrapped that grinning rascal in his swaddling clothes when he was a baby and washed him in his bath, and sat up without a wink of sleep for nights together with my widowed sister Anisya, when she was penniless and I was as poor as she; attended them when they were sick, stole wood from the porter downstairs, used to sing and crack my fingers at him with an empty belly – and this is what my nursing has come to! Here he lies, laughing at me now! What business is it of yours if I really did cross myself once for the soul of the Countess du Barry? Three days ago I read the story of her life for the first time in the dictionary. Do you know what she was, du Barry? Tell me, do you know or not?'

'Oh, of course, nobody knows but you,' the young man muttered sarcastically but unwillingly.

'She was a countess who rose from shame to a position like a queen's, and to whom a great empress wrote in her own handwriting '*ma cousine*'. A cardinal, a papal legate at a *levée du roi* (do you know what a *levée du roi* was?) himself offered to put the silk stockings on her bare legs, and even thought it an honour – a lofty and sacred personage like that! Do you know that? I see from your face you don't. Well, and how did she die? Answer if you know.'

'Get away with you! Don't pester me!'

'The way she died after such honours was that the hangman, Sampson, dragged this great lady, guiltless, to the guillotine for the diversion of Parisian *poissardes,* and she was in such terror she didn't know what was happening to her. She saw he was bending her neck down under the knife and kicking her, while the people laughed, and she fell to screaming, *Encore un moment, monsieur le bourreau, encore un moment!'* which means, "Wait one little minute, *Mr bourreau,* only one!" And perhaps for the sake of that prayer God will forgive her, for one cannot imagine a greater *misère* for a human soul than that. Do you know the meaning of the word *misère*? Well, that's what *misère* is. When I read about that countess's cry for 'one little minute', I felt as though my heart had been pinched with a pair of tongs. And what is it to a worm like you if I did, when I was going to bed, think of mentioning that sinful woman in my prayers? And perhaps the reason I mentioned her was that, ever since the beginning of the world, probably no one has crossed himself for her sake, or even thought of doing so. And it may be pleasant for her to feel in the other world that there is a sinner like herself who has uttered at least one prayer on earth for her. Why are you laughing? Don't you believe, atheist? How do you know? And you told a lie if you did hear me. I didn't only pray for the Countess du Barry; my prayer was this: "Lord, give rest to the soul of that great sinner the Countess du Barry and all like her." And that's quite a different matter, for there are many such sinful women, examples of the mutability of fortune, who have suffered much and are storm-tossed yonder, moaning and waiting. And I prayed then for you and people like you, insolent and overbearing – since you troubled to listen to my prayers...'

'That's enough, shut up! Pray for whom you like, damn you, only stop your screaming!' the nephew interrupted with vexation. 'He is mightily well read, you see. You didn't know it, did you, Prince?' he added with an awkward grin. He is always reading books and memoirs of that sort.'

'Your uncle is anyway not ... a heartless man,' Myshkin observed reluctantly.

He was beginning to feel a great aversion for the young man.

'Why, he'll be quite puffed up if you praise him like that. Look, he's licking his lips already with his hand on his heart and his mouth pursed up! He is not heartless perhaps, but he is a rogue, that's the trouble, and he is a drunkard besides. He is all to pieces, as a man who has been drinking a good many years always is; that's why nothing goes smoothly with him. He loves his children, I admit; he respected my late aunt... even loves me and has left me a share in his will, you know.'

'I won't leave you anything!' cried Lebedyev furiously.

'Listen, Lebedyev,' said Myshkin, firmly, turning away from the young man. 'I know by experience that you can be a businesslike man when you choose ... I have very little time now, and if you ... Excuse me, what is your name and your patronymic? I have forgotten.'

'Ti-ti-timofey.'

'And?'

'Lukyanovitch.'

Everyone in the room laughed again.

'A lie!' cried the nephew. 'He is lying even about that! His name is not Timofey Lukyanovitch, Prince, but Lukyan Timofeyevitch. Come, why did you tell a lie? Isn't it just the same to you if it's Lukyan or Timofey? And what does it matter to the prince? He tells lies simply from habit, I assure you.'

'Can that be true?' asked Myshkin impatiently.

'Lukyan Timofeyevitch it really is,' Lebedyev admitted, overcome with confusion, dropping his eyes humbly and again putting his hand on his heart.

'But why on earth, then, did you say that?'

'To humble myself,' whispered Lebedyev, bending his head lower and more humbly.

'Ech, what nonsense! If only I knew where to find Kolya now,' said Myshkin, and turned to go away.

'I'll tell you where Kolya is.' The young man put himself forward again.

'No, no, no!' Lebedyev flared up and flew into great excitement. 'Kolya slept here, but in the morning he went out to look for his father, whom you, Prince, have bought out of prison – God only knows why! The general promised yesterday to come here to sleep, but he hasn't come. Most likely he slept in the hotel, the Pair of Scales, close by. Kolya is probably there, or in Pavlovsk at the Epanchins'. He had the money, he meant to go yesterday, so he is probably at the Scales or at Pavlovsk.'

'He is at Pavlovsk – at Pavlovsk!… Let us go this way – this way, into the garden and … have some coffee.'

And Lebedyev took Myshkin's hand and led him away. They went out of the room, crossed the little yard, and went through a gate. Here there was a very tiny and charming garden in which, owing to the fine season, all the trees were already in leaf. Lebedyev made Myshkin sit down on a green wooden seat by a green table fixed in the ground, and seated himself facing him. A minute later coffee was brought. Myshkin did not refuse it. Lebedyev still looked eagerly and obsequiously into his face.

'I didn't know you had such an establishment,' said Myshkin with the air of a man thinking of something quite different.

'We are orphans …' Lebedyev began, wriggling, but he stopped short.

Myshkin looked absently before him and had no doubt forgotten his remark. A minute passed; Lebedyev watched him and waited.

'Well?' said Myshkin, seeming to wake up. 'Ah, yes! You know yourself, Lebedyev, what our business is. I have come in response to your letter. Speak.'

Lebedyev was confused, tried to say something, but only stuttered, no words came. Myshkin waited and smiled mournfully.

'I think I understand you perfectly, Lukyan Timofeyevitch. You probably did not expect me, and you thought I shouldn't come back from the wilds at your first message, and you wrote to clear your conscience. And here I've come. Come, give it up, don't deceive me! Give up serving two masters. Rogozhin has been here for three weeks. I know everything. Have you succeeded in selling her to him, as you did last time? Tell me the truth.'

'The monster found out of himself – of himself.'

'Don't abuse him. He has treated you badly, of course …'

'He beat me; he nearly did for me!' Lebedyev interrupted with tremendous heat. 'He set his dog on me in Moscow; it was after me the whole length of the street – a hunting bitch, a fearsome beast!'

'You take me for a child, Lebedyev. Tell me seriously, has she left him now, in Moscow?'

'Seriously, seriously, gave him the slip on the very day of the wedding again. He was counting the minutes while she made off here to Petersburg and straight to me: "Save me, protect me, Lukyan, and don't tell the prince!"… She is even more afraid of you, Prince; there's something mysterious about it!'

And Lebedyev slyly put his finger to his forehead.

'And now you have brought them together again?'

'Most illustrious prince, how could I… how could I prevent it?'

'Well, that's enough; I'll find out for myself. Only tell me, where is she now? With him?'

'Oh, no, not at all! She is still by herself. "I am free," she says, and you know, Prince, she insists strongly on that. "I am still perfectly free!" she says. She is still living at my sister-in-laws, as I wrote to you.'

'And is she there now?'

'Yes, unless she is at Pavlovsk, as the weather is so fine, at Darya Alexeyevna's villa. "I am still perfectly free," she says. She was boasting only yesterday of her freedom to Nikolay Ardalionovitch. A bad sign!'

And Lebedyev grinned.

'Is Kolya often with her?'

'He is a heedless, unaccountable fellow; he doesn't keep things secret.'

'Is it long since you have been there?'

'Every day – every day.'

'Then you were there yesterday?'

'N-no, three days ago.'

'What a pity you've been drinking, Lebedyev. Or I might have asked you something.'

'No, no, no, not a bit of it!' Lebedyev positively pricked up his ears. 'Tell me, how did you leave her?'

'S-searching.'

'Searching?'

'As though she were always searching for something, as though she had lost something. She is sick at the thought of the marriage and looks upon it as an insult. She thinks no more of him than of a bit of orange peel. Yes, she does though, for she thinks of him with fear and trembling; she won't hear his name even, and they don't meet if it can be helped ... and he feels it only too well. But there's no getting out of it. She is restless, sarcastic, double-tongued, violent...'

'Double-tongued and violent?'

'Yes, violent, for she almost pulled my hair last time over one conversation. I tried to bring her round with the Apocalypse.'

'What do you say?' Myshkin asked, thinking he had not heard him rightly.

'By reading the Apocalypse. She is a lady with a restless imagination. Ha-ha! And I've noticed too that she has a great partiality for serious subjects, however remote they may be. She likes such talk – she likes it and takes it as a mark of special respect. Yes, I am a great hand at interpreting the Apocalypse; I've been interpreting it for the last fifteen years. She agreed with me that we are living in the age of the third horse, the black one, and the rider who has the balance in his hand, seeing that everything in the present age is weighed in the scales and by agreement, and people are seeking for nothing but their rights – "a measure of wheat for a penny and three measures of barley for a penny"; and yet they want to keep a free spirit and a pure heart and a sound body and all the gifts of God. But by rights alone they won't keep them, and afterwards will follow the pale horse and he whose name was Death and with whom hell followed... We talk about that when we meet and... it has had a great effect on her.'

'Do you believe that yourself?' asked Myshkin, scanning Lebedyev with a strange expression.

'I believe it and explain it so. I am naked and a beggar and an atom in the vortex of humanity. No one respects Lebedyev; he is fair game for everyone's wit, and they are all ready to give him a kick. But in interpreting revelation I am equal to the foremost in the land, for I am clever at it. And a grand gentleman trembled before me, sitting in his armchair, as he took it in. His illustrious Excellency Nil Alexeyevitch sent for me the year before last, just before Easter – when I was serving in his department – and purposely sent Pyotr Zaharitch to fetch me from the office to his study. And he asked me when we were alone, "Is it true that you expound Antichrist?" And I made no secret of it. "I do," said I. I explained and interpreted, and did not soften down the horror, but intentionally increased it, as I unfolded the allegory and fitted dates to it. And he laughed, but he began trembling at the dates and correspondences, and asked me to close the book and go away. He rewarded me at Easter, but the week after he gave up his soul to God.'

'How so, Lebedyev?'

'He did. He fell out of his carriage after dinner … knocked his head against a post, and on the spot he passed away like a babe – a little babe. Seventy-three years old he was. He had a red face, grey hair, and was sprinkled all over with scent, and he was always smiling – smiling like a child. Then Pyotr Zaharitch remembered. "You foretold it," he said.'

Myshkin began getting up. Lebedyev was surprised and positively puzzled at his moving.

'You don't take much interest in things now,' he ventured to observe obsequiously.

'I really don't feel quite well; my head is heavy from the journey, perhaps,' answered Myshkin, frowning.

'You ought to be out of town,' Lebedyev hazarded timidly.

Myshkin stood pondering.

'In another three days I am going out of town with all my family, for the sake of my newborn nestling, and to have this house done up. We are going to Pavlovsk, too.'

'You are going to Pavlovsk too?' asked Myshkin suddenly. 'How is it everyone here is going to Pavlovsk? And you have a villa of your own there, you say?'

'Not everyone is going to Pavlovsk. Ivan Petrovitch Ptitsyn has let me have one of the villas he has bought up cheap. It's nice and high up, and green and cheap and *bon ton* and musical – and that's why everyone goes to Pavlovsk. I am living in a little lodge, however, and the villa itself is …'

'Let?'

'N-no … not quite.'

'Let it to me,' Myshkin proposed suddenly.

That seemed to be all Lebedyev had been working up to. The idea had entered his head three minutes before. And yet he had no need of a tenant, for he already had found someone who had told him he might perhaps take the villa. Lebedyev knew for a fact that it was not a question of "perhaps", and that he certainly would take the villa. But now he was struck by the idea, likely by his reckoning to be a profitable one, that he might let the villa to Myshkin, taking advantage of the fact that the previous tenant had not been quite definite. "A regular coincidence and quite a new turn of affairs" rose before his imagination suddenly. He received Myshkin's proposition with enthusiasm, and at his direct question as to terms he simply waved his hands.

'Well, as you like. I'll make enquiries; you shan't be a loser.'

They were both coming out of the garden.

'And I could … I could … if you liked, I could tell you something very interesting, highly honoured prince, relating to the same subject,' muttered Lebedyev, wriggling gleefully on one side of the prince.

Myshkin stopped.

'Darya Alexeyevna has a villa at Pavlovsk too.'

'Well?'

'And a certain person is a friend of hers and evidently intends to visit her frequently there, with an object.'

'Well?'

'Aglaia Ivanovna …'

'Ach, that's enough, Lebedyev!' Myshkin interrupted, with an unpleasant sensation, as though he had been touched on a tender spot. 'All that's … a mistake. I'd rather you'd tell me when are you moving? The sooner the better for me, as I am at a hotel…'

As they talked, they had left the garden and, without going back into the house, crossed the yard and reached the gate.

'Well, what could be better?' Lebedyev suggested at last. 'Come straight here to me from the hotel today, and the day after tomorrow we will all move to Pavlovsk together.'

'I'll see,' said Myshkin thoughtfully, and he went out at the gate.

Lebedyev looked after him. He was struck by Myshkin's sudden absent-mindedness. He had forgotten even to say goodbye as he went out; he did not even nod, which seemed out of keeping with what Lebedyev knew of Myshkin's graciousness and courtesy.

Chapter 3

It was past eleven. Myshkin knew that he could find at the Epanchins' house no one but the general himself, who might be kept in town by his duties and yet not be at home. He thought that the general might perhaps take him at once to Pavlovsk, but he particularly wanted to make one call before then. At the risk of missing Epanchin and putting off his visit to Pavlovsk till the next day, Myshkin decided to look for the house to which he so particularly wished to go.

This visit was, however, risky for him in one respect. He was perplexed and hesitated. He knew he would find the house in Gorohovy Street, not far from Sadovy Street, and decided to go there, hoping that on his way there he would succeed in making up his mind.

As he approached the point where the two streets intersect, he was surprised himself at his extraordinary emotion; he had not expected his heart to throb so painfully. One house attracted his attention in the distance, no doubt from its peculiar appearance, and Myshkin afterwards remembered saying to himself, 'That must be the very house!' With great curiosity he walked towards it to verify his conjecture; he felt that he would for some reason particularly dislike to have guessed right. It was a large gloomy house of three stories, of a dirty green colour and no pretensions to architecture. A few houses of this kind, built at the end of the last century, are still standing almost unchanged in those streets of Petersburg (where everything changes so quickly). They are built solidly with thick walls and very few windows, often with gratings on the ground-floor windows. Usually there is a money-changer's shop below, and the owner, of the sect of Skoptsy, serves in the shop and lodges above it. Without and within, the house is somehow inhospitable and frigid; it seems to be keeping something dark and hidden; and why it seems so from the mere look of the house it would be hard to explain. Architectural lines have, of course, a secret of their own. These houses are occupied almost entirely by tradespeople.

Going up to the gate and examining the inscription on it, Myshkin read, 'The house of the hereditary and honourable citizen Rogozhin.' Hesitating no longer, he opened the glass door, which slammed noisily behind him, and went up the great staircase to the first floor. It was a roughly made stone staircase and dark; the walls were painted red. He knew that Rogozhin with his mother and brother occupied the whole second floor of this dreary house. The servant who opened the door to Myshkin admitted him without taking in his name, and led him a long way. They passed through one grand drawing-room with walls painted to look like marble, an oak block floor, and furniture of 1820, coarse and heavy; they passed through some tiny rooms, winding and turning, mounting two or three steps and going down as many, till at last they knocked at a door. The door was opened by Parfyon Semyonovitch himself. Seeing Myshkin, he turned so pale and was so petrified that for a time he stood like a statue, gazing with fixed and frightened eyes and twisting his mouth into a strange smile of utter bewilderment, as though he felt the prince's visit something incredible and almost miraculous. Though Myshkin had expected something of the sort, he was surprised.

'Parfyon, perhaps I've come at the wrong moment? I can go away, you know,' he said at last with embarrassment.

'Not at all – not at all!' said Parfyon, recovering himself at last. 'You are welcome. Come in.'

They addressed one another like intimate friends. In Moscow they had often spent long hours together, and there had been meetings, moments of which had left a lasting memory in their hearts. Now they had not met for over three months.

Rogozhin's face did not lose its pallor and there still was a faint spasmodic twitching to be seen in it. Though he welcomed his guest, his extraordinary confusion still persisted. While he led Myshkin in and had made him sit down in an easy chair, the latter happened to turn to him and stood still, impressed by his strange and heavy gaze. Something seemed to transfix Myshkin, and at the same time some memory came back to him – something recent, painful, and gloomy. Not sitting down but standing motionless, he looked Rogozhin straight in the eyes for some time: at the first moment they seemed to gleam more brightly. At last Rogozhin smiled, though still rather disconcerted and hardly knowing what he was doing.

'Why do you stare so?' he muttered. 'Sit down.'

Myshkin sat down.

'Parfyon,' said he, 'tell me plainly, did you know that I was coming to Petersburg today or not?'

'I thought you were coming, and, you see, I was not mistaken,' Rogozhin added, smiling sarcastically. 'But how could I tell you would come today?'

Myshkin was even more struck by a certain harsh abruptness and strange irritability in the question.

'Even if you had known I should come today, why be so cross about it?' murmured Myshkin gently, in confusion.

'But why do you ask?'

'As I got out of the train this morning, I saw two eyes that looked at me just as you did just now from behind.'

'You don't say so! Whose eyes were they?' Rogozhin muttered suspiciously.

Myshkin fancied that he shuddered.

'I don't know; I almost think I fancied it in the crowd. I begin to be always fancying things. Do you know, Parfyon, my friend, I feel almost as I did five years ago, when I used to have fits.'

'Well, perhaps it was your fancy; I don't know,' muttered Parfyon.

The friendly smile on his face was very unbecoming to him at that moment, as though there were something disjointed in it, and however much he tried he could not put it together.

'Are you going abroad again?' he asked, and suddenly added: 'And do you remember how we came from Pskov in the same carriage together last autumn? I was coming here, and you … in your cloak, do you remember, and the gaiters?'

And Rogozhin suddenly laughed, this time with open malice, as though relieved that he had succeeded in expressing it in some way.

'Are you settled here for good?'

'Yes, I am at home. Where else should I be?'

'It's a long time since we've met. I've heard such things about you, not like yourself.'

'People will say anything,' Rogozhin observed drily.

'You've turned off all your followers, and you stay in your old home and live quietly. Well, that's a good thing. Is it your own house, or does it belong to all of you in common?'

'The house is my mother's. That's the way to her rooms across the corridor.'

'And where is your brother living?'

'My brother Semyon Semyonovitch is in the lodge.'

'Is he married?'

'He is a widower. Why do you want to know?'

Myshkin looked at him and did not answer; he was suddenly thoughtful and seemed not to have heard the question. Rogozhin waited and did not insist. They were silent for a little.

'I guessed it was your house a hundred paces away, as I came along,' said Myshkin.

'How was that?'

'I don't know at all. Your house has a look of your whole family and your Rogozhin manner of life, but if you ask me how I know that, I can't explain it. A disordered fancy, I suppose. It makes me uneasy indeed that it should trouble me so much. I had an idea before that you lived in such a house, but, as soon as I saw it, I thought at once, "That's just the sort of house he ought to have." '

'I say!' Rogozhin smiled vaguely, not quite understanding Myshkin's obscure thought. 'It was my grandfather built the house,' he observed. 'It was always tenanted by the Hludyakovs, who are Skoptsy, and they are our tenants still.'

'It's so dark! You are living here in darkness,' said Myshkin, looking round the room.

It was a big room, lofty and dark, filled with furniture of all sorts, for the most part big business tables, bureaux, cupboards, in which were kept business books and papers of some sort. The wide sofa, covered in red morocco, obviously served Rogozhin as a bed. Myshkin noticed two or three books lying on the table, at which Rogozhin had made him sit down; one of them, Solovyev's *History,* was open and had a bookmark in it. On the walls there were a few oil-paintings in tarnished gold frames. They were dark and grimy, and it was difficult to make out what they represented. One full-length portrait attracted Myshkin's notice. It was the portrait of a man of fifty, wearing a frock-coat, very long, though of European cut, and two medals round his neck. He had a very scanty short grey beard, a yellow wrinkled face with suspicious, secretive and melancholy eyes.

'Is that your father?' asked Myshkin.

'Yes, it is,' Rogozhin answered with an unpleasant grin, as though expecting some rude jest at his dead father's expense to follow immediately.

'He wasn't one of the Old Believers, was he?'

'No, he used to go to church, but it's true he used to say that the old form of belief was truer. He had a great respect for the Skoptsy too. This used to be his study. 'Why do you ask was he an Old Believer?'

'Will you have your wedding here?'

'Y-yes,' answered Rogozhin, almost starting at the unexpected question.

'Will it be soon?'

'You know yourself it doesn't depend on me.'

'Parfyon, I am not your enemy, and I have no intention of interfering with you in any way. I tell you that as I've told you once before, almost on a similar occasion. When your wedding was arranged in Moscow, I didn't hinder you, you know that. The first time *she* rushed to me of herself, almost on the wedding day, begging me "to save" her from you. It's her own words I am repeating to you. Afterwards she ran away from me too. You found her again and were going to marry her, and now they tell me she ran away from you again here. Is that true? Lebedyev told me so; that's why I've come. But that you'd come together again I learnt for the first time only yesterday in the train from one of your former friends, Zalyozhev, if you care to know. I came here with a purpose. I wanted to persuade her to go abroad for the sake of her health. She is not well physically or mentally – her brain especially, and, to my mind, she needs great care. I didn't mean to take her abroad myself; it was my plan for her to go without me. I am telling you the absolute truth. If it's quite true that you've made it up again, I shan't show myself to her, and I'll never come again to see you either. You know I don't deceive you, because I've always been open with you. I have never concealed from you what I think about it, and I have always said that to marry you would be her perdition. Your perdition too … even more perhaps than hers. If you were to part again, I should be very glad, but I don't intend to disturb or try to part you myself. Don't worry yourself and don't suspect me. You know yourself whether I was ever really your rival, even when she ran away to me. Now you are laughing. I know what you are laughing at. Yes, we lived apart there, in different towns, and you know all that *for a fact.* I explained to you before that I don't love her with love, but with pity. I believe I define it exactly. You said at the time that you understood what I said. Was that true? Did you understand? Here you are looking at me with hatred! I've come to reassure you, for you are dear to me too. I am very fond of you, Parfyon. But now I am going away and shall never come again. Goodbye!'

Myshkin got up.

'Stay with me a little,' said Parfyon softly, sitting still in his place with his head resting on his right hand. 'It's a long time since I've seen you.' Myshkin sat down. Both were silent again.

'When you are not before me I feel anger against you at once, Lyov Nikolayevitch. Every minute of these three months that I haven't seen you I have been angry with you, on my word, I have. I felt I could have poisoned you! I tell you now. You haven't been sitting a quarter of an hour with me, and all my anger is passing away and you are dear to me as you used to be. Stay with me a little ...'

'When I am with you, you believe me, but when I am away, you leave off believing me at once and begin suspecting me. You are like your father,' Myshkin answered, with a friendly smile, trying to hide his emotion.

'I believe your voice when I am with you. I understand, of course, we can't be put on a level, you and I...'

'Why do you add that? And now you are irritated again,' said Myshkin, wondering at Rogozhin.

'Well, brother, our opinion is not asked in the matter,' he answered. 'It's settled without consulting us. You see, we love in different ways too. There's a difference in everything,' he went on softly after a pause. 'You say you love her with pity. There's no sort of pity for her in me. And she hates me too, more than anything. I dream of her every night now, always that she is laughing at me with other men. And that's what she is doing, brother. She is going to the altar with me and she has forgotten to give me a thought, as though she were changing her shoe. Would you believe it, I haven't seen her for five days, because I don't dare to go to her. She'll ask me, "What have you come for?" She has covered me with shame.'

'Shame? How can you!'

'As though you didn't know! Why, she ran away with you from me on the very wedding day – you said so yourself just now.'

'Why, you don't believe yourself that...'

'Didn't she shame me in Moscow with that officer, Zemtyuzhnikov? I know for certain she did, and even after she had fixed the wedding day.'

'Impossible!' cried Myshkin.

'I know it for a fact,' Rogozhin persisted with conviction. 'She is not that sort of woman, you say? It's no good telling me she is not that sort of woman, brother. That's nonsense. With you she won't be that sort of woman, and will be horrified herself, maybe, at such doings. But that's just what she is with me. That's the fact. She looks on me as the lowest refuse. I know for a fact that simply to make a laughing-stock of me she got up an affair with Keller, that officer, the man who boxes ... You don't know, of course, the tricks she played me at Moscow. And the money – the money I've wasted! ...'

'And... and you are marrying her now? What will you do afterwards?' Myshkin asked in horror.

Rogozhin bent a lowering, terrible gaze on Myshkin and made no answer.

'It's five days since I've been with her,' he went on after a minute's pause. 'I am afraid of her turning me out. "I am still mistress in my own house," she says. "If I choose I will get rid of you altogether and go abroad." (She told me that already, that she will go abroad, he observed, as it were in parenthesis, with a peculiar look into Myshkin's eyes.) Sometimes, it's true, she only does this to scare me. She is always laughing at me somehow. But another time she really scowls and is sullen and won't say a word. That's what I am afraid of. The other day I thought I'd take her something every time I went to see her. It only made her laugh at me, and afterwards she was really angry about it. She made a present to her maid, Katya, of a shawl I gave her, the like of which she may never have seen before, though she did live in luxury. And as to when our wedding is to be, I dare not open my lips. A queer sort of bridegroom when I am afraid to go and see her! So here I sit, and when I can bear it no longer, I steal past her house on the sly, or hide behind some corner. The other day I was on the watch almost till daybreak at her gate. I fancied there was something going on. And she must have seen me from the window. "What would you have done to me," she said, "if you had found out I'd deceived you?" I couldn't stand it, and I said, "You know yourself." '

'What does she know?'

'And how do I know?' Rogozhin laughed angrily. 'At .Moscow I couldn't catch her with anyone, though I was always on the track. I took her aside then and said to her once, "You promised to marry me; you are entering an honest family, and do you know what you are now?" I told her what she is.'

'You told her?'

'Yes.'

'Well?'

' "I wouldn't take you for a footman now perhaps," she said, "let alone be your wife!" "And I won't go away with that," said I, "I am done for anyway." "And I'll call Keller, then," said she. "I'll tell him, and he'll throw you out by the scruff of your neck." I flew at her and beat her till she was black and blue.'

'Impossible!' cried Myshkin.

'I tell you it was so,' Rogozhin repeated quietly, but with flashing eyes. 'For thirty-six hours on end I didn't sleep nor eat nor drink – I didn't leave her room; I was on my knees before her. "If I die," I said, "I won't go away till you forgive me, and if you tell them to throw me out, I'll drown myself, for what should I do now without you?" She was like a mad woman all that day: she wept; then she was on the point of killing me with a knife; then she railed at me. She called Zalyozhev, Keller, Zemtyuzhnikov, and all of them, showed me to them, put me to shame. "Let's make up a party and all go to the theatre tonight, gentlemen. Let him stay here if he won't go; I am not bound to stay for him. They'll bring you tea, Parfyon Semyonovitch, when I am out; you must be hungry by now." She came back from the theatre alone. "They are cowards and sneaks," she said. "They are afraid of you, and they frighten me. They say, 'He won't go away like that. He will cut your throat, maybe.' But I'll go into my bedroom and not even lock the door – so much for my being afraid of you! So that you may see and know it. Have you had any tea?" "No," I said, "and I am not going to" "I've done my part, and this behaviour doesn't suit you at all." And she did as she said, she didn't lock her door. In the morning she came out and laughed. "Have you gone crazy?" she asked. "Why, you'll die of hunger!" "Forgive me," said I. "I don't want to forgive you. I won't marry you, I've said so. Have you been sitting on that chair all night? Haven't you been asleep?" "No," said I, "I haven't been asleep." "How stupid!

And you won't have breakfast or dinner again, I suppose?" "I told you I won't. Forgive me." "If only you knew how ill this suits you! It's like a saddle on a cow. You don't fancy you are going to scare me by that? What does it matter to me that you are hungry? As though that would frighten me!" She was angry, but not for long, she soon began gibing at me again, and I wondered how it was that there was no anger in her, for she'll resent a thing a long time, she'll resent a thing with other people for a long time. Then it entered my head that she thinks so poorly of me that she can't even feel much resentment against me. And that's the truth! "Do you know what the Pope of Rome is?" she asked. "I've heard," I said. "You've never learnt any universal history, Parfyon Semyonovitch," said she. "I never learnt anything," I said. "I'll give you a story to read then," she said. "There was once a Pope, and he was angry with an emperor, and that emperor knelt barefoot before his palace for three days without eating or drinking till he forgave him. What do you suppose that emperor thought to himself, and what vows did he take while he was kneeling there? Stay," she said, "I'll read it to you myself." She jumped up and brought the book. "It's poetry," she said, and began reading me in verse how that emperor had vowed during those three days to avenge himself on the Pope for it. "Don't you like that, Parfyon Semyonovitch?" said she. "That's all true," said I, "that you've read." "Aha! You say it's true yourself. Then perhaps you are making vows: 'When she is married to me I'll make her remember it all! I'll humble her to my heart's content!'" "I don't know," said I, "perhaps I am thinking so." "How can you say you don't know?" "Why, I don't know," said I, "I have no thoughts for that now." "What are you thinking of now?" "Well, you'll get up and walk past me, and I'm looking at you and watching you. Your skirt rustles, and my heart sinks; you go out of the room, and I remember every little word of yours, your voice and what you said. And all last night I thought of nothing; I listened all the while how you were breathing in your sleep, and twice you stirred." "And I dare say you don't think, and you don't remember, how you beat me?" she said. "Perhaps I do think of it; I don't know." "And if I don't forgive you and I won't marry you?" "I've told you I'll drown myself." "Perhaps you'll murder me first ..." she said, and seemed to ponder. Then she was angry and went out. An hour later she came in to me so gloomy. "I will marry you, Parfyon Semyonovitch," she said, "and not because I am afraid of you; there's nothing but ruin anyway. What's better? Sit down," she said, "they'll bring you dinner directly. And if I marry you I'll be a faithful wife to you," she added, "don't doubt of that and don't be uneasy." Then she was silent, and said, "Anyway you are not a flunkey. I used to think that you were a regular flunkey." Then she fixed the wedding day, and a week later she ran away from me to Lebedyev here. When I came she said, "I don't give you up altogether; I only want to wait as long as I like, because I am still my own mistress. You can wait too if you like." That's how we stand now ... What do you think of all that, Lyov Nikolayevitch?'

'What do you think yourself?' Myshkin questioned back, looking sorrowfully at Rogozhin.

'Do you suppose I drink?' broke from the latter.

He would have added something, but paused in hopeless dejection.

Myshkin stood up and would again have taken leave.

'I won't hinder you, anyway,' he said softly, almost dreamily, as though replying to some secret inner thought of his own.

'Do you know what!' said Rogozhin, suddenly more eager, and his eyes kindled. 'How is it you give in to me like this? Have you quite got over loving her? You used to be miserable, anyway; I saw that. Then why is it you've come here in such haste? From pity?' and his face worked with spiteful mockery. 'Ha, ha!'

'You think I am deceiving you now?' Myshkin enquired.

'No, I believe you, but I can't make it out. One might almost believe that your pity is greater than my love.'

A certain malice and an urgent desire to express himself at once glowed in his face.

'Well, there's no distinguishing your love from hate,' said Myshkin, smiling. 'It will pass, and then perhaps the trouble will be worse. I tell you this, brother Parfyon 'That I shall murder her?'

Myshkin started.

'You will hate her bitterly for this love, for all this torture you are suffering now. What is strangest of all to me is that she can again mean to marry you. When I heard it yesterday, I scarcely believed it, and it made me so unhappy! You see, she has thrown you up twice and run away on the wedding day, so she has some foreboding. What does she find in you now? It's not your money, that's nonsense. And no doubt you've wasted a good deal of it by now. Can it be simply to get a husband? Why, she could find plenty of others. Any man would be better than you, because you really may murder her, and she knows that only too well now, perhaps. Is it because you love her so passionately? It's true that may be it. I've heard there are women who want just that sort of love … Only …' Myshkin stopped and sank into thought.

'Why are you smiling at my father's portrait again?' asked Rogozhin, who was watching every movement, every change in Myshkin's face with extraordinary intentness.

'Why did I smile? Oh, it struck me that if it were not for this burden laid upon you, if it were not for this love, you would most likely have become exactly like your father, and in a very short time too. You would have settled down quietly in this house with an obedient and submissive wife; you would have been stern and sparing of words, trusting no one and feeling no desire to; doing nothing but heap up money in dreary silence. At the most you would sometimes have praised the old books and been interested in the Old Believers' fashion of crossing themselves, and that only in your old age …'

'Laugh away, but, do you know, she said the very same thing not long ago, when she too was looking at that portrait! It's queer how you both say the same thing now.'

'Why, has she been in your house?' asked Myshkin with interest.

'Yes. She looked a long time at the portrait and asked me about my father. "You'd be just such another," she laughed to me afterwards. "You have strong passions, Parfyon Semyonovitch," she said, "such passions that you might have been carried by them straight off to Siberia, if you weren't intelligent too. For you have a great deal of intelligence," she said. (Those were her words. Would you believe it? It was the first time I'd heard her say such a thing.) "You would have soon given up all this silliness, and as you are quite an uneducated man, you would have begun saving money and have settled down like your father in this house with your Skoptsy. Maybe you would have gone over to their faith in the end, and have grown so fond of your money that you would have heaped up not two but ten million perhaps, and have died of hunger on your bags of money. For you are passionate in everything: you push everything to a passion." That was just how she talked, almost in those very words. She had never talked to me like that before. You know she always talks nonsense with me, or jeers at me, and indeed, she began laughing this time, but then she grew so dejected, she walked all over the house, looked at everything, and seemed scared. "I'll change all this and do it up, or if you like I'll buy another house before we are married." "No, no," she said, "nothing must be changed here, we'll live like this. I want to live with your mother," she said, "when I become your wife." I took her to my mother. She was respectful to her, as if she had been her own daughter. For the last two years mother has not been quite in her right mind (she is ill), and since my father died she's become quite like a child: she can't talk, she can't walk, and only bows to everyone she sees. If we didn't feed her, I believe she wouldn't notice it for three days. I took my mother's right hand, folded her fingers. "Bless her, mother," said I "she is going to the altar with me." Then she kissed my mother's hand with feeling. "Your mother must have had a great deal of sorrow to bear," said she. She saw this book here. "What, have you begun reading Russian history?" (She said to me herself in Moscow once, "You should educate yourself. You might at least read Solovyev's Russian history. You know nothing at all.") "That's right," she said, "go on reading. I'll write you a list myself of the books you ought to read first, shall I?" And never, never before had she talked to me like that, so that I was positively amazed. For the first time I breathed like a living man.'

'I am very glad of that, Parfyon,' said Myshkin with sincere feeling, 'very glad. Who knows, after all perhaps God will bring you together.'

'That will never be!' Rogozhin cried hotly.

'Listen, Parfyon. Since you love her so, surely you want to gain her respect? And if you want to, you can't be without hope? I said just now that I was unable to comprehend what makes her marry you. But though I can't understand it, I have no doubt that there must be a sufficient, sensible reason. She is convinced of your love, but she must believe in some of your good qualities also. It can't be otherwise. What you said just now confirms this. You told me yourself that she has found it possible to speak to you in quite a different way from how she has spoken and behaved to you before. You are suspicious and jealous, and that has made you exaggerate everything you've noticed amiss. Of course she doesn't think so ill of you as you say. If she did, it would be as good as deliberately going to be drowned or murdered to marry you. Is that possible? Who would deliberately go to be drowned or murdered?'

Parfyon listened with a bitter smile to Myshkin's eager words. His conviction, it seemed, was not to be shaken.

'How dreadfully you look at me now, Parfyon!' broke from Myshkin with a feeling of dread.

'To be drowned or murdered!' said Rogozhin at last. 'Ha! Why, that's just why she is marrying me, because she expects to be murdered! Do you mean to say, Prince, you've never yet had a notion of what's at the root of it all?'

'I don't understand you.'

'Well, perhaps you really don't understand. Ha, ha! They do say you are ... *not quite right*. She loves another man – take that in! Just as I love her now, she loves another man now. And do you know who that other man is? *It's, you!* What! You didn't know?'

'Me?'

'You. She has loved you ever since that day – her birthday. Only she thinks it's out of the question to marry you, because she thinks she would disgrace you and ruin your whole life. "Everyone knows what I am," she says. She still harps upon that. She told me all this straight out to my face. She is afraid of ruining and of disgracing you, but I don't matter, she can marry me. So much for what she thinks of me! Notice that too.'

'But why did she run away from you to me and ... from me ...'

'And from you to me! Ha! Why, all sorts of things come into her head. She is always in a sort of fever now. One day she'll cry out, "I'll make an end of myself and marry you! Let the wedding be soon." She hurries things on, fixes the day, but when the time comes near, she takes fright, or other ideas come to her, God knows! You've seen it; she cries and laughs and shakes with fever. And what is there strange in her having run away from you? She ran away from you then, because she realised how much she loved you. It was too much for her to stay with you. You said just now that I sought her out in Moscow. That's not true; she ran to me straight from you of herself. "Fix the day," she said. "I am ready! Give me champagne! Let's go to the gypsies ..." she cries. She would have drowned herself long ago, if she had not had me; that's the truth. She doesn't do that because, perhaps, I am more dreadful than the water. It's from spite she is marrying me. If she marries me, I tell you for sure it will *be from spite* ...'

'But how can you ... how can you!' cried Myshkin, but broke off. He looked at Rogozhin with horror.

'Why don't you finish?' the latter replied, grinning. 'Would you like me to tell you what you are thinking to yourself at this very moment? "How can she be his wife after this? How can I let her come to that?" I know you think that...'

'I didn't come here with that idea, Parfyon; I tell you it was not that I had in my mind ...'

'It may be that you didn't come with that idea and that wasn't in your mind, but now it certainly has become your idea. Ha-ha! Well, that's enough! Why are you so upset? Can you really not have know it? You surprise me!'

'That's all jealousy, Parfyon; it's all morbidness. You have exaggerated it all immensely,' Myshkin muttered in violent agitation. 'What are you doing?'

'Leave it alone,' said Parfyon, and he quickly snatched from Myshkin's hand a knife which the latter had picked up from the table, and put it back where it had been before, beside the book.

'I feel as though I had known when I was coming to Petersburg, as though I had foreseen it,' Myshkin went on. 'I didn't want to come here; I wanted to forget everything here, to root it out of my heart! Well, goodbye! ... But what are you doing?'

As he talked Myshkin had absent-mindedly again picked up the same knife from the table, and again Rogozhin took it out of his hands and threw it on the table. It was a plain knife that wouldn't shut up, with a horn handle, and a blade seven inches long and of about the usual breadth.

Seeing that Myshkin had specially noticed that the knife had been twice taken out of his hands, Rogozhin snatched it up in angry vexation, put it in the book, and flung the book on another table.

'Do you cut the pages with it?' Myshkin asked, but almost mechanically, still apparently absorbed in deep thought.

'Yes.'

'But it's a garden knife?'

'Yes, it is. Can't one cut a book with a garden knife?'

'But it's ... quite a new one.'

'What if it is new? Mayn't I buy a new knife?' Rogozhin cried in a perfect frenzy at last, growing more exasperated at every word.

Myshkin started and looked intently at Rogozhin.

'Ach, we are a pair!' he laughed suddenly, rousing himself completely. 'Excuse me, brother, when my head is heavy, as it is now, and my illness ... I become utterly, utterly absent-minded and ridiculous. I meant to ask you about something quite different ... I've forgotten it now. Goodbye!...'

'Not that way,' said Rogozhin.

'I've forgotten.'

'This way, this way, come, I'll show you.'

Chapter 4

They went through the same rooms that Myshkin had passed through already; Rogozhin walked a little in front, Myshkin followed him. They went into a big room. On the walls there were several pictures, all of them portraits of bishops or landscapes in which nothing could be distinguished. Over the door leading into the next room there hung a picture of rather strange shape, about two yards in breadth and not more than a foot high. It was a painting of our Saviour who had just been taken from the cross. Myshkin glanced at it as though recalling something, but he was about to pass through the door without stopping. He felt very depressed and wanted to get out of this house as soon as possible. But Rogozhin suddenly stopped before the picture.

'All these pictures here were bought for a rouble or two by my father at auctions,' he said. 'He liked pictures. A man who knows about paintings looked at all of them. "They are rubbish," he said, "but that one, that picture over the door there, which was bought for a couple of roubles too," he said, "is of value." When my father was alive one man turned up who was ready to give three hundred and fifty roubles for it, but Savelyev, a merchant who is very fond of pictures, went up to four hundred for it, and last week he offered my brother Semyon Semyonovitch five hundred for it. I've kept it for myself.'

'Why, it... it's a copy of a Holbein,' said Myshkin, who had by now examined the picture, 'and, though I don't know much about it, I think it's a very good copy. I saw the picture abroad and I can't forget it. But... what's the matter?'

Rogozhin suddenly turned away from the picture and went on. No doubt his preoccupation and a peculiar, strangely irritable mood which had so suddenly shown itself in him might have explained this abruptness. Yet it seemed strange to Myshkin that the conversation, which had not been begun by him, should have been broken off so suddenly without Rogozhin's answering him.

'And by the way, Lyov Nikolayevitch, I've long meant to ask you, do you believe in God?' said Rogozhin suddenly, after having gone on a few steps.

'How strangely you question me and … look at me!' Myshkin could not help observing.

'I like looking at that picture,' Rogozhin muttered after a pause, seeming again to have forgotten his question.

'At that picture!' cried Myshkin, struck by a sudden thought. 'At that picture! Why, that picture might make some people lose their faith.'

'That's what it is doing,' Rogozhin assented unexpectedly.

They were just at the front door.

'What?' Myshkin stopped short. 'What do you mean? I was almost joking, and you are so serious! And why do you ask whether I believe in God?'

'Oh, nothing. I meant to ask you before. Many people don't believe nowadays. Is it true – you've lived abroad – what a man told me when he was drunk – that there are more who don't believe in God among us in Russia than in all other countries? 'It's easier for us than for them," he said, "because we have gone further than they have"…'

Rogozhin smiled bitterly. When he had asked his question, he suddenly opened the door and, holding the handle, waited for Myshkin to go out. Myshkin was surprised, but he went out. Rogozhin followed him on to the landing and closed the door behind him. They stood facing one another, as though neither knew where they were and what they had to do next.

'Goodbye, then,' said Myshkin, holding out his hand.

'Goodbye,' said Rogozhin, pressing tightly though mechanically the hand that was held out to him.

Myshkin went down a step and turned round.

'As to the question of faith,' he began, smiling (he evidently did not want to leave Rogozhin like that) and brightening up at a sudden reminiscence, 'as to the question of faith, I had four different conversations in two days last week. I came in the morning by the new railway and talked for four hours with a man in the train; he made friends on the spot. I had heard a great deal about him beforehand and had heard he was an atheist, among other things. He really is a very learned man, and I was delighted at the prospect of talking to a really learned man. What's more, he is a most unusually well-bred man, so that he talked to me quite as if I were his equal in ideas and attainments. He doesn't believe in God. Only, one thing struck me: that he seemed not to be talking about that at all, the whole time; and it struck me just because whenever I have met unbelievers before, or read their books, it always seemed to me that they were speaking and writing in their books about something quite different, although it seemed to be about that on the surface. I said so to him at the time, but I suppose I didn't say so clearly, or did not know how to express it, for he didn't understand. In the evening I stopped for the night at a provincial hotel, and a murder had just been committed there the night before, so that everyone was talking about it when I arrived. Two peasants, middle-aged men, friends who had known each other for a long time and were not drunk, had had tea and were meaning to go to bed in the same room. But one had noticed during those last two days that the other was wearing a silver watch on a yellow bead chain, which he seems not to have seen on him before. The man was not a thief; he was an honest man, in fact, and by a peasant's standard by no means poor. But he was so taken with that watch and so fascinated by it that at last he could not restrain himself. He took a knife, and when his friend had turned away, he approached him cautiously from behind, took aim, turned his eyes heavenwards, crossed himself, and praying fervently "God forgive me for Christ's sake!" he cut his friend's throat at one stroke like a sheep and took his watch.'

Rogozhin went off into peals of laughter; he laughed as though he were in a sort of fit. It was positively strange to see such laughter after the gloomy mood that had preceded it.

'I do like that! Yes, that beats everything!' lie cried convulsively, gasping for breath. 'One man doesn't believe in God at all, while the other believes in Him so thoroughly that he prays as he murders men! ... You could never have invented that, brother! Ha-ha-ha! That beats everything.'

'Next morning I went out to walk about the town,' Myshkin went on, as soon as Rogozhin was quiet again, though his lips still quivered with spasmodic convulsive laughter. 'I saw a drunken soldier in a terribly disorderly state staggering about the wooden pavement. He came up to me. "Buy a silver cross, Sir?" said he. "I'll let you have it for twenty kopecks. It's silver." I saw in his hands a cross – he must have just taken it off – on a very dirty blue ribbon, but one could see at once that it was only tin. It was a big one with eight corners, of a regular Byzantine pattern. I took out twenty kopecks and gave them to him, and at once put the cross round my neck; and I could see from his face how glad he was that he had cheated a stupid gentleman, and he went off immediately to drink what he got for it, there was no doubt about that. At that time, brother, I was quite carried away by the rush of impressions that burst upon me in Russia; I had understood nothing about Russia before. I had grown up as it were inarticulate, and my memories of my country were somehow fantastic during those five years abroad. Well, I walked on, thinking, "Yes, I'll put off judging that man who sold his Christ. God only knows what's hidden in those weak and drunken hearts." An hour later, when I was going back to the hotel, I came upon a peasant woman with a tiny baby in her arms. She was quite a young woman and the baby was about six weeks old. The baby smiled at her for the first time in its life. I saw her crossing herself with great devotion. "What are you doing, my dear?" (I was always asking questions in those days.) "God has just such gladness every time he sees from heaven that a sinner is praying to Him with all his heart, as a mother has when she sees the first smile on her baby's face." That was what the woman said to me almost in those words, this deep, subtle and truly religious thought – a thought in which all the essence of Christianity finds expression; that is the whole conception of God as our Father and of God's gladness in man, like a father's in his own child – the fundamental idea of Christ! A simple peasant woman! It's true she was a mother … and who knows, very likely that woman was the wife of that soldier. Listen, Parfyon. You asked me a question just now; here is my answer. The essence of religious feeling does not come under any sort of reasoning or atheism, and has nothing to do with any crimes or misdemeanours. There is something else here, and there will always be something else – something that the atheists will for ever slur over; they will always be talking of something else. But the chief thing is that you will notice it more clearly and quickly in the Russian heart than anywhere else. And this is my conclusion. It's one of the chief convictions which I have gathered from our

Russia. There is work to be done, Parfyon! There is work to be done in our Russian world, believe me! Remember how we used to meet in Moscow and talk at one time ... and I didn't mean to come back here now, and I thought to meet you not at all like this! Oh, well!... Goodbye till we meet again! May God be with you!'

He turned and went down the stairs.

'Lyov Nikolayevitch!' Parfyon shouted from above when Myshkin had reached the first half-landing. 'Have you that cross you bought from that soldier on you?'

'Yes,' and Myshkin stopped again.

'Show me.'

Something strange again! He thought a moment, went upstairs again, and pulled out the cross to show him without taking it off his neck.

'Give it me,' said Rogozhin.

'Why? Would you...' Myshkin did not want to part with the cross.

'I'll wear it, and give you mine for you to wear.'

'You want to exchange crosses? Certainly, Parfyon, I am delighted. We will be brothers!'

Myshkin took off his tin cross, Parfyon his gold one, and they exchanged. Parfyon did not speak. With painful surprise Myshkin noticed that the same mistrustfulness, the same bitter, almost ironical smile still lingered on the face of his adopted brother; at moments, anyway, it was plainly to be seen. In silence at last Rogozhin took Myshkin's hand and stood for some time as though unable to make up his mind. At last he suddenly drew him after him, saying in a scarcely audible voice, 'Come along.' They crossed the landing of the first floor and rang at the door facing the one they had come out of. It was soon opened to them. A bent old woman, wearing a black knitted kerchief, bowed low to Rogozhin without speaking. He quickly asked her some question, and without waiting for an answer led Myshkin through the rooms. Again they went through dark rooms of an extraordinary chilly cleanliness, coldly and severely furnished with old-fashioned furniture under clean white covers. Without announcing their arrival, Rogozhin led Myshkin into a small room like a drawing-room, divided in two by a polished mahogany wall with doors at each end, probably leading to a bedroom. In the corner of the drawing-room by tire stove a little old woman was sitting in an armchair. She did not look very old; she had a fairly healthy, pleasant round face, but she was quite grey, and it could be seen from the first glance that she had become quite childish. She was wearing a black woollen dress, a large black kerchief on her shoulders, and a clean white cap with black ribbons. Her feet were resting on a footstool. Another clean little old woman, rather older, was with her. She too was in mourning, and she too wore a white cap; she was silent, knitting a stocking, and was probably some sort of a companion. It might be fancied that they were both always silent. The first old woman, seeing Rogozhin and Myshkin, smiled to them, and nodded her head several times to them as a sign of satisfaction.

'Mother,' said Rogozhin, kissing her hand, 'this is my great friend, Prince Lyov Nikolayevitch Myshkin. I've exchanged crosses with him. He was like a brother to me at one time in Moscow, he did a great deal for me. Bless him, mother, as though it were your own son you were blessing. Nay, old mother, like this. Let me put your fingers right...'

But before Parfyon had time to touch her, the old woman had raised her right hand, put her two fingers against her thumb, and three times devoutly made the sign of the cross over Myshkin. Then she nodded kindly, affectionately to him again.

'Come along, Lyov Nikolayevitch,' said Parfyon, 'I only brought you here for that ...' When they came out on to the staircase again, he added, 'You know she understands nothing that's said to her, and she didn't understand a word I said, but she blessed you, so she wanted to do it of herself... Well, goodbye, it's time you were going, and I too.'

And he opened his door.

'At least let me embrace you at parting, you strange fellow,' cried Myshkin, looking at him with tender reproach; and he would have embraced him.

But Parfyon had scarcely raised his arms when he let them fall again. He could not bring himself to it. He turned away so as not to look at Myshkin; he didn't want to embrace him.

'Don't be afraid! Though I've taken your cross, I won't murder you for your watch!' he muttered indistinctly, with a sudden strange laugh.

But all at once his whole face changed; he turned horribly pale, his lips trembled, his eyes glowed. He raised his arms, embraced

Myshkin warmly, and said breathlessly, 'Well, take her then, since it's fated! She is yours! I give in to you! ... Remember Rogozhin!'

And turning from Myshkin without looking at him, he went hurriedly in and slammed the door after him.

Chapter 5

It was by now late, almost half-past two, and Myshkin did not find General Epanchin at home. Leaving a card, he made up his mind to go to the hotel the Scales, and enquire for Kolya, and if he were not there, to leave a note for him. At the Scales they told him that Nikolay Ardalionovitch 'had gone out in the morning, but as he went out he left word that if anyone should ask for him, they were to say that he might be back at three o'clock. But if he were not back by half-past three, it would mean that he had taken the train to Pavlovsk to Madame Epanchin's villa and would dine there.' Myshkin sat down to wait for him, and, as he was there, asked for dinner.

Kolya had not made his appearance at half-past three, nor even at four. Myshkin went out and walked away mechanically. At the beginning of summer in Petersburg there are sometimes exquisite days – bright, still and hot. By good fortune this day was one of those rare days. For some time Myshkin wandered aimlessly. He knew the town very little. He stood still sometimes in squares, on bridges, or at cross roads facing certain houses; once he went into a confectioner's to rest. Sometimes he began watching the passers-by with great interest, but most of the time he scarcely noticed the people in the street, nor where he was going. He was painfully strained and restless, and at the same time he felt an extraordinary craving for solitude. He longed to be alone and to give himself up quite passively to this agonising emotion without seeking to escape from it. He loathed the thought of facing the questions that were surging in his heart and his mind. 'Am I to blame for all this?' he muttered to himself, almost unconscious of his own words.

Towards six o'clock he found himself at the railway station of the Tsarskoe Syelo line. Solitude had soon become unbearable; a new warm impulse seized upon his heart, and for one moment the darkness in which his soul was steeped was lighted up by a ray of brightness. He took a ticket to Pavlovsk and was in impatient haste to get off, but, of course, he was pursued by something, and that something was a reality and not a fancy, as he was perhaps inclined to imagine. He had almost taken his seat in the train, when he suddenly flung the ticket he had only just taken on the floor and went back out of the station, pondering and confused. Some time later in the street he seemed suddenly to recall something; he seemed suddenly to grasp something very strange, something that had long worried him. He suddenly realised that he had been doing something which he had been doing for a long time, though he had not been aware of it till that minute. For some hours previously, even at the Scales, and even before he went there, he had at intervals begun suddenly looking for something. He would forget it for a long while, half an hour at a time, and then begin looking about him again uneasily.

But he had no sooner observed in himself this morbid and till then quite unconscious impulse, when there flashed upon his mind another recollection which interested him extremely. He remembered that, at the moment when he became aware that he was absorbed in looking for something, he was standing on the pavement before a shop window, examining with great interest the goods exposed in it. He felt he must find out whether he really had stood before that shop window just now, five minutes, perhaps, before; whether he hadn't dreamed it; whether he wasn't mistaken. Did that shop really exist with the goods in its window? He certainly felt specially unwell that day, almost as he used in the past when an attack of his old disease was coming on. He knew that at such times he used to be exceptionally absent-minded, and often mixed up things and people, if he did not look at them with special strained attention. But there was another special reason why he wanted to find out whether he really had been standing then before that shop. Among the things in the shop window was one thing he had looked at, he had even mentally fixed the price of it at sixty kopecks. He remembered that in spite of his absent-mindedness and agitation. If, then, that shop existed and that thing really was in the window, he must have stopped simply to look at that thing. So it must have interested him so much that it attracted his attention, even at the time when he was in such distress and confusion, just after he had come out of the railway station. He walked almost in anguish, looking to the right and his heart beat with uneasy impatience. But here was the shop, he had found it at last! He had been five hundred paces from it when he had felt impelled to turn back. And there was the article worth sixty kopecks. 'It would be certainly sixty kopecks, it's not worth more,' he repeated now and laughed. But his laughter was hysterical; he felt very wretched. He remembered clearly now that just when he had been standing here before this window he had suddenly turned round, as he had done that morning when he caught Rogozhin's eyes fixed upon him. Making certain that he was not mistaken (though he had felt quite sure of it before), he left the shop and walked quickly away from it. He must certainly think it all over. It was clear now that it had not been his fancy at the station either, that something real must have happened to him, and that it must be connected with all his former uneasiness. But he was overcome again by a sort of insuperable inner loathing: he did not want to think anything out, and he did not; he fell to musing on something quite different.

He remembered among other things that he always had one minute just before the epileptic fit (if it came on while he was awake), when suddenly in the midst of sadness, spiritual darkness and oppression, there seemed at moments a flash of light in his brain, and with extraordinary impetus all his vital forces suddenly began working at their highest tension. The sense of life, the consciousness of self, were multiplied ten times at these moments which passed like a flash of lightning. His mind and his heart were flooded with extraordinary light; all his uneasiness, all his doubts, all his anxieties were relieved at once; they were all merged in a lofty calm, full of serene, harmonious joy and hope. But these moments, these flashes, were only the prelude of that final second (it was never more than a second) with which the fit began. That second was, of course, unendurable. Thinking of that moment later, when he was all right again, he often said to himself that all these gleams and flashes of the highest sensation of life and self-consciousness, and therefore also of the highest form of existence, were nothing but disease, the interruption of the normal condition; and if so, it was not at all the highest form of being, but on the contrary must be reckoned the lowest. And yet he came at last to an extremely paradoxical conclusion. 'What if it is disease?' he decided at last. 'What does it matter that it is an abnormal intensity, if the result, if the minute of sensation, remembered and analysed afterwards in health, turns out to be the acme of harmony and beauty, and gives a feeling, unknown and undivined till then, of completeness, of proportion, of reconciliation, and of ecstatic devotional merging in the highest synthesis of life?' These vague expressions seemed to him very comprehensible, though too weak. That it really was 'beauty and worship,' that it really was the 'highest synthesis of life' he could not doubt, and could not admit the possibility of doubt. It was not as though he saw abnormal and unreal visions of some sort at that moment, as from hashish, opium, or wine, destroying the reason and distorting the soul. He was quite capable of judging of that when the attack was over. These moments were only an extraordinary quickening of self-consciousness – if the condition was to be expressed in one word – and at the same time of the direct sensation of existence in the most intense degree. Since at that second, that is at the very last conscious moment before the fit, he had time to say to himself clearly and consciously, 'Yes, for this moment one might give one's whole life!' then without doubt that moment was really worth the whole of life. He did not insist on the dialectical part of his argument, however. Stupefaction, spiritual darkness, idiocy stood before him conspicuously as the consequence of these 'higher moments; seriously, of course, he could not have disputed it. There was undoubtedly a mistake in his conclusion – that is, in his estimate of that minute, but the reality of the sensation somewhat perplexed him. What was he to make of that reality? For the very thing had happened; he actually had said to himself at that second, that, for the infinite happiness he had felt in it, that second really might well be worth the whole of life. 'At that moment,' as he told Rogozhin one day in Moscow at the time when they used to meet there, 'at that moment I seem somehow to understand the extraordinary saying that *there shall be no more time.* Probably,' he added, smiling, 'this is the very second which was not long enough for the water to be spilt out of Mahomet's pitcher, though the epileptic prophet had time to gaze at all the habitations of Allah.'

Yes, he had often met Rogozhin in Moscow, and they had not talked only of this. 'Rogozhin said just now that I had been a brother to him then; he said that for the first time today,' Myshkin thought to himself.

He thought this, sitting on a seat under a tree in the Summer Garden. It was about seven o'clock. The Garden was empty; a shadow passed over the setting sun for an instant. It was sultry and there was a feeling in the air like a foreboding of a thunderstorm in the distance. His present contemplative mood had a certain charm for him. His mind and memory seemed to fasten upon every external object about him, and he found pleasure in it. He was yearning all the while to forget something in the present, something grave, but at the first glance about him he was aware again at once of his gloomy thought, the thought he was so longing to get away from. He recalled that he had talked at dinner to the waiter at the restaurant of a very strange murder which had excited much talk and sensation. But he had no sooner recollected it than something strange happened to him again.

An extraordinary, overwhelming desire, almost a temptation, suddenly paralysed his will. He got up from the seat, walked straight from the Garden towards the Petersburg Side. Not long ago he had asked a passer-by on the bank of the Neva to point out to him across the river the Petersburg Side. It was pointed out to him, but he had not gone there then. And in any case it would have been useless to go that day, he knew it. He had long had the address; he could easily find the house of Lebedyev's relation, but he knew almost for certain that he would not find her at home. 'She certainly is gone to Pavlovsk, or Kolya would have left word at the Scales, as he had agreed.' So if he went there now, it was certainly not with the idea of seeing her. A gloomy, tormenting curiosity of another sort allured him now. A sudden new idea had come into his mind.

But it was enough for him that he had set off and that he knew where he was going; though a minute later he was walking along again almost unconscious of his surroundings. Further consideration of his 'sudden idea' became all at once intensely distasteful to him, almost impossible. He stared with painfully strained attention at every object that met his eye: he gazed at the sky, at the Neva. He spoke to a little boy he met. Perhaps his epileptic condition was growing more and more acute. The storm was certainly gathering, though slowly. It was beginning to thunder far away. The air had become very sultry …

For some reason he was continually haunted now, as one is sometimes haunted by an annoying and stupidly persistent tune, by the image of Lebedyev's nephew, whom he had seen that morning. Strange to say, he kept seeing him as the murderer of whom Lebedyev had spoken that morning, while introducing his nephew to Myshkin. Yes, he had read quite a little while ago about that murder; he had read and heard much since he had been in Russia of such cases, and always followed them. And that evening he had been extremely interested in his talk with the waiter about that same murder – the murder of the Zhemarins. The waiter agreed with him, he remembered that. He remembered the waiter too. He was an intelligent fellow, staid and careful; though 'God only knows what he is like really; it's hard to make new people out in a new country.' Yet he was beginning to have a passionate faith in the Russian soul. Oh, in those six months he had passed through a great deal – a great deal that had been quite new to him, unguessed, unknown and unexpected! But the soul of another is a dark place, and the Russian soul is a dark place – for many it is a dark place. He had long been friends with Rogozhin, for instance, they had been intimate, they had been like brothers, but did he know Rogozhin? And what chaos one found here sometimes in all this! What a muddle, what hideousness! And what a repulsive and self-satisfied pimple that nephew of Lebedyev's was! 'What am I saying though?' (Myshkin went on dreaming.) 'Did he kill those creatures, those six people? I seem to be mixing it up... How strange it is! I am rather giddy... And what a charming, what a sweet face Lebedyev's eldest daughter had – the one standing up with the baby! What an innocent, what an almost childish expression! What an almost childish laugh! Strange that he had nearly forgotten that face and now he could think of nothing else. Lebedyev, who stamped his feet at them, probably adored them all. But what was certain as that twice two make four was that Lebedyev adored his nephew too!

But how could he venture to criticise them so positively, he who had only come that day? How could he pass such judgements?

Why, Lebedyev had been a riddle to him that day. Had he expected a Lebedyev like that? Had he known a Lebedyev like that before? Lebedyev and Du Barry – heavens! If Rogozhin did commit murder, though, at last, it would not be such a senseless murder. There would not be the same chaos. A weapon made to a special pattern and the murder of six people perpetrated in complete delirium... Had Rogozhin a weapon made to a special pattern? Had he ... But... was it certain that Rogozhin would commit murder? Myshkin suddenly started. 'Isn't it criminal, isn't it base on my part to make such a supposition with cynical openness!' he cried, and a flush of shame instantly overspread his face. He was astounded; he stood still, as though struck dumb in the road. He remembered all at once the Pavlovsk station that afternoon and the station at which he had arrived that morning, and Rogozhin's question asked to his face about the *eyes*-, and Rogozhin's cross, which he was wearing now; and the blessing of his mother, to whom Rogozhin had taken him himself; and that last convulsive embrace, that last renunciation of Rogozhin's on the stairs – and after all that, to catch himself incessantly looking about him for something, and that shop and that object... What baseness! And, after all that, he was going now with a 'special purpose,' with a 'special sudden idea'! His whole soul was overwhelmed with despair and suffering. Myshkin wanted to turn back at once and go home to the hotel. He even turned and walked that way, but a minute later he stood still, reflected, and went back again to where he had been going.

Yes, he was already on the Petersburg Side; he was near the house. It was not with that same purpose he was going there now; it was not with that special idea! And how could it be? Yes, his illness was coming back, there was no doubt of that; perhaps he would even have the fit that day. All this darkness was owing to that; 'the idea,' too, was owing to that! Now the darkness was dispelled, the demon had been driven away, doubt did not exist, there was joy in his heart! And – it was so long since he had seen her, he wanted to see her, and... Yes, he would have liked to meet Rogozhin now; he would have taken him by the hand and they would have gone together. His heart was pure; he was not Rogozhin's rival! The next day he would go himself and tell Rogozhin that he had seen her. Why, he had flown here, as Rogozhin said, that afternoon simply to see her! Perhaps he would find her! It was not certain after all that she was at Pavlovsk.

Yes, all this must be made clear now, that all might see clearly into each other's hearts, that there might be no more such gloomy and passionate renunciations as Rogozhin's that day; and all this must be done in freedom and ... light. Surely Rogozhin too could walk in the light. He said he did not love her like that; that he had no compassion for her, no 'sort of pity.' It is true he had added afterwards that 'your pity perhaps is stronger than my love', but he had been unjust to himself. Hm! ... Rogozhin reading – was not that 'pity'? The beginning of 'pity'? Did not the very presence of that book prove that he was fully conscious of his attitude to her? And all he had told him that morning? Yes, that was deeper than mere passion. And does her face inspire no more than passion? Can that face indeed inspire passion now? It excites grief, it clutches the whole soul, it... and a poignant, agonising memory suddenly passed through Myshkin's heart.

Yes, agonising. He remembered how he had suffered not long ago when first he had noticed in her symptoms of insanity?. Then he had been almost in despair. And how could he have left her when she ran away from him to Rogozhin? He ought to have run after her himself without waiting for news of her. But... was it possible Rogozhin had not yet noticed insanity in her? Hm! Rogozhin sees other causes for everything passions! And what insane jealousy? What did he mean by his supposition that morning? (Myshkin suddenly flushed and there was a sort of shudder at his heart.)

But what use was it to think of that? There was insanity on both sides. And for him, Myshkin, to love that woman with passion was almost unthinkable, would have been almost cruelty, inhumanity. Yes, yes! No, Rogozhin was unfair to himself; he had a great heart which could suffer and be compassionate. When he knew all the truth, when he realised what a piteous creature that broken, insane woman was, wouldn't he forgive her all the past, all his agonies? Wouldn't he become her servant, her brother, her friend, her Providence? Compassion would teach even Rogozhin and awaken his mind. Compassion was the chief and perhaps only law of all human existence. Ah, how unpardonably and dishonourably he had wronged Rogozhin! No, it was not that 'the Russian soul was a dark place,' but that in his own soul there was darkness, since he could imagine such horrors! Because of a few warm words from the heart in Moscow Rogozhin had called him his brother; while he ... But that was sickness and delirium. That would all come right! ... Plow gloomily Rogozhin had said that morning that he was 'losing his faith'! That man must be suffering terribly! He had said that 'he liked looking at that picture'; it was not that he liked it, but that he felt drawn to it. Rogozhin was not merely a passionate soul; he was a fighter, anyway: he wanted by force to get back his lost faith. He had an agonising need of it now ... Yes, to believe in something! To believe in someone! How strange that picture of Holbein's was, though!... Ah, here is the street! And here must be that house.

Yes, it was it, No. 16, 'the house of Madame Filisov.' It was here! Myshkin rang and asked for Nastasya Filippovna.

The mistress of the house herself answered him that Nastasya Filippovna had gone to Pavlovsk that morning to stay? with Darya Alexeyevna, 'and it may be that she will stay there some days.' Madame Filisov was a little, keen-eyed, sharp-faced woman about forty, with a sly and watchful expression. She asked his name, and there was an apparently intentional air of mystery in the question. Myshkin was at first unwilling to answer, but immediately turned back and asked her emphatically to give his name to Nastasya Filippovna. Madame Filisov received this emphatic request with great attention and an extraordinary air of secrecy, by which she evidently meant to suggest, 'Set your mind at rest; I understand.' Myshkin's name obviously made a very great impression on her. He looked absent-mindedly at her, turned, and went back to his hotel. But he looked quite different now. An extraordinary change had come over him again and apparently in one instant. He walked along once more pale, weak, suffering, agitated; his knees trembled and a vague bewildered smile hovered about his blue lips. His 'sudden idea' was at once confirmed and justified, and he believed in his demon again.

But was it confirmed? But was it justified? Why that shiver again, that cold sweat, that darkness and chill in his soul? Was it because he had once more seen those eyes? But he had gone out of the Summer Garden on purpose to see them! That was what his idea' amounted to. He had intensely desired to see 'those eyes' again, so as to make quite certain that he would meet them *there,* at that house. He had desired it passionately, and why was he so crushed and overwhelmed now by the fact that he had actually just seen them? As though he had not expected it! Yes, those were the *same eyes* (and there could be no doubt now that they were the same eyes) which had gleamed at him in the morning, in the crowd when he got out of the train from Moscow; they were the same (absolutely the same) which he had caught looking at him from behind that afternoon just as he was sitting down at Rogozhin's. Rogozhin had denied it at the time; he had asked with a wry and frozen smile 'whose eyes were they?' And not many hours ago, when Myshkin was getting into the Pavlovsk train to go down to see Aglaia, and suddenly caught sight of those eyes again for the third time that day, he had an intense desire to go to Rogozhin and to tell *him* whose eyes they were. But he had run out of the station and had been hardly conscious of anything, till the moment when he found himself standing, at the cutler's shop and thinking an object with a stag-horn handle would cost sixty kopecks. A strange and dreadful demon had got hold of him for good and would not let him go again. That demon had whispered to him in the Summer Garden, as he sat lost in thought under a lime tree, that if Rogozhin had felt obliged to follow him that day and to dog his footsteps, he would certainly, on finding Myshkin had not gone to Pavlovsk (which was of course a terrible fact for Rogozhin) have gone there to Filisov's house and would certainly have watched there for him, Myshkin, who had given him his word of honour only that morning that he would not see her and that he had not come to Petersburg for that. And here was Myshkin hurrying feverishly to that house! And what if he really did meet Rogozhin there? He had only seen an unhappy man whose state of mind was gloomy, but very easy to understand. That unhappy man did not even conceal himself now. Yes, that morning Rogozhin had for some reason denied it and told a lie, but at the station he stood almost unconcealed. Indeed, it was rather he, Myshkin, had concealed himself, and not Rogozhin. And now at the house he stood on the other side of the street fifty paces away on the opposite pavement, waiting with his arms folded. There too he had been quite conspicuous and seemed to wish to be conspicuous on purpose. He stood like an accuser and a judge and not like … what?

And why had he, Myshkin, not gone up to him now? Why had he turned away from him, as though noticing nothing, though their eyes had met? (Yes, their eyes had met; they had looked at one another.) Why, he himself had wanted to take Rogozhin by the hand and to go *there* with him. He had meant to go to him next day and to tell him he had been to see her. He had refused to follow his demon when, halfway there, joy had suddenly flooded his soul. Or was there really something in Rogozhin – that is, in the whole image of the man *that day,* in all his words, movements, actions, looks, taken together, that could justify Myshkin's awful misgivings and the revolting promptings of his inner voice? Something that can be seen, but is difficult to analyse and describe; something impossible to justify on sufficient grounds, though it yet, in spite of all that difficulty and impossibility, makes a complete and compelling impression which involuntarily becomes a firm conviction? …

Conviction – of what? (Oh, how Myshkin was tortured by the hideousness, the 'degradingness' of this conviction, of 'that base foreboding,' and how he had reproached himself.) 'Say of what if you dare,' he kept telling himself continually with reproach and challenge. 'Formulate all your thought, dare to express it clearly, precisely, without faltering! Oh, I am ignoble!' he repeated with indignation and a flush on his face. 'With what eyes shall I look upon that man for the rest of my life! Oh, what a day! Oh, God, what a nightmare!'

There was a moment at the end of that long, miserable walk back from the Petersburg Side when an irresistible desire seized Myshkin to go straightway to Rogozhin, to wait for him, to embrace him with shame, with tears, to tell him everything and to end it all at once. But he was already standing at his hotel ... How he had disliked that hotel in the morning, those corridors, all that house, his room – disliked it at first sight! Several times during the day he had thought with disgust that he would have to return there ... 'Why, like a sick woman, I am believing in every presentiment today!' he thought with irritable irony, standing still at the gate. One circumstance that had happened that day rose before his mind at that moment, but he thought of it 'coldly,' 'with perfect composure,' 'without nightmare.' He suddenly recalled the knife he had seen on Rogozhin's table that morning. 'But why shouldn't Rogozhin have as many knives as he likes on his table?' he asked, greatly astounded at himself and at that point, petrified with amazement, he suddenly recalled how he had stopped at the cutler's shop. 'But what connection can there be in that?' he cried out at last, but stopped short. A new unbearable shock of shame, almost of despair, held him rooted to the spot just outside the gate. He stood still for a minute. People are sometimes held like this by sudden and unbearable memories, especially when they are associated with shame. 'Yes, I am a man of no heart and a coward,' he repeated gloomily, and abruptly moved to go on, but... he stopped short again.

The gateway, which was always dark, was particularly dark at that moment; the storm-cloud had crept over the sky and engulfed the evening light, and at the very moment that Myshkin approached the house the storm broke and there was a downpour. He was just at the entrance of the gateway when he moved on abruptly after his momentary halt. And he suddenly saw in the half dark under the gateway close to the stairs a man. The man seemed to be waiting for something, but he vanished at once. Myshkin had only caught a glimpse of him and could not see him distinctly and could not have told for certain who he was. Besides, numbers of people might be passing here; it was a hotel and people were continually running in and out. But he suddenly felt a complete and overwhelming conviction that he recognised the man and that it was certainly Rogozhin. A moment after, Myshkin rushed after him up the stairs. His heart sank. 'Everything will be decided now,' he repeated to himself with strange conviction.

The staircase up which Myshkin ran from the gateway led to the corridors of the first and second floors, on which were the rooms of the hotel. As in all old houses, the staircase was of stone, dark and narrow, and it turned round a thick stone column. On the first half-landing there was a hollow like a niche in the column, not more than half a yard wide and nine inches deep. Yet there was room for a man to stand there. Dark as it was, Myshkin, on reaching the half-landing, at once discovered that a man was hiding in the niche. Myshkin suddenly wanted to pass by without looking to the right. He had taken one step already, but he could not resist turning round.

Those two eyes, *the same two eyes,* met his own. The man hidden in the niche had already moved one step from it. For one second they stood facing one another and almost touching. Suddenly Myshkin seized him by the shoulders and turned him back towards the staircase, nearer to the light; he wanted to see his face more clearly.

Rogozhin's eyes flashed and a smile of fury contorted his face. His right hand was raised and something gleamed in it; Myshkin did not think of checking it. He only remembered that he thought he cried out, 'Parfyon, I don't believe it!' Then suddenly something seemed torn asunder before him; his soul was flooded with intense *inner* light. The moment lasted perhaps half a second, yet he clearly and consciously remembered the beginning, the first sound of the fearful scream which broke of itself from his breast and which he could not have checked by any effort. Then his consciousness was instantly extinguished and complete darkness followed.

It was an epileptic fit, the first he had had for a long time. It is well known that epileptic fits come on quite suddenly. At the moment the face is horribly distorted, especially the eyes. The whole body and the features of the face work with convulsive jerks and contortions. A terrible, indescribable scream that is unlike anything else breaks from the sufferer. In that scream everything human seems obliterated and it is impossible, or very difficult, for an observer to realise and admit that it is the man himself screaming. It seems indeed as though it were someone else screaming from within the man. That is how many people at least have described their impression. The sight of a man in an epileptic fit fills many people with positive and unbearable horror, in which there is a certain element of the uncanny. It must be supposed that some such feeling of sudden horror, together with the other terrible sensations of the moment, had suddenly paralysed Rogozhin and so saved Myshkin from the knife with which he would have stabbed him. Then before he had time to grasp that it was a fit, seeing that Myshkin had staggered away from him and fallen backwards downstairs, knocking his head violently against the stone step, Rogozhin flew headlong downstairs, avoiding the prostrate figure, and, not knowing what he was doing, ran out of the hotel.

Struggling in violent convulsions, the sick man slipped down the steps, of which there were about fifteen, to the bottom of the staircase. Very soon, not more than five minutes later, he was noticed and a crowd collected. A pool of blood by his head raised the doubt whether the sick man had hurt himself, or whether there had been some crime. It was soon recognised, however, that it was a case of epilepsy; one of the people at the hotel recognised Myshkin as having arrived that morning. The difficulty was luckily solved by a fortunate circumstance.

Kolya Ivolgin, who had promised to be back at the Scales at four and had instead gone to Pavlovsk, had on a sudden impulse refused to dine at Madame Epanchin's, had come back to Petersburg and hurried to the Scales, where he had turned up about seven o'clock. Learning from the note that Myshkin had left for him that the latter was in town, he hastened to find him at the address given in the note. Being informed in the hotel that Myshkin had gone out, he went downstairs to the restaurant and waited for him there, drinking tea and listening to the organ. Happening to overhear that someone had had a fit, he was led by a true presentiment to run out to the spot and recognised Myshkin. Suitable steps were taken at once. Myshkin was carried to his room. Though he regained consciousness, he did not fully come to himself for a long time. A doctor who was sent for to look at his injured head said there was not the least danger, and ordered a lotion. An hour later, when Myshkin began to be able to understand pretty well what was going on, Kolya took him in a covered carriage from the hotel to Lebedyev's. Lebedyev received the sick man with bows and extraordinary warmth. For his sake he hastened his removal, and three days later they were all at Pavlovsk.

Chapter 6

Lebedyev's villa was not a large one, but was comfortable and even pretty. The part of it which was to let had been newly decorated. On the rather spacious verandah by which the house was entered from the street, orange trees, lemons and jasmines had been placed in large green wooden tubs, which in Lebedyev's opinion gave the place a most seductive appearance. He had bought some of those trees with the villa and was so enchanted by the effect they produced in the verandah that he resolved to take advantage of an opportunity to buy some more of the same kind at an auction. When all the shrubs had been brought to the villa and put in their places, Lebedyev had several times that day run down the steps of the verandah to admire the effect from the street, and every time he mentally increased the sum which he proposed to ask from his future tenant.

Myshkin, worn out, depressed, and physically shattered, was delighted with the villa. But on the day of arriving at Pavlovsk – that is, three days after the fit, Myshkin looked almost well again, though inwardly he still felt ill-effects. He was glad to see everyone who was about him during those three days; he was glad of Kolya, who hardly left his side; glad to see the Lebedyev family (the nephew had gone off somewhere); he was glad to see Lebedyev himself, and even welcomed with pleasure General Ivolgin, who had visited him before he left Petersburg. On the evening they arrived at Pavlovsk a good many guests were assembled on the verandah about him. The first to arrive was Ganya, whom Myshkin hardly recognised, he had changed so much and grown so much thinner in those six months. Then came Varya and Ptitsyn, who also had a villa at Pavlovsk. General Ivolgin was almost always at Lebedyev's and had apparently moved with him. Lebedyev tried to keep him in his own part of the house and to prevent his going to see Myshkin. He treated the general like a friend; they seemed to have known each other a long time. Myshkin noticed during those three days that they were frequently engaged in long conversations together; that they often shouted and argued, even about learned subjects, which evidently gave Lebedyev great satisfaction. One might have thought that the general was necessary to him. From the time they moved to Pavlovsk Lebedyev began to be as careful about his own family, as he had been about the general. On the pretext of not disturbing Myshkin, he would not let anyone go to see him. He stamped his feet, rushed at his daughters and chased them all away, even Vera with the baby, at the least suspicion that they were going on to the verandah where Myshkin was, in spite of Myshkin's begging him not to send anyone away.

'In the first place, there will be no respect shown if you let them do what they like; and, in the second place, it's really improper for them,' he explained at last in reply to Myshkin's direct question.

'But why so?' protested Myshkin. 'Really you only Worry me with all these attentions and watchfulness. It's dull for me alone, I've told you so several times; and you depress me more than ever by the way you are always waving your hands and walking about on tiptoe.'

Myshkin hinted at the fact that, though Lebedyev chased away all his household on the pretext that quiet was necessary for the invalid, he had been coming in himself every minute, and always first opened the door, poked his head in, looked about the room, as though he wished to make sure that he was there and had not run away, and then slowly, on tiptoe, with stealthy steps, approached the armchair, so that he sometimes startled his lodger. He was continually enquiring if he wanted anything, and when Myshkin began asking him at last to leave him alone, he turned away obediently without a word, stole on tiptoe to the door, waving his hands at every step, as though to say that he had only just looked in, that he would not say a word, that he had already gone out and would not come back; yet within ten minutes, or at most a quarter of an hour, he would reappear. The fact that Kolya had free access to Myshkin was a source of the deepest mortification and even of resentful indignation to Lebedyev. Kolya noticed that Lebedyev used to stand at the door for half an hour at a time listening to what he and Myshkin were talking about, and of course he informed Myshkin of the fact.

'You seem to have appropriated me, since you keep me under lock and key,' Myshkin protested. 'At the villa, anyway, I want it to be different: and, let me tell you, I shall see anyone I like and go anywhere I choose.'

'Without the faintest doubt!' Lebedyev protested, waving his hands.

Myshkin scanned him intently from head to foot.

'And have you brought the little cupboard here that was hanging at the head of your bed?'

'No, I haven't.'

'Have you left it there?'

'It was impossible to bring it, I should have to wrench it from the wall... It's fixed firmly, firmly.'

'But perhaps there's another one like it here?'

'A better one – a better one! It was there when I bought the villa.'

'A-ah! Who was it you wouldn't admit to see me an hour ago?'

'It... it was the general. It's true I didn't let him in, and he ought not to come. I have a great respect for that man, Prince, he ... he is a great man. Don't you believe me? Well, you will see, but yet... it's better, illustrious prince, for you not to receive him.'

'But why so, allow me to ask? And why are you standing on tiptoe now, Lebedyev, and why do you always approach me as though you wanted to whisper a secret in my ear?'

'I am abject, abject, I feel it,' Lebedyev replied unexpectedly, striking himself on the chest with feeling. 'And won't the general be too hospitable for you?'

'Too hospitable?'

'Yes, hospitable. To begin with, he is intending to live with me; that he might do, but he is always in extremes, he is claiming to be a relation at once. We've been into the question of relationship several times already; it appears that we are connected by marriage. You are a second cousin of his too, on the mother's side; he explained it to me only yesterday. If you are his cousin, then you and I must be relations too, illustrious prince. That's no matter, it's a trifling weakness, but he assured me just now that all his life, ever since he was an ensign up to the eleventh of June last year, he had never sat down to dinner with less than two hundred people at his table. He went so far at last as to say they never got up from the table, so they had dinner and supper and tea for fifteen hours out of four-and-twenty for thirty years on end without a break, so that they scarcely had the time to change the tablecloths. One would get up and go, and another would come, and on holidays there would be as many as three hundred, and on the thousandth anniversary of the foundation of Russia he counted seven hundred people. It's a passion with him; such assertions are a very bad symptom. One is quite afraid to have such hospitable people in one's house, and I've been thinking, "Won't a man like that be too hospitable for you and me?" '

'But you are on excellent terms with him, I believe?'

'We are like brothers, and I take it as a joke. Let us be connections. What does it matter? It's an honour to me. Even through the two hundred people at dinner and the thousandth anniversary of Russia I can see he is a very remarkable man. I mean it sincerely. You have spoken about secrets just now – that is, that I approach you every time as if I had a secret to tell you; and as it happens there is a secret. A person you know of has just sent word that she would very much like to have an interview with you in secret.'

'Why in secret? Not at all. I'll go and see her myself today, if you like.'

'Not at all, not at all!' Lebedyev waved his hands in protest. 'It's not what you suppose that she is afraid of. By the way, the monster comes every day to ask after your health. Did you know it?'

'You really call him "monster" so often it makes me quite suspicious.'

'You can feel no sort of suspicion – no sort of suspicion at all,' said Lebedyev, hurriedly dismissing the subject. 'I only wanted to explain that a certain person is not afraid of him, but of something very different, very different.'

'Why, of what? Tell me quickly!' Myshkin questioned impatiently, looking at Lebedyev's mysterious contortions.

'That's the secret.' And Lebedyev laughed.

'Whose secret?'

'Your secret. You forbade me yourself to speak of it before you, most illustrious prince,' Lebedyev muttered; and having thoroughly enjoyed the fact that he had excited his hearer's curiosity to painful impatience, he suddenly concluded: 'She is afraid of Aglaia Ivanovna.'

Myshkin frowned and was silent for a minute.

'Oh dear, Lebedyev, I'll give up your villa!' he said suddenly. 'Where are the Ptitsyns, Gavril Ardalionovitch? You've enticed them away too.'

'They are coming – they are coming. And even General Ivolgin after them. I'll open all the doors and I'll call my daughters too – everyone, everyone, at once, at once,' Lebedyev whispered in alarm, brandishing his arms and rushing from one door to another.

At that moment Kolya entered the verandah from the street and announced that visitors – Madame Epanchin and her three daughters – were just coming to call.

'Shall I admit the Ptitsyns and Gavril Ardalionovitch, or not? Shall I admit the general or not?' said Lebedyev, skipping up, impressed by the news.

'Why not? Let anyone come who likes. I assure you, Lebedyev, you've had some wrong idea about my attitude from the very beginning; you are making a mistake all the time. I have not the slightest reason for hiding and concealing myself from anyone,' laughed Myshkin.

Looking at him, Lebedyev felt it his duty to laugh too. In spite of his great agitation, he also seemed extremely pleased.

The news brought by Kolya was true. He had come only a few steps in advance of the Epanchins to announce their arrival, so that the visitors arrived on the verandah from both sides at once: the Epanchins from the street, and the Ptitsyns, Ganya, and General Ivolgin from indoors.

The Epanchins had only just heard from Kolya that Myshkin was ill and that he was in Pavlovsk. Till then Madame Epanchin had been in painful perplexity. Two days before, the general had passed on Myshkin's card to his family. The sight of that card awakened in Lizaveta Prokofyevna a firm conviction that Myshkin would promptly follow it to Pavlovsk to call on them. It was in vain that her daughters assured her that a man who had not written for six months would perhaps be far from being in such a hurry now, and that he very likely had a great deal to do in Petersburg apart from them. How could they know what he was about? Madame Epanchin was positively angry at these remarks and was ready to wager that Myshkin would make his appearance next day at latest, though even that would be rather late! The next day she had been expecting him all the morning; they expected him to dinner, to spend the evening, and when it got quite dark Lizaveta Prokofyevna was cross with everything and quarrelled with everyone, making of course no allusion to Myshkin as the occasion of quarrel. Not one word was spoken of him on the third day either. When at dinner Aglaia let drop the remark that *Maman* was angry because the prince had not come – to which her father immediately replied that it was not his fault – Lizaveta Prokofyevna got up and left the table in wrath. At last towards evening Kolya arrived and gave them a full description of all Myshkin's adventures so far as he knew them. Lizaveta Prokofyevna was triumphant, but yet Kolya came in for a good scolding. 'He hangs about here for days together and there's no getting rid of him, and now he might at least have let us know, if he did not think fit to come himself.' Kolya was on the point of being angry at the words 'no getting rid of him,' but he put it off for another time; if the phrase had not been too offensive, he would perhaps have forgiven it altogether, for he was so pleased with Lizaveta Prokofyevna's agitation and anxiety on hearing of Myshkin's illness. She insisted for a long time on the necessity of sending a special messenger to Petersburg to get hold of a medical celebrity of the first magnitude and to carry him away by the first train. But her daughters dissuaded her from this. They were unwilling, however, to be left behind by their mamma when she instantly got ready to visit the invalid.

'He is on his deathbed,' said Lizaveta Prokofyevna in a fluster, 'and fancy our standing on ceremony! Is he a friend of the family or not?'

'But we mustn't rush in before we know how the land lies,' observed Aglaia.

'Very well, then, don't come. You will do well indeed; if Yevgeny Pavlovitch comes, there will be no one to receive him.'

At those words Aglaia, of course, set off at once with the others: though indeed she had intended to do so before. Prince S—, who had been sitting with Adelaïda, at her request instantly agreed to escort the ladies. He had been much interested when he heard of Myshkin from the Epanchins before, at the very beginning of his acquaintance with them. It appeared that he was acquainted with him; that they had met somewhere lately and had spent a fortnight together in some little town three months before. Prince S— had told them a great deal about Myshkin, indeed, and had spoken of him in a very friendly way, so it was with genuine pleasure that he went to call on him. General Epanchin was not at home that evening; Yevgeny Pavlovitch had not yet arrived either.

It was not more than three hundred paces to Lebedyev's villa. Lizaveta Prokofyevna's first disappointment was to find quite a party of visitors with Myshkin, to say nothing of the fact that among them were two or three persons for whom she had a positive hatred. Her *second* disappointment was the surprise of finding a young man to all appearance in perfect health and fashionably dressed, who came to meet them laughing, instead of the invalid whom she had expected to find on his deathbed. She actually stopped short in bewilderment, to the intense delight of Kolya, who of course might perfectly well have explained before she set out that no one was dying and that it was not a case of a deathbed. But he had not explained it, slyly foreseeing the comic wrath of Madame Epanchin when, as he reckoned, she would certainly be angry at finding Myshkin, for whom she had real affection, in good health. Kolya was so tactless, indeed, as to speak of his surmise aloud, so as to put the finishing touch to Lizaveta Prokofyevna's irritation. He was always sparring with her, and sometimes very maliciously, in spite of their affection for one another.

'Wait a bit, my young friend, don't be in a hurry! Don't spoil your triumph,' answered Lizaveta Prokofyevna, sitting down in the armchair that Myshkin set for her.

Lebedyev, Ptitsyn and General Ivolgin flew to put chairs for the young ladies. General Ivolgin gave Aglaia a chair. Lebedyev set a chair for Prince S— too, expressing profound respectfulness by the very curve of his back as he did so. Varya greeted the young ladies as usual in an ecstatic whisper.

'It's the truth, Prince, that I expected to find you almost in bed. I exaggerated things so in my fright, and I am not going to tell a lie about it. I felt dreadfully vexed just now at the sight of your happy face, but I swear it was only for a minute, before I had time to think. I always act and speak more sensibly when I have time to think. I think it's the same with you. And yet really I should be less pleased perhaps at the recovery of my own son than I am at yours; and if you don't believe me, the shame is yours and not mine. And this spiteful boy dares to play worse jokes than this at my expense. I believe he is a *protégé* of yours, so I warn you that one fine morning I shall deny myself the pleasure of enjoying the honour of his further acquaintance.'

'But what have I done?' cried Kolya. 'However much I had assured you that the prince was almost well again, you would not have been willing to believe me, because it was much more interesting to imagine him lying on his deathbed.'

'Have you come to us for long?' Lizaveta Prokofyevna asked Myshkin.

'The whole summer, and perhaps longer.'

'You are alone, aren't you? Not married?'

'No, not married,' Myshkin smiled at the simplicity of the taunt. 'There's nothing to smile at; it does happen. I was thinking of this villa. Why haven't you come to us? We have a whole wing empty. But do as you like. Have you hired it from him? That person?' she added in an undertone, nodding at Lebedyev. 'Why does he wriggle about like that?'

At that moment Vera came out of the house on to the verandah as usual with the baby in her arms. Lebedyev, who was wriggling around the chairs at a complete loss what to do with himself and desperately anxious not to go, immediately flew at Vera. He gesticulated at her and chased her off the verandah and, forgetting himself, even stamped with his feet.

'He is mad?' observed Madame Epanchin suddenly.

'No, he is ...'

'Drunk, perhaps? Your party is not attractive,' she snapped, after glancing at the other guests also. 'But what a nice girl though! Who is she?'

'That's Vera Lukyanovna, the daughter of Lebedyev here.'

'Ah! ... She is very sweet. I should like to make her acquaintance.'

But Lebedyev, hearing Madame Epanchin's words of approval, was already dragging his daughter forward to present her.

'My motherless children!' he wailed as he came up. 'And this baby in her arms is motherless, her sister, my daughter Lubov – born in most lawful wedlock from my departed wife Elena, who died six weeks ago in childbirth, by the will of God. Yes... she takes her mother's place to the baby, though she is a sister and no more ... no more, no more ...'

'And you, Sir, are no more than a fool, if you'll excuse me! That's enough, you know it yourself, I suppose,' Lizaveta Prokofyevna rapped out in extreme indignation.

'Perfectly true,' Lebedyev assented with a low and respectful bow.

'Listen, Mr Lebedyev, is it true what they say, that you interpret the Apocalypse?' asked Aglaia.

'Perfectly true ... for fifteen years.'

'I've heard about you. I think there was something in the newspapers about you?'

'No, that was about another interpreter, another one, but he is dead. I've succeeded him,' said Lebedyev, beside himself with delight.

'Be so good as to interpret it to me some day soon, as we are neighbours. I don't understand anything in the Apocalypse.'

'I must warn you, Aglaia Ivanovna, that all this is mere charlatanism on his part, believe me,' General Ivolgin put in quickly. He was sitting beside Aglaia, and tingling all over with eagerness to enter into conversation. 'Of course there are certain privileges on a holiday,' he went on, 'and certain pleasures, and to take up such an extraordinary *intrus* for the interpretation of the Apocalypse is a diversion like any other, and even a remarkably clever diversion, but I... I think you are looking at me with surprise? General Ivolgin. I have the honour to introduce myself. I used to carry you in my arms, Aglaia Ivanovna.'

'Very glad to meet you. I know Varvara Ardalionovna and Nina Alexandrovna,' Aglaia muttered, making desperate efforts not to burst out laughing.

Lizaveta Prokofyevna flushed. The irritation that had been accumulating for a long time in her heart suddenly craved for an outlet. She could not endure General Ivolgin, with whom she had been acquainted, but very long ago.

'You are lying, Sir, as usual. You have never carried her in your arms,' she snapped out indignantly.

'You've forgotten, *Maman*, he really did, at Tver,' Aglaia suddenly asserted. 'We were living at Tver then. I was six years old then, I remember. He made me a bow and arrow and taught me to shoot, and I killed a pigeon. Do you remember we killed a pigeon together?'

'And you brought me a helmet made of cardboard, and a wooden sword, I remember, too!' cried Adelaïda.

'I remember it too,' Alexandra chimed in. 'You quarrelled over the wounded pigeon. You were put in separate corners. Adelaïda stood in the corner wearing the helmet and the sword.'

When General Ivolgin told Aglaia that he had carried her in his arms, he said it without meaning it, merely to begin the conversation, and because he always began a conversation in that way with young people, if he wanted to make their acquaintance. But this time, as it happened, he was speaking the truth, though, as it happened, he had forgotten it. So when Aglaia declared that they had shot a pigeon together, it revived his memory of the past, and he recalled every detail himself, as elderly people often do remember something in the remote past. It is hard to say what there was in that reminiscence to produce so strong an effect on the poor general, who was, as usual, a little drunk, but he was all at once greatly moved.

'I remember, I remember it all!' he cried. 'I was a captain then. You were such a pretty little mite ... Nina Alexandrovna ... Ganya ... I used to be ... a guest in your house, Ivan Fyodorovitch

'And see what you've come to now!' put in Madame Epanchin. 'So you haven't drunk away all your better feeling, it affects you so much? But you've worried your wife to death! Instead of looking after your children, you sit in a debtors' prison. Go away, my friend; stand in some corner behind the door and have a cry. Remember your innocence in the past, and maybe God will forgive you. Go along, go along, I mean it. Nothing helps a man to reform like thinking of the past with regret.' But to repeat that she was speaking seriously was unnecessary. General Ivolgin, like all drunkards, was very emotional, and, like all drunkards who have sunk very low, he was much upset by memories of the happy past. He got up and walked humbly to the door, so that Lizaveta Prokofyevna was at once sorry for him.

'Ardalion Alexandrovitch, my dear man!' she called after him. 'Stop a minute; we are all sinners. When you feel your conscience more at ease, come and see me; we'll sit and chat over the past. I dare say I am fifty times as great a sinner myself. But now, goodbye; go along, it's no use your staying here.' she added suddenly, afraid he was coming back.

'You'd better not go after him for a while,' said Myshkin, checking Kolya, who was about to run after his father, 'or he will be vexed directly and all this minute will be spoiled for him.'

'That's true; don't disturb him; go in half an hour,' Lizaveta Prokofyevna decided.

'See what comes of speaking the truth for once in his life; it reduced him to tears,' Lebedyev ventured to comment.

'You are another pretty one, my man, if what I've heard is true,' said Lizaveta Prokofyevna, suppressing him at once.

The mutual relations of the guests about Myshkin gradually became evident. Myshkin was, of course, able to appreciate and did appreciate to the full the sympathy shown to him by Madame Epanchin and her daughters, and he told them with truth that before they came he had intended to have paid them a visit that day in spite of his invalid state and the late hour. Lizaveta Prokofyevna, looking at his visitors, observed that it Was still possible to carry out his intention. Ptitsyn, who was a very polite and tactful person, promptly retreated to Lebedyev's quarters, and was very anxious to get Lebedyev away with him. The latter promised to follow him quickly. Varya, meanwhile, had got into talk with the girls, and remained, and she and Ganya were greatly relieved by the departure of the general. Ganya himself withdrew soon after Ptitsyn. For the few minutes that he was in the verandah with the Epanchins, he had behaved modestly and with dignity, and was not in the least disconcerted by the determined air with which Madame Epanchin twice scanned him from head to foot. Anyone who had known him before would certainly have thought that there was a great change in him. Aglaia Was very much pleased at it.

'Was that Gavril Ardalionovitch who went out?' she asked suddenly, as she was fond of doing sometimes, interrupting the general conversation by her loud abrupt question, and addressing no one in particular.

'Yes,' answered Myshkin.

'I hardly knew him. He is very much changed and ... greatly for the better.'

'I am very glad,' said Myshkin.

'He has been very ill,' added Varya, in a tone of glad commiseration.

'How has he changed for the better?' Lizaveta Prokofyevna asked with angry perplexity and almost in dismay. 'What an idea! There's nothing better. What improvement do you see?'

'There is nothing better than the "poor knight," ' Kolya, who had been standing by Madame Epanchin's chair, brought out suddenly.

'That's exactly what I think,' said Prince S—, and he laughed.

'I am precisely of the same opinion,' Adelaïda declared solemnly.

'What poor knight?' asked Madame Epanchin, staring at all who had spoken, with perplexity and vexation, but seeing that Aglaia flushed hotly, she added angrily, 'Some nonsense, of course! Who is this "poor knight" ?'

'It's not the first time that urchin, your favourite, has twisted other people's words awry!' answered Aglaia, with haughty indignation.

In every outburst of anger from Aglaia (and she was very often angry) there was apparent, in spite of her evident seriousness and severity, something childish and impatiently schoolgirlish, so naïvely disguised that it was sometimes impossible not to laugh when one looked at her, though this was the cause of extreme indignation to Aglaia, who could not understand what people were laughing at, and 'how they could, how they dared, laugh.' Her sisters and Prince S— laughed now, and even Myshkin smiled, though he, too, flushed at something. Kolya roared with laughter, and was triumphant. Aglaia was *angry* in earnest, and looked twice as pretty. Her confusion was very becoming to her, and so was her vexation at her own confusion.

'He has twisted so many of your words awry, too!' she added.

'I based it on your own exclamation!' cried Kolya. 'A month ago you were looking through "Don Quixote," and you cried out those very words, that there was nothing better than the "poor knight." I don't know whom you were talking of, whether it was Don Quixote or Yevgeny Pavlovitch or some other person, but you were talking of someone and the conversation lasted a long while.'

'I see you allow yourself to go too far, young man, with your conjectures,' Lizaveta Prokofyevna checked him with vexation.

'But am I the only one?' Kolya persisted. 'Everybody said so, and they are saying so still. Why Prince S— and Adelaïda Ivanovna and everyone declared just now that they stood up for the "poor knight." So there must be a "poor knight", and he does exist, and I believe if it Were not for Adelaïda Ivanovna, we should have known long ago who the "poor knight" was.'

'What have I done?' laughed Adelaïda.

'You wouldn't draw his portrait, that's what you did! Aglaia Ivanovna begged you then to draw the portrait of the "poor knight," and described the whole subject of the picture. She made the subject up herself, you remember. You wouldn't.'

'But how could I draw it? According to the poem, that "poor knight"

"no more in sight of any
Raised the visor from his face."

'How could I draw the face then? What was I to draw – the visor? – The anonymous hero?'

'I don't understand what you mean by the visor,' said Madame Epanchin angrily, though she was beginning to have a very clear idea who was meant by the nickname (probably agreed upon long ago) of the 'poor knight.' But what specially angered her was that Prince Lyov Nikolayevitch was also disconcerted, and at last quite abashed like a boy of ten.

'Well, will you put a stop to this foolishness or not? Will they explain to me this "poor knight"? Is it such an awful secret that one can't approach it?'

But they only went on laughing.

'The fact is, there is a strange Russian poem about a poor knight,' Prince S— began at last, obviously anxious to suppress the subject and change the conversation, 'a fragment without a beginning or an end. About a month ago we were all laughing after dinner and trying as usual to find a subject for Adelaïda Ivanovna's next picture. You know that the whole family is always trying to find subjects for Adelaïda Ivanovna's pictures. Then we hit on the "poor knight," which of us first I don't remember.'

'Aglaia Ivanovna!' cried Kolya.

'Perhaps, I dare say, only I don't remember,' Prince S— went on. 'Some of us laughed at the subject, others declared that nothing could be better, but that to paint the "poor knight" we must find a face for him. We began to go over the faces of all our friends. Not one was suitable, and there we left it, that was all. I don't know why Nikolay Ardalionovitch thought fit to recall it all and bring it up again. What was amusing and appropriate at the time is quite uninteresting now.'

'Because some fresh foolishness is meant, mischievous and offensive,' Lizaveta Prokofyevna snapped out.

'There's no foolishness in it, nothing but the deepest respect,' Aglaia suddenly brought out, quite unexpectedly, in a grave and earnest voice.

She had mastered her confusion by now and completely recovered from it. What's more, one might, looking at her, have supposed from certain signs that she was positively glad that the jest was going so far; and this revulsion of feeling took place in her at the very moment when Myshkin's increasing and overwhelming embarrassment had become unmistakably evident to everyone.

'At one time they are laughing like mad things, and then they talk of the deepest respect! Crazy creatures! Why respect? Tell me at once, what makes you drag in deepest respect when it's neither here nor there?...'

'Deepest respect,' Aglaia went on as gravely and earnestly in response to her mother's almost spiteful questions, 'because that poem simply describes a man who is capable of an ideal, and what's more, a man who having once set an ideal before him has faith in it, and having faith in it gives up his life blindly to it. This does not always happen in our day. We are not told in that poem exactly what the "poor knight's" ideal was, but one can see it was some vision, some image of "pure beauty," and the knight in his loving devotion has put a rosary round his neck instead of a scarf. It's true that there is some obscure device of which we are not told in full, the letters A.N.B. inscribed on his shield ...'

'A.M.D.,' Kolya corrected her.

'But I say A.N.B., and that's what I want to say,' Aglaia interrupted with vexation. 'Anyway, it's clear that that poor knight did not care what his lady was, or what she did. It was enough for him that he had chosen her and put faith in her "pure beauty" and then did homage to her for ever. That's just his merit, that if she became a thief afterwards, he would still be bound to believe in her and be ready to break a spear for her pure beauty. The poet seems to have meant to unite in one striking figure the grand conception of the platonic love of mediaeval chivalry, as it was felt by a pure and lofty knight. Of course all that's an ideal. In the "poor knight" that feeling reaches its utmost limit in asceticism. It must be admitted that to be capable of such a feeling means a great deal, and that such feelings leave behind a profound impression, very, from one point of view, laudable, as with Don Quixote, for instance. The poor knight is the same Don Quixote, only serious and not comic. I didn't understand him at first, and laughed, but now I love the "poor knight," and what's more, respect his exploits.'

This was how Aglaia concluded, and, looking at her, it was difficult to tell whether she was in earnest or laughing.

'Well, he must have been a fool anyway, he and his exploits,' was her mother's comment. 'And you are talking nonsense, my girl, a regular tirade. It's not quite nice of you, to my thinking. In any case, it's not good manners. What poem? Read it; no doubt you know it! I must hear it. I've always disliked poetry; I knew no good would come of it. For goodness' sake, put up with it, Prince! You and I have got to put up with things together, it seems,' she added, addressing Myshkin.

She was very much annoyed. Myshkin tried to say something, but was still too embarrassed to speak. But Aglaia, who had taken such liberties in her tirade, was not in the least confused, but seemed pleased indeed. She got up at once, still grave and earnest as before, looking as though she had prepared herself and was only waiting to be asked, stepped into the middle of the verandah, and stood facing Myshkin, who was still sitting in his armchair. Everyone stared at her with some surprise, and almost all of them, Prince S—, her sisters and her mother, looked with an uncomfortable feeling at this new prank, which had already gone too far. But it was evident that what delighted Aglaia was just the affectation with which she was beginning the ceremony of reading. Her mother was on the point of sending her back to her seat, but at the very instant when Aglaia began to recite the well-known ballad, two more visitors entered the verandah from the street, talking loudly. These visitors were General Epanchin and a young man who followed him. Their entrance caused a slight commotion.

Chapter 7

The young man, accompanying the general, was about twenty-eight, tall and well built, with a fine and intelligent face and a humorous and mocking look in his big shining black eyes. Aglaia did not even look round at him. She went on reciting the verses, still affecting to look at no one but Myshkin and addressing him only. He realised that she was doing it all with some object. But the new arrivals did, at any rate, somewhat lessen the awkwardness of his position. Seeing them, he stood up, nodded cordially to the general from a distance, signed to them not to interrupt the recitation, and succeeded in retreating behind his armchair. Then leaning with his arm on the back of it, he was able to listen to the ballad in a more convenient and less 'absurd' position than before. Lizaveta Prokofyevna for her part motioned twice peremptorily to the visitors to stand still. Myshkin was much interested in his new visitor, the young man who was with General Epanchin. He knew he must be Yevgeny Pavlovitch Radomsky, of whom he had heard a good deal already, and thought more than once. He was only perplexed at his civilian dress; he had heard that Yevgeny Pavlovitch was a military man. A mocking smile played about the young man's lips all the time the poem was being recited, as though he too had heard something about the 'poor knight'.

'Perhaps it was his idea,' thought Myshkin to himself.

But it was quite different with Aglaia. The affectation and pompousness with which she began the recitation was replaced by earnestness and a deep consciousness of the spirit and meaning of the poem. She spoke the lines with such noble simplicity that by the end of the recitation she not only held the attention of all, but, by her interpretation of the lofty spirit of the ballad, she had, as it were, to some extent justified the exaggerated, affected gravity with which she had so solemnly stepped into the middle of the verandah. That gravity might now be taken to have been only due to the depth, and perhaps even simplicity, of her respect for the poem she had undertaken to interpret. Her eyes shone and a faint, scarcely perceptible shiver of inspiration and ecstasy passed twice over her handsome face. She recited:

'Lived a knight once, poor and simple,
Pale of face with glance austere,
Spare of speech, but with a spirit
Proud, intolerant of fear.
He had had a wondrous vision:
Ne'er could feeble human art
Gauge its deep, mysterious meaning,
It was graven on his heart.
And since then his soul had quivered
With an all-consuming fire,

Never more he looked on women,
Speech with them did not desire.
But he dropped his scarf thenceforward,
Wore a chaplet in its place,
And no more in sight of any
Raised the visor from his face.
Filled with purest love and fervour,
Faith which his sweet dream did yield,
In his blood he traced the letters
N.F.B. upon his shield.
When the Paladins proclaiming
Ladies' names as true love's sign,
Hurled themselves into the battle
On the plains of Palestine,
Lumen coeli, Sancta Rosa!
Shouted he with flaming glance,
And the fury of his menace
Checked the Mussulman's advance.
Then returning to his castle
In far distant country side,
Silent, sad, bereft of reason,
In his solitude he died.'

Recalling that moment later, Myshkin was long after greatly perplexed and tormented by a question to which he could find no answer: how could such a genuine and noble feeling be associated with such unmistakable malice and mockery? Of the existence of the mockery he had no doubt; he understood that clearly and had grounds for it. In the course of the recitation Aglaia had taken the liberty of changing the letters A.M.D. into N.F.B. That he had not misunderstood or misheard this he could have no doubt (it was proved to him afterwards). In any case Aglaia's performance – a joke of course, though too ruthless and thoughtless – was premeditated. Everyone had been talking (and 'laughing') about the poor knight for the last month. And yet as Myshkin recalled afterwards, Aglaia had pronounced those letters without any trace of jest or sneer, without indeed any special emphasis on those letters to suggest their hidden significance. On the contrary, she had uttered those letters with such unchanged gravity, with such innocent and naïve simplicity that one might have supposed that those very letters were in the ballad and printed in the book. Myshkin felt a pang of discomfort and depression.

Lizaveta Prokofyevna, of course, did not notice or understand the change in the letters, nor the allusion in it. General Epanchin understood nothing more than that a poem was being recited. Many of the other listeners understood and were surprised at the boldness of the performance, and also at the motive underlying it, but they were silent and tried to conceal it. But Myshkin was ready to wager that Yevgeny Pavlovitch had not only understood, but was even trying to show he had understood: he smiled with too mocking an air.

'How splendid!' cried Madame Epanchin in genuine enthusiasm, as soon as the recitation was over. 'Whose poem is it?'

'Pushkin's, *Maman*, don't put us to shame, it's a disgrace!' cried Adelaïda.

'It's a wonder I am no sillier with such daughters!' Lizaveta Prokofyevna responded bitterly. 'It's a disgrace! Give me that poem of Pushkin's, as soon as we get home.'

'But I don't believe we've got a Pushkin!'

'There have been two untidy volumes lying about ever since I can remember,' added Alexandra.

'We must send someone, Fyodor or Alexey, by the first train to town to buy one – Alexey would be best. Aglaia, come here! Kiss me, you recited it splendidly, but if you recited it sincerely,' she added almost in a whisper, 'I am sorry for you; if you did it to make fun of him, I can't help blaming your feelings, so that in any case it would have been better not to recite it at all. Do you understand? Go along, miss, I shall have something to say to you presently, we've stayed too long.'

Meanwhile Myshkin greeted General Epanchin, and the general was introducing Yevgeny Pavlovitch Radomsky to him.

'I picked him up on the way here, he was coming from the station, he heard that I was coming here and all the rest were here …'

'I heard that you were here too,' Yevgeny Pavlovitch interrupted, 'and as I had long meant to try and gain not only your acquaintance but your friendship, I didn't want to lose time. You are unwell? I have only just heard …'

'I am perfectly well and very glad to make your acquaintance. I've heard a great deal about you, and even talked about you to Prince S—,' answered Myshkin, holding out his hand.

Mutual courtesies were exchanged, they pressed each other's hands and looked intently into each other's eyes. At once the conversation became general. Myshkin noticed (and he was noticing everything now, rapidly and eagerly, and possibly noticed what was not there at all) that Yevgeny Pavlovitch's civilian dress excited general and very marked surprise, so much so, that for a time all other impressions were effaced and forgotten. It might be conjectured that this change implied something of great consequence. Adelaïda and Alexandra questioned Yevgeny Pavlovitch in perplexity, Prince S—, his relation, even with great uneasiness, and General Epanchin spoke almost with emotion. Aglaia was the only one who looked with perfect composure though with curiosity at Yevgeny Pavlovitch for a moment, as though she were simply trying to decide whether the civilian dress or the military suited him best, but a minute later she turned away and did not look at him again. Lizaveta Prokofyevna, too, did not care to ask any questions, though perhaps she too was rather uneasy. Myshkin fancied that Yevgeny Pavlovitch was not in her good books.

'He has surprised me, amazed me,' Ivan Fyodorovitch repeated in answer to all enquiries. 'I wouldn't believe him when I met him a little while ago in Petersburg. And why so suddenly, that's the puzzle! He is always saying himself there's no need to break the furniture.'

From the conversation that followed, it appeared that Yevgeny Pavlovitch had long ago announced his intention of resigning his commission, but had always spoken of it so flippantly that it had been impossible to take his words seriously. He always talked, indeed, with such a jesting air of serious things that it was impossible to make him out, especially if he didn't want to be made out.

'It's only for a time, for some months. A year at most, that I shall be on the retired list,' laughed Radomsky.

'But there is no need of it whatever, as far as I understand your position, at least,' General Epanchin kept urging hotly.

'But to visit my estates? You advised it yourself; besides, I want to go abroad …'

But the subject was soon changed; though the over-prominent and still persistent uneasiness seemed excessive to Myshkin, as he watched it, and he divined that there was some special reason for it.

'So the "poor knight" is on the scene again?' Yevgeny Pavlovitch queried, approaching Aglaia.

To Myshkin's surprise she looked at him perplexed and questioning, as though to give him to understand that the 'poor knight' -was a subject which she could not possibly touch upon with him, and that she did not even comprehend his question.

'But it's too late, too late to send to town for a copy of Pushkin tonight, it's too late,' Kolya maintained in exasperation to Lizaveta Prokofyevna. 'I've told you three thousand times it's too late.'

'Yes, it really is too late to send to town now,' Yevgeny Pavlovitch intervened here, too, hurriedly leaving Aglaia, 'I believe the shops are shut by now in Petersburg, it's past eight,' he declared, looking at his watch.

'Since you have waited so long without missing it, you can wait till tomorrow,' put in Adelaïda.

'And it's not the thing for people of the best society to be too much interested in literature,' added Kolya. 'Ask Yevgeny Pavlovitch. It's more correct to be keen on a yellow charabanc with red wheels.'

'You are talking in quotations again, Kolya,' observed Adelaïda.

'But he never speaks except in quotations,' chimed in Yevgeny Pavlovitch, 'he takes whole phrases out of the reviews. I've long had the pleasure of knowing Nikolay Ardalionovitch's conversation, but this time he is not talking in quotations. Nikolay Ardalionovitch is plainly alluding to my yellow charabanc with red wheels. But I have exchanged it, you are behind the times.'

Myshkin listened to what Radomsky was saying. He thought that his manners were excellent, modest and lively, and he was particularly pleased to hear him reply with perfect equality and friendliness to the gibes of Kolya.

'What is it?' asked Lizaveta Prokofyevna, addressing Vera, Lebedyev's daughter, who was standing before her with some large, almost new and finely bound volumes in her hands.

'Pushkin,' said Vera, 'our Pushkin. Father told me to offer it to you.'

'How is this? How can it be?' cried Lizaveta Prokofyevna in surprise.

'Not as a present, not as a present! I wouldn't take the liberty!' Lebedyev skipped forward from behind his daughter. 'At cost price. This is our own Pushkin handed down in the family, Annenkov's edition, which cannot be bought nowadays – at cost price. I offer it with veneration, wishing to sell it and so to satisfy the honourable impatience of your excellency's most honourable literary feelings.'

'Well, if you'll sell it, thank you. You won't be a loser by it, you may be sure. Only don't play the fool, please sir. I've heard that you are very well read, we'll have a talk one day. Will you bring them yourself?'

'With veneration and ... respectfulness!' Lebedyev grimaced with extraordinary satisfaction, taking the books from his daughter.

'Well, mind you don't lose them! Take them, even without respectfulness, but only on condition,' she added, scanning him carefully, 'that I only admit you to the door and don't intend to receive you today. Send your daughter Vera at once, if you will, I like her very much.'

'Why don't you tell him about those people?' said Vera, addressing her father impatiently, 'they'll come in of themselves, if you don't, they've begun to be noisy. Lyov Nikolayevitch,' she said, addressing Myshkin, who had already taken his hat, 'there are four men come to see you, they've been waiting a long time, scolding, but father won't let them in to you!'

'Who are they?' asked Myshkin.

'They've come on business, they say, only if you don't let them in now, they'll be sure to stop you on the way. You'd better see them, Lyov Nikolayevitch, and then you'll be rid of them. Gavril Ardalionovitch and Ptitsyn are talking to them – but they won't listen to them.'

'The son of Pavlishtchev, the son of Pavlishtchev! They are not worth it, they are not worth it!' said Lebedyev, waving his hands, 'they are not worth listening to and it would be out of place for you to disturb yourself on their account, most illustrious prince, they are not worth it...'

'The son of Pavlishtchev! Good heavens!' cried Myshkin extremely disconcerted. 'I know but... you see, I... I asked Gavril Ardalionovitch to attend to that. Gavril Ardalionovitch told me just now ...'

But Gavril Ardalionovitch had already come out of the house on to the verandah. Ptitsyn followed him. In the next room there were sounds of uproar and the loud voice of General Ivolgin, who seemed to be trying to shout down several of the others. Kolya ran indoors at once.

'This is very interesting!' observed Yevgeny Pavlovitch aloud.

'So he knows about it!' thought Myshkin.

'What son of Pavlishtchev? … And what son of Pavlishtchev can there be?' General Epanchin asked, in amazement, looking at everyone with curiosity, and observing with surprise from their faces that he was the only one who knew nothing about this new development.

The excitement and expectation was general indeed. Myshkin was profoundly astonished that such an entirely personal affair could already have roused so much interest in everyone here.

'It will be a very good thing if you put a stop to this at once and yourself!' said Aglaia, going up to Myshkin with particular earnestness, 'and allow us all to be your witnesses. They are trying to throw mud at you, Prince, you must defend yourself triumphantly, and I am awfully glad for you.'

'I want this disgusting claim to be stopped at last, too,' cried Madame Epanchin. 'Give it to them well, Prince, don't spare them! My ears have been tingling with this business, and it's been spoiling my temper on your account. Besides, it will be interesting to look at them. Call them in and we'll sit down. It's a good idea of Aglaia's. You've heard something about it, Prince?' she added addressing Prince S—.

'Of course I have; in your house. But I am particularly anxious to have a look at these young people,' answered Prince S—.

'These are what are meant by nihilists, aren't they?'

'No! They are not to say nihilists,' said Lebedyev, stepping forward, and almost shaking with excitement. 'They are different, a special sort. My nephew tells me they have gone far beyond the nihilists. You are wrong if you think you'll abash them by your presence, your excellency, they won't be abashed. Nihilists are sometimes well informed people, anyway, even learned, but these have gone further because they are first of all men of business. This is a sort of sequel to nihilism, not in a direct line, but obliquely, by hearsay, and they don't express themselves in newspaper articles, but directly in action. It's not a question of the irrationality of Pushkin, or someone, for instance, nor the necessity of the breaking up of Russia into parts, no, now they claim as a right that, if one wants anything very much, one is not to be checked by any obstacles, even though one might have to do for half a dozen people to gain one's ends. But all the same, Prince, I should not advise you …'

But Myshkin had already gone to open the door to the visitors.

'You are slandering them, Lebedyev,' he said, smiling, 'your nephew has hurt your feelings very much. Don't believe him, Lizaveta Prokofyevna. I assure you that Gorskys and Danilovs are only exceptions, and these are only. . mistaken. But I should have preferred not to see them here, before everyone. Excuse me, Lizaveta Prokofyevna, they'll come in, I'll show them to you and then take them away. Come in, gentlemen!'

He was more worried by another painful thought. He wondered: had not someone arranged this business beforehand for that time, for that hour, in the presence of those witnesses and perhaps in anticipation of his shame rather than his triumph? But he felt too sad at the thought of his 'monstrous and wicked suspiciousness.' He felt that he would have died if anyone had known he had such an idea in his head, and at the moment when his guests walked in, he was genuinely ready to believe that he was lower in a moral sense than the lowest around him.

Five persons entered, four new arrivals followed by General Ivolgin in a state of heated agitation and violent loquacity. 'He is on my side, no doubt,' thought Myshkin, with a smile. Kolya slipped in among them; he was talking hotly to Ippolit, who was one of the visitors. Ippolit listened grinning.

Myshkin made his visitors sit down. They all looked so young, hardly grown up indeed, that their visit and the attention paid them seemed strange. Ivan Fyodorovitch, for instance, who knew nothing about this 'new development,' and could not make it out, was quite indignant at the sight of their youthfulness, and would certainly have made some sort of protest, had he not been checked by his wife's unaccountable eagerness on behalf of Myshkin's private affairs. He remained, however, partly out of curiosity, and partly from kind-heartedness, hoping to help, or at least to be of use by the exercise of his authority. But General Ivolgin's bow to him, from the distance, roused his indignation again; he frowned and made up his mind to be consistently silent.

Of the four young men who came in, one, however, was a man of thirty, the retired lieutenant, who had been one of Rogozhin's crew, the boxer, 'who had in his time given as much as fifteen roubles each to beggars.' It could be guessed that he had come to stand by the others as a faithful friend, and if necessity arose, to support them. The foremost and most prominent of the others was the young man to whom the designation 'the son of Pavlishtchev' had been given, though he introduced himself as Antip Burdovsky. He was a young man poorly and untidily dressed. The sleeves of his coat shone like a mirror; his greasy waistcoat was buttoned up to the neck; his linen had disappeared entirely; his incredibly dirty black silk scarf was twisted like a rope. His hands were unwashed, he was fair and his face, which was covered with pimples, had, if one may so express it, an air of innocent insolence. He was about twenty-two, thin and not short. There was not a trace of irony or introspection in his face, nothing but a complete blank conviction of his own rights; and, at the same time, something like a strange and incessant craving to be and feel insulted. He spoke with excitement, hurrying and stuttering, hardly articulating the words, as though he had an impediment in his speech, or even were a foreigner, though he was, as a fact, entirely Russian by birth. He was accompanied, first, by Lebedyev's nephew, already known to the reader, and, secondly, by Ippolit. The latter was a very young man, seventeen or possibly eighteen, with an intelligent but always irritable expression, and terrible signs of illness in his face. He was thin as a skeleton, pale and yellow, his eyes gleamed, and two hectic spots glowed on his cheeks. He coughed incessantly; every word, almost every breath, was followed by gasping. He was evidently in the last stage of consumption. He looked as though he could scarcely live for more than another two or three weeks. He was very tired and before anyone else he sank into a chair. The other visitors were rather ceremonious and even a little embarrassed on entering; they had an important air, however, and were obviously afraid of failing to keep up their dignity in some way, which was strangely out of harmony with their reputation for despising all useless worldly trivialities, conventions and almost everything in the world except their own interests.

'Antip Burdovsky,' said 'the son of Pavlishtchev,' in a hurried stutter.

'Vladimir Doktorenko,' Lebedyev's nephew introduced himself clearly, distinctly, as though boasting of the fact that his name was Doktorenko.

'Keller,' muttered the retired lieutenant.

'Ippolit Terentyev,' squeaked the last of the party in an unexpectedly shrill voice.

All of them were sitting at last on chairs facing Myshkin; they had all introduced themselves, frowned and shifted their caps from one hand to the other to keep themselves in countenance. All of them seemed on the point of speaking, but remained silent, waiting for something with a defiant air, which seemed to say, 'no, my friend, you are wrong there, you won't take us in.' One felt that someone had only to utter one word to start them, and they would all begin talking at once, interrupting and tripping each other up.

Chapter 8

'Gentlemen, I did not expect any of you,' Myshkin began, 'I've been ill till today, and I asked Gavril Ardalionovitch Ivolgin to deal with your business (he turned to Antip Burdovsky) a month ago, as I informed you at the time. However, I have no objection to a personal explanation, but you must admit that such a time ... I suggest you should go with me into another room, if you won't keep me long ... My friends are here now, and believe me ...'

'As many friends as you like, but allow us,' Lebedyev's nephew broke in in a very reproving tone, though he did not raise his voice, 'allow us to point out that you might have treated us more politely, and not have left us waiting two hours in your servants' room ...'

'And of course ... I too ... this is behaving like a prince ... and this is ... I suppose you are the general! But I am not your servant! And ... I...' Antip Burdovsky muttered, spluttering with extraordinary excitement, with trembling lips and a voice broken with resentment. He seemed suddenly to burst or explode, but was at once in such a hurry that at the tenth word one could not follow him.

'It was like a prince!' Ippolit cried in a shrill cracked voice.

'If I were treated like that,' muttered the boxer, 'that is, if it were my personal affair, as a man of honour, if I were in Burdovskv's place ... I...'

'Gentlemen I only heard this minute that you were here, I assure you,' Myshkin repeated again.

'We are not afraid of your friends, Prince, whoever they may be, for we are within our rights,' Lebedyev's nephew declared again.

'But what right had you, let me ask,' Ippolit squeaked again, by now extremely excited, 'to submit Burdovsky's case to the judgement of your friends; anyone can see what the judgement of your friends would be!'

'But if you don't wish to speak here, Mr Burdovsky,' Myshkin succeeded in interpellating at last, staggered by such an opening, 'I tell you, let us go into another room at once, and I repeat that I only heard of you all this very minute ...'

'But you've no right to, you've no right, you've no right! Your friends ... So there!' Burdovsky gabbled suddenly again, looking wildly and apprehensively about him, and the more shy and mistrustful he was, the more heated he became. 'You have no right.'

And having uttered those words he stopped abruptly, as it were with a sudden snap, and fixing his short-sighted, extremely prominent and bloodshot eyes on Myshkin, he stared at him with dumb enquiry, his whole body bent forward. This time Myshkin was so surprised that he too was speechless, and gazed open-eyed, unable to utter a word.

'Lyov Nikolayevitch!' Lizaveta Prokofyevna called to him suddenly, 'read this at once, this minute, it has to do with your business.'

She hurriedly held out to him a weekly comic paper, and pointed with her finger at the article. As soon as the visitors came in, Lebedyev had skipped sideways up to Lizaveta Prokofyevna, with whom he was trying to ingratiate himself, and without uttering a word he had pulled this paper out of his side-pocket and had put it just before her eyes, pointing to a marked passage. What Lizaveta Prokofyevna had had time to read had excited and upset her extremely.

'But wouldn't it be better not aloud,' faltered Myshkin, very much embarrassed, 'I could read it alone ... afterwards.'

'Then you had better read it, read it at once, aloud!' said Lizaveta Prokofyevna, addressing Kolya, impatiently snatching the paper from Myshkin, almost before he had time to touch it. 'Read it aloud to all, so that everyone may hear.'

Lizaveta Prokofyevna was an excitable lady, and readily carried away, so that sometimes she would all of a sudden, without stopping to think, heave all anchors, and launch into the open sea regardless of the weather. Ivan Fyodorovitch moved uneasily. While all involuntarily stopped for the first minute and waited in perplexity,

Kolya opened the newspaper and began aloud at the passage which Lebedyev darted up to point out to him, 'Proletarians and noble scions, an episode of daily and everyday robbery! Progress! Reform! Justice!

'Strange things happen in our so-called holy Russia, in our age of reforms and of joint-stock enterprises, the age of national movements and of hundreds of millions of roubles sent abroad every year, the age of encouraging commerce and of the paralysis of industry, and so on and so on, one cannot enumerate all, gentlemen, and so – straight to the point. Here is a strange anecdote about a scion of our decaying nobility *(de profundis)*, one of those scions whose grandfathers were ruined by roulette, whose fathers have to serve as lieutenants and ensigns in the army, and usually die charged with some innocent misuse of public money; while they themselves, like the hero of our story, either grow up idiots, or are mixed up in criminal cases, in which, however, they are acquitted by the jury in the hope of their reformation, or else they end by perpetrating one of those pranks which amaze the public and disgrace our already degraded age. Our scion, wearing gaiters like a foreigner, and shivering in an unlined cloak, arrived about six months ago in Russia from Switzerland, where he had been under treatment for idiocy (*sic!*). It must be confessed that he was a lucky fellow, so that – to say nothing of the interesting malady for which he was undergoing treatment in Switzerland (can there be a treatment for idiocy, just imagine!) – he may serve as an illustration of the truth of the Russian proverb that a certain class of persons are lucky. Only think. Left a baby at his father's death – they say he was a lieutenant, who died while on his trial for a sudden disappearance at cards of all the company's money, or possibly for an excessive use of the rod on some subordinate (you remember what it was like in old days, gentlemen), our baron was taken and brought up by the charity of a very rich Russian landowner. This Russian landowner, we will call him P—, was the owner in the old golden days of four thousand souls. (The owner of four thousand souls! Do you understand, gentlemen, such an expression? I don't. One must consult an explanatory dictionary, "the tale is new, yet it's hard to believe!") He was apparently one of those drones and sluggards who spend their idle lives abroad, in summer at the waters, and in winter at the Parisian Chateau-de-Fleurs, where in the course of their lives they have left incredible sums. One may say with certainty that at least one third of the tribute paid in old days by the serfs went into the pockets of the proprietor of the Parisian Chateau-de-Fleurs (he must have been a fortunate man!). Be that as it may, the light-hearted P— brought up the noble orphan like a prince, engaged tutors and governesses for him (no doubt pretty ones) whom he brought himself by the way from Paris. But the last scion of the noble house was an idiot. The governesses from the Chateau-de-Fleurs were of no use, and up to his twentieth year our scion could not be taught to speak any language, not even his native Russian; though the latter, of course, is excusable. At last the happy whim entered the heart of the Russian serf-owner P—, that the idiot might be taught sense in Switzerland – a logical whim, however: an idle capitalist might naturally suppose that for money one might buy even sense, especially in Switzerland. Five years were spent in Switzerland under the care of a celebrated doctor, and thousands were spent on it. The idiot, of course, did not become sensible, but still, they say, he became like a human being, no great shakes, of course. Suddenly P— died, leaving no will of course. His affairs were as usual in disorder. There was a crowd of greedy heirs, who took not the slightest interest in the last scions of noble families who are treated out of charity in Switzerland for congenital idiocy. The scion, though an idiot, made an effort to deceive his doctor, and succeeded in being treated gratis for two years, so we are told, concealing from him the death of his benefactor. But the doctor was a bit of a rogue himself. Alarmed at the absence of cash and still more at the appetite of his twenty-five-year-old do-nothing, he dressed him up in his old gaiters, made him a present of his worn-out cloak, and out of charity sent him third-class *nach Russland* – to get rid of him. Luck seemed to have turned its back on our hero. But not a bit of it: fortune, which kills off whole provinces with famine, showered all her gifts on this aristocrat, like the cloud in Krylov's fable that passed over the parched fields to empty itself into the ocean. Almost at the very moment of his arrival in Petersburg, a relation of his mother's (who had, of course, been of a merchant's family) died in Moscow, a childless old bachelor, a merchant of the old school and an Old Believer. He left a good round fortune of several millions in hard cash (if it had only been for you and me, readers!) and it all came without dispute to our scion, our baron, who had been cured of idiocy in Switzerland!

Well, it was a very different tune then. A crowd of friends and acquaintances gathered about our gaitered baron, who ran after a notorious beauty of easy virtue. He even picked up relations, and above all he was pursued by perfect crowds of young ladies, hungering and thirsting for lawful matrimony. And, indeed, what could be better? An aristocrat, a millionaire and an idiot – all the qualifications at once, a husband you couldn't come across the like of if you searched for him with the lantern of Diogenes.'

'That ... that passes my comprehension!' shouted Ivan Fyodorovitch, roused to the last pitch of indignation.

'Leave off, Kolya!' Myshkin cried in a supplicating voice.

Exclamations were uttered on all sides.

'Read it! Read it, whatever happens!' Lizaveta Prokofyevna rapped out, evidently making a desperate effort to restrain herself. 'Prince! If you stop him reading, we shall quarrel!'

There was no help for it. Kolya, heated, flushed and agitated, went on reading in a troubled voice.

'But while our quickly made millionaire was floating, so to speak, in the empyrean, quite a new development came on the scene. One morning a visitor called on him with a composed and stern face, dressed modestly and like a gentleman, and evidently of progressive tendencies. In courteous, but dignified, reasonable language, he briefly explained the reason of his visit. He was a well-known lawyer. He had been instructed by a young man and was appearing on his behalf. This young man was neither more nor less than the son of the deceased P—, though he bore a different name. The licentious P— had in his youth seduced a virtuous young girl, a house-serf, but of European education (taking advantage no doubt of his seignorial rights in the old serf days) and remarking the inevitable but approaching consequence of the liaison, he made haste to get her married to a man of honourable character who was engaged in commerce, and even in the service, and had long been in love with the girl. At first he helped the young couple, but soon assistance from him was refused, owing to the honourable character of the husband. Some time passed and P— gradually forgot the girl and the son she had borne him, and afterwards, as we know, he died without making provision for him. Meanwhile his son who was born in lawful wedlock, but grew up under a different name, and completely adopted by the honourable character of his mother's husband, who had, none the less, in the course of time, also died, was thrown entirely on his own resources with an invalid, bedridden, grieving mother, in one of the remote provinces of Russia. He earned his living in the capital by his honourable daily labour, giving lessons in merchant families, and in that way supported himself, first at school, and afterwards while attending courses of profitable lectures with a view to his future advancement, but one can't earn much by lessons at a few coppers an hour, and with an invalid, bedridden mother to keep, though her death at last in the remote province was hardly an alleviation to him. Now the question arises, what would have been a just decision for our noble scion to make? You would doubtless, reader, expect him to say to himself: "I have all my life enjoyed all the gifts of P—; tens of thousands went to Switzerland for my education, governesses and treatment for idiocy; and here I am now with millions while P—'s son is wasting his noble talents giving lessons, though he is not to blame for the misconduct of the wanton father who forgot him. All that has been spent on me ought, by right, to have been spent on him. The vast sums that have been spent on me are, in reality, not mine. It was only the blind mistake of fortune; they ought to have come to the son of P—; they ought to have been used for his benefit, and not for mine, as was done by the fantastic caprice of the frivolous and forgetful P—. If I were quite noble, delicate, just, I ought to give up to his son half of my fortune, but as I am first of all a prudent person, and know only too well that he has no legal claim, I am not going to give him half my millions. But, at any rate, it would be too base and shameless on my part (the scion forgot that it would not be prudent either) if I don't give back now to P—'s son the tens of thousands that were spent by P— on my idiocy. That would only be right and just! For what would have become of me, if P— had not brought me up and had looked after his son instead of me?"

'But no! That is not how such fine gentlemen look at it. In spite of the representations of the young man's lawyer, who had undertaken his cause solely from friendship, and almost against his will, almost by force, in spite of his pointing out the obligations of honesty, honour, justice and even of simple prudence, the Swiss patient remained inflexible, and what do you think? All that would have been nothing, but here we come to what was really unpardonable and not to be excused by any illness, however interesting, this millionaire, who had only just cast off the gaiters of his professor, could not even discern that this noble character, who was wearing himself out giving lessons, was not asking for charity, was not asking for assistance, but for his right and his due, even though he has no legal claim; he does not ask for it even, but his friends demand it on his account. With a majestic air, revelling in the power of using his millions to crush people with impunity, our scion pulls out a fifty-rouble note and sends to the noble young man by way of insulting charity. You refuse to believe it. You are disgusted, you are pained, you utter exclamations of indignation, but that was what he did! The money was, of course, returned to him at once, so to speak, flung back in his face! What resource have we left us? There is no legal claim, there is no resource but publicity. We present the story to the public, guaranteeing its authenticity. One of our well-known humorous writers has perpetrated a charming epigram on the subject which deserves to take a place not only in provincial sketches of Russian life, but even in the capital:

> Dear little Lyov for five long years,
> Wrapped warm in Schneider's cloak,
> Lived like a child and often played
> Some simple foolish joke.
> Then home he came in gaiters tight,
> And found himself an heir,
> And gaily he the students robbed,
> The idiot millionaire!

When Kolya had finished reading, he handed the paper to Myshkin, and without saying a word, rushed away, buried himself in a corner and hid his face in his hands. He felt insufferably ashamed, and his boyish sensitiveness, unaccustomed to such nastiness, was wounded beyond endurance. It seemed to him as though something extraordinary had happened, which had shattered everything, and that he was almost the cause of it by the very fact of having read it aloud.

But everyone seemed to be feeling something of the same sort.

The girls felt very awkward and ashamed. Lizaveta Prokofyevna was struggling with violent anger. She, too, perhaps, was bitterly regretting that she had meddled. Now she was silent. Myshkin felt, as oversensitive people often do in such cases; he was so much ashamed of the conduct of others, he felt such shame for his visitors, that for the first moment he was ashamed to look at them. Ptitsyn, Varya, Ganya, even Lebedyev – all had rather an embarrassed air. The strangest thing was that Ippolit and 'the son of Pavlishtchev' both seemed surprised. Lebedyev's nephew, too, was obviously displeased. The boxer was the only one who sat quite serene, twisting his moustache, with a dignified air and eyes cast down, not from embarrassment, but apparently from modest pride and unmistakable triumph. It was clear that he was delighted with the article.

'This is beyond anything,' General Epanchin muttered in an undertone, 'as though fifty lackeys had met together and composed it.'

'Allow me to ask you, my dear sir, how dare you make such insulting suppositions?' cried Ippolit, trembling all over.

'This, this, this for an honourable man ... you must admit yourself, General, that if it's an honourable man, it's insulting!' muttered the boxer, who also seemed suddenly roused, twisting his moustache and twitching his shoulders and body.

'In the first place, I am not "your dear sir", and in the second place, I have no intention of giving you any explanation,' Ivan Fyodorovitch answered harshly. He was awfully annoyed; he got up from his seat and without saying a word went to the entrance of the verandah and stood on the top step with his back to the party – in violent indignation with his wife, who even now did not think fit to move.

'Friends, friends, allow me to speak at last,' Myshkin exclaimed in distress and agitation, 'and I beg you, let us talk so that we may understand one another. I say nothing about the article, gentlemen, let it alone; only one thing, friends, it's all untrue, what is said in the article; I say so, because you know that yourselves; it's shameful, in fact, so that I should be greatly surprised if any one of you has written it.'

'I knew nothing about the article till this moment,' Ippolit announced. 'I don't approve of the article.'

'Though I knew it was written, I ... I too wouldn't have advised its being published, because it's premature,' added Lebedyev's nephew.

'I knew, but I have the right... I...' muttered 'the son of Pavlishtchev.'

'What! Did you make all that up yourself?' asked Myshkin, looking with curiosity at Burdovsky. 'But it's impossible!'

'We may refuse to recognise your right to ask such questions!' Lebedyev's nephew put in.

'I only wondered that Mr Burdovsky could bring himself... but... I mean to say, since you have given publicity to the case, why were you so offended just now at my talking about it before my friends?'

'At last!' muttered Lizaveta Prokofyevna indignantly.

'And, Prince, you are pleased even to forget,' Lebedyev, unable to restrain himself, threaded his way between the chairs, almost in a fever. 'You are pleased to forget that it was only through your kindness, and the infinite goodness of your heart, you received them and listened to them, and that they have no right to demand anything, especially as you have already put the matter into the hands of Gavril Ardalionovitch, and that, too, you did through your excessive kindness. And now, most illustrious prince, in the midst of your chosen friends, you cannot sacrifice such a company to these gentlemen, and you might, so to speak, turn all these gentlemen out at once into the street, and I, as master of the house, would with the greatest pleasure ...'

'Perfectly right!' General Ivolgin thundered suddenly from the back of the room.

'Enough, Lebedyev, enough, enough,' Myshkin was beginning, but his words were lost in a perfect explosion of indignation.

'No, excuse me, Prince, excuse me, that's not enough now,' bawled Lebedyev's nephew, shouting above everyone. 'Now we must put the case on a firm and clear basis, for it is evidently not understood. There is some legal quibble involved, and on account of that quibble, they threaten to turn us into the street! But is it possible, Prince, you can think us such fools as not to understand that we have no legal claim whatever, and that if the case is analysed from a legal point of view, we have no right to ask for a single rouble? But we thoroughly grasp that, though there is no legal claim, there is a human, natural claim, the claim of common sense and the voice of conscience. And though that claim may not be written in any rotten human code, yet a generous and honest man, in other words, a man of common sense, is bound to remain generous and honest even on points that are not written in the codes. That's why we've come here without any fear of being turned out into the street (as you've threatened just now) because we don't *beg* but demand, and because of the impropriety of our visit at such a late hour (though we didn't come at a late hour, but you kept us waiting in the servants' room). We came, I say, without fear, because we assumed you to be a man of common sense, that is of honour and conscience. Yes, it's true we came in not humbly, not as beggars or cadgers, but with our heads erect, like free men, not a bit with a petition, but with a free and proud request (you hear, not with a petition, but with a request, take that in) we put the question to you directly and with dignity: do you consider yourself right or wrong in Burdovsky's case? Do you admit that you were benefited and perhaps saved from death by Pavlishtchev? If you admit it (and it's evident), do you, after receiving millions, intend or think it just to compensate Pavlishtchev's son in his poverty, even though he does bear the name of Burdovsky? Yes or no? If yes, that is, in other words, if you have what you call in your language honour and conscience, and what we more exactly describe by the term common sense, then satisfy us, and the matter is finished. Satisfy us without entreaties or gratitude on our part; don't expect them of us, for you are doing it not for our sake, but for the sake of justice. If you are unwilling to satisfy us, that is answer *no*, we go away at once and the case is over and we tell you to your face before all your witnesses, that you are a man of coarse intelligence and low development; that for the future you dare not call yourself a man of honour and conscience, and have no right to do so, that you are trying to buy that right too cheap. I've finished. I have put the question. Turn us into the street now, if you dare. You can do it, you have the power. But remember all the same that we demand and we don't beg. We demand, we do not beg!'

Lebedyev's nephew stopped, much excited.

'We demand, we demand, we demand, we don't beg,' Burdovsky gabbled thickly and turned red as a crab.

After the speech made by Lebedyev's nephew, there was a general movement and even a murmur of protest, though everyone in the party was evidently anxious to avoid meddling, except perhaps Lebedyev, who seemed in a perfect fever (strange to say, Lebedyev, though evidently on Myshkin's side, seemed to feel a glow of family pride at the speech of his nephew; anyway, he looked at the company present with a certain peculiar air of satisfaction).

'In my opinion,' Myshkin began in rather a low voice, 'in my opinion, Mr Doktorenko, in half of what you said just now, you are quite right and in the greater half, in fact. And I should agree with you entirely if you hadn't left something out in your speech. I can't tell you what you've left out exactly, I am not capable, but to make your speech quite just, something more is wanted. But we had better turn to the case, gentlemen; tell me, what made you publish that article? There isn't a word in it that isn't slander, so that to my thinking, gentlemen, you've done something mean.'

'Excuse me!'

'My dear sir!'

'This ... this ... this,' was heard at the same time from the excited visitors.

'As for the article,' Ippolit put in, shrilly, 'as for that article, I have told you already that I and the rest don't approve of it! It was written by him here' (he pointed to the boxer, who was sitting beside him); 'it's written disgracefully, I admit, it's written illiterately, and in the jargon used by retired army men like him. He is stupid, and, besides that, is a mercenary fellow, I agree. I tell him so to his face every day, but yet in half of it he was right. Publicity is the legal right of all, and therefore of Burdovsky. He must answer himself for his absurdities. As for my protesting in the name of all against the presence of your friends, I think it necessary to inform you, gentlemen, that I protested simply to assert our rights, but in reality we positively prefer that there should be witnesses, and on our way here we all four agreed that whoever your witnesses might be, if even they were your friends, they could not fail to recognise Burdovsky's claim (because it's a mathematical certainty) so that it's even better that these witnesses are your friends; it will make the truth even more evident.'

'That's true, we agreed about that,' Lebedyev's nephew assented.

'But why did you begin by making such a fuss and outcry about it, if you wanted it?' asked Myshkin in surprise.

'And as for the article, Prince,' put in the boxer, becoming agreeably excited and desperately anxious to put in his word (it might be suspected that the presence of the ladies had a strong and unmistakable effect on him), 'as for the article, I confess that I am the author of it, though my sick friend, whom I am accustomed to excuse on account of his affliction, has just criticised it. But I wrote and I published it in the journal of a friend in the form of a letter.

Only the verses are not mine and really come from the pen of a well-known satirist. I only read it through to Mr Burdovsky, and not all of it, and he at once agreed to let me publish it, but you can see for yourself that I could have published it without his consent. The right to publicity is the right of all, and it's an honourable and beneficial right. I hope you, Prince, are progressive enough not to deny that…'

'I am not going to deny anything, but you must admit that your article …'

'Is severe, you mean? But you know it's for the public benefit, so to say, and, besides, how can one let such a flagrant case pass? So much the worse for the guilty, but the public benefit before everything. As for a little inaccuracy, hyperbole so to say, you wall admit that what matters most is the motive; the object, the intention comes first. What matters is the beneficial example and one can go into the individual case afterwards. And besides there's the style and the comic value of it – and in fact, everybody writes like that, as you know yourself. Ha-ha!'

'But you are quite on a false tack, I assure you, gentlemen,' cried Myshkin. 'You published that article on the supposition that nothing would induce me to satisfy Mr Burdovsky and so you tried to frighten me and revenge yourselves. But how do you know -I may have decided to satisfy Mr Burdovsky's claim. I tell you plainly before everyone here that I will…'

'Come, that's a wise and generous saying from a wise and very generous man!' announced the boxer.

'Heavens!' broke from Lizaveta Prokofyevna.

'This is insufferable,' muttered the general.

'Allow me, friends, allow me, I'll explain the case,' Myshkin besought them. 'Your agent and representative, Tchebarov, came to see me five weeks ago, Mr Burdovsky. Your description of him, Mr Keller, is much too flattering,' Myshkin added, addressing the boxer, and suddenly laughing. 'I didn't like him at all. I realised from the first moment that this Tchebarov was at the bottom of it and that, to speak candidly, he had taken advantage of your simplicity, Mr Burdovsky, to set you on to making this claim.'

'You've no right to … I … am not simple … it's …' Burdovsky stuttered in excitement.

'You've no sort of right to make such suppositions,' Lebedyev's nephew put in sententiously.

'This is insulting in the highest degree,' squeaked Ippolit, 'the supposition is insulting, false and irrelevant!'

'I am sorry, gentlemen, I am sorry,' Myshkin apologised hurriedly, 'please excuse me; it's because I thought it might be better for us to be perfectly open with one another, but it's for you to decide, as you please! I told Tchebarov that, as I was not in Petersburg, I would at once authorise a friend to go into the case, and would let you, Mr Burdovsky, know. I tell you plainly, gentlemen, that the case struck me as simply a swindle, just because of Tchebarov's share in it ... Oh, don't take offence, gentlemen! For goodness' sake, don't take offence,' Myshkin cried in alarm, seeing again the signs of resentment in Burdovsky and of excitement and protest in his friends. 'It can have no reference to you if I do say the case was a swindle. I didn't know any one of you personally then, I didn't even know your names; I only judged by Tchebarov; I speak generally because ... if only you knew how horribly I've been taken in, since I came into my fortune!'

'Prince, you are wonderfully naïve,' Lebedyev's nephew observed ironically.

'Besides, you are a prince and a millionaire! You may possibly be kind-hearted and simple, but even if you are, you can't be an exception to the general law,' Ippolit declared.

'Possibly, gentlemen, very possibly,' Myshkin said hurriedly, 'though I don't know what general law you are speaking of. But let me go on and don't take offence about nothing; I swear I haven't the faintest wish to insult you. And really, gentlemen, one can't say one word sincerely without your being offended at once! But in the first place, it was a great shock to hear of the existence of a son of Pavlishtchev, and in such a terrible situation, as Tchebarov explained to me. Pavlishtchev was my benefactor and my father's friend. Ach, why did you write such falsehoods about my father in your article, Mr Keller? There never was any misappropriation of the company's money, nor ill-treatment of subordinates – of that I am absolutely convinced – and how could you lift your hand to write such a calumny? And what you've said about Pavlishtchev is past all endurance. You speak of that noble man as a frivolous libertine, with as much boldness and positiveness as though you were really speaking the truth, and yet he was one of the most virtuous men in the world! He was a remarkably learned man, he used to correspond with numbers of distinguished men of science, and he spent a great deal of money for the advancement of science. As for his heart and his benevolence, oh, no doubt you were quite right in saying that I was almost an idiot at that time and had no understanding of anything (though I could talk Russian and could understand it), but I can now appreciate all I remember at its true value ...'

'Excuse me,' Ippolit squeaked, 'isn't this too sentimental? We are not children. You meant to come straight to the point; it's going on for ten, remember that.'

'Very well, gentlemen,' Myshkin agreed at once. 'After my first mistrustfulness, I decided that I might have made a mistake and that Pavlishtchev might really have had a son. But I was very much amazed that that son should so readily, that is, I mean so publicly, give away the secret of his birth and disgrace his mother's name. For even at that time Tchebarov threatened me with publicity ...'

'How ridiculous!' cried Lebedyev's nephew.

'You've no right... you've no right!' cried Burdovsky.

'The son is not responsible for the immoral conduct of his father and the mother is not to blame,' Ippolit shrieked hotly.

'All the more reason for sparing her, I should have thought,' Myshkin ventured timidly.

'You are not simply naïve, Prince, you go beyond that, perhaps,' Lebedyev's nephew sneered spitefully.

'And what right had you!' Ippolit squeaked in a most unnatural voice.

'None whatever, none whatever,' Myshkin hurriedly put in. 'You are right there, I admit it, but I couldn't help it. And I said to myself at once, at the time, that I ought not to let my personal feeling come into the case, for if I consider myself bound to satisfy Mr Burdovsky's demands for the sake of my feeling for Pavlishtchev, I ought to satisfy them in any case, that is whether I respected or did not respect Mr Burdovsky. I only began about this, gentlemen, because it did all the same seem to me unnatural for a son to betray his mother's secret so publicly... in fact it was chiefly on that ground that I made up my mind that Tchebarov was a scoundrel and had egged Mr Burdovsky on to such a fraud by deceit.'

'But this is intolerable!' broke from his visitors, some of whom even leapt up from their seats.

'Gentlemen, it was just because of that I decided that poor Mr

Burdovsky must be a simple and helpless person, easily imposed upon by swindlers, and therefore I was all the more bound to help him as a 'son of Pavlishtchev' – first, by opposing Mr Tchebarov, secondly, by my friendly good offices and guidance, and thirdly, I decided to give him ten thousand roubles, that is all that by my reckoning Pavlishtchev could have spent upon me.'

'What, only ten thousand!' shouted Ippolit.

'Well, Prince, you are not at all good in arithmetic or else you are too good at it, though you do pretend to be a simpleton,' cried Lebedyev's nephew.

'I won't agree to take ten thousand,' said Burdovsky.

'Antip, take it!' the boxer prompted him in a clear and rapid whisper, bending across to him over the back of Ippolit's chair. 'Take it, and afterwards we shall see.'

'Listen, Mr Myshkin,' shrieked Ippolit, 'understand that we are not fools, not vulgar fools, as we are probably thought to be by all your visitors, and by these ladies who sneer at us so indignantly, and especially by that grand gentleman' – he pointed to Yevgeny Pavlovitch – 'whom I have not, of course the honour of knowing, though I believe I have heard something about him.'

'Allow me, gentlemen, you misunderstand me again!' Myshkin addressed them in agitation. 'In the first place you, Mr Keller, in your article have described my fortune very inaccurately; I didn't inherit millions at all. I've only perhaps an eighth or a tenth part of what you suppose, and in the next place, tens of thousands were not spent on me in Switzerland. Schneider was paid six hundred roubles a year and he only received that for the first three years, and Pavlishtchev never went to Paris to find pretty governesses, that's a calumny again. In my opinion very much less than ten thousand was spent on me altogether, but I propose to give ten thousand, and you'll admit that I could not offer Mr Burdovsky more in payment of what's due to him, even if I were awfully fond of him, and I could not do so from a feeling of delicacy alone, just because it's paving what is due and not making him a present. I don't know how you can fail to understand that, gentlemen, but still I did mean later on, by my friendship and active sympathy, to compensate the unhappy Mr Burdovsky, who has evidently been deceived, for he could not otherwise have agreed to anything so low as, for instance, publishing this scandal about his mother in Mr Keller's article ... But why are you getting angry again, gentlemen? We shall completely misunderstand each other. Why, it's turned out to be as I thought! I am convinced now by what I see myself that my guess was correct,' Myshkin tried eagerly to persuade them, anxious to pacify their excitement, and not noticing that he was only increasing it.

'Convinced now of what?' They fell upon him almost in a fury.

'Why, in the first place, I've had time to see clearly what Mr Burdovsky is myself, I see now myself what he is ... He is an innocent man, taken in by everyone! A helpless man ... and therefore I ought to spare him, and in the second place, Gavril Ardalionovitch – to whom the case has been entrusted and from whom I heard nothing for a long time, because I was travelling, and afterwards was for three days ill in Petersburg – has just now, an hour ago, at our first interview, told me that he has seen through Tchebarov's schemes, that he has proofs, and that Tchebarov is just what I took him to be. I know, gentlemen, that many people look upon me as an idiot and, owing to my reputation for giving away money freely, Tchebarov thought that he could easily impose upon me, and he reckoned just on my feeling for Pavlishtchev. But the chief point is – hear me out, gentlemen, hear me out! – the chief point is that it appears now that Mr Burdovsky is not a son of Pavlishtchev at all. Gavril Ardalionovitch has just told me, and he assures me that he has positive proof of it. Well, what do you think of that! One can scarcely believe it after all the to-do that has been made! And listen, there are positive proofs! I can't believe it yet, I don't believe it myself, I assure you I am still doubting, because Gavril Ardalionovitch has not had time to give me all the details yet, but that Tchebarov is a scoundrel there can be no doubt at all now! He has imposed upon poor Mr Burdovsky and on all of you, gentlemen, who have so nobly come to support your friend (for he obviously needs support, I understand that, of course!); he has imposed upon all of you, and has involved you all in a fraudulent business, for you know it really is fraud, it's swindling!'

'How swindling?... Not the son of Pavlishtchev? How is it possible?' exclamations were heard on all sides.

All Burdovsky's party were in inexpressible perturbation.

'Yes, of course, it's swindling! For if Mr Burdovsky turns out to be not the son of Pavlishtchev, his claim is simply fraudulent (that is, of course, if he knew the truth), but the fact is he has been deceived, that's why I insist on his character's being cleared; that's why I say that he deserves to be pitied for his simplicity, and can't be left without help; if it were not so, he would be a scoundrel too. But I am convinced that he did not understand! I was just in the same state before I went to Switzerland; I too, used to mutter incoherently – one tries to express oneself and can't. Understand that I can sympathise very well because I am almost the same, so I may be allowed to speak of it. And all the same – although there is no 'son of Pavlishtchev,' and it all turns out to be humbug – I haven't changed my mind and am ready to give up ten thousand in memory of Pavlishtchev. Before Mr Burdovsky came on the scene I meant to devote ten thousand to founding a school in memory of Pavlishtchev, but it makes no difference now whether it's for a school or for Mr Burdovsky, for though Mr Burdovsky is not the son of Pavlishtchev, he is almost as good as a son of his, because he has been so wickedly deceived; he genuinely believed himself to be the son of Pavlishtchev! Listen to Gavril Ardalionovitch, friends, let us make an end of this, don't be angry, don't be excited, sit down! Gavril Ardalionovitch will explain everything to us directly, and I confess I shall be very glad to hear all the details myself. He says he has even been to Pskov to see your mother, Mr Burdovsky, who hasn't died at all, as they've made you say in the article … Sit down, gentlemen, sit down!'

Myshkin sat down and succeeded in making Burdovsky and his friends, who had leapt up from their seats, sit down again. For the last ten or twenty minutes he had been talking eagerly and loudly, with impatient haste, carried away and trying to talk above the rest, and he couldn't of course help bitterly regretting afterwards some assumptions and some phrases that escaped him now. If he hadn't himself been worked up and roused almost beyond control, he would not have allowed himself so baldly and hurriedly to utter aloud certain conjectures and unnecessarily candid statements. He had no sooner sat down in his place than a burning remorse set his heart aching. Besides the fact that he had 'insulted' Burdovsky by so publicly assuming that he had suffered from the same disease for which he himself had been treated in Switzerland, the offer of the ten thousand that had been destined for a school had been made to his thinking coarsely and carelessly, like a charity, and just because it had been spoken of aloud before people. 'I ought to have waited and offered it to him tomorrow, alone,' Myshkin thought at once, 'now, perhaps, there will be no setting it right! Yes, I am an idiot, a real idiot!' he decided in a paroxysm of shame and extreme distress.

Meanwhile Gavril Ardalionovitch, who had hitherto stood on one side persistently silent, came forward at Myshkin's invitation, took up his stand beside him and began calmly and clearly giving an account of the case that had been entrusted to him by the prince. All talk was instantly silenced. Everyone listened with extreme curiosity, especially Burdovsky's party.

Chapter 9

'You certainly will not deny,' Gavril Ardalionovitch began, directly addressing Burdovsky, who was listening to him intently, and obviously in violent agitation, his eyes round with wonder, 'you will not attempt, and will not wish seriously to deny, that you were born just two years after your worthy mother was legally married to Mr Burdovsky, your father. The date of your birth can be too easily proved, so that the distortion of this fact – so insulting to you and your mother – in Mr Keller's article must be ascribed simply to the playfulness of Mr Keller's own imagination; he, no doubt, supposed he was making your claim stronger by this statement, and so promoting your interest. Mr Keller says that he read some of the article to you beforehand, but not the whole of it… there can be no doubt that he did not read so far as that passage …'

'No, I didn't as a fact,' the boxer interrupted, 'but all the facts were given me by a competent person, I…'

'Excuse me, Mr Keller,' interposed Gavril Ardalionovitch, 'allow me to speak. I assure you, your article will have its turn later, and then you can make your explanation, but now we had better take things in their proper order. Quite by chance with the help of my sister, Varvara Ardalionovna Ptitsyn, I obtained from her intimate friend, Madame Zubkov, a widow lady who has an estate in the country, a letter written to her by the late Mr Pavlishtchev from abroad, twenty-four years ago. Making Madame Zubkov's acquaintance, I applied, at her suggestion, to a distant relation who was in his day a great friend of Mr Pavlishtchev, the retired Colonel Vyazovkin. I succeeded in getting from him two more letters of Mr Pavlishtchev's, also written from abroad. From these three letters, from the facts and dates mentioned in them, it can be positively proved beyond all possibility of doubt or dispute, that he had gone abroad just a year and a half before you were born, Mr Burdovsky, and that he remained abroad for three years. Your mother, as you know, has never been out of Russia. For the present I will not read these letters. It's late now; I simply announce the fact. But if you care to fix a time to see me, tomorrow morning if you like, Mr Burdovsky, and bring your witnesses – as many as you please – and experts to examine the handwriting, I have no doubt that you cannot but be convinced of the obvious truth of the facts I have laid before you. If this is so, the whole case of course, falls to the ground and is over.'

Again general commotion and intense excitement followed. Burdovsky himself suddenly got up from his chair.

'If it's so, I've been deceived, deceived, not by Tchebarov, but long, long before. I don't want any experts, I don't want to see you, I believe you, I withdraw my claim ... I won't agree to the ten thousand ... Goodbye.'

He took up his cap and pushed away his chair to go out.

'If you can, Mr Burdovsky,' Gavril Ardalionovitch stopped him softly and sweetly, 'stay another five minutes. Some other extremely important facts have come to light in this case, for you at any rate they are very interesting. To my thinking, you should not remain in ignorance of them, and perhaps it will be pleasanter for you if the case can be completely cleared up ...'

Burdovsky sat down without speaking, with his head bowed, seemingly lost in thought. Lebedyev's nephew, who had got up to follow him, sat down too; though he had not lost his self-possession and his boldness, he seemed greatly perplexed. Ippolit was scowling, dejected, and apparently very much astonished. But at that moment he was coughing so violently that he stained his handkerchief with blood. The boxer was almost in dismay.

'Ech, Antip!' he cried, bitterly. 'I told you at the time ... the day before yesterday, that perhaps you really weren't Pavlishtchev's son!'

There was a sound of smothered laughter, two or three laughed louder than the rest.

'The fact you stated just now, Mr Keller,' Gavril Ardalionovitch caught him up, 'is very valuable. Nevertheless, I have a right to assert, on the most precise evidence, that though Mr Burdovsky of course knew very well the date of his birth, he was in complete ignorance of the circumstance of Mr Pavlishtchev's residence abroad, where he spent the greater part of his life, only returning to Russia at brief intervals. Besides, the fact of his going away at that time was not so remarkable as to be remembered twenty years after, even by those who knew Pavlishtchev well, to say nothing of Mr Burdovsky, who was not born at the time. It has turned out, of course, not impossible to establish the fact, but I must own that the facts I've collected came to me quite by chance, and might well not have come into my hands. So that this evidence was really almost impossible for Mr Burdovsky, or even Tchebarov, to obtain, even if they had thought of obtaining it. But they may well not have thought of it…'

'Allow me, Mr Ivolgin,' Ippolit suddenly interrupted, irritably, 'what's all this bobbery for, if I may ask. The case has been cleared up, we agree to accept the most important fact, why drag out a tedious and offensive rigmarole about it? You want, perhaps, to brag of your cleverness in investigation, to display before us and the prince what a fine detective you are? Or are you undertaking to excuse and justify Mr Burdovsky by proving that he got mixed up in this business through ignorance? But that impudence, Sir! Burdovsky has no need of your apologies and your justification, let me tell you! It's painful for him, it's trying for him; anyway, he is in an awkward position, you ought to see that and understand it.'

'Enough, Mr Teremyev, enough,' Gavril Ardalionovitch succeeded in interrupting, 'be calm, don't excite yourself, I am afraid you are not at all well? I feel for you. If you like, I've finished, or rather I am obliged to state briefly only those facts which I am convinced it would be a good thing to know in full detail,' he added, noticing a general movement suggestive of impatience. 'I only want to state, with proofs, for the information of all that are interested, that Mr Pavlishtchev bestowed so much kindness and care on your mother, Mr Burdovsky, only because she was the sister of a serf-girl with whom Mr Pavlishtchev was in love in his early youth, and so much so that he would certainly have married her if she had not died suddenly. I have proofs that this perfectly true and certain fact is very little known, or perhaps quite forgotten. Further, I could inform you how your mother was taken by Pavlishtchev at ten years old, and brought up by him as though she had been a relation, that she had a considerable dowry set apart for her, and that the trouble he took about her gave rise to extremely disquieting rumours among Pavlishtchev's numerous relations. It was even thought that he was going to marry his ward, but it ended by her marrying in her twentieth year, by her own choice (and that I can prove in a most certain way) a surveying clerk called Burdovsky. I have collected some well-authenticated facts to prove that your father, Mr Burdovsky, who was anything but a business man, gave up his post on receiving your mother's dowry of fifteen thousand roubles, entered upon commercial speculations, was deceived, lost his capital, took to drink to drown his grief, and fell ill in consequence and finally died prematurely, eight years after marrying your mother. Then, according to your mother's own testimony, she was left utterly destitute, and would have come to grief entirely, if it had not been for the constant and generous assistance of Mr Pavlishtchev, who allowed her six hundred roubles a year. There is ample evidence too, that he was extremely fond of you as a child. From this evidence, and from what your mother tells me, it seems that he was fond of you chiefly because you looked like a wretched, miserable child, and had the appearance of a cripple and could not speak plainly, and as I have learnt on well-authenticated evidence, Pavlishtchev had all his life a specially tender feeling for everything afflicted and unfairly treated by nature, particularly children – a fact of great importance in our case, to my thinking. Finally, I can boast of having found out a fact of prime importance, that is, that this extreme fondness of Pavlishtchev for you (by his efforts you were admitted to the gymnasium and taught under special supervision), little by little led the relations of Pavlishtchev and the members of his household to imagine that you were his son, and that your father was deceived by his wife. But it's noteworthy that this idea only grew into a general conviction in the latter years of Pavlishtchev's life when all his relations were alarmed about his will, and when the original facts were forgotten and it was impossible to investigate them. No doubt that idea came to your ears too, Mr Burdovsky, and took complete possession of you. Your mother, whose acquaintance I've had the honour of making, knew of these rumours, but to this day she does not know (I concealed it from her too) that you, her son, were dominated by this idea. I found your much respected mother, Mr Burdovsky, in Pskov, ill and extremely poor, as she has been ever since the death of Pavlishtchev. She told me with tears of gratitude that she was only supported by you and your help. She expects a great deal of you in the future, and believes earnestly in your future success ...'

'This is really insupportable!' Lebedyev's nephew exclaimed loudly and impatiently. 'What's the object of this romance?'

'It's disgusting, it's unseemly!' said Ippolit with an abrupt movement.

But Burdovsky noticed nothing and did not stir.

'What's the object of it? What's it for?' said Gavril Ardalionovitch with sly wonder, maliciously preparing for his conclusion. 'Why, in the first place, Mr Burdovsky is perhaps now fully convinced that Mr Pavlishtchev loved him from generosity and not as his son. This fact alone it was essential that Mr Burdovsky should know, since he upheld Mr Keller and approved of him when his article was read just now. I say this because I look upon you as an honourable man, Mr Burdovsky. In the second place, it appears that there was not the least intention of robbery or swindling in the case, even in Tchebarov; that's an important point for me too, because the prince, speaking warmly just now, mentioned that I shared his opinion of the dishonest and swindling element in the case. On the contrary, there was absolute faith in it on all sides, and though Tchebarov may really be a great rogue, in this case he appears as nothing worse than a sharp and scheming attorney. He hoped to make a good deal out of it, as a lawyer, and his calculation was not only acute and masterly, it was absolutely safe; it was based on the readiness with which the prince gives away his money and his gratitude and respect for Pavlishtchev, and what is more, on the prince's well-known chivalrous views as to the obligations of honour and conscience. As for Mr Burdovsky, personally, one may even say that, thanks to certain ideas of his, he was so worked upon by Tchebarov and his other friends that he took up the case hardly from self interest, but almost as a service to truth, progress, and humanity. Now after what I have told you, it has become clear to all that Mr Burdovsky is an innocent man, in spite of all appearances, and the prince, more readily and zealously than before, will offer him his friendly assistance, and that substantial help to which he referred just now when he spoke of schools and of Pavlishtchev.'

'Stay, Gavril Ardalionovitch, stay!' cried Myshkin, in genuine dismay, but it was too late.

'I have said, I have told you three times already,' cried Burdovsky irritably, 'that I don't want the money, I won't take it… why… I don't want to … I am going!'

And he was almost running out of the verandah. But Lebedyev's nephew seized him by the arm and whispered something to him. Burdovsky quickly turned back, and pulling a big unsealed envelope out of his pocket, threw it on a table near Myshkin.

'Here is the money! How dared you! How dared you! The money!'

'The two hundred and fifty roubles which you dared to send him as a charity by Tchebarov!' Doktorenko explained.

'The article said fifty!' cried Kolya.

'It's my fault,' said Myshkin, going up to Burdovsky. 'I've done you a wrong, Burdovsky, but I didn't send it you as a charity, believe me. I am to blame now… I was to blame before.' (Myshkin was much distressed, he looked weak and exhausted, and his words were disconnected.) 'I talked of swindling, but I didn't mean you, I was mistaken. I said that you … were afflicted as I am. But you are not like me, you … give lessons, you support your mother. I said that you cast shame on your mother's name, but you love her, she says so herself… I didn't know, Gavril Ardalionovitch had not told me everything. I am to blame. I ventured to offer you ten thousand, but I am to blame, I ought to have done it differently, and now … it can't be done because you despise me …'

'This is a madhouse!' cried Lizaveta Prokofyevna.

'Of course it's a house of madmen!' Aglaia could not refrain from saying, sharply.

But her words were lost in the general uproar; all were talking loudly and discussing, some disputing, others laughing. Ivan Fyodorovitch Epanchin was roused to the utmost pitch of indignation, and with an air of wounded dignity he waited for Lizaveta Prokofyevna. Lebedyev's nephew put in the last word, 'Yes, Prince, one must do you justice, you do know how to make use of your … well, illness (to express it politely); you've managed to offer your friendship and money in such an ingenious way that now it's impossible for an honourable man to take it under any circumstances. That's either a bit too innocent or a bit too clever … You know best which.'

'Excuse me, gentlemen!' cried Gavril Ardalionovitch, who had meantime opened the envelope, 'there are not two hundred and fifty roubles here, there's only a hundred. I say so, Prince, that there may be no misunderstanding.'

'Let it be, let it be!' cried Myshkin, waving his hands at Gavril Ardalionovitch.

'No, don't let it be.' Lebedyev's nephew caught it up at once. 'Your "let it be" is an insult to us, Prince. We don't hide ourselves, we declare it openly, yes, there are only a hundred roubles in it, instead of two hundred and fifty, but isn't it just the same ...'

'N-no, it's not just the same,' Gavril Ardalionovitch managed to interpolate, with an air of naïve perplexity.

'Don't interrupt me; we are not such fools as you think, Mr Lawyer,' cried Lebedyev's nephew, with spiteful vexation. 'Of course a hundred roubles is not two hundred and fifty, and it's not just the same, but the principle is what matters. The initiative is the great thing, and that a hundred and fifty roubles are missing is only a detail. What matters is, that Burdovsky does not accept your charity, your excellency, that he throws it in your face, and in that sense it makes no difference whether it's a hundred or two hundred and fifty. Burdovsky hasn't accepted the ten thousand, as you've seen; he wouldn't have brought back the hundred roubles, if he had been dishonest. That hundred and fifty roubles has gone to Tchebarov for his journey to see the prince. You may laugh at our awkwardness, at our inexperience in business; you've tried your very utmost to make us ridiculous, but don't dare to say we are dishonest. We'll all club together, Sir, to pay back that hundred and fifty roubles to the prince, we'll pay it back if it has to be a rouble at a time and we'll pay it back with interest. Burdovsky is poor, Burdovsky hasn't millions, and Tchebarov sent in his account after his journey. We hoped to win the case ... who would not have done the same in his place?'

'Who would not?' exclaimed Prince S—.

'I shall go out of my mind here!' cried Madame Epanchin.

'It reminds me,' laughed Yevgeny Pavlovitch, who had long been standing there watching, 'of the celebrated defence made recently by a lawyer who, bringing forward in justification the poverty of his client as an excuse for his hating murdered and robbed six people at once, suddenly finished up with something like this: "It was natural," said he, "that in my client's poverty the idea of murdering six people should have occurred to him;

and to whom indeed would it not have occurred in his position?" Something of that sort, very amusing.'

'Enough!' Lizaveta Prokofyevna announced suddenly, almost shaking with anger. 'It's time to cut short this nonsense.'

She was in terrible excitement; she flung back her head menacingly, and with flashing eyes and an air of haughty, fierce, and impatient defiance, she scanned the whole part', scarcely able at the moment to distinguish between friends and foes. She had reached that pitch of long-suppressed but at last irrepressible wrath when the craving for immediate conflict, for immediate attack on someone becomes the leading impulse. Those who knew Madame Epanchin felt at once that something unusual had happened to her. Ivan Fyodorovitch told Prince S— next day that 'she has these attacks sometimes, but such a pitch as yesterday is unusual, even with her; it happens to her once in three years or so, but not oftener. Not oftener!' he added emphatically.

'Enough, Ivan Fyodorovitch! Let me alone,' cried Lizaveta Prokofyevna, 'why are you offering me your arm now? You hadn't the sense to take me away before! You are the husband, you are the head of the family, you ought to have taken me by the ear and led me out if I were so silly as not to obey you and go. You might think of your daughters, anyhow! Now, we can find the way without you! I've had shame enough to last me a year. Wait a bit, I must still thank the prince! Thank you for your entertainment, Prince. I've been staying on to listen to the young people … It's disgraceful, disgraceful! It's chaos, infamy! It's worse than a dream. Are there many like them? … Be quiet, Aglaia! Be quiet, Alexandra, it's not your business! Don't fuss round me, Yevgeny Pavlovitch, you bother me! … So you are asking their forgiveness, my dear?' she went on, addressing Myshkin again. ' "It's my fault," says he, "for daring to offer you a fortune." … And what are you pleased to be laughing at, you braggart?' she pounced suddenly on Lebedyev's nephew. ' "We refuse the fortune," says he, "we demand, we don't ask!" As though he didn't know that this idiot will trail off tomorrow to them to offer his friendship and his money to them again. You will, won't you? You will? Will you or not?'

'I shall,' said Myshkin, in a soft and humble voice.

'You hear! So that's what you are reckoning on,' she turned again to Doktorenko. 'The money is as good as in your pocket, that's why you boast and try to impress us ... No, my good man, you can find other fools, I see through you ... I see all your game!'

'Lizaveta Prokofyevna!' cried Myshkin.

'Come away, Lizaveta Prokofyevna, it's time we went, and let us take the prince with us,' Prince S— said, smiling as calmly as he could.

The girls stood on one side, almost scared, General Epanchin was genuinely alarmed, everyone present was amazed. Some of those standing furthest away whispered together and smiled on the sly; Lebedyev's face wore an expression of perfect rapture.

'There's chaos and infamy to be found everywhere, madam,' said Lebedyev's nephew, though he was a good deal disconcerted.

'But not so bad! Not so bad as yours, my man,' Lizaveta Prokofyevna retorted with almost hysterical vindictiveness. 'Let me alone!' she cried to those who tried to persuade her. 'Well, since you yourself, Yevgeny Pavlovitch, have just told us that even a lawyer in court declared that nothing is more natural if one is poor than to butcher six people, it simply means the end of all things; I never heard of such a thing. It's all clear now! And this stuttering fellow, wouldn't he murder anyone?' (She pointed to Burdovsky, who was gazing at her in extreme bewilderment.) 'I am ready to bet that he will murder someone! Maybe he won't take your money, your ten thousand, maybe he won't take it for conscience' sake, but he'll come at night and murder you and take the money out of your cash box, he'll take it for conscience' sake! That's not dishonest to him. It's just an outburst of "noble indignation", it's a "protest", or goodness knows what ... Tfoo! Everything is topsy-turvy, everything is upside down. A girl grows up at home, and suddenly in the middle of the street she jumps into a cab: "Mother, I was married the other day to some Karlitch or Ivanitch, goodbye." And is it the right thing to behave like that, do you think? Is it natural, is it deserving of respect? The woman question? This silly boy – she pointed to Kolya – 'even he was arguing the other day that that's what "the woman question" means. Even though the mother was a fool, you must behave like a human being to her! Why did you come in tonight with your heads in the air? "Make way, we are coming! Give us every right and don't you dare breathe a word before us. Pay us every sort of respect, such as no one's heard of, and we shall treat you worse than the lowest lackey!" They strive for justice, they stand on their rights, and yet they've slandered him like infidels in their article. We demand, we don't ask, and you will get no gratitude from us, because you are acting for the satisfaction of your own conscience! Queer sort of reasoning! Why, if he'll get no gratitude from you, the prince may tell you in answer that he feels no gratitude to Pavlishtchev, because Pavlishtchev too did good for the satisfaction of his own conscience, and you know it's just his gratitude to Pavlishtchev you've been reckoning on! He has not borrowed money from you, he doesn't owe you anything, so what are you reckoning on, if not his gratitude? So how can you repudiate it? Lunatics! They regard society as savage and inhuman, because it cries shame on the seduced girl, but if you think society inhuman, you must think that the girl suffers from the censure of society, and if she does, how is it you expose her to society in the newspapers and expect her not to suffer! Lunatics! Vain creatures! They don't believe in God, they don't believe in Christ! Why, you are so eaten up with pride and vanity that you'll end by eating up one another, that's what I prophesy. Isn't that topsy-turvydom, isn't it chaos, isn't it infamy? And after that, this disgraceful creature must needs go and beg their pardon too! Are there many more like you? What are you laughing at? At my disgracing myself with you? Why, I've disgraced myself already, there's no help for it now! Don't you go grinning, you sweep!' she pounced upon Ippolit. 'He is almost at his last gasp, yet he is corrupting others! You've corrupted this silly boy' – she pointed to Kolya again – 'he does nothing but rave about you, you teach him atheism, you don't believe in God, and you are not too old for a whipping yourself, Sir! Fie upon you! ... So you'll go to them tomorrow, Prince Lyov Nikolayevitch?' she asked the prince again, almost breathless.

'Yes.'

'Then I don't want to know you!' she turned quickly to go out, but at once turned back again. 'And you'll go to this atheist too?' she pointed to Ippolit. 'How dare you laugh at me!' she cried in an unnatural scream, and darted at Ippolit unable to endure his sarcastic grin.

'Lizaveta Prokofyevna! Lizaveta Prokofyevna! Lizaveta Prokofyevna!' was heard on all sides at once.

'*Maman*, this is shameful,' Aglaia cried aloud.

'Don't worry yourself, Aglaia Ivanovna,' Ippolit answered calmly. Lizaveta Prokofyevna had dashed up to him and had seized him by the arm, and for some inexplicable reason was still holding it tight. She stood before him, her wrathful eyes fastened upon his. 'Don't worry yourself, your *maman* will see that she cannot attack a dying man … I am ready to explain why I laughed … I shall be very glad of permission to do so.'

Here he coughed terribly and could not leave off for a full minute.

'He is dying, yet he must hold forth!' cried Lizaveta Prokofyevna, letting go his arm, and looking almost with horror at the blood he wiped from his lips. 'You are not fit for talking! You simply ought to go and lie down.'

'So I shall,' Ippolit answered in a low husky voice, almost a whisper. 'As soon as I get home today, I'll go to bed … In another fortnight I shall die, as I know. B— himself told me so a week ago … So that if you allow me, I should like to say two words to you at parting.'

'Are you crazy? Nonsense! You want nursing, it's not the time to talk! Go along, go to bed!' lizaveta Prokofyevna cried in horror.

'If I go to bed, I shan't get up again till I die,' said Ippolit, smiling. 'I was thinking of going to bed and not getting up again yesterday, but I decided to put it off till the day after tomorrow, since I still could stand on my legs… so as to come here with them today… Only I am awfully tired …'

'Sit down, sit down, why are you standing! Here's a chair.' Lizaveta Prokofyevna flew up to him and set a chair for him herself.

'Thank you,' Ippolit went on softly, 'and you sit down opposite and we can talk … we must have a talk, Lizaveta Prokofyevna, I insist on it now,' he smiled at her again. 'Think, this is the last time I shall be out in the air and with people, and in a fortnight I shall certainly be underground. So that this will be like a farewell to men and to nature. Though I am not very sentimental, yet would you believe it, I am awfully glad that all this has happened at Pavlovsk; one can see the trees in leaf anyway.'

'You can't talk now,' said Lizaveta Prokofyevna, growing more and more alarmed. 'You are in a perfect fever. You were screeching and squeaking before, and now you can scarcely breathe, you are gasping!'

'I shall be better in a minute. Why do you want to refuse my last wish? Do you know, I have been dreaming of making your acquaintance for a long time, Lizaveta Prokofyevna? I have heard a great deal about you… from Kolya; he is almost the only one who hasn't given me up … You are an original woman, an eccentric woman, I've seen that for myself now … do you know, that I was rather fond of you even.'

'Good heavens, and I was positively on the point of striking him!'

'Aglaia Ivanovna held you back, I am not mistaken, am I? This is your daughter, Aglaia Ivanovna? She is so beautiful that I guessed who she was at first sight, though I'd never seen her. Let me at least look at a beautiful woman for the last time in my life.' Ippolit smiled a sort of awkward, wry smile. 'Here, the prince is here, and your husband, and the whole party. Why do you refuse my last wish?'

'A chair!' cried Lizaveta Prokofyevna, but she seized one herself and sat down opposite Ippolit. 'Kolya,' she commanded, 'you must go with him, take him, and tomorrow I'll certainly go myself …'

'If you allow me, I would ask the prince for a cup of tea … I am very tired. Do you know, Lizaveta Prokofyevna, I believe you meant to take the prince back to tea with you; stay here instead, let us spend the time together, and I am sure the prince will give us all tea. Excuse my arranging it all… But I know you, you are good-natured, the prince is good-natured too … we are all ridiculously good-natured people.'

Myshkin made haste to give orders. Lebedyev flew headlong out of the room, Vera ran after him.

'That's true,' Madame Epanchin decided abruptly, 'talk, only quietly, don't get excited. You've softened my heart … Prince! You don't deserve that I should drink tea with you but so be it, I'll stay, though I am not going to apologise to anyone! Not to anyone! It's nonsense! Still, if I've abused you, Prince, forgive me – as you like, though. But I am not keeping anyone,' she turned with an expression of extraordinary wrath to her husband and daughters, as though they had treated her disgracefully. 'I can find my way home alone.'

But they didn't let her finish. They all drew up around her readily. Myshkin at once began pressing everyone to stay to tea and apologised for not having thought of it before. Even General Epanchin was so amiable as to murmur something reassuring, and asked Lizaveta Prokofyevna politely whether it was not too cold for her on the verandah. He almost came to the point of asking Ippolit how long he had been at the university, but he didn't ask him. Yevgeny Pavlovitch and Prince S— became suddenly extremely cordial and good-humoured. A look of pleasure began to mingle with astonishment on the faces of Adelaïda and Alexandra; in fact all seemed delighted that Madame Epanchin's paroxysm was over. Only Aglaia still frowned and sat in silence at a little distance. All the rest of the party remained, no one wanted to go away, not even General Ivolgin, to whom, however, Lebedyev whispered in passing something, probably not quite pleasant, for the general at once effaced himself in the corner. Myshkin included in his invitation Burdovsky and his friends, without exception. They muttered with a constrained air that they would wait for Ippolit, and at once withdrew to the furthest corner of the verandah, where they sat down all in a row again. Probably the tea had been got ready for Lebedyev himself long before, for it was brought in almost immediately! It struck eleven.

Chapter 10

Ippolit moistened his lips with the cup of tea handed to him by Vera Lebedyev, put down the cup on the little table, and seemed suddenly embarrassed, and looked about him almost in confusion.

'Look at these cups, Lizaveta Prokofyevna,' he began with a sort of strange haste; 'these china cups – and I think they are very good china – are never used and always stand in Lebedyev's sideboard under glass, locked up, as the custom is; they are part of his wife's dowry… it's their custom to keep them locked up … and here he's brought them out for us – in your honour, of course, he is so pleased to see you …'

He meant to say more but could not think of anything.

'He is feeling awkward; I thought he would,' Yevgeny Pavlovitch whispered suddenly in Myshkin's ear. 'It's dangerous, isn't it? It's a sure sign that now he'll do something out of spite so eccentric that it will be too much for even Lizaveta Prokofyevna, perhaps.'

Myshkin looked at him enquiringly.

'You are not afraid of eccentricity,' added Yevgeny Pavlovitch, 'I am not either; I should like it, in fact. I am only anxious that our dear Lizaveta Prokofyevna should be punished – and today too, this minute – and I don't want to go till she has been. You seem feverish.'

'Afterwards, don't bother me. Yes, I am not well,' Myshkin answered carelessly and even impatiently.

He caught his own name. Ippolit was speaking of him.

'You don't believe it?' Ippolit laughed hysterically. 'You'd be sure not to, but the prince will believe it at once and not be a bit surprised.'

'Do you hear, Prince,' said Lizaveta Prokofyevna, turning to him, 'do you hear?'

People laughed round them. Lebedyev kept officiously putting himself forward and fussing about Lizaveta Prokofyevna.

'He was saying that this clown here, your landlord ... corrected the article for this gentleman, the one they read this evening about you.'

Myshkin looked at Lebedyev in surprise.

'Why don't you speak?' cried Lizaveta Prokofyevna, stamping her foot.

'Well,' muttered Myshkin, scanning Lebedyev, 'I see now that he did.'

'Is it true?' Lizaveta Prokofyevna turned quickly to Lebedyev.

'It's the holy truth, your excellency,' answered Lebedyev firmly, without hesitation, laying his hand on his heart.

'He seems to be proud of it!' she cried, nearly jumping up from her chair.

'I am a poor creature,' muttered Lebedyev. His head sank lower and lower, and he began to smite himself on the breast.

'What do I care if you are a poor creature? He thinks he'll get out of it by saying he is a poor creature! And aren't you ashamed, Prince, to have to do with such contemptible people. I ask you once again? I shall never forgive you!'

'The prince will forgive me,' said Lebedyev sentimentally and with conviction.

'Simply from good feeling,' Keller said in a loud ringing voice, suddenly darting up to them and addressing Lizaveta Prokofyevna directly, 'simply from good feeling, madam, and to avoid giving away a friend who is compromised, I said nothing this evening about the corrections, although he did suggest kicking us downstairs, as you heard yourself. To put things in their true light, I confess that I really did apply to him as a competent person and offered him six roubles, not to correct the style, but simply to give me the facts, which were for the most part unknown to me.

The gaiters, the appetite at the Swiss professor's, the fifty roubles instead of two hundred and fifty; in fact all that arrangement, all that belongs to him. He sold it me for six roubles, but he did not correct the style.'

'I must observe,' Lebedyev interposed with feverish impatience and in a sort of crawling voice, while the laughter grew louder and louder, 'that I only corrected the first half of the article, but as we didn't agree in the middle and quarrelled over one idea, I didn't correct the second half, so that everything that is bad grammar there (and some of it is bad grammar!) mustn't be set down to me ...'

'That's what he is worried about!' cried Lizaveta Prokofyevna.

'Allow me to ask you,' said Yevgeny Pavlovitch, addressing Keller, 'when was the article corrected?'

'Yesterday morning,' answered Keller, 'we met together promising on our honour to keep the secret on both sides.'

'This was while he was crawling before you protesting his devotion. A nice set of people! I don't want your Pushkin, and don't let your daughter come and see me!'

Lizaveta Prokofyevna was on the point of getting up, but suddenly turned irritably to Ippolit, who was laughing.

'Have you put me here to be a laughing-stock, young man?'

'Heaven forbid,' said Ippolit with a wry smile, 'but what strikes me most of all is your extraordinary eccentricity, Lizaveta Prokofyevna. I confess I led up the conversation to Lebedyev on purpose; I knew the effect it would have on you and on you only, for the prince will certainly forgive it, and has probably forgiven it already ... he has found an excuse for him in his own mind by now most likely; that's true, Prince, isn't it?'

He was breathless; his strange excitement grew greater at every word.

'Well!' said Lizaveta Prokofyevna wrathfully, wondering at his tone, 'Well?'

'I've heard a great deal about you of the same sort of thing ... with great pleasure ... I've learnt to respect you extremely,' Ippolit went on.

He said one thing, but said it as though he meant something quite different by the words. He spoke with a shade of mocker)': yet, at the same time, was unaccountably excited. He looked about him uneasily. He was obviously muddled, and lost the thread of what he was saying at every word. All this, together with his consumptive appearance and strange, glittering, and almost frenzied eyes, could not fail to hold the general attention.

'I should have been surprised, though I know nothing of the world (I am aware of that), at your not only remaining yourself in our company – though we were not fit company for you – but even allowing these ... young ladies to listen to a scandalous business, though they have read it all in novels already. Though I don't know, perhaps ... because I am muddled, but in any case, who could have stayed except you ... at the request of a boy (well, yes, a boy, I confess it again) to spend the evening with him and to take ... part in everything ... though you knew you would be ashamed next day... (I must admit I am not expressing myself properly). I commend all this extremely and respect it profoundly, though one can see from the very countenance of his excellency, your husband, how improper all this seems to him. Ha-ha!' he chuckled, completely at a loss; and he suddenly coughed, so that for two minutes he could not go on.

'Now he is choking!' Lizaveta Prokofyevna pronounced coldly and sharply, scanning him with stem curiosity. 'Well, my dear fellow, we've had enough of you. We must be going.'

'Allow me too, Sir, to tell you for my part,' Ivan Fyodorovitch broke out irritably, losing patience, 'that my wife is here, visiting Prince Lyov Nikolayevitch, our friend and neighbour, and that in any case it's not for you, young man, to criticise Lizaveta Prokofyevna's actions, nor to refer aloud, and to my face, to what is written on my countenance. No, Sir. And if my wife has remained here,' he went on, his irritation increasing almost at every word, 'it's rather from amazement, Sir, and from an interest, comprehensible nowadays to all, in the spectacle of strange young people. I stopped myself, as I sometimes stop in the street when I see something at which one can look as... as ... as ...'

'As a curiosity,' Yevgeny Pavlovitch prompted him.

'Excellent and true.' His excellency, rather at a loss for a comparison, was delighted. 'Precisely, as a curiosity. But in any case, what is more amazing than anything, and even regrettable to me, if it is grammatical so to express oneself, is that you are not even able, young man, to understand that Lizaveta Prokofyevna has stayed with you now because you are ill – if only you really are dying – so to say from compassion, for the sake of your piteous appeal, Sir, and that no kind of slur can in any case attach to her name, character, and consequence … Lizaveta Prokofyevna!' the general concluded, with a crimson face, 'if you mean to go, let us take leave of our dear prince …'

'Thank you for the lesson, General,' Ippolit interrupted suddenly, speaking earnestly and looking thoughtfully at him.

'Let's go, *Maman.* How much longer is this to go on!' Aglaia said wrathfully and impatiently, getting up from her chair.

'Two minutes more, dear Ivan Fyodorovitch, if you allow it.' Lizaveta Prokofyevna turned with dignity to her husband. 'I believe he is in a fever and simply delirious; I am sure of it from his eyes; he can't be left like this. Lyov Nikolayevitch, could he stay the night with you, that he needn't be dragged to Petersburg tonight? *Cher Prince* I hope you are not bored,' she added, for some reason suddenly addressing Prince S—, 'Come here, Alexandra; put your hair tidy, my dear.'

She did something to Alexandra's hair, which was already perfectly tidy, and kissed her; that was all she had called her for.

'I thought you were capable of development,' Ippolit began again, coming out of his reverie. 'Yes, this was what I meant to say.' He was delighted, as though suddenly remembering something. 'Burdovsky here genuinely wants to protect his mother, doesn't he? And it turns out that he has disgraced her. The prince here wants to help Burdovsky, and in all sincerity offers him his tender friendship and a fortune, and perhaps he is the only one of us who does not feel an aversion for him, and yet they stand facing one another like actual enemies. Ha ha ha! You all hate Burdovsky because to your thinking he has behaved in an ugly and unseemly way to his mother; isn't that so? Isn't it? Isn't it? You are all awfully fond of external beauty and seemliness, and that's all you care for; that's true, isn't it? I've suspected that was all you care for, for a long time. Well, let me tell you that very likely not one of you has loved his mother as Burdovsky has! I know, Prince, you've sent money to Burdovsky's mother on the sly, through Ganya, and I'll bet, ha ha ha!' – he laughed hysterically – 'I'll bet that now Burdovsky will accuse you of indelicacy and disrespect to his mother. I swear that's how it will be. Ha ha ha!'

At this point he choked again and coughed.

'Well, is that all? That's all now; you've said everything? Well, now go to bed; you are in a fever,' Lizaveta Prokofyevna interrupted impatiently, keeping her eyes fixed anxiously on him. 'Good heavens, he is speaking again!'

'I think you are laughing. Why do you keep laughing at me? I notice that you are laughing at me all the time,' he said, turning with a sudden and uneasy irritation to Yevgeny Pavlovitch.

The latter really was laughing. 'I only wanted to ask you, Mr … Ippolit… excuse me, I've forgotten your name.'

'Mr Terentyev,' said Myshkin.

'Yes, Terentyev. Thank you, Prince. It was mentioned before, but it escaped my memory… I wanted to ask you, Mr Terentyev, is it true what I've heard, that you believe that you have only to talk to the peasants out of the window for a quarter of an hour and they'll agree with you and follow you at once?'

'It's quite possible I've said so,' answered Ippolit, seeming to recall something. 'I certainly did say so,' he added suddenly, growing eager again and looking at Yevgeny Pavlovitch. 'What of it?'

'Absolutely nothing; I simply wanted to know, to put the finishing touch.'

Yevgeny Pavlovitch was silent, but Ippolit still looked at him in impatient expectation.

'Well, have you finished?' Lizaveta Prokofyevna asked Yevgeny Pavlovitch. 'Make haste and finish, my friends; he ought to be in bed. Or don't you know how to?'

She was in terrible vexation.

'I am very much tempted to add,' Yevgeny Pavlovitch went on, smiling, 'that everything I've heard from your companions, Mr Terentyev, and everything you've said just now, and with such unmistakable talent, amounts in my opinion to the theory of the triumph of right before everything and setting everything aside, and even to the exclusion of everything else, and perhaps even before finding out what that right consists in. Perhaps I am mistaken.'

'Of course you are mistaken; I don't even understand you… Further?'

There was a murmur in the corner, too. Lebedyev's nephew was muttering something in an undertone.

'Why, scarcely anything further,' Yevgeny Pavlovitch went on. 'I only meant to observe that from that position one may easily make a jump to the right of might, that is, to the right of the individual fist and of personal caprice, as indeed has often happened in the history of the world. Proudhon arrived at the right of might. In the American War,? I many of the most advanced Liberals declared themselves on the side of the planters on the ground that negroes are negroes, lower than the white race, and therefore that right of might was on the side of the white men …'

'Well?'

'So then you don't deny that might is right?'

'Further?'

'I must say you are logical. I only wanted to observe that from the right of might to the right of tigers and crocodiles, and even to the right of Danilovs and Gorskys, is not a long step.'

'I don't know. Further?'

Ippolit scarcely heard what Yevgeny Pavlovitch said, and asked 'Well?' and 'Further?' more from a habit he had formed in arguments than from attention or curiosity.

'Nothing more … that's all.'

'I am not angry with you, though,' Ippolit concluded suddenly and quite unexpectedly, and, hardly knowing what he was doing, he held out his hand, even smiling.

Yevgeny Pavlovitch was surprised at first, but with a most serious air touched the hand which was offered to him as though accepting forgiveness.

'I must add,' he said in the same equivocally respectful tone, 'my gratitude to you for the attention with which you have listened to me, for, from my numerous observations, our Liberals are never capable of letting anyone else have a conviction of his own without at once meeting their opponent with abuse or even something worse.'

'You are perfectly right there,' observed General Epanchin, and, folding his hands behind his back, he retreated with a bored air to the steps of the verandah, where he yawned with vexation.

'Well, that's enough of you, my friend,' Lizaveta Prokofyevna announced suddenly to Yevgeny Pavlovitch, 'I am tired of you.'

'It's late!' Ippolit suddenly got up, looking preoccupied and almost alarmed, gazing about him in perplexity. 'I've kept you; I wanted to tell you everything… I thought that everyone for the last time … that was fancy…'

It was evident that he revived by fits and starts. He would suddenly come to himself from actual delirium for a few minutes; he would remember and talk with complete consciousness, chiefly in disconnected phrases which he had perhaps thought out and learnt by heart in the long weary hours of his illness, in his bed, in sleepless solitude.

'Well, goodbye,' he said suddenly and abruptly. 'Do you think it's easy for me to say goodbye to you? Ha ha!' He laughed angrily at his *awkward* question, and, seeming suddenly to grow furious at continually failing to say what he wanted to say, he said loudly and irritably: 'Your excellency, I have the honour of inviting you to my funeral if only you think me worthy of such an honour, and … all of you, ladies and gentlemen, in the wake of the general!'

He laughed again, but it was the laugh of a madman. Lizaveta Prokofyevna moved towards him in alarm and took him by the arm. He looked at her intently with the same laugh which seemed to have stopped short and frozen on his face.

'Do you know I came here to see the trees? These here' – he pointed to the trees in the park – 'that's not ridiculous, is it? There is nothing ridiculous in it?' he asked Lizaveta Prokofyevna seriously, and suddenly he sank into thought; then a minute later raised his head and began inquisitively looking about in the company. He was looking for Yevgeny Pavlovitch, who was standing quite near on the right of him in the same place as before, but he had already forgotten and looked round. 'Ah, you've not gone away!' He found him at last. 'You were laughing just now at my wanting to talk out of the window for a quarter of an hour … But do you know I am not eighteen? I've lain so much on that pillow and looked out of that window and thought so much … about everyone … that… a dead man has no age, you know. I thought that last week when I woke up in the night… And do you know what you are more afraid of than anything? You are more afraid of our sincerity than of anything, though you do despise us! I thought that too, lying on my pillow, that night… You think I meant to laugh at you, Lizaveta Prokofyevna? No, I was not laughing at you, I only wanted to praise you. Kolya told me the prince said you were a child…that's good… Yes, what was it?…I was going to say something more …' He hid his face in his hands and pondered. 'Oh yes, when you were saying "Goodbye" just now I suddenly thought: these people here, there never will be any more of them, never! And the trees too … there will be nothing but the redbrick wall, the wall of Meyer's house … opposite my window … Well, tell them about all that… try to tell them; here's a beauty … you are dead, you know. Introduce yourself as a dead man; tell them that the dead may say anything and that the Princess Darya Alexeyevna ... won't find fault. Ha ha! You don't laugh? ...' He scanned them all mistrustfully. 'You know a great many ideas have come into my head as I lay on the pillow ... do you know, I am convinced that Nature is very ironical... You said just now that I am an atheist, but do you know this Nature ... Why are you laughing again? You, are horribly cruel!' he pronounced suddenly with mournful indignation, looking at all of them. 'I have not corrupted Kolya,' he concluded in quite a different tone, earnest and convinced, as though remembering something again.

'Nobody, nobody is laughing at you here; don't worry yourself,' said Lizaveta Prokofyevna in distress. 'A new doctor shall come tomorrow; the other one was mistaken. Sit down you can hardly stand on your legs! You are delirious ... Ah, what are we to do with him now?' she asked anxiously, making him sit down in an armchair.

A tear gleamed on her cheek. Ippolit stopped, almost amazed. He raised his hand, stretched it out timidly, and touched the tear. He smiled a childlike smile.

'I ... you,' he began joyfully, 'you don't know how I ... he has always talked to me so enthusiastically about you, he there,' he pointed to Kolya. 'I like his enthusiasm. I've never corrupted him! He is the only friend I leave behind ... I should like to have left everyone friends, everyone ... but I had none ... I meant to do so much, I had the right ... Oh, how much I wanted! Now I want nothing. I don't want to want anything, I promised myself not to want anything; let them seek the truth without me! Yes, Nature is ironical. Why,' he resumed with heat, 'why does she create the best beings only to laugh at them afterwards? It is her doing that the sole creature recognised on earth as perfection... it is her doing that, showing him to men, she has decreed for him to say words for which so much blood has been shed, that if it had been shed at once, men must have been drowned in it... Ah, it's a good thing that I am dying! Perhaps I too should utter some horrible lie, Nature would beguile me into it... I have not corrupted anyone ... I wanted to live for the happiness of all men, to discover and proclaim the truth ... I gazed out of window on Meyer's wall and dreamed of only speaking for a quarter of an hour and convincing everyone, everyone, and for once in my life I have met... you, though I haven't others, and see what has come of it? Nothing! All that has come of it is that you despise me! So then I am a fool, so then I am not needed, so then it's time for me to go! And I haven't succeeded in leaving any memory behind me – not a sound, not a trace, not one deed; I haven't preached one truth! ... Don't laugh at the foolish fellow! Forget! Forget it all. Forget it, please; don't be so cruel! Do you know that if this consumption hadn't turned up, I should have killed myself.'

He seemed wanting to say a great deal more but did not say it; he sank back in the chair, covered his face with his hands, and began crying like a little child.

'Well, what are we to do with him now!' exclaimed Lizaveta Prokofyevna. She darted up to him, took his head, and pressed it close to her bosom. He sobbed convulsively. 'There, there, there! Come, don't cry. Come, that's enough. You are a good boy. God will forgive you because of your ignorance! Come, that's enough, be a man. Besides, you'll feel ashamed.'

'Up there,' said Ippolit, trying to raise his head, 'I've a brother and sisters, little children, poor, innocent... *She* will corrupt them! You are a saint, you... are a child yourself – save them! Get them away from that woman ... she ... a disgrace ... Oh, help them, help them! God will repay you a hundredfold. For God's sake, for Christ's sake!'

'Do tell me, Ivan Fyodorovitch, what is to be done now,' Lizaveta Prokofyevna cried irritably. 'Be so good as to break your majestic silence. If you don't decide something, you may as well know that I shall stay the night here myself; you've tyrannised over me enough with your despotism!'

Lizaveta Prokofyevna spoke with excitement and anger, and awaited an immediate reply. But in such cases those present, if there are many of them, usually receive such questions in silence and with passive interest, unwilling to take anything upon themselves, and only express their opinions long afterwards. Among those present on this occasion there were some who were capable of sitting there till morning without uttering a word. Varvara Ardalionovna, for instance, had been sitting at a little distance all the evening, listening in silence with an extraordinary interest, for which there were perhaps special reasons.

'My opinion, my dear,' the general expressed himself at last, 'is that a nurse is more needed here than our agitation, and perhaps a trustworthy, sober person for the night. In any case the prince must be asked, and ... the invalid must have rest at once. And tomorrow we can show interest in him again.'

'It's twelve o'clock. We are going. Is he coming with us or is he staying with you?' Doktorenko asked Myshkin, irritably and angrily.

'If you like, you can stay here with him,' said Myshkin; 'there'll be room.'

'Your excellency!' Mr Keller suddenly and enthusiastically flew up to General Epanchin. 'If a satisfactory man is wanted for the night, I am ready to sacrifice myself for a friend ... he is such a soul! I've long considered him a great man, your excellency! My education has been defective, of course, but his criticisms – they are pearls, pearls, your excellency!'

The general turned away in despair.

'I shall be very glad if he will stay, of course; it's difficult for him to be moved,' Myshkin replied to Lizaveta Prokofyevna's irritable questions.

'Are you asleep? If you don't want him, my friend, I'll take him home with us. My goodness, he can hardly stand upright himself! Why, you are ill?'

Earlier in the evening Lizaveta Prokofyevna, not finding Myshkin at death's door, had been misled by appearances into exaggerating his strength, but his recent illness, the painful recollections associated with it, the fatigue of this strenuous evening, the incident with 'the son of Pavlishtchev,' and the to-do with Ippolit now, all worked upon the morbid sensitiveness of Myshkin and excited him almost into a fever. Another anxiety, almost a fear, could moreover be discerned in his eyes; he looked apprehensively at Ippolit, as though expecting something more from him.

Suddenly Ippolit got up, horribly pale and with an expression of terrible, almost despairing, shame on his distorted face. It was expressed chiefly in his eyes, which looked with fear and hatred at the company, and in the vacant, twisted, and abject grin on his quivering lips. He dropped his eyes at once and strolled, staggering and still with the same smile, up to Burdovsky and Doktorenko, who were standing at the verandah steps; he was going away with them.

'Ah, that's what I was afraid of!' cried Myshkin; 'that was bound to happen!'

Ippolit turned quickly to him with frenzied anger, and every feature in his face seemed to be quivering and speaking.

'Ah, you were afraid of that, were you? That was bound to happen, you say? Then let me tell you, if I hate anyone here,' he yelled, spluttering, with a hoarse shriek, 'I hate you all, every one of you! – it's you, Jesuitical, treacly soul, idiot, philanthropic millionaire; I hate you more than everyone and everything in the world! I understood and hated you long ago, when first I heard of you; I hated you with all the hatred of my soul… This has all been your contriving. You led me on to breaking down! You drove a dying man to shame! You, you, you are to blame for my abject cowardice! I would kill you if I were going to remain alive! I don't want your benevolence, I won't take anything – anything, do you hear? – from anyone! I was in delirium, and don't you dare to triumph! I curse every one of you, once for all!'

Here he choked completely.

'He is ashamed of his tears,' Lebedyev whispered to Lizaveta Prokofyevna. 'That was bound to happen. Bravo, the prince! he saw right through him.'

But Lizaveta Prokofyevna did not deign to glance at him. She was standing proudly erect, with her head thrown back, scanning 'these miserable people' with contemptuous curiosity. When Ippolit had finished, General Epanchin shrugged his shoulders; his wife looked him up and down wrathfully, as though asking an explanation of his movement, and at once turned to Myshkin.

'We must thank you, Prince, the eccentric friend of our family, for the agreeable evening you have given us all. I suppose your heart is rejoicing now at having succeeded in dragging us into your foolery… Enough, my dear friend. Thank you for having let us have a clear view at last of what you are, anyway.'

She began indignantly setting straight her mantle, waiting for 'those people' to get off. A cab drove up at that moment to take them. Doktorenko had sent Lebedyev's son, the schoolboy, to fetch it a quarter of an hour before. Immediately after his wife, General Epanchin managed to put in his word too.

'Yes indeed, Prince, I should never have expected it … after everything, after all our friendly relations … and then Lizaveta Prokofyevna …'

'How can you! How can you!' cried Adelaïda. She walked quickly up to Myshkin and gave him her hand.

Myshkin smiled at her with a bewildered face. Suddenly a rapid, excited whisper seemed to scorch his ear.

'If you don't throw up these nasty people at once, I shall hate you all my life, all my life!' Aglaia whispered to him.

She seemed in a sort of frenzy, but she turned away before he had time to look at her. However, he had by now nothing and no one to throw up: they had by this time succeeded somehow in getting the invalid into the cab, and it had driven away.

'Well, how much longer is this going on, Ivan Fyodorovitch? What do you say to it? How long am I to be tormented by these spiteful boys?'

'Well, my dear ... I am ready, of course, and ... the prince ...'

Ivan Fyodorovitch held out his hand to Myshkin, however, but, without staying to shake hands, ran after Lizaveta Prokofyevna, who descended the terrace steps, rustling and wrathful.

Alexandra, Adelaïda, and her betrothed took leave of Myshkin with genuine affection. Yevgeny Pavlovitch did the same, and he alone was in good spirits.

'It happened as I thought it would, only I am sorry you – poor fellow – have had such a bad time!' he whispered, with a most charming smile.

Aglaia went away without saying goodbye.

But the adventures of that evening were not yet over. Lizaveta Prokofyevna had still to face a very unexpected meeting.

Before she had descended the verandah steps to the road, which ran along the edge of the park, a magnificent carriage, drawn by two white horses, came dashing by Myshkin's villa. Two gorgeously dressed ladies were sitting in it. But the carriage suddenly pulled up not ten paces beyond the house. One of the ladies turned round quickly, as though she had suddenly caught sight of a friend she must speak to.

'Yevgeny Pavlovitch, is that you, dear?' cried a beautiful ringing voice, which made Myshkin, and perhaps someone else too, start. 'Oh, how glad I am I've found you at last! I sent a messenger to you in town, two of them; they've been looking for you all day!'

Yevgeny Pavlovitch stood on the verandah steps as though thunderstruck. Lizaveta Prokofyevna too stood still, but not in horror and petrifaction like Yevgeny Pavlovitch; she looked at the audacious person with the same pride and cold contempt as she had five minutes before at 'these miserable people,' and at once turned her steady gaze on Yevgeny Pavlovitch.

'I have news!' the ringing voice continued. 'Don't worry about Kupfer's IOUs. Rogozhin has bought them up for thirty; I persuaded him. You can be easy for another three months, and we'll manage Biskup and all those wretches through friends. Do you see? Everything is all right. Keep up your spirits, dear. Till tomorrow.'

The carriage set off and quickly disappeared.

'It's a madwoman,' exclaimed Yevgeny Pavlovitch at last, flushing with indignation and looking round him bewildered. 'I haven't an idea what she was talking about. What IOUs? Who is she?'

Lizaveta Prokofyevna went on looking at him for another two seconds. At last she set off quickly and abruptly towards her villa, and all the rest followed her. One minute later Yevgeny Pavlovitch came back to Myshkin on the verandah, extremely agitated.

'Prince, tell the truth. Do you know what it means?'

'I know nothing about it,' answered Myshkin, who was himself in a state of extreme and painful tension.

'No?'

'No.'

'And I don't know.' Yevgeny Pavlovitch laughed suddenly. 'I swear I've had nothing to do with any IOUs; you may believe my word of honour! But what's the matter? You are fainting?'

'Oh no, no, I assure you, no …'

Chapter 11

It was not until three days afterwards that the Epanchins were quite gracious again. Though Myshkin, as usual, took a great deal of blame on himself and genuinely expected to be punished, yet he had at first the fullest inward conviction that Lizaveta Prokofyevna could not be seriously angry with him, and was really more angry with herself. And so such a long period of animosity reduced him by the third day to the most gloomy bewilderment. Other circumstances contributed to this, and one especially so. To Myshkin's sensitiveness it went on gaining in significance during those three days (and of late he had blamed himself for two extremes, for his excessive 'senseless and impertinent' readiness to trust people and at the same time for his gloomy suspiciousness). In short, by the end of the third day the incident of the eccentric lady who had accosted Yevgeny Pavlovitch had taken in his imagination alarming and mysterious proportions. The essence of the riddle, apart from other aspects of the affair, lay for Myshkin in the mortifying question, was he to blame for this new 'monstrosity,' or was it… But he did not say who else. As for the letters 'N.F.B.,' he saw in that nothing but an innocent piece of mischief – the most childish mischief, indeed, so that it would have been a shame and even in one way almost dishonourable, to think much about it.

However, on the day after the scandalous evening for the disgraceful incidents of which he was the chief 'cause,' Myshkin had the pleasure of a morning visit from Prince S— and Adelaïda. 'They had come *principally* to enquire after his health'; they were out for a walk together. Adelaïda had just noticed in the park a tree, a wonderful spreading old tree with long twisted branches, with a big crack and hollow in it, and covered with young green leaves. She must, she positively must paint it! So that they scarcely spoke of anything else for the whole half-hour of their visit. Prince S— was as usual cordial and amiable; he questioned Myshkin about the past, and referred to the circumstances of their first acquaintance, so that hardly anything was said of the events of yesterday.

At last Adelaïda could not keep it up and admitted with a smile that they had come incognito. But her confession ended there, though from that word 'incognito' it might be judged that he was in special disfavour with her parents, or rather with her mother. But neither Adelaïda nor Prince S— uttered one word about her or Aglaia, or even General Epanchin, during their visit. When they went away to continue their walk, they did not ask Myshkin to accompany them. There was no hint of an invitation to the house either. One very suggestive phrase escaped Adelaïda indeed. Telling him about a watercolour she had been painting, she suddenly expressed a great desire to show it to him. 'How can that be done soon? Stay! I'll either send it to you today by Kolya, if he comes, or I'll bring it to you myself tomorrow when I am out for a walk with the prince,' she concluded at last, glad that she had succeeded in getting out of the difficulty so cleverly and comfortably for everyone.

At last, as he was about to take leave, Prince S— seemed suddenly to recollect. 'Ah, yes,' he asked, 'do you, perhaps, dear Lyov Nikolayevitch, know who that person was who shouted yesterday from the carriage?'

'It was Nastasya Filippovna,' said Myshkin. 'Haven't you found out yet that it was she? But I don't know who was with her.'

'I know; I've heard!' Prince S— caught him up. 'But what did that shout mean? It is, I must own, a mystery to me ... to me and to others.'

Prince S— spoke with extreme and evident perplexity.

'She spoke of some bills of Yevgeny Pavlovitch's,' Myshkin answered very simply, 'which by her request had come from some moneylender into Rogozhin's hands, and that Rogozhin will wait his convenience.'

'I heard, I heard it, my dear prince, but you know that couldn't be so! Yevgeny Pavlovitch cannot possibly have given any such bills with a fortune like his... He has, it is true, been careless in the past; and indeed I have helped him out ... But with his fortune to give IOUs to a moneylender and be worried about them is impossible. And he cannot be on such familiar and friendly terms with Nastasya Filippovna; that's what is most mysterious. He swears he knows nothing about it, and I trust him entirely. But the fact is, dear prince, I want to ask you if you know anything. I mean, has no rumour, by some marvel, reached you?'

'No, I know nothing about it, and I assure you I had nothing to do with it.'

'Ach! How strange you are, Prince! I really don't know you today. As though I could suppose you had anything to do with an affair of that kind! But you are out of sorts today.'

He embraced and kissed him.

'Had anything to do with an affair of what "kind"? I don't see that it is an "affair of that kind".'

'There is no doubt that person wished to damage Yevgeny Pavlovitch in some way by attributing to him in the eyes of those present qualities which he has not and cannot have,' Prince S— answered rather drily.

Myshkin was confused, yet he continued to gaze steadily and enquiringly at Prince S—, but the latter did not speak.

'And weren't there simply bills? Wasn't it literally as she said yesterday?' Myshkin muttered at last in a sort of impatience.

'But I tell you – judge for yourself – what can there be in common between Yevgeny Pavlovitch and … her, and above all with Rogozhin? I repeat he has an immense fortune, and I know it for a fact, and he expects another fortune from his uncle. It's simply that Nastasya Filippovna …'

Prince S— suddenly paused again, obviously because he did not care to go on speaking of Nastasya Filippovna to Myshkin.

'Then he knows her, anyway?' Myshkin asked suddenly after a minute's silence.

'That was so, I believe; he's a giddy fellow! But if it was so, it was long ago in the past – that is, two or three years back. You see, he used to know Totsky. Now, there could be nothing of the sort; they could never have been on intimate terms! You know yourself that she hasn't been here either; she hasn't been anywhere. Many people don't know yet that she has turned up again. I have noticed the carriage for the last three days, not more.'

'A splendid carriage!' said Adelaïda.

'Yes, the carriage was splendid.'

They took leave, however, on the most friendly, one might say the most brotherly, terms with Prince Lyov Nikolayevitch.

But there was something of vital importance to our hero in this visit. He had indeed suspected a good deal himself, ever since the previous evening (possibly even earlier), but till their visit he had not brought himself to justify his apprehensions completely. But now it had become clear. Prince S—, of course put a mistaken interpretation on the incident, but still he was not far from the truth; he realised, anyway, that there was an intrigue in it. ('Perhaps though, he understands it quite correctly,' thought Myshkin, 'but only does not want to speak out, and so puts a false interpretation on it on purpose.') What was clearer than anything was that they had come to see him just now (Prince S— certainly had) in the hope of getting some sort of explanation. If that were so, then they plainly looked on him as being concerned in the intrigue. Besides, if this were all so and really were of consequence, then she must have some dreadful object. What object? Horrible! 'And hows one to stop *her*? There is no possibility of stopping *her* when she is determined on her object.' That Myshkin knew by experience. 'She is mad! She is mad!'

But that morning was crowded with far too many other unexplained incidents, all coming at once and all requiring to be settled at once, so that Myshkin was very sad. His attention was distracted a little by Vera Lebedyev, who came to see him with Lubotchka, and, laughing, told him a long story. She was followed by her open-mouthed sister. They were followed by the schoolboy, Lebedyev's son, who informed him that the 'star that is called Wormwood' in the Apocalypse, 'that fell upon the fountains of waters', was, by his father's interpretation, the network of railways spread over Europe. Myshkin did not believe that Lebedyev did interpret it in this way, and resolved to ask him about it at the first convenient opportunity.

From Vera Lebedyev, Myshkin learned that Keller had taken up his quarters with them the previous day and showed every sign of not leaving them for a long time, since he found company in their house and had made friends with General Ivolgin. He declared, however, he was remaining with them solely to complete his education. On the whole Myshkin began to like Lebedyev's children more and more every day. Kolya had not been there all day – he had set off to Petersburg early in the morning. Lebedyev, too, had gone away as soon as it was light to see after some little business of his own. But Myshkin impatiently expected a visit from Gavril Ardalionovitch, who was to come to see him without fail that day.

He came just after dinner, about six o'clock in the afternoon. At the first glance at him, the thought struck Myshkin that that gentleman at least must know every detail of the affair thoroughly. How could he fail to, indeed, with people like Varvara Ardalionovna and her husband to help him? But Myshkin's relations with Ganya were somewhat peculiar. Myshkin had, for instance, entrusted him with the management of Burdovsky's affair, and particularly asked him to look after it. But in spite of the confidence he put in him over this, and in spite of something that had happened before, certain points always remained between them about which it was, as it were, mutually agreed not to speak. Myshkin fancied sometimes that Ganya would perhaps for his part have liked the fullest and most friendly candour. Now, for instance, Myshkin felt, as soon as Ganya entered, that he was fully persuaded that that moment was the time to break down the ice between them at all points. Gavril Ardalionovitch was in haste, however. His sister was awaiting him with the Lebedyevs, and they were both in a hurry over something they were doing.

But if Ganya really was expecting a whole series of impatient questions, impulsive confidences, friendly outpourings, he was certainly much mistaken. During the twenty minutes his visit lasted, Myshkin was positively dreamy, almost absent-minded. There was no possibility of the expected questions – or rather of the one principal question Ganya was expecting. Then Ganya too decided to speak with great reserve. He talked away for the whole twenty minutes without stopping, laughed, kept up a very light, charming and rapid chatter, but did not touch on the chief point.

Ganya told him among other things that Nastasya Filippovna had only been four days here in Pavlovsk and was already attracting general attention. She was staying at Darya Alexeyevna's, in a clumsy-looking little house in Matrossky Street, but her carriage was almost the finest in Pavlovsk. A perfect crowd of followers, old and young, had gathered about her already. Her carriage was sometimes escorted by gentlemen, on horseback. Nastasya Filippovna was, as she always had been, very capricious in her choice of friends and only received those she fancied. And yet a perfect regiment was forming round her; she had plenty of champions, if she needed them. One gentleman staying in a summer villa, had already on her account quarrelled with the young lady to whom he was formally betrothed; and one old general had all but cursed his son because of her. She often took out driving with her a charming little girl, a distant relative of Darya Alexeyevna's, who was only just sixteen. This girl sang very well, so their little house attracted general attention in the evenings. Nastasya Filippovna, however, behaved with extreme propriety, dressed quietly but with extraordinarily good taste, and all the ladies were 'envying her taste, her beauty and her carriage.'

'The eccentric incident yesterday,' Ganya ventured, 'was, of course, premeditated, and, of course, must not be counted. To find any fault with her, people will have to seek it out on purpose, or to invent it; which they would not be slow to do, however,' Ganya concluded, expecting Myshkin would be sure to ask him at that point why he called yesterday's incident 'premeditated', and why they would not be slow to do so.

But Myshkin did not ask it.

Ganya talked freely about Yevgeny Pavlovitch without being questioned, which was very strange, for he brought him into the conversation without any pretext for doing so. In Gavril

Ardalionovitch's opinion, Yevgeny Pavlovitch had not known Nastasya Filippovna; he scarcely knew her even now, for he had only been introduced to her four days ago when out walking, and had probably not been once at her house. As for the IOUs, it might be so too: Ganya knew that for a positive fact. Yevgeny Pavlovitch's fortune was, of course, a large one, but some business connected with his estate really was rather in a muddle. At this interesting point Ganya suddenly broke off. He said nothing about Nastasya Filippovna's prank of the previous evening, except the passing reference above.

At last Varvara Ardalionovna came in to look for Ganya. She stayed a minute, announced (also without being asked) that Yevgeny Pavlovitch was in Petersburg today and would perhaps be there tomorrow too; that her husband, Ivan Petrovitch Ptitsyn, was also in Petersburg and also probably on Yevgeny Pavlovitch's business; that something had really happened there. As she was going, she added that Lizaveta Prokofyevna was in a fiendish temper today, but, what was most odd, Aglaia had quarrelled with her whole family, not only her father and mother, but even with her two sisters, and 'that was anything but a good sign.' After giving him, as it were in passing, this last piece of news (which was of extreme importance to Myshkin), the brother and sister departed. Ganya had, possibly from false modesty, possibly to 'spare the prince's feelings,' not uttered one word about the case of 'Pavlishtchev's son.' Myshkin thanked him, however, once more for the careful way he had managed the affair.

Myshkin was very glad to be left alone at last. He walked off the verandah, crossed the road and went into the park. He longed to think over and decide upon one step. Yet that 'step' was not one of those that can be thought over, but one of those which are simply decided upon without deliberation. A terrible longing came upon him to leave everything here and to go back to the place from which he had come, to go away into the distance to some remote region, to go away at once without even saying goodbye to anyone. He had a foreboding that if he remained here even a few days longer he would be drawn into this world irrevocably and that his life would be bound up with it for ever. But he did not consider it for ten minutes; he decided at once that it would be 'impossible' to run away, that it would be almost cowardice, that he was faced with such difficulties that it was his duty now to solve them, or at least to do his utmost to solve them. Absorbed in such thoughts, he returned home after a walk of less than a quarter of an hour. He was utterly unhappy at that moment.

Lebedyev was still away from home, so that towards evening Keller succeeded in bursting in on Myshkin, brimming over with confidences and confessions, though he was not drunk. He openly declared that he had come to tell Myshkin the whole story of his life, and that it was to do so that he had remained in Pavlovsk. There was not the faintest possibility of getting rid of him; nothing would have induced him to go. Keller had come prepared to talk at great length and with great incoherence. But suddenly, almost at the first word, he skipped to the conclusion and announced that he had so completely lost 'every trace of morality' (solely through lack of faith in the Almighty) that he had positively become a thief.

'Can you fancy that!'

'Listen, Keller. If I were in your place I wouldn't confess that without special need,' Myshkin began. 'But perhaps you make things up against yourself on purpose?'

'To you alone, and solely to promote my own development. To no one else. I shall die and bear my secret to the coffin! But, Prince, if you knew, if only you knew how hard it is to get money nowadays! How is one to get it, allow me to ask you? The answer is always the same: "Bring gold or diamonds and we'll give you something for them." That's just what I haven't got. Can you fancy that? I lost my temper at last, after waiting and waiting. "Will you give me something for emeralds?" said I. "Yes, for emeralds too," said he. "Well, that's all right," said I, and I put on my hat and walked out. "You're a set of scoundrels, damn you! Yes, by Jove!" '

'Had you any emeralds, then?'

'A likely story! Oh, Prince, what a sweet and innocent, pastoral, one may say, idea of life you have!'

Myshkin began at last to feel not exactly sorry for him, but, as it were, vaguely ill at ease on his account. It occurred to him to wonder, indeed, whether anything could be made of the man by any good influence. His own influence he considered for various reasons quite unsuitable; and this was not due to self-depreciation, but to a peculiar way of looking at things. By degrees they got into talk, so much so that they did not want to part. Keller, with extraordinary readiness, confessed to actions of which it seemed inconceivable anyone could be willing to speak. At every fresh story he asserted positively that he was penitent and 'full of tears'; yet he told it as though he were proud of his action, and sometimes too so absurdly that he and Myshkin laughed at last like madmen.

'The great thing is that you have a sort of childlike trustfulness and extraordinary truthfulness,' said Myshkin at last. 'Do you know that by that alone you make up for a very great deal?'

'Generous, chivalrously generous!' Keller assented, much touched. 'But you know, Prince, it is all in dreams and, so to say, in bravado; it never comes to anything in action! And why is it? I can't understand.'

'Don't despair. Now, one can say positively that you have given me a full account of everything. I fancy anyway that it's impossible to add anything more to what you've told me, isn't it?'

'Impossible?' Keller exclaimed, almost compassionately. 'Oh, Prince, how completely, *à la Suisse,* if I may say so, you still interpret human nature!'

'Can you really have more to add?' Myshkin brought out with timid wonder. 'Then tell me, please, what did you expect of me, Keller, and why have you come to me with your confession?'

'From you? What did I expect? In the first place, it is pleasant to watch your simplicity; it's nice to sit and talk to you. I know there is a really virtuous person before me, anyway; and, secondly ... secondly ...' he was confused.

'Perhaps you wanted to borrow money?' Myshkin prompted very gravely and simply, and even rather shyly.

Keller positively started. He glanced quickly with the same wonder straight into Myshkin's face, and brought his fist down violently on the table.

'Well, that's how you knock a fellow out completely! Upon my word, Prince, such simplicity, such innocence, as was never seen in the Golden Age – yet all at once you pierce right through a fellow like an arrow with such psychological depth of observation. But allow me, Prince. This requires explanation, for I'm ... simply bowled over! Of course, in the long run my object was to borrow money, but you ask me about it as if you saw nothing reprehensible in that, as though it were just as it should be.'

'Yes ... from you it is just as it should be.'

'And you're not indignant?'

'No ... Why?'

'Listen, Prince. I've been staying here since yesterday evening: first, from a special respect for the French archbishop Bourdaloue (we were pulling corks in Lebedyev's room till three in the morning); and secondly, and chiefly (and here I'll take my oath I am speaking the holy truth!), I stayed because I wanted, by making you a full, heartfelt confession, so to speak, to promote my own development. With that idea I fell asleep, bathed in tears, towards four o'clock. Would you believe on the word of a man of honour, now at the very minute I fell asleep, genuinely filled with inward and, so to say, outward tears (for I really was sobbing, I remember), a hellish thought occurred to me: "Why not, when all's said and done, borrow money of him after my confession?" So that I prepared my confession, so to say, as though it were a sort of "fricassee with tears for sauce," to pave the way with those tears so that you might be softened and fork out one hundred and fifty roubles. Don't you think that was base?'

'But most likely that's not true; it's simply both things came at once. The two thoughts came together; that often happens. It's constantly so with me. I think it's not a good thing, though; and, do you know, Keller, I reproach myself most of all for it. You might have been telling me about myself just now. I have sometimes even fancied,' Myshkin went on very earnestly, genuinely and profoundly interested, 'that all people are like that, so that I was even beginning to excuse myself because it is awfully difficult to struggle against these *double* thoughts; I've tried. God knows how they arise and come into one's mind. But you call it simply baseness! Now, I'm beginning to be afraid of those thoughts again. Anyway, I am not your judge. Yet to my mind one can't call it simply baseness. What do you think? You were acting deceitfully to obtain my money by your tears, but you swear yourself that there was another motive too for your confession – an honourable motive as well as a mercenary one. As for the money, you want it for riotous living, don't you? And after such a confession, that's feebleness, of course. But yet how are you to give up riotous living all in a minute? That's impossible, I know. What's to be done? It had better be left to your own conscience, don't you think?'

Myshkin looked with great interest at Keller. The problem of double ideas had evidently occupied his mind for some time.

'Well, I don't understand why they call you an idiot after that!' cried Keller.

Myshkin flushed a little.

'Even the preacher, Bourdaloue, would not have spared a man, but you've spared one, and judged me humanely! To punish myself and to show that I am touched, I won't take a hundred and fifty roubles; give me only twenty-five, and it will be enough! That's all I want, for a fortnight, at any rate. I won't come for money within a fortnight. I did mean to treat Agashka, but she's not worth it. Oh, God bless you, dear prince!'

Lebedyev came in at last immediately on his return from town. Noticing the twenty-five rouble note in Keller's hand, he frowned. But the latter was in a hurry to get away as soon as he was provided with funds, and promptly took his departure. Lebedyev at once began to speak ill of him.

'You're unjust, he really was genuinely penitent,' Myshkin observed at last.

'What does his penitence amount to? It's just like me saying, "I am abject, I am abject!" yesterday. You know it's only words.'

'So that was only words? I thought you ...'

'Well, to you, only to you, I will tell the truth, because you see through a man. Words and deeds and lies and truth are all mixed up in me and are perfectly sincere. Deeds and truth come out in my genuine penitence, I swear it, whether you believe it or not; and words and lies in the hellish (and always present) craving to get the better of a man, to make something even out of one's tears of penitence. It is so, by God! I wouldn't tell another man – he'd laugh or curse. But you, Prince, judge humanely.'

'Why, that's exactly what he told me just now,' cried Myshkin, 'and you both seem to be proud of it! You positively surprise me, only he's more sincere than you are, and you've turned it into a regular trade. Come, that's enough. Don't crease up your face, Lebedyev, and don't lay your hands on your heart. Haven't you something to say to me? You don't come in for nothing ...'

Lebedyev grimaced and wriggled.

'I've been waiting for you all day to put a question to you. Tell me the truth straight off for once in your life. Had you anything to do with that carriage stopping here yesterday or not?'

Lebedyev grimaced again, began tittering, rubbing his hands even sneezing at last, but still he could not bring himself to speak.

'I see you had.'

'But indirectly, only indirectly! It's the holy truth I'm telling you! The only part I had in it was letting a certain personage know in good time that I had such a company in my house and that certain persons were present.'

'I knew you sent your son *there,* he told me so himself just now, but what intrigue is this?' Myshkin cried impatiently.

'It's not my intrigue, not mine,' Lebedyev protested, gesticulating. 'There are others, others in it, and it is rather a fantasy, so to speak, than an intrigue.'

'But what's the meaning of it? For heaven's sake, do explain! Is it possible you don't understand that it concerns me directly? You see, it is blackening Yevgeny Pavlovitch's character.'

'Prince! Most illustrious prince!' Lebedyev began wriggling again. 'You won't allow me to tell the whole truth, you know. I've tried to already more than once. You wouldn't allow me to go on ...'

Myshkin paused, and thought a little.

'Very well, tell the truth,' he said dejectedly, evidently after a severe struggle.

'Aglaia Ivanovna ...' Lebedyev promptly began.

'Be silent, be silent!' Myshkin cried furiously, flushing all over with indignation and perhaps with shame too. 'It's impossible, it's all nonsense! You invented all that yourself or some madmen like you. And let me never hear of it from you again!'

Late in the evening, after ten o'clock, Kolya arrived with a whole budget of news. His news was of two kinds: of Petersburg and of Pavlovsk. He hastily related the chief items of the Petersburg news (mainly about Ippolit and the scene of the previous day) and passed quickly to the Pavlovsk tidings, meaning to return to the former subject again later. He had returned from Petersburg three hours before and had gone straight to the Epanchins' before coming to Myshkin. 'It's awful the to-do there!' Of course the carriage incident was in the foreground, but no doubt something else had happened – something he and Myshkin knew nothing about. 'I didn't spy, of course, and didn't care to question anyone. They received me well, however, better than I'd expected, indeed, but of you not a word, Prince!'

The most important and interesting fact was that Aglaia had been quarrelling with her people about Ganya. He did not know the details of the quarrel but only that it was over Ganya (fancy that!), and it had been a terrible quarrel, so it must be something important. The general had come in late, had come in frowning; had come in with Yevgeny Pavlovitch, who met with an excellent reception, and had been wonderfully gay and charming. The most striking piece of news was that Lizaveta Prokofyevna had without any fuss sent for Varvara Ardalionovna, who was sitting with the young ladies, and had once for all turned her out of the house, in a very polite manner, however. 'I heard it from Varya herself.' But when Varya came out of Madame Epanchin's room and said goodbye to the young ladies, they did not know she had been forbidden the house for ever, and that she was taking leave of them for the last time.

'But Varvara Ardalionovna was here at seven o'clock,' said Myshkin, astonished.

'She was turned out at eight o'clock or just before. I am very sorry for Varya. I am sorry for Ganya ... No doubt they have always got some intrigues in hand; they can't get on without it. I never could make out what they were hatching, and I don't want to know. But I assure you, my dear, kind prince, that Ganya has a heart. He's a lost soul in many respects, no doubt, but he has points on other sides worth finding out, and I shall never forgive myself for not having understood him before ... I don't know whether to go on now, after the fuss with Varya. It's true I introduced myself from the very first quite independently and separately, but all the same I must think it over.'

'You need not be too sorry for your brother,' Myshkin observed. 'If it has come to that, Gavril Ardalionovitch must be dangerous in Madame Epanchin's eyes, and that means that certain hopes of his have been encouraged.'

'How, what hopes?' Kolya said in amazement. 'Surely you don't think that Aglaia .., That's impossible!'

Myshkin did not speak.

'You're an awful sceptic, Prince,' Kolya added two minutes later. 'I have noticed that for some time past you've become a great sceptic; you're beginning to believe in nothing, and are always imagining things ... Did I use the word "sceptic" correctly in this case?'

'I believe you did, though I really don't know for certain myself.'

'But I give up the word sceptic myself, I've found another explanation,' Kolya cried suddenly. 'You're not a sceptic, but you're jealous! You're fiendishly jealous of Ganya over a certain proud young lady!'

Saying this, Kolya jumped up and began laughing, as perhaps he had never laughed before. Seeing that Myshkin blushed all over, Kolya laughed more than ever. He was highly delighted with the idea that Myshkin was jealous over Aglaia, but he ceased at once on observing that the prince was really wounded. After that, they talked very earnestly and anxiously for another hour or hour and a half.

Next day Myshkin had to spend the whole morning in Petersburg on urgent business. It was past four o'clock in the afternoon when, on the way back to Pavlovsk, he met General Epanchin at the railway station. The latter seized him hurriedly by the arm, looked about him as though in alarm, and drew Myshkin after him into a first-class compartment that they might travel together. He was burning with impatience to discuss something important.

'To begin with, dear prince, don't be angry with me, and if there's been anything on my side – forget it. I should have come to see you myself yesterday, but I didn't know how Lizaveta Prokofyevna would take it … It's simply hell in my home … An inscrutable sphinx is settled there, and I wander about and can't make head or tail of it. As for you, to my thinking you're less to blame than any of us; though, of course, a great deal has happened through you. You see, Prince, it's nice to be a philanthropist, but not too much so. You've tasted the fruits of it already, maybe. I like kind-heartedness, of course, and respect Lizaveta Prokofyevna, but…'

The general continued for a long time in this style, but his words were astonishingly incoherent. It was evident that he was extremely upset and puzzled by something utterly beyond his comprehension.

'I have no doubt that you had nothing to do with it,' he spoke out at last more clearly, 'but I beg you as a friend not to visit us for some time, till the wind's changed. As for Yevgeny Pavlovitch,' he cried with extraordinary warmth, 'it's all senseless slander – the most slanderous of slanders! It's a plot, it's an intrigue, an attempt to destroy everything and to make us quarrel. You see, Prince, I'll whisper in your ear, there hasn't been a single word said between Yevgeny Pavlovitch and us yet. You understand? We're not bound in any way. But that word may be said, and very shortly, perhaps, in fact! So this is an attempt to spoil it all! But with what object, what for I can't make out! She's a marvellous woman, an eccentric woman. I'm so afraid of her I can hardly sleep at night. And what a carriage! – White horses, real *chic*. Yes, it's just what is called in French *"chic"*! Who's provided it? I did wrong, by jove – the day before yesterday my thoughts fell on Yevgeny Pavlovitch. But it turns out that it can't be so. And if it can't, what's her object in interfering? That's the riddle, that's the mystery! To keep Yevgeny Pavlovitch for herself? But I tell you again, and I'm ready to swear it, that he doesn't know her, and that those IOUs were an invention! And with what insolence she shouted "Dear" to him across the street! It's a regular plot! It's clear that we must dismiss it with contempt and treat Yevgeny Pavlovitch with redoubled respect. That's what I've said to Lizaveta Prokofyevna. Now I'll tell you my private opinion. I'm positively convinced that she's doing this to revenge herself on me personally for the past, d'you remember, though I've never done anything to her. I blush at the very thought of it. Now she's turned up again, you see; I thought she'd disappeared for good. Where's this Rogozhin hiding? Tell me that, if you please. I thought she'd been Madame Rogozhin long ago.'

The man was completely bewildered in fact. He talked alone for the whole journey, which lasted almost an hour, asked questions, answered them himself, pressed Myshkin's hand, and did at any rate convince the prince that he did not dream of suspecting him.

This was what mattered to Myshkin. He finished up by telling him about Yevgeny Pavlovitch's uncle, who was chief of some department in Petersburg. 'In a conspicuous position, seventy years old, a *viveur*, a gourmand – altogether an old gentleman with habits ... Ha ha! I know he'd heard of Nastasya Filippovna, and in fact was after her. I went to see him not long ago; he didn't see me. He was unwell, but he is a wealthy man, very wealthy, a man of consequence and ... please God, he will go on flourishing for years, but Yevgeny Pavlovitch will come in for his money in the end. Yes, yes ... But yet I'm afraid, I don't know why, but I'm afraid. It's as though there were something in the air, some trouble hovering like a bat, and I'm afraid, I'm afraid!'

And it was only on the third day, as we have said already, that the formal reconciliation of the Epanchins with Myshkin took place at last.

Chapter 12

It was seven o'clock in the evening. Myshkin was getting ready to go into the park. All of a sudden Lizaveta Prokofyevna walked alone on to his verandah.

'To begin with, don't you dare to imagine,' she began, 'that I've come to beg your pardon. Nonsense! It was entirely your fault.'

Myshkin did not speak.

'Was it your fault or not?'

'As much mine as yours, though neither I nor you was intentionally to blame. I did think myself to blame the day before yesterday, but now I've come to the conclusion that it's not so.'

'So that's what you say! Very well; listen and sit down, for I don't intend to stand.'

They both sat down. 'Secondly, not one word about mischievous urchins! I'll sit and talk to you for ten minutes; I've come to make an enquiry (and you are fancying all sorts of things, I expect?). And if you drop a single word about insolent urchins, I shall get up and go away and break with you completely.'

'Very well,' answered Myshkin.

'Allow me to ask you: did you two months or two and a half ago, about Easter, send Aglaia a letter?'

'I did write to her.'

'With what object? What was in the letter? Show me the letter!'

Lizaveta Prokofyevna's eyes glowed, she was almost quivering with impatience.

'I haven't got the letter.' Myshkin was surprised and horribly dismayed. 'If it still exists, Aglaia Ivanovna has it.'

'Don't wriggle out of it. What did you write about?'

'I'm not, and I'm not afraid of anything. I don't see any reason why I shouldn't write …'

'Hold your tongue! You shall speak afterwards. What was in the letter? Why are you blushing?'

Myshkin thought a little.

'I don't know what's in your mind, Lizaveta Prokofyevna. I only see that you don't like the letter. You must admit that I might refuse to answer such a question, but to show you that I'm not uneasy about the letter and don't regret having written it, and am not blushing in the least on account of it' – Myshkin blushed at least twice as red – 'I'll repeat that letter to you, for I believe I know it by heart.'

Saying this, Myshkin repeated the letter almost word for word as he had written it.

'What a string of nonsense! What can be the meaning of such twaddle, according to you?' Lizaveta Prokofyevna asked sharply, after listening to the letter with extraordinary attention.

'I can't quite tell myself; I know that my feeling was sincere. At that time I had moments of intense life and extraordinary hopes.'

'What hopes?'

'It's hard to explain, but not what you're thinking of now, perhaps. Hopes ... well, in one word, hopes for the future and joy that perhaps I was not a stranger, not a foreigner, *there.* I took suddenly a great liking to my own country. One sunny morning I took up a pen and wrote a letter to her; why to her – I don't know. Sometimes one longs for a friend at one's side, you know; and I suppose I was longing for a friend Myshkin added after a pause.

'Are you in love?'

'N-no. I... I wrote to her as to a sister; I signed myself her brother, indeed.'

'Hm! On purpose; I understand.'

'It's very unpleasant for me to answer these questions, Lizaveta Prokofyevna.'

'I know it's unpleasant, but it doesn't matter to me in the least whether it is unpleasant. Listen, tell me the truth as you would before God. Are you telling me lies or not?'

'I'm not.'

'Are you speaking the truth saying that you are not in love?'

'I believe quite the truth.'

'Upon my word, "you believe"! Did the urchin give it her?'

'I asked Nikolay Ardalionovitch ...'

'The urchin! The urchin!' Lizaveta Prokofyevna interrupted vehemently. 'I know nothing about any Nikolay Ardalionovitch! The urchin!'

'Nikolay Ardalionovitch ...'

'The urchin, I tell you!'

'No, not the urchin, but Nikolay Ardalionovitch,' Myshkin answered at, last, firmly though rather softly.

'Oh, very well, my dear, very well! I shall keep that against you.' For a minute she overcame her emotion and was calm.

'And what's the meaning of the "poor knight"?'

'I don't know at all; I had nothing to do with it. Some joke.'

'Pleasant to hear it all at once! Only, could she have been interested in you? Why, she has called you a freak and an idiot.'

'You need not have told me that,' Myshkin observed reproachfully, though almost in a whisper.

'Don't be angry. She's a wilful, mad, spoilt girl – if she cares for anyone she'll be sure to rail at him aloud and abuse him to his face; I was just such another. Only please don't be triumphant, my dear fellow, she's not yours. I won't believe that, and it never will be! I speak that you may take steps now. Listen, swear you're not married to that woman.'

'Lizaveta Prokofyevna, what are you saying? Upon my word!' Myshkin almost jumped up in amazement.

'But you were almost *marrying* her, weren't you?'

'I was almost marrying her,' Myshkin whispered, and he bowed his head.

'Well, are you in love with *her*, then? Have you come here now on *her* account – for *her* sake?'

'I have not come to get married,' answered Myshkin.

'Is there anything in the world you hold sacred?'

'Yes.'

'Swear that it was not to get married to her.'

'I'll swear by anything you like!'

'I believe you. Kiss me. At last I can breathe freely, but let me tell you: Aglaia doesn't love you, you must be warned of that, and she won't marry you while I'm alive; do you hear?'

'I hear.' Myshkin blushed so much that he could not look at Lizaveta Prokofyevna.

'Make a note of it. I've been looking for you back as my Providence (you're not worth it!). I've been watering my pillow with my tears at night. Not on your account, my dear – don't be uneasy. I have my own grief – a very different one, everlasting and always the same. But this is why I've been looking for you back with such impatience. I still believe that God himself has sent you to me as a friend and brother. I have no one else, except old Princess Byelokonsky, and she's gone away; and besides, she's as stupid as a sheep in her old age. Now answer me simply: yes or no. Do you know why she shouted from her carriage the day before yesterday?'

'On my word of honour, I had nothing to do with it, and know nothing about it!'

'That's enough; I believe you. Now I have other ideas about that, but only yesterday morning I put the whole blame of it on Yevgeny Pavlovitch – all the day before yesterday and yesterday morning'. Now, of course, I can't help agreeing with them. It's perfectly obvious that he was being turned into ridicule like a fool on some account, for some reason, with some object. Anyway, it's suspicious! And it doesn't look well! But Aglaia won't marry him, I can tell you that! He may be a nice man, but that's how it's to be. I was hesitating before, but now I've made up my mind for certain: "You can lay me in my coffin and bury me in the earth and then you can marry your daughter"; that's what I said straight out to Ivan Fyodorovitch today. You see that I trust you. D'you see?'

'I see and I understand.'

Lizaveta Prokofyevna looked penetratingly at Myshkin. Perhaps she keenly desired to find out what impression this news about Yevgeny Pavlovitch made upon him.

'Do you know nothing about Gavril Ivolgin?'

'You mean … I know a great deal.'

'Did you know or didn't you that he was in correspondence with Aglaia.'

'I didn't know at all,' said Myshkin, surprised and even startled. 'What! You say Gavril Ardalionovitch in correspondence with Aglaia Ivanovna? Impossible!'

'Quite lately. His sister has been paving the way for him here all the winter. She's been working like a rat.'

'I don't believe it,' Myshkin repeated firmly, after some reflection and uneasiness. 'If it had been so I should certainly have known it.'

'I dare say he'd have come of himself and made a tearful confession on your bosom! Ach, you're a simpleton, a simpleton! Everyone deceives you like a … like a … And aren't you ashamed to trust him? Surely you must see that he's cheating you all round?'

'I know very well he does deceive me sometimes,' Myshkin brought out reluctantly in a low voice, 'and he knows that I know it…' and he broke off.

'Knows it and goes on trusting him! That's the last straw! It's just what one would expect of you, though, and there's no need for me to be surprised at it. Good Lord! Was there ever such a man! Oh dear, oh dear! And do you know that this Ganya or this Varya has put her into correspondence with Nastasya Filippovna?'

'Put whom?'

'Aglaia.'

'I don't believe it! It's impossible! With what object?' He leapt up from his chair.

'I don't believe it either, though there are proofs. She is a wilful girl, a whimsical girl, a mad girl! She's a wicked girl, wicked, wicked! I'm ready to repeat it for a thousand years – she's a wicked girl. They are all like that now, even that wet hen, Alexandra, but this one's out of all bounds. Yet I don't believe it either! – Perhaps because I don't want to believe it,' she added, as though to herself. 'Why haven't you been to see us?' She turned again suddenly to Myshkin. 'Why haven't you been for the last three days?' she cried impatiently once more.

Myshkin began telling her his reasons, but she interrupted him again.

'They all look upon you as a fool and deceive you! You went to town yesterday; I'll bet you've been on your knees, begging that scoundrel to take your money, your ten thousand!'

'Not at all; I never thought of it indeed. I haven't seen him; and besides, he's not a scoundrel. I've had a letter from him.'

'Show me the letter!'

Myshkin took a note out of his portfolio and handed it to Lizaveta Prokofyevna. The note ran:

> Dear Sir – I have, of course, in other people's eves not the faintest right to have any pride. In people's opinion I'm too insignificant for that. But that's in other people's eyes and not in yours. I am quite persuaded, my dear sir, that you are perhaps better than other men. I don't agree with Doktorenko, and differ from him in this conviction. I shall never take a farthing from you, but you have helped my mother, and for that I am bound to be grateful to you, even though it be weakness. In any case, I look upon you differently and think it only right to tell you so. And

thereafter I suppose there can be no more relations of any sort between us.

Antip Burdovsky

PS. The missing two hundred roubles will be repaid you correctly in course of time.

'What stuff and nonsense!' Lizaveta Prokofyevna commented, flinging back the note. 'It's not worth reading. What are you grinning at?'

'You must admit that you were glad to read it, too.'

'What! That pack of nonsense, rotting with vanity! Why, don't you see they're all crazy with pride and vanity?'

'Yes, but yet he's owned himself wrong, has broken with Doktorenko, and the vainer he is, the more it must have cost his vanity. Oh, what a child you are, Lizaveta Prokofyevna!'

'Do you want me to slap you at last?'

'No, not at all. But because you're glad of the note and conceal it. Why are you ashamed of your feelings? You're like that in everything.'

'Don't dare to come a step to see me,' cried Lizaveta Prokofyevna, jumping up and turning pale with anger. 'Never let me set eyes upon you again!'

'In another three days you'll come of your own accord and invite me ... Come, aren't you ashamed? These are your best feelings; why are you ashamed of them? You only torment yourself, you know.'

'I'll never invite you if I die for it! I'll forget your name! I have forgotten it!!'

She rushed away from Myshkin.

'I've been forbidden to come already, apart from you!' Myshkin called after her.

'Wha-at? Who's forbidden you?' She turned in a flash, as though pricked with a needle. Myshkin hesitated to answer; he felt he had made a serious slip.

'Who has forbidden you?' Lizaveta Prokofyevna cried violently.

'Aglaia Ivanovna forbids ...'

'When? Do spe-eak!!!'

'She sent word this morning that I must never dare come and see you again.'

Lizaveta Prokofyevna stood as though petrified, but she was reflecting.

'What did she send? Whom did she send? By the urchin? A verbal message?' she exclaimed suddenly again.

'I had a note,' said Myshkin.

'Where? Give it here! At once!'

Myshkin thought a minute, yet he pulled out of his waistcoat pocket an untidy scrap of paper on which was written:

> Prince Lyov Nikolayevitch! – If, after all that's happened you propose to astonish me by a visit to our villa, you won't, let me tell you, find me among those pleased to see you.
>
> Aglaia Epanchin

Lizaveta Prokofyevna reflected a minute; then she rushed at Myshkin, seized him by the hand, and drew him after her.

'Come along! At once! It must be at once, this minute!' she cried in an access of extraordinary excitement and impatience.

'But you're exposing me to ...'

'To what? You innocent ninny! You're not like a man! Well, now I shall see it all for myself, with my own eyes.'

'But you might let me take my hat, anyway

'Here's your horrid hat! Come along! Can't even choose his clothes with taste! ... She wrote that... hm! After what had happened ... in a fever,' muttered Lizaveta Prokofyevna, dragging Myshkin along and not for one minute releasing his hand. 'I stood up for you just now – said aloud you were a fool not to come ... But for that, she wouldn't have written such a senseless note! An improper note! Improper, for a well-bred, well-brought-up, clever girl! Hm!' she went on, 'Or... or perhaps... perhaps she was vexed herself at your not coming, only she didn't consider that it wouldn't do to write like that to an idiot, because he'd take it literally, as he has done. Why are you listening?' she cried, flaring up, realising that she had said too much. 'She wants someone to laugh at like you. It's long since she's seen such a one, that's why she's asking you! And I'm glad, very glad, that she'll make fun of you now – very glad; it's just what you deserve. And she knows how to do it. Oh, she knows how! ...'

PART THREE

Chapter 1

We are constantly hearing complaints that there are no practical people in Russia; that there are plenty of politicians, plenty of generals, that any number of business men of all sorts can be found at a moment's notice, but that there are no practical men – at least, everyone is complaining of the lack of them. There are not even efficient railway servants, we hear, on some of the lines; it's not even possible to get a steamship company decently managed. You hear of a railway collision or of a bridge that breaks under a train on a newly opened railway-line. Or you hear of a train's wintering in a snowdrift: the journey should have lasted a few hours and the train was snowed up for five days. One hears of hundreds of tons of goods lying rotting for two or three months at a time before they are dispatched. And I am told (though it is hardly credible) that a merchant's clerk who persisted in worrying for the dispatch of his goods got a box on the ear from the superintendent, who justified this display of efficiency on his part on the ground that he lost his patience. There are so many government offices that it staggers one to think of them; everyone has been in the service, is in the service, or intends to be in the service – so that one wonders how, with such an abundance of material, a decent board of management cannot be made up to run a railway or a line of steamers.

This question is often met by a very simple answer – so simple, in fact, that the explanation seems hardly credible. It's true, we are told, everyone has been or is in government service in Russia, and this system has been going on for two hundred years on the most approved German pattern from grandfather to grandson – but officials are the most unpractical of people, and things have come to such a pass that a purely theoretical character and lack of practical knowledge were only lately regarded, even in official circles as almost the highest qualification and recommendation. But there's no need to discuss officials; we set out to talk about practical men. There's no doubt that diffidence and complete lack of initiative have always been considered the chief sign of a practical man, and indeed are so regarded still. But why blame ourselves only – if this opinion is regarded as an accusation? From the beginning, all the world over, lack of originality has been reckoned the chief characteristic and best recommendation of an active, businesslike and practical man, and at least ninety-nine per cent of mankind – and that's a low estimate – have always held that opinion, and at most one per cent looks at it differently.

Inventors and geniuses have almost always been looked on as no better than fools at the beginning of their career, and very frequently at the end of it also; this is the most hackneyed observation, familiar to everyone. If, for instance, for scores of years, everybody had been putting their money into a bank and millions had been invested in it at 4 per cent, and then the bank ceased to exist and people were left to their own initiative, the greater part of those millions would infallibly be lost in wild speculation or in the hands of swindlers – and in fact this is only in accordance with the dictates of propriety and decorum. Yes, decorum; if a proper diffidence and decorous lack of originality have been universally accepted as the essential characteristics of a practical man and a gentleman, a sudden transformation would be quite ungentlemanly and almost indecent. What tender and devoted mother wouldn't be dismayed and ill with terror at her son's or daughter's stepping one hair's-breadth off the beaten track. 'No, better let him be happy and live in comfort without originality,' is what every mother thinks as she rocks the cradle. And our nurses have from the earliest times sung as they dandle their babies, 'He shall dress in gold, the pet-wear a general's epaulette.' Thus even with our nurses the rank of general has been considered the highest pinnacle of Russian happiness, and so has been the most popular national ideal of peaceful and contented bliss. And, indeed, after passing an examination without distinction and serving thirty-five years, who can fail to become at last a general and to have invested a decent sum in the bank? So that a Russian attains the position of a practical and business man without the slightest effort. The only person among us who can fail to reach the general's rank is the original man – in other words, the man who won't be quiet. Possibly there is some mistake about this, but, speaking generally, this is true, and our society has been perfectly correct in its definition of a practical man.

But much of this is superfluous; I had intended simply to say a few words of explanation about our friends the Epanchins. That family, or at any rate the more reflective members of it, suffered continually from a common family characteristic, the very opposite of the virtues we've been discussing above. Though they did not clearly understand the fact (for it is difficult to understand it), they yet sometimes suspected that everything in their family was unlike what is found in all other families. In other families everything went smoothly, with them it was all ups and downs; other people seemed to follow routine – they always seemed to be doing something exceptional. Other people were always decorously timid, but they were not. Lizaveta Prokofyevna was, indeed, liable to alarms – too much so, in fact, but it was not the decorous, worldly timidity for which they longed. But perhaps it was only Lizaveta Prokofyevna who was worried about it; the girls were too young, though they were penetrating and ironical; and though the general penetrated (not without some strain, however), he never said anything more than 'Hm' in perplexing circumstances and put all his trust in his wife. So the responsibility rested on her. It was not that this family was distinguished by marked initiative or was drawn out of the common rut by any conscious inclination towards originality, which would have been a complete breach of the proprieties. Oh no! There was really nothing of the sort, that is, there was no conscious purpose in it, and yet, in spite of all, the Epanchin family, though highly respectable, was not quite what every respectable family ought to be. Of late Lizaveta Prokofyevna had begun to blame herself alone and her 'unfortunate' character for this state of affairs, which increased her distress. She was continually reproaching herself with being 'a silly and eccentric old woman who didn't know how to behave,' and she worried over imaginary troubles, was in a continual state of perplexity, was at a loss how to act in the most ordinary contingencies, and always magnified every misfortune.

At the beginning of our narrative we mentioned that the Epanchin family enjoyed the sincere esteem of all. Even General Epanchin, although a man of obscure origin, was received everywhere and treated with respect. He did, in fact, deserve respect – in the first place, as a man of wealth and of some standing, and secondly, as a very decent fellow, though by no means of great intellect. But a certain dullness of mind seems an almost necessary qualification, if not for every public man, at least for everyone seriously engaged in making money. Finally, General Epanchin had good manners, was modest, knew how to hold his tongue, and yet would not allow himself to be trampled upon, not simply because he was a general, but also because he was an honest and honourable man. As for his wife, she was, as we have explained already, of good family, though that is not a matter of great consideration among us, unless there are powerful friends as well. But she had acquired a circle of such friends; she was respected, and in the end loved by persons of such consequence that it was natural that everyone should follow their example in respecting and receiving her. There could be no doubt that her anxieties about her family were groundless; there was very little cause for them and they were ridiculously exaggerated. But if you have a wart on the forehead or on the nose, you always fancy that no one has anything else to do in the world than stare at your wart, make fun of it, and despise you for it, even though you have discovered America. No doubt Lizaveta Prokofyevna was generally considered 'eccentric', yet there could be no question about her being esteemed, but she came at last to cease to believe in that esteem, and the whole trouble lay in that. Looking at her daughters, she was fretted by the suspicion that she was continually ruining their prospects, that she was ridiculous, insupportable, and did not know how to behave, for which, of course, she was always blaming her daughters and her husband, and quarrelling with them all day long, though she loved them with a self-sacrificing and almost passionate affection.

What worried her most of all was the suspicion that her daughters were becoming just as eccentric as she was and that girls in society were not and ought not to be like them. 'They are growing into nihilists, that's what it comes to!' she repeated to herself every minute. For the last year, and especially of late, this melancholy notion had grown more and more fixed in her mind. 'To begin with, why don't they get married?' she kept asking herself. 'To torment their mother – they make that the object of their existence; and it all comes from these new ideas, these cursed women's rights!

Didn't Aglaia take it into her head six months ago to cut off her magnificent hair? (Heavens, even I hadn't hair like that when I was young!) She had the scissors in her hand; I had to go down on my knees to her! ... Well, she did it out of spite, no doubt, to torment her mother, for she is a spiteful, self-willed, spoiled girl, and above all spiteful, spiteful, spiteful! But didn't that fat Alexandra mean to follow her example and try to cut off her fleece, and not from spite, not from caprice, but in all simplicity, like a fool, because Aglaia persuaded her that without hair she would sleep better and be free from headache? And the numbers and numbers of suitors they have had in these last five years! And there really were nice men, first-rate men, among them! What are they waiting for? Why don't they get married? Simply to annoy their mother – there's no other reason for it, none whatever!'

At last the sun seemed to be dawning even for her maternal heart, at least one daughter, at least Adelaïda, would be settled. 'There's one off our hands,' said Madame Epanchin, when she had occasion to refer to the event aloud (in her thoughts she expressed herself with far greater tenderness). And how well how suitably, the whole thing had come about! Even in society, it was talked of with respect. He was a distinguished man, a prince, a man of fortune, and a nice man, and, what's more, it was a marriage of inclination. What could be better? But she had always been less anxious about Adelaïda than about the other two, though her artistic proclivities sometimes gravely troubled the mother's apprehensive heart. 'But she is of a cheerful disposition and has plenty of sense, too – she's a girl that will always fall on her legs,' was her consoling reflection. She was more afraid for Aglaia than for any of them. About the eldest girl, Alexandra, her mother could not make up her mind whether to be afraid or not. Sometimes she fancied the girl was 'utterly hopeless.'

'She is twenty-five so she will be an old maid, and with her looks!' Lizaveta Prokofyevna positively shed tears at night thinking of her, while Alexandra herself lay sleeping tranquilly. 'What is one to make of her? Is she a nihilist or simply a fool?' That she was not a fool even Lizaveta Prokofyevna had no doubt, she had the greatest respect for Alexandra's judgement and was fond of asking her advice. But that she was 'a wet hen' she did not doubt for a moment, 'so calm that there's no making her out. Though wet hens are not calm – foo, I am quite muddled over them!'

Lizaveta Prokofyevna had an inexplicable feeling of sympathy and commiseration for Alexandra – more, in fact, than for Aglaia, whom she idolised. But the bitter sallies (in which her maternal solicitude and sympathy chiefly showed itself), her taunts and names, such as 'wet hen,' only amused Alexandra. It came to such a pass that at times the most trivial matters made Madame Epanchin dreadfully angry and drove her to perfect frenzy. Alexandra, for instance, was fond of sleeping late and had a great many dreams, but her dreams were always marked by an extraordinary ineptitude and innocence – they might have been the dreams of a child of seven. And the very innocence of her dreams became a source of irritation to her mother. Once Alexandra dreamed of nine hens, and it had been the cause of a regular quarrel between her and her mother – why it would be difficult to explain. Once, and once only, she had succeeded in dreaming of something that might be called original – she dreamed of a monk who was all alone in a dark room into which she was afraid to go. The dream was at once reported with triumph to their mother by her two laughing sisters, but their mother was angry again and called them all three a set of fools.

'Hm! She is as calm as a fool and a regular wet hen; there's no waking her up; and yet she is sad, she looks quite sad sometimes! What is she grieving over? What is it?' Sometimes she put that question to her husband, and, as usual, she asked it hysterically, threateningly, expecting an immediate reply. Ivan Fyodorovitch said 'Hm,' frowned, shrugged his shoulders, and with a despairing gesture delivered himself of the dictum, 'She needs a husband.'

'Only God grant her one unlike you, Ivan Fyodorovitch!' Lizaveta Prokofyevna burst out like a bomb at last, 'unlike you in his thoughts and judgements, Ivan Fyodorovitch. Not a churlish churl like you, Ivan Fyodorovitch ...'

Ivan Fyodorovitch promptly made his escape, and Lizaveta Prokofyevna calmed down after her 'explosion.' The same evening, of course, she would invariably be particularly attentive, gentle, affectionate to her husband, 'the churlish churl,' Ivan Fyodorovitch, to her kind, dear, and adored Ivan Fyodorovitch, for she had been fond of him and even in love with him all her life – a fact of which he was well aware himself, and he had a boundless respect for her.

But her chief and continual anxiety was Aglaia.

'She is exactly, exactly like me, the very picture of me in every respect,' the mother used to say to herself. 'Self-willed, horrid little imp! Nihilist, eccentric, mad and spiteful, spiteful, spiteful! Good Lord, how unhappy she will be!'

But, as we have said already, a spell of sunshine had softened and lighted up everything for a moment. For almost a whole month Lizaveta Prokofyevna had a complete respite from her anxieties. Adelaïda's approaching marriage made people in society talk about Aglaia too, and Aglaia's manner had been so good, so even, so clever, so enchanting; rather proud, but that suited her so well! She had been so affectionate, so gracious to her mother all that month! ('It's true it was necessary to be very, very careful about Yevgeny Pavlovitch, to get to the bottom of him, and Aglaia doesn't seem to favour him much more than the rest.') Anyway, she had suddenly become such a delightful girl; and how handsome she was – mercy on us, how handsome! She grew more beautiful day by day. And here …

And here this wretched little prince, this miserable little idiot, had hardly made his appearance and everything was in a turmoil again, everything in the house was topsy-turvy.

What had happened, though?

Nothing would have happened to other people, that was certain. But it was Lizaveta Prokofyevna's peculiarity that in the combinations and concatenations of the most ordinary things she managed to see, through her ever-present anxiety, something which alarmed her at times till it made her ill and inspired in her a terror absolutely exaggerated and inexplicable, and for that reason all the harder to bear. What must have been her feelings when suddenly now, through the tangle of absurd and groundless worries, something actually became apparent that really seemed important – something that might in all seriousness call for anxiety, hesitation, and suspicion!

'And the insolence of writing me that accursed anonymous letter about that *hussy,* that she is in communication with Aglaia,' Lizaveta Prokofyevna was thinking all the way home, as she drew Myshkin along, and afterwards, as she made him sit down at the round table about which all the family was assembled. 'How did they dare to think of such a thing! I should die of shame if I believed a syllable of it, or if I were to show Aglaia that letter. It's making a laughing-stock of us, of the Epanchins! And it's all

Ivan Fyodorovitch's fault; it's all your fault, Ivan Fyodorovitch! Ah, why didn't we spend the summer at Yelagin Island? I said we ought to have gone to Yelagin. It may be that horrid Varya wrote the letter, or perhaps… it's all Ivan Fyodorovitch's fault, it's all his fault! It's for his benefit that *hussy* got this up, as a souvenir of their former relations, to make him look a fool, just as she made fun of him as a fool before and led him by the nose when he used to be taking her pearls … And yet the long and short of it is that we all are brought into it; your daughters are brought into it, Ivan Fyodorovitch – young girls, young ladies, young ladies moving in the best society, marriageable girls; they were there, they were standing by, they heard it all, and they were dragged into the scene with those nasty boys too. You may congratulate yourself, they were there too and heard it! I won't forgive, I won't forgive, I'll never forgive this wretched little prince! And why has Aglaia been hysterical for the last three days? Why is it she has been on the point of quarrelling with her sisters, even with Alexandra, whose hands she always kisses as though she were her mother she has such a respect for her? Why has she behaved so enigmatically with everyone for the last three days? What has Gavril Ivolgin to do with it? Why is it that she praised Ivolgin today and yesterday too, and burst out crying? Why is it that that cursed "poor knight" is mentioned in that anonymous letter, and she never even showed her sisters the prince's letter? And why …what, what induced me to run to him like a cat in a fit and to drag him here with me! Mercy on us, I must have taken leave of my senses to do this! To talk to a young man about my daughter's secrets … and about secrets that almost concern him! Good heavens, it's a blessing he is an idiot and … and … a friend of the family. But is it possible Aglaia is fascinated by such a queer fish! Heavens, what am I babbling! Oh dear, oh dear! We are a set of originals … they ought to put us all in a glass case – me especially – and exhibit us at twopence a head. I shall never forgive you for this, Ivan Fyodorovitch, never! And why is it she doesn't make fun of him now? She declared she'd make fun of him and now she doesn't! There she is, gazing at him, all eyes; she doesn't speak, she doesn't go away, she stands there, yet she told him not to come herself … He sits there quite pale. And that confounded chatterbox, Yevgeny Pavlovitch, keeps the whole conversation to himself. How he does run on! – Doesn't let one get a word in edgeways. I could have found out everything at once, if I could only turn the conversation on it…'

Myshkin really was almost pale, as he sat at the round table, and he seemed to be at the same time in a state of great uneasiness, and at moments in a rapture that flooded his soul, though he could not comprehend it himself. Oh, how he feared to glance towards the corner from which two dark eyes were intently watching him, and at the same time how his heart throbbed with delight that he was sitting among them again, that he would hear her familiar voice – after what she had written to him! Heavens, what would she say to him now! He had not uttered one word yet, and he listened with strained attention to the 'running on' of Yevgeny Pavlovitch, who had rarely been in such a happy and excited mood as that evening. Myshkin listened to him, but for a long time scarcely took in a word of what he was saying. Except Ivan Fyodorovitch, who had not yet returned from Petersburg, all the family was assembled. Prince S— was there too. They seemed to be meaning in a little time to go and listen to the band before tea. The conversation had evidently begun before Myshkin arrived. A little later Kolya made his appearance on the verandah. 'So he is received here as before,' Myshkin thought to himself.

The Epanchins' villa was a luxurious one, built as a Swiss chalet and was picturesquely covered with flowering creepers. It was surrounded on all sides by a small but charming flower garden. They all sat on the verandah as at Myshkin's, only the verandah was rather wider and more sumptuous.

The subject of the conversation appeared to be to the taste of few of the party. It had apparently arisen out of a heated argument, and no doubt everyone would have been glad to change the subject. But Yevgeny Pavlovitch seemed to persist all the more obstinately, regardless of the impression he was making; Myshkin's arrival seemed to make him even more eager. Lizaveta Prokofyevna frowned, though she did not quite understand it. Aglaia, who was sitting on one side, almost in a corner, remained listening, obstinately silent.

'Allow me,' Yevgeny Pavlovitch was protesting warmly. 'I say nothing against Liberalism. Liberalism is not a sin; it is an essential part of the whole, which without it would drop to pieces or perish; Liberalism has just as much right to exist as the most judicious Conservatism. But I am attacking Russian Liberalism, and I repeat again I attack it just for the reason that the Russian Liberal is not a Russian Liberal, but an un-Russian Liberal. Show me a Russian Liberal and I'll kiss him in front of you all.'

'That is, if he cares to kiss you,' said Alexandra, who was exceptionally excited, so much so that her cheeks were redder than usual.

'There,' thought Lizaveta Prokofyevna to herself, 'she goes on sleeping and eating, and you can't rouse her, and then suddenly, once a year, she pops up and begins talking in such a way that one can only gape at her.'

Myshkin momentarily noticed that Alexandra seemed particularly to dislike Yevgeny Pavlovitch's talking too light-heartedly; he was talking about a serious subject, and seemed to be hot about it, and at the same time he seemed to be making a joke of it.

'I was maintaining just now, just before you came in, Prince,' Yevgeny Pavlovitch went on, 'that Liberals so far have come only from two classes of society – from the old landowning class, that's now a thing of the past, and from clerical families. And as those two classes have become regular castes, something quite apart from the nation, and more and more so from generation to generation, so everything they have done and are doing is absolutely non-national.'

'What? So everything that has been done is un-Russian?' protested Prince S—.

'Non-national; though it's Russian, it's not national. The Liberals among us are not Russian, and the Conservatives are not Russian either, any of them… And you may be sure that the nation will accept nothing of what has been done by landowners and divinity students, either now or later …'

'Well, that's too much! How can you maintain such a paradox, that is, if you are speaking in earnest. I must protest against such wild statements about the Russian landowner; you are a Russian landowner yourself,' Prince S— objected warmly.

'But I didn't speak of the Russian landowner in the sense in which you are taking it. It's the most respectable class, if only because I belong to it; especially now, since it has ceased to be a caste …'

'Do you mean to say there has been nothing national in literature?' Alexandra interposed.

'I am not an authority on literature, but even Russian literature is in my opinion not Russian at all, unless perhaps Lomonosov, Pushkin, and Gogol are national.'

'That's not bad, to begin with; and besides, one of those was a peasant and the other two were landowners,' said Adelaïda, laughing.

'Quite so, but don't be triumphant. As, of all Russian writers, these three are the only ones that have so far been able to say something of their own, something not borrowed, they have by this fact become national. Any Russian who says or writes or does anything of his own – something original, not borrowed – inevitably becomes national, even if he can't speak Russian properly. That I regard as an axiom. But we were not talking of literature at first; we were talking of Socialists, at the beginning. Well, I maintain that we haven't one single Russian Socialist; there are none and there have never been, for all our Socialists are also landowners or divinity students. All our notorious and professed Socialists, both here and abroad, are nothing more than Liberals from the landed gentry of the serf-owning days. Why are you laughing? Show me their books, show me their theories, their memoirs; and, though I am no literary critic, I can write you the most convincing criticism, in which I'll show you as clear as daylight that every page of their books, pamphlets, and memoirs has been written by Russian landowners of the old school. Their anger, their indignation, their wit, are all typical of that class, as it was even in pre-Famusov" times; their raptures, their tears are perhaps real, genuine tears, but they are landowners' tears – landowners' or divinity students' ... You are laughing again, and you are laughing too, Prince? You don't agree either, then?'

They really were all laughing, and Myshkin smiled too.

'I can't say offhand yet whether I agree or not,' Myshkin brought out, suddenly leaving off smiling and starting with the air of a schoolboy caught in a fault, 'but I assure you I am listening to you with the greatest pleasure ...'

He was almost breathless, as he said this, and cold sweat came out on his forehead. They were the first words he had uttered since he had sat down. He tried to look round at the company and had not the courage; Yevgeny Pavlovitch caught his movement and smiled.

'I will tell you a fact, gentlemen,' he went on in the same tone as before, that is, with extraordinary gusto and warmth, though at the same time he seemed almost laughing, possibly at his own words – 'a fact, the observation and discovery of which I have the honour of ascribing to myself and to myself alone; nothing has been said or written about it, anyway. This fact expresses the whole essence of Russian Liberalism of the sort of which I am speaking. In the first place, what is Liberalism, speaking generally, but an attack (whether judicious or mistaken is another question) on the established order of things? That's so, isn't it? Well, my fact is that Russian Liberalism is not an attack on the existing order of things, but is an attack on the very essence of things, on the things themselves, not merely on the order of things; not on the Russian *regime*, but on Russia itself. My Liberal goes so far as to deny even Russia itself, that is, he hates and beats his own mother. Every unhappy and disastrous fact in Russia excites his laughter and almost his delight. He hates the national habits, Russian history, everything. If there is any justification for him, it is that he doesn't know what he is about and takes his hatred of Russia for Liberalism of the most fruitful kind. (Oh, you often meet among us Liberals who are applauded by the rest and who are perhaps the most absurd, the most stupid and dangerous of Conservatives, and they are unaware of it themselves.) This hatred of Russia was quite lately almost regarded by some of our Liberals as sincere love for their country. They boasted that they knew better than other people how that love ought to show itself, but now they have become more candid and are ashamed of the very idea of "loving" one's country; the very conception of it they have dismissed and banished as trivial and pernicious. This is a fact; I insist on that and ... and the truth must be told sooner or later fully, simply, and openly. But it's a fact that has never been heard of and has never existed in any other people since the world began, and so it is an accidental phenomenon and may not be permanent, I admit. There cannot be a Liberal anywhere else who hates his own country. How can we explain it among us? Why, by the same fact as before, that the Russian Liberal hitherto has not been Russian; nothing else explains it, to my thinking.'

'I take all that you have said as a joke, Yevgeny Pavlovitch,' Prince S— replied earnestly.

'I haven't seen every Liberal, so I can't undertake to judge,' said Alexandra, 'but I've listened to your ideas with indignation: you've taken an individual case and generalised from it, and so you've been unjust.'

'An individual case? Ah! The word has been uttered,' Yevgeny Pavlovitch caught her up. 'Prince, what do you think? Have I taken an individual case or not?'

'I ought to say, too, that I have been very little with Liberals and seen very little of them,' said Myshkin, 'but I fancy that you may be partly right and that the sort of Russian Liberalism of which you are speaking really is disposed to hate Russia itself, not only its institutions. Of course, this is only partly true ... of course, this cannot be true of all.'

He broke off in confusion. In spite of his excitement, he was greatly interested in the conversation. One of Myshkin's striking characteristics was the extraordinary *naïveté* of the attention, with which he always listened to anything that interested him, and of the answers he gave when anyone asked him questions. His face, and even his attitude, somehow reflected that *naïveté*, that good faith, unsuspicious of mockery or humour. But though Yevgeny Pavlovitch had for a long time past always behaved to him with a certain shade of mockery, now, on hearing his answer, he looked very gravely at him, as though he had not expected such an answer from him.

'So ... how strange it is of you, though!' he said. 'Did you really answer me in earnest, Prince?'

'Why, didn't you ask me in earnest?' replied Myshkin in surprise.

Everyone laughed.

'Trust him,' said Adelaïda. 'Yevgeny Pavlovitch always makes fun of everyone! If you only knew what stories he tells sometimes with perfect seriousness!'

'I think this is a tedious conversation and there was no need to have begun it,' Alexandra observed abruptly. 'We meant to go for a walk.'

'And let us go! It's an exquisite evening,' cried Yevgeny Pavlovitch. 'But to show you that this time I was speaking quite seriously, and still more to show the prince so (you have interested me extremely, Prince, and I assure you I am not quite such a silly fellow as I must seem to you – though I really am a silly fellow!), and if you'll allow me, ladies and gentleman, I will ask the prince one last question to satisfy my own curiosity, and then we will leave off. This question occurred to me very appropriately two hours ago. You see, Prince, I sometimes think of serious things too. I answered it, but let us see what the prince will say. He spoke just now about an "individual case." This phrase of ours is a very significant one; one often hears it. Everyone has been talking and writing of late about that dreadful murder of six persons by that … young man and of the strange Speech made by the counsel for the defence, in which it was said that, considering the poverty of the criminal, it must have been *natural* for him to think of murdering these six people. Those are not precisely the words used, but the sense, I think, is that or very much like it. It's my private opinion that the lawyer who gave expression to this strange idea was under the conviction that he was expressing the most liberal, the most humane and progressive sentiment that could be uttered in our day. Well, what do you make of it? Is this corruption of ideas and convictions, is the possibility of such a distorted and extraordinary view an 'individual case' or a typical example?'

Everyone laughed again.

'Individual, of course, individual,' laughed Alexandra and Adelaïda.

'And let me warn you again, Yevgeny Pavlovitch,' said Prince S'—, 'that your joke is growing very stale.'

'What do you think, Prince?' Yevgeny Pavlovitch went on, not listening, but catching Myshkin's earnest and interested eyes fixed on him. 'Does it seem to you to be an individual case or typical? I'll own it was on your account I thought of the question.'

'No, not individual,' Myshkin said gently but firmly.

'Upon my word, Lyov Nikolayevitch,' cried Prince S— with some vexation, 'don't you see that he is trying to catch you? He is certainly in fun and he means to make game of you.'

'I thought Yevgeny Pavlovitch was in earnest,' said Myshkin, blushing and dropping his eyes.

'My dear prince,' Prince S — went on, 'remember what we were talking about once, three months ago; you said that one could point to so many remarkable and talented lawyers in our new-established law courts, and how many highly remarkable verdicts had been given by the juries! How pleased you were about it, and how pleased I was at the time seeing your pleasure! We said that we had a right to be proud … And this inept defence, this strange argument, is, of course, a casual exception, the one among thousands.'

Myshkin thought a moment, but with an air of perfect conviction, though speaking softly and even, it seemed, timidly, he answered, 'I only meant to say that a perversion of ideas and conceptions – as Yevgeny Pavlovitch expressed it – is very often to be met with, is, unhappily, far more the general rule than an exceptional case. And so much so that if this perversion were not such a general phenomenon, perhaps there would not be such impossible crimes as these …'

'Impossible crimes! But I assure you that just such crimes, and perhaps still more awful ones, have existed in the past and at all times, and not only among us but everywhere, and, in my opinion, will occur again and again for a very long time. The difference is that there was much less publicity in Russia in old days, while now people have begun to talk and even to write of such cases, so that it seems as though these criminals were a recent phenomenon. That's how your mistake arises – an extremely naïve mistake, Prince, I assure you,' said Prince S—, with a mocking smile.

'I know that there were very many crimes and just as awful ones in the past. I have been lately in the prisons and succeeded in making acquaintance with some criminals and convicts. There are even more terrible criminals than that one, men who have committed a dozen murders and feel no remorse whatever. But I tell you what I noticed: that the most hardened and unrepentant murderer knows all the same that he is a "criminal", that is, he considers in his conscience that he has acted wrongly, *even* though he *is* unrepentant. And every one of them was like that; while those of whom Yevgeny Pavlovitch was speaking refuse even to consider themselves as criminals and think that they are in the right and … that they have even acted well – it almost comes to that. That's, to my thinking, where the terrible difference lies. And observe, they are all young, that is, they are all of the age in which one may most easily and helplessly fall under the influence of perverted ideas.'

Prince S— had ceased laughing and listened to Myshkin with a puzzled air. Alexandra, who had been on the point of saying something, held her peace, as though some special thought made her pause. Yevgeny Pavlovitch looked at Myshkin in genuine surprise, with no tinge of mockery.

'But why are you so surprised at him, my good sir?' said Lizaveta Prokofyevna, breaking in unexpectedly. 'Why did you think he was not so clever as you and could not reason as well as you can?'

'No, I didn't mean that,' said Yevgeny Pavlovitch. 'Only, how is it, Prince – excuse the question – if you see this so clearly, how is it that you (excuse me again) did not notice the same perversion of ideas and moral convictions in that strange case … the other day, you know … of Burdovsky's, wasn't it? It's exactly the same. I fancied at the time that you didn't see it at all?'

'But let me tell you, my dear man,' said Lizaveta Prokofyevna, getting hot, 'we all noticed it. We sit here feeling superior to him. But he got a letter from one of them today, from the worst of the lot, the pimply one – do you remember, Alexandra? He begs his pardon in the letter – in a fashion of his own, of course – and says he has broken with the companion who egged him on at the time – do you remember, Alexandra? – and that he puts more faith now in the prince. But we haven't had such a letter, though we know how to turn up our noses at him.'

'And Ippolit has just moved to our villa, too,' cried Kolya.

'What? Is he there already?' said Myshkin, taken aback.

'He arrived just after you had gone out with Lizaveta Prokofyevna. I brought hint.'

'Well, I'll bet anything,' Lizaveta Prokofyevna fired up suddenly, quite forgetting that she had just been praising Myshkin, 'I'll bet that he went last night to see him in his garret and begged his pardon on *his* knees, so that that spiteful spitfire might deign to move to his villa. Did you go yesterday? You've confessed it yourself. Is it true? Did you go on your knees?'

'He didn't do anything of the kind,' cried Kolya, 'quite the contrary. Ippolit seized the prince's hand yesterday and kissed it twice. I saw it myself. That's how the interview ended, except that the prince told him simply that he would be more comfortable at the villa, and he instantly agreed to come as soon as he felt better.'

'There's no need, Kolya …' murmured Myshkin, getting up and taking his hat. 'Why are you talking about this? I…'

'Where are you going?' said Lizaveta Prokofyevna, stopping him.

'Don't trouble, Prince,' Kolya went on in his excitement. 'Don't go and disturb him; he is having a nap after the journey. He is very pleased, and you know, Prince, I think it will be much better if you don't meet today, if you put it off till tomorrow, or else he'll be uncomfortable again. He said this morning that he hadn't felt so strong and well for the last six months, he isn't coughing half as much.'

Myshkin noticed that Aglaia suddenly left her place and came to the table. He dared not look at her, but he felt in his whole being that she was looking at him at that moment and was perhaps looking at him wrathfully, that there must be indignation in her black eyes and that her face was flushed.

'But I think, Nikolay Ardalionovitch, that you made a mistake in bringing him here, if you mean that consumptive boy who cried then and invited us to his funeral,' observed Yevgeny Pavlovitch. 'He talked so eloquently of the wall of the house opposite that he will certainly be homesick for that wall; you may be sure of that.'

'That's the truth; he will quarrel, break with you and go away – that will be the end of it.'

And Lizaveta Prokofyevna drew her work-basket near her with an air of dignity, forgetting that everyone was preparing to go for a walk.

'I remember that he bragged a lot of that wall,' Yevgeny Pavlovitch put in again. 'He can't die eloquently without that wall, and he is very anxious for an eloquent death-scene.'

'What of it?' muttered Myshkin. 'If you won't forgive him, he'll die without your forgiveness ... Now he has come here for the sake of the trees.'

'Oh, for my part I forgive him everything; you can tell him so.'

'That's not the way to take it,' Myshkin answered softly and, as it were, reluctantly, looking at one spot on the floor and not raising his eyes. 'You ought to be ready to receive his forgiveness too.'

'How do I come in? What wrong have I done him?'

'If you don't understand, then ... But you do understand; he wanted... to bless you all then and to receive your blessing, that was all.'

'Dear prince,' Prince S— hastened to interpose somewhat apprehensively, exchanging glances with some of the others, 'it's not easy to reach paradise on earth, but you reckon on finding it; paradise is a difficult matter, Prince, much more difficult than it seems to your good heart. We had better drop the subject, or else we may all feel uncomfortable too and then ...'

'Let's go and hear the band,' said Lizaveta Prokofyevna sharply, getting up from her place angrily.

The others followed her example.

Chapter 2

All at once Myshkin went up to Yevgeny Pavlovitch.

'Yevgeny Pavlovitch,' he said with strange heat, seizing his hand, 'believe that I look upon you as the best and most honourable of men in spite of everything. Be sure of that …'

Yevgeny Pavlovitch positively drew back a step with surprise. For a moment he was struggling with an irresistible desire to laugh, but looking closer he saw that Myshkin seemed not himself, or at least was in a peculiar state of mind.

'I don't mind betting, Prince,' he cried, 'that you didn't mean to say that, nor perhaps to speak to me at all. But what's the matter with your Are you feeling ill?'

'That may be, that may well be. And you were very clever to notice that perhaps it was not you I meant to address.'

He said this with a strange and even absurd smile, but, seeming suddenly excited, he cried, 'Don't remind me of my conduct three days ago! I've been very much ashamed for the last three days… I know that I was to blame …'

'But… but what have you done so dreadful?'

'I see that you are perhaps more ashamed of me than anyone, Yevgeny Pavlovitch. You are blushing; that's the sign of a good heart. I'm going away directly, you may be sure of that.'

What's the matter with him? Do his fits begin like this?' Lizaveta Prokofyevna asked Kolya in alarm.

'Don't be uneasy, Lizaveta Prokofyevna. I'm not in a fit, and I'm just going. I know that I am … afflicted. I've been ill for twenty-four years, from my birth till I was twenty-four years old. You must take what I say as from a sick man now. I'm going directly – directly. You may be sure of that. I'm not ashamed, for it would be strange to be ashamed of that, wouldn't it? But I'm out of place in society … I'm not speaking from wounded vanity … I've been reflecting during these three days and I've made up my mind that I ought to explain things sincerely and honourably to you at the first opportunity. There are ideas, very great ideas, of which I ought not to begin to speak, because I should be sure to make everyone laugh. Prince S— has warned me of that very thing just now … My gestures are unsuitable. I've no right sense of proportion. My words are incongruous, not befitting the subject, and that's a degradation for those ideas. And so I have no right … Besides, I'm morbidly sensitive… I am certain that no one would hurt my feelings in this house, and that I am more loved here than I deserve. But I know (I know for certain) that twenty years' illness must leave traces, so that it's impossible not to laugh at me … sometimes … It is so, isn't it?'

He looked about him as though expecting an answer.

All were standing in painful perplexity at this unexpected, morbid, and in any case apparently causeless, outbreak. But this outbreak gave rise to a strange episode.

'But why are you saying that here?' cried Aglaia suddenly. 'Why do you say it to *them?* Them! Them!'

She seemed to be stirred to the highest pitch of indignation. Her eyes flashed fire. Myshkin stood facing her, dumb and speechless, and he suddenly turned pale.

'There's not one person here who is worth such words,' Aglaia burst out. 'There's no one here, no one, who is worth your little finger, nor your mind, nor your heart! You are more honourable than any of them, nobler, better, kinder, cleverer than any of them! Some of them are not worthy to stoop to pick up the handkerchief you have just dropped … Why do you humble yourself and put yourself below them? Why do you distort everything in yourself? Why have you no pride?'

'Mercy on us! Who could have expected this?' cried Lizaveta Prokofyevna, throwing up her hands.

' "The poor knight." Hurrah!' cried Kolya, enchanted.

'Be silent! … How dare they insult me in your house!' cried Aglaia, suddenly flying out at her mother. She was by now in that hysterical state when no line is drawn and no check regarded. 'Why do you all torture me, every one of you? Why have they been pestering me for the last three days on your account, Prince? Nothing will induce me to marry you! Let me tell you that I never will on any consideration. Understand that. As though one could marry an absurd creature like you! Look at yourself in the looking-glass, what do you look like standing there? Why, why do they tease me and say I'm going to marry you? You ought to know that. You are in the plot with them too!'

'No one has ever teased you about it,' muttered Adelaïda in alarm.

'No one has ever thought of such a thing. No one has said a word about it!' cried Alexandra.

'Who has been teasing her? When has she been teased? Who can have said such a thing? Is she raving?' Lizaveta Prokofyevna addressed the room, quivering with anger.

'Everyone has been talking about it, everyone, for the last three days! I will never, never marry him!'

As she cried this, Aglaia burst into bitter tears, hiding her face in her handkerchief, and sank into a chair.

'But he hasn't even ...'

'I haven't asked you, Aglaia Ivanovna,' broke suddenly from Myshkin.

'Wha-a-t?' Lizaveta Prokofyevna brought out in indignation, amazement and horror. 'What's that?'

She could not believe her ears.

'I meant to say... I meant to say,' faltered Myshkin, 'I only wanted to explain to Aglaia Ivanovna ... to have the honour to make clear to her that I had no intention ... to have the honour of asking for her hand ... at any time. It's not my fault – it's not my fault indeed, Aglaia Ivanovna. I've never wanted to, it never entered my head. I never shall want to, you'll see that for yourself. Be sure of that. Some spiteful person must have slandered me to you. Don't worn about it!'

As he said this, he went up to Aglaia.

She removed the handkerchief with which she was covering her face, stole a hasty glance at his panic-stricken countenance, took in the meaning of his words, and went off into a sudden fit of laughter in his face, such gay and irresistible laughter, such droll and mocking laughter that Adelaïda could not contain herself, especially when she too looked at Myshkin. She rushed up to her sister, embraced her, and broke into the same irresistible schoolgirlish and merry laughter. Looking at them, Myshkin too began to smile, and with a joyful and happy expression repeated, 'Well, that's all right! That's all right!'

At that point Alexandra too gave way and laughed heartily. It seemed as though the three girls would never stop laughing.

'Ah, tire mad things!' muttered Lizaveta Prokofyevna. 'First they frighten one, and then ...'

But Prince S— was laughing too, and so was Yevgeny Pavlovitch. Kofya laughed without stopping, and Myshkin laughed also looking at them all.

'Let's go for a walk – let's go for a walk!' cried Adelaïda 'AH of us, and the prince must go with us. There's no need for you to go away, you dear person. Isn't he a dear, Aglaia? Isn't he, mother? What's more, I must, I must kiss him and embrace him for… for his explanation to Aglaia just now. *Maman* dear, will you let me kiss him? Aglaia, let me kiss *your* prince,' cried the mischievous girl; and she actually skipped up to the prince and kissed him on the forehead.

He snatched her hands, squeezed them so tightly that Adelaïda almost cried out, looked at her with infinite gladness, and quickly raised her hand to his lips and kissed it three times.

'Come along!' Aglaia called to them. 'Prince, you shall escort me. May he, *Maman*, after refusing me? You've refused me for good, haven't you, Prince? That's not the way to offer your arm to a lady. Don't you know how to give your arm to a lady? That's right. Come along, we'll lead the way. Would you like us to go on ahead, *tête-à-tête*?'

She talked incessantly, still laughing spasmodically.

'Thank God – thank God!' repeated Lizaveta Prokofyevna, though she did not know herself what she was rejoicing at.

'Extraordinarily queer people!' thought Prince S— perhaps for the hundredth time since he had known them, but… he liked these queer people. As for Myshkin, he was perhaps not greatly attracted by him. Prince S— looked rather gloomy and, as it were, preoccupied, as they set off.

Yevgeny Pavlovitch seemed in the liveliest humour. All the way to the railway station he was amusing Adelaïda and Alexandra, who laughed at his jokes with such extreme readiness that he began to be a trifle suspicious that perhaps they were not listening to him at all. At this thought he suddenly broke into violent and perfectly genuine laughter without explaining the reason. His amusement was characteristic of the man. Though the sisters were in the most hilarious mood, they kept looking at Aglaia and Myshkin in front of them. It was evident that their younger sister's conduct was a complete enigma to them. Prince S— kept trying to talk about other subjects to Lizaveta Prokofyevna, perhaps to distract her mind, and bored her horribly. She seemed completely dazed, answered at random, and sometimes did not answer at all. But that was not the end of Aglaia's enigmas that evening. The last of them fell to the lot of Myshkin alone. When they had got about a hundred paces from the house, Aglaia said in a rapid half-whisper to her obstinately silent cavalier, 'Look there, to the right.'

Myshkin looked.

'Look more carefully. Do you see that seat in the park, over there where those three big trees are ... a green seat?'

Myshkin answered that he did.

'Do you like the place? I sometimes come and sit here alone at seven o'clock in the morning, when everyone else is asleep.'

Myshkin murmured that it was a charming spot.

'And now you can leave me. I don't want to walk arm-in-arm with you any further. Or, better, walk arm-in-arm with me, but don't speak to me – not a word. I want to think by myself.'

This warning was unnecessary, however. Myshkin would not have uttered a word in any case. His heart began throbbing violently when she spoke of the seat in the park. After a minute's deliberation he dismissed the foolish idea with shame.

It is a well-known fact remarked by everyone that the public about the Pavlovsk bandstand is more 'select' on weekdays than on Sundays and holidays, when 'all sorts of people' flock there from town. The ladies, though not in holiday attire, are more elegant. It is the correct thing to gather about the bandstand. The orchestra is about the best of our park bands, and often plays new pieces. There is great decorum and propriety of behaviour in the gardens, though there is a general air of homeliness, and even intimacy. Summer visitors go there to look at their acquaintances. Many do this with genuine pleasure and frequent the gardens for that purpose alone. But there are some who only go for the music. Unpleasant scenes are rare, though of course they occasionally occur even on weekdays. But that, to be sure, is inevitable.

It was an exquisite evening, and there were a good many people in the gardens. All the places round the orchestra were taken. Our party sat down on chairs rather apart, close to the left-hand exit from the station. The crowd and the music revived Lizaveta Prokofyevna a little and diverted the young ladies. They had already exchanged glances with some of the visitors and had already nodded affably to several of their acquaintances; they had scrutinised the dresses, detected some eccentricities, and discussed them with sarcastic smiles. Yevgeny Pavlovitch too bowed frequently to acquaintances. Aglaia and Myshkin, who were still together, had already attracted some attention. Soon several young men went up to the young ladies and their mother; two or three remained to talk to them. They were all friends of Yevgeny Pavlovitch's. Among them was a very handsome, good-humoured and talkative young officer. He hastened to address Aglaia and did his utmost to engage her attention. She was particularly gracious and sprightly with him. Yevgeny Pavlovitch asked Myshkin to let him introduce this friend. Myshkin hardly took in what was wanted of him, but the introduction took place, both bowed and shook hands. Yevgeny Pavlovitch's friend asked a question, but Myshkin either did not answer or mumbled something so strangely to himself that the officer stared at him, then glanced at Yevgeny Pavlovitch, at once saw why the introduction had been made, smiled slightly and turned to Aglaia again. Only Yevgeny Pavlovitch noticed that Aglaia suddenly flushed at this.

Myshkin did not even observe that other people were talking and paying attention to Aglaia. He was perhaps at moments even unconscious that he was sitting beside her. Sometimes he longed to get away, to vanish from here altogether. He would have been positively glad to be in some gloomy, deserted place, only that he might be alone with his thoughts and no one might know where he was. Or at least to be at home in the verandah, with no one else there, not Lebedyev nor the children; to throw himself on the sofa and bury his head in the pillow, and to lie like that for a day and a night and another day. At moments he dreamed of the mountains, and especially one familiar spot which he always liked to think of, a spot to which he had been fond of going and from which he used to look down on the village, on the waterfall gleaming like a white thread below, on the white clouds and the old ruined castle. Oh, how he longed to be there now, and to think of one thing! – Oh, of nothing else for his whole life, and a thousand years would not be too long! And let him be utterly forgotten here. Oh, that must be! It would have been better indeed if they had never known him, and if it had all been only a dream. And wasn't it just the same, dream and reality? Sometimes he began looking at Aglaia, and for five minutes at a time did not take his eyes off her face. But the look in his eyes was too strange. He seemed to be looking at her as at an object a mile away, or as at her portrait, not herself.

'Why are you looking at me like that, Prince?' she asked him suddenly, interrupting her lively talk and laughter with the group around her. 'I am afraid of you; I feel as though you meant to put out your hand and touch my face and feel it with your fingers. He does look like that, doesn't he, Yevgeny Pavlovitch?'

Myshkin seemed surprised to hear that he was being spoken to, pondered, though perhaps he did not quite understand, and did not answer. But seeing that she and all the rest were laughing, he opened his mouth and began to laugh too. The laughter grew louder; the officer, who must have been of a mirthful disposition, simply shook with laughter. Aglaia suddenly whispered to herself wrathfully, 'Idiot!'

'Good heavens! Surely she can't be … a man like that… is she utterly mad?' her mother muttered to herself.

'It's a joke. The same as that about the "poor knight," nothing more,' Alexandra whispered firmly in her ear. 'She's making fun of him again, as she always does. But the joke has gone too far. We must put a stop to it, *Maman*. She went on like an actress and scared us out of pure mischief…'

'It's a good thing she's pitched on an idiot like that,' her mother whispered back.

But her daughter's remark had relieved her.

Myshkin heard them call him an idiot, however, and started, but not at being called an idiot. He forgot the word immediately. But in the crowd not far from where he was sitting – he could not have pointed out the exact spot – he caught a glimpse of a face – a pale face, with curly black hair, with a familiar, a very familiar smile and expression; he caught a glimpse of it and it vanished. Very likely it was only his fancy; all that remained with him was an impression of a wry smile, the eyes, and the jaunty pale green necktie of the apparition. Whether the figure had disappeared in the crowd, or whether it had slipped into the station Myshkin could not decide.

But a minute later he began quickly and uneasily looking about him; this first apparition might be the forerunner of a second. That must certainly be so. Could he have forgotten the possibility of a meeting when he went into the gardens? It is true that when he went to the gardens he had no idea that he was coming there – he was in such a troubled state of mind.

If he had been more capable of observing, he might have noticed for the last quarter of an hour that Aglaia too was looking round uneasily from time to time; she too seemed to be on the lookout for someone. Now, when his uneasiness had become very marked, Aglaia's excitement and uneasiness also increased, and as soon as he looked round him, she at once looked about too. The explanation of their uneasiness followed quickly.

Quite a number of persons, at least a dozen, suddenly appeared from the side entrance, near which Myshkin and the Epanchins and their friends were sitting. The foremost of the group were three women, two of them remarkably good-looking; and it was not strange that they were followed by so many admirers. But there was something peculiar about the women and the men who were with them, quite unlike the rest of the crowd gathered to listen to the music. They were at once noticed by almost everyone, but most people tried to look as though they had not seen them at all, and only some of the young men smiled at them, whispering something to one another. It was impossible to avoid seeing them: they displayed themselves conspicuously, talking loudly and laughing. It might well have been thought that many of them were drank, though some of them were smartly and fashionably dressed. Yet there were among them persons of very strange appearance, in strange clothes, with strangely flushed faces. There were some officers among them; some were not young; some were solidly dressed in well-cut, comfortably fitting clothes, with rings and studs, and splendid pitch-black wigs and whiskers, with especially stately though rather grumpy dignity in their faces, yet they would have been shunned in society like the plague. Among our suburban places of resort there are, of course, some distinguished for exceptional respectability and enjoying a particularly good reputation. But even the most cautious person may sometimes be struck by a tile from a neighbour's roof. Such a tile was now about to fall on the decorous public who had gathered to listen to the band.

On the way from the station to the bandstand there were three steps. The group stopped just at the top of these steps; they hesitated whether to go down, but one woman stepped forward; only two of her suite ventured to follow her. One was a middle-aged man of rather modest appearance. He looked like a gentleman in all respects, yet he had the forlorn air of one of those men whom nobody knows and who know nobody. The other was a most dubious figure, completely out at elbows. Nobody else followed the eccentric lady. But going down the steps she did not look back, as though she did not care whether she were followed or not. She laughed and talked loudly as before. She was dressed richly and with excellent taste, but somewhat too splendidly. She turned towards the other side of the bandstand, where a private carriage was waiting for somebody.

Myshkin had not seen *her* for more than three months. Ever since he had arrived in Petersburg, he had been intending to go and see her, but perhaps a secret presentiment had deterred him. He could not in any case gauge what impression meeting her would make upon him, and he often tried with dread to imagine it. One thing was clear to him – that the meeting would be painful. Several times during those six months he had recalled the first impression made on him by that woman's face, when he had only seen it in the photograph. But even the impression made by the photograph was, he remembered, extremely painful. That month in the provinces, when he had been seeing her almost every day, had had a fearful effect upon him, so much so that he sometimes tried to drive away all recollection of it. There was something which always tortured him in the very face of this woman. Talking to Rogozhin, he had put down this sensation to his infinite pity for her, and that was the truth. That face, even in the photograph, had roused in him a perfect agony of pity: the feeling of compassion and even of suffering over this woman never left his heart, and it had not left it now. Oh no, it was stronger than ever! But Myshkin was dissatisfied with what he had said to Rogozhin; and only now at the moment of her sudden appearance he realised, perhaps through his immediate sensation, what had been lacking in his words. Words had been lacking which might have expressed horror – yes, horror. Now at this moment he felt it fully. He was certain, he was fully convinced for reasons of his own, that that woman was mad. If, loving a woman more than anything in the world, or foreseeing the possibility of loving her thus, one were suddenly to see her in chains behind an iron grating and beneath the rod of a prison warder, one would feel something like what Myshkin felt at that moment.

'What's the matter with you?' Aglaia whispered quickly, looking round at him and naïvely pulling at his arm.

He turned his head, looked at her, glanced into her black eyes which flashed at that moment with a light he could not understand, tried to smile at her, but immediately, as though forgetting her, turned his eyes to the right and again began watching the startling apparition.

Nastasya Filippovna was at that moment walking close by the young ladies' chairs. Yevgeny Pavlovitch went on telling Alexandra something which must have been very amusing and interesting. He talked rapidly and eagerly. Myshkin remembered that Aglaia had uttered in a whisper the words: 'What a ...' – a vague, unfinished phrase.

She instantly checked herself and said no more, but that was enough.

Nastasya Filippovna, who was walking by, seeming to notice no one in particular, suddenly turned towards them, and seemed only now to observe Yevgeny Pavlovitch.

'B-bah! Why here he is!' she exclaimed, suddenly standing still. 'One might have sent a special messenger to look for him and never find him, and here he sits where you'd never expect him ... I thought you were there at your uncle's.'

Yevgeny Pavlovitch flushed, looked furiously at Nastasya Filippovna, but hurriedly turned away from her again.

'What! Don't you know? Only fancy, he doesn't know yet! He has shot himself! Your uncle shot himself this morning. I was told this morning at two o'clock, and half the town knows it by now. Three hundred and fifty thousand roubles of government money are missing, they say; some say five hundred. And I always counted on his leaving you a fortune. He's whisked it all away. He was a dissipated old fellow. Well, goodbye, *bonne chance*. Aren't you really going there? You sent in your papers in good time, you sly fellow. Nonsense; he knew, he knew! Very likely he knew yesterday.'

Though in her insolent persistence in this public proclamation of an acquaintance and intimacy which did not exist, there was certainly a motive, and of that there could be no doubt now, yet Yevgeny Pavlovitch had thought at first of escaping without noticing his assailant. But Nastasya Filippovna's words fell on him like a thunderbolt. Hearing of his uncle's death, he grew white as a sheet and turned towards his informant. At that moment Lizaveta Prokofyevna got up quickly from her seat, made everyone behind her get up, and almost ran away. Only Myshkin stayed for a moment in indecision, and Yevgeny Pavlovitch still remained standing, unable to collect himself. But the Epanchins were scarcely twenty paces away, when an outrageously scandalous incident followed.

The officer, who was a great friend of Yevgeny Pavlovitch's and had been talking to Aglaia, was highly indignant.

'One wants a whip, there's no other way of dealing with such a hussy!' he said almost loudly. (He had apparently been Yevgeny Pavlovitch's confidant in the past.)

Nastasya Filippovna instantly turned to him. Her eyes flashed. She rushed up to a young man, a complete stranger, who was standing a couple of paces from her, snatched a thin plaited riding-whip out of his hand, and struck the offender with all her might across the face. All this happened in one moment... The officer, beside himself, flew at her. Nastasya Filippovna's followers were no longer beside her. The decorous middle-aged gentleman had managed to disappear altogether; while the festive gentleman stood aside, laughing heartily. In another minute the police would have appeared, and Nastasya Filippovna would have fared badly, if unexpected help had not been at hand. Myshkin, who was also standing two steps away, succeeded in seizing the officer by the arms from behind. Wresting away his arms, the officer gave him a violent push in the chest. Myshkin was flung three paces back and fell on a chair. But two other champions had come forward to protect Nastasya Filippovna. Facing the attacking officer stood the boxer, the author of the article already known to the reader and formerly one of Rogozhin's retinue.

'Ex-lieutenant Keller!' he introduced himself forcibly. 'If you want to fight, captain, I'll replace the weaker sex, at your service. I've been through a course of English boxing. Don't push, captain. I feel for the deadly insult you've received, but I can't allow you to use your fists on a woman in public. If, like an honourable man and a gentleman, you prefer some other method, you know what I mean, captain.'

But the captain had recovered himself and was not listening. At that instant Rogozhin made his appearance in the crowd, and seizing Nastasya Filippovna by the arm, led her away. Rogozhin too seemed terribly shaken, he was white and trembling. As he led Nastasya Filippovna away, he had time to laugh malignantly in the officer's face, and with vulgar triumph said, 'Whew! He's caught it! His mug's all over blood! Whew!'

Recovering himself and completely realising with whom he had to deal, the officer (though covering his face with his handkerchief) turned politely to Myshkin, who had got up from his chair.

'Prince Myshkin, whose acquaintance I have had the pleasure of making just now?'

'She's mad! She's insane! I assure you!' responded Myshkin in a shaking voice, for some reason holding out his trembling hands to him.

'I, of course, cannot boast of so much knowledge on that subject. But I had to know your name.'

He nodded and walked away. The police hurried up five seconds after the last of the persons concerned had disappeared. But the scene had not lasted more than two minutes. Some of the audience had got up from their chairs and gone away; some had simply moved from one place to another; while some were delighted at the scene, and others were eagerly talking and enquiring about it. The incident, in fact, passed off in the usual way. The band began playing again. Myshkin followed the Epanchins. If he had thought, or had had time to look to the left as he was sitting there, after he had been pushed away, he might have seen, twenty paces from him, Aglaia, who had stood still to watch the scandalous scene, regardless of her mother's and sisters' calls to her. Prince S— had run up to her and at last persuaded her to come quickly away. Her mother remembered that she had returned to them so excited that she could scarcely have heard their calling her. But within two minutes, when they were walking back into the park, Aglaia said in her usual careless and capricious tone: 'I wanted to see how the farce would end.'

Chapter 3

The scene in the gardens had impressed both mother and daughters almost with horror. Excited and alarmed, Lizaveta Prokofyevna had literally almost run all the way home with her daughters. According to her notions and ideas, so much had happened, and so much had been brought to light by the incident, that certain ideas had taken definite shape in her brain, in spite of her confusion and alarm. But everyone realised that something peculiar had happened, and that perhaps, and fortunately too, some extraordinary secret was on the verge of being disclosed.

In spite of all Prince S—'s former assurances and explanations, Yevgeny Pavlovitch had been 'unmasked,' exposed, detected, 'and publicly found out in his connection with that creature.' So thought the mother and both her elder daughters. The only effect of that conclusion was to intensify the mystery. Though the girls were secretly somewhat indignant with their mother for her extreme alarm and too conspicuous flight, yet they did not venture to worry her with questions during the first shock of the disturbance. Moreover something made them fancy that their sister Aglaia knew more of the matter than their mother and all of them put together. Prince S—, too, looked black as night; he too seemed plunged in thought. Lizaveta Prokofyevna did not say a word to him all the way home, and he did not seem to be aware of it. Adelaïda made an attempt to ask him. 'What uncle had been spoken of just now and what had happened in Petersburg?' But with a very sour face he muttered something vague in reply about making enquiries, and its being all nonsense.

'No doubt of that,' assented Adelaïda, and she asked nothing more.

Aglaia became exceptionally quiet, and only observed on the way that they were hurrying too fast. Once she turned round and caught sight of Myshkin, who was hastening after them. She smiled ironically at his efforts to overtake them, and did not look round at him again.

At last, when they were nearly reaching their villa, they saw Ivan Fyodorovitch, who had just arrived from Petersburg, coming to meet them. His first word was to ask after Yevgeny Pavlovitch. But his wife walked by him wrathfully, without answering or even looking at him. From the faces of his daughters and Prince S— he guessed at once there was a storm brewing. But apart from this, there was an unusual uneasiness in his expression. He took Prince S—'s arm, stopped him at the entrance, and exchanged a few words with him almost in a whisper. From the troubled air of both as they walked afterwards on to the verandah and went up to Lizaveta Prokofyevna's room it might be surmised that they had heard some extraordinary news. By degrees, they were all gathered in Lizaveta Prokofyevna's room upstairs, and no one but Myshkin was left at last on the verandah. Though he had no conscious motive for staying, yet he sat on in the corner as though expecting something. It did not occur to him, as they seemed so upset, that he had better go away. He seemed oblivious of the whole universe, and ready to go on sitting for the next two years, wherever he might be put. From time to time, sounds of anxious conversation reached him from above. He could not have said how long he had been sitting there. It had grown late and was quite dark when Aglaia suddenly came out on to the verandah. She looked calm, though she was rather pale. Seeing Myshkin, whom she apparently had not expected to find sitting there in the corner, Aglaia smiled, as though perplexed.

'What are you doing here?' she asked, going up to him.

Myshkin muttered something in confusion, and jumped up from his seat. But Aglaia at once sat down beside *him, and he sat* down again. Suddenly she examined him attentively, then looked as though aimlessly at the window, and then again at him.

'Perhaps she wants to laugh at me,' Myshkin thought. 'No, she'd have laughed at me then.'

'Perhaps you'd like some tea. I'll order some,' she said, after a silence. 'N-no. I don't know ...'

'How do you mean – you don't know? Oh, by the way, listen. If someone challenged you to a duel, what would you do? I wanted to ask you before.'

'Why ... who ... no one will challenge me to a duel.'

'But if they did? Would you be very much frightened?'

'I think I should be very... much afraid.'

'You mean it? Then you are a coward?'

'N-no. Perhaps not. A coward is a man who's afraid and runs away. If one's afraid and doesn't run away, one's not a coward,' said Myshkin, smiling, after a moment's thought.

'And you wouldn't run away?'

'Perhaps I shouldn't run away.' He laughed at last at Aglaia's questions.

'Though I'm a woman, nothing would make me run away,' she observed, almost offended. 'But you're laughing at me and pretending, as you usually do, to make yourself more interesting. Tell me, they fire at twelve paces, don't they, sometimes at ten, so they must be killed or wounded?'

'People are not often killed at duels, I imagine.'

'Not often? Pushkin was killed.'

'That may have been accidental.'

'It wasn't an accident. It was a duel to the death and he was killed.'

'The bullet struck him so low down that no doubt Dantes aimed higher, at his head or at his chest; no one aims like that, so it's most likely that the bullet hit Pushkin by accident. People who understand told me so.'

'But a soldier I talked to once told me that they were ordered by the regulations to fire halfway-up, that's their phrase "halfway-up." So they're not ordered to fire at the head or the chest, but "halfway-up". I asked an officer afterwards and he told me it was perfectly true.'

'That's probably because they fire from a long distance.'

'But can you shoot?'

'I never have shot.'

'Don't you even know how to load a pistol?'

'No. That is, I know how it's done, but I've never done it myself.'

'Well, that means you don't know, for it wants practice. Listen and remember: first you must buy some good gunpowder, not damp (they say it must not be damp, but very dry), very fine powder, you must ask for that sort, not what's used in cannons. The bullet, I'm told, people make themselves somehow. Have you pistols?'

'No, and I don't want them,' laughed Myshkin.

'Oh, what nonsense! You must buy a good one, French or English. I'm told they're the best. Then take a thimbleful of powder, or two thimblefuls, perhaps, and sprinkle it in. Better put plenty. Ram it in with felt (they say that felt is necessary for some reason); you can get that out of some mattress, or doors are sometimes covered with felt. Then, when you've poked the felt in, put in the bullet – do you hear, the bullet afterwards, the powder first, or it won't shoot. Why are you laughing? I want you to practise shooting every day, and to learn to hit a mark. Will you?'

Myshkin laughed. Aglaia stamped her foot with vexation. The earnest air with which she carried on such a conversation somewhat surprised him. He rather felt that he must find out something, ask about something; something more serious anyway than the loading of a pistol. But everything had flown out of his head except the one fact, that she was sitting beside him, and that he was looking at her, and. it made no difference to him at that moment what she talked about.

Ivan Fyodorovitch, himself, came downstairs and on to the verandah at last. He was going out with a frowning, anxious and resolute face.

'Ah, Lyov Nikolayevitch, that's you ... Where are you going now?' he asked, though Myshkin showed no signs of moving. 'Come along, I've a word to say to you,'

'Goodbye,' said Aglaia, and held out her hand to Myshkin.

It was rather dark on the verandah by now. He could not make out her face quite clearly. A minute later, when he had left the villa with the general, he suddenly flushed hotly, and squeezed his right hand tightly.

It appeared that Ivan Fyodorovitch had to go the same way. In spite of the late hour, he was hurrying to discuss something with someone. But meanwhile, on the way, he began talking to Myshkin, quickly, excitedly, and somewhat incoherently, frequently mentioning Lizaveta Prokofyevna. If Myshkin could have been more observant at that moment, he might perhaps have guessed that the general wanted to find out something from him, or rather, wanted to ask him a plain question, but could not bring himself to the real point. Myshkin was so absent-minded that at first he heard nothing at all, and when the general stopped before him with some excited question, to his shame he was forced to confess that he had not understood a word.

The general shrugged his shoulders.

'You're all such queer people all about one,' he began again. 'I tell you that I am at a loss to understand the notions and alarms of Lizaveta Prokofyevna. She's in hysterics, crying and declaring that we've been disgraced, shamed. Who? How? By whom? When and why? I confess I am to blame (I recognise it), I'm very much to blame, but the persecutions of... this troublesome woman (who's misconducting herself into the bargain) can be restrained, by the police at the worst, and I intend to see someone today and take steps. Everything can be done quietly, gently, kindly even, in a friendly way and without a breath of scandal. I admit that many things may happen in the future, and that there's a great deal that's unexplained; there's an intrigue in it, but if they know nothing about it here, they can make no explanation there. If I've heard nothing and you've heard nothing, he's heard nothing, and she's heard nothing, who has heard, I should like to ask you? How is it to be explained, do you suppose, except that half of it is mirage, unreal, something like moonshine or some hallucination.'

'She is mad,' muttered Myshkin, recalling with pain the recent scene.

'That's just what I say, if you're talking of her. That idea has occurred to me too, and I slept peacefully. But now I see that their opinion is more correct, and I don't believe in madness. She's a nonsensical woman, I grant, but she's artful as well, and far from mad. Her freak today about Kapiton Alexeyitch shows that too clearly. It's a fraudulent business, or at least a Jesuitical business for objects of her own.'

'What Kapiton Alexeyitch?'

'Ah, mercy on us, Lyov Nikolayevitch, you don't listen. I began by telling you about Kapiton Alexeyitch; I was so upset that I'm all of a tremble still. That's what kept me so long in town today. Kapiton Alexeyitch Radomsky, Yevgeny Pavlovitch's uncle …'

'Ah!' cried Myshkin.

'Shot himself at daybreak this morning, at seven o'clock. A highly-respected old man, seventy, a free-liver. And it's just exactly as she said – a large sum of government money missing.'

'Where could she have …'

'Heard of it? Ha-ha! Why, she had a whole regiment around her, as soon as she arrived here. You know what sort of people visit her now and seek "the honour of her acquaintance." She might naturally have heard it this morning from someone coming from town, for all Petersburg knows it by now, and half Pavlovsk, or perhaps the whole of it. But what a sly remark it was she made about the uniform, as it was repeated to me, about Yevgeny Pavlovitch's having sent in his papers in the nick of time! What a fiendish hint! No, that doesn't smack of madness. I refuse to believe, of course, that Yevgeny Pavlovitch could have known of the catastrophe beforehand, that is, that at seven o'clock on a certain day, and so on. But he may have had a presentiment of it all. And I, and all of us, and Prince S—, reckoned that he would leave him a fortune. It's awful! Awful! But understand me, I don't charge Yevgeny Pavlovitch with anything, and I hasten to make that clear, but still, it's suspicious, I must say. Prince S— is tremendously struck by it. It's all fallen out so strangely.'

'But what is there suspicious about Yevgeny Pavlovitch's conduct?'

'Nothing. He's behaved most honourably. I haven't suggested anything of the sort. His own property, I believe, is untouched. Lizaveta Prokofyevna, of course, won't listen to anything. But, what's worse, all this family upset, or rather, all this tittle-tattle, really one doesn't know what to call it ... You're a friend of the family in a real sense, Lyov Nikolayevitch, and would you believe it, it appears now, though it's not known for certain, that Yevgeny Pavlovitch made Aglaia an offer a month ago, and that she refused him point-blank.'

'Impossible!' cried Myshkin warmly.

'Why, do you know anything about it? You see, my dear fellow,' cried the general, startled and surprised, stopping short as though petrified, 'I may have chattered on to you more than I should. That's because you ... because you ... are such an exceptional fellow, one may say. Perhaps you know something?'

'I know nothing ... about Yevgeny Pavlovitch,' muttered Myshkin.

'I don't either. As for me, my boy, they certainly want to see me dead and buried, and they won't consider how hard it is for a man, and that I can't stand it. I've just been through an awful scene! I speak to you as though you were my son. The worst of it is that Aglaia seems to be laughing at her mother. Her sisters told their mother, as a guess, and a pretty certain one, that she'd refused Yevgeny Pavlovitch and had a rather formal explanation with him a month ago. But she's such a wilful and whimsical creature, it's beyond words. Generosity and every brilliant quality of mind and heart she has, but capricious, mocking – in fact, a little devil, and full of fancies, too. She laughed at her mother to her face just now, at her sisters too, and at Prince S— I don't count, of course, for she never does anything but laugh at me. But yet, you know, I love her; I love her laughing even – and I believe she, little devil, loves me specially for it, that is, more than anyone else, I believe. I'll bet anything she's made fun of you too. I found her talking to you just now after the storm upstairs; she was sitting with you, as though nothing had happened.'

Myshkin flushed crimson, and squeezed his right hand, but said nothing.

'My dear, good Lyov Nikolayevitch,' the general began with warmth and feeling again, 'I ... and Lizaveta Prokofyevna too (though she's begun to abuse you again, and me, too, on your account, though I don't understand why), we love you, we love you truly and respect you, in spite of everything, I mean of all appearances. But you'll admit yourself, my dear boy, that it is mystifying and irritating to hear that cold-blooded little devil suddenly (for she stood before her mother with a look of profound contempt for all our questions, mine especially, for, confound it all, I was fool enough to take it into my head to make a show of sternness, seeing I'm the head of the family – well, I made a fool of myself), that cold-blooded little devil suddenly declare with a laugh that that "mad woman" (that was her expression, and it strikes me as queer that she agrees with you: "How can you have failed to see it till now," she says) "has taken it into her head at all costs to marry me to Prince Lyov Nikolayrevitch, and for that purpose to get Yevgeny Pavlovitch turned out of our house." … She simply said that, she gave no further explanation, she went on laughing and we simply gaped at her; she slammed the door and went out. Then they told me of what passed between her and you this afternoon. And … and listen, dear prince, you're a sensible man and not given to taking offence. I've observed that about you, but … don't be angry: I'll be bound she's making fun of you. She laughs like a child, so don't be angry with her, but that's certainly it. Don't think anything of it – she's simply making a fool of you and all of us, out for mischief. Well, goodbye. You know our feelings, our genuine feelings for you, don't you? They'll never change in any respect… but now I must go this way. Goodbye! I've not often been in such a tight hole (what's the expression?) as I am now … A pretty summer holiday!'

Left alone at the crossroads, Myshkin looked round him, rapidly crossed the road, went close up to the lighted window of a villa, unfolded the little piece of paper which he had held tight in his right hand all the time he had been talking to Ivan Fyodorovitch, and by a faint beam of light, read:

> Tomorrow morning at seven o'clock I will be on the green seat in the park waiting for you. I have made up my mind to talk to you about an exceedingly important matter which concerns you directly.
>
> PS. I hope you will show no one this letter. Though I'm ashamed to give you such a caution, I think that you deserve it and I write it, blushing with shame at your absurd character.
>
> PPS. I mean the green seat I pointed out to you this morning. You ought to be ashamed that I should have to write this, too.

The letter had been scribbled in haste and folded anyhow, most likely just before Aglaia came out on to the verandah. In indescribable agitation, that was almost like terror, Myshkin held the paper clenched tightly in his right hand again, and hastily leapt away from the window, from the light, like a frightened thief, but in doing so he ran full-tilt into a gentleman who was standing just behind his back.

'I have been following you, Prince,' said the gentleman.

'Is that you, Keller?' cried Myshkin, surprised.

'I was looking for you, Prince. I've been watching for you by the Epanchins'. Of course, I couldn't go in. I walked behind you while you were with the general. I am at your service, Prince, you may dispose of me. I am ready for any sacrifice, even death, if need be.'

'Oh ... what for?'

'Why, no doubt a challenge will follow. That Lieutenant... I know him, though not personally ... he won't accept an affront. The likes of us, that is, Rogozhin and me, he is inclined to look upon as dirt, and perhaps deservedly, so you are the only one called upon. You'll have to pay the piper, Prince. He's been enquiring about you, I hear, and no doubt, a friend of his will call on you tomorrow, or he may be waiting for you now. If you do me the honour to choose me for your second, I'm ready to be degraded to the ranks for you. That's why I've been looking for you, Prince.'

'So you're talking of a duel too!' laughed Myshkin, to Keller's great surprise.

He laughed heartily. Keller, who had been on tenterhooks until he had satisfied himself by offering to be Myshkin's second, was almost offended at the sight of the prince's light-hearted mirth.

'But you seized him by the arms, this afternoon, Prince. That's hard for a man of honour to put up with in a public place.'

'And he gave me a push in the chest!' cried Myshkin, laughing. 'There's nothing for us to fight about! I'll beg his pardon, that's all. But if we must fight, we will! Let him shoot, I should like it. Ha-ha! I know how to load a pistol now. Do you know I've been taught how to load a pistol? Can you load a pistol, Keller? First you have to buy powder, pistol powder, not damp, and not as coarse as for cannon. Then you have to put the powder in first, and get some felt off a door. And then you have to put the bullet in afterwards, and not the bullet before the powder, or it won't go off. Do you hear, Keller? Or else it won't go off. Ha-ha! Isn't that a magnificent reason, friend Keller? Ach, Keller, do you know I must hug you and give you a kiss this minute! Ha-ha-ha! How was it that you turned up so suddenly this afternoon? Come and see me sometime soon and have some champagne. We'll all get drunk! Do you know I've twelve bottles of champagne at home in Lebedyev's cellar? They came into his hands somehow and he sold them to me the day before yesterday; the very day after I moved into his house, I bought them all. I'll get the whole party together. Are you going to sleep tonight?'

'As I do even night, Prince.'

'Well, pleasant dreams, then. Ha-ha!'

Myshkin crossed the road and vanished into the park, leaving Keller somewhat perplexed. He had never yet seen Myshkin in such a strange mood, and could not have imagined him like this.

'Fever, perhaps, for he's a nervous man, and all this has affected him, but yet he won't be frightened. I am sure that sort are not cowards, by Jove!' Keller was thinking to himself. Hm! Champagne! An interesting fact, though! Twelve bottles, a dozen; a decent provision. I'll bet that Lebedyev got that champagne as a pledge from someone. Hm! He's rather nice, that prince; I like such fellows; there's no time to lose though, and ... if there's champagne, it's the moment for it...'

That Myshkin was almost in a fever was, of course, a correct surmise.

He wandered a long while about the dark park, and at last 'found himself' walking along an avenue. The impression was left on his consciousness of having walked thirty or forty times up and down that avenue from the seat to a tall and conspicuous old tree, a distance of a hundred paces. He could not, if he had tried, have remembered what he had been thinking all that time, which must have been at least an hour. He caught himself, however, thinking one thought which made him burst out laughing; though there was nothing to laugh at, he kept wanting to laugh. It occurred, to him that the suggestion of a duel might have arisen not only in Keller's mind, and that, therefore, the conversation about the loading of pistols was not without motive.

'Bah!' He stopped suddenly. Another idea dawned upon him. 'She came out on to the verandah just now when I was sitting there in the corner, and was awfully surprised to find me there and – how she laughed ... she talked about tea; and she had that note in her hands all the while, of course. So she must have known I was sitting on the verandah. Why then was she surprised? Ha-ha!'

He took the letter out of his pocket and kissed it, but at once stopped short and pondered.

'How strange it is! How strange it is!' he said, a minute later, even with a certain sadness. In moments of intense joy he always grew sad, he could not himself have said why. He looked round attentively and was surprised that he had come there. He was very tired; he went to the seat and sat down on it. There was an extraordinary stillness all round. The music in the gardens had ceased, there was perhaps no one left in the park. It must have been at least half-past eleven. It was a soft, warm, clear night – a Petersburg night in early June, but in the thick shady avenue where he was sitting it was almost dark.

If anyone had told him at that moment that he had fallen in love, that he was passionately in love, he would have rejected the idea with surprise and perhaps with indignation. And if anyone had added that Aglaia's letter was a love-letter, arranging a tryst with a lover, he would have been hotly ashamed of such a man, and would perhaps have challenged him to a duel. All this was perfectly sincere, and he never once doubted it, or admitted the slightest 'double' thought of a possibility of the girl's loving him or even of his loving her. He would have been ashamed of such an idea. The possibility of love for him, 'for such a man as he was,' he would have looked upon as a monstrous thing. He fancied that, if it really meant anything, it was only mischief on her part. But he was quite unconcerned by that consideration, and thought it all in the natural order of things. He was occupied and absorbed with something quite different. He fully believed the statement dropped by the excited general that she was making fun of everyone, and of him, Myshkin, particularly. He did not feel in the least insulted at this; to his thinking, it was quite as it should be. To him the chief thing was that tomorrow he would see her again early in the morning, would sit beside her on the green seat, would learn how to load a pistol, and would look at her. He wanted nothing more. It did once or twice occur to him to wonder what she meant to say to him, and what was this important matter which concerned him so directly. Moreover, he never had a moment's doubt of the real existence of that 'important matter' for which he was summoned. But he was far from considering that 'important matter' now. He did not feel indeed, the slightest inclination to think about it.

The crunch of slow footsteps on the sand of the avenue made him raise his head. A man whose face was difficult to distinguish in the dark came up to the seat and sat down beside him. Myshkin turned quickly, almost touching him, and discerned the pale face of Rogozhin.

'I knew you were wandering about here somewhere. I haven't been long finding you,' Rogozhin muttered through his teeth.

It was the first time they had seen each other since their meeting in the corridor of the hotel. Amazed at Rogozhin's sudden appearance, Myshkin could not for some time collect his thoughts and an agonising sensation rose up again in his heart. Rogozhin saw the effect he had produced, but although he was at first taken aback and talked with an air of studied ease, Myshkin fancied soon that there was nothing studied about him, nor even any special embarrassment. If there were any awkwardness in his gestures and words, it was only on the surface. The man could not change at heart.

'How did … you find me here?' asked Myshkin, in order to say something.

'I heard from Keller (I was going to see you), "he's gone into the park," he said. Well, thought I, so that's how it is.'

'What is?' Myshkin anxiously caught up the phrase he had dropped.

Rogozhin laughed but gave no explanation.

'I got your letter, Lyov Nikolayevitch. It's all of no use … and I wonder at you. But now I've come to you from *her*. She bade me bring you without fail. She is very anxious to say something to you. She wanted to see you today.'

'I'll go tomorrow. I'm going home directly. Are you … coming to me?'

'Why should I? I've said all I had to say. Goodbye.'

'Won't you corner' Myshkin asked gently.

'You're a strange fellow, Lyov Nikolayevitch. One can't help wondering at you.'

Rogozhin laughed malignantly.

Why so? Why are you so bitter against me now?' asked Myshkin, sadly and warmly. 'You know yourself now that all you thought was untrue. But yet I fancy that you are still angry with me. And do you know why? You're still angry because you attacked me. I tell you I only remember that Parfyon Rogozhin, with whom I exchanged crosses that day. I wrote to you last night to forget all that madness and not to speak of it again. Why do you turn away from me? Why do you hide your hand? I tell you, I look upon all that happened then simply as madness. I understand what you were feeling, that day, as though it were myself. What you fancied did not exist and could not exist. Why should there be anger between us?'

'As though you could feel anger!' Rogozhin laughed again, in response to Myshkin's sudden and heated speech.

He had moved two steps away, and was actually standing with his face averted from Myshkin and his hands hidden behind him.

'It's not the thing for me to come and see you now, Lyov Nikolayevitch,' he added, slowly and sententiously in conclusion.

'You still hate me so?'

'I don't like you, Lyov Nikolayevitch, so why should I come and see you! Ah, Prince, you're like a child; you want a plaything, and you must have it at once, but you don't understand things. You are saying just what you wrote in your letter. Do you suppose I don't believe you? I believe every word – you never have deceived me, and never will in the future. But I don't like you all the same. You wrote that you've forgotten everything and you only remember the brother Rogozhin with whom you exchanged crosses, and not that Rogozhin who raised his knife against you. But how do you know my feelings?' (Rogozhin smiled again.) 'Why, perhaps I've never once repented of it, while you've already sent me your brotherly forgiveness. Perhaps I was already thinking of something else that evening, but about that...'

'You had forgotten to think!' Myshkin put in. 'I should think so! I bet that you went straight then to the train, and flew off here to Pavlovsk, to the bandstand to follow her about in the crowd and watch her as you did today. That doesn't surprise me! If you hadn't been in such a state at that time, that you could think of nothing else, perhaps you wouldn't have attacked me with the knife. I had a presentiment from the first, looking at you; do you know what you were like then? When we changed crosses, that idea may have been already at the back of my mind. Why did you take me to your mother then? Did you think to put a check on yourself by that? No, you cannot have thought of it, but you felt it just as I did ... We were feeling just the same. If you had not made that attack (which

God averted), what should I have been then? I did suspect you of it, our sin was the same, in fact. (Yes, don't frown. And why do you laugh?) You've "not repented"! Perhaps even if you wanted to, you couldn't regret it, because you don't like me, besides. And if I were like an innocent angel to you, you'd still detest me so long as you think she loves me and not you. That must be jealousy. But I've thought something about that this week, Parfyon, and I'll tell it you. Do you know that she may love you now more than anyone, and in such a way that the more she torments you, the more she loves you? She won't tell you so, but you must know how to see it. When all's said and done, why else is she going to marry you? Some day she will tell you so herself. Some women want to be loved like that, and that's just her character. And your love and your character must impress her! Do you know that a woman is capable of torturing a man with her cruelty and mockery without the faintest twinge of conscience, because she'll think every time she looks at you: "I'm tormenting him to death now, but I'll make up for it with my love, later".'

Rogozhin laughed, as he listened to Myshkin.

'But, I say, Prince, have you come in for the same treatment? I've heard something of the sort about you, if it's true.'

'What, what could you have heard?' Myshkin started, and stopped in extreme confusion.

Rogozhin went on laughing. He had listened with curiosity and perhaps with some pleasure to Myshkin, whose joyful and impulsive warmth had greatly impressed and encouraged him.

'And I've not merely heard it; I see now it's true,' he added. 'When have you talked like this before? I never heard you say such things before. If I hadn't heard something of the sort about you, I shouldn't have come here: to a park, too, and at midnight.'

'I don't understand you at all, Parfyon Semyonitch.'

'She told me about it a long time ago, and I saw it for myself today as you sat listening to the band this afternoon with the young lady. She's been vowing, she swore to me today and yesterday, that you were head over ears in love with Aglaia Epanchin. That's nothing to me, Prince, and it's no business of mine. If you have left off loving her, she still loves you. You know that she's set on marrying you to her. She has sworn to do it, ha-ha! She says to me: "Tell them I won't marry you without that. When they've gone to church, we'll go to church." I can't make out what it means, and I never have understood: she either loves you beyond all reckoning, or... if she does love you, why does she want to marry you to someone else? She says, "I want to see him happy," so she must love you.'

'I've told you and written to you that she's ... out of her mind,' said Myshkin, who had listened to Rogozhin with distress.

'The Lord knows! You may be mistaken ... But today she fixed the wedding-day when I brought her home from the gardens: in three weeks' time or perhaps sooner, she said, we will certainly be married; she swore it, and kissed the ikon. It all rests with you now, it seems, Prince. Ha-ha!'

'That's all madness. What you've said about me will never be! I'll come and see you tomorrow.'

'How can you call her mad?' observed Rogozhin. 'How is it she seems sane to everyone else, and only mad to you? How could she write letters to her? If she had been mad, they'd have noticed it in her letters!'

'What letters?' asked Myshkin in alarm.

'Why to *her,* to the young lady, and she reads them. Don't you know? Well then, you'll find out. Of course she'll show you them herself.'

'I can't believe that!' cried Myshkin.

'Ach! Lyov Nikolayevitch! You've only gone a little way along that path, as far as I can see. You're only beginning. Wait a bit: you'll keep your own detectives yet and be on the watch day and night too; and know of every step she takes, if only ...'

'Stop, and never speak of that again!' cried Myshkin. 'Listen, Parfyon, just before you appeared I came here and suddenly began laughing – I don't know what about. The only reason was that I remembered it was my birthday tomorrow. It seems to have come on purpose. It's almost twelve o'clock. Come, let us meet the day! I've got some wane. Let's drink some. Wish for me what I don't know how to wish for myself. You wish it, and I'll wish all happiness to you. If not, give back the cross. You didn't send the cross back to me next day! You've got it on now, haven't you?'

'Yes,' said Rogozhin.

'Well, then, come along. I don't want to meet my new life without you, for my new life has begun. You don't know Parfyon that my new life has begun today.'

'I see for myself now, and know that it has begun, and I'll tell *her* so. You're not like yourself at all, Lyov Nikolayevitch!'

Chapter 4

As he drew near his villa Myshkin noticed with great surprise that his verandah was brightly lighted up, and that a large and noisy company was assembled there. The party was a merry one, laughing and shouting; they seemed to be arguing at the top of their voices; the first glance suggested that they were having an hilarious time. And when he mounted to the verandah he found that in fact they had all been drinking, and drinking champagne, and apparently had been drinking for some time, so that many of the revellers had become very agreeably exhilarated by now. They were all people he knew, but it was strange that they should all have come together at once, as though by invitation, though Myshkin had not invited them, and had only by chance recollected that it was his birthday.

'No doubt you told someone you'd uncork the champagne, and so they've all run in,' muttered Rogozhin, following Myshkin to the verandah. 'We know their ways. You've only to whistle to them …' he added, almost angrily, doubtless recalling his own recent past.

They all greeted Myshkin with shouts and good wishes, and surrounded him. Some were very noisy, others much quieter, but hearing that it was his birthday, all in turn hastened to congratulate him. Myshkin was puzzled at the presence of some persons, for instance, Burdovsky, but what was most surprising was that Yevgeny Pavlovitch turned out to be among them. Myshkin could scarcely believe his eyes, and was almost scared at seeing him.

Lebedyev, flushed and almost ecstatic, ran up with explanations; he was pretty far gone already. From his babble it appeared that the party had come together quite naturally, and in fact by chance. First of all, towards the evening, Ippolit had arrived, and feeling much better, had expressed the desire to wait for Myshkin on the verandah. He had installed himself on the sofa; then Lebedyev had gone down to join him and then all his household – that is, his daughters and General Ivolgin. Burdovsky had come with Ippolit, to bring him. Ganya and Ptitsyn seemed to have called in later, as they passed by, at about the time of the incident in the gardens. Then Keller had turned up, told them it was Myshkin's birthday, and asked for champagne. Yevgeny Pavlovitch had only arrived half an hour ago. Kolya too had insisted vigorously on their bringing champagne and celebrating the occasion. Lebedyev had readily produced the wine.

'But my own! My own!' he murmured to Myshkin. 'At my own expense, to celebrate your birthday and congratulate you; and there'll be some supper, some light refreshments, my daughter is seeing to that. But, Prince, if only you knew the subject they're discussing! Do you remember in "Hamlet," "to be or not to be"? The subject of the day! Questions and answers ... And Mr Terentyev's at the utmost pitch ... He won't go to bed! And he's only had a sip of the champagne it won't hurt him ... Come along, Prince, you settle it! They've all been waiting for you, all been waiting for your happy wit...'

Myshkin met the sweet and kindly eyes of Vera Lebedyev, who was also trying to get to him through the crowd. Passing over the rest, he held out his hand first to her. She flushed with pleasure, and wished him 'a happy life *from that day forward..'* Then she rushed full speed to the kitchen; there she was preparing some supper. But even before Myshkin had arrived – whenever she could tear herself for a minute from her work – she had run out to the verandah and listened, all ears, to the heated discussion that never paused among the exhilarated guests concerning subjects of the most abstract nature, mysterious to her. Her open-mouthed younger sister was asleep on a chest in the next room, but the boy, Lebedyev's son, was standing by Kolya and Ippolit, and the look on his eager face showed that he was ready to stand there, listening and enjoying himself for another ten hours at a stretch.

'I have been waiting particularly to see you, and I'm very glad that you've come in such a happy mood,' said Ippolit, when Myshkin went up to shake his hand, immediately after Vera's.

'How do you know I'm in a happy mood?'

'One can see it from your face. Finish greeting the company and make haste and sit here. I've been waiting particularly to see you,' he added, seeming to lay stress on the fact that he had been waiting. In reply to an enquiry from Myshkin whether it were not bad for him to be sitting up so late, he answered that he could not help wondering himself how it was that he had been almost dying three days ago, and yet he had never felt better in his life than that evening.

Burdovsky jumped up from his chair and muttered that he 'had only brought Ippolit,' and that he was glad; that he had 'written nonsense' in his letter, but now was 'simply glad …' Without finishing his sentence, he warmly pressed Myshkin's hand and sat down on a chair.

Last of all Myshkin went up to Yevgeny Pavlovitch; the latter at once took his arm.

'I have a couple of words to say to you,' he whispered, 'and about a very important circumstance. Let us move aside for a moment.'

'A couple of words,' whispered another voice in Myshkin's other ear; and another hand took his arm on the other side.

With surprise Myshkin observed a terribly unkempt figure with a flushed, winking and laughing face, in which he instantly recognised Ferdyshtchenko, who had turned up from goodness knows where.

'Do you remember Ferdyshtchenko?' he asked Myshkin.

'Where have you come from?' cried Myshkin.

'He is sorry,' cried Keller, running up. 'He was hiding. He didn't want to come out to us. He was hiding in the corner there. He's sorry, Prince, he feels himself to blame.'

'But what for? What for?'

'I met him, Prince. I met him just now and brought him along. He is one of the rarest men among my friends. But he's sorry.'

'Delighted, gentlemen; go and sit down with the rest. I'll come directly,' said Myshkin, getting away at last and hurrying to Yevgeny Pavlovitch.

'It's very interesting here,' observed the latter. 'I've enjoyed the half-hour I've been waiting for you. Look here dear Lyov Nikolayevitch, I've settled everything with Kurmyshov and I've come to set your mind at rest. You have no need to be uneasy. He is taking the thing very very sensibly, especially as to my thinking, it was more his fault.'

'What Kurmyshov?'

'Why, the fellow whose arms you held this afternoon. He was so furious that he meant to come to you for an explanation tomorrow.'

'You don't mean it! What nonsense!'

'Of course it is nonsense, and could only end in nonsense, but these people …'

'You've come about something else, too, perhaps, Yevgeny Pavlovitch?'

'Oh, of course, I have,' replied the other, laughing. 'I'm setting off at daybreak tomorrow, dear prince, for Petersburg, about that unhappy business, about my uncle, you know. Would you believe it, it's all true, and everybody knew it except me. I feel so overwhelmed by it that I haven't been able to go to *them* (the Epanchins). I can't go tomorrow either, because I shall be in Petersburg. Do you understand? I may not be here for three days perhaps. In short, things are in a bad way with me. Though the matter is of the utmost importance, yet I decided that I must speak quite openly with you about something, and without delay – that is, before I go. I'll sit and wait, if you like, till your party has broken up; besides, I've nowhere else to go. I'm so excited that I couldn't go to bed. Moreover, though it's an unconscionable proceeding, and not at all the thing to pursue a man like this, I tell you straight out, I have come to ask for your friendship, my dear prince. You're a unique sort of person – that is you don't tell a lie at every turn, perhaps not at all, and I want a friend and adviser in a certain matter, for there's not a doubt I'm one of the unlucky, now...'

He laughed again.

'The trouble is this,' said Myshkin, thinking for an instant. 'You want to wait till they have gone, but God knows when that will be. Wouldn't it be better for us to take a walk in the park now? They'll wait for me, of course; I'll excuse myself.'

'No, no! I have my own reasons for not letting them suspect that we're talking apart for some object. There are people here who are very inquisitive about our relations with one another. Don't you know that, Prince? And it will be much better if they see that we are on the most friendly terms without any private understanding. Do you understand? They'll break up in another two hours; I'll ask you to give me twenty minutes or half an hour then ...'

'By all means, you are very welcome. I am delighted to see you without explanations, and thank you for your kind words about our friendly relations. Pardon me for having been inattentive today; do you know, I somehow can't pay attention just now.'

'I see, I see,' muttered Yevgeny Pavlovitch, with a faint smile.

He was ready to laugh at anything that evening.

'What do you see?' said Myshkin, startled.

'But you don't suspect, dear prince,' said Yevgeny Pavlovitch, still smiling, and not answering his direct question, 'you don't suspect that I've simply come to take you in and, incidentally, to get something out of you, eh?'

'That you have come to get something out of me I have no doubt,' said Myshkin, laughing too at last, 'and perhaps you have planned to deceive me a little, too. But what of it? I am not afraid of you. Besides, I somehow don't mind now. Would you believe it? And … and … and as I am convinced above all that you're a splendid fellow, we shall perhaps end by really becoming friends. I like you very much, Yevgeny Pavlovitch. You are, in my opinion … a thorough gentleman.'

'Well, anyway, it's very nice to have to do with you in anything, whatever it may be,' said Yevgeny Pavlovitch in conclusion. 'Come, I'll drink a glass to your health. I'm awfully glad I came to you. Ah!' he stopped suddenly, 'that Mr Ippolit has come to stay with you, hasn't he?'

'Yes.'

'He isn't going to die directly, I imagine?'

Why do you ask?'

'Oh, nothing; I have been spending half an hour with him here…'

Ippolit had been waiting for Myshkin and watching him and Yevgeny Pavlovitch all the while they had been talking aside. He became feverishly excited when they came up to the table. He was uneasy and agitated. Sweat stood out on his forehead. In his glittering eyes could be seen a sort of vague impatience, as well as a continual wandering uneasiness. His eyes strayed aimlessly from object to object, from face to face. Though he took a leading part in the noisy general conversation, his excitement was simply feverishness. He paid little heed to the conversation itself. His arguments were incoherent, ironical and carelessly paradoxical. He broke off in the middle and did not finish what he had begun with fervent heat. To his surprise and regret, Myshkin learnt that he had been allowed without protest that evening to drink two glasses of champagne, and that the glass that stood empty before him was the third. But he learnt this only later; at the moment he was not very observant.

'Do you know I'm awfully glad that your birthday is today,' cried Ippolit.

'Why?'

'You'll see; make haste and sit down. In the first place, because your... people have all come here tonight. I'd reckoned there'd be a lot of people, for the first time in my life I've been right in my reckoning! It's a pity I didn't know it was your birthday. I'd have brought you a present... Ha-ha! But perhaps I have brought you a present! Is it long till daylight?'

'It's not two hours now to sunrise,' observed Ptitsyn, looking at his watch.

'What need of daylight, when one can read out of doors without it?' remarked someone.

'Because I want to see the sun rise. Can we drink to the health of the sun, Prince? What do you think?'

Ippolit spoke abruptly, addressing the whole company unceremoniously, as though he were giving orders, but he was apparently unconscious of doing so himself.

'Let's drink to it, if you like. Only you ought to keep quieter, Ippolit, oughtn't you?'

'You're always for sleep; you might be my nurse, Prince! As soon as the sun shows itself and "resounds" in the sky (who was it wrote the verse, "the sun resounded in the sky"? There's no sense in it, but it's good) then we'll go to bed. Lebedyev, the sun's the spring of life, isn't it? What's the meaning of "springs of life" in the Apocalypse? Have you heard of the "star that is called Wormwood," prince?'

'I've heard that Lebedyev identifies the "star that is called Wormwood" with the network of railways spread over Europe,'

'No, excuse me, that won't do!' cried Lebedyev, leaping up and waving his arms, as though he were trying to stop the general laughter that followed. 'Excuse me! With these gentlemen ... all these gentlemen!' he turned suddenly to Myshkin, 'I tell you on certain points, it's simply this ..."

And he rapped the table twice without ceremony, which increased the general mirth.

Though Lebedyev was in his usual 'evening' condition, he was on this occasion over-excited and irritated by the long and learned discussion that had taken place, and on such occasions he treated his opponents with undisguised and unbounded contempt.

'That's not right! Half an hour ago, Prince, we made a contract not to interrupt, not to laugh while anyone was speaking but to leave him free to express himself; and then let the atheists answer him, if they like. We chose the general as president. For else, anyone can be shouted down in a lofty idea, a profound idea …'

'But speak, speak! Nobody is shouting you down,' cried voices.

'Talk, but don't talk nonsense.'

'What is "the star that is called Wormwood"?' asked somebody.

'I haven't the slightest idea,' answered General Ivolgin, returning with an important air to his former seat as president.

'I'm wonderfully fond of all these arguments and disputations, Prince – learned ones, of course,' Keller was muttering meantime, positively fidgeting on his chair with impatience and excitement. 'Learned and political,' he added, suddenly and unexpectedly addressing Yevgeny Pavlovitch, who was sitting almost next to him. 'Do you know, I'm awfully fond of reading in the papers about the English Parliament. I don't mean what they discuss (I'm not a politician, you know), but I like the way they speak to one another, and behave like politicians, so to speak: "the noble viscount sitting opposite", "the noble earl who is upholding my view", "my honourable opponent who has amazed Europe by his proposal" – all those expressions, all this parliamentarism of a free people, that's what's so fascinating to people like us. I'm enchanted, Prince. I've always been an artist at the bottom of my soul; I swear I have, Yevgeny Pavlovitch.'

'Why, then,' cried Ganya hotly, in another corner, 'it would follow from what you say that railways are a curse, that they are the ruin of mankind, that they are a plague that has fallen upon the earth to pollute the "springs of life"?'

Gavril Ardalionovitch was in a particularly excited state that evening, and in gay, almost triumphant spirits, so Myshkin fancied. He was joking, of course, with Lebedyev, egging him on, but soon he got hot himself.

'Not railways, no,' retorted Lebedyev, who was at the same time losing his temper and enjoying himself tremendously.

'The railways alone won't pollute the "springs of life", but the whole thing is accursed; the whole tendency of the last few centuries in its general, scientific and materialistic entirety, is perhaps really accursed.'

'Certainly accursed, or only perhaps? It's important to know that, you know,' queried Yevgeny Pavlovitch.

'Accursed, accursed, most certainly accursed!' Lebedyev maintained with heat.

'Don't be in a hurry, Lebedyev, you're much milder in the morning,' put in Ptitsyn with a smile.

'But in the evening more open! In the evening more hearty and open!' Lebedyev turned to him warmly. 'More open-hearted and definite, more honest and honourable; and although I am exposing my weak side to you, no matter. I challenge you all now, all you atheists. With what will you save the world, and where have you found a normal line of progress for it, you men of science, of industry, of co-operation, of labour-wage, and all the rest of it? With what? With credit? .What's credit? Where will credit take you?'

'Ach! You are inquisitive!' observed Yevgeny Pavlovitch.

'Well, my opinion is that anyone who is not interested in such questions is a fashionable "*chenapan*".

'But at least it leads to general solidarity and a balance of interests,' observed Ptitsyn.

'That's all! That's all! Without recognising any moral basis except the satisfaction of individual egoism and material necessity! Universal peace, universal happiness, from necessity! Do I understand you right, my dear sir, may I venture to ask?'

'But the universal necessity of living, eating, and drinking, and a complete, scientific in fact, conviction that these necessities are not satisfied without association and solidarity of interests is, I believe, a sufficiently powerful idea to serve as a basis and "spring of life" for future ages of humanity,' observed Ganya, who was excited in earnest.

'The necessity of eating and drinking, that is merely the instinct of self-preservation ...'

'But isn't that instinct of self-preservation a sufficient matter? Why, the instinct of self-preservation is the normal law of humanity...'

'Who told you that?' cried Yevgeny Pavlovitch suddenly. 'It's a law, that's true, but it's no more normal than the law of destruction, or even self-destruction. Is self-preservation the whole normal law of mankind?'

'A-ha!' cried Ippolit, turning quickly to Yevgeny Pavlovitch and scrutinising him with wild curiosity, but seeing that he was laughing, he too laughed, nudged Kolya who was standing beside him, and asked him again what o'clock it was, and even took hold of Kolya's silver watch himself and looked eagerly at the hands. Then, as though forgetting everything, he stretched himself on the sofa, placed his arms behind his head, and stared at the ceiling; half a minute later, he sat down again at the table, drawing himself up, and listening to the babble of Lebedyev, who was intensely excited.

'An artful and ironical idea, insidious as a larding-needle!' Lebedyev greedily caught up Yevgeny Pavlovitch's paradox; 'an idea expressed with the object of provoking opponents to battle – but a true idea! For you, a worldly scoffer and cavalry officer (though not without brains), are not yourself aware how true and profound your idea is. Yes, Sir, the law of self-destruction and the law of self-preservation are equally strong in humanity! The devil has equal dominion over humanity till the limit of time which we know not. You laugh? You don' t believe in the devil? Disbelief in the devil is a French idea, a frivolous idea. Do you know who the devil is? Do you know his name? Without even knowing his name, you laugh at the form of him, following Voltaire's example, at his hoofs, at his tail, at his horns, which you have invented, for the evil spirit is a mighty menacing spirit, but he has not the hoofs and horns you've invented for him. But he's not the point now.'

'How do you know that he's not the point now?' cried Ippolit suddenly, and laughed as though in hysterics.

'A shrewd and insinuating thought!' Lebedyev approved. 'But, again, that's not the point. Our question is whether the "springs of life" have not grown weaker with the increase of...'

'Railways?' cried Kolya.

'Not railway communication, young but impetuous youth, but all that tendency of which railways may serve, so to speak, as the artistic pictorial expression. They hurry with noise, clamour and haste, for the happiness of humanity, they tell us. "Mankind has grown too noisy and commercial; there is little spiritual peace," one secluded thinker has complained. "So be it, but the rumble of the wagons that bring bread to starving humanity is better, maybe, than spiritual peace," another thinker, who is always moving among his fellows, answers him triumphantly, and walks away from him conceitedly. But, vile as I am, I don't believe in the wagons that bring bread to humanity. For the wagons that bring bread to humanity, without any moral basis for conduct, may coldly exclude a considerable part of humanity from enjoying what is brought, so it has been already…'

'The wagons can coldly exclude?' someone repeated.

'And so it has been already,' repeated Lebedyev, not deigning to notice the question. 'We've already had Malthus, the friend of humanity. But the friend of humanity with shaky moral principles is the devourer of humanity, to say nothing of his conceit; for, wound the vanity of anyone of these numerous friends of humanity, and he's ready to set fire to the world out of petty revenge – like all the rest of us, though, in that, to be fair; like myself, vilest of all, for I might well be the first to bring the fuel and run away myself. But that's not the point again!'

'What is it, then?'

'You're boring us.'

'The points lie in what follows, in an anecdote of the past, for I absolutely must tell you a story of ancient times. In our times, and in our country, which I trust you love, gentlemen, as I do, for I am ready to shed the last drop of my blood for …'

'Get on, get on!'

'In our country, as well as in the rest of Europe, widespread and terrible famines visit humanity, as far as they can be reckoned, and as far as I can remember, not oftener now than four times a century, in other words, every twenty-five years. I won't dispute the exact number, but they are comparatively rare.'

'Compared with what?'

'Compared with the twelfth century, or those near it, before or after. For then, as they write and as writers assert, widespread famines came usually every two years, or at least every three years, so that in such a position of affairs men even had recourse to cannibalism, though they kept it secret. One of these cannibals announced, without being forced to do so, as he was approaching old age, that in the course of his long and needy life he had killed and eaten by himself in dead secret sixty monks and a few infant laymen, a matter of six, but not more. That is extraordinarily few compared with the immense mass of ecclesiastics he had consumed. Grown-up laymen, it appeared, he had never approached with that object.'

'That can't be true!' cried the president himself, the general in an almost resentful voice. 'I often reason and dispute with him, gentlemen, always about such things, but usually he brings forward such absurd stories, that it makes your ears ache, without a shred of probability.'

'General, remember the siege of Kars! And let me tell you, gentlemen, that my story is the unvarnished truth. I will only observe that every reality, even though it has its unalterable laws, is almost always difficult to believe and improbable, and sometimes, indeed, the more real it is the more improbable it is.'

'But could he eat sixty monks?' they asked, laughing round him.

'He didn't eat them all at once, that's evident. But if he consumed them in the course of fifteen or twenty years, it is perfectly comprehensible and natural...'

'Natural?'

'Yes, natural,' Lebedyev repeated, with pedantic persistence, 'Besides, a Catholic monk is, from his very nature, easily led and inquisitive, and it wouldn't be hard to lure him into the forest, or to some hidden place, and there to deal with him as aforesaid. But I don't deny that the number of persons devoured seems excessive to the point of greediness.'

'It may be true, gentlemen,' observed Myshkin suddenly.

Till then he had listened in silence to the disputants and had taken no part in the conversation; he had often joined heartily in the general outbursts of laughter. He was evidently delighted that they were so gay and so noisy; even that they were drinking so much. He might perhaps not have uttered a word the whole evening, but suddenly he seemed moved to speak. He spoke with marked gravity, so that everyone turned to him at once with interest.

'What I mean, gentlemen, is, that famines used to be frequent. I have heard of that, though I know little history. But I think they must have been. When I was among the Swiss mountains I was surprised at the ruins of feudal castles, built on the mountain slopes or precipitious rocks at least half a mile high (which means some miles of mountain path). You know what a castle is: a perfect mountain of stones. They must have meant an awful, incredible labour. And, of course, they were all built by the poor people, the vassals. Besides which, they had to pay all the taxes and support the priesthood. How could they provide for themselves and till the land? They must have been few in number at that time; they died off terribly from famine, and there may have been literally nothing to eat. I've sometimes wondered, indeed, how it was that the people didn't become extinct altogether; how it was that nothing happened to them, and how they managed to endure it and survive. No doubt Lebedyev is right in saying that there were cannibals, and perhaps many of them; only I don't understand why he brought monks into the story, and what he means by that.'

'Probably because in the twelfth century it was only the monks who were fit to eat, because they were the only people that were fat,' observed Gavril Ardalionovitch.

'A magnificent and true idea!' cried Lebedyev, 'seeing he didn't touch laymen – not one layman to sixty ecclesiastics; and that's a frightful thought, an historical thought, a statistical thought indeed, and such facts make history for one who understands. For it follows with arithmetical exactitude that the ecclesiastics lived at least sixty times as happily and comfortably as all the rest of mankind at that period. And perhaps they were at least sixty times as fat...'

'An exaggeration! An exaggeration, Lebedyev!' they all laughed.

'I agree that is an historical thought, but what are you leading up to?' Myshkin enquired again. (He spoke with such gravity and so absolutely without mocking or jeering at Lebedyev, at whom all the rest were laughing, that in contrast with the general tone his words could not help sounding comic. They were almost on the verge of laughing at him, but he did not notice it.)

'Don't you see, Prince, that he's a madman?' said Yevgeny Pavlovitch, bending down to him. 'I was told here just now that he's mad on being a lawyer and making lawyers' speeches, and wants to go in for an examination. I'm expecting a glorious burlesque.'

'I am leading up to vast issues,' Lebedyev was roaring meanwhile. 'But let us first of all analyse the psychological and legal position of the criminal. We see that the criminal, or, as I might call him, my client, in spite of the impossibility of finding any other comestible, several times in the course of his interesting career, showed signs of a desire to repent and shun the clergy. We see this clearly from the facts. It will be remembered that he did at any rate consume five or six infants – a number relatively insignificant, yet remarkable from another point of view. It is evident that, tormented by terrible pangs of conscience (for my client is a religious man and conscientious, as I shall prove later), and to minimise his sin as far as possible, he, by way of experiment, changed his diet from the clergy to the laity. That it was by way of experiment is beyond doubt again, for had it been simply for the sake of gastronomic variety, the number six would be too insignificant. Why only six? Why not thirty? (Half, half of one and half of the other.) But if it were only an experiment, arising simply from despair and the fear of sacrilege, and of offending the Church, the number six becomes quite intelligible, for six attempts to appease the pangs of conscience are more than enough, as the attempts could not but be unsuccessful. And in the first place, in my opinion, an infant is too small – that is, insufficient, so that he would need three times or five times as many infant laymen for the same period of time as one ecclesiastic. So that the sin, though less on the one side, would be greater on the other – not in quality, but in quantity. In this reflection, gentlemen, I am of course entering into the feelings of a criminal of the twelfth century. As for me, a man of the nineteenth century, I should have reasoned differently, I beg to inform you, so you need not grin at me, gentlemen, and it's not at all the thing for you to do, General. In the second place, an infant, in my opinion, would be not sufficiently nutritious, and perhaps too sweet and mawkish, so that his appetite would be unsatisfied, while the pangs of conscience would remain. Now for the conclusion, the finale, gentlemen, in which lies the solution of one of the greatest questions of that age and of this! The criminal ends by going and giving information against himself to the clergy and gives himself up to the authorities. One wonders what tortures awaited him in that age – the wheel, the stake and the fire. Who was it urged him to go and inform against himself? Why not simply stop short at sixty and keep the secret till his dying breath? Why not simply relinquish the clergy and live in penitence as a hermit? Why not, indeed, enter a monastery himself? Here is the solution. There must have been something stronger than stake and fire, stronger even than the habit of twenty years! There must have been an idea stronger than any misery, famine, torture, plague, leprosy, and all that hell, which mankind could not have endured without that idea, which bound men together, guided their hearts, and fructified the springs of life. Show me anything like such a force in our age of vices and railways ... I should say of steamers and railways, but I say vices and railways, because I'm drunk but truthful. Show me any idea binding mankind together today with anything like the power it had in those centuries. And dare to tell me that the springs of life have not been weakened and muddied beneath the "star," beneath the network in which men are enmeshed. And don't try to frighten me with your prosperity, your wealth, the infrequency of famine and the rapidity of the means of communication. There is more wealth, but there is less strength. There is no uniting idea; everything has grown softer, everything is limp, and everyone is limp! We've all, all of us grown limp ... But that's enough. That's not the point now. The point is, honoured Prince, whether we shouldn't see to getting ready the supper, that's being prepared for your visitors.'

Lebedyev had roused several of his hearers to positive indignation. (It must be noted that corks were being drawn incessantly all the time.) But his unexpected reference to supper conciliated all his opponents at once. He called such a conclusion 'a smart, lawyer-like wind-up.' Good-humoured laughter rang out again, the guests grew more festive, and they all got up from the table to stretch their legs and take a turn on the verandah. Only Keller was still displeased with Lebedyev's speech, and was much excited.

'He attacks enlightenment and upholds the bigotry of the twelfth century. He's attitudinising; it's not through simple-heartedness. How did he himself come by this house, allow me to ask?' he said aloud, appealing to each and all.

'I used to know a real interpreter of the Apocalypse,' the general was saying in another corner to another group of listeners, among them Ptitsyn, whom he had buttonholed – 'the late Grigory Semyonovitch Burmistrov. He used to make your heart glow. First, he'd put on his spectacles, and open a big old book in a black leather binding, and he'd a grey beard and two medals in recognition of his munificent charities. He used to begin sternly and severely. Generals would bow down before him, and ladies fell into swoons. But this fellow winds up with supper! It's beyond anything.'

Ptitsyn listened to the general, smiled, and made towards his hat, as though meaning to go, but seemed to be undecided, or to have forgotten his intention. Ganya had left off drinking and pushed away his glass even before they got up from the table. A shade of gloom came over his face. When they rose from the table, he went up to Rogozhin and sat down beside him. They might have been supposed to be on the friendliest terms. Rogozhin, who had also at first been several times on the point of getting up and slipping away, sat now motionless with his head bowed. He too seemed to have forgotten his intention. He had not drunk a drop of wine all the evening, and was very thoughtful. From time to time he raised his eyes and gazed at everyone. It might have been supposed now that he was expecting something of great importance to him and had made up his mind to wait for it.

Myshkin had drunk no more than two or three glasses, and was only light-hearted. As he rose from the table, he caught the eye of Yevgeny Pavlovitch. He remembered the explanation they were to have, and smiled cordially. Yevgeny Pavlovitch nodded to him and indicated Ippolit, whom he was intently watching at the moment. Ippolit was asleep at full length on the sofa.

'Tell me, Prince, why has this wretched boy forced himself upon your' he asked suddenly, with such undisguised annoyance and even malice, that Myshkin was surprised. 'I'll bet he's got some mischief in his mind!'

'I have noticed,' said Myshkin, 'I have fancied, at any rate, that he is in your thoughts a great deal today, Yevgeny Pavlovitch, isn't he?'

'And you may say too I've enough to think about in my own position, so that I'm surprised myself at not being able to get away from that detestable countenance all the evening.'

'He has a handsome face ...'

'Look, look!' cried Yevgenv Pavlovitch, pulling Myshkin by the arm. 'Look!

Myshkin gazed at Yevgeny Pavlovitch with wonder again.

Chapter 5

Ippolit, who had suddenly fallen asleep on the sofa, towards the end of Lebedyev's harangue, now as suddenly waked up, as though someone had poked him in the ribs.

He started, sat up, looked round him, and turned pale; he seemed to gaze about him as it were in alarm. There was almost a look of horror on his face when he remembered everything and reflected.

'What, are they going? Is it over? Is it all over? Has the sun risen?' he kept asking in agitation, clutching Myshkin's hand.

'What's the time? For God's sake, what's the time? I've overslept myself. Have I been asleep long?' he added, with an almost desperate air, as though he had missed something on which his whole fate at least depended.

'You've been asleep seven or eight minutes,' answered Yevgeny Pavlovitch.

Ippolit looked greedily at him and reflected for some moments.

'Ah ... That's all! Then I...'

And he drew a deep, eager breath, as though casting off some heavy weight. He realised at last that nothing 'was over,' that it was not yet daybreak, that the guests had got up from the table only on account of supper, and that Lebedyev's chatter was the only thing that was over. He smiled and a hectic flush came out in two bright spots on his cheeks.

'And you've been counting the minutes while I was asleep, Yevgeny Pavlovitch,' he commented, ironically. 'You couldn't tear yourself away from me all the evening, I've seen that. Ah! Rogozhin! I was dreaming about him just now,' he whispered to Myshkin, frowning, and nodding towards Rogozhin, who was sitting at the table. 'Ah! Yes!' he flew off to another subject, 'where's the orator? Where's Lebedyev? Has he finished then? What was he talking about? Is it true, Prince, that you said once that "beauty" would save the world? Gentlemen!' he shouted loudly, addressing the whole company, 'the prince asserts that beauty will save the world! But I assert that the reason he has such playful ideas is that he is in love; I was certain of it when he came in just now. Don't blush, Prince, it makes me sorry for you. What sort of beauty will save the world? Kolya told me ... Are you a zealous Christian? Kolya says that you say you're a Christian yourself.'

Myshkin looked at him attentively and made no answer.

'You don't answer? Perhaps you think I'm very fond of you?' Ippolit added suddenly, abruptly.

'No, I don't think so. I know you don't like me.'

'What, after yesterday? Was I honest with you yesterday?'

'I knew yesterday that you didn't like me.'

'Is that because I envy ... envy you? You always thought that and think so still, but... but why do I speak of that to you? I want some more champagne; pour some out, Keller.'

'You musn't drink any more, Ippolit, I won't let you ...'

And Myshkin moved away the glass.

'You're right,' he agreed immediately, as it were, dreamily. 'Maybe they'll say… it doesn't matter a damn to me what they say? … Does it? Does it? Let them say so afterwards, eh, Prince? What does it matter to any of us what happens *afterwards*? But I'm half asleep. What an awful dream I had. I've only just remembered it. I don't wish you such dream, Prince, though perhaps I really don't like you. But why should one wish a man harm, even if one doesn't like him, eh? How is it I keep asking questions – I keep asking questions? Give me your hand; I'll press it warmly, like this … You hold out your hand to me, though! So you know that I shall shake hands sincerely. I won't drink any more if you like. What time is it? But you needn't tell me, I know what time it is. The hour has come! Now is the very time. Why are they laying supper over there, in the corner? This table is free, then? Good! Gentlemen, I … But all these gentlemen are not listening … I intend to read an essay, Prince; supper, of course, is more interesting, but…'

And suddenly, quite unexpectedly, he pulled out of his breast pocket a large envelope, sealed with a large red seal. He laid it on the table before him.

This unexpected action produced a sensation in the company, who were unprepared for it, and were by now far from sober. Yevgeny Pavlovitch positively started up on his chair. Ganya moved quickly to the table; Rogozhin did the same, but with a sort of peevish vexation, as though he understood what was coming. Lebedyev, who happened to be close by, came up with inquisitive eyes and stared at the envelope, trying to guess what it meant.

'What have you there?' Myshkin asked, uneasily.

'At the first peep of sunshine I shall go to rest, Prince. I've said so; on my honour, you shall see!' cried Ippolit. 'But… but… Do you imagine that I'm not capable of breaking open that envelope?' he added, turning his eyes from one to another, with a sort of challenge, and apparently addressing all without distinction.

Myshkin noticed that he was trembling all over.

'None of us imagine such a thing,' Myshkin answered for all. 'And why should you suppose that anyone thinks so? And what… what a strange idea to read to us? What have you there, Ippolit?'

'What is it?'

'What's happened to him now?' they were asking on all hands.

All the party came up, some of them still eating. The envelope with the red seal drew them all like a magnet.

'I wrote it yesterday, myself, directly after I'd promised I would come to live with you, Prince. I was writing it all day yesterday, and all night, and finished it this morning; in the night, towards morning, I had a dream.'

'Wouldn't it be better tomorrow?' Myshkin interposed timidly.

'Tomorrow there will be "no more time",' Ippolit laughed hysterically. 'But don't be uneasy. I'll read it in forty minutes, or, well – an hour … And see how interested they all are; they've all come up, they're all staring at my seal, and if I hadn't sealed the article up in an envelope, there'd have been no sensation! Ha-ha! You see what mystery does! Shall I break the seal or not, gentlemen?' he shouted, laughing his strange laugh, and staring at them with glittering eyes. 'A secret! A secret! And do you remember, Prince, who proclaimed that there will be "no more time"? It was proclaimed by the great and mighty angel in the Apocalypse.'

'Better not read it!' Yevgeny Pavlovitch cried suddenly, but with a look of uneasiness so unexpected in him that it struck many persons as strange.

'Don't read it,' cried Myshkin, too, laying his hand on the envelope.

'Why read? It's rime for supper now,' observed someone.

'An article? A magazine article?' enquired another.

'Dull, perhaps,' added a third.

'What's it all about?' enquired the rest.

But Myshkin's timid gesture seemed to have intimidated Ippolit himself.

'So… I'm not to read it?' he whispered to him, almost apprehensively, with a wry smile on his blue lips, 'not to read it?' he muttered, scanning his whole audience, all their eyes and faces, and as it were catching at them all again, with the same aggressive effusiveness. 'Are you … afraid?' he turned again to Myshkin.

'What of?' asked the latter, his face changing more and more.

'Has anyone got a twenty-kopeck piece?' Ippolit leapt up from his chair as though he had been pulled up. 'Or any coin?'

'Here you are,' Lebedyev gave it him at once.

The idea occurred to him that the invalid had gone out of his mind.

'Vera Lukyanovna!'Ippolit hurriedly begged her, 'Take it, throw it on the table – heads or tails? Heads – I read it!'

Vera looked in alarm at the coin, at Ippolit, and then at her father, and awkwardly throwing back her head, as though she felt she ought not to look at the coin, she tossed it. It came up heads.

'I read it!' whispered Ippolit, as though crushed by the decision of destiny. He could not have turned more pale, if he had heard his death sentence.

'But,' he started suddenly, after half a minute's silence, 'what? Can I really have tossed up?' With the same appealing frankness he scrutinised the whole circle. 'But, you know, that's an amazing psychological fact!' he cried suddenly, addressing Myshkin in genuine astonishment. 'It's ... it's an incredible fact, Prince,' he repeated, reviving, and seeming to recover himself. 'You must make a note of this, Prince, remember it, for I believe you are collecting facts relating to capital punishment... I've been told so, ha-ha! Oh, my God, what senseless absurdity!'

He sat down on the sofa, put his elbows on the table, and clutched at his head. 'Why it's positively shameful! But what the devil do I care if it is shameful!' he raised his head almost at once. 'Gentlemen, gentlemen! I will break the seal of my envelope!' he declared, with sudden determination. 'I... I don't compel you to listen though!'

With hands trembling with excitement he opened the envelope, took out several sheets of notepaper covered with small handwriting, put them before him, and began to arrange them.

'What is it? 'What's the matter? What's he going to read?' some people muttered gloomily; others were silent.

But they all sat down and stared inquisitively. Perhaps they really did expect something unusual. Vera caught hold of her father's chair, and was almost crying with fright. Kolya was hardly less alarmed. Lebedyev, who had already sat down, rose and moved the candles nearer to Ippolit to give him more light.

'Gentlemen this ... you'll see directly what it is,' Ippolit added for some reason, and he suddenly began reading: ' "An essential explanation! Motto: *après moi le déluge.* 'Oh dear, oh dear! Damn it!' he cried out, as though he had been scalded. 'Can I seriously have written such a stupid motto?... Listen, gentlemen!... I assure you that all this is perhaps after all the most fearful nonsense! It's only some thoughts of mine ... If you think there's anything mysterious about it... anything prohibited ... in fact...'

'If you'd only read it without a preface!' interrupted Ganya.

'It's affectation!' someone added.

'There's too much talk,' put in Rogozhin, who had been silent till then.

Ippolit suddenly looked at him, and when their eyes met, Rogozhin gave a bitter and morose grin, and slowly pronounced a strange sentence.

'It's not the way to set about this business, lad, it's not the way …'

No one, of course, knew what Rogozhin meant, but his words made rather a strange impression on everyone; everyone seemed to catch a passing glimpse of a common idea. On Ippolit these words made a terrible impression; he trembled so much that Myshkin put out his arm to support him, and he would certainly have cried out but that his voice failed him. For a whole minute he could not speak, and stared at Rogozhin, breathing painfully. At last, gasping for breath, with an immense effort he articulated, 'So it was you … you … it was you?'

'What was I? What about me?' answered Rogozhin, amazed.

But Ippolit, firing up and suddenly seized almost with fury, shouted violently: 'You were in my room last week at night, past one o'clock, on the day I had been to you in the morning, *you* Confess, it was you.'

'Last week, at night? Have you gone clean out of your senses, lad?'

The 'lad' was silent again for a minute, putting his forefinger to his forehead, and seeming to reflect. But there was gleam of something sly, almost triumphant, in his pale smile that was still distorted by fear.

'It was you!' he repeated, almost in a whisper, but with intense conviction. 'You came to me and sat in my room without speaking, on the chair by the window, for a whole hour; more, between twelve and two o'clock at night. Then afterwards, between two and three, you got up and walked out… It was you, it was you! Why did you frighten me? Why did you come to torment me? I don't understand it, but it was you.'

And there was a sudden flash of intense hatred in his eyes, though he was still trembling with fear.

'You shall know all about it directly, gentlemen … I… I… listen…'

Once more, and with desperate haste, he clutched at the sheets of paper. They had slipped and fallen apart. He attempted to put them together. They shook in his shaking hands. It was a long time before he could get them right.

'He's gone mad, or delirious,' muttered Rogozhin, almost inaudibly.

The reading began at last. At the beginning, for the first five minutes, the author of the unexpected *article* still gasped for breath, and read jerkily and incoherently, but as he went on his voice grew stronger and began to express the sense of what he was reading. But he was sometimes interrupted by a violent fit of coughing; before he was halfway through the article, he was very hoarse. His feverish excitement, which grew greater and greater as he read, reached an intense pitch at last, and so did the painful impression on his audience. Here is the whole article:

An Essential Explanation.
Après moi le déluge!

The prince was here yesterday morning. Among other things he persuaded me to move to his villa. I knew that he would insist upon this, and felt sure that he would blurt straight out that it would be 'easier to die among people and trees,' as he expresses it. But today, he did not say 'die', but said 'it will be easier to live', which comes to much the same thing, however, in my position. I asked him what he meant by his everlasting 'trees', and why he keeps pestering me with those 'trees', and learnt to my surprise that I had myself said on that evening that I'd come to Pavlovsk to look at the trees for the last time. When I told him I should die just the same, looking at trees, or looking out of my window at brick walls, and that there was no need to make a fuss about a fortnight, he agreed at once, but the greenness and the fresh air will be sure, according to him, to produce a physical change in me, and my excitement and my *dreams* will be affected and perhaps relieved. I told him again, laughing, that he spoke like a materialist. He answered with his smile that he had always been a materialist. As he never tells a lie, that saying means something. He has a nice smile; I have examined him carefully now. I don't know whether I like him or not; I haven't time now to bother about it. The hatred I have felt for him for five months has begun to go off this last month, I must observe. Who knows, maybe I came to Pavlovsk chiefly to see him. But... why did I leave my room then? A man condemned to death ought not to leave his corner. And if I had not now taken my final decision, but had intended to linger on till the last minute, nothing would have induced me to leave my room, and I should not have accepted his invitation to go to him, to die in Pavlovsk. I must make haste and finish this 'explanation' before tomorrow, anyway. So I shan't have time to read it over and correct it. I shall read it over tomorrow, when I'm going to read it to the prince and two or three witnesses, whom I mean to find there. Since there will not be one word of falsehood in it, but everything is the simple truth, the last and solemn truth, I feel curious to know what impression it will make on myself, at the hour and minute when I shall read it over. I was wrong in writing, though, that it was the 'last and solemn truth'; it's not worth telling lies for a fortnight, anyway, for it's not worth while living a fortnight. That's the best possible proof that I shall write nothing but the truth. (NB – Not to forget the thought: am I not mad at this minute, or rather these minutes? I was told positively that in the last stage consumptives sometimes go out of their minds for a time. Must verify this tomorrow from the impression made on my audience. I must settle that question absolutely, or else I cannot act.)

I believe I have just written something awfully stupid, but as I said, I've no time to correct it; besides, I've promised myself on purpose not to correct one line in this manuscript, even if I notice that I contradict myself every five lines. What I want to decide after the reading tomorrow is just whether the sequence of my ideas is correct; whether I shall notice my mistakes, and therefore whether all I have thought over in this room for the last six months is true, or delirium.

If I had had to leave my rooms two months ago and say goodbye to Meyer's wall, I'm certain I should have been sorry. But now I feel nothing, yet tomorrow I am leaving my room and the wall or *ever!* So my conviction, that a fortnight is not worth regretting or feeling anything about, has mastered my whole nature, and can dictate to my feelings. But is it true? Is it true that my nature is completely vanquished now? If somebody began torturing me now, I should certainly begin to scream, and I shouldn't say that it was not worth while screaming and feeling pain, because I only had a fortnight more to live.

But is it true that I have only a fortnight left to live, not more? I told a lie that day at Pavlovsk. B— told me nothing and never saw me, but a week ago they brought me a student called Kislorodov; by his convictions he is a materialist, an atheist, and a nihilist, that's why I sent for him. I wanted a man to tell me the naked truth at last, without any softening or ado about it. And so he did, and not only readily and without any fuss, but with obvious satisfaction (which was going too far to my thinking). He blurted out that I had about a month left to live, perhaps a little more, if my circumstances were favourable, but I may die much sooner. In his opinion I might die suddenly, for instance, tomorrow. There are such cases. Only the day before yesterday in Kolumna a young lady, in consumption, whose condition was similar to mine, was just starting for the market to buy provisions, when she suddenly felt ill, lay down on the sofa, uttered a sigh and died. All this Kislorodov told me with a sort of jauntiness, carelessly and unfeelingly, as though he were doing me an honour by it, that is, as though showing me that he takes me, too, for the same sort of utterly sceptical superior creature, as himself, who, of course, cares nothing about dying. Anyway, the fact is authenticated; a month and no more! I am quite sure he's not mistaken.

I wondered very much how the prince guessed that I had 'bad dreams'. He used those very words, that in Pavlovsk 'my excitement and *dreams'* would change. And why dreams? He's either a doctor, or exceptionally intelligent, and able to see things. (But that he is, after all said and done, an 'idiot' there can be no doubt.) Just before he came in, I had, as though purposely, a pretty dream (though, as a matter of fact I have hundreds of dreams like that, now.) I fell asleep -I believe about an hour before he came in – and dreamt that I was in a room, but not my own. The room was larger and loftier than mine, better furnished, and lighter. There was a wardrobe, a chest of drawers, a sofa, and my bed, which was big and broad and covered with a green silk quilted counterpane. But in the room I noticed an awful animal, a sort of monster. It was like a scorpion, but was not a scorpion, it was more disgusting, and much more horrible, and it seemed it was so, just because there was nothing like it in nature, and that it had come *expressly* to me, and that there seemed to be something mysterious in that. I examined it very carefully: it was brown, and was covered with shell, a crawling reptile, seven inches long, two fingers thick at the head, and tapering down to the tail, so that the point of the tail was only about the sixth of an inch thick. Almost two inches from the head, at an angle of forty-five degrees to the body, grew two legs, one on each side, nearly four inches long, so that the whole creature was in the shape of a trident, if looked at from above. I couldn't make out the head but I saw two whiskers, short, and also brown, looking like two strong needles. There were two whiskers of the same sort at the end of the tail, and at the end of each of the legs, making eight whiskers in all. The beast was running about the room, very quickly, on its legs and its tail, and, when it ran, the body and legs wriggled like little snakes, with extraordinary swiftness in spite of its shell, and that was very horrible to look at. I was awfully afraid it would sting me; I had been told it was poisonous, but what worried me most of all was the question who had sent it into my room, what they meant to do to me, and what was the secret of it? It hid under the chest of drawers, under the cupboard, crawled into corners. I sat on a chair, and drew my legs up under me. It ran quickly right across the room and disappeared near my chair. I looked about in terror, but as I sat with my legs curled up I hoped that it would not crawl up the chair. Suddenly I heard behind me, almost at my head, a sort of scraping rustle. I looked round, and saw that the reptile was crawling up the wall, and was already on a level with my head and was positively touching my hair with its tail, which was twirling and wriggling with extraordinary rapidity. I sprang up, and the creature disappeared. I was afraid to lie down on the bed for fear it should creep under the pillow. My mother came into the room with some friend of hers. They began trying to catch the creature, but were cooler than I was, and were not, in fact, afraid of it. But they didn't understand. Suddenly the reptile crawled out again. It seemed to have some special design and crawled, this time very slowly, across the room towards the door, wriggling slowly, which was more revolting than ever. Then, my mother opened the door and called Norma, our dog – a huge, shaggy, black Newfoundland; it died five years ago. It rushed into the room and stopped short before the reptile. The creature stopped too, but still wriggled and scraped the ground with its paws and tail. Animals cannot feel terror of the mysterious, unless I'm mistaken, but at that moment it seemed to me that there was something very extraordinary in Norma's terror, as though there were something uncanny in it, as though the dog too felt that there was something ominous, some mystery in it. She moved back slowly facing the reptile, which crept slowly and cautiously towards her, it seemed meaning to dart at her, and sting her. But in spite of her fear, Norma looked very fierce, though she was trembling all over. All at once she slowly bared her terrible teeth and opened her huge red jaws, crouched, prepared for a spring, made up her mind, and suddenly seized the creature with her teeth. The reptile must have struggled to slip away, so that Norma caught it once more as it was escaping, and twice over got it full in her jaws, seeming to gobble it up as it ran. Its shell cracked between her teeth, the tail and legs hanging out of the mouth moved at a tremendous rate. All at once Norma gave a piteous squeal: the reptile had managed to sting her tongue. Whining and yelping she opened her mouth from the pain, and I saw that the creature, though bitten in two, was still wriggling in her mouth, and was emitting, from its crushed body, on to the dog's tongue, a quantity of white fluid such as comes out of a squashed black-beetle … Then I waked up and the prince came in.

'Gentlemen,' said Ippolit, suddenly breaking off from his reading, and seeming almost ashamed, 'I haven't read this over, but I believe I have really written a great deal that's superfluous. That dream …'

'That's true enough,' Ganya hastened to put in.

'There's too much that's personal in it, I must own, that is, about myself…'

As he said this, Ippolit had a wear)' and exhausted air, and wiped the sweat off his forehead with his handkerchief.

'Yes, you're too much interested in yourself,' hissed Lebedyev.

'I don't force anyone, let me say again, gentlemen. If anyone doesn't want to hear, he can go away.'

'He turns them out... of another man's house,' Rogozhin grumbled, hardly audibly.

'And how if we all get up and go away?' said Ferdyshtchenko suddenly. He had till then not ventured to speak aloud.

Ippolit dropped his eyes suddenly and clutched his manuscript. But at the same second he raised his head again, and with flashing eyes and two patches of red on his cheeks, he said, looking fixedly at Ferdyshtchenko, 'You don't like me at all.'

There was laughter; most of the party did not laugh, however. Ippolit flushed horribly.

'Ippolit,' said Myshkin, 'fold up your manuscript, and give it to me, and go to bed here in my room. We'll talk before you go to sleep, and tomorrow, but on condition that you never open these pages. Will you?'

'Is that possible?' Ippolit looked at him in positive amazement. 'Gentlemen!' he cried, growing feverishly excited again, 'this is a stupid episode, in which I haven't known how to behave. I won't interrupt the reading again. If anyone wants to listen, let him.'

He took a hurried gulp of water from the glass, hurriedly put his elbows on the table to shield his face from their eyes, and went on, obstinately reading. But his shame soon passed off.

'The idea,' he went on, 'that it's not worth while to live a few weeks began to come over me really, I fancy, a month ago, when I had four weeks to live, but it only took complete possession of me three days ago, when I came back from that evening at Pavlovsk. The first moment that I fully directly grasped that thought was on the prince's verandah, at the instant when I was meaning to make a last trial of life, when I wanted to see people and trees (granted I said that myself), when I got excited, insisted on the rights of Burdovsky "my neighbour", and dreamed that they would all fling wide their arms, and clasp me in them, and beg my forgiveness for something, and I theirs; in short, I behaved like a stupid fool. And it was at that time that a "last conviction" sprang up in me. I wondered how I could have lived for six months without that conviction! I knew for a fact that I had consumption and it was incurable. I didn't deceive myself, and understood the case clearly. But the more clearly I understood it, the more feverishly I longed to live: I clutched at life, I wanted to live whatever happened. Admitting that I might well have resented the dark and obscure lot which was to crush me like a fly, and, of course, with no reason, yet why couldn't I have stopped at resentment? Why did I actually *begin* living, knowing that I couldn't begin it now. Why did I try it, knowing that it was useless for me to try anything? And yet I could not even read, and gave up books. What use to read, what use to learn for six months? More than once that thought drove me to fling aside a book.

'Yes, that wall of Meyer's could tell a story! I have written a great deal on it. There isn't a spot on that filthy wall which I haven't studied. Cursed wall! And yet it's dearer to me than all the trees of Pavlovsk, that is, it would be dearer than all, if everything were not all the same to me now.

'I remember now with what greedy interest I began, at that time, watching *their* life: I had had no such interest in the past. I used to look forward with cursing and impatience to seeing Kolya, when I was too ill to go out myself. I pried into every detail, and was so interested in every rumour that I believe I became a regular gossip. I couldn't understand, for instance, why people who had so much life before them did not become rich (and, indeed, I don't understand it now). I knew one poor fellow, who, I was told afterwards, died of hunger, and I remember that it made me furious: if it had been possible to bring the poor devil back to life, I believe I'd have had him executed. I was sometimes better for weeks at a time and able to go out of doors, but the street exasperated me at last to such a degree that I purposely sat indoors for days together, though I could have gone out like anyone else. I couldn't endure the scurrying, bustling people, everlastingly dreary, worried and preoccupied, flitting to and fro about me on the pavement. Why their everlasting gloom, uneasiness, and bustle, their everlasting sullen spite (for they are spiteful, spiteful, spiteful). Whose fault is it that they are miserable and don't know how to live, though they've sixty years of life before them? Why did Zarnitzyn let himself die of hunger when he had sixty years of life before him? And each one points to his rags, his toil-worn hands, and cries savagely: "We toil like cattle, we labour, we are poor and hungry as dogs! Others don't toil, and don't labour, and they are rich!" (The everlasting story!) Among them, running and struggling from morning to night, is some miserable sniveller like

Ivan Fomitch Surikov "a gentleman born" – he lives in our block over my head – always out at elbows, with his buttons dropping off, running errands, and taking messages for all sorts of people, from morning till night. Talk to him – he's poor, destitute, starving, his wife died, he couldn't buy medicine for her, his baby was frozen to death in the winter; his elder daughter is a "kept mistress" ... he's for ever whimpering and complaining. Oh, I've never felt the least, the least pity for these fools, and I don't now -I say so with pride! Why isn't he a Rothschild? Whose fault is it that he hasn't millions, like Rothschild, that he hasn't a heap of golden imperials and napoleon-d'ors, a perfect mountain, as high as the mounds made in carnival week. If he's alive he has everything in his power! Whose fault is it he doesn't understand that?

'Oh, now I don't care, now I've no time to be angry, but then I repeat, I literally gnawed my pillow at night and tore my quilt with rage. Oh, how I used to dream then, how I longed to be turned out into the street at eighteen, almost without clothing, almost without covering, to be deserted and utterly alone, without lodging, without work, without a crust of bread, without relations, without one friend in a great town, hungry, beaten (so much the better) but healthy – and then I would show them ...

'What would I show?

'Oh, no doubt you think I don't know how I've humiliated myself as it is by my "Explanation"! Oh, everyone of course will look upon me as a sniveller who knows nothing of life, forgetting that I'm not eighteen now, forgetting that to live as I have lived for these six months means as much as living to grey old age! But let them laugh and say that this is all fairytales. It's true, I have told myself fairytales, I have filled whole nights in succession with them, I remember them all now.

'But is it for me to tell them now, now when the time for fairytales is over, even for me? And to whom? I amused myself with them when I saw clearly that I was forbidden even to learn the Greek grammar, as I once thought of doing. "I shall die before I get to the syntax," I thought at the first page, and threw the book under the table. It's lying there still. I've forbidden Matryona to pick it up.

'Anyone into whose hands my "Explanation" falls, and who has the patience to read it through, may look upon me as a madman, or as a schoolboy, or, more likely still, as a man condemned to death, for whom it's natural to believe that everyone else thinks too little of life and is apt to waste it too cheaply, and to use it too lazily, too shamelessly, that they're none, not one of them, worthy of it. Well, I protest that my reader will be mistaken; and that my conviction has nothing to do with my being sentenced to death. Ask them, ask them what they all, every one of them understand by happiness. Oh, you may be sure that Columbus was happy not when he had discovered America, but when he was discovering it. Take my word for it, the highest moment of his happiness was just three days before the discovery of the New World, when the mutinous crew were on the point of returning to Europe in despair. It wasn't the New World that mattered, even if it had fallen to pieces.

'Columbus died almost without seeing it; and not really knowing what he had discovered. It's life that matters, nothing but life – the process of discovering, the everlasting and perpetual process, not the discovery itself, at all. But what's the use of talking! I suspect that all I'm saying now is so like the usual commonplaces that I shall certainly be taken for a lower-form schoolboy sending in his essay on "sunrise," or they'll say perhaps that I had something to say, but that I did not know how to "explain" it. But I'll add though that there is something at the bottom of every new human thought, every thought of genius, or even every earnest thought that springs up in any brain, which can never be communicated to others, even if one were to write volumes about it and were explaining one's idea for thirty-five years; there's something left which cannot be induced to emerge from your brain, and remains with you for ever; and with it you will die, without communicating to anyone perhaps, the most important of your ideas. But if I too have failed to convey all that has been tormenting me for the last six months, it will, anyway, be understood that I have paid very dearly for attaining my present "last conviction." This is what I felt necessary, for certain objects of my own, to put forward in my "Explanation". However, I will continue.'

Chapter 6

'I don't want to tell "a" lie; reality has caught me too on its hook in the course of these six months, and sometimes so carried me away that I forgot my death sentence, or rather did not care to think of it, and even did work. About my circumstances then, by the way. When eight months ago I became very ill I broke off all my ties and gave up all who had been my comrades. As I had always been a rather glum sort of person, my comrades easily forgot me; of course, they'd have forgotten me even apart from that circumstance. My surroundings at home – that is, in my "family," were solitary too. Five months ago I shut myself up once for all and cut myself off completely from the rooms of the family. They always obeyed me, and no one dared to come in to me, except at a fixed time to tidy my room and bring me my dinner. My mother obeyed me in fear and trembling and did not even dare to whisper in my presence when I made up my mind sometimes to let her come to me. She was continually beating it into the children not to make a noise and disturb me. I'll own I often complained of their shouting; they must be fond of me by now! I think I tormented "faithful Kolya," as I called him, pretty thoroughly too. Latterly even he's worried me. All that is natural: men are created to torment one another. But I noticed that he put up with my irritability as though he had determined beforehand not to be hard on an invalid. Naturally that irritated me, but I believe he had taken it into his head to imitate the prince in "Christian meekness," which was rather funny. He's a boy, young and eager, and of course imitates everything. But I have felt occasionally that it was high time for him to take his own line. I'm very fond of him. I tormented Surikov too, who lives above us and runs errands from morning till night. I was continually proving to him that he was to blame for his own poverty, so that he was scared at last and gave up coming to see me. He's a very meek man, the meekest of beings. (N.B. They say meekness is a tremendous power. I must ask the prince about that, it's his expression.) But in March, when I went upstairs to see "the frozen" baby, as he called it, and accidentally smiled at the corpse of his baby, for I began to explain to Surikov again that it was "his own fault," the sniveller's lips began trembling, and seizing my shoulder with one hand, he pointed to the door with the other, and softly, almost in a whisper in fact, said: 'Go, Sir!'

'I went away, and I liked that very much, liked it at the time, even at the very minute when he showed me out. But for long afterwards his words produced a painful impression on me when

I remembered them: a sort of contemptuous pity for him, which I didn't want to feel at all. Even at the moment of such an insult (I felt that I had insulted him, though I didn't mean to), even at such a moment he could not get angry! His lips trembled, not from anger, I swear. He seized my arm and uttered his magnificent "Go, Sir!" absolutely without anger. There was dignity, a good deal of it, indeed, quite incongruous with him, in fact (so that, to tell the truth, there was something very comical about it), but there was no anger. Perhaps it was simply that he suddenly felt contempt for me. When I've met him two or three times on the stairs since then, he began taking off his hat to me, which he never used to do before, but he didn't stop as he used to, but ran by in confusion. If he did despise me it was in his own fashion: he despised me *meekly.* But perhaps he simply took off his hat to me as to the son of a creditor. For he always owes my mother money and can never extricate himself from his debts. And, in fact, that's the most likely explanation. I meant to have it out with him, and I know he would have begged my pardon within ten minutes, but I decided it was better to let him alone.

'It was just at that time – that is, about the time that Surikov "froze his baby", about the middle of March, I suddenly felt much better, I don't know why, and it lasted for a fortnight. I began going out, especially at dusk. I loved the March evenings when it began freezing and the gas was lighted. I sometimes walked a long way. One evening I was overtaken in the dark by a "gentleman." I didn't see him distinctly. He was carrying something wrapped up in paper and wore some sort of an ugly little overcoat, too short for him, too thin for the time of year. Just as he reached a street lamp ten paces ahead of me, I noticed something fell out of his pocket. I made haste to pick it up, and was only just in the nick of time, for someone in a long kaftan sprang forward, but seeing the thing in my hand did not quarrel over it; he stole a glance at what was in my hand and slipped by. It was an old morocco pocketbook of old-fashioned make, stuffed full, but I guessed at the first glance that it might be with anything else but not with notes. The man who had lost it was already forty paces ahead of me, and was soon lost to sight in the crowd. I ran and began shouting after him, but as I had nothing to shout but "hi!" he did not turn round. Suddenly he whisked round to the left in at the gate of a house. When I turned in at the gateway, which was very dark, there was no one there. It was a house of immense size – one of those monsters built by speculators for low-class tenements, and sometimes containing as many as a hundred flats. When I ran in at the gate, I fancied I saw a man in the furthest right-hand corner in the huge yard, though in the darkness I could scarcely distinguish him. Running to that corner, I saw the entrance to the stairs. The staircase was narrow, extremely dirty, and not lighted up at all. But I heard a man still on the stairs above, and I mounted the staircase, reckoning that while the door was being opened to him, I should have time to overtake him. And so I did. Each flight of stairs was short; they seemed endless in number, so that I was fearfully out of breath. A door was opened and shut on the fifth storey. I could make that out while I was three flights below. While I ran up, while I was getting my breath and feeling for the bell, several minutes passed. The door was opened at last by a peasant woman, who was blowing up a samovar in a tiny kitchen. She heard my enquiries in silence, not understanding a word I said, of course, and in silence opened the door into the next room, which was also a tiny and fearfully low-pitched room, wretchedly furnished with the barest essentials. There was an immensely wide bed with curtains in it, on which lay "Terentyitch" (as the woman called him), a man apparently drunk. There was a candle-end burning in an iron candlestick on the table, and there was a bottle beside it nearly empty. Terentyitch grunted something and waved towards another door, while the woman went away, so there was nothing for me to do but to open that door. I did so and walked into the next room.

'The next room was even smaller and more cramped than the other, so that I did not know which way to turn; the narrow single bed in the corner took up a great deal of the space. The rest of the furniture consisted of three plain chairs, heaped up with rags of all sorts, and a cheap kitchen table in front of a little old sofa covered with American leather, so that there was scarcely room to pass between the table and the bed. On the table there was a lighted tallow candle in a similar iron candlestick, and on the bed was a tiny baby, crying. It could not have been more than three weeks old, to judge from the sound it made. It was being "changed" by a pale, sickly looking woman. She was apparently young, in complete *déshabillé,* and looked as though she had only just got up after a confinement. But the child was not comforted, but went on crying, clamouring for the emaciated mother's breast. On the sofa there was another child, a girl about three years old, asleep, covered, I think, with a man's dress-coat. At the table stood a gentleman in a very tattered coat (he had taken off the overcoat and it was lying on the bed). He was undoing a blue paper parcel which contained about two pounds of wheat bread and two little sausages. There was besides a teapot on the table with tea in it, and a few crusts of black bread. A partly opened trunk and two bundles of rags poked out from under the bed.

'In fact, there was the greatest disorder. It struck me at the first glance that the man and the woman were people of some breeding who had been reduced by poverty to that degrading condition when disorder gets the upper hand of every effort to contend with it, and even drives people to a bitter impulse to find in the daily increasing disorder a sort of fierce and, as it were, vindictive satisfaction.

'When I went in, the gentleman, who had only entered just before me and had unwrapped his provisions, was talking rapidly and excitedly to his wife. Though she had not finished attending to the baby, she had already begun whimpering; the news must have been bad as usual. The face of the man, who looked about eight-and-twenty, was dark and lean, with black whiskers and cleanly shaved chin. It struck me as rather refined and even agreeable. The face was morose, with a morose look in the eyes, and with a morbid shade of over-sensitive pride. A strange scene followed my entrance.

'There are people who derive extraordinary enjoyment from their irritable sensitiveness, especially when it reaches a climax, as it very quickly does with them. At that moment I believe they would positively prefer to have been insulted rather than not. These irritable people are always horribly fretted by remorse afterwards, if they have sense, of course, and are capable of realising that they have been ten times as excited as they need have been.

'The gentleman stared at me for some time in amazement, and his wife in alarm, as though there were something monstrous in anyone's coming to see them. But all at once he flew at me almost with fury. I had not had time to mumble two words, yet seeing I was decently dressed, he felt, I suppose, fearfully insulted at my daring to peep into his den so unceremoniously, and to see the hideous surroundings of which he was so ashamed. He was glad, no doubt, of an opportunity of venting on anyone his rage at his own ill-luck.

For one minute I even thought he would attack me. He turned white as a woman in hysterics, and alarmed his wife dreadfully.

' "How dare you come in like this? Get out!" he shouted, trembling, and scarcely able to pronounce the words. But suddenly he saw his pocketbook in my hands.

' "I believe you dropped this," I said as calmly and drily as I could (that was the best thing to do, in fact).

'He stood facing me in absolute terror, and for some time seemed unable to take it in. Then he snatched at his side pocket, opened his mouth in dismay, and clapped his hand to his forehead.

' "Good God! Where, how did you find it?"

'I explained in the briefest words and, if possible, still more drily how I'd picked up the pocketbook, how I'd run after him, calling and how at last, on the chance and almost feeling my way, I had followed him up the stairs.

' "Oh heavens!" he cried, turning to his wife, "here are all our papers, the last of my instruments – everything... Oh, my dear sir, do you know what you've done for me? I should have been lost!"

'Meanwhile I had taken hold of the door handle to go out without answering. But I was out of breath myself, and my excitement brought on such a violent fit of coughing that I could scarcely stand. I saw the gentleman rushing from side to side to find an empty chair, and finally snatching the rags off one, he flung them on to the floor, and hurriedly handing it to me, carefully helped me to sit down. But my cough went on without stopping for three minutes and more.

'When I recovered he was sitting beside me on another chair, from which he had also flung the rags on to the floor, looking intently at me.

' "You seem to be ill," he said, in the tone in which doctors usually open proceedings with a patient. "I am a medical man myself" (he didn't say "doctor"), and as he said it, something made him point to the room, as though protesting against his surroundings. I see that you ...'

"I'm in consumption," I said as curtly as possible, and I got up.

'He jumped up too at once.

' "Perhaps you are exaggerating and ... if you take proper care ..." '

'He had been so overwhelmed that he still seemed unable to pull himself together; the pocketbook was still in his left hand.

' "Oh, don't trouble yourself," I interposed again, taking hold of the door handle. "B— examined me last week, and my business is settled." (I brought B— in again.) "Excuse me ..."

'I tried again to open the door and leave the embarrassed and grateful doctor crushed with shame, but the cursed cough attacked me once more. Then the doctor insisted that I should sit down again and rest. He turned to his wife, and, without moving from her place, she uttered a few grateful and cordial words. She was so embarrassed as she spoke that a red flush suffused her thin, pale, yellow cheeks. I remained, but with an air of being horribly afraid I was in their way (which was the proper thing). My doctor began at last to be fretted by remorse, I saw that.

' "If I..." he began, breaking off and moving restlessly about every moment. "I am so grateful to you, and I behaved so badly to you... I... you see ..." again he indicated the room, "at the present moment I am placed in such a position ..."

' "Oh," said I, 'there's no need to see; it's the usual thing. I expect you've lost your post, and have come up here to go into the case, and try to get another post."

' "How did you ... know?" he asked in surprise.

' "It's obvious from the first glance," I said with involuntary irony. 'Lots of people come up from the provinces full of hope and run about and live like this."

'He suddenly began speaking with warmth and with quivering lips; he began complaining, he began telling his story, and I must own he moved me. I stayed nearly an hour with him. He told me his story, a very common one. He had been a provincial doctor, had a government post, but some intrigues were got up against him, in which even his wife was involved. His pride was touched; he lost his temper. A change in the governing authorities favoured the designs of his enemies; they undermined his reputation, made complaints against him. He lost his post, and had spent all his savings on coming to Petersburg to get the case taken up. Here, of course, for a long time he could get no hearing; then he got a hearing; then he was answered by a refusal; then he was deluded with promises; then he was answered with severity; then he was directed to write something by way of explanation; then they refused to take what he had written, and ordered him to file a petition – in short, he had been driven from pillar to post for the last five months, and had spent his last farthing. His wife's last rags were in pawn, and now there was a new baby, and, and ... "today a final refusal of my petition, and I've hardly bread – nothing – my wife just confined. I... I..."

'He jumped up from his chair and turned away. His wife was crying in the corner, the baby began squealing again. I took out my notebook and began writing in it. When I had finished and stood up, he was standing before me, looking at me with timid curiosity.

' "I have put down your name," I said, "and all the rest of it: the place where you served, the name of the governor, the day of the month. I have a comrade, an old schoolfellow called Bahmutov, and his uncle, Pyotr Matvyeitch Bahmutov, is an actual state councillor and director ..."

' "Pyotr Matvyeitch Bahmutov!" exclaimed my doctor, almost trembling. "Why, it almost entirely depends upon him!"

'Everything about my doctor's story and its successful conclusion, which I chanced to assist in bringing about, fell out and fitted in as though by design, exactly as in a novel. I told these poor people that they must try not to build any hopes on me; that I was a poor schoolboy myself. (I intentionally exaggerated my powerlessness; I finished my studies long ago and am not a schoolboy.) I told them that it was no good for them to know my name, but that I'd go at once to Vassilyevsky Island to my schoolfellow Bahmutov; and as I knew for a fact that his uncle, the actual state councillor, being a bachelor without children, positively worshipped his nephew, loving him passionately as the last representative of the family, "My comrade may perhaps be able to do something for you, and for me, with his uncle, of course."

' "If only they would allow me an explanation with his excellency! If only they would vouchsafe me the honour of a personal explanation!" he exclaimed, with glittering eyes, shivering as though he were in a fever.

'That was what he said, "vouchsafe." Repeating once more that it would be sure to come to nothing, I added that if I didn't come to see them next morning, it Would mean that everything was over and they had nothing to expect. They showed me out with bows; they were almost beside themselves. I shall never forget the expression of their feces. I took a cab and at once set off for Vassilyevsky Island.

'At school I had been for years on bad terms with Bahmutov. He was considered an aristocrat among us, or I at least used to call him one. He was very well dressed and drove his own horses, but was not a bit stuck-up. He was always a good comrade, and exceptionally good-humoured, sometimes even witty. He hadn't a very far-reaching intelligence, though he was always top of the class. I was never top in anything. All his schoolfellows liked him, except me. He had several times made overtures to me during those years, but I had always turned away from him with sullen ill-humour. Now I had not seen him for a year; he was at the university. When towards nine o'clock I went in to him, I was announced with great ceremony. He met me at first with amazement, and far from affably, but he soon brightened up and, looking at me, burst out laughing.

' "What possessed you to come and see me, Terentyev?" he cried with his invariable good-natured ease which was sometimes impudent but never offensive, which I liked so much in him and for which I hated him so much. "But hows this?" he exclaimed with dismay. "You're very ill!"

'My cough racked me again. I dropped into a chair and could scarcely get my breath.

' "Don't trouble. I'm in consumption," I said. "I've come to you with a request."

'He sat down, wondering, and I told him at once the whole story of the doctor, and explained that, having an influence over his uncle, he might be able to do something.

' "I'll do it. Certainly I'll do it," he said. "I'll attack my uncle tomorrow. And indeed I'm glad to do it; and you've told it all so well... But what put it into your head, Terentyev, to come to me?"

"So much depends upon your uncle in this case. And since we were always enemies, Bahmutov, and as you're an honourable man, I thought you wouldn't refuse an enemy," I added with irony.

' "As Napoleon appealed to England!" he cried, laughing. "I'll do it! I'll do it! I'll go at once if I can," he added hastily, seeing that I was gravely and sternly getting up from my chair.

'And indeed the affair was unexpectedly arranged among us in the most successful way. Within six weeks our doctor was appointed to a post in another province, and had received help in money, as well as his travelling expenses. I suspect that Bahmutov, who had taken to visiting the doctor pretty often (I purposely did not do so, and even received the doctor coolly when he came to see me), I suspect that Bahmutov had induced the doctor to accept a loan from him. I saw Bahmutov about twice in the course of the six weeks, and we met for the third time when we saw the last of the doctor. Bahmutov got up a dinner with champagne for him at parting, at which the doctor's wife too was present, though she left early to go home to her baby. It was at the beginning of May. It was a fine evening. The huge ball of the sun was sinking on the water. Bahmutov saw me home; we went by the Nikolaevsky Bridge; we were both a little drunk. Bahmutov spoke of his delight at the successful conclusion of the business, thanked me for something, said how happy he felt after a good deed, declared that the credit of it all was mine, and that people were wrong in preaching and maintaining, as many do now, that individual benevolence was of no use. I had a great longing to speak too.

' "Anyone who attacks individual charity," I began, "attacks human nature and casts contempt on personal dignity. But the organisation of 'public charity' and the problem of individual freedom are two distinct questions, and not mutually exclusive. Individual kindness will always remain, because it's an individual impulse, the living impulse of one personality to exert a direct influence upon another. There was an old fellow at Moscow, a 'General' – that is, an actual state councillor, with a German name. He spent his whole life visiting prisons, and prisoners; every party of exiles to Siberia knew beforehand that the 'old General' would visit them on the Sparrow Hills. He carried out this good work with the greatest earnestness and devotion. He would turn up, walk through the rows of prisoners, who surrounded him, stop before each, questioning each as to his needs, calling each of them 'my dear,' and hardly ever preaching to anyone. He used to give them money, send them the most necessary articles – leg-wrappers, under garments, linen, and sometimes took them books of devotion, which he distributed among those who could read, firmly persuaded that they would read them on the way, and that those who could read would read them to those who could not. He rarely asked a prisoner about his crime; he simply listened if the criminal began speaking of it. All the criminals were on an equal footing with him, he made no distinction between them. He talked to them as though they were brothers, and they came in the end to look on him as a father. If he saw a woman with a baby among the prisoners, he would go up, fondle the child, and snap his fingers to make it laugh. He visited the prisoners like this for many years, up to the time of his death, so much so that he was known all over Russia and Siberia – that is, by all the criminals. A man who had been in Siberia told me that he had seen himself how the most hardened criminals remembered the general; yet the latter could rarely give more than twenty farthings to each prisoner on his visits. It's true they spoke of him without any great warmth, or even earnestness. Some one of these 'unhappy' creatures, a man who had murdered a dozen people and slaughtered six children solely for his own pleasure (for there are such men, I am told), would suddenly, once in twenty years, apropos of nothing, heave a sigh, and say, ' "What about that old general, is he still alive, I wonder?"

' "Perhaps he smiles as he says it. And that's all. But how can you tell what seed may have been dropped in his soul for ever by that old general, whom he hasn't forgotten for twenty years? How can you tell, Bahmutov, what significance such an association of one personality with another may have on the destiny of those associated?... You know it's a matter of a whole lifetime, an infinite multitude of ramifications hidden from us. The most skilful chess-player, the cleverest of them, can only look a few moves ahead; a French player who could reckon out ten moves ahead was written about as a marvel. How many moves there are in this, and how much that is unknown to us! In scattering the seed, scattering your 'charity,' your kind deeds, you are giving away, in one form or another, part of your personality, and taking into yourself part of another; you are in mutual communion with one another, a little more attention and you will be rewarded with the knowledge of the most unexpected discoveries. You will come at last to look upon your work as a science; it will lay hold of all your life, and may fill up your whole life. On the other hand, all your thoughts, all the seeds scattered by you, perhaps forgotten by you, will grow up and take form. He who has received them from you will hand them on to another. And how can you tell what part you may have in the future determination of the destinies of humanity? If this knowledge and a whole lifetime of this work should make you at last able to sow some mighty seed, to bequeath the world some mighty thought, then ..." and so on. I talked a great deal.

' "And to think that you, talking like this, are condemned to death!" cried Bahmutov, with a warm note of reproach against someone in his voice.

'At that moment we were standing on the bridge, and leaning our elbows on the rail, we looked into the Neva.

' "And do you know what's just struck me?" I said, bending lower over the rail.

' "Not to throw yourself into the water!" cried Bahmutov, almost in alarm. Perhaps he read my thought in my face.

' "No, for the time being, only the following reflection: here I have two or three months left to live, perhaps four, but when I've only two months, for instance, left, if I'm terribly anxious to do a good deed which requires a great deal of work, activity, and bother, like our business with the doctor, I ought to refuse it because I haven't time enough left, and seek some other good work on a smaller scale, and more within my means (if I am still so drawn to good deeds). You must own that's an amusing idea."

'Poor Bahmutov was much distressed on my account. He took me home to my very door, and was for the most part silent, having too much tact to attempt to console me. As he said "goodbye" to me he pressed my hand warmly and asked permission to come and see me. I answered that if he came to comfort me (and that, even if he were silent, he would come to comfort me, I explained that to him) each time by doing so, he would remind me of death more than ever. He shrugged his shoulders, but agreed with me. We parted fairly civilly, which was more than I had expected.

'But that evening and that night there was sown the first seed of my "last conviction." I clutched eagerly at this new idea and eagerly analysed it in all its branches, in all its aspects. I didn't sleep all night, and the more deeply I went into it, the more I absorbed it, the more frightened I became. An awful terror came over me and haunted me continually for the following days. Sometimes, thinking of that continual terror of mine, I shivered suddenly with another dread. From that dread I could not but conclude that my "last conviction" had taken too grave a hold upon me, and must lead to its logical conclusion. But I had not resolution enough for that conclusion. Three weeks later it was all over and that resolution came to me, but it was through a very strange circumstance.

'Here in my explanation I note down all these dates and numbers. Of course it will make no difference to me, but *now* (and perhaps only for this moment) I should like those who will judge of my action to be able to see what long chain of logical reasoning led to my "last conviction." I have just written above that the final resoluteness, which I had lacked for carrying out my "last conviction," seemed to come to me, not from logical reasoning, but from a strange shock, from a strange circumstance, perhaps quite irrelevant. Ten days ago Rogozhin came to see me about an affair of his own, which there is no need to go into. I had never seen Rogozhin before, but I had heard a great deal about him. I gave him the necessary information. He soon went away, and as he had simply come for the information, our acquaintance might have ended there. But he interested me too much, and all that day I was possessed by strange ideas, so that I made up my mind to go to him next day, to return his visit. Rogozhin was evidently not pleased to see me, and even dropped a "delicate" hint that it was no good for us to continue the acquaintance; yet I spent a very interesting hour, and probably he did the same. The contrast between us was so great that it could not be ignored by us, especially by me. I was a man whose days were numbered, while he was living the fullest, the most actual life, absorbed in the moment, entirely unconcerned about "final" deductions, numbers, or anything whatever except what... what... what he was mad upon, in fact. Mr Rogozhin must forgive me that expression, if only because I'm a poor hand at literature and don't know how to express my ideas. In spite of his unfriendliness, I thought he was a man of intelligence and capable of understanding much, though he had few outside interests. I gave him no hint of my "final conviction," but yet I fancied that he guessed it as he listened to me. He did not speak; he is awfully silent. As I took leave I hinted that, in spite of all the difference and the contrast between us – *les extrémités se touchent* (I explained that in Russian for him), and that perhaps he was by no means so far from my "final conviction" as he seemed. To that he responded with a very grim and sour grimace, got up, himself handed me my cap, making it appear as though I -were going away of my own accord, and without more ado led me out of his gloomy house, pretending to see me out from politeness. His house impressed me; it's like a graveyard, and I believe he likes it, which is very natural, indeed; such a full, vivid life as he leads is too full in itself to need a setting.

'That visit to Rogozhin exhausted me very much, and I had felt very unwell all that morning. Towards the evening I was very weak and lay down on my bed; from time to time I was in a high fever, and even delirious. Kolya was with me till eleven o'clock.

I remember everything he talked of, however, and everything we spoke about. But when at moments a mist passed before my eyes I kept seeing Ivan Fomitch, who seemed to be receiving millions of money and not to know where to put it, to be worried about it, terrified that it would be stolen, and at last he seemed to decide to bury it in the earth. Finally I advised him, instead of digging such a mountain of gold into the earth, to have the whole heap melted down into a golden coffin for the frozen baby and to have the baby dug up for the purpose. This sarcasm of mine seemed to be accepted by Surikov with tears of gratitude, and he went at once to carry out the plan, and I thought I left him with a curse.

'Kolya assured me, when I was quite myself again, that I had not slept at all, but that I had been talking to him all the time about Surikov. At moments I was in great misery and in a state of collapse, so that Kolya was uneasy when he left me. When I got up myself to lock the door after him, I suddenly recalled a picture I had seen at Rogozhin's, over the door of one of the dreariest of his rooms. He showed it me himself in passing. I believe I stood before it for five minutes. There was nothing good about it from an artistic point of view, but it produced a strange uneasiness in me.

'The picture represented Christ who has only just been taken from the cross. I believe artists usually paint Christ, both on the cross and after He has been taken from the cross, still with extraordinary beauty of face. They strive to preserve that beauty even in His most terrible agonies. In Rogozhin's picture there's no trace of beauty. It is in every detail the corpse of a man who has endured infinite agony before the crucifixion; who has been wounded, tortured, beaten by the guards and the people when He carried the cross on His back and fell beneath its weight, and after that has undergone the agony of crucifixion, lasting for six hours at least (according to my reckoning). It's true it's the face of a man *only just* taken from the cross – that is to say, still bearing traces of warmth and life. Nothing is rigid in it yet, so that there's still a look of suffering in the face of the dead man, as though he were still feeling it (that has been very well caught by the artist). Yet the face has not been spared in the least. It is simply nature, and the corpse of a man, whoever he might be, must really look like that after such suffering. I know that the Christian Church laid it down, even in the early ages, that Christ suffering was not symbolical but actual, and that His body was therefore fully and completely subject to the laws of nature on the cross. In the picture the face is fearfully crushed by blows, swollen, covered with fearful, swollen and blood-stained bruises, the eyes are open and squinting: the great wide-open whites of the eyes glitter with a sort of deathly, glassy light. But, strange to say, as one looks at this corpse of a tortured man, a peculiar and curious question arises: if just such a corpse (and it must have been just like that) was seen by all His disciples, by those who were to become His chief apostles, by the women that followed Him and stood by the cross, by all who believed in Him and worshipped Him, how could they believe that that martyr would rise again? The question instinctively arises: if death is so awful and the laws of nature so mighty, how can they be overcome? How can they be overcome when even He did not conquer them, He who vanquished nature in His lifetime, who exclaimed, "Maiden, arise!" and the maiden arose – "Lazarus, come forth!" and the dead man came forth? Looking at such a picture, one conceives of nature in the shape of an immense, merciless, dumb beast, or more correctly, much more correctly, speaking, though it sounds strange, in the form of a huge machine of the most modern construction which, dull and insensible, has aimlessly clutched, crushed and swallowed up a great priceless Being, a Being worth all nature and its laws, worth the whole earth, which was created perhaps solely for the sake of the advent of that Being. This picture expresses and unconsciously suggests to one the conception of such a dark, insolent, unreasoning and eternal Power to which everything is in subjection. The people surrounding the dead man, not one of whom is shown in the picture, must have experienced the most terrible anguish and consternation on that evening, which had crushed all their hopes, and almost their convictions. They must have parted in the most awful terror, though each one bore within him a mighty thought which could never be wrested from him. And if the Teacher could have seen Himself on the eve of the crucifixion, would He have gone up to the cross and have died as He did? That question too rises involuntarily, as one looks at the picture.

'All this floated before my mind by snatches, perhaps in actual delirium, for fully an hour and a half before Kolya went away, sometimes taking definite shape. Can anything that has no shape appear in a shape? But I seemed to fancy at times that I saw in some strange, incredible form that infinite power, that dull, dark, dumb force. I remember that someone seemed to lead me by the hand, holding a candle, to show me a huge and loathsome spider, and to assure me, laughing at my indignation, that this was that same dark, dumb and almighty power. There is always a little lamp lighted at night before the ikon in my room. It is a dim and feeble light, yet one can make out everything, and even read just under the lamp. I believe it must have been after midnight. I had not slept at all and lay with wide-open eyes. Suddenly my door opened and Rogozhin walked in.

'He walked in, shut the door, looked at me without speaking, and went quietly to the chair standing just under the lamp. I was awfully surprised and looked at him in suspense. Rogozhin put his elbows on the little table and began to stare at me without speaking. So passed two or three minutes, and I remember his silence greatly offended and annoyed me. Why wouldn't he talk? His coming so late at night did strike me as strange, of course, but I remember that I was not so tremendously taken aback by it. Rather the other way, indeed, for though I had not put my thought clearly into words in the morning, I know he understood it; and it was a thought that one might well come to talk over once more, even at a very late hour. I took it for granted he had come for that. Our parting in the morning had been rather unfriendly, and I remember that he looked at me once or twice very sarcastically. I saw the same sarcastic look in his face now, and it was that which offended me. That it actually was Rogozhin and not an apparition, an hallucination, I had not the slightest doubt at the beginning. I never thought of it, in fact.

'Meanwhile he went on sitting there and still staring at me with the same sarcastic look. I turned angrily on my bed, leaned with my elbow on the pillow, and made up my mind to be silent too, even if we had to sit like that all the time. I was set on his beginning first. I think twenty minutes must have passed in that way. Suddenly the idea occurred to me: what if it's not Rogozhin, but only an apparition?

'I had never once seen an apparition, during my illness or before it. But I had always felt as a boy, and now too – that is, quite lately – that if I should ever see such a thing I should die on the spot, although I don't believe in ghosts. Yet when the idea struck me that it was not Rogozhin but only an apparition, I remember I wasn't in the least frightened. In fact it made me feel angry. Another strange thing was that I was not nearly so concerned and anxious to decide whether it was Rogozhin or an apparition, as I should have been. I believe I was thinking of something else at the time. I was much more interested, for instance, in the question why Rogozhin, who had been in his dressing-gown and slippers earlier in the day, was now wearing a dress-coat, a white waistcoat, and a white tie. The thought struck me too: if it is an apparition and I'm not afraid of it why not get up, go to him, and make sure? Perhaps I didn't dare and was afraid. But I'd no sooner thought of being afraid than an icy shiver ran all down me; I felt a cold chill at my spine and my knees trembled. At that very instant, as though guessing that I was afraid, Rogozhin moved away the hand on which he was leaning, drew himself up, and his lips began to part, as though he were going to laugh; he stared at me persistently. I was seized with such fury that I longed to fall upon him, but as I had vowed not to be the first to speak, I remained in bed. Besides, I was still not sure whether it was Rogozhin or not.

'I don't remember exactly how long it lasted; I can't be quite sure either whether I didn't lose consciousness from time to time. But at last Rogozhin got up and looked at me as deliberately and intently as he had on coming in. He no longer grinned at me, and softly, almost on tiptoe, went to the door, opened it, and went out. I did not get out of bed. I don't know how long I lay with my eyes open, thinking. Goodness knows what I thought about. I don't remember either how I lost consciousness. But I waked next morning at ten o'clock when they knocked at my door. I have arranged that, if I don't open the door myself before ten o'clock and call for tea to be brought to me, Matryona should knock. When I opened the door to her, the thought occurred to me at once: how could he have come in when the door was locked? I made enquiries, and convinced myself that Rogozhin in the flesh could not have come in, as all our doors are locked at night.

'Well, this peculiar incident which I have described so minutely was the cause of my making up my mind. What helped to bring about that "final decision" was not logic, not a logical conviction, but a feeling of repulsion. I could not go on living a life which was taking such strange, humiliating forms. That apparition degraded me. I am not able to submit to the gloomy power that takes the shape of a spider. And it was only when I felt at last, as it was getting dark, that I had reached the final moment of full determination that I felt better. But that was only the first stage; for the second stage I had to go to Pavlovsk. But all that I have explained sufficiently already.

Chapter 7

'I had a little pocket-pistol; I got it when I was quite a child, at that absurd age when one is delighted at the story of a duel or of an attack by robbers, at imagining how one might be challenged to a duel and how bravely one would face the pistol-shot. A month ago I looked at it, and got it ready. In the box where it lay I found two bullets, and in the powder-horn there was powder enough for three charges. It's a miserable pistol, it doesn't aim straight, and wouldn't kill further than fifteen paces. But, of course, it would blow one's skull off, if one put it right against the temple.

'I decided to die at Pavlovsk at sunrise, and I meant to go into the park, so as not to upset anyone in the villa. My "Explanation" will explain things sufficiently to the police. Lovers of psychology, and anyone else who likes, are welcome to get anything they can out of it. But I don't want this manuscript to be made public. I beg the prince to keep one copy for himself, and to give another to Aglaia Ivanovna Epanchin. Such is my will. I bequeath my skeleton to the Medical Academy, for the good of science.

'I don't admit the right of any man to judge me, and I know that I am now beyond the reach of all judgement. Not long ago I was much amused by imagining – what if the fancy suddenly took me to kill someone, a dozen people at once, or to do something awful, something considered the most awful crime in the world – what a predicament my judges would be in, with my having only a fortnight to live, now that corporal punishment and torture is abolished. I should die comfortably in hospital, warm and snug, with an attentive doctor, and very likely much more snug and comfortable than at home. I wonder that the idea doesn't strike people in my position, if only as a joke. But perhaps it does; there are plenty of people fond of a joke, even among us.

'But though I don't recognise the right of any to judge me I know that I shall be judged when I am dumb, and have no voice to defend myself. I don't want to go away without leaving some word of defence – a free defence, not forced out of me, not to justify myself – oh, no! I have no one's forgiveness to ask, and nothing to ask forgiveness for – it's simply because I want to.

'Here, at the outset, a strange question arises: by what right, with what motive could anyone presume to dispute my right to dispose of my last fortnight? Whose business is it to judge? What is it to anyone that I should not only be condemned, but should conscientiously endure my sentence to the end? Can it really matter to anyone? From the ethical point of view? I quite understand that if, in the bloom of health and strength, I were to take my life, which might be "of use to my neighbour," and all the rest of it, morality might reproach me on traditional lines for disposing of my life without asking leave, or for some other reason of its own. But now, now that the term of my sentence has been pronounced? What moral obligation demands, not only your life, but the last gasp with which you give up your last atom of life, listening to words of comfort from the prince, whose Christian arguments are bound to bring him to the happy thought that it is really for the best that you should die. (Christians like him always do come to that idea. It's their favourite tack.) And what does he want to bring in his ridiculous "trees of Pavlovsk" for? To soften the last hours of my life? Don't they understand, that the more I forget myself, the more I give myself up to the last semblance of life and love, with which they are trying to screen from me Meyer's wall and all that is so openly and simply written on it, the more unhappy they make me? What use to me is your nature, your Pavlovsk park, your sunrises and sunsets, your blue sky, and your contented faces, when all this endless festival has begun by my being excluded from it? What is there for me in this beauty when, every minute, every second I am obliged, forced, to recognise that even the tiny fly, buzzing in the sunlight beside me, has its share in the banquet and the chorus, knows its place, loves it and is happy; and I alone am an outcast, and only my cowardice has made me refuse to realise it till now. Oh, I know how the prince and all of them would have liked, from principle and for the triumph of morality, to lead me on to singing Millevoix' celebrated classical verse.

Ah, puissent voir longtemps votre beauté sacrée
Tant d'amis sourds à mes adieux!

Qu'ils meurent pleins de jours, que leur mort soit pleurée,
Qu'un ami leur ferme les yeux!

instead of these "corrupting and wicked words". But believe me, believe me, simple-hearted souls, that those edifying lines, that academic benediction of the world in French verse, contains so much concealed bitterness, such irreconcilable malice, revelling in rhyme, that perhaps, even the poet himself was muddled and took that malice for tears of tenderness, and died in that faith; peace be to his ashes! Let me tell you, there is a limit of ignominy in the consciousness of one's own nothingness and impotence beyond which a man cannot go, and beyond which he begins to feel immense satisfaction in his very degradation ... Oh, of course humility is a great force in that sense, I admit that – though not in the sense in which religion accepts humility as a force.

'Religion! Eternal life I can admit, and perhaps I always have admitted it. Let consciousness, kindled by the will of a higher Power, have looked round upon the world and have said – "I am!" and let it suddenly be doomed by that Power to annihilation, because it's somehow necessary for some purpose – and even without explanation of the purpose – so be it, I admit it all, but again the eternal question: what need is there of my humility? Can't I simply be devoured without being expected to praise what devours me? Can there really be Somebody up aloft who will be aggrieved by my not going on for a fortnight longer? I don't believe it; and it's a much more likely supposition that all that's needed is my worthless life, the life of an atom, to complete some universal harmony, for some sort of plus and minus, for the sake of some sort of contrast, and so on, just as the life of millions of creatures is needed every day as a sacrifice, as, without their death, the rest of the world couldn't go on (though that's not a very grand idea in itself, I must observe). But so be it! I admit that otherwise, that is without the continual devouring of one another, it would have been impossible to arrange the world. I am even ready to admit that I can't understand anything about that arrangement. But this I do know for certain: that if I have once been allowed to be conscious that "I am," it doesn't matter to me that there are mistakes in the construction of the world and that without them it can't go on. Who will condemn me after that, and on what charge? Say what you like, it's all impossible and unjust.

'And yet, in spite of all my desire to do it, I could never conceive of there being no future life, no Providence. It seems most likely that they do exist, but that we don't understand anything about the future life or its laws. But if this is so difficult and even impossible to understand, surely I shan't be held responsible for not being able to comprehend the inconceivable. It's true, they tell me, and the prince, of course, is with them there, that submissive faith is needed, that one must obey without reasoning, simply from piety, and that I shall certainly be rewarded in the next world for my humility.

'We degrade God too much, ascribing to Him our ideas, in vexation at being unable to understand Him. But, again, if it's impossible to understand Him, I repeat it's hard to have to answer for what it is not given to man to understand. And, if it is so, how shall I be judged for being unable to understand the will and laws of Providence? No, we'd better leave religion on one side.

'And I've said enough, indeed. When I reach these lines, the sun will, no doubt, be rising, and "resounding in the sky", and its vast immeasurable power will be shed upon the earth. So be it! I shall be looking straight at the source of power and life; I do not want this life! If I'd had the power not to be born, I would certainly not have accepted existence upon conditions that are such a mockery. But I still have power to die, though the days I give back are numbered. It's no great power, it's no great mutiny.

'My last "Explanation": I am dying, not because I am not equal to bearing these three weeks. Oh, I should have the strength, and, if I cared to, I should be comforted enough by the recognition of the wrong done me, but I'm not a French poet, and I do not care for such consolation. Finally, there's temptation too. Nature has so limited my activity by its three weeks' sentence, that perhaps suicide is the only action I still have time to begin and end by my own will. And, perhaps I want to take advantage of the last possibility of *action*. A protest is sometimes no small action ...'

The Explanation was over. Ippolit at last stopped.

There is, in extreme cases, a pitch of cynical frankness when a nervous man, exasperated, and beside himself, shrinks from nothing, and is ready for any scandal, even glad of it. He falls upon people with a vague but firm determination to fling himself from a belfry a minute later, and so settle any difficulties that may arise. And the approaching physical exhaustion is usually the symptom of this condition. The extreme, almost unnatural tension which had kept Ippolit up till that moment had reached that fatal pitch. This eighteen-year-old boy, exhausted by illness, seemed as weak as a trembling leaf torn from a tree. But as soon as – for the first time in the course of the last hour – he looked round upon his audience, the most haughty, most disdainful and resentful repugnance was at once apparent in his eyes and his smile. He made haste with his challenge. But his listeners too were very indignant. They were all noisily and angrily getting up from the table. Weariness, wine, nervous strain increased the disorderliness and, as it were, foulness of the impression, if one may so express it.

Suddenly Ippolit leapt up, as though he had been thrust from his seat.

'The sun has risen,' he cried to Myshkin, seeing the treetops lighted up, and pointing to them as though to a marvel. 'It has risen!'

'Why, did you think it wasn't going to rise?' observed Ferdyshtchenko.

'It will be baking hot again, all day,' muttered Ganya, with careless annoyance, stretching and yawning, with his hat in his hands. 'What if there's a month of this drought!... Are we going or not, Ptitsyn?'

Ippolit listened with an astonishment that approached stupefaction. He suddenly turned fearfully pale and began trembling all over.

'You act your indifference very awkwardly to insult me,' he said, staring at Ganya. 'You're a cur!'

'Well, that's beyond anything, to let oneself go like that!' roared Ferdyshtchenko. 'What phenomenal feebleness!'

'He's simply a fool,' said Ganya.

Ippolit pulled himself together a little.

'I understand, gentlemen,' he began, trembling as before, and stuttering at every word – 'that I may deserve your personal resentment, and ... I'm sorry I've distressed you with these ravings (he pointed to the manuscript), or rather I'm sorry that I haven't distressed you at all' ... (he smiled stupidly). 'Have I distressed you, Yevgeny Pavlovitch?' he darted across to him with the question. 'Did I distress you or not, tell me?'

'It was rather drawn out, still it was...'

'Speak out! Don't tell lies for once in your life!' Ippolit insisted trembling.

'Oh! It's absolutely nothing to me! I beg you to be so good as to leave me alone,' Yevgeny Pavlovitch turned away disdainfully.

'Good night, Prince,' said Ptitsyn, going up to Myshkin.

'But he's going to shoot himself directly! What are you thinking of? Look at him,' cried Vera, and she flew to Ippolit in great alarm; she even clutched at his arms. 'Why, he said he Would shoot himself at sunrise! What are you about!'

'He won't shoot himself.' several voices, among them Ganya's, muttered malignantly.

'Gentlemen, take care!' cried Kolya, and he, too, caught at Ippolit's arm. 'Only look at him. Prince, Prince, what are you thinking of?' Ippolit was surrounded by Vera, Kolya, Keller and Burdovsky. They all caught hold of him.

'He has the right… the right…' Burdovsky murmured, though he, too, seemed quite beside himself.

'Excuse me, Prince, what arrangements do you propose to make?' said Lebedyev, going up to Myshkin. He was drunk and so enraged that he was insolent.

'What arrangements?'

'Net, Sir; excuse me; I'm the master of the house, though I don't wish to be lacking in respect to you… Granting that you are master here too, still I don't care in my own house …'

'He won't shoot himself! The wretched boy is fooling!' General Ivolgin cried unexpectedly, with indignation and aplomb.

'Bravo, General!' Ferdyshtchenko applauded.

'I know he won't shoot himself, General, honoured general, but all the same … seeing I'm master of the house.'

'Listen, I say, Mr Terentyev,' said Ptitsyn suddenly, holding out his hand to Ippolit, after saying goodbye to Myshkin. 'I believe you speak in your manuscript of your skeleton and leave it to the Academy? You mean your own skeleton, your bones you mean, isn't it?'

'Yes, my bones …'

'That's all right then. I asked for fear there should be a mistake; I've been told there was such a case.'

'How can you tease him?' cried Myshkin suddenly.

'You've made him cry,' added Ferdyshtchenko.

But Ippolit was not crying. He tried to move from his place, but the four standing about him seized his hands at once. There was a sound of laughter.

'That's what he's been after, that they should hold his hands; that's what he read his confession for,' observed Rogozhin. 'Goodbye, Prince. Ech, we've been sitting too long – my bones ache.'

'If you really did mean to shoot yourself, Terentyev,' laughed Yevgeny Pavlovitch – 'after such compliments, if I were you, I should make a point of not doing it, to tease them.'

'They're awfully eager to see me shoot myself!' cried Ippolit, flying out at his words.

He spoke as though he were attacking someone. 'They're annoyed that they won't see it.'

'So you think they won't see it? I'm not egging you on; quite the contrary; I think it's very likely you will shoot yourself. The great thing is not to lose your temper ...' said Yevgeny Pavlovitch in a patronising drawl.

'I only see now that I made a fearful mistake in reading them my Explanation,' said Ippolit, looking at Yevgeny Pavlovitch with a sudden trustfulness, as though asking the confidential advice of a friend.

'It's an absurd position, but... I really don't know what to advise you,' answered Yevgeny Pavlovitch, smiling.

Ippolit bent a stem, persistent gaze at him, and did not answer. It might have been supposed that he was unconscious at some moments.

'No, excuse me, it's a strange way of doing things,' said Lebedyev. ' "I'll shoot myself in the park," ' says he, ' "so as not to upset anyone." That's his notion, that he won't upset anyone if he goes down three steps a few feet into the park.'

'Gentlemen ...' began Myshkin.

'No, allow me, honoured prince,' Lebedyev interrupted furiously, 'as you can see for yourself that it's not a joke, and as half your guests at least are of the same opinion, and are convinced that, after what he has said, he will feel bound in honour to shoot himself, I, as master of the house, and as a witness of it, call upon you to assist me!'

'What's to be done, Lebedyev? I am ready to assist you.'

'I'll tell you what. In the first place he must give up the pistol he boasted about before us all, and all the ammunition too. If he gives it up, I consent to let him stay the night in this house, in consideration of his invalid state, under my own supervision, of course. But tomorrow he must certainly go about his business. Excuse me, Prince! If he won't give up his weapon, I shall at once take hold of him, I on one side, and the general on the other, and send at once to inform the police; and then the affair can be left for the police to deal with. Mr Ferdyshtchenko, as a friend, will go for them.'

An uproar followed. Lebedyev was excited, and threw aside all restraint. Ferdyshtchenko prepared to go for the police. Ganya insisted frantically that no one meant to shoot himself. Yevgeny Pavlovitch said nothing.

'Prince, have you ever jumped from a belfry?' Ippolit whispered to him, suddenly.

'N-no,' answered Myshkin, naïvely.

'Did you imagine that I did not foresee all this hatred!' Ippolit whispered again, looking at Myshkin with flashing eyes, as though he really expected an answer from him.

'Enough!' he cried, suddenly, to the whole party. 'It's my fault … more than anyone's. Lebedyev, here's the keys (he took out his purse and from it a steel ring with three or four keys upon it). 'Here, the last but one … Kolya will show you … Kolya, where is Kolya?' cried he, looking at Kolya, and not seeing him. 'Yes… he'll show you. He packed my bag with me, yesterday. Take him, Kolya. In the prince's study, under the table … is my bag… with this key… at the bottom in a little box… my pistol and powder-horn. He packed it himself, Mr Lebedyev; he'll show you. But on condition that tomorrow, early, when I start for Petersburg, you'll give me back my pistol. Do you hear? I do it for the prince, not for you.'

'Well, that's better,' said Lebedyev, snatching at the key; and, laughing viciously, he ran into the next room.

Kolya would have remained, he tried to say something, but Lebedyev drew him away.

Ippolit looked at the laughing revellers. Myshkin noticed that his teeth were chattering, as though he were in a terrible chill.

'What wretches they all are!' Ippolit whispered to Myshkin, in a frenzy.

When he spoke to Myshkin he bent right over and whispered to him.

'Leave them. You're very weak…'

'In a minute, in a minute … I'm going in a minute.'

Suddenly he put his arms round Myshkin.

'You think I am mad perhaps?' He looked at him strangely, laughing.

'No, but you ...'

'In a minute, in a minute, be quiet; don't say anything, stand still. I want to look you in the eyes ... Stand like that, and let me look. I say goodbye to man.'

He stood and looked fixedly at Myshkin for ten seconds without speaking. Very pale, his hair soaked with sweat, he caught somehow strangely at Myshkin's hand with his as though afraid to let him go.

'Ippolit, Ippolit, what is the matter with you?' cried Myshkin.

'Directly... Enough ... I'm going to bed. I'll have one drink to greet the sun ... I want to, I want to ... let me be.'

He quickly caught up a glass from the table, sprang up from his seat, and in one instant he was at the verandah steps. Myshkin was about to run after him, but it happened, as though by design, that, at that moment Yevgeny Pavlovitch held out his hand to say goodbye to him. One second after, there was a general outcry on the verandah. Then followed a minute of extreme consternation.

This was what had happened. On reaching the verandah steps, Ippolit had stopped short, with his left hand holding the glass and his right hand in his coat pocket. Keller afterwards declared that Ippolit had that hand in his right hand pocket before, while he was talking to Myshkin, and clutching at his shoulder and his collar with his left hand, and that that right hand in his pocket, so Keller declared, had first raised a faint suspicion in him. However that may have been, some uneasiness made him run after Ippolit. But he was too late. He only saw something suddenly shining in Ippolit's right hand, and at the same second, a little pocket pistol was against his temple. Keller rushed to seize his hand, but, at that second, Ippolit pressed the trigger. There was the sound of the sharp, short click of the trigger, but no shot followed. When Keller seized Ippolit, the young man fell into his arms, apparently unconscious, perhaps really imagining that he was killed. The pistol was already in Keller's hand. Ippolit was held up, a chair was brought. They sat him down on it, and all crowded round, shouting and asking questions. All had heard the click of the trigger, and saw the man alive without a scratch. Ippolit himself sat, not understanding what was going on, staring blankly at all around him. Lebedyev and Kolya ran up at that instant.

'Did it miss fire?' people were asking.

'Perhaps it was not loaded?' others surmised.

'It was loaded,' Keller pronounced, examining the pistol, 'but

'Can it have missed fire?'

'There was no cap in it,' Keller announced.

It is hard to describe the piteous scene that followed. The general pause of the first moment was quickly succeeded by laughter. Some of the party positively roared, and seemed to find a malignant pleasure in the position. Ippolit sobbed as though he were in hysterics, wrung his hands, rushed up to everyone, even to Ferdyshtchenko, whom he clutched with both hands, swearing that he had forgotten, 'forgotten quite accidentally and not on purpose', to put in the cap; that 'he had all the caps here, in his waistcoat pocket, a dozen of them (he showed them to everyone about him). But he hadn't put them in before, for fear of its going off by accident in his pocket; that he had counted on always having time to put a cap in, and he had suddenly forgotten it.' He rushed up to Myshkin, to Yevgeny Pavlovitch, besought Keller to give him back the pistol, that he might show them all that 'his honour, his honour'... that he was now 'dishonoured for ever'.

He fell unconscious at last. He was carried into Myshkin's study and Lebedyev, completely sobered, sent at once for a doctor, while he himself remained by the invalid's bedside with his daughter, his son, Burdovsky, and the general. When Ippolit had been carried out unconscious, Keller stood in the middle of the room, and with positive inspiration pronounced, dwelling on every word, and emphasising it so that all might hear.

'Gentlemen! If any one of you ever once insinuates in my presence that the cap was forgotten intentionally, and maintains that the unhappy young man was acting a farce, he will have to deal with me.'

But no one answered him. The guests were at last leaving in a crowd and in haste. Ptitsyn, Ganya, and Rogozhin set off together.

Myshkin was much surprised that Yevgeny Pavlovitch had changed his mind and was going away without speaking to him.

'You wanted to speak to me when the others had gone, didn't you?' he asked him.

'Just so,' said Yevgeny Pavlovitch, suddenly sitting down and making Myshkin sit beside him. 'But now I have changed my mind for a time. I confess that I have had rather a shock, and so have you.

My thoughts are in a tangle. Besides, what I want to discuss with you is too important a matter to me and to you too. You see, Prince, for once in my life, I want to do something absolutely honest, that is, something absolutely without any ulterior motive; and, well, I think I'm not quite capable of doing anything perfectly honest at this moment, and you too perhaps … and so … well, we'll discuss it later. Perhaps the matter will be made more plain later to both of us, if we wait another three days which I shall spend now in Petersburg.'

Then he got up from his chair again, so that it seemed strange he should have sat down. Myshkin, fancied, too, that Yevgeny Pavlovitch was annoyed and irritated, that there was a hostile look in his eyes which had not been there before.

'By the way, are you going to the patient now?'

'Yes … I'm afraid,' said Myshkin.

'Don't be afraid. He'll live another six weeks, and he may even get well here. But the best thing you can do is to get rid of him tomorrow.'

'Perhaps I really did egg him on by … not saying anything. He may have thought I didn't believe he would shoot himself? What do you think, Yevgeny Pavlovitch?'

'Not at all. It's too good-natured of you to worry about it. I've heard tell of such things, but I've never in real life seen a man shoot himself on purpose to win applause, or from spite because he was not applauded for it. And, what's more, I wouldn't have believed in such an open exhibition of feebleness. But you'd better get rid of him tomorrow all the same.'

'Do you think he'll shoot himself again?'

'No, he won't do it now. But be on your guard with these home-bred Lasseners of ours. I repeat, crime is only too often the refuge of these mediocre, impatient and greedy nonentities.'

'Is he a Lassener?'

'The essence is the same, though the *emplois* are different, perhaps. You'll see whether this gentleman isn't capable of murdering a dozen people simply as a "feat", as he read us just now in his explanation. Those words of his won't let me sleep now.'

'You are too anxious perhaps.'

'You're a wonderful person, Prince. You don't believe he's capable of killing a dozen persons *now.*'

'I'm afraid to answer you. It's all very strange, but …'

'Well, as you like, as you like!' Yevgeny Pavlovitch concluded irritably. 'Besides, you're such a valiant person. Don't you be one of the dozen, that's all!'

'It's most likely he won't kill anyone,' said Myshkin, looking dreamily at Yevgeny Pavlovitch.

The latter laughed angrily.

'Goodbye! It's time I was off. Did you notice he bequeathed a copy of his "Explanation" to Aglaia Ivanovna?'

'Yes, I did, and ... I am thinking about it.'

'That's right, in case of the "dozen,"' laughed Yevgeny Pavlovitch again, and he went out.

An hour later, when it was already past three o'clock, Myshkin went out into the park. He had tried to sleep, but was kept awake by the violent throbbing of his heart. Everything was quiet in the house, and, as far as possible, tranquillity had been restored. The sick boy had fallen asleep, and the doctor declared that there was no special danger. Lebedyev, Kolya, and Burdovsky lay down in the invalid's room, so as to take turns in watching him. There was nothing to be afraid of.

But Myshkin's uneasiness grew front moment to moment. He wandered in the park, looking absently about him, and stopped in surprise when he reached the open space before the station, and saw the rows of seats, and the music-stands of the orchestra.

He was impressed by the scene, which struck him as horribly squalid. He turned back, and going by the path along which he had walked the day before with the Epanchins, he reached the green seat which had been fixed as the trysting place; sat down on it, and suddenly laughed out loud, which at once made him feel extremely indignant with himself. His dejection persisted; he longed to go away ... he knew not where. In a tree overhead a bird was singing, and he began looking for it among the leaves. All at once the bird darted out of the tree, and at the same instant he recalled the 'fly in the warm sunshine', of which Ippolit had written, that 'it knew its place and took part in the general chorus, but he alone was an outcast'. The phrase had struck him at the time; and he recalled it now. One long-forgotten memory stirred within him, and suddenly rose up clear before him.

It was in Switzerland, during his first year, in the early part of it, in fact. Then he was almost like an idiot; he could not even speak properly – and sometimes could not understand what was wanted of him. He once went up into the mountain-side, on a bright, sunny day, and walked a long time, his mind possessed with an agonising but unformulated idea. Before him was the brilliant sky, below, the lake, and all around an horizon, bright and boundless which seemed to have no ending. He gazed a long time in distress. He remembered now how he had stretched out his hands to that bright, infinite blue, and had shed tears. What tortured him Was that he was utterly outside all this. What was this festival? What was this grand, everlasting pageant to which there was no end, to which he had always, from his earliest childhood, been drawn and in which he could never take part? Every morning the same bright sun rises, every morning the same rainbow in the waterfall, every evening that highest snow mountain glows, with a flush of purple against the distant sky, every 'little fly that buzzes about him in the hot sunshine has its part in the chorus; knows its place, loves it and is happy.' Every blade of grass grows and is happy! Everything has its path, and everything knows its path, and with a song goes forth, and with a song returns. Only he knows nothing, and understands nothing, neither men nor sounds; he is outside it all, and an outcast. Oh, of course he could not say it then in those words, could not utter his question. He suffered dumbly, not comprehending, but now it seemed to him that he had said all this at the time, those very words, and that that phrase about the fly Ippolit took from him; from his words then and his tears. He felt sure of it, and for some reason the thought set his heart beating.

He dropped asleep on the seat, but his agitation still persisted. Just as he was falling asleep he remembered that Ippolit was to kill a dozen people, and smiled at the absurdity of the notion. There was an exquisite brightness and stillness all round him only broken by the rustle of the leaves which seemed to make it even more silent and solitary. He had many dreams, and all were disquieting, and at times made him start uneasily. At last a woman came to him; he knew her, and knowing her was torture; he knew her name, and would have known her anywhere – but strange to say – her face now was not the same as he had always known it, and he felt an agonising reluctance to acknowledge her as the same woman. There was such remorse and horror in this face that it seemed as though she must be a fearful criminal, and had just committed some awful crime. Tears quivered on her pale cheeks; she beckoned to him and put her finger to her lips, as though to warn him to follow her quietly. His heart turned cold; nothing, nothing on earth would induce him to admit that she was a criminal, but he felt that something awful was about to happen, that would ruin his whole life. She seemed anxious to show him something not far off, in the park. He got up to follow her, and suddenly he heard beside him the sound of a gay, fresh laugh; he felt a hand in his. He seized the hand, pressed it tight and waked up. Aglaia was standing before him, laughing aloud.

Chapter 8

She was laughing, but she was indignant.

'Asleep! You were asleep!' she cried with disdainful wonder.

'It's you!' muttered Myshkin, hardly awake, and recognising her with surprise. 'Oh, yes! We were going to meet… I've been asleep here.'

'So I see.'

'Did no one wake me but you? Has no one been here but you? I thought there was… another woman here.'

'Another woman's been here?'

At last he was wide awake.

'It was only a dream,' he said pensively. 'Strange at such a moment to have such a dream … Sit down!'

He took her hand and made her sit down on the seat; he sat beside her and sank into thought. Aglaia did not begin the conversation, but scrutinised her companion intently. He gazed at her too, though sometimes his eyes looked as though he did not see her. She began to flush.

'Oh, yes,' said Myshkin, starting, 'Ippolit shot himself.'

'When? In your rooms?' she asked, but without great surprise. 'He was alive only yesterday evening, wasn't he? How could you sleep after such a thing?' she cried, with sudden animation.

'But he's not dead, you know. The pistol did not go off.'

Aglaia insisted on Myshkin's at once giving her a minute account of what had happened the previous evening. She continually urged him on in his story, though she kept interrupting him with questions, almost always irrelevant. She listened with great interest to what Yevgeny Pavlovitch had said, and several times asked him to repeat it.

'Well, that's enough! We must make haste,' she ended, after hearing everything. 'We've only an hour to be here, till eight o'clock. For at eight I must be at home, so that they mayn't know I've been sitting here, and I've come out with an object. I have a great deal to tell you. Only you've quite put me out now. About Ippolit, I think that his pistol was bound not to go off. It's just like him. But you're sure that he really meant to shoot himself, and that there was no deception about it?'

'There was no deception.'

'That's more likely, indeed. So he wrote that you were to bring me his confession? Why didn't you bring it?'

'Why, he's not dead. I'll ask him for it.'

'Be sure to bring it. And there is no need to ask him. He'll certainly be delighted, for perhaps it was with that object he shot at himself, that I might read his confession afterwards. Please don't laugh at me, I beg you, Lyov Nikolayevitch, because it may very well be so.'

'I'm not laughing, for I'm convinced myself that that may very likely be partly the reason.'

'You're convinced! Do you really think so, too?'

Aglaia was extremely surprised.

She asked rapid questions, talked quickly, but sometimes seemed confused, and often did not finish her sentences. At times she seemed in haste to warn him of something. Altogether she was in extraordinary agitation, and, though she looked very bold and almost defiant, she was perhaps a little scared too. She was wearing a very plain everyday dress, which suited her extremely well. She was sitting on the edge of the seat, and she often started and blushed. Myshkin's confirmation of her idea, that Ippolit had shot himself that she might read his confession afterwards, surprised her very much.

'Of course,' Myshkin explained, 'he wanted us all to praise him, as well as you …'

'Praise him?'

'That is … how shall I tell you … it is very difficult to explain. Only he certainly wanted everyone to come round him and tell him that they loved him very much and respected him; he longed for them all to beg him to remain alive. It may very well be that he had you in his mind more than anyone, because he mentioned you at such a moment ... though, perhaps, he didn't know himself that he had you in mind.'

'That I don't understand at all; that he had it in his mind and didn't know he had it in his mind. I think I do understand, though. Do you know that thirty times I dreamed of poisoning myself, when I was only thirteen, and writing it all in a letter to my parents. And I, too, thought how I would lie in my coffin, and they would all weep over me, and blame themselves for having been too cruel to me ... Why are you smiling again?' she added quickly, frowning. 'What do you think about when you dream by yourself? Perhaps you fancy yourself a field-marshal, and dream you've conquered Napoleon?'

'Well, honour bright, I do dream of that, especially when I'm dropping asleep,' said Myshkin, laughing. 'Only it's always the Austrians I conquer, not Napoleon.'

'I'm in no mood for joking with you, Lyov Nikolayevitch. I'll see Ippolit myself. I beg you to tell him so. I think it's very horrid on your part, for it's very brutal to look on and judge a man's soul, as you judge Ippolit. You have no tenderness, nothing but truth, and so you judge unjustly.'

Myshkin pondered.

'I think you're unfair to me,' he said. 'Why, I see no harm in his thinking in that way, because all people are inclined to think like that. Besides, perhaps he didn't think like that at all, but only wanted it... He longed for the last time to come near to men, to win their respect and love. Those are very good feelings, you know. Only it somehow all went wrong. It's his illness, and something else, perhaps! Besides, everything always goes right with some people, while with others nothing ever comes off...'

'You mean that for yourself, I suppose?' observed Aglaia.

'Yes, I do,' answered Myshkin, not conscious of any sarcasm in the question.

'But I wouldn't have fallen asleep in your place, anyway. It shows that wherever you pitch you fall asleep on the spot. It's not at all nice of you.'

'But I haven't slept all night; I walked and walked afterwards. I've been where the music was.'

'What music?'

'Where the band was playing, yesterday. Then I came here, sat down, thought and thought, and fell asleep.'

'Oh, so that's how it was! That makes it a little better. But why did you go to the bandstand?'

'I don't know. I happened to.'

'Very well, very well, afterwards; you keep interrupting me. And what does it matter to me if you did go to the bandstand? What woman was it you were dreaming about?'

'It was … you've seen her.'

'I understand. I quite understand. You think a lot … How did you dream of her? What was she doing? Though I don't care to know,' she snapped out, with an air of vexation. 'Don't interrupt me …'

She waited a little, as though to pluck up her courage or to overcome her vexation.

'I'll tell you what I asked you to come for; I want to make a proposition that you should be my friend. Why are you staring at me all of a sudden?' she asked, almost wrathfully.

Myshkin certainly was watching her very intently at that moment, observing that she had begun to flush hotly again. In such cases, the more she blushed, the more angry she seemed with herself, and it was unmistakably apparent in her flashing eyes. Usually she transferred her anger to the person she was talking to, whether he were to blame or not, and would begin quarrelling with him. Being aware of her own awkwardness and desperate shyness and very conscious of it, she was, as a rule, not very ready to enter into conversation, and was more silent than her sisters, sometimes too silent, indeed. When, particularly in such delicate cases, she was positively obliged to speak, she would begin the conversation with marked haughtiness and with a sort of defiance. She always felt beforehand when she was beginning or about to begin to blush.

'Perhaps you don't care to accept my proposition?' She looked haughtily at Myshkin.

'Oh, yes, I should like to. Only it was quite unnecessary … That is, I shouldn't have thought you need make such a proposition,' said Myshkin in confusion.

'What did you think then? What do you suppose I asked you to come here for? What's in your mind? But perhaps you look on me as a little fool, as they all do at home?'

'I didn't know that they look on you as a fool. I … I don't look on you so.'

'You don't look on me so? Very clever on your part. Particularly cleverly expressed.'

'I think you may be quite clever at times,' Myshkin went on. 'You said something very clever just now. You were speaking of my uncertainty about Ippolit. "There's nothing but truth in it, and so it's unjust." I shall remember that and think it over.'

Aglaia suddenly crimsoned with pleasure. All such transitions of feeling were artlessly apparent in her, and followed one another with extraordinary rapidity. Myshkin, too, was delighted, and positively laughed with pleasure, watching her.

'Listen,' she began again. 'I've been waiting for a long time to tell you all about it. I've been wanting to, ever since you wrote me that letter, and even before then ... You heard half of it yesterday. I consider you the most honest and truthful of men, more honest and truthful than anyone; and if they do say that your mind ... that is, that you're sometimes afflicted in your mind, it's unjust. I made up my mind about that, and disputed with others, because, though you really are mentally afflicted (you won't be angry at that, of course; I'm speaking from a higher point of view), yet the mind that matters is better in you than in any of them. It's something, in fact, they have never dreamed of. For there are two sorts of mind: one that matters, and one that doesn't matter. Is that so? That is so, isn't it?'

'Perhaps it is,' Myshkin articulated faintly. His heart was trembling and throbbing violently.

'I was sure you would understand,' she went on impressively. 'Prince S— and Yevgeny Pavlovitch don't understand about those two sorts of mind, nor Alexandra either, but, only fancy, *Maman* understood.'

'You're very like Lizaveta Prokofyevna.'

'How so? Really?' Aglaia asked, surprised.

'Yes, really.'

'Thank you,' she said, after a moment's thought. 'I am very glad I'm like *Maman*. You have a great respect for her, then?' she added, quite unconscious of the *naïveté* of the question.

'Very great. And I'm glad you saw it so directly.'

'And I'm glad, because I've noticed that people sometimes... laugh at her. But let me tell you what matters most. I've been thinking a long time, and at last I've picked you out. I don't want them to laugh at me at home. I don't want them to look on me as a little fool. I don't want them to tease me ... I realised it all at once, and refused Yevgeny Pavlovitch point-blank, because I don't want to be continually being married! I want... I want... Well, I want to run away from home, and I've chosen you to help me.'

'Run away from home!' cried Myshkin.

'Yes, yes, yes! Run away from home,' she cried, at once flaring up with extraordinary anger. 'I can't bear, I can't bear their continually making me blush there. I don't want to blush before them, or before Prince S— or before Yevgeny Pavlovitch, or before anyone, and so I've chosen you. To *you* I want to tell everything, everything, even the most important thing, when I want to, and you must hide nothing from me on your side. I want, with one person at least, to speak freely of everything, as I can to myself. They suddenly began saying that I was waiting for you, and that I loved you. That began before you came here, though I didn't show them the letter. And now they're all talking about it. I want to be bold, and not to be afraid of anything. I don't want to go to their balls. I want to be of use. I've been wanting to get away for a long time. For twenty years I've been bottled up at home, and they keep trying to marry me. I've been thinking of running away since I was fourteen, though I was a silly. Now I've worked it all out, and was waiting for you to ask you all about foreign countries. I have never seen a Gothic cathedral. I want to go to Rome. I want to visit all the learned societies. I want to study in Paris. I was preparing myself and studying all last year, and I've read a great many books. I have read all the forbidden books. Alexandra and Adelaïda read any books – they're allowed to. But I am not allowed to read all of them; they supervise me. I don't want to quarrel with my sisters, but I told my father and mother long ago that I want to make a complete change in my social position. I propose to take up teaching, and I've been reckoning on you because you said you were fond of children. Couldn't we go in for education together, not at once perhaps, but in the future? We should be doing good together. I don't want to be a general's daughter. Tell me, are you a very learned person?'

'Oh, not at all.'

'That's a pity, for I thought... how was it I thought so? You'll be my guide all the same because I have chosen you.'

'That's absurd, Aglaia Ivanovna.'

'I want to run away from home – I want to,' she cried, and again her eyes flashed. 'If you won't consent, I shall marry Gavril Ardalionovitch. I don't want to be looked upon as a horrid girl at home, and be accused of goodness knows what.'

'Are you mad!' cried Myshkin, almost leaping up from his seat. 'What are you accused of? Who accuses you?'

'Everyone at home. Mother, my sisters, father, Prince S—, even your horrid Kolya. If they don't say so straight out, they think so. I told them all so to their faces, mother and father too. *Maman* was ill for a whole day afterwards. And next day Alexandra and Papa told me that I didn't understand what nonsense I was talking and what words I was speaking. And I told them straight out that I understood everything; all sorts of words; that I'm not a little girl; that I read two novels of Paul de Kock two years ago, so as to find out everything. *Maman* almost fainted when she heard me.'

A strange idea suddenly occurred to Myshkin. He looked intently at Aglaia and smiled.

He could scarcely believe that the haughty girl who had once so proudly and disdainfully read him Gavril Ardalionovitch's letter was actually sitting before him. He could not conceive that the disdainful, stern beauty could turn out to be such a baby, a baby, who perhaps did not even now understand some words.

'Have you always lived at home, Aglaia Ivanovna?' he asked. 'I mean, did you never go to school or study at an institute?'

'I've never been anywhere. I've always sat at home, as though I were corked up in a bottle, and I'm to be married straight out of the bottle. Why are you laughing again? I notice that you, too, seem to be laughing at me, and taking their part,' she added, frowning menacingly. 'Don't make me angry, I don't know what's the matter with me as it is. I'm certain you came here fully persuaded that I am in love with you, and was making a tryst with you,' she snapped out irritably.

'I certainly was afraid of that yesterday,' Myshkin blurted out with simplicity. (He was very much confused.) 'But I am convinced today that you …'

'What?' cried Aglaia, and her lower lip began trembling. 'You were afraid that I … You dared to imagine that I … Good heavens! You suspected perhaps that I invited you here to ensnare you, so that we might be found here afterwards, and that you might be forced to marry me.'

'Aglaia Ivanovna! Aren't you ashamed? How could such a nasty idea arise in your pure, innocent heart? I'd swear that you don't believe one word of it… and you don't know what you're saving!'

Aglaia sat, looking doggedly at the ground, as though frightened herself at what she had said.

'I'm not ashamed at all,' she muttered. 'How do you know that my heart is so innocent? How dared you send me a love letter, that time?'

'A love-letter? My letter – a love-letter! That letter was most respectful; that letter was the outpouring of my heart at the bitterest moment of my life! I thought of you then as of some light… I…'

'Oh, very well, very well,' she interrupted suddenly, in a quite different, completely penitent and almost frightened tone. She turned to him, though still trying to avoid looking at him, and seemed on the point of touching his shoulder, to beg him more persuasively not to be angry with her.

'It's all right,' she added, terribly shamefaced. 'I feel I used a very stupid expression. I said that just … to test you. Take it as though it were unsaid. If I offended you, forgive me. Don't look straight at me, please. Turn away. You said that was a very nasty idea. I said it on purpose to vex you. Sometimes I'm afraid of what I'm going to say myself, then all at once I say it. You said just now that you wrote that letter at the most painful moment of your life. I know what moment it was,' she said softly, looking at the ground again.

'Oh, if you could know everything!'

'I do know everything!' she cried, with renewed excitement. 'You'd been living for a whole month in the same flat with that horrid woman with whom you ran away …'

She did not turn red this time, but turned pale as she uttered the words, and she stood up as though she did not know what she was doing, but recollecting herself, sat down again; for a long time her lip was still quivering. The silence lasted a minute. Myshkin was greatly taken aback by the suddenness of her outburst, and did not know how to account for it.

'I don't love you at all,' she said suddenly, as though rapping out the phrase.

Myshkin made no answer; again they were silent for a minute.

'I love Gavril Ardalionovitch …' she said, speaking hurriedly, but scarcely audibly, bending her head still lower.

'That's not true,' answered Myshkin, also almost whispering.

'Then I'm lying? That's true. I gave him my word the day before yesterday, on this very seat.'

Myshkin was frightened, and pondered a minute.

'That's not true,' he repeated, with decision. 'You've invented all that.'

'You're wonderfully polite. Let me tell you he's reformed. He loves me more than his life. He burnt his hand before my eyes to show me that he loved me more than his life.'

'Burnt his hand?'

'Yes, his hand. You may believe it or not – I don't care.'

Myshkin was silent again. There was no trace of jesting in Aglaia's words. She was angry.

'Why, did he bring a candle with him, if he did it here? I don't see how else he could ...'

'Yes ... he did. What is there unlikely about it?'

'A whole one, in a candlestick?'

'Oh, well... no ... half a candle ... a candle-end ... a whole one. It doesn't matter. Let me alone! He brought matches, too, if you like. He lighted the candle, and he left his finger in it for half an hour. Is there anything impossible in that?'

'I saw him yesterday. His fingers were all right.'

Aglaia suddenly went off into a peal of laughter, like a child.

'Do you know why I told you that fib, just now?' She suddenly turned to Myshkin with childlike confidence, and the laugh still quivering on her lips. 'Because, when you are lying, if you skilfully put in something not quite ordinary, something eccentric, something, you know, that never has happened, or very rarely, it makes the lie sound much more probable. I've noticed that. It didn't answer with me because I didn't do it properly ...'

Suddenly she frowned again, as though recollecting herself.

'When,' she turned to Myshkin, looking seriously and even mournfully at him, When I read you about the "poor knight", though I did mean to applaud you for one thing, yet I wanted also to put you to shame for your behaviour, and to show you I knew all about it.'

'You are very unjust to me ... to that unhappy woman of whom you spoke so horribly just now, Aglaia.'

'It's because I know all about it, all about it. That's why I spoke like that! I know that six months ago you offered her your hand in the presence of everyone. Don't interrupt me. You see, I speak without comment. After that she ran away with Rogozhin; then you lived with her in some country place or in the town, and she went away from you to someone else (Aglaia blushed painfully); then she went back again to Rogozhin who loves her like ... like a madman. Then you a very clever person, too ... galloped after her here, as soon as you heard she had gone back to Petersburg. Yesterday evening you rushed to defend her, and just now you were dreaming about her... You see, I know all about it; it was for her sake, for her sake you came here, wasn't it?'

'Yes, for her sake,' Myshkin answered softly, looking down mournfully and dreamily, not suspecting with what burning eyes Aglaia glared at him.

'For her sake, to find out... I don't believe in her being happy with Rogozhin though ... In short, I don't know what I could do for her here, or how I could help her, but I came.'

He started and looked at Aglaia; she was listening to him with a look of hatred.

'If you came, not knowing why, then you love her very much,' she brought out at last.

'No,' answered Myshkin, 'no, I don't love her. Oh, if you only knew with what horror I recall the time I spent with her!'

A shudder ran down him, as he uttered the words.

'Tell me all,' said Aglaia.

'There is nothing in it you might not hear about. Why I wanted to tell you all about it, and only you, I don't know. Perhaps because I really did love you very much. That unhappy woman is firmly convinced that she is the most fallen, the most vicious creature in the whole world. Oh, don't cry shame on her, don't throw stones at her! She has tortured herself too much from the consciousness of her undeserved shame! And my God, she's not to blame! Oh, she's crying out every minute in her frenzy that she doesn't admit going wrong, that she was the victim of others, the victim of a depraved and wicked man. But whatever she may say to you, believe me, she's the first to disbelieve it, and to believe with her whole conscience that she is... to blame. When I tried to dispel that gloomy delusion, it threw her into such misery that my heart will always ache when I remember that awful time. It's as though my heart had been stabbed once for all. She ran away from me. Do you know what for? Simply to show me that she was a degraded creature. But the most awful thing is that perhaps she didn't even know herself that she only wanted to prove that to me, but ran away because she had an irresistible inner craving to do something shameful, so as to say, to herself at once, "There, you've done something shameful again, so you're a degraded creature!" Oh, perhaps you won't understand this, Aglaia. Do you know that in that continual consciousness of shame there is perhaps a sort of awful, unnatural enjoyment for her, a sort of revenge on someone. Sometimes I did bring her to seeing light round her once more, as it were. But she would grow restive again at once, and even came to accusing me bitterly of setting myself up above her (though I had no thought of such a thing) and told me in so many words at last, when I offered her marriage, that she didn't want condescending sympathy or help from anyone, nor to be elevated to anyone's level. You saw her yesterday. Do you think she's happy with that set, that they are fitting company for her? You don't know how well educated she is, and what she can understand! She really surprised me sometimes.'

'Did you ever then preach her such … sermons?'

'Oh, no,' Myshkin went on dreamily, not observing the tone and the question. 'I hardly ever spoke. I often wanted to speak, but I really didn't know sometimes what to say. You know, in some cases it is better not to speak at all. Oh, I loved her; oh, I loved her very much, but afterwards … afterwards … afterwards she guessed it all.'

'What did she guess?'

'That I only pitied her, but that I… don't love her any more.'

'How do you know? Perhaps she really fell in love with that … landowner she went away with?'

'No, I know all about it. She was only laughing at him.'

'And did she never laugh at you?'

'N-no. She used to laugh in anger. Oh, then she would reproach me horribly, in a fury – and she was wretched herself! But… afterwards … Oh, don't remind me, don't remind me of that!'

He hid his face in his hands.

'And do you know that she writes letters to me almost every day?'

'Then it is true!' cried Myshkin, in dismay. 'I heard so, but I wouldn't believe it.'

'From whom did you hear it?' Aglaia asked, scared.

'Rogozhin said so yesterday, but not quite definitely.'

'Yesterday? Yesterday morning? What time yesterday? Before the band played, or after?'

'Afterwards. In the evening, past eleven.'

'Oh, if it was Rogozhin… But do you know what she writes to me in these letters?'

'I shouldn't be surprised at anything. She's insane.'

'Here are the letters.' Aglaia pulled three letters in three envelopes out of her pocket and threw them down before Myshkin. 'For the last week, she's been beseeching, imploring, coaxing me to marry you. She … Oh, well, she's clever, though she's insane. And you're right in saying she's much cleverer than I am … She writes that she's in love with me, that she tries every day to get a chance of seeing me even in the distance. She writes that you love me, that she knows it, that she noticed it long ago, that you used to talk to her about me then. She wants to see you happv. She's certain that only I can make you happy … She writes so wildly … so strangely … I haven't shown her letters to anyone. I've been waiting for you. Do you know what this means? Can you guess?'

'It's madness, a proof of her insanity,' Myshkin brought out, and his lips began to tremble.

'You're not crying now, are you?'

'No, Aglaia. No. I'm not crying.' Myshkin looked at her.

'What am I to do about it? What do you advise me? I can't go on getting these letters!'

'Oh, leave her alone, I entreat you!' cried Myshkin. 'What can you do in this darkness? I'll do all I can to prevent her writing to you again.'

'Then you're a man of no heart!' cried Aglaia. 'Surely you must see that she's not in love with me, but that she loves you, only you. How can you have noticed everything in her and not have seen that? Do you know what it is, what these letters mean? It's jealousy. It's more than jealousy! She … do you suppose she'd really marry Rogozhin as she writes here in her letters? She'd kill herself the day after our wedding!'

Myshkin started; his heart stood still. But he gazed in amazement at Aglaia. It was strange to him to realise that the child was so fully a woman.

'God knows, Aglaia, that to bring peace back to her and make her happy, I would give up my life. But… I can't love her now, and she knows it!'

'Then sacrifice yourself, it's just in your line! You're such a charitable person! And don't call me Aglaia ... You called me simply Aglaia just now. You ought to raise her up, you are bound to. You ought to go away with her again so as to give peace and calm to her heart. Why, you love her, you know!'

'I can't sacrifice myself like that, though I did want to at one time ... and perhaps I want to still. But I know *for certain* that with me she'll be lost, and so I leave her. I was to have seen her today at seven o'clock, but perhaps I won't go now. In her pride she will never forgive me for my love – and we shall both come to ruin. That's abnormal, but everything here is abnormal. You say she loves me, but is this love? Can there be such love after what I have gone through? No, it's something else, not love!'

'How pale you've grown!' Aglaia cried, in sudden dismay.

'It's nothing. I've not had much sleep. I'm exhausted ... We really did talk about you then, Aglaia ...'

'So that's true? You actually *could talk to her about me* and ... and how could you care for me when you had only seen me once?'

'I don't know how. In my darkness then I dreamed ... I had an illusion perhaps of a new dawn. I don't know how I thought of you at first. It was the truth I wrote you then, that I didn't know. All that was only a dream, from the horror then ... Afterwards I began to work. I shouldn't have come here for three years ...'

'Then you've come for her sake?'

And there was a quiver in Aglaia's voice.

'Yes, for her sake.'

Two minutes of gloomy silence on both sides followed. Aglaia got up from the seat.

'You may say,' she began in an unsteady voice, 'you may believe that that ... your woman ... is insane, but I have nothing to do with her insane fancies ... I beg you, Lyov Nikolayevitch, to take these three letters and fling them back to her from me! .And if,' Aglaia cried suddenly, 'and if she dares write me a single line again, tell her I shall complain to my father, and have her put into a House of Correction ...'

Myshkin jumped up, and gazed in alarm at Aglaia's sudden fury; a mist seemed to fall before his eyes.

'You can't feel like that... It's not true!' he muttered.

'It's the truth! It's the truth!' screamed Aglaia, almost beside herself.

'What's the truth? What truth?' they heard a frightened voice saying near them.

Lizaveta Prokofyevna stood before them.

'It's the truth that I'm going to marry Gavril Ardalionovitch! That I love Gavril Ardalionovitch, and that I'm going to run away from home with him tomorrow!' cried Aglaia, flying out at her. 'Do you hear? Is your curiosity satisfied? Is that enough for you?'

And she ran home.

'No, my friend, don't you go away,' said Lizaveta Prokofyevna, detaining him, 'you'll be so good as to give me an explanation. What have I done to be so worried? I've been awake all night as it is.'

Myshkin followed her.

Chapter 9

On reaching home Lizaveta Prokofyevna stopped in the first room; she could get no further and sank on the couch, perfectly limp, forgetting even to ask Myshkin to sit down. It was a rather large room, with a round table in the middle of it, with an open fireplace, with quantities of flowers on an *étagère* in the window, and with another glass door leading into the garden in the opposite wall. Adelaïda and Alexandra came in at once, and looked enquiringly and with perplexity at their mother and Myshkin.

At their summer villa the girls usually got up about nine o'clock, but for the last three days Aglaia had been getting up earlier and going for a walk in the garden, not at seven o'clock, but at eight or even later. Lizaveta Prokofyevna, who really had been kept awake all night by her various worries, got up about eight o'clock on purpose to meet Aglaia in the garden, reckoning on her being up already, but she did not find her either in the garden or in her bedroom. At last she grew thoroughly alarmed and waked her daughters. From the servants she learnt that Aglaia Ivanovna had gone out into the park at seven o'clock. The girls laughed at their whimsical sister's new whim, and observed to their mother that Aglaia might very likely be angry, if she went to look for her in the park, and that she was probably with a book sitting on the green seat of which she had been talking the day before yesterday, and about which she had almost quarrelled with Prince S— because he saw nothing particularly picturesque about it. Coming upon the couple, and hearing her daughter's strange words, Lizaveta Prokofyevna was greatly alarmed for many reasons, but when she brought Myshkin home with her, she felt uneasy at having spoken openly about it. 'After all, why should Aglaia not meet the prince in the park and talk to him, even if the interview had been arranged between them beforehand?'

'Don't imagine, my good friend,' she braced herself to say, 'that I brought you here to cross-examine you. After what happened yesterday I might well not have been anxious to see you for some time …'

She could not go on for a moment.

'But you would very much like to know how I came to meet Aglaia Ivanovna this morning?' Myshkin completed her sentence with perfect serenity.

'Well, I did want to!' Lizaveta Prokofyevna flared up at once. 'I am not afraid of speaking plainly. For I'm not insulting anyone, and I don't want to offend anyone …'

'To be sure, you naturally want to know, without any offence; you are her mother. I met Aglaia Ivanovna this morning at the green seat, at seven o'clock, as she invited me to do so yesterday. She let me know by a note yesterday evening that she wanted to meet me to talk of an important matter. We met and had been talking for a whole hour of matters that only concerned Aglaia Ivanovna. That's all.'

'Of course it's all, my good sir, and without a shadow of doubt,' Madame Epanchin assented with dignity.

'Capital, Prince,' said Aglaia, suddenly entering the room, 'I thank you with all my heart for not believing that I would condescend to lie about it. Is that enough, *Maman*, or do you intend to cross-examine him further?'

'You know that I have never yet had to blush for anything before you, though you would perhaps be glad if I had.' Lizaveta Prokofyevna replied impressively. 'Goodbye, Prince. Forgive me for having troubled you. And I hope you will remain convinced of my unchanged respect for you.'

Myshkin at once bowed to right and to left, and silently withdrew. Alexandra and Adelaïda laughed and whispered together. Their mother looked sternly at them.

'*Maman,*' laughed Adelaïda, 'it was only that the prince made such magnificent bows; sometimes he's so clumsy, but he was suddenly just like ... like Yevgeny Pavlovitch.'

'Delicacy and dignity are taught by the heart and not by the dancing-master,' Lizaveta Prokofyevna summed up sententiously. And she went up to her room without even looking at Aglaia.

When Myshkin got home about nine o'clock he found Vera Lukyanovna and the servant on the verandah. They were sweeping up and clearing away after the disorder of the previous evening.

'Thank goodness, we've had time to finish before you came!' said Vera joyfully.

'Good morning; I feel a little giddy, I didn't sleep well. I should like a nap.'

'Here, in the verandah, as you did yesterday? Good. I'll tell them all not to wake you. Father's gone off somewhere.'

The maid went away. Vera was about to follow her, but she turned and went anxiously up to Myshkin.

'Prince, don't be hard on that... poor fellow; don't send him away today.'

'I won't on any account. It's as he chooses.'

'He won't do anything now, and ... don't be severe with him.'

'Certainly not, why should I?'

'And don't laugh at him, that's the chief thing.'

'Oh, I shouldn't think of it.'

'I'm silly to speak of it to a man like you,' said Vera, flushing. 'Though you're tired,' she laughed, half turning to go away, 'your eyes are so nice at this moment... they look happy.'

'Do they, really?' Myshkin asked eagerly, and he laughed, delighted.

But Vera, who was as simple-hearted and blunt as a boy, was suddenly overcome with confusion, she turned redder and redder, and, still laughing, she went hurriedly away.

'What a ... jolly girl,' thought Myshkin, and immediately forgot her. He went to the corner of the verandah where there stood a sofa with a little table beside it; he sat down, hid his face in his hands and sat so for some ten minutes. All at once, with haste and agitation, he took three letters out of his coat-pocket.

But again the door opened and Kolya came out. Myshkin was, as it were, relieved that he had to replace the letters in his pocket and put off the evil moment.

'Well, what an adventure!' said Kolya, sitting down on the sofa and going straight for the subject, as boys like him always do. 'What do you think of Ippolit now? Have you no respect for hint?'

'Why not … but, Kolya, I'm tired … Besides, it's too sad to begin about that again … How is he, though?'

'He's asleep and won't wake for another two hours. I understand; you haven't slept at home. You've been in the park… it was the excitement, of course … and no wonder!'

'How do you know that I have been walking in the park and haven't been asleep?'

Vera said so just now. She tried to persuade me not to come, but I couldn't resist coming for a minute. I've been watching for the last two hours by his bedside; now Kostya Lebedyev is taking his turn. Burdovsky has gone. Then lie down, Prince, good night… or rather day! Only, do you know, I'm amazed!'

'Of course … all this …'

'No, Prince, no. I'm amazed at his "confession". Especially the part in which he spoke of Providence and the future life. There's a gigantic thought in it!'

Myshkin looked affectionately at Kolya who had no doubt come in to talk at once about the 'gigantic thought.'

'But it was not only the thought; it was the whole setting of it! If it had been written by Voltaire, Rousseau, Proudhon, I shouldn't have been so much struck. But for a man who knows for certain that he has only ten minutes to talk like that – isn't that pride? Why, it's the loftiest assertion of personal dignity, it's regular defiance … Yes, it's titanic strength of will! And after that to declare he left the cap out on purpose – it's base, incredible! But you know, he deceived us yesterday; he was sly. I didn't pack his bag with him, and I never saw the pistol. He packed everything up himself, so he took me quite off my guard. Vera says that you're going to let him stay here; I swear there'll be no danger, especially as we shall never leave him.'

'And which of you have been with him in the night?'

'Kostya Lebedyev, Burdovsky, and I. Keller was there a little while, but he went off to Lebedyev's part to sleep, because there wasn't room for us all to lie down. Ferdyshtchenko, too, slept in Lebedyev's part of the house. He went off at seven. The general sleeps always at Lebedyev's – he's gone too … Lebedyev will come out to you presently. He's been looking for you, I don't know why; he asked for you twice. Shall I let him in or not, as you want to sleep? I'm going to have a sleep, too. Oh, by the way, I should like to tell you one thing. I was surprised at the general this morning. I came out for a minute and suddenly met the general, and still so drunk that he didn't know me: he stood before me like a post; he fairly flew at me when he came to himself. "Hows the invalid?" said he, "I came to ask after the invalid ..." I reported this and that. "Well, that's all right," he said, "but what I really came out for, what I got up for was to warn you. I have reasons for supposing that one can't say everything before Mr Ferdyshtchenko and ... one must be on one's guard." Do you understand, Prince?'

'Really? But... it doesn't matter to us.'

'Of course it doesn't. We're not masons! So I felt surprised at the general's getting up on purpose in the night to wake me to tell me so.'

'Ferdyshtchenko has gone, you say?'

'At seven o'clock. Lie came in to see me on the way. I was sitting up with Ippolit. He said he was going to spend the day with Vilkin – there's a drunken fellow here called Vilkin. Well, I'm off! And here's Lukyan Timofeyitch ... The prince is sleepy, Lukyan Timofeyitch, right about face!'

'Only for a moment, much honoured prince, on a matter of great consequence to me,' Lebedyev, coming in, pronounced in a forced undertone of great significance, and he bowed with dignity.

He had only just come in, and still held his hat in his hand. His face looked preoccupied and wore a peculiar, unusual expression of personal dignity. Myshkin asked him to sit down.

'You've enquired for me twice already? You are still anxious, perhaps, on account of what happened yesterday?'

'You mean on account of that boy, Prince? Oh, no; yesterday my ideas were in confusion ... but today I don't intend to contradict your propositions in any way whatever.'

'Contra – ? What did you say?'

'I said "contradict", a French word, like many other words that have entered into the composition of the Russian language, but I don't defend it.'

'What's the matter with you this morning, Lebedyev? You're so dignified and formal, and you speak with such solemnity and as if you were spelling it out,' said Myshkin, laughing.

'Nikolay Ardalionovitch!' Lebedyev addressed Kolya in a voice almost of emotion – 'having to acquaint the prince with a matter affecting myself alone …'

'Of course, of course, it's not my business! Goodbye, Prince!' Kolya retired at once.

'I like the child for his tact,' pronounced Lebedyev, looking after him, 'a quick boy, but inquisitive. I've encountered a severe calamity, respected prince, last night or this morning at daybreak; I hesitate to determine the precise hour.'

'What is it?'

'I have lost four hundred roubles from my coat-pocket, much honoured prince. We were keeping the day!' added Lebedyev with a sour smile.

'You've lost four hundred roubles? That's a pity.'

'Particularly for a poor man honourably maintaining his family by his own labour.'

'Of course, of course. How did it happen?'

'The fruits of drinking. I have come to you as my Providence, much honoured prince. I received a sum of four hundred roubles in silver from a debtor yesterday, at five o'clock in the afternoon, and I came back here by train. I had my pocketbook in my pocket. When I changed my uniform for my indoor-coat, I put the money in the coat-pocket, intending that very evening to meet a call with it… I was expecting an agent.'

'By the way, Lukyan Timofeyitch, is it true you put an advertisement in the papers that you would lend money on gold or silver articles?'

'Through an agent; my own name does not appear, nor my address. The sum at my disposal is paltry, and in view of the increase of my family you will admit that a fair rate of interest…'

'Quite so, quite so. I only asked for information; forgive my interrupting.'

'The agent did not turn up. Meantime the wretched boy was brought here. I was already in an over-elevated condition, after dinner; the visitors came, we drank … tea, and … and I grew merry to my ruin. When Keller came in late and announced your fête day and the order for champagne, since I have a heart, dear and much-honoured prince (which you have probably remarked already, seeing that I have deserved you should), since I have a heart, I will not say feeling, but grateful – and I am proud of it –

I thought, well, to do greater respect to the coming festivity and, in expectation of congratulating you, by going to change my old housecoat, and putting on the uniform I had taken off on my return – which indeed I did, as you, Prince probably observed, seeing me the whole evening in my uniform. Changing my attire, I forgot the pocketbook in the coat-pocket … so true it is that when God will chastise a man, He first of all deprives him of his reason; and only this morning, at half-past seven, on waking up, I jumped up like a madman, and snatched first thing at my coat – the pocket was empty! The pocketbook had vanished!'

'Ach, that is unpleasant!'

'Unpleasant indeed; and with true tact you have at once found the right word for it,' Lebedyev added, not without slyness.

'Well, but … 'Myshkin said uneasily, pondering. 'It's serious, you know.'

'Serious indeed. Again, Prince, you have found the very word to describe …'

'Ach, don't go on, Lukyan Timofeyitch. What is there to find. Words are not what matter. Do you think you could have dropped it out of your pocket when you were drunk?'

'I might have. Anything may happen when one is drunk as you so sincerely express it, much honoured prince. But I beg you to consider if I had dropped the article out of my pocket when I changed my coat, the dropped article would have been on the floor. Where is that article?'

'Did you put it away perhaps in a drawer, in a table?'

'I've looked through everything, I've rummaged everywhere, though I hadn't hidden it anywhere and hadn't opened any drawer, as I distinctly remember.'

'Have you looked in your cupboard?'

'The first thing I did was to look in the cupboard, and I've looked there several times already … And how could I have put it in the cupboard, truly honoured prince?'

'I must own, Lebedyev, this distresses me. Then someone must have found it on the floor?'

'Or picked it out of my pocket! Two alternatives.'

'This distresses me very much, for who … That's the question!'

'Not a doubt of it. That is the great question; you find the very word, the very notion, with wonderful exactitude, and you define the position, most illustrious prince.'

'Ach, Lukyan Timofeyitch, give over scoffing, this …'

'Scoffing!' cried Lebedyev, clasping his hands.

'Well, well, that's all right. I'm not angry. It's quite another matter … I'm afraid for people. Whom do you suspect?'

'A most difficult and complicated question! The servant I can't suspect; she was sitting in the kitchen. Nor my own children either …'

'I should think not!'

'One of the visitors then.'

'But is that possible?'

'Utterly, and in the highest degree impossible, but so it must be. I'm prepared to admit, however, I'm convinced, indeed that it is a case of theft; it could not have been committed in the evening when we were all together, but in the night or even in the morning by someone who passed the night here.'

'Ach, my God!'

'Burdovsky and Nikolay Ardalionovitch I naturally exclude; and they didn't even come into my room.'

'I should think so! Even if they had come! Who spent the night there?'

'Counting me, there were four of us in two adjoining rooms: the general, Keller, Mr Ferdyshtchenko, and I. So it must have been one of us four!'

'Of the three, then. But which?'

'I counted myself for correctness and accuracy, but you will admit, Prince, that I could hardly have robbed myself, though such cases do happen …'

'Ach, Lebedyev, how wearisome this is!' cried Myshkin. 'Come to the point. Why do you drag it out?'

'So that leaves three, and first, Mr Keller, an unsteady, drunken fellow, and in certain respects liberal, that is, as regards the pocket, but in other respects rather with chivalrous than liberal tendencies. He slept here in the sick man's room, and only in the night came in here on the pretext of the bare floor being hard to sleep on.'

'You suspect him?'

'I did suspect him. When at eight o'clock I jumped up like a madman and struck myself on the forehead with my hands, I at once waked the general, who was sleeping the sleep of innocence. Taking into consideration the strange disappearance of Ferdyshtenko, which of itself had aroused our suspicions, we both resolved to search Keller, who was lying sleeping like a top. We searched him thoroughly: he hadn't a farthing in his pockets, and we couldn't find one pocket without a hole in it. He'd a blue check cotton handkerchief in a disgusting condition; then a love-letter from a housemaid, threatening him and asking for money, and some bits of the article you heard. The general decided that he was innocent. To complete our investigation we waked the man himself by poking him violently. He could hardly understand what was the matter. He opened his mouth with a drunken air; the expression of his face was absurd and innocent, foolish even – it was not he!'

'Well, I am glad!' Myshkin sighed joyfully. 'I was so afraid for him!'

'You were afraid? Then you had some grounds for it?' Lebedyev screwed up his eyes.

'Oh, no, I meant nothing,' faltered Myshkin. 'I was very stupid to say I was afraid for him. Do me the favour, Lebedyev, not to repeat it to anyone…'

'Prince, Prince! Your words are in my heart… at the bottom of my heart! It is a tomb!…' said Lebedyev ecstatically, pressing his hat to his heart.

'Good, good … Then it must have been Ferdyshtchenko? That is, I mean you suspect Ferdyshtchenko?'

'Who else?' Lebedyev articulated softly, looking intently at Myshkin.

'To be sure … Who else is there … but I mean again, what evidence is there?'

'There is evidence. First his disappearance at seven o'clock, or before seven in the morning.'

'I know; Kolya told me that he went in to him, and said that he was going to spend the day with … I forget with whom … some friend of his.'

'Vilkin. So Nikolay Ardalionovitch has told you already?'

'He told me nothing about the theft.'

'He doesn't know, for I've kept it secret for the time being. And so he went to Vilkin's. It would seem there's nothing strange in a drunken man's going to see another drunken fellow like himself, even before daybreak, and without any reason. But here we have a clue: as he went he left the address … Now, Prince, follow up the question: why did he leave an address? Why did he purposely go out of his way to Nikolay Ardalionovitch to tell him, "I'm going to spend the day at Vilkin's." Who would care to know that he was going away and to Vilkin's? Why announce it? No, here we have the cunning, the cunning of a thief! It's as much as to say, "I purposely don't cover up my traces, so how can I be a thief? Would a thief leave word where he was going?" It's an excess of anxiety to avert suspicion, and to efface, so to say, his footprints in the sand ... Do you understand me, honoured prince?'

'I understand, I quite understand, but you know that's not enough.'

'A second clue. The track turns out to be a false one, and the address given was not exact. An hour later, that is, at eight o'clock, I was knocking at Vilkin's; he lives here in Fifth Street, and I know him too. There was no sign of Ferdyshtchenko, though I did get out of the servant who was stone deaf that someone really had knocked one hour before, and been pretty vigorous, too, so that he broke the bell. But the servant wouldn't open the door, not wishing to wake Mr Vilkin, and perhaps not anxious to get up herself. It does happen so.'

'And is that all your evidence? It's not much.'

'Prince, but who is there to suspect? Judge for yourself,' Lebedyev concluded, persuasively, and there was a gleam of something sly in his grin.

'You ought to search your rooms once more and look in every drawer,' Myshkin pronounced anxiously, after some pondering.

'I have searched them,' Lebedyev sighed, still more insinuatingly.

'H'm! ... And what did you want to change that coat for?' cried Myshkin, thumping the table in vexation.

'That's a question from an old-fashioned comedy. But, most kind prince, you take my misfortune too much to heart. I don't deserve it. I mean I alone don't deserve it, but you are worried about the criminal... About that good-for-nothing Mr Ferdyshtchenko?'

Well, yes. You certainly have worried me,' Myshkin cut him short absently and with dissatisfaction. 'So what do you intend to do ... if you are so convinced it is Ferdyshtchenko?'

'Prince, honoured prince, who else could it be?' said Lebedyev, wriggling with growing persuasiveness. 'You see, the lack of any other on whom to fix, and, so to say, the complete impossibility of suspecting anybody but Mr Ferdyshtchenko, is, so to say, another piece of evidence, the third against Mr Ferdyshtchenko. For, I ask again, who else could it be? You wouldn't have me suspect Mr Burdovsky, I suppose? Ha-ha-ha!'

'What nonsense!'

'Nor the general? Ha-ha-ha!'

'What folly!' Myshkin said, almost angrily, turning impatiently in his seat.

'Folly, and no mistake! Ha-ha-ha! And he amused me, too. I mean the general did! I went with him just now, while the track was fresh, to Vilkin's … and you must note that the general was even more struck than I was when, first thing after finding out my loss, I waked him up. His face changed. He turned red and pale, and at last flew into violent and righteous indignation beyond anything I should have suspected of him. He is a most honourable man! He tells lies continually, from weakness, but he's a man of the loftiest sentiments. A man, too, of no guile, who inspires the fullest confidence by his artlessness. I have told you already, honoured Prince, that I've more than a weakness, I've an affection for him. He suddenly stopped in the middle of the street, unbuttoned his coat, uncovered his chest. "Search me!" he said. "You searched Keller. Why don't you search me? That's only justice!" said he. And his arms and legs were trembling; he was quite pale; he looked so threatening. I laughed and said, "Listen, General, if anyone else had said such a thing about you, I'd have taken my head off with my own hands; I'd have put it on a big dish, and would have carried it myself to everyone who doubted you: do you see this head? I would say. I'll answer for him with this head, and not only so, but I'd go through fire for him. That's what I'd do," said I. Then he threw his arms round me, there in the street, burst into tears, trembling, and squeezed me so tight that it made me cough. "You're the only friend left me in my misfortunes," said he. Lie's a man of feeling! Then, of course, he told me an anecdote on the spot, of how he had once been suspected of stealing five hundred thousand roubles in his youth, but that next day he had thrown himself into a house on fire, and had dragged out of the flames the count who had suspected him, and Nina Alexandrovna, who was a girl at the time. The count embraced him, and so his marriage followed with Nina Alexandrovna. And next day, in the ruins of the house, they found a box with the lost money in it. It was an iron box of English make, with a secret lock, and it had somehow got under the floor so that no one noticed it, and it was only found after the fire. A complete lie. But when he spoke of Nina Alexandrovna he positively blubbered. A most honourable lady, Nina Alexandrovna, though she is angry with me.'

'You don't know her, do you?'

'Scarcely at all, but I should be heartily glad to, if only to justify myself to her. Nina Alexandrovna has a grievance against me, pretending that I lead her spouse astray into drunkenness. But far from leading him astray, I restrain him. I perhaps entice him away from more pernicious society. Besides, he's my friend and, I confess it to you, I won't desert him now. In fact, it's like this: where he goes there I go. For you can only manage him through his sensibility. He's quite given up visiting his captain's widow now, though he secretly longs for her, and even sometimes moans for her, especially in the morning when he puts on his boots. I don't know why it's at that time. He's no money, that's the trouble, and there's no going to see her without. Hasn't he asked you for money, honoured prince?'

'No, he hasn't.'

'He's ashamed to. He did mean to. He owned to me, in fact, that he meant to trouble you, but he's bashful, seeing you obliged him not long ago, and besides he thinks you wouldn't give it him. He told me this as his friend.'

'But you don't give him money?'

'Prince! Honoured prince! For that man I'd give not money, alone, but, so to say, my life ... But no, I don't want to exaggerate, not my life, but if it were a case of fever, an abscess, or even a cough, I'd be ready to bear it for him, I really would. For I look upon him as a great, though fallen man! Yes, indeed, not only money.'

'Then, you do give him money?'

'N-no; money I have not given him, and he knows himself that I won't give it him. But that's solely with a view to his elevation and reformation. Now he is insisting on coming to Petersburg with me. You see, I'm going to Petersburg to find Mr Ferdyshtchenko while the tracks are fresh. For I know for a fact that he is there by now. My general is all eagerness, but I suspect that he'll give me the slip in Petersburg to visit his widow. I'm letting him go on purpose, I must own, as we've agreed to go in different directions, as soon as we arrive, so as to catch Mr Ferdyshtchenko more easily. So I shall let him go, and then fall on him all of a sudden, like snow on the head, at the widow's – just to put him to shame, as a family man, and as a man, indeed, speaking generally.'

'Only don't make a disturbance, Lebedyev. For goodness' sake, don't make a disturbance,' Myshkin said in an undertone with great uneasiness.

'Oh, no, simply to put him to shame and see what sort of a face he makes, for one can judge a great deal from the face, honoured prince, especially with a man like that! Ah, Prince! Great as my own trouble is now, I cannot help thinking of him and the reformation of his morals. I have a great favour to ask of you, Prince, and I must confess it was expressly for that I have come to you. You are familiar with their home, you have even lived with them; so, if you would decide to assist me, honoured prince, entirely for the sake of the general and his happiness ...'

Lebedyev positively clasped his hands, as though in supplication.

'Assist you? Assist you how? Believe me, I am extremely anxious to understand you, Lebedyev.'

'It was entirely with that conviction I have come to you! We could act through Nina Alexandrovna, constantly watching over, and, so to speak, tracking his excellency in the bosom of his family. I don't know them, unluckily... moreover Nikolay Ardalionovitch adores you, so to speak, with every fibre of his youthful heart, he could help, perhaps...'

'No, to bring Nina Alexandrovna into this business ... Heaven forbid! Nor Kolya either ... But perhaps I still fail to understand you, Lebedyev.'

'Why, there's nothing to understand!' Lebedyev sprang up from his chair. 'Sympathy, sympathy, and tenderness – that's all the treatment our invalid requires. You, Prince, will allow me to think of him as an invalid?'

'Yes, it shows your delicacy and intelligence.'

'For the sake of clearness, I will explain to you by an example taken from my practice. You see the kind of man he is: his only weakness now is for that widow, who won't let him come without money, and at whose house I mean to discover him today, for his own good, but supposing it were not only the captain's widow, supposing he had committed an actual crime, or anyway a most dishonourable action (though of course he's incapable of it), even then, I tell you, you could do anything with him simply by generous tenderness, so to speak, for he is the most sensitive of men! Believe me, he wouldn't hold out for five days; he would speak out of himself; he would weep and confess, especially if one went to work cleverly, and in an honourable style, by means of his family's vigilant watch, and yours, over his comings and goings ... Oh, most noble-hearted prince!' Lebedyev leapt up in a sort of exaltation. 'Of course I'm not asserting that he ... I am ready to shed my last drop of blood, so to speak, for him at this moment, though his incontinence and drunkenness and the captain's widow, and all that, taken together, may lead him on to anything.'

'In such a cause I am always ready to assist,' said .Myshkin, getting up. 'Only, I confess, Lebedyev, I am dreadfully uneasy: tell me, do you still ... In one word you say yourself that you suspect Mr Ferdyshtchenko.'

'Why, who else? Who else, true-hearted prince?' Again Lebedyev clasped his hands ingratiatingly, with a sugary smile.

Myshkin frowned and got up from his place.

'Look here, Lukyan Timofeyitch, a mistake here would be a dreadful thing. This Ferdyshtchenko ... I should not like to speak ill of him ... This Ferdyshtchenko ... well, who knows, perhaps it is he!... I mean to say that perhaps he really is more capable of it than ... anyone else.'

Lebedyev opened his eyes and pricked up his ears.

'You see,' said Myshkin, stumbling and frowning more and more, as he walked up and down the verandah, trying not to look at Lebedyev – 'I was given to understand ... I was told about Mr Ferdyshtchenko that he was a man before whom one must be careful not to say anything ... too much – you understand? I say this to show that perhaps he really is more capable of it than anyone else ... so as not to make a mistake, that's the great thing – do you understand?'

'Who told you that about Mr Ferdyshtchenko?' Lebedyev caught him up instantly.

'Oh, it was whispered to me. I don't believe it myself, though ... I'm awfully vexed to be obliged to tell you ... I assure you I don't believe it myself ... it's some nonsense ... Oh dear, oh dear! How stupid I've been!'

'You see, Prince,' Lebedyev was positively quivering all over, 'this is important. This is extremely important now. I don't mean as to Mr Ferdyshtchenko, but as to the way this information reached you' – saying this Lebedyev ran backwards and forwards after Myshkin, trying to keep step with him – 'I've something to tell you now, Prince: just now, when I was going with the general to Vilkin's, after he told me about the fire, he was boiling over, of course, with anger, and suddenly began dropping the same hint to me about Mr Ferdyshtchenko, but so strangely and incoherently that I couldn't help asking him some questions, and in the end I was fully convinced that all the whole thing was solely an inspiration of his excellency's, solely arising, so to speak, front his generous heart. For he lies entirely because he can't restrain his sentimentality. Now, kindly consider this: if he told a he, and I'm sure he did, how could you have heard of it? It was the inspiration of the moment, you understand, Prince – so who could have told you? That's important, that... That's very important, and ... so to say ...'

'Kolya told me it just now, and he was told it this morning by his father whom he met at six o'clock – between six and seven – in the passage, when he came out for something.'

And Myshkin told the story in detail.

'Ah, well, that's what's called a clue.' Lebedyev laughed noiselessly, rubbing his hands. 'Just as I thought! That means that his excellency waked from his sleep of innocence at six o'clock, expressly to go and wake his darling son and warn him of the great danger of associating with Mr Ferdyshtchenko. What a dangerous man Mr Ferdyshtchenko must be! And what parental solicitude on the part of his excellency!'

'Listen, Lebedyev,' Myshkin was utterly confused, 'listen, keep quiet about it! Don't make an uproar! I beg you, Lebedyev, I entreat you. In that case I swear I'll help you, but on condition that nobody, nobody knows!'

'Rest assured, most noble-hearted, most sincere and generous prince,' cried Lebedyev in perfect exaltation – 'rest assured that all this will be buried in my loyal heart. I'd give every drop of my blood ... Illustrious prince, I'm a poor creature in soul and spirit, but ask any poor creature, any scoundrel even, which he'd rather have to do with, a scoundrel like himself, or a noble-hearted man like you, most true-hearted prince, he'll answer that he prefers the noble-hearted man, and that's the triumph of virtue! Goodbye honoured prince! Treading softly ... treading softly, and ... hand in hand.'

Chapter 10

Myshkin understood at last why he turned cold every time he touched those three letters, and why he had put off reading them until the evening. When, in the morning, he had sunk into a heavy sleep on the lounge in the verandah without having brought himself to open those three envelopes, he had another painful dream, and again the same 'sinful woman' came to him. Again she looked at him with tears sparkling on her long eyelashes, again beckoned him to follow her, and again he waked up, as he had done before, with anguish recalling her face. He wanted to go to *her* at once, but could not. At last, almost in despair he opened the letters and began reading them.

These letters too were like a dream. Sometimes one dreams strange, impossible and incredible dreams; on awakening you remember them and are amazed at a strange fact. You remember first of all that your reason did not desert you throughout the dream; you remember even that you acted very cunningly and logically through all that long, long time, while you were surrounded by murderers who deceived you, hid their intentions, behaved amicably to you while they had a weapon in readiness, and were only waiting for some signal; you remember how cleverly you deceived them at last, hiding from them; then you guessed that they'd seen through your deception and were only pretending not to know where you were hidden, but you were sly then and deceived them again; all this you remember clearly. But how was it that you could at the same time reconcile your reason to the obvious absurdities and impossibilities with which your dream was overflowing? One of your murderers turned into a woman before your eyes, and the woman into a little, sly, loathsome dwarf – and you accepted it all at once as an accomplished fact, almost without the slightest surprise, at the very time when, on another side, your reason was at its highest tension and showed extraordinary power, cunning, sagacity, and logic? And why, too, on waking up and fully returning to reality, do you feel almost every time, and sometimes with extraordinary intensity, that you have left something unexplained behind with the dream? You laugh at the absurdities of your dream, and at the same time you feel that interwoven with those absurdities some thought lies hidden, and a thought that is real, something belonging to your actual life, something that exists and has always existed in your heart. It's as though something new, prophetic, that you were awaiting, has been told you in your dream. Your impression is vivid, it may be joyful or agonising, but what it is, and what was said to you, you cannot understand or recall.

It was almost like this, after reading these letters. But even before he had unfolded them, Myshkin felt that the very fact of the existence and the possibility of them was like a nightmare. How could *she* have brought herself to write to *her,* he asked himself as he wandered about alone that evening (at times not knowing where he was going). How could she write of *that,* how could such a mad fantasy have arisen in her mind? But that fantasy had by now taken shape, and the most amazing thing of all for him was that, as he read those letters, he himself almost believed in the possibility and the justification of that fantasy. Yet, of course, it was a dream, a nightmare, a madness, but there was something in it tormentingly real, and agonisingly true, which justified the dream and the nightmare and the madness. For several hours together he seemed to be haunted by what he had read, every minute recalling fragments of it; brooding over them, pondering them. Sometimes he was even inclined to tell himself that he had foreseen all this and known it beforehand. It even seemed to him as though he had read it all before, some time very long ago, and that everything that he had grieved over since, everything that had been a pain or a dread to him had all lain hidden in those letters he had read long ago.

'When you open this letter' – so the first epistle began – 'you will look first of all at the signature. The signature will tell you all, and explain all, so there's no need to make any defence or explanation. If I were in any way on a level with you, you might be offended at such impertinence. But, who am I, and who are you? We are two such opposite extremes, and I am so infinitely below you that I cannot insult you, even if I wanted to.'

In another place she wrote, 'Don't consider my words the sick ecstasy of a sick mind, but you are for me perfection! I have seen you, I see you every day. I don't judge you; I have not come by reason to believe that you are perfection; I simply have faith in it. But one wrong I do you: I love you. Perfection should not be loved; one can only look on perfection as perfection. Is that not so? Yet I am in love with you. Though love makes equal, yet don't be uneasy; I have not put myself on an equality with you even in my most secret thought. I have written, "don't be uneasy." Can you possibly be uneasy? I would kiss your footprints if I could. Oh, I don't put myself on a level with you ... Look at my signature, you need only look at my signature!'

'I notice, however,' she wrote in another letter, 'that I join your name with his, and I have never once asked myself whether you love him. He loved you, though he had seen you only once. He thought of you as of "light". Those are his own words, I heard them from him. But without words I knew that you were "light" for him. I've lived a whole month beside him, and understood then that you love him too. To me you and he are one.'

'What does this mean?' she wrote again. 'Yesterday I passed by you and you seemed to blush. It can't be so. It was my fancy. If you were brought to the filthiest den and shown vice in its nakedness, you should not blush; you are too lofty to resent an insult. You can hate everyone base and low, not for your own sake, but for the sake of others, those whom they wrong. You no one can wrong. Do you know I think you even ought to love me? You are for me the same as for him – a ray of light. An angel cannot hate, cannot help loving. Can one love everyone, all men, all one's neighbours? I have often asked myself that question. Of course not. It's unnatural indeed. In abstract love for humanity one almost always loves no one but oneself. But that's impossible for us and you are different. How could you not love anyone, when you cannot compare yourself with anyone, and when you are above every insult, every personal resentment. You alone can love without egoism, you alone can love, not for yourself, but for the sake of him whom you love. Oh, how bitter it would be for me to find out that you feel shame or anger on account of me. That would be your ruin. You would sink to my level at once.

'Yesterday, after meeting you I went home and invented a picture. Artists always paint Christ as he appears in the Gospel stories. I would paint Him differently. I would imagine Him alone, His disciples must have sometimes left Him alone. I would leave only a little child beside Him. The child would be playing beside Him, perhaps be telling Him something in his childish words. Christ has been listening, but now He is thoughtful, His hand still resting unconsciously on the child's fair little head. He is looking into the distance at the horizon; thought, great as the whole world, dwells in His eyes. His face is sorrowful. The child leans silent with his elbow on Christ's knees, his cheek on his little hand and his head turned upwards and looks intently at Him, pondering as little children sometimes ponder. The sun is setting ... That is my picture. You are innocent, and in your innocence lies all your perfection. Oh, only remember that! What have you to do with my passion for you? You are now altogether mine, I shall be all my life beside you ... I shall soon die.'

Finally, in the very last letter stood the words:

'For God's sake, think nothing of me, and don't think that I am abasing myself by writing to you like this, or that I belong to the class of people who enjoy abasing themselves, even if from pride. No, I have my consolation, but it is difficult for me to explain it to you. It would be difficult for me to explain it clearly even to myself, although it torments me that I cannot. But I know that I cannot abase myself, even from an access of pride; and of self-abasement from purity of heart I am incapable. And so I do not abase myself at all.

'Why do I so want to bring you together – for your sake, or for my own? For my own sake, of course; for myself, of course, it would solve all my difficulties, I have told myself so long ago. I have heard that your sister Adelaïda said of my portrait then that with such beauty one might turn the world upside down. But I have renounced tire world. Does it amuse you to hear that from me, meeting me decked in lace and diamonds, in the company of drunkards and profligates? Don't mind that, I have almost ceased to exist and I know it. God knows what in my stead lives within me. I read that every day in two terrible eyes which are always gazing at me, even when they are not before me. Those eyes are *silent* now (they are always silent), but I know their secret. His house is gloomy, and there is a secret in it. I'm sure that he has, hidden in his box, a razor, wrapped in silk like that murderer in Moscow, he too lived in the same house with his mother, and kept a razor wrapped in silk to cut a throat with. All the time I was in their house, I kept fancying that somewhere under the floor there might be a corpse hidden there by his father perhaps, wrapped in American leather, like the corpse in the Moscow case, and surrounded in the same way with jars of Zhdanov's fluid. I could show you the corner. He is always silent: but I know he loves me so much that he can't help hating me. Your marriage and ours are to take place together: we have fixed that. I have no secrets from him. I should kill him from terror … But he will kill me first. He laughed just now and said I was raving: he knows I am writing to you.'

And there was much, much more of the same kind of raving in those letters. One of them, the second, written in a small hand, covered two large sheets of notepaper.

At last Myshkin came out of the darkness of the park, where he had been wandering a long time, as he had the previous night. The clear limpid night seemed to him lighter than ever.

'Can it still be so early?' he thought. (He had forgotten to take his watch.) He fancied he heard music somewhere in the distance. 'It must be at the station,' he thought, 'they've certainly not gone there today.' As he made the reflection, he saw that he was standing close to the Epanchins' villa. He knew quite well that he was bound to find himself there at last, and with a beating heart he went up to the steps of the verandah. No one met him. The verandah was empty. He waited, and opened the door into the room. 'They never shut that door,' the thought flickered through his mind, but the room was empty too. It was almost dark in it.

He stood still in the middle of the room in perplexity. Suddenly the door opened and Alexandra came in, with a candle in her hand. On seeing Myshkin she was surprised and stopped short before him enquiringly. Obviously she was simply crossing the room from one door to the other, with no idea of finding anyone there.

'How do you come here?' she asked at last.

'I… came in …'

Maman is not quite well, nor Aglaia either. Adelaïda is going to bed, I'm going too. We've been at home by ourselves all the evening. Papa and the prince are in Petersburg.'

'I've come … I've come to you … now…'

'Do you know what the time is?'

'N-no.'

'Half-past twelve. We always go to bed by one.'

'Why, I thought it was half-past nine.'

'It doesn't matter!' she laughed. 'And why didn't you come in before? We may have been expecting you.'

'I… thought…' he faltered, moving away.

'Goodbye. Tomorrow I shall make them all laugh.'

He went homewards by the road that encircled the park. His heart was beating, his thoughts were in a maze, and everything round him became like a dream. And suddenly, just as yesterday he had twice waked up at the same dream, the same apparition rose again before him. The same woman came out of the park and stood before him, as though she had been waiting for him there. He started, and stood still. She snatched his hand and pressed it tight. 'No, this was not an apparition!'

And at last she stood before him, face to face for the first time since their parting. She was saying something to him, but he looked at her in silence; his heart was too full, and ached with anguish. Oh, never could he forget that meeting with her and he always remembered it with the same anguish. She sank on her knees before him on the spot, in the street, like one demented. He stepped back in horror, and she tried to catch his hand to kiss it, and just as in his dream that night, the tears glistened on her long eyelashes.

'Stand up! Stand up!' he said in a frightened whisper, raising her. 'Stand up, at once!'

'Are you happy? Happy?' she asked. 'Only say one word to me, are you happy now? Today, this minute? Have you been with her? What did she say?'

She did not get up. She did not hear him. She questioned him hurriedly, and was in haste to speak, as though she were being pursued.

'I'm going tomorrow as you told me. I won't ... It's the last time I shall see you. The last time! Now it's absolutely the last time!'

'Calm yourself, stand up!' he said in despair.

She looked greedily at him, clutching at his hands.

'Goodbye,' she said at last, she got up and went quickly away from him, almost running. Myshkin saw that Rogozhin had suddenly appeared beside her, that he had taken her arm, and was leading her away.

'Wait a minute, Prince,' cried Rogozhin, 'I'll be back in five minutes.'

Five minutes later he did, in fact, return. Myshkin was waiting for him at the same place.

'I've put her in the carriage,' he said. 'It's been waiting there at the corner since ten o'clock. She knew you'd be at the young lady's all the evening. I told her exactly what you wrote to me today. She won't write to the young lady again, she's promised; and she'll go away from here tomorrow as you wish. She wanted to see you for the last time, though you refused her. We've been waiting for you here, on that seat there, to catch you as you came back.'

'Did she take you with her of her own accord?'

'Why not?' grinned Rogozhin. 'I saw what I knew before. You've read the letters I suppose?'

'Have you really read them?' asked Myshkin, struck by that idea.

'Rather! She showed me each one of them herself. About the razor, too, do you remember, ha-ha!'

'She's mad!' cried Myshkin, wringing his hands.

'Who knows about that? Perhaps not,' Rogozhin said softly, as though to himself. Myshkin did not answer.

'Well, goodbye,' said Rogozhin. 'I'm going away tomorrow too: don't remember evil against me! And I say, brother,' he added, turning quickly, 'why didn't you answer her question: are you happy or not?'

'No, no, no!' cried Myshkin, with unspeakable sadness.

'I should think not, indeed,' laughed Rogozhin maliciously, and he went away without looking back.

PART FOUR

Chapter 1

About a week had passed since the meeting of the two persons of our story on the green seat. One bright morning about half-past ten Varvara Ardalionovna Ptitsyn was returning from visiting some friends, plunged in mournful reflection.

There are people whom it is difficult to describe completely in their typical and characteristic aspect. These are the people who are usually called 'ordinary,' 'the majority,' and who do actually make up the vast majority of mankind. Authors for the most part attempt in their tales and novels to select and represent vividly and artistically types rarely met with in actual life in their entirety, though they are nevertheless almost more real than real life itself. Podkolyosin as a type is perhaps exaggerated, but not at all unreal. What numbers of clever people after being introduced by Gogol to Podkolyosin at once discovered that tens and hundreds of their friends and acquaintances were extraordinarily like him. They knew before reading Gogol that their friends were like Podkolyosin, only they did not know what name to give them. In real life, extremely few bridegrooms jump out of window just before their wedding, for, apart from other considerations, it's not a convenient mode of escape. Yet how many men, even intelligent and virtuous persons, on the eve of their wedding day have been ready to acknowledge at the bottom of their hearts that they were Podkolyosins. Not all husbands exclaim at every turn *'Tu l'a voulu, Georges Dandin!'* But how many millions and billions of times that cry from the heart has been uttered by husbands all the world over after the honeymoon, or – who knows? — even perhaps the day after the wedding!

Without entering into deeper considerations, we will simply point out that in actual life typical characteristics are apt to be watered down, and that Georges Dandins and Podkolyosins exist and are moving before our eyes every day, only in a less concentrated form. With the reservation that Georges Dandin in full perfection, as Moliere has portrayed him, may also be met with in real life, though not frequently, we will conclude our reflections, which are beginning to be suggestive of newspaper criticism.

Yet the question remains! What is an author to do with ordinary people, absolutely 'ordinary,' and how can he put them before his readers so as to make them at all interesting? It is impossible to leave them out of fiction altogether, for commonplace people are at even moment the chief and essential links in the chain of human affairs; if we leave them out, we lose all semblance of truth. To fill a novel completely with types or, more simply, to make it interesting with strange and incredible characters, would be to make it unreal and even uninteresting. To our thinking a writer ought to seek out interesting and instructive features even among commonplace people. When, for instance, the very nature of some commonplace persons lies just in their perpetual and invariable commonplaceness, or better still, when, in spite of the most strenuous efforts to escape from the daily round of commonplaceness and routine, they end by being left invariably for ever chained to the same routine, such people acquire a typical character of their own – the character of a commonplaceness desirous above all things of being independent and original without the faintest possibility of becoming so.

To this class of 'commonplace' or 'ordinary' people belong certain persons of my tale, who have hitherto, I must confess, been insufficiently explained to the reader. Such were Varvara Ardalionovna Ptitsyn, her husband, Mr Ptitsyn, and her brother, Gavril Ardalionovitch.

There is, indeed, nothing more annoying than to be, for instance, wealthy, of good family, nice-looking, fairly intelligent, and even good-natured, and yet to have no talents, no special faculty, no peculiarity even, not one idea of one's own, to be precisely 'like other people.' To have a fortune, but not the wealth of Rothschild; to be of an honourable family, but one which has never distinguished itself in any way; to have a pleasing appearance expressive of nothing in particular; to have a decent education, but to have no idea what use to make of it; to have intelligence, but *no ideas of one's own* to have a good heart, but without any greatness of soul; and so on and so on. There is an extraordinary multitude of such people in the world, far more than appears. They may, like all other people, be divided into two classes: some of limited intelligence; others much cleverer. The first are happier. Nothing is easier for 'ordinary' people of limited intelligence than to imagine themselves exceptional and original and to revel in that delusion without the slightest misgiving. Some of our young ladies have only to crop their hair, put on blue spectacles, and dub themselves Nihilists, to persuade themselves at once that they have immediately gained 'convictions' of their own. Some men have only to feel the faintest stirring of some kindly and humanitarian emotion to persuade themselves at once that no one feels as they do, that they stand in the foremost rank of culture. Some have only to meet with some idea by hearsay, or to read some stray page, to believe at once that it is their own opinion and has sprung spontaneously from their own brain. The impudence of simplicity, if one may so express it, is amazing in such cases. It is almost incredible, but yet often to be met with. This impudence of simplicity, this unhesitating confidence of the stupid man in himself and his talents, is superbly depicted by Gogol in the wonderful character of Lieutenant Pirogov. Pirogov has no doubt that he is a genius, superior indeed to any genius. He is so positive of this that he never questions it; and, indeed, he questions nothing. The great writer is forced in the end to chastise him for the satisfaction of the outraged moral feeling of the reader, but, seeing that the great man simply shook himself after the castigation and fortified himself by consuming a pie, he flung up his hands in amazement and left his readers to make the best of it. I always regretted that Gogol took his great Pirogov from so humble a rank, for he was so self-satisfied that nothing could be easier for him than to imagine himself, as his epaulettes grew thicker and more twisted with years and promotion, an extraordinary military genius; or rather, not imagine it, but simply take it for granted. Since he had been made a general, he must have been a military genius! And how many such have made terrible blunders afterwards on the field of battle! And how many Pirogovs there have been among our writers, savants and propagandists! I say 'have been,' but of course we have them still.

Gavril Ardalionovitch Ivolgin belonged to the second category. He belonged to the class of the 'much cleverer' people, though he was infected from head to foot with the desire for originality. But that class, as we observed above, is far less happy than the first, for the *clever* 'commonplace' man, even if he occasionally or even always fancies himself a man of genius and originality, yet preserves the worm of doubt gnawing in his heart, which in some cases drives the *clever* man to utter despair. Even if he submits, he is completely poisoned by his vanity's being driven inwards. But we have taken an extreme example. In the vast majority of these *clever* people, things do not end so tragically. Their liver is apt to be affected in their declining years, that's all. But before giving in and humbling themselves, such men sometimes play the fool for years, all from the desire of originality. There are strange instances of it, indeed; an honest man is sometimes, for the sake of being original, ready to do something base. It sometimes happens that one of these luckless men is not only honest but good, is the guardian angel of his family, maintains by his labour outsiders as well as his own kindred, and yet can never be at rest all his life! The thought that he has so well fulfilled his duties is no comfort or consolation to him; on the contrary, it irritates him. 'This is what I've wasted all my life on,' he says; 'this is what has fettered me, hand and foot; this is what has hindered me from doing something great! Had it not been for this, I should certainly have discovered – gunpowder or America, I don't know precisely what, but I would certainly have discovered it!' What is most characteristic of these gentlemen is that they can never find out for certain what it is that they are destined to discover and what they are within an ace of discovering. But their sufferings, their longings for what was to be discovered, would have sufficed for a Columbus or a Galileo.

Gavril Ardalionovitch had taken the first step on that road, but he was only at its beginning; he had many years of playing the fool before him. A profound and continual consciousness of his own lack of talent, and at the same time the overwhelming desire to prove to himself that he was a man of great independence, had rankled in his heart almost from his boyhood up. He was a young man of violent and envious cravings, who seemed to have been positively born with his nerves overwrought. The violence of his desires he took for strength. His passionate craving to distinguish himself sometimes led him to the brink of most ill-considered actions, but our hero was always at the last moment too sensible to take the final plunge. That drove him to despair. He could perhaps have made up his mind to anything extremely base to attain what he dreamed of. But as fate would have it, he always turned out to be too honest for any great meanness. (Small meannesses he was, however, prepared for.) He looked with loathing and hatred on the downfall and poverty of his family. He treated even his mother haughtily and contemptuously, though he knew perfectly well that his mother's reputation and character were the pivot on which his future rested.

When he entered General Epanchin's house he said to himself at once, 'Since I must be mean, let me be so thoroughly, if only I win my game' – and was scarcely ever thoroughly mean. And why should he imagine that he would certainly need to be mean? Of Aglaia he was simply frightened at the time, but he kept on with her on the off-chance, though he never seriously believed that she would stoop to him. Afterwards at the time of his affair with Nastasya Filippovna, he suddenly imagined that money would be the means of attaining *everything*. 'If I must be mean, well then I will,' he repeated to himself every day with satisfaction, but with a certain dismay. 'If one must be mean, let us be first-rate at it,' he urged himself continually. 'Commonplace people are afraid to be, but I am not.'

Losing Aglaia and crushed by circumstances, he completely lost heart, and actually brought Myshkin the money flung him by a mad woman to whom it had been given by a madman. A thousand times afterwards he regretted having returned that money, though he was continually priding himself upon it. He did actually shed tears for three days while Myshkin was in Petersburg, but in those three days he grew to hate the prince because the latter looked at him too compassionately, though 'not everyone would have had the strength' for such a deed as returning that money. But the frank confession to himself that his misery was due to nothing but the continual mortification of his vanity distressed him horribly.

Only long afterwards he saw and realised what a different ending an affair with such a strange and innocent creature as Aglaia might have had. He was consumed by regrets; he threw up his post and sank into despondency and dejection. He lived with his father and mother in Ptitsyn's house and at the latter's expense, and openly despised Ptitsyn, although he followed his advice and had the sense almost always to ask it. Gavril Ardalionovitch was angry, for instance, with Ptitsyn for not aiming at becoming a Rothschild. 'If you go in for usury, do it thoroughly – squeeze people, coin money out of them, show willpower, be a king among the Jews.'

Ptitsyn was unassuming and quiet; he did nothing but smile. But once he thought it necessary to have a serious explanation with Ganya, and he carried out the task with a certain degree of dignity. He had proved to Ganya that he was doing nothing dishonest and that he had no right to call him a grasping Jew; that it was not his fault that money was so valuable; that he was acting honestly and justly, and that in reality he was only an intermediary in these affairs, and that finally, thanks to his accuracy in business, he was already favourably known to first-rate people and his business was increasing. 'I shall never be a Rothschild, and I don't want to be,' he said, smiling; 'but I shall have a house in Liteyny, perhaps two even, and there I shall stop.'

'And who knows, perhaps even three,' he thought to himself, but he never uttered this aloud, he concealed that daydream.

Nature loves such people and is kind to them; she will reward Ptitsyn not with three but with four houses, and just because he has realised from childhood that he will never become a Rothschild. But beyond four houses nature will not go, and Ptitsyn's success will end there.

Gavril Ardalionovitch's sister was quite a different person. She too was possessed with strong desires, but they were rather persistent than impulsive. She had plenty of common-sense in emergencies, and was not devoid of it indeed in everyday life. It is true that she also was one of the ordinary people who dream of being original; yet she very soon found out that she had no particular originality, and did not take it too much to heart, perhaps – who knows? – from pride of a sort. She took her first practical step with great decision in marrying Ptitsyn. But in getting married she did not say to herself, 'If I must be mean, I will be mean so long as I gain my end,' as her brother Ganya would certainly have said to himself, and may possibly have said aloud to her, when he gave his approval as elder brother to the match. Quite the contrary, in fact: Varvara Ardalionovna married after having convinced herself that her future husband was a pleasant, unassuming, almost educated man, who could never be induced to do anything very dishonourable. As for minor acts of meanness, Varvara Ardalionovna did not worry about such trifles; and, in fact, one can find such trifles everywhere. It's no good looking for an ideal being! She knew, besides, that by marrying she would provide a refuge for her mother, her father and her brothers. Seeing her brother in trouble, she wanted to help him in spite of all their previous misunderstandings.

Ptitsyn sometimes urged Ganya, in a friendly way, of course, to take another post. 'You despise generals and being a general,' he would say to him sometimes in joke; 'but mind, "they" will all finish by being generals; if you live long enough you will see.'

'But what makes them think that I despise generals and being a general?' Ganya thought ironically to himself.

For her brother's sake Varvara Ardalionovna made up her mind to enlarge her circle of acquaintance. She managed to get a footing at the Epanchins'. The memories of childhood stood her in good stead there, for she and Ganya had played with the Epanchins as children. We may observe here that if Varvara Ardalionovna had visited the Epanchins in pursuit of some fantastic dream, by that very fact she would have excluded herself from that class of people with whom she mentally ranked herself. But she was not pursuing a dream; she was working on a fairly firm basis: she was reckoning on the peculiarities of the Epanchin family. She was never tired of studying Aglaia's character. The task she set before herself was to bring those two, Aglaia and her brother, together again. Possibly she actually did attain this object to some extent; possibly she made blunders, building perhaps too much on her brother and expecting from him what he could not under any circumstances have given. In any case she behaved with considerable art at the Epanchins': for weeks together she made no allusion to her brother; she was always extremely truthful and sincere; she behaved simply but with dignity. As for the depths of her conscience, she was not afraid to look into them, and she did not reproach herself for anything in the least. It was that that gave her power. There was only one thing she noticed in herself, that she too was spiteful; that she too had a great deal of *amour propre,* and one might almost say of mortified vanity. She noticed it particularly at certain moments, especially almost every time she was walking home from the Epanchins'.

And just now she was on her way back from them, and, as we have said already, she was dejected and preoccupied. A shade of bitter mockery was apparent in her dejection. At Pavlovsk Ptitsyn occupied a roomy but not very attractive-looking house in a dusty street, which would within a short period become his own property, so that he was already negotiating for the sale of it. As she was going up the steps, Varvara Ardalionovna heard an extraordinary noise from upstairs and caught the voices of her father and brother shouting at one another. Going to the drawing-room and seeing Ganya running to and fro, white with fury and almost tearing his hair, she frowned and, with a weary air, sank on the sofa without taking off her hat. Knowing that if she let a minute pass without asking her brother why he was in such a state, he would certainly be angry with her, Varya hastened to observe, in the form of a question: 'The usual story?'

'The usual story indeed!' cried Ganya. 'The usual story! No! The devil only knows what is happening here, it's not the same as usual. The old man is getting perfectly frantic... Mother's in floods of tears. Upon my word, Varya, I'll turn him out, say what you like, or ... or I'll go away myself,' he added, probably recollecting that it was not possible to turn anyone out of another person's house.

'You must make allowances,' murmured Varya.

'What allowances? For whom?' cried Ganya, firing up. 'For his filthy habits? No, you may say what you like, that's impossible. Impossible, impossible, impossible! And what a way to behave: he is in fault, and it makes him all the more stuck up. "The gate is not good enough for him, we must pull the wall down!" Why are you sitting there like that? You don't look yourself.'

'I look as I always do,' Varya answered with displeasure.

Ganya looked at her more carefully.

'Have you been there?' he asked suddenly.

'Yes.'

'Stay, shouting again! What a disgrace, and at such a time too!'

'What sort of time? It's no such special time.'

Ganya looked more intently than ever at his sister.

'Have you found out something more?' he asked.

'Nothing unexpected, anyway. I found out that it's all a fact. My husband was nearer the truth than either of us; it's turned out just as he predicted from the beginning. Where is he?'

'Not at home? What's turned out?'

'The prince is formally betrothed to her. The thing is settled. The elder girls told me. Aglaia consents; they have even left off keeping it dark. (There's always been so much mystery till now.) Adelaïda's wedding will be put off again so that the two weddings may be on one day. Such a romantic notion! Quite poetical! You'd better be writing a poem for the occasion than running about the room to no purpose. Princess Byelokonsky will be there this evening; she's come in the nick of time; there are to be visitors. He is to be presented to the Princess Byelokonsky, though she knows him already. I believe the engagement will be publicly announced. They are only afraid he may let something drop or break something when he walks into the drawing-room, or else flop down himself; it's quite in his line.'

Ganya listened very attentively, but to his sister's surprise this news, which ought to have overwhelmed him, seemed to have by no means an overwhelming effect on him.

'Well, that was clear,' he said after a moment's thought. 'So it's the end,' he added, with a strange smile, glancing slyly into his sister's face and still walking up and down the room, but much more quietly.

'It's a good thing you take it like a philosopher. I am glad, really,' said Varya.

'Yes, it's a load off one's mind; off yours, anyway.'

'I think I've served you sincerely without criticising or annoying you. I didn't ask you what sort of happiness you expected with Aglaia.'

'Why, was I expecting ... happiness from Aglaia?'

'Oh, please don't discuss it philosophically! Of course you were. It's all over and there's nothing more for us to do. We've been fools. I must own I could never take the thing quite seriously. It was simply on the off-chance that I took it up. I was reckoning on her ridiculous character, and my chief object was to please you. It was ten to one it would come to nothing. I don't know to this day what you have been hoping for.'

'Now your husband and you will be trying to make me get a job; you'll give me lectures on perseverance and strength of will, and not despising small profits, and all the rest of it. I know it by heart,' laughed Ganya.

'He has something new in his mind,' Varya thought to herself.

'How are they taking it? Are they pleased, the father and mother?' Ganya asked suddenly.

'N-no, I think not. However, you can judge for yourself. Ivan Fyodorovitch is pleased. The mother is uneasy; she's always viewed him with dislike as a suitor, we know that.'

'I don't mean that. He is an impossible suitor, unthinkable, that's evident. I was talking about their attitude now. What's their line now? Has she given her formal consent?'

'She hasn't so far said no, that's all, but that's all one could expect from her. You know how insanely shy and bashful she still is. When she was a child she would creep into a cupboard and sit there for two or three hours, simply to escape seeing visitors. Though she has grown such a maypole, she is just the same now. You know, I believe there really is something in it even on her side. They say she is laughing at the prince from morning till night, so as to hide her feelings, but she must manage to say something on the sly to him every day, for he looks as though he were in heaven, he is beaming. He is fearfully funny, they say. I heard it from them. I fancied too that they laughed at me to my face, the elder girls.'

Ganya at last began to frown; perhaps Varya went on enlarging on the subject on purpose to get at his real view. But they heard a shout again upstairs.

'I'll turn him out!' Ganya fairly roared, as though glad to vent his annoyance.

'And then he will go disgracing us everywhere, as he did yesterday.'

'Yesterday? What do you mean? Why, did he ... Ganya seemed dreadfully alarmed all of a sudden.

'Oh dear, didn't you know?' Varya pulled herself up.

'What! Surely it isn't true that he has been there?' cried Ganya, flushing crimson with shame and anger. 'Good heavens! Why you've come from there! Have you heard something about it? Has the old man been there? Has he, or not?'

And Ganya rushed to the door. Varya flew at him and clutched him with both hands.

'What are you about? Where are you going?' she said. 'If you let him out now, he will do more harm than ever; he will go to everyone.'

'What did he do there? What did he say?'

'Well, they couldn't tell me themselves, they hadn't understood it; he only frightened them all. He went to see Ivan Fyodorovitch; he was out. He asked to see Lizaveta Prokofyevna. First he asked her about a post – wanted to get a job; and then he began complaining of us, of me, of my husband, of you especially ... He talked a lot of stuff.'

'You couldn't find out what?' Ganya was quivering hysterically.

'How could I? He scarcely knew what he was saying himself; and perhaps they did not tell me everything.'

Ganya clutched at his head and ran to the window. Varya sat down at the other window.

'Aglaia is an absurd creature,' she observed suddenly. 'She stopped me and said "Please give your parents my special respects. I shall certainly have an opportunity of seeing your father one of these days." .And she said that so seriously; it was awfully queer...'

'Not in derision? Not in derision?'

'That's just it, it wasn't. That is what was so queer.'

'Does she know about the old man, or not, what do you think?'

'There's no doubt in my mind that they don't know in the family. But you've given me an idea: Aglaia perhaps does know. She is the only one who does know perhaps, for her sisters were surprised too when she sent her greeting to father so seriously. And why to him particularly? If she does know, the prince must have told her.'

'It's not difficult to guess who told her! A thief! It's the last straw. A thief in our family, "the head of the house"!'

'That's nonsense!' cried Varya, losing patience. 'A drunken prank, that's all. And who made up the story? Lebedyev, the prince ... they are a nice lot themselves; they are wise people! Don't believe a word of it.'

'The old man is a thief and a drunkard,' Ganya went on bitterly, 'I am a beggar, my sister's husband is a moneylender – an alluring prospect for Aglaia! A lovely state of things and no mistake!'

'That sister's husband who is a moneylender is ...'

'Keeping me, you mean? Don't mince matters, please.'

'Why are you so cross?' said Varya, restraining herself. 'You are a regular schoolboy, you don't understand anything. You think all this might injure you in Aglaia's eyes? You don't know her. She'd refuse the most eligible suitor and run off delighted with some student to starve in a garret – that's her dream! You've never been able to understand how interesting you would have become in her eyes, if you had been able to bear our surroundings with pride and fortitude. The prince has hooked her, in the first place, because he wasn't fishing for her; and secondly, because he is looked upon by everyone as an idiot. The very fact that she is upsetting her family about him is a joy to her. Ah, you don't understand!'

'Well, we shall see whether I understand or not,' Ganya muttered enigmatically. 'Still, I shouldn't like her to know about the old man. I thought Myshkin would have been able to hold his tongue. He made Lebedyev keep quiet; he didn't want to speak out to me when I insisted on knowing.'

'So you see that, apart from him, it has leaked out. And what does it matter to you now? What are you hoping for? And even if you had any hope left, it would only make her look on you as a martyr.'

'Well, even she would be a coward about a scandal, in spite of all her romantic notions. It's all up to a certain point, and everyone draws the line somewhere. You are all alike.'

'Aglaia would be a coward?' Varya fired up, looking contemptuously at her brother. 'You've got a mean little soul! You are all a worthless lot. She may be absurd and eccentric, but she is a thousand times more generous than any of us.'

'Well, never mind, never mind, don't be cross,' Ganya murmured again complacently.

'I am sorry for mother, that's all,' Varya went on. 'I am so afraid this scandal about father may reach her ears. Ach! I am afraid it will!'

'No doubt it has reached her,' observed Ganya.

Varya had risen to go upstairs to Nina Alexandrovna, but, stopping short, she looked attentively at her brother.

'Who could have told her?'

'Ippolit, most likely. It would have been the greatest satisfaction to him to report the matter to mother, as soon as he moved here, I expect.'

'But how does he know? Tell me that, pray. The prince and Lebedyev made up their minds to tell nobody; Kolya knows nothing.'

'Ippolit? He found it out for himself. You can't imagine what a sly beast he is; what a gossip he is; how quick he is at sniffing out anything bad, any sort of scandal. You may not believe it, but I am sure he has succeeded in getting a hold on Aglaia; and if he hasn't, he will. Rogozhin has got to know him too. How is it the prince does not notice it? And how eager he is to score off me now! He looks upon me as his personal enemy, I've seen that a long time – why and with what object, since he is dying, I can't make out. But I'll get the better of him. You will see that I'll score off him, not he off me!'

'What made you, then, entice him here, if you hate him so? And is he worth scoring off?'

'You advised me to entice him here.'

'I thought he would be of use. But do you know that he has fallen in love with Aglaia himself now, and has been writing to her? They asked me about him … He may even have written to Lizaveta Prokofyevna.'

'He is not dangerous in that way,' said Ganya, with a spiteful laugh, 'but most likely you are mistaken. It's very possible he is in love, for he is a boy. But… he wouldn't write anonymous letters to the old lady. He is such a spiteful, insignificant, self-satisfied mediocrity!… I am convinced, I know, that he represented me to her as a scheming adventurer; that's what he began with. I must own that, like a fool, I talked to him freely at first. I thought that, simply to revenge himself on the prince, he'd work in my interests. He is such a sly beast! At, I have seen through him now completely! And he heard about that theft from his mother, the captain's widow. If the old man did bring himself to it, it was for that woman's sake. He suddenly told me, apropos of nothing, that the general had promised his mother four hundred roubles; and he told me that without the least ceremony, absolutely apropos of nothing. Then I understood it all. And he peered right in my face with a sort of glee. He's told mother too, most likely, for the mere pleasure of breaking her heart. And why on earth doesn't he die, pray? He promised to die in three weeks, and here he is getting fatter! He is coughing less; he said himself last night that he hadn't brought up blood for two days.'

'Turn him out.'

'I don't hate him, I despise him!' Ganya pronounced proudly. 'Well, yes, I do hate him then, I do,' he shouted suddenly with extraordinary fury, 'and I'll tell him so to his face, even if he lies dying on his bed! If you'd read his confession – good Lord, the *naïveté* of its insolence! He is a regular Lieutenant Pirogov, a Nozdryov turned tragic, and, above all, he is a puppy! Oh, how I should have enjoyed thrashing him, simply to surprise him! Now he wants to pay everyone out because he failed to … But what's that? A noise again? What can it be, really? I won't put up with it, Ptitsyn!' he cried to his brother-in-law who came into the room. 'What's the meaning of this? What are we coming to? This is … this is …'

But the noise was quickly coming nearer, the door was suddenly flung open, and old Ivolgin, wrathful, crimson in the face, and beside himself with agitation, attacked Ptitsyn too. The old man was followed by Nina Alexandrovna, Kolya and last of all Ippolit.

Chapter 2

It was five days since Ippolit had moved to Ptitsyn's house. This had happened naturally, without any break between him and Myshkin. Far from quarrelling, they appeared to part as friends. Gavril Ardalionovitch, who had been so antagonistic to Ippolit on that evening, came of himself, three days afterwards, however to see him, probably moved to do so by some sudden idea. Rogozhin too, for some reason, took to visiting the invalid. It seemed to Myshkin at first that it would be better for the 'poor boy himself if he were to move out of his (Myshkin's) house. But at the dine of his removal Ippolit observed that he was going to stay with Ptitsyn, 'who was so kind as to give him a corner,' and, as though purposely, he never once put it that he was going to stay with Ganya, though it was Ganya who had insisted on his being received into the house. Ganya noticed it at the time, and it rankled in his heart.

He was right when he told his sister that the invalid was better. Ippolit was somewhat better than before, and the improvement was evident at the first glance. He came into the room after everyone else, with a sarcastic and malignant smile on his face. Nina Alexandrovna came in, very much frightened. She was thinner and had greatly changed during the last six months; since she had moved to her daughter's house on the latter's marriage, she had almost given up outwardly taking any part in her children's affairs. Kolya was worried and seemed puzzled; there was a great deal he did not understand in the 'general's madness,' as he expressed it, being, of course, unaware of the reasons of this last upset in the house. But it was clear to him that his father was quarrelling everywhere and all day long, and had suddenly so changed that he was not like the same man. It made him uneasy, too, to see that the old man had, for the last three days, entirely given up drinking. He knew that his father had fallen out and even quarrelled with Lebedyev and Myshkin. Kolya had just returned home with a pint bottle of vodka, paid for out of his own pocket.

'Really, mother,' he had assured Nina Alexandrovna upstairs, 'really it's better to let him drink. It's three days since he touched a drop, he must be feeling wretched. It's really better; I used to take it him to the prison.'

The general flung the door wide open, and stood in the doorway, seeming to quiver with indignation.

'Sir!' he shouted in a voice of thunder to Ptitsyn. 'If you have really decided to sacrifice to a milksop and an atheist a venerable old man, your father, that is, at least, the father of your wife, who has served his sovereign, I will never set my foot within your doors from this hour. Choose, Sir, choose at once; it's either me or that... screw! Yes, a screw! I said it without thinking, but he is a screw, for he probes into my soul with a screw, and with no sort of respect... With a screw!'

'Don't you mean a corkscrew?' Ippolit put in.

'No, not a corkscrew! For I stand before you, a general, not a bottle. I have decorations, the rewards of distinction ... and you have less than nothing. It's either he or I. Make up your mind, Sir, at once, at once!' he shouted frantically again to Ptitsyn.

At that moment Kolya set a chair for him and he sank on to it exhausted.

'You really had better... have a nap,' muttered Ptitsyn, overwhelmed.

'Fancy him threatening!' Ganya said to his sister in an undertone.

'Have a nap!' shouted the general. 'I am not drunk, Sir, and you insult me. I see,' he went on, getting up, 'that everything is against me here, everything and everybody. Enough! I am going... But you may be sure, Sir, you may be sure ...'

He was not allowed to finish. They made him sit down again; and began begging him to be calm. Ganya, in a fury, retired into a corner. Nina Alexandrovna was trembling and weeping.

'But what have I done to him? What's he complaining of?' cried Ippolit, grinning.

'As though you had done nothing!' Nina Alexandrovna observed suddenly. 'It's particularly shameful of you ... and inhuman to torment an old man ... and in your place, too.'

'To begin with, what is my place, Madam? I respect you very much, you personally, but…'

'He's a screw!' bawled the general. 'He probes into my soul and heart. He wants me to believe in atheism. Let me tell you, young whipper-snapper, that before you were born I was loaded with honours. And you're only an envious man, torn in two with coughing and dying of spite and infidelity. And why has Gavril brought you here? They're all against me, even to my own son.'

'Oh, leave off, you've got up a tragedy!' cried Ganya. 'If you didn't put us to shame all over the town, it would be better.'

'What, I put you to shame, milksop, you? I can only do you credit, I can't dishonour you!'

He began shouting, and they could not restrain him, but Gavril Ardalionovitch could not control himself either.

'You talk about honour!' he shouted angrily.

'What do you say?' thundered the general, turning pale and taking a step towards him.

'That I need only open my mouth to…' Ganya roared suddenly, and broke off.

They stood facing one another, both excessively agitated, especially Ganya.

'Ganya, what are you about!' cried Nina Alexandrovna, rushing to restrain her son.

'How senseless it is of you all,' Varya snapped out in indignation. 'Be quiet, mother,' she said, taking hold of her.

'Only for mother's sake, I spare him,' Ganya brought out tragically.

'Speak!' roared the general in a perfect frenzy. 'Speak, on pain of your father's curse! Speak!…'

'As though I were frightened of your curse! And whose fault is it that you've been like a madman for the last eight days? Eight days, you see I keep a reckoning. Mind you don't drive me too far. I'll tell everything… Why did you go stumping off to the Epanchins' yesterday? And you call yourself an old man, grey haired, the father of a family! He's a pretty one!'

'Shut up, Ganya!' shouted Kolya.

'Shut up, you fool!'

'But how have I, how have I insulted him?' Ippolit persisted, but still in the same jeering voice. 'Why did he call me a screw, you heard him? He came pestering me; he was here just now, talking of some Captain Eropyegov. I don't desire your company at all, General, I've always avoided it, as you know yourself. I have nothing to do with Captain Eropyegov, you will admit. I didn't come here for the sake of Captain Eropyegov. I simply expressed my opinion that this Captain Eropyegov may possibly never have existed. He raised the devil.'

'He certainly never has existed,' Ganya rapped out.

But the general stood looking stupefied, and gazed blankly about him. His son's words had impressed him by their extraordinary openness. For the first instant he could not even find words. And at last, only when Ippolit burst out laughing in response to Ganya and cried out: 'There, did you hear, your own son, too, says there was no such person as Captain Eropyegov,' the old man muttered, completely disconcerted, 'Kapiton Eropyegov, not Captain ... Kapiton... the retired Lieutenant-Colonel Eropyegov ... Kapiton.'

'And there was never a Kapiton, either,' cried Ganya, thoroughly exasperated.

'Why ... wasn't there?' muttered the general, and a flush overspread his whole face.

'Oh, leave off!' Ptitsyn and Varya tried to repress them.

'Hold your tongue, Ganya!' Kolya shouted again.

But this intercession seemed to bring the general to himself.

'How can you say there wasn't? Why didn't he exist?' he flew out menacingly at his son.

'Oh, because there wasn't. There wasn't and that's all, and there couldn't be! So there. Leave me alone, I tell you.'

'And this is my son ... my own son, whom I... Oh, Heavens!... No such person as Eropyegov, Eroshka Eropyegov!'

'There you are, now he's Eroshka, before he was Kapitoshka!' put in Ippolit.

'Kapitoshka, Sir, Kapitoshka, not Eroshka. Kapiton, Kapiton Alexeyevitch, I mean, Kapiton ... Lieutenant-Colonel on half-pay ... he was married to Marya ... to Marya ... Petrovna. Su ... su ... a friend and comrade ... Sutugov ... from the time of the cadets' For his sake I shed ... I screened... killed. No such person as Kapitoshka Eropyegov! No such person." the general shouted wildly, yet it might be assumed that what he was shouting about was not what really mattered. Another time he would, of course, have put up with something far more insulting than the assertion of Kapiton Eropyegov's absolute non-existence. He would have shouted, made a fuss, been moved to frenzy, but yet, in the end, he would have gone upstairs to bed. But now, such is the fantastic strangeness of the human heart, it happened that a slight, such as the doubt about Eropyegov, was the last drop in his cup. The old man turned crimson, raised his arms and shouted, 'Enough! My curse! ... Out of this house! Nikolay, bring me my bag ... I am going ... away!'

He went out in haste and extreme wrath. Nina Alexandrovna, Kolya and Ptitsyn rushed after him.

'Well, what have you done now!' Varya said to her brother. 'He'll be off there again most likely. The disgrace of it!'

'He shouldn't steal,' cried Ganya, almost spluttering with anger. Suddenly his eyes met Ippolit's. Ganya positively shook. 'As for you, Sir,' he shouted, 'you ought to remember, anyway, that you're in another person's house and ... enjoying his hospitality, and not to irritate an old man who has obviously gone out of his mind.'

Ippolit too felt a qualm, but he instantly controlled himself.

'I don't quite agree with you that your papa has gone out of his mind,' he answered calmly, 'on the contrary, it seems to me that he has had more sense of late, really; don't you think so? He has become so cautious, suspicious. He pries into everything, weighs every word. He began talking to me about that Kapitoshka with an object, you know. Only fancy, he wanted to lead me on to ...'

'Aïe, what the devil do I care what he wanted to lead you on to? I beg you not to try your shifty dodges on me, Sir,' shrieked Ganya. 'If you, too, know the real cause why the old man is in such a state (and you've been spying here these five days to such a degree that you certainly do know) you ought not to have irritated ... the unhappy man, and worried my mother by exaggerating the matter, for it's all nonsense, simply a drunken freak, nothing more, not proved either, and I don't think it's worth a thought... but you must sting and spy because you ... you are ...'

'A screw!' laughed Ippolit.

'Because you are an abject creature, because you worried people for half an hour, thinking to frighten them by shooting yourself with an unloaded pistol, making such a shameful exhibition of yourself, you walking mass of jaundiced spite, who can't even commit suicide without making a mess of it! I have given you hospitality, you've grown fat, you've left off coughing, and you repay it'

'Allow me, two words only; I am in Varvara Ardalionovna's house, not yours, and I imagine indeed that you yourself are enjoying the hospitality of Mr Ptitsyn. Four days ago I begged my mother to find lodgings for me in Pavlovsk and to move here herself, because I certainly feel better here, though I have not grown fat at all and am still coughing. Mother let me know yesterday evening that the lodging was ready, and I hasten to inform you on my side, that thanking your mother and sister for their kindness, I will move there today, as I decided to do last night. Excuse me, I interrupted you, I believe you wanted to say a great deal more.'

'Oh, if that's so,' said Ganya quivering.

'If that's so, allow me to sit down,' added Ippolit, seating himself with perfect composure in the chair where the general had been sitting. 'After all I am ill, you know; well, now I'm ready to listen to you, especially as this is our last conversation, perhaps indeed our last meeting.'

Ganya suddenly felt ashamed.

'You may be sure I won't demean myself by settling accounts with you,' said he, 'and if you …'

'You need not be so lofty,' interrupted Ippolit, 'on the very first day of my coming here, I vowed I would not deny myself the satisfaction of paying off all scores with you, and in the most thoroughgoing way, when we came to part. I intend to do this now, but after you, of course.'

'I beg you to leave the room.'

'You'd better speak. You'll only regret not having had it out, you know.'

'Leave off, Ippolit, it's all so horribly undignified; do me the favour to be quiet,' said Varya.

'Only to oblige a lady,' laughed Ippolit, getting up. 'Certainly, Varvara Ardalionovna, for you I am ready to cut it short, but only that, for some explanation between me and your brother is absolutely essential, and nothing would induce me to go away leaving a misunderstanding.'

'In plain words you're a scandalmonger,' screamed Ganya, 'and so you won't go away without a scandal.'

'There, you see,' Ippolit observed coolly, 'you're at it again, already. You certainly will regret not speaking out. Once more I make way for you. I await your words.'

Gavril Ardalionovitch looked at him contemptuously, without speaking.

'You won't speak. You mean to keep up your part – please yourself. On my side I will be as brief as possible. Two or three times today I have been reproached with accepting your hospitality. That's unfair. By inviting me to stay with you, you tried to entrap me yourself, you reckoned I should want to pay out the prince. You heard, besides, that Aglaia Ivanovna had shown sympathy for me and read my confession. Supposing for some reason that I was ready to devote myself altogether to your interests, you hoped that you might get help from me. I won't explain more in detail! I do not demand assurances or confessions from you either; enough that I leave you to your conscience, and that now we thoroughly understand each other.'

'Goodness knows what you make out of the most ordinary thing!' cried Varya.

'I told you: he's a scandalmonger and a nasty schoolboy,' said Ganya.

'Allow me, Varvara Ardalionovna, I'll go on. The prince, of course, I can neither like nor respect, but he is certainly a kind man, though … rather ridiculous. But I've certainly no reason to hate him; I didn't let on when your brother tried to set me against the prince; I was looking forward to having a laugh at him afterwards. I knew that your brother would make a blunder and give himself away to me shockingly. And so it has turned out… I am ready to spare him now, simply out of respect for you, Varvara Ardalionovna. But since I have made it clear that it is not so easy to catch me, I'll explain why I was so anxious to make your brother look a fool. You must know that I've done it because I hate him, I confess it openly. When I die (for I am dying even if I have grown fatter as you say), when I die, I feel I shall go to paradise with my heart incomparably more at ease, if I succeed in making a fool of one at least of the class of people who have persecuted me all my life, whom I have hated all my life, and of which your excellent brother is a conspicuous example. I hate you, Gavril Ardalionovitch, simply *because* – this will perhaps seem marvellous to you – simply because you are the type, the incarnation, the acme of the most insolent and self-satisfied, the most vulgar and loathsome commonplaceness. Yours is the commonplaceness of pomposity, of self-satisfaction and Olympian serenity. You are the most ordinary of the ordinary! Not the smallest idea of your own will ever take shape in your heart or your mind. But you are infinitely envious; you are firmly persuaded that you are a great genius, but yet doubt does visit you sometimes at black moments, and you grow spiteful and envious. Oh, there are still black spots on your horizon; they will pass when you become quite stupid, and that's not far off, but a long and chequered path lies before you; I can't call it a cheerful one and I'm glad of it. In the first place I predict that you won't gain a certain lady ...'

'Oh, this is unbearable!' cried Varya. 'Will you leave off, you horrid, spiteful creature?'

Ganya turned white, quivered and kept silent. Ippolit stopped, looked intently and with relish at him, turned his eyes to Varya, bowed and went out, without adding another word.

Gavril Ardalionovitch might with justice have complained of his lot and of his ill-success. For some time Varya did not venture to speak to him, she did not even glance at him as he paced to and fro before her with long strides; at last he walked away to the window and stood with his back to her. Varya thought of the Russian proverb about 'a knife that cuts both ways.' A noise began again overhead.

'Are you going?' Ganya asked suddenly, hearing her get up from her seat. 'Wait a bit. Look at this.'

He went up and threw on the chair before her a piece of paper folded into the shape of a tiny note.

'Good heavens!' cried Varya, clasping her hands.

There were just seven lines in the note:

> Gavril Ardalionovitch! As I am convinced of your friendly feeling for me I venture to ask your advice in a matter of great importance to me. I should like to meet you tomorrow morning at seven o'clock at the green seat. It's not far from our villa. Varvara Ardalionovna who *must* accompany you knows the place well.
>
> A. E.

'Good heavens, what will she do next?' Varvara Ardalionovna flung up her hands.

Little as Ganya was inclined to be boastful at that moment, he could not help showing his triumph, especially after Ippolit's humiliating predictions. A self-satisfied smile lit up his face, and Varya, too, beamed all over with delight.

'And that on the very day when her betrothal is to be announced! Well, there's no knowing what she'll do next!'

'What do you think? What does she mean to speak about tomorrow?' asked Ganya.

'That doesn't matter. What matters is that she wants to see you for the first time after six months. Listen to me, Ganya, whatever's happened, whatever turn it takes, I tell you it's *important!* It's tremendously important! Don't swagger, don't make another blunder, and don't be faint-hearted either, mind that. She must have guessed why I've been trudging off there for the last six months? And fancy, she didn't say a word to me today, she made no sign. I've been to them on the sly, you know. The old woman did not know I was there, or maybe she'd have sent me packing. I risked it for your sake, to find out at all costs ...'

Again there was shouting and uproar overhead. Several persons were coming downstairs.

'This mustn't be allowed now on any account!' cried Varya, flurried and alarmed. 'Not a shadow of a scandal! Go, ask his forgiveness!'

But the head of the family was already in the street. Kolya was dragging his bag after him. Nina Alexandrovna was standing on the steps, crying; she would have run after him, but Ptitsyn held her back.

'You only make him worse like that,' he said to her. 'He has nowhere to go. He'll be brought back again in half an hour. I've spoken to Kolya already; let him play the fool.'

'Why these heroics? Where can you go?' Ganya shouted from the window. 'You've nowhere to go!'

'Come back, father!' cried Varya, 'the neighbours will hear.'

The general stopped, turned round, stretched out his hand, and exclaimed, 'My curse on this house!'

'He must take that theatrical tone!' muttered Ganya, closing the window with a slam.

The neighbours certainly were listening. Varya ran out of the room.

When Varya had gone out, Ganya took the note from the table, kissed it, gave a click of satisfaction and pirouetted round.

Chapter 3

The scene with the general would never have come to anything in other circumstances. He had had sudden outbursts of temper of the same kind before, though not often; for, generally speaking, he was a very good-tempered man, and of a rather kindly disposition. A hundred times perhaps he had struggled against the bad habits that had gained the mastery of him of late years, hie used suddenly to remember that he was the head of a family, would make it up with his wife, and shed genuine tears. He respected and almost worshipped Nina Alexandrovna, for having forgiven him so much in silence, and for loving him, even though he had become a grotesque and degraded figure. But his noble-hearted efforts to overcome his failings did not usually last long. The general was besides of a too 'impulsive' character, though in his ow n peculiar fashion. He could not stand for long his empty mode of life as a penitent in his family and ended by revolting. He flew into a paroxysm of excitement, for which, perhaps he was inwardly reproaching himself at the very moment, though he could not restrain himself: he quarrelled, began talking eloquently and rhetorically, insisting upon being treated with the most exaggerated and impossible respect and finally would disappear from the house, sometimes remaining absent for a long time. For the last two years he had only a vague idea from hearsay of the circumstances of the family. He had given up going farther into matters, feeling not the slightest impulse to do so.

But this time there was something exceptional in the 'general's outbreak'. Everyone seemed to be aware of something, and everyone seemed afraid to speak of it. The general had 'formally' presented himself to his family, that is to Nina Alexandrovna, only three days before, but not humble and penitent as on all previous 'reappearances,' but on the contrary – with marked irritability. He was loquacious, restless, talked heatedly to all, and, as it were, hurled himself upon everyone he met, but always speaking of such irrelevant and unexpected subjects that it was impossible to get to the bottom of what was worrying him. At moments he was cheerful, but for the most part he was thoughtful, though he did not know himself what he was thinking about. He would suddenly begin to talk of something – of the Epanchins, of Myshkin, of Lebedyev – and then he would suddenly break off and cease speaking, and only responded to further questions with a vacant smile, without being conscious himself that he was being questioned or that he was smiling. He had spent the previous night moaning and groaning and had exhausted Nina Alexandrovna, who had been up all night, preparing fomentations. Towards morning he had suddenly fallen asleep; he slept for four hours and waked up with a most violent and irrational attack of hypochondria, which ended in a quarrel with Ippolit and 'a curse on this house.' They noticed, too, that for those three days he had been liable to violent attacks of self-esteem, which made him morbidly ready to take offence. Kolya assured his mother and insisted that this was all due to a craving for drink, and perhaps for Lebedeyev, with whom the general had become extraordinarily friendly of late. But, three days before, he had suddenly quarrelled with Lebedyev, and had parted from him in a terrible fury. There had even been some sort of a scene with Myshkin. Kolya begged Myshkin for an explanation, and began at last to suspect that he too knew something he did not want to tell him. If, as Ganya, with every possibility of correctness, supposed, some special conversation had taken place between Ippolit and Nina Alexandrovna, it seemed strange that this spiteful youth, whom Ganya called so openly a 'scandalmonger,' had not found satisfaction in initiating Kolya into the secret in the same way. It was very possible that he was not such a malicious and nasty 'puppy' as Ganya had described him in speaking to his sister, but was malicious in a different way. And he could hardly have informed Nina Alexandrovna of what he had observed simply in order 'to break her heart.' Don't let us forget that the causes of human actions are usually immeasurably more complex and varied than our subsequent explanations of them. And these can rarely be distinctly defined. The best course for the storyteller at times is to confine himself to a simple narrative of events. And this is the line we will adopt in the rest of our account of the present catastrophe with the general; for, do what we may, it is absolutely inevitable we should bestow rather more space and attention than we had originally proposed on this person of secondary importance in our story.

These events had succeeded one another in the following order.

When Lebedyev on the same day returned with the general from his visit to Petersburg to look for Ferdyshtchenko, he told Myshkin nothing particular. If Myshkin had not been at the time too busy and preoccupied with other impressions of great importance to him, he might soon have noticed that during the two following days Lebedyev, far from giving him any kind of explanation, seemed, for some reason, to be trying to avoid meeting him. When Myshkin did at last turn his attention to the subject, he was surprised that he could not remember during those three days having met Lebedyev in any but the most blissful state of mind, and almost always in company with the general. They were never apart for a moment. Myshkin sometimes heard the sound of loud and rapid talk and merry laughing dispute from overhead. Once, very late at night, the strains of a martial and Bacchanalian song had suddenly and unexpectedly burst upon his ears, and he recognised at once the husky bass of the general. But the song ceased suddenly before the end. Then for about another hour an extremely animated, and from all signs, drunken conversation followed. It might be conjectured that the friends were embracing one another, and one of them finally began to weep. Then followed a violent quarrel, which also ceased suddenly soon after. All this time Kolya seemed peculiarly preoccupied. Myshkin was generally not at home, and returned sometimes very late. He was always told that Kolya had been looking for him all day, and asking for him. But when they met, Kolya had nothing special to tell him except that he was 'dissatisfied' with the general and his goings on at present: 'They wander about together, get drunk in a tavern close by, embrace one another and quarrel in the street. They make each other worse, and can't be parted.' When Myshkin observed that it had been just the same every day before, Kolya was quite unable to find an answer, and could not explain the cause of his present uneasiness.

The morning after the Bacchic song and quarrel, Myshkin was leaving the house about eleven o'clock when he was suddenly confronted by the general, who seemed greatly excited, almost overwhelmed, by something.

'I've long been seeking the honour of meeting you, honoured Lyov Nikolayevitch, very long,' he muttered, squeezing Myshkin's hand very tightly, almost hurting him. 'A very, very long time.'

Myshkin begged him to sit down.

'No, I won't sit down. Besides, I'm keeping you. I'll come another time. I believe I may take the opportunity of congratulating you on ... the fulfilment of your heart's desire.'

'What heart's desire?'

Myshkin was disconcerted. Like many people in his position he fancied that nobody saw, guessed, or understood anything about him.

'Never mind, never mind! I would not wound your most delicate feelings. I have known them, and I know what it is when another man ... pokes his nose ... as the saying is... where it isn't wanted. I feel that every morning. I have come about another matter, an important one. A very important matter, Prince.'

Myshkin once more begged him to be seated and sat down himself.

'Perhaps for one second ... I have come to ask advice. I have, of course, no practical aim in life, but as I respect myself and ... business habits in which the Russian as a rule, is so conspicuously deficient... I wish to place myself and my wife and my children in a position ... in fact, Prince, I want your advice.'

Myshkin warmly applauded his intention.

'Well, that's all nonsense,' the general interrupted suddenly, 'that's not what I want to say, but something else, something important. I simply want to explain to you, Lyov Nikolayevitch, as a man in the sincerity of whose heart and the nobility of whose feelings I have complete confidence, as ... as ... You are not surprised at my words, Prince?'

Myshkin observed his visitor, if not with surprise, at least with extreme attention and curiosity.

The old man was rather pale, his lips quivered slightly at times, his hands seemed unable to find a resting-place. He only remained a few minutes in his seat, and had twice already got up from his chair for some reason, and sat down again, obviously not paying the slightest attention to what he was doing. There were books lying on the table: he took up one, and still talking, glanced at the opened page, shut it again at once, and laid it back on the table, snatched up another book which he did not open, and held it all the rest of the time in his right hand, waving it continually in the air.

'Enough!' he shouted suddenly. 'I see that I have been disturbing you shockingly.'

'Oh, not in the least, please go on. Quite the contrary. I'm listening and trying to guess ...'

'Prince! I am anxious to gain for myself a position of respect... I am anxious to respect myself and ... my rights.'

'A man animated by such a desire is deserting of respect, if only on that ground.'

The prince brought out his copybook phrase in the firm conviction that it would have an excellent effect. He guessed instinctively that some such hollow but agreeable phrase uttered at the right moment might immediately have an irresistible and soothing influence on the mind of such a man, especially in such a position as the general. In any case it was necessary to send such a visitor away with a lighter heart, and that was the problem.

The phrase flattered and touched and greatly pleased General Ivolgin: he suddenly melted, instantly changed his tone, and went off into a long, enthusiastic explanation. But, however intently Myshkin listened, he could make literally nothing of it. The general talked for ten minutes, heatedly, rapidly, as though he could not get out his crowding thoughts quickly enough. Tears positively shone in his eyes towards the end, yet it was nothing but sentences without beginning or end, unexpected words and unexpected ideas, bursting out rapidly and unexpectedly and stumbling over one another.

'Enough! You have understood me, and I am satisfied,' he concluded, suddenly getting up. 'A heart such as yours cannot fail to understand a suffering man. Prince, you are ideally generous. What are other men beside you? But you are young and I bless you. The long and short of it is I came to ask you to appoint an hour for an important conversation with me, and on that I rest my chief hope. I seek for nothing but friendship and sympathy, Prince. I have never been able to master the yearnings of my heart.'

'But why not at once? I am ready to listen ...'

'No, Prince, no!' the general interrupted hotly. 'Not now! Now is a vain dream! It is too, too important! Too important! The hour of that conversation will be an hour of irrevocable destiny. That will be my hour, and I should not wish it to be possible for us to be interrupted at such a sacred moment by any chance corner, any impudent fellow, and there are plenty of such impudent fellows.' He bent down suddenly to Myshkin, with a strange, mysterious, and almost frightened whisper. 'Such impudent fellows, not worthy the heel ... of your shoe, adored prince. Oh! I don't say of my shoe. Note particularly that I don't refer to my own shoe, for I have too much self-respect to say that straight out... but you alone are able to understand that in waiving my heel in such a case I show perhaps the utmost pride of worth. Except you, no one will understand it, *he* least of all. *He* understands nothing, Prince; he is utterly, utterly incapable of understanding. One must have a heart to understand!'

At last Myshkin was almost alarmed and he made an appointment with General Ivolgin for the same hour next day.

The latter went out with a confident air, greatly comforted, and almost reassured. In the evening between six and seven Myshkin sent to ask Lebedyev to come to him for a minute.

Lebedyev made his appearance with great alacrity, 'esteemed it an honour,' as he began at once on entering. There was not the shadow of a hint that he'd been as it were in hiding for the last three days, and was obviously trying to avoid meeting Myshkin. He sat down on the edge of the chair, with smiles and grimaces, with laughing and watchful little eyes, rubbing his hands and assuming an air of the most naïve expectation of hearing something, of receiving some communication of the first importance, long expected and guessed by everyone. Myshkin winced again. It became clear to him that everyone had suddenly begun to expect something of him, that everyone looked at him, as though wanting to congratulate him with hints, smiles, and winks. Keller had run in two or three times for a minute already, also with an evident desire to congratulate him; each time he began vaguely and enthusiastically but did not finish, and quickly disappeared again. (He had been drinking particularly heavily of late, and making a sensation in some billiard-room.)

Even Kolya, in spite of his sadness, had also attempted once or twice to begin upon some subject with Myshkin.

Myshkin asked Lebedyev directly and somewhat irritably what he thought of General Ivolgin's state of mind, and why the latter seemed so uneasy. In a few words he told him of the scene that morning.

'Everyone has his own reasons for uneasiness, Prince ... and ... especially in our strange and uneasy age, you know,' Lebedyev answered with a certain dryness, and relapsed into offended silence, with the air of a man deeply deceived in his expectations.

'What philosophy!' said Myshkin smiling.

'Philosophy would be useful, very useful in our age in its practical application, but it's despised, that's how it is. For my part, honoured Prince, though I have respected your confidence to me on a certain point you know of, yet only to a certain degree, and no further than circumstances relating to that point especially… that I understand, and I don't in the least complain.'

'Lebedyev, you seem to be angry about something?'

'Not at all, not in the least, honoured and resplendent prince … not in the least!' Lebedeyev cried passionately, laying his hand upon his heart. 'On the contrary, I realised at once, that, neither by my position in the world, nor by the qualities of my mind or my heart, nor the amount of my fortune, nor my former behaviour, nor my knowledge – in no way do I deserve the confidence with which you honour me, so far above my hopes, and that if I can serve you it is as a slave and hireling. Nothing else. I am not angry, but Fm sad.'

'Come, come, Lukyan Timofeyitch!'

'Nothing else! So it is in the present case. Meeting you, fixing my heart and thought upon you, I said to myself: "I am unworthy of your confidence as a friend, but as the landlord of your house perhaps I may receive at the fitting time, before the anticipated event, so to speak, a warning, or at least an intimation in view of certain changes expected in the future …" '

As he uttered this, Lebedyev positively fastened his sharp little eyes on Myshkin, who was looking at him in astonishment. He was still in hopes of satisfying his curiosity.

'I don't understand a word!' cried Myshkin, almost with anger, 'and … you're an awful intriguer!' he suddenly broke into a most genuine laugh. Instantly Lebedeyev laughed too, and his beaming face showed clearly that his hopes were confirmed, and even redoubled.

'And do you know what I have to tell you, Lukyan Timofeyitch? Don't be angry with me, but I wonder at your simplicity, and not only yours! You are expecting something of me with such simplicity now, at this very moment, that I feel positively ashamed and conscience-stricken at hating nothing to satisfy you with, but I swear that I really have nothing. Can you fancy that?' Myshkin laughed again.

Lebedyev put on a dignified air. It was true that he was sometimes too naïve and intrusive in his curiosity, but at the same time he was a rather cunning and wily man, and in some cases even too artfully silent. Myshkin had almost made an enemy of him by continually putting him off. But Myshkin put him off, not because he despised him, but because the subject of his curiosity was a delicate one. Myshkin had only a few days before looked on some of his own dreams as a crime, while Lukyan Timofeyitch took Myshkin's rebuffs simply as a proof of personal aversion and mistrust, withdrew, cut to the heart and jealous not only of Kolya and of Keller, but even of his own daughter, Vera. Even at that very moment, he could, perhaps, have told Myshkin a piece of news of the greatest interest to him and perhaps sincerely desired to do so, but he remained gloomily silent and did not tell him.

'In what way can I be of use to you, honoured prince, since anyway you ... called me just now,' he said at last after a brief silence.

'Why, I asked you about the general,' Myshkin, who had been musing for a moment, too, answered hurriedly, 'and ... in regard to that theft you told me about.'

'In regard to what?'

'Why, as though you don't understand me now! Oh, dear, Lukyan Timofeyitch, you're always acting a part! The money, the money, the four hundred roubles you lost that day in your pocketbook, and about which you came to tell me in the morning, as you were setting off for Petersburg. Do you understand at last?'

'Ah, you're talking about that four hundred roubles!' drawled Lebedyev, as though he had only just guessed. 'I thank you, Prince, for your sincere sympathy; it is too flattering to me, but... I've found it some time since.'

'Found it! Ah, thank God!'

'That exclamation is most generous on your part, for four hundred roubles is no small matter for a poor man who lives by his hard work, with a large family of motherless children ...'

'But I didn't mean that! Of course, I am glad you found the money,' Myshkin corrected himself quickly, 'but how did you find it?'

'Very simply. I found it under the chair on which my coat had been hung, so that the pocketbook must have slipped out of the pocket on to the floor!'

'Under a chair? It's impossible! Why, you told me yourself you had hunted in every corner. How was it you came to overlook the most obvious place?'

'I should think I did look! I remember only too well how I looked! I crawled on all fours, felt the place with my hands, moving back the chairs because I couldn't trust my own eyes: I saw there was nothing there for the place was as smooth and empty as my hands, and yet I went on fumbling. You always see that weakness in anyone who is very anxious to find anything, when anything serious and important has been lost. A man sees there's nothing there, the place is empty, and yet he peeps into it a dozen times.'

'Yes, I dare say; only, how was it seen? ... I still don't understand,' muttered Myshkin, disconcerted. 'You told me before it wasn't there, and you had looked in that place, and then it suddenly turned up!'

'And then it suddenly turned up.'

Myshkin looked strangely at Lebedyev.

'And the general?' he asked suddenly.

'What about the general? ...' Lebedyev seemed at a loss again.

'Oh, dear! I ask you what did the general say when you found the pocketbook under the chair? You looked for it together, you know.'

'We did look together before. But that time, I confess, I held my tongue, and preferred not to tell him that the pocketbook had been found by me and alone.'

'But... why? And the money? Was it all there?'

'I opened the pocketbook. The money was untouched, every rouble of it.'

'You might have come to tell me,' Myshkin observed thoughtfully.

'I was afraid to disturb you, Prince, in your personal, and, so to say, absorbing interests, and besides, I made as though I had found nothing. I opened the pocketbook and looked at it, then I shut it and put it back under the chair.'

'But what for?'

'Oh, n-nothing, from curiosity,' chuckled Lebedyev, rubbing his hands.

'Then it has been lying there since the day before yesterday?'

'Oh, no; it only lay there for a day and a night. You see, it was partly that I wanted the general to find it. For since I had found it, why should not the general notice the object, which lay conspicuous under the chair, so to speak, catching the eye. I lifted that chair several times and put it so that the pocketbook was completely in view, but the general simply didn't notice it, and so it went on for twenty-four hours. He seems to be extraordinarily unobservant now, and there's no making him out. He talks, tells stories, laughs, chuckles, and then flies into a violent temper with me. I don't know why. At last, as we were going out of the room, I left the door open on purpose; he hesitated, would have said something, most likely he was uneasy about the pocketbook with such a sum of money in it, but suddenly flew into an awful rage and said nothing. Before we had gone two steps in the street, he left me and walked away in the other direction. We only met in the evening in the tavern.'

'But in the end you did take the pocketbook from under the chair?'

'No, it vanished from under the chair that same night.'

'Then where is it now?'

'Oh, here,' cried Lebedyev, laughing suddenly, drawing himself up to his full height and looking amiably at Myshkin. 'It suddenly turned up, here, in the lappet of my coat. Here; won't you look, feel.'

The left lappets of the coat had indeed been formed into something like a bag in front, in the most conspicuous place, and it was clear at once to the touch that there was a leather pocketbook there that had fallen down from a torn pocket.

'I took it out and looked. The money's all there. I dropped it in again, and so I've been walking about since yesterday morning. I carry it in my coat and it knocks against my legs.'

'And you take no notice of it?'

'And I take no notice of it. Ha-ha! And would you believe it, honoured prince, though the subject is not worthy of so much notice on your part, my pockets were always perfectly good, and then a hole like that, all of a sudden, in one night! I began to look at it more curiously; it's as though someone had cut it with a penknife. Isn't it almost incredible?'

'And ... the general?'

'He's been angry all day; both yesterday and today; fearfully ill-humoured. At one time he'd be beaming and hilarious till he began to pay me compliments, then he'd be sentimental to tears, then suddenly angry, so much so, that I'd be frightened really, for I'm not a military man, after all. We were sitting yesterday in the tavern, and the lappet of my coat stood out as though by chance, in the most prominent way; a perfect mountain. He looked at it on the sly, and was angry. He hasn't looked me straight in the face for a long time, unless he's *very* drunk or sentimental, but yesterday he gave me a look that made a shudder run down my spine. Tomorrow, though, I mean to find the pocketbook, but I shall have an evening's fun with him before then.'

'Why are you tormenting him so?' cried Myshkin.

'I'm not tormenting him, Prince, I'm not tormenting him,' Lebedyev replied with warmth. 'I sincerely love and ... respect him; and now, whether you believe it or not, he's dearer to me than ever. I have come to appreciate him even more.'

Lebedyev said all this so earnestly and sincerely that Myshkin was positively indignant.

'You love him and you torment him like this! Why, by the very act of putting the lost pocketbook where it could be seen under the chair and in your coat, by that alone he shows you that he doesn't want to deceive you, but with open-hearted simplicity asks your forgiveness. Do you hear? He's asking your forgiveness! So he relies on the delicacy of your feelings, so he believes in your friendship for him. And yet you reduce to such humiliation a man like that... a most honest man!'

'Most honest, Prince, most honest!' Lebedyev assented with sparkling eyes. 'And you, most noble prince, are the only person capable of uttering that true word about him! For that, I am devoted to you and ready to worship you, though I am rotten to the core with vices of all sorts! That's settled it! I will find the pocketbook now, at once, not tomorrow. Look, I take it out before your eyes; here it is. Here's the money, untouched, here. Take it, most noble prince, take care of it till tomorrow. Tomorrow or next day I'll have it. And, do you know, Prince, it's evident that it must have been lying somewhere in my garden, hidden under some stone, the first night it was lost. What do you think?'

'Mind you don't tell him directly to his face that you've found the pocketbook. Let him simply see that there's nothing in the lappet of your coat, and he'll understand.'

'You think so? Wouldn't it be better to tell him I have found it, and to pretend I had not guessed about it till now? '

'N-no,' Myshkin pondered, 'N-no; it's too late for that now. That's more risky. You'd really better not speak of it! Be kind to him, but... don't show too much, and ... and ... You know ...'

'I know, Prince, I know. That is I know that I shan't do it properly, perhaps. For one needs to have a heart like yours to do it. Besides he's irritable and prone to it himself, he has begun to treat me too superciliously sometimes of late. One minute he is whimpering and embracing me, and then he'll suddenly begin to snub me, and sneer at me contemptuously, and then I just show him the lappet on purpose. Ha-ha! Goodbye, Prince, for it's clear I'm keeping you and interrupting you in your most interesting feelings, so to say ...'

'But for goodness' sake, the same secrecy as before!'

'Treading softly, treading softly!'

But, though the matter was settled, Myshkin remained almost more puzzled than before. He awaited with impatience his interview with the general next day.

Chapter 4

The hour fixed was twelve, but Myshkin was, quite unexpectedly, late. On his return home he found the general waiting for him. He saw at the first glance that the old man was displeased, and very likely, just because he had been kept waiting. Apologising, Myshkin made haste to sit down, but he felt strangely timid, as though his guest were made of porcelain and he were afraid of breaking him. He had never felt timid with the general before; it had never entered his head to feel so. Myshkin soon perceived that he was a perfectly different man from what he had been yesterday. Instead of agitation and incoherence, there was an unmistakable, a visible and marked reserve; it could he seen that this was a man who had taken an irrevocable decision. But his composure was more apparent than real. In any case the visitor displayed a gentlemanly ease of manner, though with reserved dignity. He even treated Myshkin at first with an air of condescension, as proud people who have been gratuitously insulted sometimes do behave with gentlemanly ease. He spoke affably, though with a certain aggrieved intonation.

'Your book, which I borrowed from you the other day,' he said, nodding significantly at a book he had brought which was lying on the table. 'I thank you.'

'Oh, yes. Have you read that article, General? How did you like it? It's interesting, isn't it?' Myshkin was delighted at the chance of beginning to talk on an irrelevant subject.

'Interesting, perhaps, but crude, and of course absurd. Probably a lie in every sentence.'

The general spoke with aplomb, and even drawled his words a little.

'Ah, it's such an unpretentious story; the story of an old soldier who was an eyewitness of the arrival of the French in Moscow; some things in it are charming. Besides, every account given by an eyewitness is precious, isn't it, whoever he may be?'

'Had I been the editor, I would not have printed it; as for the descriptions of eyewitnesses in general, people are more ready to believe crude liars, who are amusing, than a man of worth who has seen service. I know some descriptions of the year 1812 which ... I've come to a determination, Prince, I am leaving this house ... the house of Mr Lebedyev.'

The general looked significantly at .Myshkin.

'You have your own rooms at Pavlovsk at... at your daughter's ...' said Myshkin, not knowing what to say.

He remembered that the general had come to ask his advice about a most important matter, on which his fate depended.

'At my wife's; in other words, at home, in my daughter's house.'

'I beg your pardon. I...'

'I am leaving Lebedyev's house, because, dear prince, because I have broken with that man. I broke with him yesterday evening and regret I did not do so before. I insist on respect, Prince, and I wish to receive it even from those, upon whom I bestow, so to speak, my heart. Prince, I often bestow my heart, and I am almost always deceived. That man is not worthy of what I gave him.'

'There's a great deal in him that's extravagant,' Myshkin observed discreetly, 'and some traits... but in the midst of it all one can perceive a good heart, and a sly, and sometimes amusing intelligence.'

The nicety of the expressions and the respectfulness of the tone flattered the general, though he still looked at Myshkin sometimes with sudden mistrustfulness. But Myshkin's tone was so natural and sincere that he could not suspect it.

'That he has good qualities,' the general assented, 'I was the first to declare, when I almost bestowed my friendship on that individual. I have no need of his house and his hospitality, having a family of my own. I do not justify my failings. I am weak; I have drunk with him, and now perhaps I am weeping for it. But it was not for the sake of the drink alone (excuse, Prince, the coarseness of candour in an irritated man), it was not for the sake of the drink alone I became friendly with him. What allured me was just, as you say, his qualities. But all only to a certain point, even his qualities; and if he suddenly has the impudence to declare to one's face, that in 1812, when he was a little child he lost his left leg, and buried it in the Vagankovsky cemetery in Moscow, he is going beyond the limit, showing disrespect and being impertinent…'

'Perhaps, it was only a joke to raise a laugh.'

'I understand. An innocent lie, however crude, to raise a laugh, does not wound a human heart. One man will tell a lie, if you like, simply from friendship, to please the man he is talking to, but if there's a suspicion of disrespect, if he means to show just by such disrespect that he is weary of the friendship, there's nothing left for a man of honour but to turn away and break off all connection, putting the offender in his proper place.'

The general positively flushed as he spoke.

'Why, Lebedyev could not have been in Moscow in 1812. He's not old enough. It's absurd.'

'That's the first thing, but even supposing he could have been born then, how can he declare to one's face that the French *chasseur* aimed a cannon at him and shot off his leg, just for fun; that he picked the leg up and carried it home, and afterwards buried it in the Vagankovsky cemetery; and he says that he put a monument over it with an inscription on one side: 'Here lies the leg of the collegiate secretary, Lebedyev,' and on the other: 'Rest, beloved ashes, till the dawn of a happy resurrection,' and that he had a service read over it every year (which is nothing short of blasphemy), and that he goes to Moscow every year for the occasion. To prove it he invites me to go to Moscow to show me the tomb, and even the very cannon taken from the French, now in the Kremlin. He declares it's the eleventh from the gate, a French *falconet* of an old-fashioned pattern.'

'And besides, he has both his legs, uninjured, apparently,' laughed Myshkin. 'I assure you it was harmless jest. Don't be angry.'

'But allow me to have my own opinion; as for his appearing to have two legs, that's not altogether improbable; he declares that he got his leg from Tchernosvitov...'

'Oh, yes, they say that people can dance with legs from that maker.'

'I'm perfectly aware of that, when Tchernosvitov invented his leg, the first thing he did was to run and show it to me. But his legs were invented much later ... What's more, he asserts that his late wife never knew, all the years they were married, that he, her husband, had a wooden leg. When I observed to him how foolish it all was, he said to me: "if you were a page of Napoleon's in 1812, you might let me bury my leg in Vagankovsky." '

'But did you really ...' Myshkin began, and broke off embarrassed.

The general too seemed a shade embarrassed, but at the same instant he looked at Myshkin with distinct condescension, and even irony.

'Go on, Prince, go on,' he drawled with peculiar suavity. 'I can make allowances, speak out; confess that you are amused at the very thought of seeing before you a man in his present degradation and... uselessness, and to hear that that man was an eyewitness of... great events. Hasn't he gossiped to you already?'

'No, I've heard nothing from Lebedyev, if it's Lebedyev you are talking about...'

'Hm! ... I had supposed the contrary. The particular conversation took place between us yesterday apropos of that strange article in the *Archives.* I remarked on its absurdity, and since I had myself been an eyewitness ... you are smiling, Prince, you are looking at my face?'

'N-no. I...'

'I am youngish looking,' the general drawled the words – 'but I am somewhat older in years than I appear. In 1812 I was in my tenth or eleventh year. I don't quite know my own age exactly. In my service list my age is less; it has been my weakness all my life to make myself out younger than I am.'

'I assure you, General, that I don't think it strange that you should have been in Moscow in 1812, and ... of course you could describe ... like everyone else who was there. One of our writers begins his autobiography by saying that, when he was a baby in arms, in Moscow, in 1812, he was fed with bread by the French soldiers.'

'There, you see,' the general condescendingly approved, 'what happened to me was of course out of the ordinary, but there is nothing incredible in it. Truth very often seems impossible. Page! It sounds strange, of course. But the adventure of a ten-year-old boy may perhaps be explained just by his age. It wouldn't have happened to a boy of fifteen, that's certain, for at fifteen, I should not, on the day of Napoleon's entry into Moscow, have run out of the wooden house in Old Bassmann Street, where I was living with my mother, who had not left the town in time and was terror-stricken. At fifteen I too should have been afraid, but at ten I feared nothing, and I forced my way through the crowd to the very steps of the palace just when Napoleon was dismounting from his horse.'

'Certainly, that's a very true remark, that at ten years old one might not be afraid ...' Myshkin assented, abashed and distressed by feeling that he was just going to blush.

'Most certainly, and it all happened as simply and naturally as possible, in reality; set a novelist to work on the subject, he would weave in all sorts of incredible and improbable details.'

'Oh, that's true!' cried Myshkin. 'I was struck by the same idea, quite lately. I know a genuine case of murder for the sake of stealing a watch – it's appearing in the newspapers now. If some author had invented it, critics and those who know the life of the people would have cried out at once that it was improbable, but reading it in the newspapers as a fact, you feel that in such facts you are studying the reality of Russian life. That's an excellent observation of yours, General,' Myshkin concluded warmly, greatly relieved at finding a refuge from his blushes.

'Isn't it? Isn't it?' cried the general, his eyes sparkling with pleasure. 'A boy, a child who knows nothing of fear, makes his way through the crowd to see the fine show, the uniforms, the suite, and the great man about whom he has heard such a lot. For at that time people had talked of nothing else for years. The world was full of that name. I drank it in with my milk, so to speak. Napoleon was two paces away when he chanced to catch my eye. I looked like a little nobleman, they dressed me well. There was no one like me in the crowd you may believe ...'

'No doubt it must have struck him and have shown him that everyone had not left Moscow, and that there were still some of the nobility there with their children.'

'Just so! Just so! He wanted to win over the boyars! When he bent his eagle glance upon me, my eye must have flashed in response. *"Voilà un garçon bien éveillé! Qui est ton père?"* I answered him at once, almost breathless with excitement: "A general who died in the field for his country." *"Le fils d'un boyard et d'un brave par-dessus le marché! J'aime les boyards. M'aimes tu, petit?"* To this rapid question I answered as rapidly: "A Russian heart can discern a great man even in the enemy of his country!" That is, I don't remember whether I literally used those words ... I was a child ... but that was certainly the drift of them! Napoleon was struck, he thought a moment and said to his suite: "I like the pride of that child! But if all Russians think like that child, then ..." He said no more, but walked into the palace. I at once mingled with the suite and ran after him. They made way for me, and already looked upon me as a favourite. But all that was only for a moment... I only remember that when the Emperor went into the first room he stopped before the portrait of the Empress Catherine, looked at it a long time thoughtfully, and at last pronounced: "That was a great woman!" and passed by. Within two days everyone knew me in the palace and the Kremlin and called me: *"le petit boyard."* I only went home to sleep. At home they were almost frantic about it. Two days later, one of Napoleon's pages, Baron de Basencour, died, exhausted by the campaign. Napoleon remembered me; they took me, brought me to him without explanation; they tried on me the uniform of the dead page – a boy of twelve, and when they had brought me, wearing the uniform to the Emperor and he had nodded to me, they announced to me that I had been found worthy of favour and appointed a page-in-waiting to his Majesty. I was glad; I had, in fact, long felt warmly attracted by him ... and besides, as you know very well, a brilliant uniform means a great deal to a child ... I wore a dark green dress-coat, with long narrow tails, gold buttons, red edgings worked with gold on the sleeves, and with a high, erect, open-collar, worked in gold, and embroidery on the tails; tight white chamois leather breeches, a white silk waistcoat, silk stockings, and buckled shoes ... and when the Emperor rode out, if I was one of the suite, I wore high top-boots. Although the situation was anything but promising, and there was a feeling of terrible catastrophe in the air, etiquette was kept up as far as possible, and in fact, the greater the foreboding of catastrophe, the more rigorous was the court punctilio.'

'Yes, of course ...' muttered Myshkin with an almost hopeless air. 'Your memoirs would be ... extremely interesting.'

The general, of course, had been repeating the story he had already told Lebedyev the day before, and so he repeated it fluently, but at this point he stole a mistrustful glance at Myshkin again.

'My memoirs,' he brought out with redoubled dignity – 'write my memoirs? That is not a temptation to me, Prince! If you will have it, my memoirs are already written, but... they are lying in my desk. When my eyes are closed for ever in the grave, then they may be published, and no doubt they will be translated into foreign languages, not for the sake of their literary value, no, but from the importance of the tremendous events of which I have been the eyewitness, though as a child; the more for that indeed. As a child I had the entry into the private bedroom, so to speak, of the "Great Man." I heard at night the groans of that "Titan in agony," he could not feel ashamed to groan and weep before a child, though I understood even then, that the cause of his distress was the silence of the Emperor Alexander.'

'To be sure, he wrote letters... with overtures of peace ...' Myshkin assented timidly.

'We don't know precisely with what overtures he wrote, but he wrote every day, every hour, letter after letter! He was fearfully agitated! One night, when we were alone, I flew to him weeping. (Oh, I loved him!) "Beg, beg forgiveness of the Emperor Alexander!" I cried to him. Of course, I ought to have used the expression: "make peace with the Emperor Alexander," but, like a child, I naïvely expressed all I felt. "Oh, my child!" he replied – he paced up and down the room. "Oh, my child!" He did not seem to notice at that time that I was only ten, and liked to talk to me. "Oh, my child, I am ready to kiss the feet of the Emperor Alexander, but then the King of Prussia, and then the Austrian Emperor. Oh, for them my hatred is everlasting and ... at last... of course you know nothing of politics." He seemed suddenly to remember to whom he was speaking, and ceased, but there were gleams of fire in his eyes long after. Well, say I describe all these facts – and I was the eyewitness of the greatest events – say I publish my memoirs now, and all the critics, the literary vanities, all the envy, the cliques ... no, your humble servant!'

'As for cliques, no doubt your observation is a true one, and I agree with you,' Myshkin observed quietly after a moment's silence. 'I read not long ago a book by Charasse, about the Waterloo campaign. It is evidently a genuine book, and experts say that it is written with great knowledge. But on every page one detects glee at the humiliation of Napoleon; and if it had been possible to dispute Napoleon's genius in every other campaign, Charasse would be extremely glad to do it. And that's not right in such a serious work, because it's the spirit of partisanship. Had you much to do in waiting on the Emperor?'

The general was delighted. The earnestness and simplicity of Myshkin's question dissipated the last traces of his mistrustfulness.

'Charasse! Oh, I was indignant myself. I wrote to him myself, at the time, but... I don't remember now ... You ask if I had much to do in Napoleon's service? Oh, no! I was called a page-in-waiting, but even at the time I did not take it seriously. Besides, Napoleon soon lost all hope of winning over the Russians, and no doubt he would have forgotten me, whom he had adopted from policy, if he had not... if he had not taken a personal fancy to me; I say that boldly now. My heart was drawn to him. My duties were not exacting; I had sometimes to be present in the palace and to ... attend the Emperor when he rode out, that was all. I rode a horse fairly well. He used to drive out before dinner. Davoust, I, and a mameluke, Roustan, were generally in his suite ...'

'Constant'. The name was pronounced almost involuntarily by Myshkin.

'N-no, Constant was not there then. He had gone with a letter ... to the Empress Josephine. His place was taken by two orderlies and some Polish ... and that made up the whole suite, except for the generals and marshals whom Napoleon took with him to explore the neighbourhood, and consult about the position of the troops. The one who was oftenest in attendance was Davoust, as I remember now; a huge, stout, coldblooded man, in spectacles, with a strange look in his eyes. He was consulted more often than anyone by the Emperor, who appreciated his judgement. I remember they were in consultation for several days; Davoust used to go in to him morning and evening. Often they even argued; at last Napoleon seemed to be brought to agree. They were alone in the Emperor's study; I was present, scarcely observed by them. Suddenly Napoleon's eye chanced to fall upon me, a strange thought gleamed in his eye. "Child," said he to me, "what do you think? If I adopt the Orthodox faith, and set free your slaves, will the Russians come over to me or not?" "Never!" I cried indignantly. Napoleon was impressed. "In the patriotism shining in that child's eyes," said he, "I read the verdict of the whole Russian people. Enough, Davoust! That's all a fantasy! Explain your other plan."'

'But there was a great idea in that plan too,' said Myshkin, evidently growing interested. 'So you would ascribe that project to Davoust?'

'At any rate, they consulted together. No doubt, the idea was Napoleon's, the idea of an eagle. But there was an idea too in the other plan ... That was the famous *"conseil du lion"*, as Napoleon himself called that advice of Davoust's. That advice was to shut himself up in the Kremlin with all the troops, to build barracks, to dig out earthworks, to place cannons, to kill as many horses as possible and salt the flesh, to procure by purchase or pillage as much corn as possible, and to spend the winter there till spring; and in the spring to fight their way through the Russians. This plan fascinated Napoleon. We used to ride round the Kremlin walls *every* day; he used to show where to demolish, where to construct lunettes, ravelins, or a row of blockhouses – he had a quick eye, swift judgement, a sure aim. Everything was settled at last. Davoust insisted on a final decision. Once more they were alone except for me. Again Napoleon paced the room with folded arms. I could not take my eyes off his face, my heart throbbed. "I am going," said Davoust. "Where?" asked Napoleon. "To salt horseflesh," said Davoust. Napoleon shuddered, it was the turning-point. "Child," said he to me, suddenly, "what do you think of our intention?" No doubt he asked me as sometimes a man of the greatest intelligence will at the last moment toss up to decide. I turned to Davoust instead of to Napoleon and spoke as though by inspiration: "You'd better cut and run home, General!" The plan was abandoned. Davoust shrugged his shoulders, and went out, muttering in a whisper: *"Bah! Il devient supérstitieux."* And the next day the retreat was ordered.'

'All that is extremely interesting,' Myshkin murmured in a very low voice, 'if it really was so ... I mean to say ...' he hastened to correct himself.

'Oh, Prince,' cried the general, so carried away by his own story that perhaps he could not stop short even of the most flagrant indiscretion, 'you say, "if it really was so"! But there was more, I assure you, far more! These are only paltry political facts. But I repeat I was the witness of the tears and groans of that great man at night; and that no one saw but I! Towards the end, indeed, he ceased to weep, there were no more tears, he only moaned at times, but his face was more and more overcast, as it were, with darkness. As though eternity had already cast its dark wings about it. Sometimes at night we spent whole hours alone together, in silence – the mameluke Roustan would be snoring in the next room, the fellow slept fearfully soundly. "But he is devoted to me and to the dynasty," Napoleon used to say about him. Once I was dreadfully grieved; and suddenly he noticed tears in my eyes. He looked at me tenderly. "You feel for me!" he cried, "you, a child, and perhaps another boy will feel for me – my son, *le roi de Rome,* all the rest, all, all hate me, and my brothers would be the first to betray me in misfortune!" I began to sob and flew to him. Then he broke down, he threw his arms round me, and our tears flowed together. "Do, do write a letter to the Empress Josephine!" I sobbed to him. Napoleon started, pondered, and said to me: "You remind me of the one other heart that loves me; I thank you, my dear!" He sat down on the spot, and wrote the letter to the Empress Josephine, which was taken by Constant next day.'

'You did splendidly,' said Myshkin 'In the midst of his evil thoughts you led him to good feelings.'

'Just so, Prince, and how well you put it! How like your own good heart!' cried the general rapturously, and, strange to say, genuine tears stood in his eyes. 'Yes, Prince, yes, that was a magnificent spectacle. And do you know I very nearly went back with him to Paris, and should no doubt have shared with him his "sultry prison isle", but alas! – Fate severed us! We were parted, he to the sultry prison isle, where, who knows, he may have recalled in hours of tragic tribulation the tears of the poor boy who embraced him and forgave him Moscow. I was sent to the cadets' corps, where I found nothing but strict discipline, the roughness of comrades, and … alas! All turned to dust and ashes! "I don't want to part you from your mother, and take you with me," he said to me on the day of the retreat, "but I should like to do something for you." He had already mounted his horse. "Write something as a souvenir for me in my sister's album," said I, timidly, for he was very troubled and gloomy. He turned, asked for a pen, took the album. "How old is your sister?" he asked me.

"Three years old," I answered. *"Une petite fille alors!"* And he wrote in the album:

> *Ne mentez jamais.*
> *Napoléon, votre ami sincère?*

'Such advice and in such a moment, Prince, you can imagine!'

'Yes, that was remarkable.'

'That page was framed in gold under glass and always used to hang on the wall in my sister's drawing-room, in the most conspicuous place, it hung there till her death; she died in childbirth; where it is now -I don't know... but... Ach, Heaven! It's two o'clock already! How I have kept you, Prince! It's unpardonable!'

The general got up from his chair.

'Oh, on the contrary,' mumbled Myshkin. 'You have so entertained me, and ... in fact, it's so interesting; I am so grateful to you!'

'Prince!' said the general again, squeezing his hand till it hurt, gazing at him with sparkling eyes, as though suddenly thunderstruck at some thought he had recollected. 'Prince! You are so kind, so good-hearted, that I'm sometimes positively sorry for you. I am touched when I look at you. Oh, God bless you! May a new life begin for you, blossoming ... with love. Mine is over! Oh, forgive me. Goodbye!'

He went out quickly, covering his face with his hands. Myshkin could not doubt the genuineness of his emotion. He realised too that the old man had gone away enraptured at his success; yet he had a misgiving that he was one of that class of liars with whom lying has become a blinding passion, though at the very acme of their intoxication they secretly suspect that they are not believed, and that they cannot be believed. In his present position the old man might be overwhelmed with shame when he returned to the reality of things. He might suspect Myshkin of too great a compassion for him and feel insulted. 'Haven't I made it worse by leading him on to such flights?' Myshkin wondered uneasily, and suddenly he could not restrain himself, and laughed violently for ten minutes. He was nearly beginning to reproach himself for his laughter, but at once realised that he had nothing to reproach himself with, since he had an infinite pity for the general.

His misgiving proved true. In the evening he received a strange letter, brief but resolute. The general informed him that he was parting from him, too, for ever, that he respected him, and was grateful to him, but that even from him he could not accept of compassion which were derogatory to the dignity of a man who was unhappy enough without that.' When Myshkin heard that the old man had taken refuge with Nina Alexandrovna, he felt almost at ease about him. But we have seen already that the general had caused some sort of trouble at Lizaveta Prokofyevna's too. Here we cannot go into the details, but we wall mention briefly that the upshot of the interview was that the general scared Lizaveta Prokofyevna, and by his bitter insinuations against Ganya had roused her to indignation. He was led out in disgrace. That was why he had spent such a night and such a morning, was completely unhinged and had run out into the street almost in a state of frenzy.

Kolya had not yet fully grasped the position, and even hoped to bring him round by severity.

'Well, where are we off to now, do you suppose, General?' he said. 'You don't want to go to the prince's. You've quarrelled with Lebedyev, you've no money, and I never have any. We are in a nice mess in the street!'

' "It's better to be of a mess than in a mess!" I made that... pun to the admiration of the officers' mess ... in forty-four... In eighteen ... forty-four, yes! ... I don't remember ... oh, don't remind me, don't remind me! "Where is my youth, where is my freshness!" as exclaimed ... who exclaimed it, Kolya?'

'Gogol, father, in "Dead Souls," ' answered Kolya, and he stole a timid glance at his father.

' "Dead Souls"! Oh, yes, dead! When you bury me, write on the tombstone. "Here lies a dead soul!" "Disgrace pursues me!" Who said that, Kolya?'

'I don't know, father.'

'There was no such person as Eropyegov? Eroshka. Eropyegov...' he cried frantically, stopping short in the street. 'And that was said by my son, my own son! Eropyegov, who for eleven months took the place to me of a brother, for whom I fought a duel... Prince Vygoryetsky, our captain said to him over a bottle: "Grisha, where did you get your Anna ribbon, tell me that?" "On the battlefield of my country, that's where I got it!' I shouted: "Bravo, Grisha!" And that led to a duel, and afterwards he was married to Marya Petrovna Su … Sutugin, and was killed in the field … A bullet glanced off the cross on my breast and hit him straight in the brow. "I shall never forget!" he cried, and fell on the spot. I… Eve served with honour, Kolya; I've served nobly, but disgrace – "disgrace pursues me!' You and Nina will come to my grave. "Poor Nina!" I used to call her so in old days, Kolya, long ago in our early days, and how she loved … Nina, Nina! What have I made of your life! For what can you love me, long-suffering soul! Your mother has the soul of an angel, Kolya, do you hear, of an angel!'

'I know that, father. Father, darling, let's go back home to mother! She was running after us! Come, why are you standing still? As though you don't understand … Why are you crying?'

Kolya shed tears himself, and kissed his father's hands.

'You're kissing my hands, mine!'

'Yes, yours, yours. What is there to wonder at? Come, why are you crying in the middle of the street? And you call yourself a general, an army man; come, let's go!'

'May God bless you, dear boy, for having been respectful to a wretched, disgraceful old man. Yes, to a wretched, disgraceful old man, your father … May you, too, have such a boy … *le roi de Rome*. O, "a curse a curse on this house!" '

'But why on earth are you going on like this?' cried Kolya, boiling over suddenly, 'what has happened? Why won't you go home now? Why have you gone out of your mind?'

'I'll explain, I'll explain to you … I'll tell you everything; don't shout, people will hear … *le roi de Rome* … Oh, I'm sick, I'm sad. "Nurse, where is thy tomb?" Who was it cried that, Kolya?'

'I don't know, I don't know who cried it! Let's go home, at once, at once! I'll give Ganya a hiding if necessary … but where are you off to again?'

But the general drew him to the steps of a house close by.

'Where are you going? That's a stranger's house!'

The general sat down on the step, still holding Kolya's hand, and drawing him to him.

'Bend down, bend down!' he muttered. 'I'll tell you everything … disgrace … bend down … your ear, your ear; I'll tell you in your ear …'

'But what is it?' cried Kolya, terribly alarmed, yet stooping down to listen.

'Le roi de Rome ...' whispered the general. He, too, seemed trembling all over.

'What? Why do you keep harping on *le roi de Rome*? ... What?'

'I ... I ...' whispered the general again, clinging more and more tightly to 'his boy's shoulder. 'I... want... I'll tell... you everything, Marya ... Marya ... Petrovna Su-su-su...'

Kolya tore himself away, seized the general by the shoulders, and looked at him frantically. The old man flushed crimson, his lips turned blue, faint spasms ran over his face. Suddenly he lurched forward and began slowly sinking into Kolya's arms.

'A stroke!' the boy shouted aloud in the street, seeing at last what was the matter.

Chapter 5

In reality Varvara Ardalionovna had in her conversation with her brother somewhat exaggerated the certainty of her news concerning Myshkin's engagement to Aglaia Epanchin.

Perhaps, like a sharp-sighted woman, she had divined what was bound to come to pass in the immediate future; perhaps, disappointed at her dream (in which, how ever, she had never really believed) passing off in smoke, she was too human to be able to deny herself the gratification of instilling added bitterness into her brother's heart, by exaggerating the calamity, even though she loved him sincerely and felt sorry for him. In any case, she could not have received such exact information from her friends, the Epanchins; there were only hints, half-uttered words, meaningful silences, and surmises. Though, perhaps, Aglaia's sisters gossiped a little with design, so that they might themselves find out something from Varvara Ardalionovna. It may have been that they, too, could not forego the feminine pleasure of teasing a friend a little, though they had known her from childhood; they could not in so long a time have failed to get at least a glimpse of what she was aiming at.

On the other hand, Myshkin, too, though he was perfectly right in assuring Lebedyev that he had *nothing to* tell him, and that nothing special had happened to him, may have been mistaken. Something very strange certainly was happening to all of them;

nothing had happened, and yet, at the same time, a great deal had happened. Varvara Ardalionovna, with her unfailing feminine instinct, had guessed this last fact.

It is very difficult, however, to explain in proper orderly fashion how it came to pass that everyone in the Epanchins' house was struck at once by the same idea, that something vital had happened to Aglaia, and that her fate was being decided. But as soon as this idea had flashed upon all of them, at once all insisted that they had felt misgivings about it and foreseen it long ago; that it had been clear since the episode of the 'poor knight', and even before, only, at that time, they were unwilling to believe in anything so absurd. So the sisters declared; Lizaveta Prokofyevna, of course, had foreseen and known everything long before anyone, and her 'heart had ached about it' long ago, but, whether she had known it long ago or not, the thought of the prince suddenly became very distasteful to her, because it threw her so completely out of her reckoning. Here was a question which required an immediate answer, but not only was it impossible to answer it, but poor Lizaveta Prokofyevna, however much she struggled, could not even see the question quite clearly. It was a difficult matter. 'Was the prince a good match, or not? Was it all a good thing, or not? If it were not a good thing (and undoubtedly it was not) in what way was it not good? And if, perhaps, it were good (and that was also possible) in what way was it good, again?' The head of the family himself, Ivan Fyodorovitch, was of course first of all surprised, but immediately afterwards made the confession that, 'By Jove, he'd had an inkling of it all this time, now and again, he seemed to fancy something of the sort.' He relapsed into silence at the threatening glances of his wife; he was silent in the morning, but, in the evening, alone with his wife and compelled to speak, suddenly and, as it were, with unwonted boldness he gave vent to some unexpected opinions. 'I say, after all, what did it amount to?' (Silence.) 'All this was very strange of course if it were true, and he didn't dispute it, but...' (Silence again.) 'And, on the other hand, if one looked at the thing without prejudice, the prince was a most charming fellow, upon my word, and... and, and – well, the name, our family name, all that would have the air, so to say, of keeping up the family name which had fallen low in the eyes of the world, that was, looking at it from that point of view because they knew what the world was; the world was the world, but still the prince was not without fortune if it was only a middling one; he had … and, and, and' (prolonged silence, and a complete collapse). When Lizaveta Prokofyevna heard her husband's words, her anger was beyond all bounds.

In her opinion all that had happened was 'unpardonable and criminal folly, a sort of fantastic vision, stupid and absurd!' In the first place, 'this little prince was a sickly idiot, and in the second place – a fool; he knew nothing of the world and had no place in it. To whom could one present him, where was one to put him? He was an impossible sort of democrat; he hadn't even got a post… and… and what would Princess Byelokonsky say? And was this, was this the sort of husband they had imagined and planned for Aglaia?' The last argument, of course, was the chief one. At this reflection the mother's heart shuddered, bleeding and weeping, though, at the same time, something quivered within it, whispering to her, 'In what way is the prince not what is wanted?' And that protest of her own heart was what gave Lizaveta Prokofyevna more trouble than anything.

Aglaia's sisters were for some reason pleased at the thought of Myshkin. It didn't even strike them as very strange; in short, they might at any moment have gone over to his side completely. But they both made up their minds to keep quiet. It had been noticed as an invariable rule in the family that the more obstinate and emphatic Lizaveta Prokofyevna's opposition and objections were on any matter of dispute, the surer sign it was for all of them that she was already almost on the point of agreeing about it. But Alexandra did not find it possible to be perfectly silent. Her mother, who had chosen her long ago as her adviser, was calling for her every minute now, and asking for her opinions and still more for her recollections; that is 'How it had all come to pass? How was it nobody saw it? Why did no one say anything? What was the meaning of that horrid "poor knight"? Why was she alone, Lizaveta Prokofyevna, doomed to worry about everything, to notice and foresee everything, while the others did nothing but count the crows,' and so on, and so on. Alexandra was on her guard at first, and confined herself to remarking that she thought her father's idea rather true, that in the eyes of the world the choice of Prince Myshkin as the husband of one of the Epanchins might seem very satisfactory. Gradually getting warmer, she even added that the prince was by no means 'a fool,' and never had been; and as for his consequence – there was no knowing what a decent man's consequence would depend upon in a few years' time among us in Russia; whether on the successes in the service that were once essential, or on something else. To all this her mamma promptly retorted that Alexandra was 'a Nihilist, and this was all their hateful "woman-question." ' Half an hour later she set off for town and from there to Kamenny Island to find Princess Byelokonsky, who happened, fortunately, to be in Petersburg at the time, though she was soon going away. Princess Byelokonsky was Aglaia's godmother.

The 'old princess' listened to Lizaveta Prokofyevna's feverish and desperate outpourings, and was not in the least moved by the tears of the harassed mother; she even looked at her sarcastically. The old lady was a terrible despot; she would not allow even her oldest friends to be on an equal footing with her, and she looked on Lizaveta Prokofyevna simply as her protégée, as she had been thirty-five years before, and she never could reconcile herself to the abruptness and independence of her character. She observed among other things that 'they were, as usual, in much too great a hurry, and were making a mountain out of a molehill; that so far as she heard, she was not convinced that anything serious had really happened; and wouldn't it be better to wait until there was something to go upon? That the prince, in her opinion, was a nice young man, though sickly, eccentric, and of little consequence. The worst point about him was that he was openly keeping a mistress.' Madame Epanchin was well aware that the princess was rather cross at the failure of Yevgeny Pavlovitch whom she had introduced to them. She went home to Pavlovsk in a state of greater irritation than when she had set out, and she fell foul of everyone at once, chiefly, on the ground that 'they'd all gone crazy,' and that things were not done like that by anyone whatever except by them. 'Why were they in such a hurry? What has happened? So far as I can judge I cannot see that anything has happened! Wait till there's something to go upon! Ivan Fyodorovitch is always fancying things and making mountains out of molehills.'

The upshot of it was that they must keep calm, wait and look on coolly. But alas! The calm did not last ten minutes. The first blow to her composure was the news of what had happened during her absence at Kamenny Island. (Madame Epanchin's visit had taken place on the day after Myshkin had paid a visit after midnight instead of at nine o'clock.) In reply to their mother's impatient questions, the sisters answered in detail to begin with that 'nothing special had happened during her absence,' that the prince had come, that for a long time, quite half an hour, Aglaia had not come down to see him, that afterwards she came down and at once asked Myshkin to play chess; that the prince did not know how to play and Aglaia had beaten him at once; that she was very lively and had scolded the prince, who was horribly ashamed of his ignorance; she had laughed at him dreadfully, so that they were sorry to look at him. Then she suggested a game of cards, 'fools'. But that had turned out quite the other way. The prince played fools in masterly fashion, like a professor; Aglaia had even cheated and changed cards, and had stolen tricks from under his very nose, and yet he had made a 'fool' of her five times running. Aglaia got fearfully angry, quite forgot herself, in fact; she said such biting and horrid things to the prince that at last he left off laughing, and turned quite pale when she told him at last that 'she wouldn't set foot in the room as long as he were there, and that it was positively disgraceful of him to come to them, especially at night, past twelve o'clock, *after all that had happened.' Then* she slammed the door and went out. The prince walked out as though from a funeral, in spite of all their efforts to console him. All of a sudden, a quarter of an hour after the prince had gone, Aglaia had run downstairs to the verandah in such haste that she had not dried her eyes, and they were still wet with tears. She ran down because Kolya had come, bringing a hedgehog. They had all begun looking at the hedgehog. Kolya explained that the hedgehog was not his; that he was out for a walk with a schoolfellow, Kostya Lebedyev, who had stayed in the street and was too shy to come in, because he was carrying a hatchet; that they had just bought the hedgehog and the hatchet from a peasant they had met. The peasant had sold them the hedgehog for fifty kopecks, and they had persuaded him to sell the hatchet, too, because 'he might just as well,' and it was a very good hatchet. All of a sudden Aglaia had begun worrying Kolya to sell her the hedgehog; she got very excited about it, and even called Kolya 'darling'. For a long time Kolya would not consent, but at last he gave way and summoned Kostya Lebedyev, who did in fact come in carrying a hatchet and very much abashed. But then it had suddenly appeared that the hedgehog was not theirs at all, but belonged to another, a third boy, called Petrov, who had given the two of them money to buy Schlosser's *History* for him from a fourth boy, which, the latter, being in want of money, was selling cheap; that they had been going to buy Schlosser's *History*, but they hadn't been able to resist buying the hedgehog, so that it followed that the hedgehog and the hatchet belonged to the third boy, to whom they were carrying them instead of Schlosser's *History*. But Aglaia had so insisted that at last they made up their minds and sold her the hedgehog. As soon as Aglaia had bought the hedgehog, she had, with Kolya's help, placed it in a wicker basket, and covered it with a table-napkin, then she began asking Kolya to take it straight to the prince from her, begging him to accept it as a sign of her 'profound respect'. Kolya agreed, delighted, and promised to do it without fail, but began immediately pestering her to know 'what was meant by the hedgehog and by making him such a present?'

Aglaia had answered that it was not his business. He answered that he was convinced there was some allegory in it. Aglaia had been angry, and flew out at him, saying that he was nothing but a 'silly boy'. Kolya at once retorted that if it were not that he respected her sex and, what was more, his own convictions, he would have shown her on the spot that he knew how to answer such insults. It had ended, however, in Kolya's carrying off the hedgehog in delight, and Kostya Lebedyev had run after him. Aglaia, seeing that Kolya was swinging the basket too much could not resist calling to him from the verandah: 'Please, don't drop it, Kolya darling!' as though she had not been quarrelling with him just before. Kolya had stopped, and he, too, as though he had not been quarrelling, had shouted with the utmost readiness: 'I won't drop him, Aglaia Ivanovna, don't you be uneasy!' and had run on again at full speed. After that Aglaia had laughed tremendously and had gone up to her own room exceedingly pleased, and had been in high spirits the rest of the day.

Lizaveta Prokofyevna was completely confounded by this account. One might ask why? But she was evidently in a morbid state of mind. Her apprehension was aroused to an extreme point, above all, by the hedgehog. What did the hedgehog mean? What compact underlay it? What was understood by it? What did it stand for? What was its cryptic message? Moreover, the luckless Ivan Fyodorovitch, who happened to be present during the inquisition, spoilt the whole business by his reply. In his opinion there was no cryptic message in it, and the hedgehog 'was simply a hedgehog and nothing more – at most it meant a friendly desire to forget the past and make it up; in a word it was all mischief, but harmless and excusable.'

We may note in parenthesis that he had guessed right. Myshkin returned home after being dismissed and ridiculed by Aglaia and sat for half an hour in the blackest despair, when Kolya suddenly appeared with the hedgehog. The sky cleared at once. Myshkin seemed to rise again from the dead; he questioned Kolya, hung on every word he said, repeated his questions ten times over, laughed like a child, and continually shook hands with the two laughing boys who gazed at him so frankly. The upshot of it was that Aglaia forgave him, and that he could go and see her again that evening, and that was for him not only the chief thing but everything.

'What children we still are, Kolya! And ... and ... how nice it is that we are such children,' he cried at last, joyfully.

'The simple fact is she's in love with you, Prince, that's all about it!' Kolya answered authoritatively and impressively.

Myshkin flushed, but this time he said nothing, and Kolya simply laughed and clapped his hands. A minute later Myshkin laughed too, and he was looking at his watch every five minutes to see how time was going and how long it was till evening.

But Madame Epanchin's mood got the upper hand of her, and at last she could not help giving way to hysterical excitement. In spite of the protests of her husband and daughters, she immediately sent for Aglaia in order to put the fatal question to her, and to extort from her a perfectly clear and final answer: 'To make an end of it once for all, to be rid of it, and not to refer to it again! I can't exist till evening without knowing!' And only then they all realised to what an absurd pass they had brought things. They could get nothing out of Aglaia except feigned amazement, indignation, laughter and jeers at the prince and at all who questioned her. Lizaveta Prokofyevna lay on her bed and did not come down till evening tea, when Myshkin was expected. She awaited his coming with a tremor, and almost went into hysterics when he appeared.

And Myshkin, for his part, came in timidly, as it were feeling his way, looking into everyone's *eyes,* and seeming to question them all because Aglaia was not in the room again, which made him uneasy at once. There were no other guests present that evening; the family was alone. Prince S— was still in Petersburg, busy over the affairs of Yevgeny Pavlovitch's uncle. 'If only he could have been here and said something, anyway,' said Lizaveta Prokofyevna to herself, deploring his absence. Ivan Fyodorovitch sat with a very puzzled air; the sisters were serious, and, as though intentionally, silent. Lizaveta Prokofyevna did not know how to begin the conversation. At last she vigorously abused the railway, and looked with resolute challenge at Myshkin.

Alas! Aglaia did not come down, and Myshkin was lost. Losing his head and hardly able to articulate, he began to express the opinion that to improve the line would be exceedingly useful, but Adelaïda suddenly laughed, and he was crushed again. At that very instant Aglaia came in. Calmly and with dignity she made Myshkin a ceremonious bow, and solemnly seated herself in the most conspicuous place at the round table. She looked enquiringly at Myshkin. Everyone realised that the moment had come when all doubts would be removed.

'Did you get my hedgehog?' Aglaia asked firmly and almost angrily.

'I did,' answered Myshkin, with a sinking heart, and he flushed red.

'Explain at once what you think about it. That's essential for the peace of mind of Mamma and all the family.'

'Come, come, Aglaia ...' began the general, suddenly uneasy.

'This is beyond everything!' said Lizaveta Prokofyevna, for some reason suddenly alarmed.

'It's not beyond anything, *Maman*,' her daughter answered sternly at once. 'I sent the prince a hedgehog today, and I want to know his opinion. Well, Prince?'

'What sort of opinion, Aglaia Ivanovna?'

'Of the hedgehog.'

'That is, I suppose, Aglaia Ivanovna, you want to know how I took... the hedgehog ... or, rather, how I regarded the ... sending ... of the hedgehog, that is ... I imagine in such a case, that is, in fact...

He gasped and was silent.

'Well, you've not said much,' said Aglaia, after waiting five seconds. 'Very well, I agree to drop the hedgehog, but I am very glad that I can put an end to all this accumulation of misunderstanding. Let me know from you personally: are you making me an offer or not?'

'Good heavens!' broke from Lizaveta Prokofyevna. Myshkin started and drew back; Ivan Fyodorovitch was petrified; the sisters frowned.

'Don't lie, Prince, tell the truth. I am persecuted with strange questionings on your account. Is there any foundation for these questionings?... Well?'

'I have not made you an offer, Aglaia Ivanovna,' said Myshkin, suddenly reviving. 'But you know how I love you and believe in you ... even now

'What I am enquiring is – do you ask for my hand, or not?'

'I do,' Myshkin answered with a sinking heart.

A general stir of agitation followed.

'All this is not the thing, my dear fellow,' said Ivan Fyodorovitch, violently agitated. 'This ... this is almost impossible if it's like this, Aglaia ... Forgive it, Prince, forgive it, my dear fellow! ... Lizaveta Prokofyevna!' he turned to his wife for assistance, 'you must ... go into it!'

'I refuse, I refuse!' cried Lizaveta Prokofyevna, waving her hands.

'Allow me to speak, *Maman*. I count for something in this business; the extreme moment of my fate is being decided (this was the expression Aglaia used) 'and I want to find out for myself, and I'm glad besides that it's before everyone ... Allow me to ask you, Prince, if you "cherish such intentions", how do you propose to secure my happiness?'

'I really don't know, Aglaia Ivanovna, how to answer you, in this question ... What is there to answer? And besides... is it necessary?'

'You seem to be embarrassed and out of breath; take a rest and pull yourself together; drink a glass of water, though they'll soon give you some tea.'

'I love you, Aglaia Ivanovna. I love you very much, I love no one but you and ... don't jest, I implore you ... I love you very much.'

'This is an important matter, though, we are not children; we must look at it practically ... Have the goodness now to explain what your fortune is?'

'Come, come, Aglaia! What are you doing! This is not the thing, not the thing,' Ivan Fyodorovitch muttered in dismay.

'Disgraceful!' said Lizaveta Prokofyevna in a loud whisper.

'She's out of her mind!' Alexandra whispered as loudly.

'My fortune ... that is, money?' said Myshkin, surprised.

'Just so.'

'I have ... I have now one hundred and thirty-five thousand,' Myshkin muttered, reddening.

'Is that all?' said Aglaia aloud, in open wonder, without the faintest blush. 'It doesn't matter though, especially with economy. Do you intend to enter the service?'

'I was thinking of preparing for an examination to become a private tutor ...'

'Very appropriate; no doubt that will increase our income. Are you proposing to be a court chamberlain?'

'A court chamberlain? I never imagined such a thing, but...'

But at this point the two sisters could not contain themselves and burst into laughter. Adelaïda had long noticed in the twitching features of Aglaia's face symptoms of imminent and irrepressible laughter, which she was, for the time, controlling with all her might. Aglaia looked menacingly at her laughing sisters, but a second later she, too, broke down, and went off into a frantic, almost hysterical, fit of laughter. At last she leapt up and ran out of the room.

'I knew it was all a joke and nothing more!' cried Adelaïda, 'from the very beginning, from the hedgehog.'

'No, this I will not allow; I will not,' cried Lizaveta Prokofyevna, suddenly boiling over with anger, and she hastened out after Aglaia. The sisters ran out immediately after her. Myshkin was left alone in the room with the head of the family.

'This is ... could you have imagined anything like it, Lyov Nikolayevitch?' General Epanchin cried abruptly, hardly knowing what he wanted to say. 'Yes, seriously, speak?'

'I see that Aglaia Ivanovna was laughing at me,' said Myshkin sadly.

'Wait a bit, my boy. I'll go and you wait a bit, because ... you at least, you at least, Lyov Nikolayevitch, explain to me how all this happened, and what does it all mean, looked at as a whole, so to say? You must admit, my boy – I'm her father; anyway I'm her father and so I don't understand anything about it; you at least let me know.'

'I love Aglaia Ivanovna; she knows that... and I think she has known it a long time.'

The general shrugged his shoulders.

'Strange, strange! ... And are you very fond of her?'

'Very.'

'This all seems so strange to me. That is, such a surprise and blow that... You see, my dear boy, it's not the fortune (though I did expect you had rather more), but... my daughter's happiness... in fact... are you in a position to secure... her happiness? And... and... what does it mean: is it a joke or real on her side? Not on your side, but on hers, I mean?'

Alexandra's voice was heard at the door, calling her father.

'Wait a bit, my boy, wait a bit! Wait a bit and think it over. I'll be back directly,' he said hurriedly, and almost in alarm he rushed out in response to the call.

He found his wife and daughter in each other's arms, mingling their tears. They were tears of bliss, tenderness, and reconciliation. Aglaia was kissing her mother's hands, cheeks and lips; they were hugging each other closely.

'Here, look at her, Ivan Fyodorovitch! There you have the whole of her,' said Lizaveta Prokofyevna.

Aglaia lifted her happy, tear-stained little face from her mother's bosom, and looked at her father; she laughed aloud, jumped up to him, embraced him warmly, and kissed him several times. Then she flung herself on her mother again and hid her face completely in her bosom so that no one could see it, and began crying again at once. Lizaveta Prokofyevna covered her with the end of her shawl.

'What are you doing with us, you cruel girl – that's what I want to know,' she said, but joyfully, as though she could breathe more easily now.

'Cruel! Yes, cruel!' Aglaia assented suddenly. 'Spoilt! Good-for-nothing! Tell Papa that. Oh, yes, he's here! Papa, you're here? Do you hear?' she laughed through her tears.

'My dear, my idol!' The general kissed her hand, beaming all over with happiness. (Aglaia did not take her hand away.) 'So you love this young man then?'

'No-no-no! I can't bear ... your young man, I can't endure him!' cried Aglaia, boiling over suddenly and raising her head. 'And if you ever dare again ... I mean it, Papa, I mean it; do you hear? I mean it.'

And she certainly did mean it; she flushed all over and her eyes gleamed. Her father was nonplussed and alarmed. But Lizaveta

Prokofyevna made a signal to him behind her daughter, and he took it to mean: 'Don't ask questions.'

'If it is so, my angel, it's as you like, it's for you to decide, he's waiting there alone. Shouldn't we give him a delicate hint to go away?'

Ivan Fyodorovitch, in his turn, winked at his wife.

'No, no, that's not necessary; especially a "delicate" one. You go to him yourself; I'll come in afterwards, directly. I want to beg that ... young man's pardon, because I hurt his feelings.'

'Yes, you did dreadfully,' Ivan Fyodorovitch assented seriously.

'Well, then ... you all had better stay here, and I'll go in first alone, you shall come directly after; come the very second after, that's better,' She had already reached the door but suddenly turned back.

'I shall laugh! I shall die of laughing!' she declared sorrowfully.

But at the same second she turned and ran in to Myshkin.

'Come, what's the meaning of it? What do you think?' Ivan Fyodorovitch began quickly.

'I am afraid to say,' Lizaveta Prokofyevna answered as quickly. 'But to my mind it's clear.'

'To mine, too. As clear as day. She loves him.'

'Not only loves; she's in love with him,' put in Alexandra. 'But what a man, when you think of it!'

'God bless her if such is her fate!' said Lizaveta Prokofyevna, crossing herself devoutly.

'It must be her fate,' the general agreed, 'and there's no escaping fate.' And they all went into the dining-room where a surprise awaited them again.

Aglaia, far from laughing as she had feared on going up to Myshkin, said to him almost shyly, 'Forgive a stupid, nasty, spoilt girl' (she took his hand), 'and believe me we all respect you immensely. And if I dared to turn into ridicule your splendid ... kind simplicity, forgive me as you'd forgive a child for being naughty. Forgive me for persisting in an absurdity, which could not, of course, have the slightest consequence.'

The last words Aglaia uttered with particular emphasis.

The father, mother, and sisters were all in the drawing-room in time to see and hear all this, and all were struck by the words, 'absurdity which cannot have the slightest consequence.' And still more so by the earnestness with which Aglaia spoke of that absurdity. They all looked at one another questioningly. But Myshkin did not seem to understand those words and was at the very summit of happiness.

'Why do you talk like that?' he muttered. 'Why do you … ask … forgiveness?'

He would have said that he wasn't worthy of her asking his forgiveness. Who knows, perhaps he did notice the meaning of the words, 'absurdity which cannot have the slightest consequence,' but being such a strange man, perhaps, he was relieved at those words. There is no doubt that the mere fact that he could come and see Aglaia, again without hindrance, that he was allowed to talk to her, sit with her, walk with her was the utmost bliss to him; and who knows, perhaps he would have been satisfied with that for the rest of his life. (It was just this contentment that Lizaveta Prokofyevna secretly dreaded; she understood him; she dreaded many things in secret, which she could not have put into words herself.)

It's difficult to describe how completely Myshkin regained his spirits and courage that evening. He was so light-hearted that they grew lighthearted watching him – as Aglaia's sisters expressed it afterwards. He was talkative, and that had not happened to him again since the morning, six months ago, when he had first made the acquaintance, of the Epanchins. On his return to Petersburg he was noticeably and intentionally silent and had quite lately said to Prince S—, in the presence of all, that he must restrain himself and be silent, that he might not degrade an idea by his expressing it. He was almost the only one who talked that evening, he described many things. He answered questions clearly, minutely, and with pleasure. But there was not a glimpse of a word approaching love-making in his conversation. He expressed earnest, sometimes profound ideas. Myshkin even expounded some of his own views, his own private observations, so that it would have been funny, if it had not been so well expressed; as all who heard him that evening agreed later on. Though General Epanchin liked serious subjects of conversation, yet both he and Lizaveta Prokofyevna secretly thought it was too intellectual, so that they felt actually sad at the end of the evening. But Myshkin went so far at last as to tell some very amusing stories, which he was the first to laugh at, so that the others laughed more at his joyful laugh than at the story itself. As for Aglaia, she hardly spoke all the evening, but she listened all the while to Lyov Nikolayevitch, and gazed at him even more than she listened.

'She looks at him and can't take her eyes off him; she hangs on every word he utters, she catches everything,' Lizaveta Prokofyevna said afterwards to her husband. 'But tell her that she loves him and you'll have the walls about your ears.'

'There's no help for it, it's fate!' said the general, shrugging his shoulders.

And long afterwards he kept repeating the phrase which pleased him. We will add that, as a business man, he too disliked a great deal in the present position, above all its indefiniteness. But he, too, resolved for the time to keep quiet, and to take his cue … from Lizaveta Prokofyevna.

The happy frame of mind of the family did not last long. Next day Aglaia quarrelled with Myshkin again, and things went on like that for several days. For hours together she would jeer at Myshkin and make him almost a laughing-stock. It is true they would sometimes sit for an hour or two together in the arbour in the garden, but it was observed that, at such times, Myshkin almost always read aloud the newspaper or some book to Aglaia.

'Do you know,' Aglaia said one day, interrupting his reading of the newspaper, 'I have noticed that you are dreadfully uneducated. You don't know anything thoroughly, if one asks you who someone is, or in what year anything happened, or the name of a treaty. You're much to be pitied.'

'I told you that I have not much learning,' answered Myshkin.

'What have you if you haven't that? How can I respect you after that? Read on; or rather, don't. Leave off reading.'

And again, that evening, there was something that mystified them all in her behaviour. Prince S— came back; Aglaia was very cordial to him, she made many enquiries about Yevgeny Pavlovitch. (Myshkin had not yet come in.) Suddenly Prince S— permitted himself an allusion to 'another approaching event in the family,' to a few words which had escaped Lizaveta Prokofyevna, suggesting that they might have to put off Adelaïda's wedding again in order that the two weddings might take place together. Aglaia flared up in a way no one could have expected at 'these stupid suppositions,' and among other things the phrase broke from her that she had 'no intention at present of taking the place of anybody's mistress.'

These words struck everybody, and above all her parents. In a secret confabulation with her husband, Lizaveta Prokofyevna insisted that he must go into the question of Nastasya Filippovna with Myshkin, once for all.

Ivan Fyodorovitch swore that all this was only 'a whim,' and put it down to Aglaia's 'delicacy'; that if Prince S— had not referred to the marriage there would not have been this outburst, because Aglaia knew herself, knew on good authority, that it was all a slander of ill-natured people, and that Nastasya Filippovna was going to marry Rogozhin, that the prince had nothing to do with it, let alone a *liaison* with her; and never had had, if one's to speak the whole truth.

Yet Myshkin went on being blissful and untroubled by anything. Oh, of course, he too noticed sometimes something gloomy and impatient in Aglaia's expression, but he had more faith in something different, and the gloom vanished of itself. Once having faith in anything, he could not waver afterwards. Perhaps he was too much at ease in his mind, so it seemed at least to Ippolit who chanced to meet him in the park.

'Well, didn't I tell you at the time that you were in love?' he began, going up to Myshkin and stopping him.

Myshkin shook hands with him and congratulated him on his 'looking so much better.' The invalid seemed hopeful himself, as consumptives are so apt to be.

He had come up to Myshkin to say something sarcastic about his happy expression, but he soon drifted off the subject and began to talk about himself. He began complaining, and his complaints were many and long-winded, and rather incoherent.

'You wouldn't believe,' he concluded, 'how irritable they all are there; how petty, how egoistic, vain, and commonplace. Would you believe it, they only took me on condition of my dying as quickly as possible, and now they're all in a fury that I am not dying, but, on the contrary, better. It's a farce! I bet you don't believe me.'

Myshkin had no inclination to reply.

'I sometimes think of moving back to you again,' Ippolit added carelessly. 'So you don't think they're capable of taking a man in on condition of his dying as quickly as possible?'

'I thought they invited you with other views.'

'Aha! You are by no means so simple as you are reputed to be! Now is not the time, or I'd tell you something about that wretched Ganya and his hopes. They're undermining your position, Prince;

they're doing it mercilessly and … it's quite pitiful to see you so serene. But, alas! You can't help it!'

'That's a funny thing to pity me for!' laughed Myshkin; 'do you think I should be happier if I were less serene?'

'Better be unhappy and know the truth, than be happy and live … like a fool. You don't seem to believe that you have a rival – and in that quarter?'

'What you say about a rival is rather cynical, Ippolit; I am sorry I have not the right to answer you. As for Gavril Ardalionovitch, judge for yourself whether he can be happy in his mind after all he has lost; that is, if you know anything at all about his affairs? It seems to me better to look at it from that point of view. There's time for him to change; he has a life before him, and life is rich … though … though …' Myshkin broke off uncertainly. 'As for undermining I don't know what you are talking about; let's drop this conversation, Ippolit.'

'We'll drop it for the time; besides you must always go in for being gentlemanly, of course. Yes, Prince, you'd have to touch it with your finger in order to disbelieve it again. Ha, ha! And do you despise me very much now, what do you think?'

'What for? Because you have suffered and are still suffering more than we?'

'No, but because I am unworthy of my suffering.'

'If anyone is able to suffer more, he must be more worthy of suffering. When Aglaia Ivanovna read your confession, she wanted to see you, but…'

'She's putting it off … she can't. I understand, I understand …' Ippolit interrupted, as though anxious to break off the conversation as quickly as possible. 'By the way, they tell me that you read all that rigmarole aloud to her yourself; it was literally in delirium that I wrote it and … did it. And I don't understand how anyone can be so -I won't say cruel (it would be humiliating for me), but so childishly vain and revengeful, as to reproach me with that confession and to use it against me as a weapon. Don't be uneasy, I'm not talking about you.'

'But I am sorry that you repudiate that manuscript, Ippolit; it is sincere, and you know that even the most absurd points in it, and there are many of them' (Ippolit scowled), 'are redeemed by suffering, because to confess them is suffering and … perhaps great manliness. The idea that animated you must have had a noble foundation, however it may seem. I see that more clearly as time goes on, I swear I do. I don't judge you. I speak to say what I think, and I'm sorry that I didn't speak at the time.'

Ippolit flushed hotly. The thought flashed through his mind that Myshkin was pretending, and taking him in. But, looking into his face he could not help being convinced of his sincerity. His face brightened.

'Yet I must die all the same!' he said, almost adding, 'a man like me!'

'And only fancy how your Ganya plagues me; the objection he has trumped up is that three or four who heard my confession will very likely die before I do. What do you say to that! He supposes that's a comfort to me, ha! ha! In the first place they haven't died yet. And even if these people did die, you'll admit that's no comfort to me. He judges by himself, but he goes further. He simply abuses me now, he says a decent man would die in silence, and that it's all egoism on my part! What do you say to that! Yes, what about egoism on his part; what refinement, and yet at the same time what ox-like coarseness of egoism, though they can't see it in themselves! Have you ever read, Prince, of the death of Stepan Glyebov in the eighteenth century? I happened to read about it yesterday…'

'What Stepan Glyebov?'

'He was impaled in the time of Peter.'

'Oh dear, yes, I know. He was fifteen hours on the stake, in the frost, in a fur coat, and died with extraordinary grandeur. Yes, I read it… what of it?'

'God grants such deaths to men, but not to us! You think, perhaps, I'm not capable of dying like Glyebov?'

'Oh, not at all!' Myshkin said, confused. 'I only meant to say that you … that is, not that you would not be like Glyebov, but… that you … that you would be more likely then to be …'

'I guess, like Osterman? And not Glyebov – that's what you meant to say?'

'What Osterman?' said Myshkin, surprised.

'Osterman, the diplomat Osterman, Peter's Osterman,' muttered Ippolit, suddenly disconcerted.

A certain perplexity followed.

'Oh, n-n-no! I didn't mean to say that,' Myshkin said emphatically, after a brief silence. 'You would never, I think … have been an Osterman.'

Ippolit frowned.

'The reason I maintain that, though,' Myshkin resumed suddenly, obviously anxious to set things right, 'is because the men of those days (I swear I've always been struck by it) were absolutely not the same people that we are now; it was not the same race as now, in our age, really, it seems we are a different species... In those days they were men of one idea, but now we are more nervous, more developed, more sensitive; men capable of two or three ideas at once ... Modern men are broader-minded and I swear that this prevents their being so all-of-a-piece as they were in those days. I... I simply said it with that idea, and not...'

'I understand; you're doing your level best to console me now for the simplicity with which you disagreed with me, ha, ha! You're a perfect child, Prince. I notice though that you all handle me like a china cup ... I'm not angry, it's all right, never mind! Anyway, we've had an awfully funny conversation; you're sometimes a perfect child, Prince. Let me tell you, though, that I should like perhaps to be something better than Osterman. It would not be worth while to rise from the dead for the sake of Osterman ... I see I ought to die as soon as possible though, or I, myself, shall... Leave me. Goodbye! Well now, come, tell me what do you think would be the best way for me to die? ... To make a virtuous ending of it as far as may be, that is? Come, tell me!'

'Pass by us, and forgive us our happiness,' said Myshkin in a low voice.

'Ha, ha, ha! Just as I thought! I knew it was sure to be something like that! Though you are ... you are ... Well, well! You are eloquent people! Goodbye! Goodbye!'

Chapter 6

What Varvara Ardalionovna had told her brother about the evening party at the Epanchins' at which Princess Byelokonsky was expected was also quite correct; the guests were expected that evening. But in this case too she had expressed herself rather too strongly. It had, indeed, all been arranged with too much hurry, and even with some quite unnecessary excitement, just because in that family 'they never could do things like other people.' It was all due to the impatience of Lizaveta Prokofyevna, who was 'anxious not to be kept longer in suspense,' and to the feverish tremors of both parental hearts concerning the happiness of their favourite daughter. Moreover, Princess Byelokonsky really was going away soon, and as her patronage certainly did carry weight in society, and as they hoped she would be well disposed to Myshkin, the parents reckoned that 'the world' would accept Aglaia's betrothed straight from the hands of the omnipotent 'old princess,' and that therefore if there were anything strange about it, it would seem much less strange under such patronage. The real fact was that the parents were quite unable to settle the question themselves whether there was anything strange in the matter, and if so how much. Or whether there were nothing strange about it at all. The candid and friendly opinion of influential and competent persons would be of use just at the present moment when, thanks to Aglaia, nothing had been finally settled. In any case, sooner or later the prince would have to be introduced into society, of which he had so far not the faintest idea. In short, they were intending to 'show him. The party arranged was, however, a simple one. Only 'friends of the family' were expected, and not many of them. One other lady besides Princess Byelokonsky was coming, the wife of a very important dignitary. Yevgeny Pavlovitch was almost the only young man expected, and he was to escort Princess Byelokonsky.

Myshkin heard that Princess Byelokonsky was coming three days beforehand; of the party he learned only the previous day. He noticed, of course, the busy air of the members of the family, and even from certain insinuating and anxious attempts to broach the subject to him, he perceived that they dreaded the impression he might make. But somehow the Epanchins, all without exception, were possessed by the idea that he was too simple to be capable of guessing that they were uneasy in this way on his account; and so, looking at him, everyone was inwardly troubled. He did in fact, however, attach scarcely any consequence to the approaching event. He was occupied with something quite different. Aglaia was becoming every hour more gloomy and capricious – that was crushing him. When he knew that they were expecting Yevgeny Pavlovitch, he was greatly delighted, and said that he had long been wishing to see him. For some reason no one liked these words. Aglaia went out of the room in vexation, and only late at night, about twelve o'clock, when Myshkin was going away, she seized an opportunity of a few words alone with him, as she saw him out.

'I should like you not to come and see us all day tomorrow, but to come in the evening when these ... visitors are here. You know that there are to be visitors?'

She spoke impatiently and with intense severity. It was the first time she had spoken to him of this 'party.' To her, too, the idea of these visitors was almost insufferable; everyone noticed it. She may have felt greatly tempted to quarrel with her parents about it, but pride and modesty kept her from speaking. Myshkin saw at once that she also was afraid on his account (and did not want to admit that she was afraid), and he too felt suddenly frightened.

'Yes, I've been invited,' he answered.

She evidently found it difficult to go on.

'Can one speak to you about anything serious? Just for once?' She grew suddenly fearfully angry, not knowing why, and not able to control herself.

'You can, and I am listening. I'm very glad,' muttered Myshkin.

Aglaia paused again for a minute, and began with evident repugnance, 'I didn't want to dispute with them about it, for you can't make them see reason about some things. Some of *Maman's* principles have always been revolting to me. I say nothing about papa; it's no use expecting anything from him. *Maman* is a noble woman, of course; if you dared to propose anything mean to her, you'd see. Yet she bows down before these ... contemptible creatures. I don't mean the old princess. She's a contemptible old woman, contemptible in character, but clever and knows how to turn them all round her finger – one can say that for her, anyway. Oh, the meanness of it! And it's ludicrous. We've always been people of the middle-class, as middle-class as could possibly be. Why force ourselves into this aristocratic circle? And my sisters are on the same tack. Prince S— has upset them all. Why are you pleased that Yevgeny Pavlovitch will be here?'

'Listen, Aglaia,' said Myshkin. 'It seems to me that you are very much afraid that I shall be floored tomorrow ... in this company.'

'Me afraid? On your account?' Aglaia flushed all over. 'Why should I be afraid on your account, even if you ... even if you do disgrace yourself utterly. What is it to me? And how can you use such words? What do you mean by being 'floored'? It's a contemptible word, vulgar!'

'It's ... a schoolboy word.'

'Quite so, a schoolboy word! Contemptible! You seem to intend to use words like that all the evening tomorrow. You can look up more of them at home in your dictionary; you'll make a sensation! It's a pity that you know how to come into the room properly. Where did you learn it? Do you know how to take a cup of tea and drink it properly, when everyone's looking at you on purpose?'

'I believe I do.'

'I'm sorry you do. It would have made me laugh if you didn't. Mind you break the Chinese vase in the drawing-room, anyway. It was an expensive one. Please do break it; it was a present. Mother would be beside herself and would cry before everyone. She's so fond of it! Gesticulate as you always do, knock it over and break it. Sit near it on purpose.'

'On the contrary, I'll sit as far from it as I can. Thank you for warning me.'

'Then you are afraid you will wave your arms about. I'll bet anything you'll begin talking on some serious, learned, lofty subject. That will be ... tactful.'

'I think that would be stupid ... if it's not appropriate.'

'Listen, once for all,' said Aglaia, losing all patience. 'If you talk about anything like capital punishment, or the economic position of Russia, or of how "beauty will save the world" ... of course I should be delighted and laugh at it... but I warn you, never show yourself before me again! Do you hear? I'm in earnest! This time I'm in earnest!'

She really was *in earnest* in her threat. Something exceptional could be heard in her words and seen in her eyes, which Myshkin had never noticed before, and which was not like a joke.

'Now, after what you've said I'm sure to talk too much ... even ... perhaps break the vase. I wasn't in the least afraid before, and now I'm afraid of everything. I shall certainly be floored.'

'Then hold your tongue. Sit quiet and hold your tongue.'

'I shan't be able to. I'm sure I shall be so alarmed that I shall begin talking and shall break the vase. Perhaps I shall fall down on the slippery floor, or something of that sort, for that has happened to me before. I shall dream about it all night. Why did you talk to me about it!'

Aglaia looked gloomily at him.

'I tell you what: I'd better not come at all tomorrow! I'll report myself ill, and that will be the end of it,' he concluded at last.

Aglaia stamped and turned positively white with anger.

'Good God! Did anyone ever see anything like it? He's not coming, when it has all been arranged on purpose for him and … my goodness! It's a treat to have to do with a senseless person like you.'

'I'll come! I'll come!' Myshkin broke in hastily. 'And I give you my word of honour that I'll sit the whole evening without opening my mouth. I'll manage it.'

'You'll do well. You said just now you'd "report yourself ill." Where do you pick up such expressions? What possesses you to talk to me in such language? Are you trying to tease me?'

'I beg your pardon; that's a schoolboy expression too. I won't use it. I quite understand that you are … anxious … on my account (yes, don't be angry), and I'm awfully glad of it. You don't know how frightened I am now – and how glad I am of your words. But I assure you, all this panic is petty and nonsensical. It really is, Aglaia. But the joy remains. I'm awfully glad that you're such a child, such a kind good child! Oh, how splendid you can be, Aglaia!'

Aglaia, of course, was on the point of flying into a rage, but suddenly a rush of quite unexpected feeling took possession of her soul in one instant.

'And you won't reproach me for my coarse words just now … someday … afterwards?' she asked suddenly.

'How can you? How can you? Why are you flaring up again? And now you're looking gloomy again. You've taken to looking too gloomy sometimes now, Aglaia, as you never used to look. I know why that is…'

'Hush! Hush!'

'No, it's better to speak. I've been wanting to say it a long time. I've said it already, but that's not enough, for you didn't believe me. There's one person who stands between us …'

'Hush, hush, hush, hush!' Aglaia interrupted suddenly, gripping his hand tightly and looking at him almost in terror.

At that moment her name was called. With an air of relief she left him at once and ran away.

Myshkin was in a fever all night. Strange to say, he had been feverish for several nights running. That night, when he was half delirious, the thought occurred to him: what if he should have a fit tomorrow before everyone? He had had fits in public. He turned cold at the thought. All night he imagined himself in a mysterious and incredible company among strange people. The worst of it was that he 'kept talking.' He knew he ought not to talk, but he went on talking all the time; he was trying to persuade them of something. Yevgeny Pavlovitch and Ippolit were of the party, and seemed extremely friendly.

He waked up at nine o'clock with a headache, with confusion in his mind and strange impressions. He felt an intense and unaccountable desire to see Rogozhin, to see him and to say a great deal to him – what about he could not himself have said – then he fully made up his mind to go and see Ippolit. There was some confused sensation in his heart, so much so that, although he felt acutely what happened to him that morning, he could not fully realise it. One thing that happened to him was a visit from Lebedyev.

Lebedyev made his appearance rather early, soon after nine, and was almost completely drunk. Although Myshkin had not been observant of late yet he could not help seeing that ever since General Ivolgin had left them – that is, for the last three days, Lebedyev had been behaving very badly. He seemed to have suddenly become extremely greasy and dirty, his cravat was on one side, and the collar of his coat was torn. In his lodge he kept up a continual storm, which was audible across the little courtyard. Vera had come in on one occasion in tears to tell him about it.

On presenting himself that morning, he talked very strangely, beating himself on the breast and blaming himself for something.

'I have received ... I have received the chastisement for my baseness and treachery – a slap in the face,' he concluded tragically at last.

'A slap in the face! From whom? And so early?'

'So early?' and Lebedyev smiled sarcastically. 'Time has nothing to do with it... even for physical chastisement... but I've received a moral, not a physical, castigation.'

He suddenly sat down without ceremony and began to tell his story. It was a very incoherent one. Myshkin frowned, and wanted to get away, but all at once some words caught his attention. He was struck dumb with amazement. Mr Lebedyev was telling of strange things.

He had apparently begun about some letter. Aglaia Ivanovna's name was mentioned. Then Lebedyev began all at once bitterly reproaching Myshkin himself; it could be gathered that he was offended with the prince. At first, he said, the prince had honoured him with his confidence in transactions with a certain 'person' (with Nastasya Filippovna), but had afterwards broken with him completely and had dismissed him with ignominy, and had even been so offensive as to repel with rudeness 'an innocent question about the approaching changes in the house.' With drunken tears, Lebedyev protested that 'after that, he could endure no more, especially as he knew a great deal... a very great deal... from Rogozhin, from Nastasya Filippovna, and from her friend, and from Varvara Ardalionovna ... herself... and from ... and from even Aglaia Ivanovna; would you believe it, through Vera, through my beloved, my only daughter ... yes ... though indeed she's not my only one, for I've three. And who was it informed Lizaveta Prokofyevna by letters, in dead secret, of course? Ha-ha! Who has been writing to her about all the shiftings and changings of the 'personage,' Nastasya Filippovna? Ha-ha-ha! Who, who is the anonymous writer, allow me to ask?'

'Can it be you?' cried Myshkin.

'Just so,' the drunkard replied with dignity, 'and this very morning at half-past eight, only half an hour – no, three-quarters of an hour ago – I informed the noble-hearted mother that I had an incident ... of importance to communicate to her. I informed her by letter through a maid at the back door. She received it.'

'You've just seen Lizaveta Prokofyevna!' cried Myshkin, unable to believe his ears.

'I saw her just now and received a blow... a moral one. She gave me back the letter; in fact she flung it in my face unopened ... and even kicked me out ... only morally speaking, not physically ... though it was almost physical too, not far off it!'

'What letter was it she flung at you unopened?'

'Why ... ha-ha-ha! Haven't I told you? I thought I'd said that already ... It was a letter I had received on purpose to give to ...'

'From whom? For whom?'

It was difficult to make head or tail of some 'explanations' of Lebedyev's, or to understand anything from them. But as far as he could make out, Myshkin gathered that the letter had been brought in the early morning to Vera Lebedyev by the servant girl, to be delivered to the person to whom it was addressed … 'just as before… just as before to a certain personage, and from the same person. (For I designate one of them a "person" and the other only a "personage," as derogatory and distinguishing, for there is a great distinction between an innocent and high-born young lady of a general's family and … a lady of the other sort.) And so the letter was from that 'person' beginning with the letter "A" …'

'How can that be? To Nastasya Filippovna? Nonsense!' cried Myshkin.

'It was, it was. Or if not to her, to Rogozhin; it's all the same, to Rogozhin … and there was even one to Mr Terentyev, to be handed on from the person beginning with "A," ' said Lebedyev, smiling and winking.

As he was continually mixing up one thing with another and forgetting what he had begun to speak about, Myshkin held his peace to let him speak out. Yet it still remained far from clear whether the correspondence had been carried on through him or through Vera. Since he himself declared that 'it was just the same whether the letters were for Rogozhin or for Nastasya Filippovna,' it seemed more likely that the letters had not passed through his hands, if there actually had been letters. How this letter had come into his hands remained absolutely inexplicable. The most probable explanation was that he had somehow snatched them from Vera … stolen them on the sly and carried them for some object to Lizaveta Prokofyevna. That was what Myshkin gathered and understood at last.

'You're out of your mind!' he cried in extreme agitation.

'Not quite, honoured prince,' Lebedyev replied, not without malice. 'It's true, I meant to hand it to you, to put it into your own hands; to do you a service … but I reflected that it was better to be of use in that quarter by revealing everything to the noble-hearted mother… as I had communicated with her before by letter anonymously; and when I wrote to her just now a preliminary note asking her to see me at twenty minutes past eight I signed myself again "your secret correspondent." I was admitted promptly with the utmost haste by the back door… to the presence of the illustrious lady.'

'Well?'

'And there, as you know already, she nearly beat me; very nearly, so that one might almost say she practically did beat me.

And she threw the letter in my face. It's true she wanted to keep it… I saw it, I noticed it, but she thought better of it and flung it in my face: "Since a fellow like you has been entrusted with it, give it!" … She was positively offended. Since she wasn't ashamed to say so before me, she must have been offended. She's a hot-tempered lady!'

'Where is the letter now?'

'Why, I've got it still. Here it is.'

And he handed Myshkin Aglaia's note to Gavril Ardalionovitch, which the latter two hours later showed to his sister with such triumph.

'That letter can't remain with you.'

'It's for you, for you. It's to you I am bringing it,' Lebedyev hastened to declare with warmth. 'Now I'm yours again, entirely yours, from head to heart, your servant after my momentary treachery. "Punish the heart, spare the beard," as Thomas More said … in England and in Great Britain. *"Mea culpa, mea culpa"*, as the Romish Pope says – that is, I mean the Pope of Rome, though I call him the Romish Pope.'

'This letter must be sent off at once,' said Myshkin anxiously. 'I'll give it.'

'But wouldn't it be better, wouldn't it be better, most highly bred prince … to do this?'

Lebedyev made a strange, expressive grimace. He fidgeted violently in his place, as though he had been suddenly pricked by a needle, and, winking slyly, made a significant gesture with his hands.

'What do you mean?' Myshkin asked severely.

'Wouldn't it be better to open it?' he whispered ingratiatingly and, as it were, confidentially.

Myshkin leapt up with such passion that Lebedyev took to his heels, but he stopped short at the door to see whether he could hope for pardon.

'Ech! Lebedyev, is it possible to sink to such abject degradation as this?' cried Myshkin bitterly.

Lebedyev's face brightened.

'I'm abject, abject!' he approached at once, with tears beating himself on the breast.

'You know this is abominable!'

'Abominable it is! That's the word for it!'

'What a horrid habit it is to behave ... in this queer way! You ...are simply a spy! Why do you write anonymously and worry such a noble and kind-hearted woman? And why has not Aglaia Ivanovna a right to write to whom she pleases? Did you go to complain of it today? Did you hope to receive a reward? What induced you to tell tales?'

'Simply agreeable curiosity and the desire of a generous heart to be of use! Now I am yours again, all yours! You may hang me!'

'Did you go to Lizaveta Prokofyevna in the condition you're in now?' Myshkin enquired with disgust.

'No, I was fresher, more decent. It was only after my humiliation that I got... into this state.'

'Well, that's enough. Leave me.'

But he had to repeat this request several times before he could induce his visitor to go. Even after he had opened the door, he came back on tiptoe into the middle of the room and gesticulated with his hands to show how to open the letter. He did not venture to put his advice into words. Then he went out with a suave and amiable smile.

All this had been extremely painful to hear. What was most evident was one striking fact: that Aglaia was in great trouble, great uncertainty, in great distress about something. ('From jealousy,' Myshkin whispered to himself.) It was evident also that she was being worried by ill-intentioned people, and what was very strange was that she trusted them in this way. No doubt that inexperienced but hot and proud little head was hatching some special schemes, perhaps ruinous, and utterly wild. Myshkin was greatly alarmed, and in his perturbation did not know what to decide upon. There was no doubt he must do something, he felt that. He looked once more at the address on the sealed letter. Oh, he had no doubt and no uneasiness on that side, for he trusted her. What made him uneasy about that letter was something different. He did not trust Gavril Ardalionovitch. And yet he was on the point of deciding to restore him the letter himself, and he even left the house with that object, but he changed his mind on the way. Almost at Ptitsyn's door, by good fortune he met Kolya, and charged him to put the letter into his brother's hands, as though it had come straight from Aglaia Ivanovna. Kolya asked no questions and delivered it, so that Ganya had no suspicion that the letter had halted so many times upon its journey. Returning home, Myshkin asked Vera Lebedyev to come to him, told her what was necessary, and set her mind at rest, for she had been all this time hunting for the letter, and was in tears. She was horrified when she learned that her father had carried off the letter. (Myshkin found out from her afterwards that she had more than once helped Rogozhin and Aglaia Ivanovna in secret, and it had never occurred to her that she could be injuring Myshkin in doing so.)

And Myshkin was at last so upset that when, two hours later, a messenger from Kolya ran in with the news of his father's illness, for the first minute the prince could not grasp what was the matter. But this event restored him by completely distracting his attention. He stayed at Nina Alexandrovna's (where the invalid, of course, had been carried) right up to the evening. He was scarcely of any use, but there are people whom one is, for some reason, glad to have about one in times of grief. Kolya was terribly distressed, he cried hysterically, but was continually being sent on errands: he ran for a doctor and hunted up three; ran to the chemist's and to the barber's. They succeeded in resuscitating the general, but he did not regain his senses. The doctors opined that the patient was in any case in danger. Varya and Nina Alexandrovna never left the sick man's side. Ganya was disconcerted and overcome, but would not go upstairs, and seemed afraid to see the invalid; he wrung his hands, and in incoherent and disconnected talk with Myshkin he let drop the phrase, 'What a calamity, and to come at such a moment!'

Myshkin fancied he understood what he meant by 'such a moment.' Myshkin did not find Ippolit at Ptitsyn's. Lebedyev, who after the morning's 'explanation' had slept all day without waking, ran in towards evening. Now he was almost sober and shed genuine tears over the sick man, as though he had been his own brother. He blamed himself aloud without explaining why, and would not leave Nina Alexandrovna, assuring her every moment that 'he, he was the cause of it; he and no one else … simply from agreeable curiosity,' and that the 'departed' (so he persisted in calling the still living general) was positively 'a man of genius!' He insisted with great seriousness on his genius, as though it might be of extraordinary service at that moment. Seeing his genuine tears, Nina Alexandrovna said to him at last with a note of reproach, and almost with cordiality, 'Well, God bless you! Don't cry. Come, God will forgive you!' Lebedyev was so much impressed by these words and the tone of them that he was unwilling to leave her side all the evening (and all the following days, from early morning till the hour of the general's death, he spent in their house). Twice during the day a messenger came from Lizaveta Prokofyevna to enquire after the invalid.

When at nine o'clock in the evening Myshkin made his appearance in the Epanchins' drawing-room, which was already full of guests, Lizaveta Prokofyevna at once began questioning him sympathetically and minutely about the patient, and replied with dignity to Princess Byelokonsky's enquiry, 'What patient, and who is Nina Alexandrovna?' Myshkin was much pleased at this. Explaining the position to Madame Epanchin, he spoke 'splendidly,' as Aglaia's sisters said afterwards, 'modestly, quietly, with dignity and without gestures or too many words.' He walked in admirably, was perfectly dressed, and far from falling down on the slippery floor, as they had all been afraid the day before, evidently made a favourable impression on everyone.

Sitting down and looking round, he for his part noticed at once that the company were not in the least like the bogies with which Aglaia had tried to frighten him, nor the nightmare figures of his last night's dreams. For the first time in his life he saw a tiny corner of what is called by the dreadful name 'society.' For some time past certain projects, considerations and inclinations had made him eager to penetrate into that enchanted circle, and so he was deeply interested by his first impression of it. This first impression was fascinating. It somehow seemed to him at once as though these people were, so to speak, born to be together; as though it were not a 'party' and no guests had been invited that evening to the Epanchins'; that these were all 'their own people,' and that he himself had long been their devoted friend and shared their thoughts, and was now returning to them after a brief separation. The charm of elegant manners, of simplicity, and of apparent frankness was almost magical. It could never have entered his head that all this simple frankness and nobility, wit, and refined personal dignity was perhaps only an exquisite artistic veneer. The majority of the guests, in spite of their prepossessing exterior, were rather empty-headed people, who were themselves unaware, however, that much of their superiority was mere veneer, for which they were not responsible indeed, as they had adopted it unconsciously and by inheritance. Myshkin, carried away by the charm of his first impression, had no inclination to suspect this. He saw, for instance, that this important and aged dignitary, who might have been his grandfather, ceased speaking in order to listen to an inexperienced young man like himself; and not only listened to him, but evidently valued his opinion, was so cordial, so genuinely kind to him, and yet they were strangers, meeting for the first time. Perhaps the refinement of this courtesy was what produced the most effect on Myshkin's eager sensitiveness. He was perhaps prejudiced and predisposed to favourable impression.

And yet all these people – though of course they were 'friends of the family' and one another – were by no means such great friends either of the family or of one another as Myshkin took them to be, as soon as he met them and was introduced to them. There were persons of the party who would never on any account have recognised the Epanchins as their equals. There were persons who absolutely detested one another: old Princess Byelokonsky had always 'despised' the wife of the 'old dignitary'; while the latter for her part had anything but friendly feelings for Lizaveta Prokofyevna. This 'dignitary,' her husband, who for some reason had been a patron of the Epanchins from their youth up, and was the leading figure present, was a personage of such vast consequence in the eyes of Ivan Fyodorovitch that the latter was incapable of any sensation except reverence and awe in his presence, and he would have had a genuine contempt for himself if he could for one moment have put himself on an equal footing with him, and have thought of him as less than the Olympian Jove. There were people who had not met one another for some years, and felt nothing but indifference if not dislike for one another; yet they greeted each other now as though they had only met yesterday in the most friendly and intimate company. Yet the party was not a large one. Besides Princess Byelokonsky and the 'old dignitary' – who really was a person of consequence – and his wife, there was in the first place a very solid military general, a count, or baron with a German name – a man of extraordinary taciturnity, with a reputation for a marvellous acquaintance with affairs of government, and almost with a reputation for learning – one of those Olympian administrators who know 'everything,' except perhaps Russia itself; a man who once in five years made some 'extraordinarily profound' remark, which inevitably became a proverb and penetrated even to the loftiest circles; one of those governing officials who usually, after an extremely, even strangely protracted term of service, die possessed of large fortunes and high honours in leading positions, though they have never performed any great exploits, and in fact have always a certain aversion for exploits. This general was next above Ivan Fyodorovitch in the service, and the latter in the zeal of his grateful heart and through a peculiar form of vanity regarded him too as his patron. Yet the general by no means considered himself Ivan Fyodorovitch's patron. He treated him with absolute coolness, and, though he gladly availed himself of his numerous services, he would have replaced him by another official at once, if any consideration, even the most trivial, had called for such exchange. There was too an elderly and important gentleman who was supposed to be a relation of Lizaveta Prokofyevna's, though this was quite untrue – a man of high rank and position, of birth and fortune. He was stout, and enjoyed excellent health; he was a great talker, and had the reputation of a discontented man (though only in the most legitimate sense of the word), even a splenetic man (though even this was agreeable in him), with the tricks of the English aristocracy and with English tastes (as regards roast beef, harness, footmen and so on). He was a great friend of the 'dignitary,' and amused him. Moreover, Lizaveta Prokofyevna for some reason cherished the strange idea that this elderly gentleman (a somewhat frivolous person with a distinct weakness for the female sex) might suddenly take it into his head to make Alexandra happy with the offer of his hand. Below this top and most solid layer of the assembly came the younger guests, though these too were conspicuous for extremely elegant qualities. To this group belonged Prince S— and Yevgeny Pavlovitch, and, moreover, the well-known and fascinating Prince N—, who had seduced and fascinated female hearts all over Europe, a man of five-and-forty though still of handsome appearance, and a wonderful storyteller; a man whose large fortune was to some extent dissipated and who usually lived abroad. There were people too who made up, indeed, a third special stratum, not belonging themselves to the 'inner circle' of society, though, like the Epanchins, they could sometimes be met in that circle. Through a certain sense of fitness which always guided them, the Epanchins liked on the rare occasions of their giving parties to mix the highest society with persons of a rather lower grade, with select representatives of the 'middling kind' of people. The Epanchins were praised indeed for doing so, and it was said of them that they understood their position and were people of tact, and they were proud of being thought so. One of the representatives of this 'middling sort' was that evening a colonel of engineers, a serious man, a very intimate friend of Prince S—, by whom he had been introduced to the Epanchins. He was silent in society, however, and wore on the big forefinger of his right hand a large and conspicuous ring, probably presented to him. There was present too a poet of German origin, but a Russian poet, and perfectly presentable, moreover, so that he could be introduced into good society without apprehension. He was of handsome, though for some reason repulsive, appearance. He was eight-and-thirty, and was irreproachably dressed. He belonged to an intensely bourgeois but intensely respectable German family. He was successful in taking advantage of every opportunity, gaining the patronage of persons in high places and retaining their favour. He had at one time made a verse translation of some important work of some important German poet, was adroit in dedicating his translations, and adroit in boasting of his friendship with a celebrated but deceased Russian poet (there's a perfect crowd of writers who love to record in print their friendship with great and deceased writers), and he had been quite recently brought to the Epanchins by the wife of the 'old dignitary.' This lady was celebrated for her patronage of literary and learned men, and had even actually procured one or two writers a pension through powerful personages with whom she had influence. She really had influence of a sort. She was a lady of five-and-forty (and therefore a very young wife for so aged a man as her husband), who had been a beauty and still, like many ladies of forty-five, had a mania for dressing far too gorgeously. She was of small intelligence, and her knowledge of literature was very dubious. But the patronage of literary men was as much a mania with her as was gorgeous array. Many books and translations had been dedicated to her. Two or three writers had, with her permission, printed letters they had written to her on subjects of the greatest importance ...

And all this society Myshkin took for true coin, for pure gold without alloy. All these people were too, as though of set purpose, in the happiest frame of mind that evening, and very well pleased with themselves. They all without exception knew that they were doing the Epanchins a great honour by their visit. But, alas! Myshkin had no suspicion of such subtleties. He did not suspect, for instance, that, while the Epanchins were contemplating so important a step as the decision of their daughter's future, they would not have dared to omit exhibiting him, Prince Lyov Nikolayevitch, to the old dignitary who was the acknowledged patron of the family. Though the old dignitary for his part would have borne with perfect equanimity the news of the most awful calamity having befallen the Epanchins, he would certainly have been offended if the Epanchins had betrothed their daughter without his advice and, so to speak, without his leave. Prince N—, that charming, unquestionably witty and open-hearted man, was firmly persuaded that he was something like a sun that had risen that night to shine upon the Epanchins' drawing-room. He regarded them as infinitely beneath him, and it was just this open-hearted and generous notion which prompted his wonderfully charming ease and friendliness with the Epanchins. He knew very well that he would have to tell some story to delight the company, and led up to it with positive inspiration. When Myshkin heard the story afterwards, he felt that he had never heard anything like such brilliant humour and such marvellous gaiety and *naïveté* almost touching, on the lips of such a Don Juan as Prince N—. If he had only known how old and hackneyed that story was, how it was known by heart, worn threadbare, stale, and a weariness in every drawing-room, and only at the innocent Epanchins' passed for a novelty, for an impromptu, genuine and brilliant reminiscence of a splendid and brilliant man! Even the little German poet, although he behaved with great modesty and politeness, was ready to believe that he was conferring an honour on the family by his presence. But Myshkin saw nothing of the other side, noticed no undercurrent. This was a mischance that Aglaia had not foreseen. She was looking particularly handsome that evening. The three young ladies were dressed for the evening, but not over smartly, and wore their hair in a particular style. Aglaia was sitting with Yevgeny Pavlovitch, and was talking to him and making jokes with exceptional friendliness. Yevgeny Pavlovitch was behaving more sedately than usual, also perhaps from respect to the dignitaries. He was already well known in society, however; he was quite at home there, though he was so young. He arrived at the Epanchins' that evening with crape on his hat, and Princess Byelokonsky remarked with approbation on it. Some fashionable young men would not under such circumstances have put on mourning for such an uncle. Lizaveta Prokofyevna too was pleased at it, though she seemed on the whole preoccupied. Myshkin noticed that Aglaia looked at him intently once or twice, and he fancied she was satisfied with him. By degrees he began to feel very happy. His recent 'fantastical' ideas and apprehensions after his conversation with Lebedyev seemed to him now, when he suddenly, at frequent intervals, recalled them, an inconceivable, incredible, even ridiculous dream! (His chief, though unconscious, impulse and desire had been all day to do something to make him disbelieve that dream!) He spoke little and only in answer to questions, and finally was silent altogether; he sat still and listened, but was evidently enjoying himself extremely. By degrees something like an inspiration was beginning to work within him too, ready to break out at the first opportunity... He began talking, indeed, by chance in answer to questions, and apparently quite without any special design.

Chapter 7

While he was enjoying himself, watching Aglaia as she talked to Prince N— and Yevgeny Pavlovitch, suddenly the elderly Anglomaniac, who was entertaining the 'dignitary' in another corner and with animation telling him some story, uttered the name of Nikolay Andreyevitch Pavlishtchev. Myshkin turned quickly in their direction and began to listen.

They were discussing public affairs and some disturbances on estates in the province. There must have been something amusing about the Anglomaniac's account for the old man began laughing at last at the little sallies of the speaker.

He was telling smoothly, and, as it were, peevishly drawling his words, with soft emphasis on the vowel sounds, how he had been obliged as a direct result of recent legislation to sell a splendid estate of his in the province and for half its value, too, though he was in no need of money, and at the same time to keep an estate that had gone to ruin, was encumbered, and a subject of litigation, and had even to spend money to do so. 'To avoid another lawsuit about the Pavlishtchev estate, I ran away from them. Another inheritance or two of that kind and I shall be ruined. I should have come in for nine thousand acres of excellent land, however.'

'Why, of course ... Ivan Petrovitch is a relation of the late Nikolay Andreyevitch ... you made a search for relations, I believe,' General Epanchin, who happened to be near and noticed Myshkin's marked attention to the conversation, said to him in an undertone.

He had till then been entertaining the general who was the head of his department, but he had for some time been noticing Myshkin's conspicuous isolation, and was becoming uneasy. He wanted to bring him to a certain extent into the conversation and in that way show him off and introduce him a second time to the 'great personages.'

'Lyov Nikolayevitch was left on the death of his parents a ward of Nikolay Andreyevitch Pavlishtchev,' he put in, meeting Ivan Petrovitch's eye.

'Delighted to hear it,' observed the latter. 'And I remember it well, indeed. When Ivan Fyodorovitch introduced us just now,I knew you at once, and from your face, too. You've changed very little, indeed, though you were only ten or eleven when I saw you. There is something one remembers about your features ...'

'Did you see me when I was a child?' Myshkin asked, with great surprise.

'Yes, very long ago,' Ivan Petrovitch went on. 'At Zlatoverhovo, where you used to live at my cousin's. In old days I used to go pretty often to Zlatoverhovo. Don't you remember me? You might very likely not remember ... You were then ... you had some sort of illness then, so much so that I was very much struck on one occasion.'

'I don't remember at all,' Myshkin asserted with warmth.

A few more words of explanation, perfectly calm on the part of Ivan Petrovitch, and betraying great agitation on the part of Myshkin, followed, and it appeared that the two elderly maiden ladies, kinswomen of Pavlishtchev, who had lived on his estate, Zlatoverhovo, and by whom Myshkin had been brought up, were also cousins of Ivan Petrovitch's. The latter was as unable as everyone else to explain what induced Pavlishtchev to take so much trouble over his *protégé,* the little prince. 'It hadn't, in fact, occurred to me to be curious about that,' but yet, it appeared that he had an excellent memory, for he remembered how severe his elder cousin, Marfa Nikitishna had been with her little pupil, 'so that on one occasion I stood up for you and attacked her system of education. For the rod, and nothing but the rod with an invalid child … you'll admit…' and how tender the younger sister, Natalya Nikitishna, was to the poor child … 'They are both,' he went on, 'in X Province now (though I'm not sure whether they're both living) where Pavlishtchev left them an extremely nice little property. I believe Marfa Nikitishna wanted to go into a convent, but I won't be sure, I may be thinking of someone else … Yes, I heard that the other day, about a doctor's wife.'

Myshkin listened to this with eyes shining with delight and emotion. With great warmth he declared that he should never forgive himself for not having seized an opportunity to seek out and visit the ladies who had brought him up, though he had been for six months in the central provinces. He had been meaning to set off every day, but had been continually occupied with other matters … But that now he was determined … he would certainly … even though it were to — Province … 'So you know Natalya Nikitishna? What a fine, what a saintly nature! But, Marfa Nikitishna, too … forgive me … but I think you are mistaken about Marfa Nikitishna! She was severe, but … how could she help losing patience… with such an idiot as I was then. Ha-ha! You know I was a complete idiot. Ha-ha! Though … you saw me then, and…how is it that I don't remember you, tell me please? So you …my God! Are you really a relation of Nikolay Andreyevitch Pavlishtchev?'

'I assure you I ant,' said Ivan Petrovitch, with a smile, scrutinising Myshkin.

'Oh, I didn't say that because I … doubted it… and, in fact, how could I doubt it… Ha-ha!… in the least? But I only mean that Nikolay Andreyevitch Pavlishtchev was such a splendid man! A most noble-hearted man, I assure you!'

Myshkin was not exactly breathless but 'choking with good-heartedness,' as Adelaïda expressed it next day to her betrothed, Prince S—.

'Mercy on us!' laughed Ivan Petrovitch. 'Why shouldn't I be a relation of a noble-hearted man, even?'

'Oh, my goodness!' cried Myshkin, overcome with confusion and growing more and more hurried and eager. 'I … I've said something stupid again, but… that's bound to happen because I…I…I… but that's out of place again! And of what consequence am I, pray, beside such interests, such vast interests? And by comparison with such a noble-hearted man! For you know, he really was a noble man, wasn't he? Wasn't he?'

Myshkin was positively trembling all over. Why he was suddenly so agitated, why he was in such a state of ecstasy and emotion quite irrelevant and as it seemed out of all proportion with the subject of conversation, it was difficult to decide. He was in such a state of mind and he almost seemed to feel the warmest and liveliest gratitude to someone for something, perhaps to Ivan Petrovitch himself, if not to the whole company. He was 'bubbling over' with happiness. Ivan Petrovitch began at last staring at him more fixedly, the 'dignitary' too began looking at him with great intentness. Princess Byelokonsky looked wrathfully at Myshkin and tightened her lips. Prince N—, Yevgeny Pavlovitch, Prince S—, the young ladies, all broke off their conversation and listened. Aglaia seemed frightened, Lizaveta Prokofyevna's heart failed her. They, too, the mother and daughters, had behaved strangely: they had foreseen and decided that it would be better for Myshkin to sit still and be silent the whole evening. But as soon as they saw him sitting in complete solitude, perfectly satisfied with his position, they were at once dreadfully upset. Alexandra had been on the point of going to him across the room and tactfully joining the company, that is Prince N—'s group, near Princess Byelokonsky. And now that Myshkin had begun talking of his own accord they were even more perturbed.

'You are right in saying that he was a most excellent man!' Ivan Petrovitch pronounced impressively, with no smile now. 'Yes, yes, he was an excellent man! Excellent, and worthy,' he added, after a pause. 'Worthy one may say, of all respect,' he added more impressively, after a third pause. 'And ... and it is very agreeable to see on your part...'

'Wasn't it that Pavlishtchev that there was a queer story about... with the abbé ... the abbé ... I've forgotten which abbé ... only everybody was talking about it at one time,' the 'dignitary brought out as though recollecting something.

'With the Abbé Goureau, a Jesuit,' Ivan Petrovitch recalled. 'Yes, there you have our most excellent and worthy people. Because he was after all a man of family and fortune, a court chamberlain, if he had ... chosen to remain in the service ... And then he suddenly threw up the service to go over to the Roman Church and become a Jesuit, and almost openly, with a sort of enthusiasm. It's true, he died in the nick of time… everybody said so …'

Myshkin was beside himself.

'Pavlishtchev … Pavlishtchev, went over to the Roman Church? Impossible!' he cried in horror.

' "Impossible," indeed!' Ivan Petrovitch drawled solidly. That's saying a good deal, and you must admit, dear prince … However you have such a high opinion of the deceased … He certainly was a most good-natured man, and to that I chiefly attribute the success of that rascal Goureau. But ask me what a fuss and bother I had afterwards over that affair … especially with that very Goureau. Only fancy,' he turned suddenly to the old man, 'they even tried to put in a claim under the will, and I was forced to have recourse to the most, that is, to vigorous measures … to bring them to their senses … for they're first-rate at that kind of thing. Won-der-ful people! But, thank goodness! It all happened in Moscow. I went straight to the court, and we soon … brought them to their senses.'

'You wouldn't believe how you grieve and astonish me,' cried Myshkin.

'I am sorry. But as a matter of fact, all this was after all a trifling business and would have ended in smoke as such things always do: I'm convinced of it. Last summer,' he went on, turning to the old man, 'Countess K., I am told, went into some Catholic convent abroad. Russians never can hold out if once they come under the influence of those … rogues… especially abroad.'

'It all comes from our … weariness,' the old dignitary mumbled authoritatively. 'And their manner of proselytising is … skilful and peculiar to them … They know how to scare people. They gave me a good scare, too, I assure you, in Vienna in 1832. But I wouldn't surrender, I ran away from them. Ha, ha! I really did run away from them…'

'I heard, my dear sir, that you ran away from Vienna to Paris with the beauty, Countess Levitzky, and that was why you flung up your post, not to escape from the Jesuits,' Princess Byelokonsky put in suddenly.

'Well, you see, it was from a Jesuit; it turns out after all that it was from a Jesuit,' the old dignitary retorted, laughing at the agreeable recollection. 'You seem to be very religious, which one doesn't often meet with nowadays in a young man,' he added, turning genially to Prince Lyov Nikolayevitch, who was listening open-mouthed and still amazed.

The old man evidently wanted to study Myshkin more closely. He had for some reason become an object of interest to him.

'Pavlishtchev was a clear-headed man and a Christian, a genuine Christian,' Myshkin brought out suddenly. 'How could he have accepted a faith ... that's unchristian? Catholicism is as good as an unchristian religion!' he added, suddenly, looking about him with flashing eyes as though scanning the whole company.

'Come, that's too much!' muttered the old man, and he looked with surprise at General Epanchin.

'How do you mean Catholicism is an unchristian religion,' said Ivan Petrovitch, turning round in his chair. 'What is it then?'

'An unchristian religion in the first place!' Myshkin began, in extreme agitation and with excessive abruptness. 'And in the second place Roman Catholicism is even worse than atheism itself, in my opinion! Yes, that's my opinion! Atheism only preaches a negation, but Catholicism goes further: it preaches a distorted Christ, a Christ calumniated and defamed by themselves, the opposite of Christ! It preaches the Antichrist, I declare it does, I assure you it does! This is the conviction I have long held, and it has distressed me, myself... Roman Catholicism cannot hold its position without universal political supremacy, and cries: *'Non possumus!'* To my thinking Roman Catholicism is not even a religion, but simply the continuation of the Western Roman Empire, and everything in it is subordinated to that idea, faith to begin with. The Pope seized the earth, an earthly throne, and grasped the sword; everything has gone on in the same way since, only they have added to the sword lying, fraud, deceit, fanaticism, superstition, villainy. They have trifled with the most holy, truthful, sincere, fervent feelings of the people; they have bartered it all, all for money, for base earthly power. And isn't that the teaching of Antichrist? How could atheism fail to come from them? Atheism has sprung from Roman Catholicism itself. It originated with them themselves. Can they have believed themselves? It has been strengthened by revulsion from them; it is begotten by their lying and their spiritual impotence! Atheism! Among us it is only the exceptional classes who don't believe, those who, as Yevgeny Pavlovitch splendidly expressed it the other day, have lost their roots. But over there, in Europe, a terrible mass of the people themselves are beginning to lose their faith – at first from darkness and lying, and now from fanaticism and hatred of the church and Christianity.'

Myshkin paused to take breath. He had been talking fearfully fast. He was pale and breathless. They all glanced at one another, and at last the old dignitary simply burst out laughing. Prince N— drew out his lorgnette, and took a prolonged stare at Myshkin. The German poet crept out of his corner, and moved nearer to the table, with a spiteful smile on his face.

'You are exaggerating very much,' Ivan Petrovitch drawled with an air of being bored, and even rather ashamed of something. 'There are representatives of that Church who are virtuous and worthy of all respect...'

'I have said nothing about individual representatives of the Church. I was speaking of Roman Catholicism in its essence. I am speaking of Rome. Can a Church disappear altogether? I never said that!'

'I agree. But all that's well known and – irrelevant, indeed, and ... it's a theological question ...'

'Oh, no, no! It's not only a theological question, I assure you it's not! It concerns us much more closely than you think. That's our whole mistake, that we can't see that this is not exclusively a theological question! Why, socialism too springs from Catholicism and the Catholic idea! Like its brother atheism, it comes from despair in opposition to Catholicism on the moral side, to replace the lost moral power of religion, to quench the spiritual thirst of parched humanity, and to save them not by Christ but also by violence. That, too, is freedom through violence, that, too, is union through sword and blood. "Don't dare to believe in God, don't dare to have property and individuality, *fraternité ou la mort* two millions of heads!" By their works ye shall know them – as it is said. And don't imagine that all this is so harmless and without danger for us. Oh, we need to make resistance at once, at once! Our Christ whom we have kept and they have never known must shine forth and vanquish the West. Not letting ourselves be slavishly caught by the wiles of the Jesuits, but carrying our Russian civilisation to them, we ought to stand before them and not let it be said among us, as it was just now, that their preaching is skilful.'

'But allow me, allow me!' said Ivan Petrovitch, growing dreadfully uneasy, looking about him, and positively beginning to be terrified. 'All your ideas, of course, are very praiseworthy and full of patriotism, but all this is exaggerated in the extreme, and... in fact, we had better drop the subject

'No, it's not exaggerated; it's even understated, positively understated, because I am not capable of expressing

'Allow me!'

Myshkin ceased speaking, and sitting upright in his chair gazed with a fixed and fervent look at Ivan Petrovitch.

'I fancy you have been too much affected by what happened to your benefactor,' the old dignitary indulgently observed, with unruffled composure. 'You have grown over-ardent... perhaps from solitude. If you were to live more among people and to see more of the world, I expect you would be welcomed as a remarkable young man; then, of course, you would grow less excitable and you would see that it is all much simpler ... and besides such exceptional cases are due in my opinion partly to our being *blasé*, partly to our being ... bored.'

'Just so, just so!' cried Myshkin. 'A splendid idea! It's just from dullness, from our dullness. Not from being *blasé*. On the contrary, from unsatisfied yearning ... not from being *blasé*. There you're mistaken. Not simply from unsatisfied yearnings, but from feverishness, from burning thirst. And ... and don't think that it's to such a slight extent that one can afford to laugh at it. Excuse me, one needs to look ahead in these things. As soon as Russians feel the ground under their feet and are confident that they have reached firm ground, they are so delighted at reaching it that they rush at once to the furthest limit. Why is that? You are surprised at Pavlishtchev, and you put it down to madness on his part, or to simplicity. But it's not that! And Russian intensity in such cases is a surprise not to us only but to all Europe. If one of us turns Catholic, he is bound to become a Jesuit, and one of the most underground. If he becomes an atheist, he's sure to clamour for the extirpation of belief in God by force, that is, by the sword. Why is this, why such frenzy? You must surely know! Because he has found the fatherland which he has missed here. He has reached the shore, he has found the land and he rushes to kiss it. Russian atheists and Russian Jesuits are the outcome not only of vanity, not only of a bad, vain feeling, but also of spiritual agony, spiritual thirst, a craving for something higher, for a firm footing, for a fatherland in which they have ceased to believe, because they have never even known it! It's easier for a Russian to become an atheist than for anyone else in the world. And Russians do not merely become atheists but they invariably *believe* in atheism, as though it were a new religion without noticing that they are putting faith in a negation. So great is our craving! "He who has no roots beneath him has no god." That's not my own saying. It was said by a merchant and Old Believer, whom I met when I was travelling. It's true he did not use those words. He said: "The man who has renounced his fatherland has renounced his god." Only think that among us, even highly educated people join the sect of Flagellants. Though why is that worse than nihilism, Jesuitism, or atheism? It may even be rather more profound! But that's what their agony has brought them to. Reveal to the yearning and feverish companions of Columbus the "New World", reveal to the Russian the "world" of Russia, let him find the gold, the treasure hidden from him in the earth! Show him the whole of humanity, rising again, and renewed by Russian thought alone, perhaps by the Russian God and Christ, and you will see into what a mighty and truthful, what a wise and gentle giant he will grow, before the eyes of the astounded world, astounded and dismayed, because it expects of us nothing but the sword, nothing but the sword and violence, because, judging us by themselves, the other peoples cannot picture us free from barbarism. That has always been so hitherto and goes on getting more so! And ...'

But at this point, an incident took place, and the speaker's eloquence was cut short in the most unexpected manner.

This wild tirade, this rush of strange and agitated words and confused, enthusiastic ideas, which seemed tripping each other up and tumbling over one another in confusion, all seemed suggestive of something ominous in the mental condition of the young man who had broken out so suddenly, apropos of nothing. Those present who knew Myshkin wondered apprehensively (and some of them with shame) at this outbreak, which was so out of keeping with his habitual diffidence and restraint, with his rare and peculiar tact in some cases, and his instinctive feeling for real propriety. They could not understand what it was due to. What had been told him about Pavlishtchev could not have been the cause of it. The ladies gazed at him from their corner, as though he had taken leave of his senses, and Princess Byelokonsky confessed afterwards that in another minute she would have taken to her heels. The old gentlemen were almost disconcerted in their first amazement; the chief of the department looked sternly and with displeasure at him from his place. The colonel of engineers sat in absolute immobility. The German positively turned pale, but still smiled his artificial smile, looking at the rest of the company to see how they were taking it. But all this and the whole 'scandal' might have ended in the most ordinary and natural way in another minute. General Epanchin, who was extremely astonished, though he grasped the situation sooner than the rest, had made several attempts to stop Myshkin already. But failing in his efforts, he was making his way towards him, with a firm and resolute design. In another minute, he would perhaps, had it been necessary, have taken the extreme step of leading Myshkin out of the room in a friendly way on the pretext of his being ill, which would, perhaps, have been the truth, and which the general fully believed himself... But the scene had a very different conclusion.

At the beginning, when Myshkin at first entered the drawing-room, he had seated himself as far as possible from the china vase about which Aglaia had so scared him. It seems almost beyond belief, but after Aglaia's words the day before a haunting conviction, a prodigious and incredible presentiment obsessed him that he would be sure to break the vase next day, however carefully he kept away from it and tried to avoid the disaster. But so it was. In the course of the evening other and brighter impressions had flowed into his soul: we have spoken of that already. He forgot his presentiment. When he had heard Pavlishtchev's name mentioned, and General Epanchin had brought him forward and introduced him again to Ivan Petrovitch, he moved nearer to the table and sat down in tire very armchair nearest to the huge and handsome china vase, which stood on a pedestal almost at his elbow and a little behind him.

At his last words he suddenly rose from his seat, and incautiously waved his arm, somehow twitching his shoulder and ... there was a general scream of horror! The vase tottered at first, as though hesitating whether to fall upon the head of some old gentleman, but suddenly inclining in the opposite direction, towards the German poet, who skipped aside in alarm, it crashed to the ground. A crash, a scream, and the priceless fragments were scattered about the carpet, dismay and astonishment – what was Myshkin's condition would be hard, and is perhaps unnecessary, to describe! But we must not omit to mention one odd sensation, which struck him at that very minute, and stood out clearly above the mass of other confused and strange sensations. It was not the shame, not the scandal, not the fright, nor the suddenness of it that impressed him most, but his foreknowledge of it! He could not explain what was so arresting about that thought, he only felt that it had gripped him to the heart, and he stood still in a terror that was almost superstitious! Another instant and everything seemed opening out before him; instead of horror there was light, joy, and ecstasy; his breath began to fail him, and … but the moment had passed. Thank God, it was not that! He drew a breath and looked about him.

He seemed for a long time unable to understand the fuss that was going on around him, or rather, he understood it perfectly and saw everything, but stood, as it were apart, as though he had no share in it, and, like someone invisible in a fairytale, had crept into the room and was watching people, with whom he had no concern though they interested him. He saw them picking up the pieces, heard rapid conversations, saw Aglaia, pale, looking strangely at him, very strangely; there was no trace of hatred, no trace of anger in her eyes, she was looking at him with a frightened expression, but there was so much affection in it and her eyes flashed so at the rest of the company… his heart ached with a sweet pain. At last he saw to his amazement that they had all sat down again and were positively laughing, as though nothing had happened! In another minute the laughter grew louder: they laughed, looking at him, at his dumb stupefaction, but their laughter was friendly and gay. Many of them addressed him, speaking so cordially, Lizaveta Prokofyevna most of all: she spoke laughingly and said something very, very kind. Suddenly he felt General Epanchin slap him amicably on the shoulder. Ivan Petrovitch, too, was laughing, but the old 'dignitary' was the most charming and sympathetic of all: he took Myshkin's hand and with a faint squeeze of it, and a light pat with the other hand, urged him to pull himself together, as though he were talking to a little frightened boy (Myshkin was highly delighted at this), and made him sit down beside him. Myshkin looked with pleasure into his face, and was somehow still unable to speak, his breath failed him; he liked the old man's face so much.

'What,' he muttered at last, 'you really forgive me? You, too, Lizaveta Prokofyevna?'

The laughter was louder than ever. Tears came into Myshkin's eyes – he could hardly believe in it; he was enchanted.

'It was a fine vase, to be sure. I can remember it here for the last fifteen years, yes … fifteen …' Ivan Petrovitch was beginning.

'A terrible disaster, indeed! Even a man must come to an end, and all this to-do about a clay pot!' said Lizaveta Prokofyevna, in a loud voice. 'Surely you're not so upset over it, Lyov Nikolayevitch?' she added, with a positive note of apprehension. 'Never mind, my dear boy, never mind! You'll frighten me, really.'

'And you forgive me for *everything*? For *everything*, besides the vase?'

Myshkin would have got up from his seat, but the old man drew him again by the arm.

He would not let him go.

'C'est très curieux et c'est très sérieux!' he whispered across the table to Ivan Petrovitch, speaking, however, rather loudly.

Myshkin may have heard it.

'So I've not offended anyone? You can't think how happy I am at the notion, but that was bound to be so! Could I possibly offend anyone here? I should be offending you again, if I could think such a thing.'

'Calm yourself, my dear boy, this is all exaggerated. And there's nothing for you to be so grateful about. That's an excellent feeling, but exaggerated.'

'I'm not thanking you, I am only … admiring you, I'm happy looking at you. Perhaps I'm talking nonsense, but I must speak, I must explain … if only from self-respect All he said and did was spasmodic, confused, feverish. It is quite likely that the words he uttered were often not those he intended to use. His eyes seemed to ask whether he might speak. His glance fell upon Princess Byelokonsky.

'It's all right, my dear boy, go on, go on, only don't be in such haste,' she observed. 'You began in such a breathless hurry just now, and you see what came of it, but don't be afraid to talk. These ladies and gentlemen have often seen queerer folk than you. They won't be surprised at you. And you are not so very remarkable, either. You've done nothing but break a vase and given us all a fright.'

Myshkin listened to her, smiling.

'Why it was you,' he began, addressing the old 'dignitary,' 'it was you who saved a student called Podkumov and a clerk called Shvabrin from exile three months ago.'

The old man positively flushed a little, and muttered that he must calm himself.

'And, I think it's you, I've heard,' he turned at once to Ivan Petrovitch, 'who gave your peasants timber to rebuild their huts when they were burnt out, though they were free and had given you a lot of trouble?'

'Oh, that's ex-ag-gera-ted,' muttered Ivan Petrovitch, though with an air of dignified pleasure.

But this time it was true that Myshkin's words were 'exaggerated"; it was only an incorrect rumour that had reached him.

'And did not you,' he went on, addressing Princess Byelokonsky, 'receive me six months ago in Moscow, as though I had been your own son, when Lizaveta Prokofyevna wrote to you. And, exactly as though I had been your own son, you gave me one piece of advice which I shall never forget. Do you remember?'

'Why are you in such a taking?' said Princess Byelokonsky, with vexation. 'You're a good-natured fellow but absurd. If someone gives you a halfpenny you thank him as though he had saved your life. You think it praiseworthy, but it's disgusting.'

She was on the verge of being angry, but suddenly burst out laughing, and this time her laughter was good-humoured. Lizaveta Prokofyevna's face brightened too; General Epanchin beamed.

'I said that Lyov Nikolayevitch was a man … a man … if only he wouldn't be in such a hurry as the princess observed …' General Epanchin murmured in rapture, repeating Princess Byelokonsky's words, which had struck him.

Only Aglaia seemed mournful, but there was a flush perhaps of indignation in her face.

'He really is very charming,' the old man muttered again to Ivan Petrovitch.

'I came here with anguish in my heart,' Myshkin went on with increasing emotion, speaking more and more quickly, more and more queerly and eagerly. 'I… I was afraid of you, afraid of myself too. Of myself most of all. When I came back here to Petersburg, I determined that I would see the best people, the people of old family, of ancient lineage, to which I belong myself, among whom I am in the front rank by birth. Now, I'm sitting with princes like myself, am I not? I wanted to get to know you, and it was necessary, very, very necessary! … I've always heard too much that was bad about you, more than what was good; of your pettiness, the exclusiveness of your interests, your stagnation, your shallow education, and your ridiculous habits. Oh, so much is said and written about you! I came here today with curiosity, with excitement. I wanted to see for myself and make up my own mind whether this upper-crust of Russian society is really good for nothing and has out-lived its time, is drained of its ancient life and only fit to die, but still persists in a petty, endless strife with the men … of the future, getting in their way and not conscious that it is dying itself. I did not quite believe in this view before, because there never has been an upper class amongst us, except, perhaps, the courtiers, by uniform or… by accident and now it has quite disappeared. That's right, isn't it?'

'No, it's not right at all,' said Ivan Petrovitch, smiling ironically.

'There, he's off again!' said Princess Byelokonsky, losing patience.

'*Laissez le dire,* he's trembling all over,' the old man warned them in an undertone.

Myshkin had completely lost control of himself.

'And what do I find? I find people elegant, simple-hearted, and clever. I meet an old man who is ready to listen to a boy like me and be kind to him. I find people ready to understand and to forgive, Russian, and kind-hearted, almost as kind and warm-hearted as I met there, and almost their equals. You can judge what a delightful surprise it is! Oh, do let me put it into words! I had heard so often and fully believed myself that society was nothing but manners, and antiquated forms, and that all reality was extinct. But I see now for myself that that cannot be so among us; that may be anywhere else but not in Russia. Can you all be Jesuits and frauds? I heard Prince N— tell a story just now. Wasn't that simple-hearted, spontaneous humour; wasn't it genuine frankness? Can such sayings come from the lips of a man … who is dead; whose heart and talent have run dry? Could the dead have treated me as you have treated me? Isn't it material… for the future, for hope? Can such people lag behind and fail to understand?'

'I beg you again; calm yourself, my dear boy. We'll talk about all this another time. I shall be delighted …' smiled the old 'dignitary.'

Ivan Petrovitch cleared his throat and turned round in his chair; General Epanchin made a movement; the chief of the department began talking to the old 'dignitary's wife, paying not the slightest attention to Myshkin, but the 'dignitary's wife frequently listened and glanced at him.

'No, it's better for me to speak, you know,' Myshkin began again, with another feverish outburst, addressing the old man with peculiar trustfulness, and as it were, confidentially. 'Yesterday, Aglaia Ivanovna told me not to talk, and even told me what subjects not to talk about; she knows I'm absurd on those subjects. Pm twenty-seven, but I know that I'm like a child. I have no right to express an opinion, I've said that long ago. It's only with Rogozhin in Moscow that I've talked openly. We read Pushkin together, the whole of him. He knew nothing of him, not even the name of Pushkin ... I'm always afraid that my absurd manner may discredit the thought or the *leading idea.* I have no elocution. My gestures are always inappropriate, and that makes people laugh, and degrades my ideas. I've no sense of proportion either, and that's the great thing; that's the chief thing in fact... I know it's better for me to sit still and keep quiet. When I persist in keeping quiet, I seem very sensible, and what's more I think things over. But now it's better for me to talk. I'm talking because you look at me so nicely; you have such a nice face! I promised Aglaia Ivanovna yesterday that I'd be silent all the evening!'

'Vraiment!' smiled the old dignitary.

'But sometimes I think that I am not right in thinking that. Sincerity is more important than elocution, isn't it? Isn't it?'

'Sometimes.'

'I want to explain everything, everything, everything! Oh, yes! You think I'm Utopian? A theorist? My ideas are really all so simple ... Don't you believe it? You smile? You know I'm contemptible sometimes, for I lose my faith. As I came here just now, I wondered: "How shall I talk to them? With what words shall I begin, so that they may understand a little?" How frightened I was, but I was more frightened for you. It was awful, awful! And yet, how could I be afraid? Wasn't it shameful to be afraid? What does it matter that for one advanced man there is such a mass of retrograde and evil ones? That's what I'm so happy about; that I'm convinced now that there is no such mass, and that it's all living material! There's no reason to be troubled because we're absurd, is there? You know it really is true that we're absurd, that we're shallow, have bad habits, that we're bored, that we don't know how to look at things, that we can't understand; we're all like that, all of us, you, and I, and they! And you are not offended at my telling you to your faces that you're absurd? Are you? And if that's so, aren't you good material? Do you know, to my thinking it's a good thing sometimes to be absurd; it's better in fact, it makes it easier to forgive one another, it's easier to be humble. One can't understand everything at once, we can't begin with perfection all at once! In order to reach perfection one must begin by being ignorant of a great deal. And if we understand things too quickly, perhaps we shan't understand them thoroughly. I say that to you who have been able to understand so much already and … have failed to understand so much. I am afraid for you now. You are not angry at a boy like me for saying such things to you? Of course you're not! Oh, you know how to forget and to forgive those who have offended you and those who have not offended you, for it's always more difficult to forgive those who have not offended one, and just because they've *not* injured one, and that therefore one's complaint of them is groundless. That's what I expected of the best people, that's what I was in a hurry to tell you as I came here, and did not know how to tell you … You are laughing, Ivan Petrovitch? You think that I was afraid for *them*, that I'm *their* champion, a democrat, an advocate of equality?' he laughed hysterically (he had been continually breaking into short laughs of delight). 'I'm afraid for you, for all of you, for all of us together. I am a prince myself, of ancient family, and I am sitting with princes. I speak to save us all, that our class may not vanish in vain; in darkness, without realising anything, abusing everything, and losing everything. Why disappear and make way for others when we might remain in advance and be the leaders? If we are advanced we shall be the leaders. Let us be servants in order to be leaders.'

He began to try to get up from his chair, but the old man still held him, though he looked at him with growing uneasiness.

'Listen! I know it's not right to talk. Better set an example, better to begin … I have already begun … and – and – can one really be unhappy? Oh, what does my grief, what does my sorrow matter if I can be happy? Do you know I don't know how one can walk by a tree and not be happy at the sight of it? How can one talk to a man and not be happy in loving him! Oh, it's only that I'm not able to express it... And what beautiful things there are at every step, that even the most hopeless man must feel to be beautiful! Look at a child! Look at God's sunrise! Look at the grass, how it grows! Look at the eyes that gaze at you and love you!...'

He had for some time been standing as he talked. The old man looked at him in alarm. Lizaveta Prokofyevna cried out, 'Ah, my God!' and threw up her hands in dismay, the first to realise what was wrong.

Aglaia quickly ran up to him. She was in time to catch him in her arms, and with horror, with a face distorted with pain, she heard the wild scream of the 'spirit tearing and casting down the unhappy man.'

The sick man lay on the carpet. Someone hastened to put a pillow under his head.

No one had expected this. A quarter of an hour later, Prince N—, Yevgeny Pavlovitch, and the old dignitary were trying to restore the liveliness of the company, but within half an hour the party had broken up. Many words of sympathy and regret were uttered, a few comments were made. Ivan Petrovitch remarked that 'the young man was a Slavophil or something of the sort, but that there was nothing very dangerous about that, however.' The old dignitary expressed no opinion. It's true that later on, next day and the day after, everyone who had been present seemed rather cross. Ivan Petrovitch was positively offended, but not seriously so. The chief of the department was for some time rather cold to General Epanchin. The old dignitary, who was their 'patron', mumbled something by way of admonition to the father of the family, though, in flattering terms he expressed the deepest interest in Aglaia's future. He really was a rather good-hearted man, but one reason of the interest he had taken in Myshkin that evening was the part that the prince had played in the scandal connected with Nastasya Filippovna. He had heard something of the story and had been much interested by it, and would have liked indeed to ask questions about it.

Princess Byelokonsky said to Lizaveta Prokofyevna as she took leave that evening, 'Well, there's good and bad in him. And if you care to know my opinion, there's more bad than good. You can see for yourselves what he is, a sick man!'

Madame Epanchin made up her mind, once for all, that as a bridegroom he was 'impossible,' and that night she vowed to herself that 'as long as she was living, he should not be the husband of Aglaia.' She got up in the same mind next morning. But in the course of the morning, by lunchtime at one o'clock, she was drawn into contradicting herself in an extraordinary way.

In reply to her sisters' carefully guarded question, Aglaia replied coldly, but haughtily, as it were, rapping it out, 'I've never given him a promise of any sort, I've never in my life looked on him or thought of him as my betrothed. He is no more to me than anyone else.'

Lizaveta Prokofyevna suddenly flared up.

'That I should never have expected of you,' she said with chagrin. 'As a suitor he's out of the question, I know, and thank God that we're agreed about it. But I didn't expect such words from you. I looked for something very different from you. I'd be ready to turn away all those people who were here last night and to keep him. That's what I think of him!

At that point she stopped short, frightened at her words. But if only she had known how unjust she was to her daughter at that moment! Everything was settled in Aglaia's mind. She too was waiting for the hour that was to decide everything and every hint, even incautious touch dealt a deep wound to her heart.

Chapter 8

For Myshkin, too, that morning began under the influence of painful forebodings; they might be explained by his invalid state, but his sadness was quite indefinite, and that was what made it most distressing to him. It is true that painful, mortifying facts stood vividly before him, but his sadness went beyond everything he remembered, and the reflections that followed that memory. He realised that he could not regain his serenity alone. By degrees the conviction took root in him that something special, something decisive, would happen to him that very day. His fit of the previous evening had been a slight one. Besides depression and a certain weariness in his head and pain in his limbs, he had nothing the matter with him. His brain worked fairly accurately, though his soul was ill at ease. He got up rather late, and at once clearly recalled the previous evening. He remembered, too, though not quite distinctly, how he had been taken home half an hour after the fit. He learnt that a messenger had already been from the Epanchins to ask after his health. At half-past eleven another called to enquire and this pleased him. Vera Lebedyev was among the first to visit him and wait upon him. She burst out crying for the first minute when she saw him, but when Myshkin at once reassured her she began laughing. He was suddenly struck by the girl's deep sympathy for him. He took her hand and kissed it. Vera flushed crimson.

'Ach, what are you doing!' she cried, drawing her hand away in dismay. She went away quickly in strange confusion. She had time though to tell him, among other things, that her father had run off very early to see the 'departed,' as he persisted in calling the general, to find out whether he had died in the night, and it was reported, so she was told, that he was at the point of death. At twelve o'clock Lebedyev himself came home, and went in to Myshkin, not merely 'for a minute to enquire after his precious health,' and so on, but also to look into the cupboard. He did nothing but sigh and groan and Myshkin soon dismissed him; yet he made an attempt to question the prince about his fit the previous evening, though it was evident he knew full details about it already. After him Kolya ran in also for a minute. He really was in a hurry, and was in great and painful agitation. He began by directly and insistently begging Myshkin for an explanation of all that they had been concealing from him, asserting that he had learnt almost everything the day before. He was deeply and violently distressed.

With all possible sympathy Myshkin told him the whole story, relating the facts with absolute exactness, and it fell like a thunderbolt on the poor boy. He could not utter a word and wept in silence. Myshkin felt that this was one of those impressions which remain for ever and make a turning-point in a young life. He hastened to give him his view of the case, adding that in his opinion the old man's death might principally be due to the horror inspired by his own action, and that not everyone was capable of such a feeling. Kolya's eyes flashed as he listened to Myshkin.

'They're a worthless lot – Ganya and Varya and Ptitsyn! I'm not going to quarrel with them, but our paths lie apart from this moment. Ah, Prince, I've had so many new feelings since yesterday!

It's a lesson for me! I consider that my mother, too, is entirely my responsibility now; though she's provided for at Varya's, that's not the thing ...'

He jumped up, remembering that he was expected at home, hurriedly asked after Myshkin's health, and listening to the answer, added in haste, 'Isn't there something else? I heard yesterday (though I've no right)... but if you ever want a devoted servant for any purpose, here he is before you. It seems as though we're both of us not quite happy, isn't that so? But... I don't ask anything, I don't ask ...'

He went away, and Myshkin sank into still deeper brooding. Everyone was predicting misfortune, everyone had already drawn conclusions, everyone looked at him, as though they knew something and something he did not know. 'Lebedyev asks questions, Kolya directly hints at it, and Vera weeps.' At last he dismissed the subject in vexation. 'It's all my accursed sickly over-sensitiveness,' he thought. His face brightened when, after one o'clock he saw the Epanchins, who came to visit him 'for a moment.' They really did come only for a moment. When Lizaveta Prokofyevna got up from lunch, she announced that they were all going for a walk at once, and all together. The announcement was made in the form of a command, dry, abrupt and unexplained. They all went out, that is the mother, the girls, and Prince S— Lizaveta Prokofyevna turned in a direction exactly opposite to that which they took every day. Everyone understood what it meant, but everyone refrained from speaking for fear of irritating Madame Epanchin, and, as though to escape from reproaches or objections, she walked in front without looking back at them. At last Adelaïda observed that there was no need to race along like that and that there was no catching Mamma up.

'Now then,' said Lizaveta Prokofyevna, turning suddenly, 'we're just passing his door. Whatever Aglaia may think, and whatever may happen afterwards, he is not a stranger, and what's more, now he's in trouble and ill. I shall go to see him anyhow. If any care to come too, they can, if not you can go on. The way is open.'

They all went in, of course. Myshkin very properly hastened to beg forgiveness once more for the vase and ... the scene.

'Oh, that's no matter,' answered Lizaveta Prokofyevna. 'I don't mind about the vase, I mind about you. So now you're aware yourself that there was a scene last night, that's how it is "the morning after." But it's all of no consequence, for everyone sees now that one mustn't be hard on you. Goodbye for the present though. If you feel strong enough, go for a little walk and then have a nap – that's my advice. And if you feel disposed, come in as usual. Be sure, once for all, that whatever happens, whatever may come you'll always be our friend, mine anyway. I can answer for myself…"

All accepted this challenge, and confirmed their mother's sentiments. They went out, but in this simple-hearted haste to say something kind and encouraging there lay hid a great deal that was cruel, of which Lizaveta Prokofyevna had no suspicion. In the words 'as usual' and 'mine at least' – there was again an ominous note. Myshkin began to drink of Aglaia. It is true that she had given him a wonderful smile on going in and again on taking leave, but she had not uttered a word, even when the others had all made their protestations of friendship, though she had looked intently at him once or twice. Her face was paler than usual, as though she had slept badly that night. Myshkin made up his mind that he would certainly go to them that evening 'as usual' and he looked feverishly at his watch. Vera came in just three minutes after the Epanchins had gone.

'Aglaia Ivanovna gave me a message for you just now, in secret, Lyov Nikolayevitch,' she said.

Myshkin positively trembled.

'A note?'

'No, a message. She had hardly time for that, even. She begs you earnestly not to be away from home for one minute all today, up till seven o'clock this evening, or till nine o'clock, I couldn't quite hear.'

'But why so? What does it mean?'

'I know nothing about it. Only she was very earnest that I should give you the message.'

'Did she say "very earnest"?'

'No, she didn't say that. She just managed to turn round and speak, as I luckily ran up to her myself. But I could see from her face whether she Was in earnest over it. She looked at me so that she made my heart stop beating…'

After asking a few more questions Myshkin was more agitated than ever, though he succeeded in learning nothing more. When he was left alone, he lay down on the sofa and fell to musing again.

'Perhaps they have a visitor there till nine o'clock and she's afraid I may do something silly before visitors again,' he thought at last, and began again impatiently waiting for evening and looking at his watch. But the mystery was solved long before the evening, and the solution also was brought by a visitor, and took the form of a new and agonising mystery.

Just half an hour after the Epanchins' visit, Ippolit came in to him, so tired and exhausted that, entering without uttering a word, he literally fell, almost unconscious, into an easy chair, and instantly broke into an insufferable cough. He coughed till the blood came. His eyes glittered and there were hectic flushes on his cheeks. Myshkin murmured something to him, but Ippolit made no reply, and for a long time could only motion to Myshkin to let him alone. At last he came to himself.

'I'm going!' he pronounced, with an effort at last, and with a husky voice.

'I'll go with you if you like,' said Myshkin, getting up from his seat and suddenly stopping short, as he recalled that he had been forbidden to leave the house.

Ippolit laughed.

'I'm not going away from you,' he went on, continually gasping and coughing, 'on the contrary, I found it necessary to come to you and about something important... but for which I would not have disturbed you. I'm going *over yonder*, and this time I believe I really am going. It's all up! I haven't come for sympathy, believe me ... I lay down at ten o'clock today meaning not to get up again till the *time came*. But you see I changed my mind and got up once more to come to you ... so you see I had to.'

'It grieves me to look at you. You'd better have sent for me instead of troubling to come here.'

'Well, that's enough. You've expressed your regret and enough to satisfy the requirements of politeness ... But I forgot: how are you yourself?'

'I'm all right. Yesterday I was ... not quite ...'

'I know, I know, the Chinese vase had the worst of it. I'm sorry I wasn't there! I've come about something. In the first place, I've had the pleasure today of seeing Gavril Ardalionovitch at a tryst with Aglaia Ivanovna on the green seat. I was astonished to see how stupid a man can look. I remarked upon it to Aglaia Ivanovna, when Gavril Ardalionovitch had gone ... You seem not to be surprised at anything, Prince,' he added, looking mistrustfully at Myshkin's calm face. 'To be surprised at nothing, they say, is a sign of great intelligence. To my mind, it might quite as well be a sign of great stupidity ... But I don't mean that for you, excuse me ... I am very unfortunate in my expressions today.'

'I knew yesterday that Gavril Ardalionlovitch

Myshkin broke off, obviously confused, though Ippolit was annoyed at his not being surprised.

'You knew it! That's something new! But don't tell me about it... You weren't a witness of the interview today, I suppose?'

'You saw that I was not there, since you were there yourself.'

'Oh, you may have been sitting behind a bush somewhere. But I'm glad, for your sake, of course, for I was beginning to think that Gavril Ardalionovitch – was the favourite.'

'I beg you not to speak of this to me, Ippolit, and in such terms.'

'Especially since you know all about it already.'

'You are mistaken, I know hardly anything about it, and Aglaia Ivanovna knows for a fact that I know nothing about it. I knew nothing about their meeting, really. You say there's been a meeting between them? Very well then, let us leave the subject 'But hows this? One minute you know, the next you don't. You say, 'very well and let us leave it.' But look here, don't be so trustful! Especially if you don't know anything about it. You are trustful because you don't know anything about it. And do you know what those two, the brother and sister, are scheming for? Perhaps you suspect that? Very well, very well, I'll drop it,' he added, noticing an impatient gesture from Myshkin. 'Well, I've come about my own affairs and I want to ... explain about it. Damn it all, one can't die without explanations. It's awful how much I explain. Do you care to hear?'

'Speak, I'm listening.'

'But I'm changing my opinion again, though, I'll begin with Ganya, all the same. Would you believe it that I had an appointment at the green seat today, too? I don't want to tell a lie, though. I insisted on an interview myself, I begged for it, I promised to reveal a secret. I don't know whether I came too early (I believe I really was early), but I had no sooner sat down beside Aglaia Ivanovna, when I saw Gavril Ardalionovitch and Varvara Ardalionovna coming along, arm in arm, as though they were out for a walk. They both seemed much amazed at meeting me. It was so unexpected that they were quite taken aback. Aglaia

Ivanovna flushed crimson, and you may not believe it, but she was rather disconcerted, whether because I was there or simply at the sight of Gavril Ardalionovitch – you know what a beauty he is – anyway she turned crimson, and ended it all in a second, very absurdly. She got up, answered Gavril Ardalionovitch's bow, and Varvara Ardalionovna's ingratiating smile, and suddenly rapped out: "I've only come to express in person my pleasure at your sincere and friendly feelings, and if I am in need of them, believe me …" Then she turned away and the two went off -I don't know whether like fools or in triumph – Ganya, of course, a fool. He couldn't make out a word, and turned as red as a lobster (he has an extraordinary expression of face sometimes). But Varvara Ardalionovna seemed to understand that they must make their escape as quickly as possible, and that this was quite enough from Aglaia Ivanovna, and she drew her brother away. She's cleverer than he is and I've no doubt she's triumphant now. I came to Aglaia Ivanovna to make arrangements about a meeting with Nastasya Filippovna.'

'With Nastasya Filippovna,' cried Myshkin.

'Aha! You seem to be losing your indifference and beginning to be surprised. I'm glad that you're ready to be like a human being at last. I'll comfort you for that. This is what comes of serving a young lady of lofty soul. I got a slap in the face from her today.'

'Morally speaking?' Myshkin could not help asking.

'Yes, not physically. I don't think anyone would raise a hand against a creature like me, even a woman would not strike me now. Even Ganya wouldn't strike me! Though I did think he was going to fly at me at one time yesterday … I'll bet you anything I know what you're thinking about now. You're thinking, "he mustn't be beaten of course, but he might be smothered with a pillow or a wet cloth in his sleep – in fact one ought to …" It's written on your face that you're thinking that at this very second.'

'I've never thought of such a thing,' Myshkin answered with disgust.

'I don't know, I dreamt last night that I was smothered with a wet cloth by… a man … I'll tell you who it was – Rogozhin! What do you think? Could a man be smothered with a wet cloth?'

'I don't know.'

'I've heard that it can be done. Very well, we'll drop it. Come, why am I a slanderer? Why did she accuse me of being a slanderer today? And take note, it was after she'd heard every word I had to say, and questioned me, too ... But that's just like a woman! For her sake I've got into communication with Rogozhin, an interesting person. In her interests I have arranged a personal interview with Nastasya Filippovna for her. Was it because I wounded her vanity by hinting that she enjoyed Nastasya Filippovna's "leavings"? Yes, I did try to impress that upon her all the time in her interest, I don't deny it. I wrote her two letters in that strain, and today for the third time, at our interview ... I began by telling her that it was humiliating for her... Though the word 'leavings' wasn't mine, but someone else's. At Ganya's, anyway, everybody was saying it, and indeed she repeated it herself. So how can she call me a slanderer? I see, I see, it's very amusing for you to look at me now, and I bet you're applying those stupid verses to me:

> And on the gloom of my declining hour
> Perchance the farewell smile of love may shine.

'Ha-ha-ha!' He went off into an hysterical laugh. 'Mark,' he gasped through a fit of coughing, 'what a fellow Ganya is, he talks about "leavings" and what does he want to take advantage of himself now!'

For a long while Myshkin was silent. He was horror-struck.

'You spoke of an interview with Nastasya Filippovna,' he murmured at last.

'Hey, are you really unaware that Aglaia Ivanovna is going to meet Nastasya Filippovna today? And that for that purpose Nastasya Filippovna has been brought, through Rogozhin, from Petersburg, at an invitation of Aglaia Ivanovna and by my efforts, and is now staying with Rogozhin, where she stayed before, very near you, in the house of that woman ... Darya Alexeyevna ... a very dubious lady, a friend of hers, and to that very doubtful house Aglaia Ivanovna is going today to have a friendly conversation with Nastasya Filippovna, and to decide various problems. They want to work at arithmetic. Didn't you know it? Honour bright?'

'That's incredible!'

'Well, that's all right if it's incredible. But how could you know? Though this is such a place, if a fly buzzes everyone knows of it. But I've warned you, and you may be grateful to me. Well, till we meet again – in the next world probably. But another thing: though I have been a cad to you, because … why should I be a loser? Kindly tell me that? For your advantage, eh? I've dedicated my "Confession" to her (you didn't know that?). And how she received it too, ha-ha! But anyway I've not behaved like a cad to her, I've not done her any harm, but she's put me to shame and snubbed me … though I've done you no harm either. If I did refer to "leavings" and things of that sort, still I am telling you the day and the hour and the address of their meeting, and I've let you into the whole game … from resentment of course, not from generosity. Goodbye, I'm as talkative as a stammerer or a consumptive. Mind you take steps at once, if you deserve to be called a man. The interview is to take place this evening, that's the truth.'

Ippolit went towards the door, but Myshkin called after him and he stopped in the doorway.

'So then, according to you, Aglaia Ivanovna is going herself today to Nastasya Filippovna?' asked Myshkin.

Patches of red came out on his forehead and cheeks.

'I don't know for a fact, but that's probably so,' answered Ippolit, looking round. 'Yes, it must be so. Nastasya Filippovna couldn't go to her? And it wouldn't be at Ganya's, where there's a man almost dead. What do you think of the general?'

'It can't be there, if only for that reason,' Myshkin put in. 'How could she get away even if she wanted to? You don't know… the habits of the household. She couldn't get away from home alone to see Nastasya Filippovna. It's nonsense.'

'Look here, Prince, nobody jumps out of window, but when the house is on fire the grandest gentleman or lady is ready to jump out of window. When it's a case of necessity, there's no help for it, and our young lady will even go to see Nastasya Filippovna. And don't they let them go anywhere, your young ladies?'

'No, I didn't mean that…'

'Well, if not, she's only to go down the steps, and go straight there, and she needn't ever go home again. There are cases when one may sometimes burn one's ships and not go home again. Life does not consist only of lunches and dinners and Prince S—'s. I fancy you take Aglaia Ivanovna for a young lady or a boarding-school miss. Wait till seven or eight o'clock. If I were in your place, I'd send someone to be on the watch there to catch the very minute when she comes down the steps. Send Kolya. He'll be delighted to play the spy, believe me, for your sake, I mean … for everything's relative … Ha-ha!'

Ippolit went out. Myshkin had no reason for asking anyone to spy for him, even if he had been capable of doing so. Aglaia's command that he should stay at home was now almost explained. Perhaps she meant to come and fetch him, or perhaps it was that she did not want him to turn up there and so had told him to stay at home. That might be so, too. His head was in a whirl; the whole room was turning round. He lay down on the sofa and closed his eyes.

In either case it was final, conclusive. Myshkin did not think of Aglaia as a young lady, or a boarding-school miss. He felt now that he had been uneasy for a long time, and that it was just something of this kind he had been dreading. But what did she want to see her for? A shiver ran over Myshkin's whole body. He was in a fever again.

No, he didn't look on her as a child! He had been horrified by some of her views, some of her sayings of late. He sometimes fancied that she had seemed too reserved, too controlled, and he remembered that this had alarmed him. He had been trying during those days not to think about it, he had dismissed oppressive ideas, but what lay hidden in that soul? The thought had worried him for a long time, though he had faith in that soul. And now all this must be settled and revealed that day. An awful thought! And again – 'that woman!' Why did it always seem to him that that woman was bound to appear at the last moment, and tear asunder his fate like a rotten thread? That it had always seemed so he was ready to swear now, though he was almost delirious. If he had tried to forget 'her' of late, it was simply because he was afraid of her. Did he love that woman or hate her? He had not put that question to himself once that day. His heart was clear on one point: he knew whom he loved … He was not so much afraid of the meeting of the two, not of the strangeness, not of the unknown cause of that meeting, not of what it might lead to, whatever it might be – he was afraid of Nastasya Filippovna. He remembered a few days later that all through those feverish hours her eyes, her glance, were before him, her words were in his ears – strange words, though little remained of them in his memory, when those feverish hours of misery were over. He scarcely remembered that Vera had brought him his dinner, that he ate it, and did not know whether he slept after dinner or not. All he knew was that he only began to see things clearly that evening, when Aglaia came towards him on the verandah, and he jumped up from the sofa and went to meet her. It was a quarter past seven. Aglaia was entirely alone, dressed simply, as it seemed hastily, in a light burnous. Her face was pale as it had been that morning, and her eyes glittered with a dry, hard light. He had never seen such an expression in her eyes. She looked at him attentively.

'You are quite ready,' she observed quietly, and with apparent composure. 'You are dressed and have your hat in your hand. So you've been warned, and I know by whom – Ippolit?'

'Yes, he told me …' muttered Myshkin, more dead than alive.

'Come along. You know that you must escort me there. You are strong enough to go out, I suppose?'

'I'm strong enough, but… is this possible?'

He broke off instantly and could say no more. This was his one attempt to restrain the mad girl, and after it he followed her like a slave. Confused as his ideas were, he realised that she would certainly go *there* even without him, and that therefore he was bound to go with her in any case. He divined how strong her determination was. It was beyond him to check this wild impulse. They walked in silence the whole way, scarcely uttering a word. He only noticed that she knew the way well, and when he wanted to go a rather longer way because the road was more deserted, and suggested this to her, she seemed to listen with strained attention and answered abruptly, 'It's all the same!'

When they had almost reached Darya Alexeyevna's abode (a big, old, wooden house) there came down the steps a gorgeously dressed lady with a young girl. They both got into an elegant carriage which stood waiting at the steps, talking and laughing loudly. They did not once glance at the approaching couple and seemed not to notice them. As soon as the carriage had driven off, the door instantly opened a second time, and Rogozhin, who had been waiting there, admitted Myshkin and Aglaia and closed the door behind them.

'There's no one in the whole house now, except us four,' he observed aloud, and looked strangely at Myshkin.

In the first room they went into, Nastasya Filippovna was waiting. She too was dressed very simply and all in black. She stood up to greet them, but did not smile or even give Myshkin her hand.

Her intent and uneasy eyes were fastened on Aglaia. The two ladies sat at a little distance from one another – Aglaia on a sofa in a corner of the room, Nastasya Filippovna at the window. Myshkin and Rogozhin did not sit down, and she did not invite them to do so. Myshkin looked with perplexity and, as it were, with pain at Rogozhin, but the latter still wore the same smile. The silence lasted some moments.

At length an ominous look passed over Nastasya Filippovna's face. Her gaze grew obstinate, hard, and full of hatred, and it was riveted all the time upon her visitors. Aglaia was evidently confused, but not intimidated. As she walked in, she scarcely looked at her rival, and, for the time, sat with downcast eyes, as though musing. Once or twice she looked, as it were, casually round the room. There was an unmistakable shade of disgust on her face, as though she were afraid of contamination here. She mechanically arranged her dress, and even once restlessly changed her seat, moving to the other end of the sofa. She was hardly perhaps conscious of her actions, but their unconsciousness made them even more insulting. At last she looked resolutely straight into Nastasya Filippovna's face and read at once all that was revealed in the ominous gleam in her rival's eyes. Woman understood woman. Aglaia shuddered.

'You know, of course, why I asked you to come,' she brought out at last, but in a very low voice, and pausing once or twice even in this brief sentence.

'No, I know nothing about it,' Nastasya Filippovna answered, drily and abruptly.

Aglaia flushed. Perhaps it struck her suddenly as strange and incredible that she should be sitting here with that woman in 'that woman's' house, and hanging upon her answer. At the first sound of Nastasya Filippovna's voice a sort of shiver ran over her. All this, of course, 'that woman' saw quite clearly.

'You understand everything… but you pretend not to understand on purpose,' said Aglaia, almost in a whisper, looking sullenly at the floor.

'Why should I?' Nastasya Filippovna smiled.

'You want to take advantage of my position, of my being in your house,' Aglaia brought out, awkwardly and absurdly.

'You're responsible for your position, not I,' said Nastasya Filippovna, suddenly flaring up. 'You're not here at my invitation, but I at yours, and I don't know to this hour with what object.'

Aglaia raised her head haughtily.

'Restrain your tongue. That is your weapon and I've not come to fight you with it.'

'Ah! You have come to fight me then! Would you believe it, I thought that you were ... cleverer

They looked at one another, no longer concealing their spite. One of them was the woman who had lately written those letters to the other. And now it all fell to pieces at their first meeting. And yet not one of the four persons in the room seemed at that moment to think it strange. Myshkin, who would not the day before have believed in the possibility of it even in a dream, now stood, gazed and listened as though he had foreseen this long ago. The most fantastic dream seemed to have changed suddenly into the most vivid and sharply defined reality. One of these women, at that moment, so despised the other, and so keenly desired to express this feeling to her (possibly she had come simply to do so, as Rogozhin said next day) that, unaccountable as the other was with her disordered intellect and sick soul, it seemed that no idea she had adopted beforehand could have been maintained against the malignant, purely feminine contempt of her rival. Myshkin felt sure that Nastasya Filippovna would not mention the letters of her own accord. He could guess from her flashing eyes what those letters must be costing her now; and he would have given half his life that Aglaia should not speak of them.

But Aglaia seemed suddenly to pull herself together, and instantly mastered herself.

'You misunderstand me,' she said. 'I have not come here to fight you, though I don't like you. I... I came ... to speak to you as one human being to another. When I sent for you, I had already made up my mind what to speak to you about, and I won't depart from that decision now, though you should not understand me at all. That will be the worse for you and not for me. I wanted to answer what you have written to me, and to answer you in person, because I thought it more convenient. Hear my answer to all your letters. I felt sorry for Prince Lyov Nikolayevitch from that day when I first made his acquaintance, and heard afterwards what happened at your party. I felt sorry for him, because he is such a simple-hearted man and in his simplicity believed that he might be happy ... with a woman ... of such a character. What I was afraid of for him came to pass. You were incapable of loving him, you tortured him and abandoned him. You could not love him, because you were too proud ... no, not proud, that's a mistake, but too vain ... that's not it, either, it's your self-love which amounts almost to madness, of which your letters to me are a proof. You couldn't love a simple-hearted man like him, and very likely you secretly despised him and laughed at him. You can love nothing but your shame and the continual thought that you've been brought to shame and humiliated. If your shame were less or you were free from it altogether, you'd be more unhappy...' (Aglaia enjoyed pronouncing these too rapidly uttered but long prepared and pondered words – words she had brooded over before she had dreamed of the present interview; with malignant eyes she watched their effect on Nastasya Filippovna's face, distorted with agitation). 'You remember,' she went on, 'he wrote me a letter then. He says that you know about that letter and have read it, in fact. From that letter I understood it all and understood it correctly. He confirmed that himself lately, that is, everything I'm telling you, word for word, indeed. After the letter I waited. I guessed that you were sure to come here, because you can't exist without Petersburg; you are still too young and too good-looking for the provinces. Though, indeed, those are not my words either,' she added, blushing hotly, and from that moment the colour did not leave her face, till she finished speaking. 'When I saw the prince again, I felt dreadfully hurt and wounded on his account. Don't laugh. If you laugh, you're not worthy to understand that.'

'You see that I'm not laughing,' Nastasya Filippovna pronounced sternly and mournfully.

'It's nothing to me, though, laugh as much as you like. When I began to question him, he told me that he had ceased to love you long ago, that even the memory of you was a torture to him, but that he was sorry for you ... and that when he thought of you, it always pierced his heart. I have to tell you, too, that I have never in my life met a man like him for noble simplicity, and boundless trustfulness. I understood from the way he talked that anyone who chose could deceive him, and that he would forgive anyone afterwards who had deceived him, and that was why I grew to love him ...'

Aglaia paused for a moment as though amazed, as though hardly able to believe her own ears that she could have uttered such words. But at the same time an infinite pride shone in her eyes.

She seemed by now to be beyond caring, even if 'that woman' did laugh at once at the avowal that had broken from her.

'I've told you all, and now, no doubt, you understand what I want of you?'

'Perhaps I do understand, but tell me yourself,' Nastasya Filippovna answered softly.

There was a glow of anger in Aglaia's face.

'I want to learn from you,' she pronounced firmly and distinctly, 'what right you have to meddle in his feelings for me? By what right you have dared to send me letters? What right you have to be continually declaring to him and to me that you love him, after abandoning him of your own accord and running away from him in such an insulting and degrading way.'

'I have never declared either to him or to you that I love him,' Nastasya Filippovna articulated with an effort, 'and ... you are right that I did run away from him,' she added, hardly audibly.

'Never declared it "to him or to me"!' cried Aglaia. 'How about your letters? Who asked you to begin matchmaking and persuading me to marry him? Wasn't that a declaration? Why do you force yourself upon us? I thought at first that you wanted to rouse in me an aversion for him by interfering with us, and so make me give him up. It was only afterwards that I guessed what it meant. You simply imagined that you were doing something wonderful and heroic with all these pretences. Why, are you capable of loving him if you love your vanity so dearly? Why didn't you simply go away from here instead of writing me absurd letters? Why don't you even now marry the generous man who loves you so much that he honours you with the offer of his hand? It's quite clear why – if you many Rogozhin, what grievance will you have to complain of? You'll have had too much honour done you. Yevgeny Pavlovitch said that you'd read too much poetry and have had "too much education for your ... position"; that you're a blue stocking and live in idleness. Add to that your vanity and one gets the full explanation of you.'

'And don't you live in idleness?'

Too hurriedly, too crudely, the contest had reached such an unexpected point, unexpected indeed, for when Nastasya Filippovna set off for Pavlovsk, she still had dreams of something different, though no doubt her forebodings were rather of ill than good. Aglaia was absolutely carried away by the impulse of the moment, as though she were falling down a precipice and could not resist the dreadful joy of vengeance. It was positively strange for Nastasya Filippovna to see Aglaia like this. She looked at her and seemed as though she could not believe her eyes, and was completely at a loss for the first moment. Whether she were a woman who had read too much poetry as Yevgeny Pavlovitch had said, or simply mad, as Myshkin was convinced, in any case this woman – though she sometimes behaved with such cynicism and impudence – was really far more modest, soft, and trustful than might have been believed. It's true that she was full of romantic notions, of self-centred dreaminess and capricious fantasy, but yet there was much that was strong and deep in her… Myshkin understood that. There was an expression of suffering in his face. Aglaia noticed this and trembled with hatred.

'How dare you address me like that?' she said, with indescribable haughtiness, in reply to Nastasya Filippovna's question.

'You must have heard me wrong,' said Nastasya Filippovna in surprise. 'How have I addressed you?'

'If you wanted to be a respectable woman, why didn't you give up your seducer, Totsky, simply … without theatrical scenes?' Aglaia said suddenly, apropos of nothing.

'What do you know of my position that you dare to judge me?' said Nastasya Filippovna, trembling, and turning terribly white.

'I know that you didn't go to work, but off with a rich man, Rogozhin, to go on posing as a fallen angel. I don't wonder that Totsky tried to shoot himself to escape from such a fallen angel!'

'Don't!' said Nastasya Filippovna with repulsion, and as though in anguish, 'you understand me about as well as … Darya Alexeyevna's housemaid, who was tried in court the other day with her betrothed. She'd have understood better than you …'

'Very likely, a respectable girl who works for her living. Why do you speak with such contempt of a housemaid?'

'I don't feel contempt for work, but for you when you speak of work.'

'If you'd wanted to be respectable, you'd have become a washerwoman.'

They both got up and gazed with pale faces at each other.

'Aglaia, leave off! It's unjust,' cried Myshkin, like one distraught.

Rogozhin was not smiling now, but was listening with compressed lips and folded arms.

'There, look at her,' said Nastasya Filippovna, trembling with anger, 'look at this young lady! And I took her for an angel! Have you come to me without a governess, Aglaia Ivanovna? ... And if you like ... if you like I'll tell you at once, directly and plainly, why you came to see me. You were afraid, that's why you came.'

'Afraid of you?' asked Aglaia, beside herself with naïve and insulting amazement that this woman dared to speak to her like this.

'Me, of course! You were afraid of me since you decided to come and see me. You don't despise anyone you're afraid of. And to think that I've respected you up to this very moment! But do you know why you are afraid of me and what is your chief object now? You wanted to find out for yourself whether he loves you more than me, or not, for you're fearfully jealous...'

'He has told me that he hates you ...' Aglaia faltered.

'Perhaps, perhaps I am not worthy of him, only... only I think you're lying! He cannot hate me and he could not have said so. But I am ready to forgive you ... seeing the position you're in ... though I did think better of you. I thought that you were cleverer and better looking even, I did indeed! ... Well, take your treasure ... here he is, he's looking at you, he is quite dazed. Take him, but on condition that you leave this house at once! This very minute!

She dropped into an easy chair and burst into tears. But suddenly there was a light of some new feeling in her face. She looked intently and fixedly at Aglaia, and rose from her seat.

'But if you like I'll tell him ... I'll order him, do you hear? I've only to tell him, and he'll throw you up at once and stay with me for ever, and marry me, and you'll have to run home alone. Shall I? Shall I?' she cried, like a mad creature, scarcely able to believe that she could be saying such things.

Aglaia ran in terror to the door, but stopped at the door and listened.

'Shall I send Rogozhin away? You thought that I was going to marry Rogozhin to please you? Here in your presence I shall cry to Rogozhin "Go away!" and say to the prince, "do you remember what you promised?" Heavens! Why have I humiliated myself so before them? Didn't you tell me yourself, Prince, that you would follow me whatever happened to me, and would never abandon me, that you love me and forgive me everything and – re ... resp ... Yes, you said that too! And it was only to set you free that I ran away from you then, but now I don't want to! Why has she treated me like a loose woman? Ask Rogozhin whether I'm a loose woman, he'll tell you! Now when she has covered me with shame and before your eyes too, will you turn away from me also, and walk away arm in arm with her? Well, curse you then, for you were the only one I trusted. Go away, Rogozhin, you're not wanted!' she went on, hardly knowing what she was doing, bringing the words out with an effort, with a distorted face and parched lips, evidently not believing a syllable of her tirade, and at the same time wishing to prolong the position if only for a second and to deceive herself. The outbreak Was so violent that it might almost have killed her, so at least it seemed to Myshkin.

'Here he is! Look at him!' she cried to Aglaia, pointing to Myshkin. 'If he doesn't come to me at once, if he does not take me, and doesn't give you up, take him for yourself, I give him up, I don't want him.'

Both she and Aglaia stood, as it were, in suspense, and both gazed like mad creatures at Myshkin. But he, perhaps, did not understand all the force of this challenge; in fact, it's certain that he didn't. He only saw before him the frenzied, despairing face, which, as he had once said to Aglaia, had 'stabbed his heart for ever.' He could bear no more and he turned, appealing and reproachful to Aglaia, pointing to Nastasya Filippovna.

'How can you! You see what an ... unhappy creature she is!'

But he could utter nothing more, petrified by the awful look in Aglaia's eyes. That look betrayed such suffering and at the same time such boundless hatred that, with a gesture of despair, he cried out and ran to her, but it was already too late. She could not endure even the instant of his hesitation. She hid her face in her hands, cried, 'Oh, my God!' and ran out of the room, Rogozhin followed to unbolt the street-door for her.

Myshkin ran too, but he felt himself clutched by two arms in the doorway. The desperate, contorted face of Nastasya Filippovna was gazing fixedly at him, and her blue lips moved, asking, 'You follow her? Her?'

She dropped senseless in his arms. He lifted her up, carried her into the room, laid her in a low chair, and stood over her in blank suspense. There was a glass of water on a little table. Rogozhin, coming back, took it up and sprinkled it in her face. She opened her eyes, and for a minute remembered nothing, but suddenly looked round her, started, cried out and threw herself in Myshkin's arms.

'Mine, mine!' she cried. 'Has the proud young lady gone? Ha-ha-ha!' she cried in hysterics. 'Ha-ha-ha! I gave him up to that young lady. And why? What for? I was mad! Mad!… Get away, Rogozhin. Ha-ha-ha!'

Rogozhin looked at them intently, and did not utter a word, but took his hat and went away. Ten minutes later Myshkin was sitting by Nastasya Filippovna, with his eyes fastened upon her, stroking her head and cheeks with both hands, as though she were a little child. He sighed in response to her laughter and was ready to cry at her tears. He said nothing, but listened intently to her broken, excited, incoherent babble. He scarcely took it in, but smiled gently to her, and as soon as he fancied she was beginning to grieve again, or to weep, to reproach him or complain, he began at once stroking her head again, and tenderly passing his hands over her cheeks, soothing and comforting her like a child.

Chapter 9

A fortnight had passed since the events narrated in the last chapter, and the positions of the persons concerned were so completely changed that it is extremely difficult for us to continue our story without certain explanations. And yet we must, as far as possible, confine ourselves to the bare statement of facts and for a very simple reason: because we find it difficult in many instances to explain what occurred. Such a preliminary statement on our part must seem very strange and obscure to the reader, who may ask how we can describe that of which we have no clear idea, no personal opinion. To avoid putting ourselves in a still more false position, we had better try to give an instance – and perhaps the kindly disposed reader will understand – of our difficulty. And we do this the more readily as this instance will not make a break in our narrative, but will be the direct continuation of it.

A fortnight later, that is at the beginning of July, and in the course of that fortnight, the history of our hero, and particularly the last incident in that history, were transformed into a strange, very diverting, almost incredible, and at the same time conspicuously actual scandal which gradually spread through all the streets adjoining Lebedyev's, Ptitsyn's, Darya Alexeyevna's and the Epanchins' villas, in short almost all over the town and even the districts adjoining it. Almost all the society of the place, the inhabitants, the summer visitors and the people who came to hear the band were all talking of the same story told in a thousand variations – how a prince, after causing a scandal in a well-known and honourable family and jilting a young girl of that family, to whom he was already betrothed, had been captivated by a well-known cocotte; had broken with all his own friends and, regardless of everything, regardless of threats, regardless of the general indignation of the public, was in a few days' time intending, with head erect, looking everyone straight in the face, to be openly and publicly married here in Pavlovsk to a woman with a disgraceful past. The story became so richly adorned with scandalous details, so many well-known and distinguished persons were introduced into it, and so many fantastic and enigmatical shades of significance were given to it, while on the other hand, it was presented with such incontestable and concrete facts that the general curiosity and gossip were, of course, very pardonable. The most subtle, artful, and at the same time probable interpretation must be put to the credit of a few serious gossips belonging to that class of sensible people who are always, in every rank of society, in haste to explain every event to their neighbours, and who find indeed their vocation and often their consolation in doing so. According to their version, the young man was of good family, a prince, and almost wealthy, a fool but a democrat, who had gone crazy over the contemporary nihilism revealed by Mr Turgenev. Though scarcely able to speak Russian, he had fallen in love with the daughter of General Epanchin, and had succeeded in being accepted as her betrothed by the family. But like the Frenchman in a story that had just appeared in print, who had allowed himself to be consecrated as a priest, had purposely begged to be consecrated, had performed all the rites, all the bowings and kissings and vows, and so on, in order to inform his bishop publicly next day, that, not believing in God, he considered it dishonourable to deceive the people and be kept by them for nothing, and so had renounced the priesthood he had assumed the day before, and sent his letter to be printed in all the liberal papers – like this French atheist, the prince had played a false part. It was said that he had purposely waited for the formal evening party given by the parents of his betrothed at which he was presented to very many distinguished personages, in order to declare his way of thinking aloud before everyone, that he had been rude to venerable old dignitaries, had renounced his betrothed publicly and insultingly; and in struggling with the servants who led him out had broken a magnificent china vase. It was stated as characteristic of the tendencies of the day that the senseless man really was in love with his betrothed, the general's daughter, and had renounced her simply on account of nihilism, and for the sake of the scandal it would lead to, so that he might have the gratification of marrying a 'lost' woman in sight of all the world and thereby proving his conviction that there were neither 'lost' nor 'virtuous' women, but that all women were alike, free; that he did not believe in the old conventional division, but had faith only in the 'woman question'; that in fact a 'lost' woman was in his eyes somewhat superior to one who was not lost. This explanation sounded extremely probable, and was accepted by the majority of the summer visitors, the more readily as it seemed to be supported by daily events. It's true that a great number of facts still remained unexplained. It was said that the poor girl so adored her betrothed – according to some people her 'seducer' – that on the day after he threw her over, she had run to find him where he was sitting with his mistress. Others maintained on the contrary that she had been purposely lured by him to his mistress's simply for the sake of nihilism, that is, for the sake of shaming and insulting her. However that may have been, the interest in the story grew greater every day, especially as there remained not the slightest doubt that the scandalous marriage really would take place.

And now, if we should be asked for an explanation – not of the nihilistic significance of the incident, oh, no! – But simply how far the proposed marriage satisfied Myshkin's real desires, what those desires actually were at that moment, how the spiritual condition of our hero was to be defined at that instant, and so on, and so on, we should, we admit, find it very difficult to answer. We can only say one thing, that the marriage really was arranged, and that Myshkin himself had authorised Lebedyev, Keller, and a friend of Lebedyev's, presented to Myshkin by the latter at this juncture, to undertake all necessary arrangements, religious and secular; that they were bidden not to spare money; that Nastasya

Filippovna was insisting on the wedding and in haste for it. That Keller, at his own ardent request, had been chosen for the prince's best man, while Burdovsky, who accepted the appointment with enthusiasm, had been chosen to perform the same office for Nastasya Filippovna, and that the wedding day had been fixed for the beginning of July. But besides these well-authenticated circumstances, some other facts are known to us which throw us completely out of our reckoning, because they are in direct contradiction of the preceding. We have a strong suspicion, for instance, that, after authorising Lebedyev and the others to make all the arrangements, Myshkin almost forgot the very same day that he had a master of the ceremonies, and a wedding and 'best men' at hand; and that his haste in handing over arrangements to others was simply to avoid thinking about it himself, and even, perhaps, to make haste to forget about it. Of what was he thinking himself in that case, what did he want to remember, and for what was he struggling? There is no doubt, moreover, that no sort of coercion, on Nastasya Filippovna's part, for instance, was applied to him; that Nastasya Filippovna certainly did desire a speedy wedding, and that it was she, and not Myshkin, who had thought of the wedding. But Myshkin had agreed of his own free will, somewhat casually indeed, and as though he had been asked for some quite ordinary thing. Such strange facts are before us in abundance, but far from making things clearer to our thinking, they positively obscure every explanation, however we take them. But we will bring forward another instance.

Thus, we know for a fact that during that fortnight Myshkin spent whole days and evenings with Nastasya Filippovna; that she took him with her for walks and to hear the band; that he drove out in her carriage with her every day; that he began to be uneasy about her if an hour passed without his seeing her (so that by every sign he loved her sincerely); that whatever she talked to him about, he listened with a mild and gentle smile for hours together, saying scarcely anything himself. But we know too that in the course of those days he had several, in fact many, times called at the Epanchins' without concealing the fact from Nastasya Filippovna, though it had driven her almost to despair. We know that, as long as the Epanchins remained at Pavlovsk, they did not receive him, and consistently refused to allow him to see Aglaia Ivanovna; that he would go away without saying a word and next day go to them again as though he had completely forgotten their refusal the day before, and, of course, be refused again. We know too, that an hour after Aglaia Ivanovna had run away from Nastasya Filippovna, perhaps even less than an hour after, Myshkin was already at the Epanchins', confident, of course, of finding Aglaia there, and that his arrival had thrown the household into extreme amazement and alarm, because Aglaia had not yet returned home. And it was only from him the Epanchins had first learned that she had been with him to Nastasya Filippovna's. It was said that Lizaveta Prokofyevna, her daughters and even Prince S— treated Myshkin on that occasion in a very harsh and hostile way; and that they had there and then in the strongest terms renounced all friendship and acquaintance with him, the more emphatically that Varvara Ardalionovna had suddenly made her appearance and announced to Lizaveta Prokofyevna that Aglaia had been in her house for the last hour in a fearful state of mind, and seemed unwilling to return home. This last piece of news affected Lizaveta Prokofyevna more than anything, and it turned out to be quite true. On coming away from Nastasya Filippovna's, Aglaia would certainly sooner have died than have faced her family, and so she flew to Nina Alexandrovna's. Varvara Ardalionovna for her part felt it essential promptly to inform Lizaveta Prokofyevna of everything. And the mother and daughters rushed off at once to Nina Alexandrovna's, followed by the head of the family, Ivan Fyodorovitch, who had just returned home. Myshkin trudged along after them, in spite of their dismissal of him and their harsh words. But Varvara Ardalionovna took care that there, too, he was not allowed to see Aglaia. The end of it was that, when Aglaia saw her mother and sisters shedding tears over her and not uttering a word of blame, she threw herself into their arms and at once returned home with them. It was said, though the story was not well authenticated, that Gavril Ardalionovitch was particularly unlucky on this occasion, too; that seizing the opportunity while Varvara Ardalionovna was running to Lizaveta Prokofyevna, and he was left alone with Aglaia, he had thought fit to begin talking of his passion; that, listening to him, Aglaia had, in spite of her tears and dejection, suddenly burst out laughing and had all at once put a strange question to him: would he, to prove his love, burn his finger in the candle? Gavril Ardalionovitch was, so the story went, petrified by the question; he was so completely taken aback, and his face betrayed such extreme amazement, that Aglaia had laughed at him as though she were in hysterics, and to get away from him ran upstairs to Nina Alexandrovna where she was found by her parents. This story was repeated to Myshkin next day by Ippolit who, being too ill to get up, sent for the prince on purpose to tell it to him. How Ippolit got hold of the story we don't know, but when Myshkin heard about the candle and the finger, he laughed so much that Ippolit was surprised. Then he suddenly began to tremble and burst into tears … Altogether, he was during those days in a state of great uneasiness, and extraordinary perturbation, vague but tormenting. Ippolit bluntly declared that he thought he was out of his mind, but it was impossible to affirm this with certainty.

In presenting all these facts and declining to attempt to explain them, we have no desire to justify our hero in the eyes of the reader. What is more we are quite prepared to share the indignation he excited even in his friends. Even Vera Lebedyev was indignant with him for a time; even Kolya was indignant; even Keller was indignant, till he was chosen as best man, to say nothing of Lebedyev himself, who even began intriguing against Myshkin, also from an indignation which was quite genuine. But of that we will speak later. Altogether, we are in complete sympathy with some forcible and psychologically deep words of Yevgeny Pavlovitch's, spoken plainly and unceremoniously by the latter in friendly conversation with Myshkin six or seven days after the incident at Nastasya Filippovna's. We must observe, by the way, that not only the Epanchins, but everyone directly or indirectly connected with them had thought proper to break off all relations with Myshkin. Prince S— for instance turned aside when he met Myshkin and did not respond to his greeting. But Yevgeny Pavlovitch was not afraid of compromising himself by visiting the prince, though he had begun visiting the Epanchins every day again, and was received by them with an unmistakable increase of cordiality. He came to see Myshkin the very day after the Epanchins had left Pavlovsk. He knew already of all the rumours that were circulating, and had, perhaps indeed, assisted to circulate them himself. Myshkin was delighted to see him and at once began speaking of the Epanchins. Such a simple and direct opening completely loosened Yevgeny Pavlovitch's tongue too, so that he went straight to the point without beating about the bush.

Myshkin did not know that the Epanchins had left. He was struck by the news, he turned pale, but a minute later he shook his head, confused and meditative, and acknowledged that 'so it was bound to be'; then he asked quickly, 'where had they gone?'

Meanwhile Yevgeny Pavlovitch watched him carefully, and he marvelled not a little at all this – the rapidity of his questions, their simplicity, his perturbation, restlessness and excitement, and at the same time a sort of strange openness. He told Myshkin about everything, however, courteously and in detail. There was a great deal the latter had not heard, and this was the first person to visit him from the Epanchins' circle. He confirmed the rumour that Aglaia really had been ill. She had lain for three days and nights in a fever without sleeping. Now she was better and out of all danger, but in a nervous and hysterical state. 'It was a good thing,' he said, 'that now there was perfect harmony in the house. They tried to make no allusion to the past, not only before Aglaia, but also among themselves. The parents had already made up their minds to a trip abroad in the autumn, immediately after Adelaïda's wedding. Aglaia had received in silence the preliminary hints at this plan. He, Yevgeny Pavlovitch, might very possibly be going abroad too. Even Prince S— might possibly go with Adelaïda for a couple of months if business permitted. The general himself would remain. They had all moved now to Kolmino, their estate fifteen miles out of Petersburg, where they had a spacious manor-house. Princess Byelokonsky had not yet returned to Moscow, and he believed she was staying on at Pavlovsk on purpose. Lizaveta Prokofyevna had insisted emphatically that they could not stay on in Pavlovsk, after what had happened. He, Yevgeny Pavlovitch, had reported to her every day the: rumours that were circulating in the town. It did not seem possible for them to move to the villa at Yelagin.'

'And indeed,' added Yevgeny Pavlovitch, 'you'll admit yourself they could hardly have faced it out ... Especially knowing what's going on here in your house every hour, Prince, and your daily calls *there* in spite of their refusing to see you ...'

'Yes, yes, yes, you're right. I wanted to see Aglaia Ivanovna,' said Myshkin, shaking his head again.

'Ah, dear prince,' cried Yevgeny Pavlovitch, with warm-hearted regret. 'How then could you allow ... all that's happened? Of course, of course, it was all so unexpected. I understand that you must have been at your wits' end and you could not have restrained the mad girl; that was not in your power. But you ought to have understood how intense and how much in earnest the girl was ... in her feeling for you. She did not care to share you with another woman and you... you could desert and shatter a treasure like that!'

'Yes, yes, you're right. I am to blame,' Myshkin began again in terrible distress. 'And do you know she alone, Aglaia alone, looked at Nastasya Filippovna like that... No one else ever looked at her like that.'

'Yes, that's just what makes it all so dreadful that there was nothing serious in it,' cried Yevgeny Pavlovitch, completely carried away. 'Forgive me, Prince, but I ... I've been thinking about it, Prince. I have thought a lot about it; I know all that happened before, I know all that happened six months ago, all – and there was nothing serious in it! It was only your head, not your heart, that was involved, an illusion, a fantasy, a mirage, and only the scared jealousy of an utterly inexperienced girl would have taken it for anything serious!

At this point, without mincing matters, Yevgeny Pavlovitch gave full vent to his indignation. Clearly and reasonably, and, we repeat, with great psychological insight, he drew a vivid picture of Myshkin's past relations with Nastasya Filippovna. He had at all times a gift for language, and at this moment he rose to positive eloquence. 'From the very first,' he declared, 'it began with falsity. What begins in a lie must end in a lie; that's a law of nature. I don't agree, and, in fact, I'm indignant when somebody calls you – well – an idiot. You're too clever to be called that. But you're so strange that you're not like other people – you must admit that yourself. I've made up my mind that what's at the bottom of all that's happened is your innate inexperience (mark that word, "innate," prince), and your extraordinary simple-heartedness, and then the phenomenal lack of all feeling for proportion in you (which you have several times recognised yourself), and finally the huge mass of intellectual convictions, which you, with your extraordinary honesty, have hitherto taken for real, innate, intuitive convictions! You must admit yourself, Prince, that from the very beginning, in your relations with Nastasya Filippovna, there was an element of *conventional democratic* feeling (I use the expression for brevity), the fascination, so to say, of the "woman question" (to express it still more briefly). I know all the details of the strange, scandalous scene that took place at Nastasya Filippovna's, when Rogozhin brought his money. If you like, I will analyse you to yourself on my fingers, I will show you to yourself as in a looking-glass, I know so exactly how it all was, and why it all turned out as it did. As a youth in Switzerland you yearned for your native country, and longed for Russia as for an unknown land of promise. You had read a great many books about Russia, excellent books perhaps, but pernicious for you. You arrived in the first glow of eagerness to be of service, so to say; you rushed, you flew headlong to be of service. And on the very day of your arrival, a sad and heart rending story of an injured woman is told you, you a virginal knight – and about a woman! The very same day you saw that woman, you were bewitched by her beauty, her fantastic, demoniacal beauty (I admit she's a beauty, of course). Add to that your nerves, your epilepsy, add to that our Petersburg thaw which shatters the nerves, add all that day, in an unknown and to you almost fantastic town, a day of scenes and meetings, a day of unexpected acquaintances, a day of the most surprising reality, of meeting the three Epanchin beauties, and Aglaia among them; then your fatigue and the turmoil in your head, and then the drawing-room of Nastasya Filippovna, and the tone of that drawing-room, and … what could you expect of yourself at such a moment, what do you think?'

'Yes, yes; yes, yes,' Myshkin shook his head, beginning to flush crimson. 'Yes, that's almost exactly how it was. And do you know I'd scarcely slept at all in the train the night before, and all the night before that, and was fearfully exhausted.'

'Yes, of course, that's just what I am driving at,' Yevgeny Pavlovitch went on warmly, 'the fact's clear that you, intoxicated with enthusiasm, so to speak, clutched at the opportunity of publicly proclaiming the generous idea, that you, a prince by birth and a man of pure life, did not regard a woman as dishonoured who had been put to shame, not through her own fault, but through the fault of a disgusting aristocratic profligate. Good heavens, of course one can understand it. But that's not the point, dear prince, the point is whether there was reality, whether there was genuineness in your emotions, whether there was natural feeling or only intellectual enthusiasm. What do you think; in the temple the woman was forgiven – just such a woman, but she wasn't told that she'd done well, that she was deserving of all respect and honour, was she? Didn't common sense tell you within three months the true state of the case? But, even granting that she's innocent now -I won't insist on that for I don't want to – but could all her adventures justify such intolerable, diabolical pride, such insolent, such rapacious egoism? Forgive me, Prince, I let myself be carried away, but…'

'Yes, all that may be so. Maybe you are right…' Myshkin muttered again, 'she certainly is very much irritated, and you're right, no doubt, but…'

'Deserving of compassion? That's what you mean to say, my kind-hearted friend? But how could you, out of compassion, for the sake of her pleasure, put to shame another, a pure and lofty girl, humiliate her in those haughty, those hated eyes? What will compassion lead you to next? It's an exaggeration that passes belief! How can you, loving a girl, humiliate her like this before her rival, jilt her for the sake of another woman, in the very presence of that other, after you had yourself made her an honourable offer … and you did make her an offer, didn't you? You said so before her parents and her sisters! Do you call yourself an honourable man after that, allow me to ask you, Prince? And … and didn't you deceive that adorable girl when you told her that you loved her?'

'Yes, yes, you're right. Ach, I feel that I am to blame!' Myshkin replied, in unutterable distress.

'But is that enough?' cried Yevgeny Pavlovitch, indignantly. 'Is it sufficient to cry out: "Ach, I'm to blame?" You are to blame, but yet you persist! And where was your heart then, your "Christian" heart? Why, you saw her face at that moment: well, was she suffering less than *the other,* that other woman who has come between you? How could you have seen it and allowed it? How could you?'

'But… I didn't allow it,' muttered the unhappy prince.

'You didn't allow it?'

'I really didn't allow anything. I don't understand to this hour how it all came to pass. I… I was running after Aglaia Ivanovna at the time, but Nastasya Filippovna fell down fainting. And since then they haven't let me see Aglaia Ivanovna.'

'Never mind! You ought to have run after Aglaia even if the other woman was fainting!'

'Yes … yes, I ought to have … She would have died you know. She would have killed herself, you don't know her, and . . it made no difference, I should have told Aglaia Ivanovna everything afterwards, and … you see, Yevgeny Pavlovitch, I see that you don't know everything. Tell me, why won't they let me see Aglaia Ivanovna? I would have explained everything to her. You see, they both talked of the wrong thing, utterly wrong ; that's why it all happened … I can't explain it to you at all, but perhaps I could explain it to Aglaia … Oh, dear; oh, dear! You speak of her face at that moment when she ran away … Oh, dear, I remember it!… Let us go, let us go!' He jumped hastily up from his seat and pulled Yevgeny Pavlovitch by the hand.

'Where are you going?'

'Let's go to Aglaia Ivanovna; let's go at once! …'

'But she's not in Pavlovsk now, I told you so. And why go to her?'

'She will understand, she will understand!' Myshkin muttered, clasping his hands imploringly. 'She would understand that it's all not *that,* but something quite different!'

'How do you mean, something quite different? Only, you're going to marry her, anyhow. So you persist in it… Are you going to be married or not?'

'Well, yes … I am; yes, I am!'

'Then how is it "not that"?'

'No, it's not that, not that, it makes no difference that I'm going to marry her. That's nothing, nothing.'

'How do you mean it makes no difference and it's nothing? Why, it's not a trifling matter, is it? You're marrying a woman you love to make her happy, and Aglaia Ivanovna sees that and knows it. How can you say it makes no difference?'

'Happy? Oh, no! I'm only just marrying her; she wants me to. And what is there in my marrying her? I … oh, well, all that's no matter! Only she would certainly have died. I see now that her marrying Rogozhin was madness. I understand now all that I didn't understand before, and, you see, when they stood there, facing one another, I couldn't bear Nastasya Filippovna's face … You don't know, Yevgeny Pavlovitch' – he dropped his voice mysteriously – 'I've never said this to anyone, not even to Aglaia, but I can't bear Nastasya Filippovna's face … It was true what you said just now about that evening at Nastasya Filippovna's, but there is one tiling you left out because you don't know it. I looked at *her face!* That morning, in her portrait, I couldn't bear the sight of it… Vera, now, Lebedyev's daughter, has quite different eyes. I … I'm afraid of her face!' he added with extraordinary terror.

'You're afraid of it?'

'Yes; she's – mad!' he whispered, turning pale.

'You're sure of that?' asked Yevgeny Pavlovitch, with extreme interest.

'Yes, sure. Now I'm sure. Now, during these last days, I've become quite sure!'

'But what are you doing, Prince?' Yevgeny Pavlovitch cried with horror. 'So you're marrying her from a sort of fear? There's no understanding it! Without even loving her, perhaps?'

'Oh, no. I love her with my whole heart! Why, she's … a child! Now she's a child, quite a child! Oh, you know nothing about it!'

'And at the same time you have declared your love to Aglaia Ivanovna?'

'Oh, yes, yes!'

'How so? Then you want to love both of them?'

'Oh, yes, yes!'

'Upon my word, Prince, think what you're saying!'

Without Aglaia I'm …I absolutely must see her! I… I shall soon die in my sleep, I thought I should have died last night in my sleep. Oh, if Aglaia only knew, if she only knew everything… absolutely everything I mean. For in this case one needs to know everything, that's what matters most. Why is it we never can know *everything* about another person, when one ought to, when that other one's to blame! … But I don't know what I'm saying. I'm muddled. You've shocked me very much … and does her face look now as it did when she ran away? Oh, yes, I am to blame! Most likely it's all my fault. I don't know quite how, but I am to blame… There's something in all this I can't explain to you, Yevgeny Pavlovitch. I can't find the words, but… Aglaia Ivanovna will understand! Oh, I've always believed that she would understand.'

'No, Prince, she won't understand. Aglaia Ivanovna loved you like a woman, like a human being, not like an abstract spirit. Do you know what, my poor prince, the most likely thing is that you've never loved either of them!'

'I don't know, perhaps so … perhaps. You're right in a great deal, Yevgeny Pavlovitch. You are very clever, Yevgeny Pavlovitch. Oh, my head is beginning to ache again. For God's sake, let's go to her! For God's sake!'

'But I tell you she's not in Pavlovsk, she's in Kolmino.'

'Let's go to Kolmino. Let's go at once!'

'That's impossible!' Yevgeny Pavlovitch said emphatically, getting up. 'Listen. I'll write to her. You take a letter!'

'No, Prince, no! Spare me such a commission. I can't!'

They parted. Yevgeny Pavlovitch went away with odd impressions, and in his judgement too the upshot of it was that Myshkin was not in his right mind. And what was the meaning of that *face* he feared so much, and yet loved! And yet perhaps he really would die without seeing Aglaia, so that Aglaia never would know how much he loved her! 'Ha-ha! And how can one love two at once? With two different sorts of love? That's interesting … poor idiot! What will become of him now?'

Chapter 10

But Myshkin did not die before his wedding, either awake or 'in his sleep,' as he had predicted to Yevgeny Pavlovitch. Perhaps he did not sleep well and had bad dreams, but by day with people, he was kind and seemed contented. At times he seemed lost in brooding, but that was only when he was alone. The wedding was being hurried on; it was fixed for about a week after Yevgeny Pavlovitch's visit. With such haste his best friends, if he had any, could hardly have 'saved the poor crazy fellow.' There were rumours that General Epanchin and his wife, Lizaveta Prokofyevna, were partly responsible for Yevgeny Pavlovitch's visit. But if, in the immense kindness of their hearts, they may both have washed to save the poor lunatic from ruin, they could hardly go beyond this feeble effort; neither their position nor, perhaps, their inclination was compatible (naturally enough) with a more pronounced action. We have mentioned already that many even of those immediately surrounding Myshkin had turned against him. Vera Lebedyev, however, confined herself to shedding a few tears in solitude, staving more in the lodge, and looking in upon Myshkin less than before. Kolya at this time was occupied with his father's funeral. The old general had died of a second stroke eight days after the first. Myshkin showed the warmest sympathy with the grief of the family, and for the first few days spent several hours daily with Nina Alexandrovna. He went to the funeral and to the service in the church. Many people noticed that Myshkin's arrival and departure were accompanied by whispers among the crowd in the church. It was the same thing in the streets and in the gardens. Wherever he walked or drove out, he was greeted by a hum of talk, his name was mentioned, he was pointed out; and Nastasya Filippovna's name, too, was audible. People looked out for her at the funeral, but she was not present. Another person conspicuously absent was the captain's widow, whom Lebedyev succeeded in preventing from coming. The burial service had a strong and painful effect on Myshkin. He whispered to Lebedyev in answer to some question that it was the first time he had been present at an Orthodox funeral, though he had a faint memory of a similar service at a village church in his childhood.

'Yes, it seems as though it's not the same man in the coffin as we elected president lately – do you remember, Prince?' Lebedyev whispered to .Myshkin. 'Whom are you looking for?'

'Oh, nothing. I fancied ...'

'Not Rogozhin?'

'Why is he here?'

'Yes, in the church.'

'I fancied I saw his eyes,' Myshkin muttered in confusion. 'But why? What's he here for? Was he invited?'

'They never thought of him. Why, they don't know him at all. There are all kinds of people in the crowd here. But why are you so astonished? I often meet him now. Why, four times in this last week I've met him in Pavlovsk.'

'I've never seen him once since ... that time,' muttered Myshkin.

As Nastasya Filippovna too had not once told him that she had met Rogozhin 'since that time,' Myshkin concluded now that Rogozhin was for some reason keeping out of sight on purpose. All that day he was lost in thought, while Nastasya Filippovna was exceptionally lively during the day and evening.

Kolya, who had made it up with Myshkin before his father's death, suggested that he should ask Keller and Burdovsky to be his best men (as the matter was urgent and near at hand). He guaranteed that Keller would behave properly and perhaps be of use, while there was no need to speak of Burdovsky, as he was a quiet and retiring person. Nina Alexandrovna and Lebedyev observed to Myshkin that if the marriage were a settled thing, there was no need for it to be at Pavlovsk, in the height of the summer season, so publicly. They urged that it would be better to have the wedding at Petersburg and even in the house. Myshkin saw only too clearly the drift of their apprehensions. He replied briefly and simply that it was Nastasya Filippovna's particular wish.

Next day Keller called on Myshkin, having been informed that he was to be a 'best man.' Before going in he stood still in the doorway, and as soon as he saw Myshkin, he raised his right hand, with the forefinger apart from the rest, and cried, as though taking a vow, 'I won't drink.'

Then he went up to Myshkin, warmly pressed and shook both his hands, and announced that certainly, when he first heard of the wedding, he felt hostile and had proclaimed the fact at billiards, and for no other reason than that he had anticipated for the prince and had daily hoped, with the impatience of a friend, to see by his side at the altar someone like the Princess de Rohan, or at least de Chabot. But now he saw for himself that Myshkin looked at things at least twelve times as nobly as all of them 'put together'! For he did not care for pomp or wealth, nor even for public esteem, but cared only for the truth! The sympathies of exalted persons were too well known, and the prince was too lofty by his education not to be an exalted person, speaking generally!

'But the common herd and rabble judge differently; in the town, in the houses, in the assemblies, in the villas, at the bandstand, in the taverns and the billiard-rooms, they were talking and shouting of nothing but the coming event. I have heard that they were even talking of getting up "rough music" under the windows – and that, so to say, on the wedding night! If you should need, Prince, the pistol of an honest man, I am ready to exchange half a dozen shots like a gentleman before you rise the morning after your nuptials.' He advised too, in anticipation of a great rush of thirsty souls on coming out of the church, to have the fire-hose ready in the courtyard. But Lebedyev opposed this. He said they would pull the house to pieces if they had the hose.

'That Lebedyev is intriguing against you, Prince, he is really. They want to put you under control. Can you believe it? With everything, your freedom and your money – that is, the two objects which distinguish every one of us from a quadruped! I've heard it, I've heard it on good authority! It's the holy truth!'

Myshkin seemed to remember having heard something of the sort himself, but of course he had paid no attention to it. Now, too, he merely laughed and forgot it again at once. Lebedyev certainly had been very busy for some time past. This man's schemes sprang up by inspiration, and in the excess of his ardour became too complex, developing into ramifications far removed from his original starting-point. This was why he generally failed in his undertakings. When, almost on the wedding-day, he came to Myshkin to express his penitence (it was his invariable habit to express his penitence to those against whom he had been intriguing, especially when he had not succeeded), he announced to him that he was born a Talleyrand and didn't know how it was he had become a mere Lebedyev. Then he disclosed his whole game, which greatly interested Myshkin. According to his story, he had begun by looking for the protection of some persons of consequence on whose support he might reckon in case of need, and he had gone to General Ivan Fyodorovitch. General Epanchin was perplexed, was full of goodwill towards the 'young man,' but declared that, 'however much he might wish to save him, it was not seemly for him to act in the matter.' Lizaveta Prokofyevna would not see him or listen to him. Yevgeny Pavlovitch and Prince S— simply waved him away. But he, Lebedyev, did not lose heart, and took the advice of a shrewd lawyer, a worthy old man and a great friend of his, almost his patron. He had given his opinion that it was only possible if they had competent witnesses as to his mental derangement and unmistakable insanity, and still more persons of consequence to back them. Even then Lebedyev was not discouraged, and had, on one occasion, even brought a doctor – also a worthy old man, with an Anna ribbon" – who was staying at Pavlovsk, to see the prince, simply, so to say, to see how the land lay, to make the prince's acquaintance, and, not officially but in a friendly way, to let him know what he thought of him.

Myshkin remembered the doctor's visit. He remembered that Lebedyev had pestered him the evening before about his not being well, and when Myshkin positively declined medical aid, Lebedyev suddenly made his appearance with a doctor, pretending that they had both just come from Ippolit Terentyev, who was much worse, and that the doctor had something to tell Myshkin about the invalid. Myshkin praised Lebedyev, and received the doctor very cordially. They began talking at once of Ippolit. The doctor asked him to give a minute account of the scene of the attempted suicide, and the prince quite delighted him by his description and explanation of the incident. They talked of the climate of Petersburg, of Myshkin's affliction, of Switzerland, and of Doctor Schneider. The discussion of Schneider's system and Myshkin's stories about him so interested the doctor that he stayed two hours with him smoking Myshkin's excellent cigars, while Lebedyev produced a delicious liqueur, which was brought in by Vera. Then the doctor, who was a married man and paterfamilias, overflowed with such compliments to Vera that he excited her intense indignation. They parted friends. On leaving Myshkin the doctor said to Lebedyev, if everyone like that were to be put under control, who would be left to control them? In reply to Lebedyev's tragic description of the imminent event, the doctor shook his head slyly and cunningly, and observed at last that, even apart from the fact that 'there's nobody a man may not marry,' the fascinating lady, besides being of incomparable beauty, which alone might well attract a wealthy man, was also – so he, at least, had heard – possessed of a fortune that had come to her from Totsky and Rogozhin, pearls and diamonds, shawls and furniture; and therefore the dear prince's choice, far from being a proof of peculiar, so to say, glaring foolishness, was rather a testimony to the shrewdness of his worldly wisdom and prudence, and therefore tended to the very opposite conclusion, completely in the prince's favour, in fact...'

This idea struck Lebedyev too, and he did not go beyond it. 'And now,' he added to Myshkin, you will see nothing from me but devotion and readiness to shed my blood for you, and I've come to tell you so.'

Ippolit too had distracted Myshkin's mind during those days; he sent for him only too often. The family was living in a little house not far off. The little ones, Ippolit's brother and sister, were glad to be at Pavlovsk, if only because they could escape from the invalid into the garden. The poor captain's widow was left at his mercy and was completely his victim. Myshkin was obliged to intervene and make peace between them every day, and the invalid still called him his 'nurse,' though at the same time he seemed to feel bound to despise him for playing the part of peacemaker. He was in high dudgeon against Kolya because the latter had scarcely visited him of late, having stayed at first beside his dying father and afterwards with his widowed mother. At last he made Myshkin's approaching marriage to Nastasya Filippovna the butt of his gibes, and ended by offending the prince and making him really angry at last. Myshkin gave up visiting him. Two days later the captain's widow trotted round in the morning and begged Myshkin, with tears, to come to them or 'that fellow would be the death of her.' She added that the invalid wanted to tell him a great secret. Myshkin went.

Ippolit wanted to make it up, wept, and after his tears, of course, felt more spiteful than ever, but was afraid to show his spite. He was very ill, and there was every sign that the end was close at hand. He had no secret to tell him, except some earnest requests – breathless, so to say, with emotion (possibly shammed) – 'to beware of Rogozhin.'

'He is a man who wall never give up his object. He's not like you and me, Prince; if he wants a thing, nothing will shake him,' &c. &c.

Myshkin began questioning him more in detail, tried to get at facts of some sort. But there were no facts except Ippolit's personal sentiments and impressions. To his intense gratification, Ippolit did, however, at last succeed in scaring Myshkin thoroughly. At first he was unwilling to respond to some of Ippolit's questions, and only smiled at his advice 'to go abroad; there were Russian priests everywhere, and he could be married there.' But Ippolit ended at last with the suggestion: 'It's for Aglaia Ivanovna I am afraid, you know; Rogozhin knows how you love her. It's a case of love for love. You have robbed him of Nastasya Filippovna, he will kill Aglaia Ivanovna; though she's not yours now, still you'd feel it, wouldn't you?'

He attained his object. Myshkin left him almost beside himself.

These warnings about Rogozhin came the day before the wedding. Myshkin saw Nastasya Filippovna that evening for the last time before the wedding. But she was not in a state to reassure him. On the contrary, she had of late made him more and more uneasy. Till then, that is a few days before, when she saw him she made every effort to cheer him up, and was dreadfully afraid of his looking sad. She even tried singing to him; most frequently she would tell him everything amusing she could think of. Myshkin almost always pretended to laugh heartily. Sometimes he did really laugh at the brilliant wit and genuine feeling with which she sometimes told stories, when she was carried away by her subject, as she often was. Seeing Myshkin's mirth, seeing the impression made on him, she was delighted, and began to feel proud of herself. But now her melancholy and brooding grew more marked every hour. His conviction of Nastasya Filippovna's condition did not waver, but for that conviction all her behaviour now would have seemed to him enigmatic and unaccountable. But he genuinely believed that her recovery was possible. He had been quite truthful in telling Yevgeny Pavlovitch that he loved her truly and sincerely, and in his love for her there was an element of the tenderness for some sick, unhappy child who could not be left to shift for itself. He did not explain to anyone his feeling for her, and, in fact, disliked speaking of it, when he found it impossible to avoid the subject. When they were together, they never discussed their 'feelings', as though they had taken a vow not to do so. Anyone might have taken part in their everyday gay and lively conversation. Darya Alexeyevna used to say afterwards that she had done nothing all this time, but wonder and rejoice, as she looked at them.

But his view of Nastasya Filippovna's spiritual and mental condition to some extent saved him from many perplexities. Now she was completely different from the woman he had known three months before. He no longer wondered, for instance, why she had run away from marrying him then with tears, with curses and reproaches, yet now she was herself insisting on the marriage. So she was no longer afraid that marriage with her would be misery for him, thought Myshkin. Such a rapid growth of self-confidence could not be natural in her, in his opinion. But, again, this self-confidence could not be due simply to her hatred for Aglaia. Nastasya Filippovna was capable of feeling too deeply for that. It could not come from dread of her fate with Rogozhin. All these causes as well as others might indeed enter into it. But what was clearest to his mind was what he had suspected long ago – that is, that the poor sick soul had broken down. Though all this saved him in one way from perplexity, it could not give him any peace or rest all that time. At times he tried, as it were, not to think of anything. He seemed really to look on his marriage as some insignificant formality, he held his own future so cheap. As for protests, conversations like the one with Yevgeny Pavlovitch, he was utterly unable to answer them, and felt himself absolutely incompetent, and so avoided all talk of the kind.

He noticed, however, that Nastasya Filippovna knew and understood quite well what Aglaia meant for him. She did not speak, but he saw her 'face,' when she found him sometimes preparing to go to the Epanchins. When the Epanchins left Pavlovsk, she was positively radiant. Unobservant and unsuspicious as he was, he had begun to be worried by the thought that Nastasya Filippovna might make up her mind to some public scandal to get Aglaia out of Pavlovsk. The talk and commotion about the wedding in all the villas was no doubt partly kept up by Nastasya Filippovna in order to irritate her rival. As it was difficult to meet the Epanchins, Nastasya Filippovna arranged to drive right in front of their windows with the prince in her carriage beside her. This was a horrible surprise for Myshkin. He realised it, as he usually did, when it was too late to set things right, when the carriage was actually passing the windows. He said nothing, but he was ill for two days afterwards. She did not repeat the experiment. During the last few days before the wedding she had frequent fits of brooding. She always ended by overcoming her melancholy, and became cheerful again, but more gently, not so noisily, not so happily cheerful as she had been of late. Myshkin redoubled his attention. It struck him as curious that she never spoke of Rogozhin. Only once, five days before the wedding, a message was suddenly brought him from Darya Alexeyevna to come at once, as Nastasya Filippovna was in a terrible state. He found her in a condition approaching complete madness. She kept screaming, shuddering, and crying out that Rogozhin was hidden in the garden, in their house, that she had seen him just now, that he would kill her in the night, that he would cut her throat! She could not be calmed all day. But that evening when Myshkin looked in on Ippolit for a moment, the captain's widow, who had only just returned from the town where she had been on some little affair of her own, told him that Rogozhin had been to her lodging that day at Petersburg and had questioned her about Pavlovsk. In answer to his enquiry she said that Rogozhin had called on her at the very time when he was supposed to have been seen in the garden by Nastasya Filippovna. It was explained as pure imagination. Nastasya Filippovna went to the captain's widow herself to question her more minutely, and was greatly relieved.

On the day before the wedding Myshkin left Nastasya Filippovna in a state of great excitement. Her wedding finery arrived from the dressmaker's in Petersburg – her wedding dress, the bridal veil, and so on. Myshkin had not expected that she would be so much excited over her dress. He praised everything, and his praises made her happier than ever. But she let slip what was in her mind. She had heard that there was indignation in the town; that the madcaps of the place were getting up some sort of charivari with music, and possibly verses composed for the occasion; and that this was more or less with the approval of the rest of Pavlovsk society. And so she wanted to hold up her head higher than ever before them, to outshine them all with the taste and richness of her attire. 'Let them shout, let them whistle if they dare!' Her eyes flashed at the very thought of it. She had another secret thought, but she did not utter that aloud. She hoped that Aglaia, or at any rate someone sent by her, would also be in the crowd incognito, in the church, would look and see, and she secretly prepared herself for it. She parted from Myshkin at eleven o'clock in the evening, absorbed in these ideas, but before it had struck midnight a messenger came running to Myshkin from Darya Alexeyevna begging him to 'come at once, she's very bad.'

Myshkin found his bride shut up in her bedroom, weeping, in despair, in hysterics. For a long time she would hear nothing that was said to her through the closed door. At last she opened it, letting no one in but Myshkin, shut the door, and fell on her knees before him. (So at least Darya Alexeyevna, who managed to get a peep, reported afterwards.)

'What am I doing? What am I doing? What am I doing to you?' she cried, embracing his feet convulsively.

Myshkin spent a whole hour with her; we do not know what they talked about. Darya Alexeyevna said that they parted peaceably and happily an hour later. Myshkin sent once more that night to enquire, but Nastasya Filippovna had dropped asleep.

In the morning before she waked, two more messengers were sent by Myshkin to Darya Alexeyevna, and it was a third messenger who was charged to report that 'there was a perfect swarm of dressmakers and hairdressers from Petersburg round Nastasya Filippovna now; that there was no trace of yesterday's upset; that she was busy, as such a beauty might well be, over dressing before her wedding; and that now, that very minute, there was an important consultation which of her diamonds to put on and how to put them on.'

Myshkin was completely reassured.

The account of what followed at the Wedding was given me by people who saw it all, and I think it is correct.

The wedding was fixed for eight o'clock in the evening; Nastasya Filippovna was quite ready by seven. From six o'clock onwards a gaping crowd began gathering round Lebdeyev's villa, and a still larger one round Darya Alexeyevna's. The church began filling up by seven o'clock. Vera Lebedyev and Kolya were in great alarm on Myshkin's account. But they had a great deal to do in the house. They were arranging for a reception and refreshments in the prince's rooms, though they hardly expected much of a gathering after the wedding. Besides the necessary persons who had to be present at the wedding, Lebedyev, the Ptitsyns, Ganya, the doctor with the Anna on his breast, and Darya Alexeyevna had been invited. When Myshkin asked Lebedyev why he had invited the doctor, 'a man he hardly knew,' the latter replied complacently, 'An order on his breast, a man who is respected, for the style of the thing.'

And Myshkin laughed. Keller and Burdovsky in evening suits, with gloves, looked quite correct, only Keller still troubled Myshkin and his supporters by a certain undisguised inclination for combat and cast very hostile looks at the sightseers who were gathering round the house. At last, at half-past seven, Myshkin set off for the church in a coach. We may observe, by the way, that he particularly wished not to omit any of the usual ceremonies. Everything was done openly, publicly, and 'in due order.' Making his way somehow or other through the crowd in the church, escorted by Keller, who cast menacing looks to right and left of him, and followed by a continual fire of whispers and exclamations, Myshkin disappeared for a time into the altar end of the church, and Keller went off to fetch the bride from Darya Alexeyevna's, where he found at the entrance a crowd two or three times as large and fully three times as free and easy as at the prince's. As he mounted the steps, he heard exclamations that were beyond endurance, and had already turned round to address an appropriate harangue to the crowd when he was luckily stopped by Burdovsky and by Darya Alexeyevna, who ran out at the door. They seized him and drew him indoors by force. Keller was irritated and hurried. Nastasya Filippovna got up, looked once more into the looking-glass, observed with a wry smile, as Keller reported afterwards, that she was 'as pale as death', bowed devoutly to the ikon, and went out on to the steps.

A hum of voices greeted her appearance. For the first moment, it is true, there were sounds of laughter, applause, even perhaps hisses, but within a moment another note was heard.

'What a beauty!' they exclaimed in the crowd.

'She's not the first and she won't be the last.'

'She'll cover it all up with the wedding ring.'

'You won't find a beauty like that again in a hurry. Hurrah!' cried those standing nearest.

'A princess! For a princess like that I'd sell my soul,' cried a clerk. ' "One night at the price of a life!" ' he quoted.

Nastasya Filippovna certainly was as white as a handkerchief when she came out, but her great black eyes glowed upon the crowd like burning coals. The crowd could not stand against them. Indignation was transformed into cries of enthusiasm. The door of the carriage was already open, Keller had already offered the bride his arm, when suddenly she uttered a cry and rushed straight into the crowd. All who were accompanying her were petrified with amazement. The crowd parted to make way for her, and five or six paces from the steps Rogozhin suddenly appeared. Nastasya Filippovna had caught his eyes in the crowd. She rushed at him like a mad creature and seized him by both arms.

'Save me! Take me away! Where you will, at once!'

Rogozhin seized her in his arms and almost carried her to the carriage. Then in a flash he pulled out a hundred-rouble note and gave it to the driver.

'To the railway station, and if you catch the train, there's another hundred for you.'

And he leapt into the carriage after Nastasya Filippovna and closed the door. The coachman did not hesitate for one moment and whipped up his horses. Keller pleaded afterwards that he was taken by surprise: 'Another second and I should have come to, and I wouldn't have let them go!' he explained, describing the adventure. He and Burdovsky would have taken another carriage that stood by and have rushed off in pursuit, but reflected as he was starting that 'it was in any case too late, and one couldn't bring her back by force!'

'And the prince won't wish it!' decided Burdovsky, greatly agitated.

Rogozhin and Nastasya Filippovna galloped to the station in time. After they had got out of the carriage, and when Rogozhin was on the point of stepping into the train he had time to stop a girl who was wearing an old but decent dark mantle and a silk kerchief on her head.

'Would you like fifty roubles for your mantle?' he cried, suddenly holding out the money to the girl. While she was still lost in amazement and trying to take it in, he had already thrust the fifty-rouble note into her hand, pulled off the mantle and kerchief, and flung them on the shoulders and head of Nastasya Filippovna. Her gorgeous array was too conspicuous, would have attracted attention on the journey, and it was only afterwards that the girl understood why her old and worthless mantle had been bought at so much profit to herself.

A rumour of what had happened reached the church with astounding rapidity. When Keller hurried to the prince, numbers of people whom he did not know rushed up to question him. There was loud talking, shaking of heads, and even laughter. No one left the church. Everyone waited to see how the bridegroom would take the news. He turned pale, but received the news quietly, saying hardly anything.

'I was afraid, but *yet* I didn't think this would happen ...' And then, after a brief silence, he added: 'However ... in her condition... this is in the natural order of things.' This comment even Keller spoke of afterwards as 'unexampled philosophy'. Myshkin came out of the church apparently calm and confident, so at least many people noticed and said afterwards. He seemed very anxious to get home and to be alone, but he was not allowed. He was followed into his room by several of the guests who had been invited – Ptitsyn, Gavril Ardalionovitch, and the doctor, who, like the others, seemed indisposed to go home. Moreover, the whole house was literally besieged by an idle crowd. From the verandah Myshkin could hear Keller and Lebedyev in angry dispute with some persons who were complete strangers, though they seemed to be of good position, and were bent on entering the verandah at any cost. Myshkin went out to the disputants, enquired what was the matter, and politely waving aside Lebedyev and Keller, he courteously addressed a stout, grey-headed gentleman who was standing on the steps at the head of a group of others, and invited him to honour him with a visit. The gentleman was somewhat disconcerted, but came in all the same, and after him came a second and a third. Out of the whole crowd seven or eight came in, trying to be as much at their ease as possible in doing so. But it turned out that no more were eager to join them, and they soon began censuring those intruders, who sat down, while a conversation sprang up and tea was offered. All this was done very modestly and decorously, to the considerable surprise of the new arrivals. There were, of course, some attempts to enliven the conversation and turn it to the theme lying uppermost in their minds. A few indiscreet questions were asked, a few risky remarks made. Myshkin answered everyone so simply and cordially, yet with so much dignity, with such confidence in the good breeding of his guests, that indiscreet questions died away of themselves. Little by little the conversation became almost serious. One gentleman, catching at a word, suddenly swore with intense indignation that he would not sell his property, whatever happened; that on the contrary he would hang on and on and that was better than money.'

'There, my dear sir, you have my system of economy, and I don't mind your knowing it.' As he was addressing Myshkin, the latter warmly commended his intention, though Lebedyev whispered in his ear that this gentleman had neither house nor home, and never had had a property of any kind. Almost an hour passed, tea was finished, and after tea the visitors began to be ashamed to stay longer. The doctor and the grey-headed gentleman took a warm farewell of Myshkin, and they all said goodbye with noisy heartiness. Good wishes were expressed, and the opinion that 'it was no use grieving, and that maybe it was all for the best,' and so on. Attempts were made, indeed, to ask for champagne, but the older guests checked the younger ones. When all were gone, Keller bent over to Lebedyev and informed him, 'You and I would have made a row, had a fight, disgraced ourselves, have dragged in the police, but he's made a lot of new friends – and what friends! I know them!' Lebedyev, who was a little 'elevated,' sighed, and articulated, ' "Thou hast hid these things from the wise and prudent, and hast revealed them unto babes." I said so about him before, but now I'll add that God has saved the babe himself from the bottomless pit, He and His saints!'

At last, about half-past ten, Myshkin was left alone. His head was aching. Kolya had helped him change his wedding clothes for his everyday suit, and was the last to leave. They parted very warily. Kolya did not speak about what had happened, but promised to come early next day. He bore witness afterwards that Myshkin had given him no hint at their last parting, and so concealed his intentions even from him. Soon there was scarcely anyone left in the house. Burdovsky went off to Ippolit's. Keller and Lebedyev went away too. Only Vera Lebedyev remained for some time in Myshkin's rooms, hurriedly restoring them to their usual order. As she went out, she glanced at Myshkin. He was sitting with both elbows on the table and his head hidden in his hands. She went softly up to him and touched him on the shoulder. Myshkin looked at her in surprise, and for a minute seemed trying to remember. But recollecting and recognising everything, he suddenly became extremely agitated, though all he did was to beg Vera very earnestly to knock at his door early next morning, at seven o'clock, in time to catch the first train. Vera promised. Myshkin begged her eagerly not to speak of this to anyone. She promised that too, and at last when she opened the door to go Myshkin stopped her for the third time, and took her hands, kissed them, then kissed her on her forehead, and with rather a 'peculiar' air, said, 'Till tomorrow!' So at least Vera described it afterwards. She went away in great anxiety about him. She felt rather more cheerful in the morning, when at seven o'clock she knocked at his door as agreed and informed him that the train for Petersburg would leave in a quarter of an hour. It seemed to her that he answered her quite in good spirits, and even with a smile. He had hardly undressed that night, though he had slept. He thought he might be back that day. It appeared therefore that he had thought it possible and necessary to tell no one but her at that moment that he was going to town.

Chapter 11

An hour later he was already in Petersburg and soon after nine he was ringing at Rogozhin's door. He went in at the visitors' entrance and for a long time there was no answer. At last the door of the flat occupied by Rogozhin's mother was opened and a trim-looking old servant appeared.

'Parfyon Semyonovitch is not at home,' she announced from the door. 'Whom do you want?'

'Parfyon Semyonovitch!'

'He is not at home.'

The old servant looked at Myshkin with wild curiosity.

'Tell me, anyway, did he sleep at home last night? And ... did he come back alone yesterday?'

The old woman went on looking at him but made no reply.

'Wasn't Nastasya Filippovna with him here ... last night?'

'But allow me to ask who may you be pleased to be?'

'Prince Lyov Nikolayevitch Myshkin, we are very intimate friends.'

'He is not at home.'

The woman dropped her eyes.

'And Nastasya Filippovna?'

'I know nothing about that.'

'Stay, stay! When is he coming back?'

'We know nothing of that either.'

The door was closed.

Myshkin determined to come back in an hour's time. Glancing into the yard he saw the porter.

'Is Parfyon Semyonovitch at home?'

'Yes.'

'How is it I was told just now that he was not at home?'

'Did his servant tell you that?'

'No, the servant at his mother's. I rang at Parfyon Semyonovitch's, but there was no answer.'

'Perhaps he's gone out,' the porter commented. 'You see, he doesn't say. And sometimes he takes the key away with him; the rooms are locked up for three days at a time.'

'Do you know for a fact that he was at home yesterday?'

'Yes, he was. Sometimes he goes in at the front door and one doesn't see him.'

'And was Nastasya Filippovna with him yesterday?'

'That I can't say. She doesn't often come; I think we should know if she had been.'

Myshkin went out and for some time walked up and down the pavement lost in thought. The windows of the rooms occupied by Rogozhin were all closed; the windows of the part inhabited by his mother were almost all open. It was a hot, bright day. Myshkin crossed to the pavement on the other side of the street and stopped to look once more at the windows. They were not only closed, but almost everywhere hung with white curtains.

He stood still a moment, and strange to say it suddenly seemed to him that the corner of one curtain was lifted and he caught a glimpse of Rogozhin's face, a momentary glimpse and it vanished. He waited a little longer and resolved to go back and ring again, but on second thoughts he put it off for one hour. 'And who knows perhaps it was only my fancy …'

What decided him was that he was in haste to get to the Izmailovsky Polk, to the lodging Nastasya Filippovna had lately occupied. He knew that when, at his request, she had left Pavlovsk three weeks before, she had settled in the house of a friend of hers, the widow of a teacher, an estimable lady with a family, who let well-furnished rooms, and in fact almost made her living by doing so. It was highly probable that, when Nastasya Filippovna moved for the second time to Pavlovsk, she had kept her lodging; it was very likely in any case that she had spent the night at those lodgings where Rogozhin, of course, would have brought her that evening. Myshkin took a cab. On the way it struck him that he ought to have begun by doing this, because it was unlikely she should have gone at night straight to Rogozhin's. He remembered the porter's words that Nastasya Filippovna did not often come. If she did not at any time come often, what would have induced her to stay at Rogozhin's now? Comforting himself with these reflections, Myshkin reached the lodgings at last more dead than alive.

To his great amazement at the widows they had heard nothing of Nastasya Filippovna either that day or the day before, but they all ran out to stare at him, as at a wonder. The lady's numerous family – all girls of every age between seven and fifteen – ran out after their mother and surrounded Myshkin, gaping. They were followed by a lean, yellow-faced aunt, and last of all the grandmother, a very aged lady in spectacles. The lady of the house earnestly begged him to go in and sit down, which Myshkin did. He saw at once that they knew quite well who he was and that his wedding was to have taken place the day before, and that they were dying to ask about the wedding and about the marvellous fact that he was enquiring of them for the woman, who should have been at that moment with him at Pavlovsk, but had too much delicacy to ask. In brief outlines he satisfied their curiosity about the wedding. Cries and exclamations of wonder and dismay followed, so that he was obliged to tell almost the whole story, in outline only, of course. Finally, the council of the sage and agitated ladies determined that the first thing certainly was to knock at Rogozhin's till he got an answer and to find out positively from him about everything. If he were not at home (and that he must ascertain for certain), or if he were unwilling to say, the prince should go to a German lady living with her mother at Semyonovsky Polk, who was a friend of Nastasya Filippovna's; possibly Nastasya Filippovna, in her excitement and desire to conceal herself, might have passed the night with them.

Myshkin got up completely crushed; they said afterwards that he had turned fearfully pale; indeed, his legs were almost giving way under him. At last, through the terrible shrill patter of their voices, he made out that they were arranging to act with him and were asking for his address in town. He had no address, it appeared; they advised him to put up at some hotel. Myshkin thought a moment and gave the address of the hotel he had stayed at before, the one where he had had a fit five weeks before. Then he set off again to Rogozhin's. This time he failed to get an answer, not only from Rogozhin's, but even from his mother's flat. Myshkin went in search of the porter and with some difficulty found him in the yard; the porter was busy and hardly answered him, hardly looked at him in fact. Yet he asserted positively that Parfyon Semyonovitch had gone out very early in the morning, had gone to Pavlovsk, and would not be home that day.

'I will wait; perhaps he will be back in the evening?'

'But he mayn't be back for a week. There's no telling.'

'So he had anyway been at home that night?'

'That he had, to be sure.'

All this was suspicious, and there was something queer about it. It was quite possible that the porter might have received fresh instructions in the interval: he had been quite talkative the first time, but now he simply turned his back on him. But Myshkin made up his mind to come back once more, two hours later, and even to keep watch on the house if necessary, but now there was still hope in the German lady and he drove off to Semyonovsky Polk.

But at the German lady's they did not even understand what he wanted. From some words they let slip, he was able to guess that the German beauty had quarrelled with Nastasya Filippovna about a fortnight before, so that she had heard nothing of her of late and exerted herself to the utmost now to make him understand that she did not care to hear anything 'if she had married all the princes in the world'. Myshkin made haste to get away. It occurred to him among other conjectures that she might have gone to Moscow as she had done before, and Rogozhin of course had gone after her or perhaps with her. 'If I could only find any traces!' He remembered, however, that he must stop at a hotel and he hurried to Liteyny; there he was at once given a room. The waiter asked him if he would not have something to eat; he answered absent-mindedly that he would. Then, realising, was furious with himself at wasting half an hour over lunch; and only later on grasped the fact that he was not obliged to remain to eat the lunch that was served to him. A strange sensation gained possession of him in that dingy and stuffy corridor, a sensation that strove painfully to become a thought, but he still could not guess what that new struggling thought was. He went out of the hotel at last, hardly knowing what he was doing; his head was in a whirl. But where was he to go? He rushed off to Rogozhin's again.

Rogozhin had not come back; there was no answer to his ring, he rang at old Madame Rogozhin's; the door was opened and he was told that Parfyon Semyonovitch was not at home and might be away for three days. Myshkin was disconcerted at being looked at as before with such wild curiosity. This time he could not find the porter at all. He crossed over to the opposite pavement as before, gazed up at the windows and walked up and down in the stifling heat for half an hour, possibly more. This time nothing was stirring; the windows did not open, the white curtains were motionless. He made up his mind that he certainly had been mistaken before, that it was his fancy; that the windows in fact were so opaque and dirty that it would have been difficult to see, even if anyone had peeped out. Relieved by this reflection he set off to the widow lady's at Izmailovsky Polk.

There they were already expecting him. The lady herself had already been to three or four places and had even been to Rogozhin's; nothing was to be seen or heard there. Myshkin listened in silence, went into the room, sat down on the sofa and gazed at them all, as though he did not understand what they were talking about. Strange to say, he was at one moment keenly observant, at the rest absent-minded to an incredible degree. All the family declared afterwards that he was an extraordinarily strange person that day, so that 'perhaps even then the end was clear.' At last he got up and asked them to show him the rooms which had been Nastasya Filippovna's. They were two large, light, lofty rooms, very nicely furnished and let at a high rent. All the ladies described afterwards how Myshkin had scrutinised every object in the room, had seen on the table a French book from the library, *Madame Bovary,* lying open, turned down the corner of the page at which the book was open, asked permission to take it with him, and not heeding the objection that it was a library book, put it in his pocket. He sat down at the open window and seeing a card-table marked with chalk, he asked who played. They told him that Nastasya Filippovna used to play every evening with Rogozhin at Fools, Preference, Millers, Whist, Your Own Trumps – all sorts of games and that they had only taken to playing cards lately, after she came back from Pavlovsk, because Nastasya Filippovna was always complaining that she was bored, that Rogozhin would sit silent all the evening and did not know how to say a word, and she would often cry; and suddenly the next evening Rogozhin had taken a pack of cards out of his pocket; then Nastasya Filippovna had laughed, and they began playing. Myshkin asked where were the cards they used to play with? But the cards were not forthcoming; Rogozhin used to bring a new pack every day in his pocket and took it away again with him.

The ladies advised him to go once more to Rogozhin's and to knock loudly once more, and to go not at once but in the evening, 'perhaps something will turn up.' The widow herself offered meanwhile to go to Pavlovsk, to Darya Alexeyevna's, to find out whether anything was known of her there. They asked Myshkin to come again in any case, at ten o'clock that evening, that they might agree on the plans for next day.

In spite of all their attempts to comfort and reassure him, Myshkin's soul was overwhelmed with absolute despair. In unutterable dejection he walked to his hotel. The dusty, stifling atmosphere of Petersburg weighed on him like a press; he was jostled by morose or drunken people, stared aimlessly at the faces, and perhaps walked much farther than he need have done; it was almost evening when he went into his room. He decided to rest a little and then to go to Rogozhin's again, as he had been advised. He sat down on the sofa, leaned his elbows on the table and sank into thought.

God knows how long and of what he thought. There were many things he dreaded and he felt painfully, agonisingly, that he was in terrible dread. Vera Lebedyev came into his mind; then the thought struck him that Lebedyev perhaps knew something about it, or, if he did not, might find out more quickly and easily than he could. Then he remembered Ippolit, and that Rogozhin used to visit Ippolit. Then he thought of Rogozhin, as he was lately at the funeral, then in the park, then suddenly as he was here in the corridor, when he hid and waited for him with a knife. He recalled his eyes now, his eyes as they looked at him there in the darkness. He shuddered: that thought which had been striving for expression suddenly came into his head.

He thought that if Rogozhin were in Petersburg, even though he were hiding for a time, he would certainly end by coming to him, Myshkin, with good or with evil intention, as he had done then. Anyway, if Rogozhin did want to see him, there would be nowhere else for him to come but here, to this corridor. He did not know his address, so he might very well suppose that Myshkin would go to the same hotel as before; anyway, he would try looking for him here if he had great need of him. And who knows, perhaps he had great need of him?

So he mused and the idea seemed to him for some reason quite possible. He could not have explained if he had probed his own thought why he should be suddenly so necessary to Rogozhin, and why it was so impossible that they should not meet. But the thought was an oppressive one: 'If he is all right, he will not come,' Myshkin went on thinking; 'he is more likely to come if he is unhappy; and he is certain to be unhappy.'

Of course, with that conviction he ought to have remained at home in his room, waiting for Rogozhin, but he seemed unable to remain with this new idea; he snatched up his hat and went out hurriedly. It was almost dark in the corridor by now. 'What if he suddenly comes out of that corner and stops me at the stairs?' flashed through his mind, as he reached the same spot. But no one came out. He passed out at the gate, went out into the street, wondered at the dense crowd of people who had flocked into the streets at sunset (as they always do in Petersburg in summertime) and turned in the direction of Gorohovy. Fifty paces from the hotel, at the first crossing someone in the crowd suddenly touched his elbow, and in an undertone said in his ear, 'Lyov Nikolayevitch, follow me, brother, I want you.'

It was Rogozhin.

Strange to say, Myshkin began telling him joyfully, gabbling at a great rate and hardly articulating the words, how he had just expected to see him at the hotel in the corridor.

'I've been there,' Rogozhin unexpectedly answered. 'Come along.'

Myshkin was surprised at his answer, but did not wonder till two minutes later at least, when he realised it. When he reflected on the answer, he was alarmed and began to look intently at Rogozhin, who was walking almost half a step in front of him, looking straight before him, not glancing at anyone they passed, making way for other people with mechanical care.

'Why didn't you ask for me at my room ... if you have been at the hotel?' asked Myshkin suddenly.

Rogozhin stopped, looked at him, thought a little, and as though he did not take in the question, said, 'I say, Lyov Nikolayevitch, you go straight along, here to the house, you know? But I'll walk on the other side. And mind that we keep together ...'

Saying this, he crossed the road to the opposite pavement, stood still to see whether Myshkin were walking on and seeing that he was standing still, gazing at him open-eyed, motioned him towards Gorohovy and walked on turning every moment to look at Myshkin and sign him to follow. He was evidently reassured by Myshkin's understanding him and following him on the other side of the pavement. It occurred to Myshkin that Rogozhin wanted to keep a look out, and not let someone pass him on the way, and that therefore he had crossed to the other side, 'Only why didn't he say whom he has to look out for?'

So they walked for five hundred paces, and all at once, for some reason, Myshkin began trembling. Rogozhin still kept looking back at him, though not so often. Myshkin could not stand it and beckoned to him. Rogozhin at once crossed the road to him.

'Is Nastasya Filippovna in your house?'

'Yes.'

'And was it you looked at me behind the curtain this morning?'

'Yes.'

'How, was it you? ...'

But Myshkin did not know what more to ask or how to finish his question. Moreover, his heart was throbbing so violently that he could scarcely speak. Rogozhin, too, was silent, and he still gazed at him as before, that is, as it were, dreamily.

'Well, I am going,' he said suddenly, preparing to cross the road again, 'and you go by yourself. Let us go separately in the street... that's better for us ... on different sides... You will see.'

When at last they turned on opposite sides of the road into Gorohovy and began to approach Rogozhin's house, Myshkin's legs began to give way under him again, so that it was almost difficult for him to walk. It was about ten o'clock in the evening. The windows in the old lady's part of the house were still open as before; in Rogozhin's they were all closed, and in the twilight the white curtains over them seemed still more conspicuous. Myshkin approached the house from the other side of the pavement. Rogozhin from his side of the pavement went straight up the steps and beckoned to him. Myshkin crossed over and joined him.

'The porter doesn't know that I've come home now. I said this morning that I was going to Pavlovsk, and I left word at my mother's, too,' he whispered, with a sly and almost pleased smile. 'We'll go in and no one will hear.'

The key was already in his hand. As he went up the staircase, he turned round and shook his finger at Myshkin to warn him to go up quietly; quietly he opened the door of his rooms, let Myshkin in, followed him in cautiously, closed the door behind him, and put the key in his pocket.

'Come along,' he articulated in a whisper.

He had not spoken above a whisper since they were in Liteyny. In spite of all his outward composure, he was inwardly in a state of intense agitation. When they went into the drawing-room, on their way to the study, he went to the window and mysteriously beckoned to Myshkin.

'When you began ringing here this morning, I guessed at once that it was you. I went on tiptoe to the door and heard you talking to Pafnutyevna. And I gave her orders as soon as it was daylight that if you or anyone from you or anyone whatever began knocking at my door, she wasn't to say I was here on any account, especially if you yourself came for me, and I gave her your name. And afterwards when you went out, the thought struck me, 'What if he stands and keeps a look-out and watches in the street.' I went up to this very window, drew aside the curtain, and there you were, standing looking straight at me ... That's how it happened.'

'Where is... Nastasya Filippovna?' Myshkin articulated breathlessly.

'She is ... here,' Rogozhin brought out slowly, after a moment's delay.

'Where?'

Rogozhin raised his eyes and looked intently at Myshkin.

'Come along ...'

He still talked in a whisper and not hurriedly, but deliberately, and still with the same strange dreaminess. Even when he told him about the curtain, he seemed to mean something quite different by his words, in spite of the spontaneousness with which he spoke.

They went into the study. There was some change in the room since Myshkin had been in it last. A heavy green silk curtain that could be drawn at either end hung right across the room, dividing the alcove where Rogozhin's bed stood from the rest of the apartment. The heavy curtain was closely drawn at both ends. It was very dark in the room. The white nights of the Petersburg summer were beginning to get darker and, had it not been for the full moon, it would have been difficult to make out anything in Rogozhin's dark rooms with the windows curtained. It is true they could still see each other's faces, though very indistinctly. Rogozhin's face was pale as usual; his glittering eyes watched Myshkin intently with a fixed stare.

'You'd better light a candle,' said Myshkin.

'No, no need,' answered Rogozhin, and taking Myshkin's hand he made him sit down on a chair; he sat opposite, moving his chair up so that he almost touched Myshkin with his knees. Between them, a little to one side, stood a small round table.

'Sit down, let's stay here a bit,' he said, as though persuading Myshkin to stay. 'I seemed to know that you would be staying at that hotel again,' he began, as people sometimes approach an important subject by beginning about quite irrelevant trifles. 'As soon as I got into the corridor I thought, what if he is sitting waiting for me, just as I am for him at this very moment? Have you been to the teacher's widow?'

'Yes,' Myshkin was hardly able to articulate from the violent throbbing of his heart.

'I thought of that, too. There'll be talk, I thought ... and then I thought again: I'll bring him here for the night, so that we may spend this night together.'

'Rogozhin! Where is Nastasya Filippovna?' Myshkin whispered suddenly, and he stood up trembling in every limb. Rogozhin got up, too.

'There,' he whispered, nodding towards the curtain.

'Asleep?' whispered Myshkin.

Again Rogozhin looked at him, intently as before.

'Well, come along then!... Only you ... well, come along!'

He lifted the curtain, stood still, and turned to Myshkin again.

'Come in,' he nodded, motioning him to go within the curtain. Myshkin went in.

'It's dark here,' he said.

'One can see,' muttered Rogozhin.

'I can scarcely see ... there's a bed.'

'Go nearer,' Rogozhin suggested softly.

Myshkin took a step nearer, then a second, and stood still. He stood still and looked for a minute or two. Neither of them uttered a word all the while they stood by the bedside. Myshkin's heart beat so violently that it seemed as though it were audible in the deathlike stillness of the room. But his eyes were by now accustomed to the darkness, so that he could make out the whole bed. Someone lay asleep on it, in a perfectly motionless sleep; not the faintest stir, not the faintest breath could be heard. The sleeper was covered over from head to foot with a white sheet and the limbs were vaguely defined; all that could be seen was that a human figure lay there, stretched at full length. All around in disorder at the foot of the bed, on chairs beside it, and even on the floor, clothes had been flung in disorder; a rich white silk dress, flowers, and ribbons. On a little table at the head of the bed there was the glitter of diamonds that had been taken off and thrown down. At the end of the bed there was a crumpled heap of lace and on the white lace the toes of a bare foot peeped out from under the sheet; it seemed as though it had been carved out of marble and it was horridly still. Myshkin looked and felt that as he looked, the room became more and more still and deathlike. Suddenly there was the buzz of a fly which flew over the bed and settled on the pillow. Myshkin started.

'Let's go.' Rogozhin touched his arm. They went out, and sat down on the same chairs, facing one another again. Myshkin trembled more and more violently, and never took his questioning eyes off Rogozhin's face.

'I notice you are trembling, Lyov Nikolayevitch,' Rogozhin said at last, 'almost as much as you did when you had your illness. Do you remember, in Moscow? Or as you had once before a fit? I can't think what I should do with you now Myshkin listened, straining every effort to understand, and still his eyes questioned him.

'Was it... you?' he brought out at last, nodding towards the curtain.

'It was I,' Rogozhin whispered, and he looked down.

They were silent for five minutes.

'For if,' Rogozhin began, continuing suddenly as though his speech had not been interrupted, 'you are ill, have your fit and scream, someone may hear from the street or the yard, and guess that there are people in the flat. They'll begin knocking and come in ... for they all think I am not at home. I haven't lighted a candle for fear they should guess from the street or the yard. For when I am away, I take the key and no one ever comes in to tidy the place for three or four days in my absence. That's my habit. So I took care they shouldn't find out we are here ...'

'Stay,' said Myshkin. 'I asked the porter and the old woman this morning whether Nastasya Filippovna hadn't stayed the night here. So they must know already.'

'I know that you asked them. I told Pafnutyevna that Nastasya Filippovna came here yesterday and went away to Pavlovsk and that she was only here ten minutes. And they don't know she stayed the night here – no one knows it. I came in with her yesterday quite secretly, as we did just now. I'd been thinking on the way that she wouldn't care to come in secretly, but not a bit of it! She whispered, she walked on tiptoe, she drew her skirts round her, and held them in her hand that they might not rustle. She shook her finger at me on the stairs – it was you she was afraid of. She was mad with terror in the train, and it was her own wish to stay the night here. I thought of taking her to her lodgings at the widows – but not a bit of it! "He'll find me there as soon as it's daylight," she said, "but you will hide me and early tomorrow morning we'll set off for Moscow," and then she wanted to go somewhere to Orel. And as she went to bed she kept saying we'd go to Orel ...'

'Stay; what are you going to do now, Parfyon. What do you want to do?'

'I wonder about you, you keep trembling. We'll stay the night here together. There is no bed but that one, and I thought we might take the pillows off the two sofas and make up a bed here for you and me beside the curtain, so that we can be together. For if they come in and begin looking round or searching, they'll see her at once and take her away. They'll begin questioning me, I shall say it was me, and they'll take me away at once. So let her lie here now beside us, beside you and me …'

'Yes, yes!' Myshkin agreed warmly.

'So we won't confess and let them take her away.'

'Not on any account!' Myshkin decided. 'Certainly not.'

'That's what I decided, lad, not to give her up on any account to anyone! We'll keep quiet all night. I only went out for an hour this morning, except for that I've been with her all the time. And then I went to find you in the evening. Another thing I am afraid of is that it's so hot and there may be a smell. Do you notice a smell?'

'Perhaps I do, I don't know. There certainly will be by the morning.'

'I covered her with American leather, good American leather, and put the sheet over it, and I put four jars of Zhdanov's disinfectant there uncorked, they are standing there now.'

'Just as they did that time … at Moscow?'

'On account of the smell, brother. And you see how she is lying … You must look in the morning when it's light. What's the matter, can't you stand up?' Rogozhin asked with apprehensive wonder, seeing that Myshkin was trembling so much that he could not get up.

'My legs won't move,' muttered Myshkin, 'it's from terror, I know … When the fear is over I shall get up.'

'Stay, I'll make up our bed and you'd better lie down … and I'll lie down too … and we'll listen, for I don't know yet, lad, for I don't understand it all yet, I warn you of that beforehand, so that you may know all about it beforehand …'

Muttering these unintelligible words, Rogozhin began making up the beds. It was evident that he had thought of these beds, possibly even that morning. The previous night he had lain on the sofa. But there was not room for two on the sofa, and he was set on their sleeping side by side, that was why, with much effort, he now dragged, right across the room, the various cushions off the two sofas and laid them by the curtain. He made the bed after a fashion; he went up to Myshkin, tenderly and eagerly took him by the arm, raised him and led him to the bed, but Myshkin found he could walk by himself, so his terror was passing off, and yet he still was trembling.

'Because,' Rogozhin began making Myshkin lie down on the left on the best cushions, while without undressing he stretched himself out on the right, clasping his hands behind his head, 'because it's hot, brother, and you know there may be a smell... I am afraid to open the windows; my mother has got jars of flowers, heaps of flowers and they have such a delicious smell; I thought of bringing them in, but Pafnutyevna would have been suspicious, she is inquisitive.'

'She is inquisitive,' Myshkin assented.

'Shall we buy nosegays and put flowers all round her? But I think, friend, it will make us sad to see her with flowers round her!'

'Listen!' said Myshkin uncertainly, as though he were looking for what he meant to ask and at once forgetting it again, 'listen, tell me what did you do it with? A knife? The same one?'

'The same one.'

'There's something else; I want to ask you something else, Parfyon ... I want to ask you a great many questions, all about it... but you had better tell me first, to begin with, so that I may know; did you mean to kill her before my wedding, at the church door ... with a knife?'

'I don't know whether I meant to or not,' Rogozhin answered drily, seeming somewhat surprised at the question and not understanding it. 'Did you ever take the knife with you to Pavlovsk?'

'No, never. All I can tell you about the knife is this, Lyov Nikolayevitch,' he added after a pause, 'I took it out of a locked drawer this morning, for it all happened this morning, about four o'clock. It had been lying in a book all the time ... And ... and ... another thing seems strange: the knife went in three or four inches ... just under the left breast ... and there wasn't more than half a tablespoonful of blood flowed on to her chemise, there was no more ...'

'That, that, that,' Myshkin sat up suddenly in great agitation, 'that I know, I've read about it, that's called internal bleeding ... Sometimes there's not one drop. That's when the stab goes straight to the heart.'

'Stay, do you hear?' Rogozhin interrupted quickly, all of a sudden, sitting up in terror on the cushions. 'Do you hear?'

'No!' answered Myshkin, as quickly and fearfully looking at Rogozhin.

'Steps! Do you hear? In the drawing-room ...' They both began listening.

'I hear,' said Myshkin decidedly.

'Footsteps?'

'Footsteps.'

'Shall we shut the door or not?'

'Shut it...'

They shut the door and both lay down again.

They were silent for a long time.

'Ah, yes,' Myshkin began suddenly in the same excited and hurried whisper, as though he had caught his thought and were dreadfully afraid of losing it again; he sat up on the bed. 'It's ... I wanted ... those cards! Cards ... They said you played cards with her?'

'Yes I did,' said Rogozhin, after a brief silence.

'Where are ... the cards?'

'They are here,' Rogozhin brought out after a longer silence, 'here ...'

He brought a pack of cards wrapped up in paper out of his pocket and held them out to Myshkin. He took it, but with a sort of wonder. A new feeling of hopeless sadness weighed on his heart; he realised suddenly that at that moment and a long time past he had been saying not what he was wanting to say and had been doing the wrong thing, and that the cards he was holding in his hands and was so pleased to see were no help, no help now. He stood up and clasped his hand. Rogozhin lay without movement and seemed not to hear and see his action, but his eyes glittered in the darkness and were wide open and staring fixedly. Myshkin sat down on a chair and began looking at him with terror. Half an hour passed; suddenly Rogozhin cried out aloud and began laughing, as though he had forgotten they must speak in a whisper, 'That officer, that officer ... do you remember how she switched that officer at the bandstand, ha-ha-ha! And there was a cadet... a cadet... a cadet, too, who rushed up ...'

Myshkin jumped up from the chair in new terror. When Rogozhin was quiet (and he suddenly ceased), Myshkin bent softly over him, sat beside him and with his heart beating violently and his breath coming in gasps, he began looking at him. Rogozhin did not turn his head towards him and seemed indeed to have forgotten him. Myshkin looked and waited; time was passing, it began to get light. From time to time Rogozhin began suddenly and incoherently muttering in a loud harsh voice, he began shouting and laughing. Then Myshkin stretched out his trembling hand to him and softly touched his head, his hair, stroking them and stroking his cheeks … he could do nothing else! He began trembling again, and again his legs seemed suddenly to fail him. Quite a new sensation gnawed at his heart with infinite anguish. Meanwhile it had become quite light; at last he lay down on the pillow as though utterly helpless and despairing and put his face close to the pale and motionless face of Rogozhin; tears flowed from his eyes on to Rogozhin's cheeks, but perhaps he did not notice then his own tears and was quite unaware of them.

Anyway, when after many hours the doors were opened and people came in, they found the murderer completely unconscious and raving. Myshkin was sitting beside him motionless on the floor, and every time the delirious man broke into screaming or babble, he hastened to pass his trembling hand softly over his hair and cheeks, as though caressing and soothing him. But by now he could understand no questions he was asked and did not recognise the people surrounding him; and if Schneider himself had come from Switzerland to look at his former pupil and patient, remembering the condition in which Myshkin had sometimes been during the first year of his stay in Switzerland, he would have flung up his hands in despair and would have said as he did then, 'An idiot!'

Chapter 12

Conclusion

The schoolmaster's widow, hurrying off to Pavlovsk, had gone straight to see Darya Alexeyevna, who was agitated by the events of the previous day, and telling her all that she knew threw her into a regular panic. The two ladies decided at once to get into communication with Lebedyev, who as a householder and a friend of his lodger, was also in agitation. Vera Lebedyev told them all that she knew. By Lebedyev's advice they decided to set off to Petersburg all three together, in order as quickly as possible to prevent what might very easily come to pass. So it came about that at about eleven o'clock next morning Rogozhin's flat was broken open in the presence of the police, of Lebedyev, of the ladies, and of Rogozhin's brother, Semyon Semyonovitch, who lived in the lodge. Matters were greatly facilitated by the evidence of the porter, that he had seen Parfyon Semyonovitch the previous evening going in at the front door with a visitor and seemingly in secret.

For two months Rogozhin was prostrate with inflammation of the brain, and he was tried as soon as he recovered. He gave straightforward, exact, and fully satisfactory evidence on every point, in consequence of which from the very first Myshkin's name was not brought into the case. Rogozhin was taciturn during his trial. He did not contradict his adroit and eloquent counsel, who proved clearly and logically that the crime committed was a consequence of the brain fever which had set in long before its perpetration, as a result of the troubles of the accused. But he added nothing of his own to confirm that contention, and as before, clearly and precisely maintained and recollected the minutest circumstances connected with the crime. In view of extenuating circumstances he was sentenced to only fifteen years penal servitude in Siberia, and heard his sentence grimly, silently, and 'dreamily.' All his vast fortune, except the comparatively small part that he had squandered in the first few months of debauchery, passed to his brother Semyon Semyonovitch, to the great satisfaction of the latter. Rogozhin's old mother is still living, and seems from time to time to remember her favourite son, Parfyon, though only vaguely. God has saved her mind and her heart from the knowledge of the blow that has fallen on her melancholy house.

Lebedyev, Keller, Ganya, Ptitsyn, and many of the other persons of our story go on living as before and have changed but little. There is scarcely anything to be said about them. Ippolit died in a state of terrible excitement somewhat sooner than he had expected, a fortnight after the death of Nastasya Filippovna. Kolya was greatly affected by what had happened; he attached himself more closely than ever to his mother. Nina Alexandrovna is uneasy at his being too thoughtful for his years; he may become an active and useful man. Among other things, the arrangement of Myshkin's future was partly due to his efforts; he had long before noticed Yevgeny Pavlovitch Radomsky as different from the other persons he had made friends with of late; he was the first to go and tell him all he knew about the case and Myshkin's present condition. He was not mistaken in his estimate of him. Yevgeny Pavlovitch took the warmest interest in the luckless 'idiot's' fate and by his care and efforts Myshkin was taken back to Dr Schneider's in Switzerland. As Yevgeny Pavlovitch has gone abroad and intends to spend a long time in Europe, openly declaring that he is a superfluous man in Russia, he visits his sick friend at Schneider's pretty often, at least once every few months. But Schneider frowns and shakes his head more ominously every time; he hints at a permanent derangement of the intellect; he does not yet say positively that recovery is out of the question, but he allows himself phrases suggestive of most melancholy possibilities. Yevgeny Pavlovitch takes this very much to heart; he has a heart, which is evident from the fact that Kolya writes to him, and that he even sometimes answers him. Another curious fact is known about him, and as it shows a kindly trait in his character, we hasten to mention it. After every visit to Dr Schneider, Yevgeny Pavlovitch, besides writing to Kolya, sends a letter to another person in Petersburg giving the most sympathetic and minute account of Myshkin's state of health. Together with the most respectful expression of devotion those letters sometimes (and more and more frequently) contain a frank statement of views, ideas, and feelings – in fact something approaching a feeling of warm friendship is revealed by them. The person who is in correspondence with him (though the letters are not very frequent) and who has won so much attention and respect from him is Vera Lebedyev. We have never been able to ascertain how such relations arose between them. No doubt they began at the time of Myshkin's breakdown, when Vera Lebedyev was so distressed that she fell positively ill. But exactly what incident brought about his acquaintance and friendship we do not know.

We have alluded to these letters chiefly because they contained news of the Epanchins, and especially of Aglaia. Of her Yevgeny Pavlovitch wrote in a rather disconnected letter from Paris that after a brief and extraordinary attachment to an exile, a Polish count, she had suddenly married him against the wishes of her parents, who had only given their consent at last because there were possibilities of a terrible scandal. Then after almost six months' silence Yevgeny Pavlovitch gave his correspondent a lengthy and detailed account of how, on his last visit to Dr Schneider's, he had met there Prince S— and all the Epanchin family (except, of course, Ivan Fyodorovitch who was kept in Petersburg by business). It was a strange meeting; they had all met Yevgeny Pavlovitch with extraordinary delight; Adelaïda and Alexandra were unaccountably grateful to him 'for his angelic kindness to the unhappy prince.' Lizaveta Prokofyevna wept bitterly at the sight of Myshkin in his afflicted and humiliated condition. Obviously everything had been forgiven him. Prince S— had made a few just and true observations. It seemed to Yevgeny Pavlovitch that Adelaïda and he were not yet in perfect harmony, but that inevitably in the future Adelaïda would spontaneously and ungrudgingly allow her impetuous temper to be guided by Prince S—'s good sense and experience. Moreover, the painful experiences the family had been through, especially Aglaia's recent adventure with the exile, had made a profound impression upon her. Everything that the family had dreaded in giving Aglaia to the Polish count had within six months come to pass, together with fresh surprises of which they had never dreamed. It turned out that the count was not even a count, and if he were really an exile, it was owing to some dark and dubious incident in the past. He had fascinated Aglaia by the extraordinary nobility of his soul, which was torn with patriotic anguish, and fascinated her to such a degree that even before she married him she became a member of a committee for the restoration of Poland and had, moreover, visited the confessional of a celebrated Catholic priest, who gained a complete ascendancy over her mind. The vast estates of the Polish count, of which he had given Lizaveta Prokofyevna and Prince S— almost incontestable evidence, turned out to be a myth. What was more, within six months of the wedding the count and his friend the celebrated confessor had succeeded in setting Aglaia completely against her family, so that for some months they had not even seen her …

There was, in fact, a great deal to say, but Lizaveta Prokofyevna, her daughters, and even Prince S— had been so much distressed by all this 'terrible business,' that they were reluctant even to allude to some points in conversation with Yevgeny Pavlovitch, though they were aware that he already knew the story of Aglaia's latest infatuation. Poor Lizaveta Prokofyevna was longing to be back in

Russia, and according to Yevgeny Pavlovitch's account she was bitter and unfair in her criticism of everything in Europe.

'They can't make decent bread anywhere; in winter they are frozen like mice in a cellar,' she said, 'here, at any rate, I've had a good Russian cry over this poor fellow,' she added pointing to Myshkin, who did not even recognise her. 'We've had enough of following our whims; it's time to be reasonable. And all this, all this life abroad, and this Europe of yours is all a fantasy, and all of us abroad are only a fantasy... remember my words, you'll see it for yourself!' she concluded almost wrathfully, as she parted from Yevgeny Pavlovitch.

Other Titles Available In This Series

9 739353 763619

9 789352 762729

9 789352 762736

9 789352 766833

9 789352 762897

9 789352 763153

9 789352 762910

9 789352 762767

9 789352 766443

9 789352 766475

9 789352 763332

9 789352 763399